Praise for *Shadows of the Apt*

'A novel brimming with imagination and execution'   *SciFiNow*

'Epic fantasy at its best. Gripping, original and multi-layered story-telling from a writer bursting with lots of fascinating ideas'
WalkerofWorlds.com

'Superb world building, great characters and extreme inventiveness'
FantasyBookCritic blog

'Adrian is continuing to go from strength to strength. Magic'
FalcataTimes blog

'Reminiscent of much that's gone before from the likes of Gemmel, Erikson, Sanderson and Cook but with its own unique and clever touch, this is another terrific outing from Mr Tchaikovsky'
Sci-Fi-London.com

'I still cannot deny the greatness of Adrian Tchaikovsky's books . . . a glorious success of fantasy literature'   *LECBookReviews.com*

'Tchaikovsky's series is a pretty great one – he has taken some classic fantasy elements and added a unique (as far as I'm aware) twist and element to his characters and the world . . . Tchaikovsky has created a world that blends epic fantasy and technology'
CivilianReader blog

'Tchaikovsky manages to blend these insect characteristics with human traits convincingly, giving a fresh slant to the inhabitants of his classic tale'   *SFReader.com*

War Master's Gate

Adrian Tchaikovsky was born in Woodhall Spa, Lincolnshire before heading off to Reading to study psychology and zoology. For reasons unclear even to himself he subsequently ended up in law and has worked as a legal executive in both Reading and Leeds, where he now lives. Married, he is a keen live role-player and occasional amateur actor, has trained in stage-fighting, and keeps no exotic or dangerous pets of any kind, possibly excepting his son.

Catch up with Adrian at www.shadowsoftheapt.com for further information plus bonus material including short stories and artwork.

War Master's Gate is the ninth novel in the Shadows of the Apt series.

BY ADRIAN TCHAIKOVSKY

Shadows of the Apt

SHADOWS OF THE APT
BOOK NINE

War Master's Gate

ADRIAN
TCHAIKOVSKY

TOR

First published in 2013 by Tor
an imprint of Pan Macmillan, a division of Macmillan Publishers Limited
Pan Macmillan, 20 New Wharf Road, London N1 9RR
Basingstoke and Oxford
Associated companies throughout the world
www.panmacmillan.com

ISBN 978-0-230-75701-1

Typeset by Ellipsis Digital Limited, Glasgow
Printed and bound by CPI Group (UK) Ltd, Croydon, CR0 4YY

*Dedicated to the memory of Robert Holdstock,
one of the true masters.*

Acknowledgements

The same giants whose shoulders I have clambered up for previous volumes remain very much in support for this one: Annie, my wife; Simon Kavanagh, my agent; Peter Lavery, my line editor; and all the many useful people at Tor. I would also like to thank Keris McDonald for getting me and the Second Army out of a bit of a tactical dilemma partway into the plot.

At this stage, though, drawing towards the conclusion of a series, I sometimes feel that the people I need to thank the most are the characters themselves, who by now are really writing large swathes of the plot without much intervention needed by me. For which their reward, all too often, is a final one.

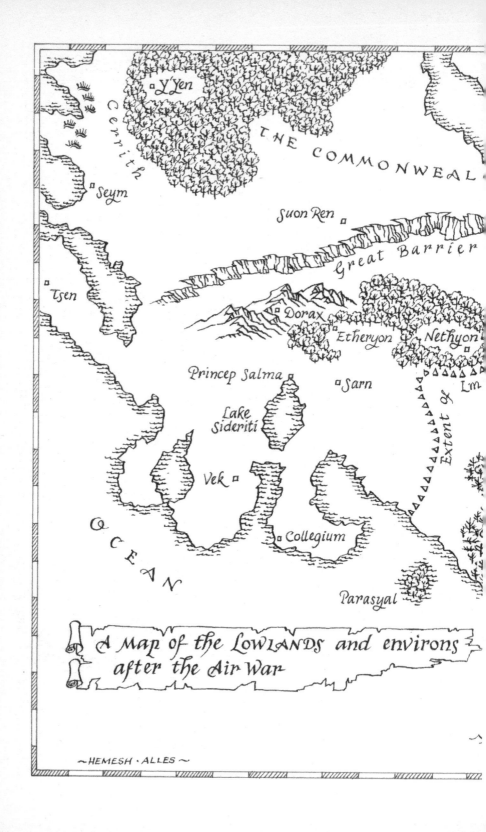

Y'Yen

Cerrith

Seym

THE COMMONWEAL

Suon Ren

Great Barrier

Tsen

Dorax

Etheryon   Nethyon

Lm

Princep Salma   Sarn

Lake
Sideriti

Extent of

Vek

OCEAN

Collegium

Parasyal

A Map of the Lowlands and environs
after the Air War

~ HEMESH · ALLES ~

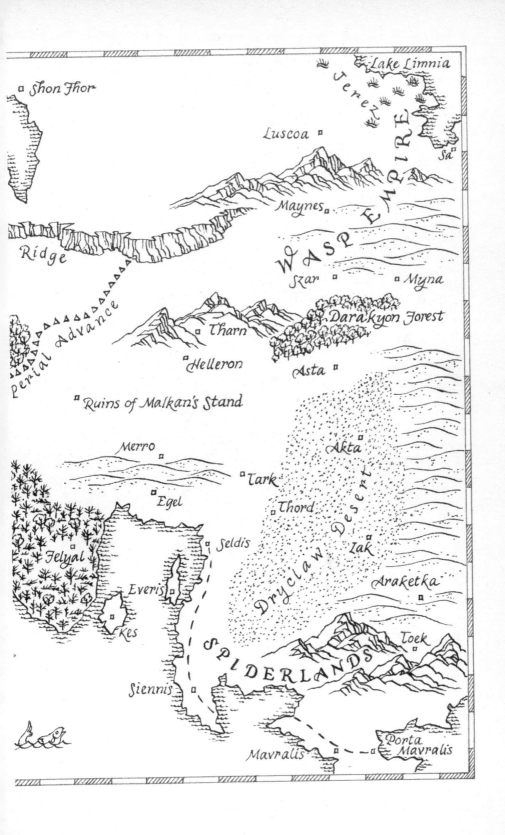

Principal Cast

The Collegiate Front

Collegiate Forces

Stenwold Maker, War Master
Jodry Drillen, Speaker for the Assembly
Taki, Solarnese pilot
Elder Padstock, chief officer, Maker's Own
Kymene, leader of the free Mynan forces
Eujen Leadswell of the Student Company
Laszlo, Fly-kinden, former *Tidenfree* pirate
Straessa 'the Antspider', officer, Coldstone Company
Gerethwy, Woodlouse soldier, Coldstone Company
Sartaea te Mosca, Fly-kinden lecturer and healer
Averic, Wasp soldier, Student Company
Madagnus, chief officer, Coldstone Company
Remas Boltwright, chief officer, Fealty Street Company
Willem Reader, aviation artificer
Tomasso, Fly-kinden, pirate
Castre Gorenn, Dragonfly soldier, Coldstone Company
Jons Allanbridge, aviator
Helmess Broiler, Assembler, Wasp sympathizer
Termes, Vekken commander

Imperial and Allied Forces

General Tynan, Second Army
Mycella of the Aldanrael
Colonel Cherten, Army Intelligence/Rekef
Major Oski, Fly-kinden, Engineers
Captain-Auxillian Ernain, Bee-kinden, Engineers
Captain Bergild, Air Corps
Jadis of the Melisandyr, Mycella's bodyguard
Morkaris, mercenary adjutant
Captain Vrakir, Red Watch
Captain Nistic, Hornet-kinden specialist

The Sarnesh Front

Sarnesh and Allied Forces

Tactician Milus
Commander Sentius
Zerro, Fly-kinden Scout

Balkus, renegade Sarnesh Ant, Princep Commander
Syale, Roach-kinden, Princep ambassador
Helma Bartrer, Collegiate Assembler and Master of the College
Amnon, former Khanaphir First Soldier
Laszlo, Fly-kinden, Collegiate agent
Terastos, Moth-kinden, Dorean agent
Grief, Monarch of Princep Salma

Cheerwell Maker, Stenwold's niece
Tynisa, Stenwold's ward
Thalric, renegade Wasp
Maure, halfbreed necromancer

Imperial Forces

Empress Seda
General Roder, Eighth Army
Gjegevey, Woodlouse adviser
Tisamon, Empress's bodyguard
Esmail/Ostrec, spy, Red Watch
Yraea, Tharen agent
Tegrec, Tharen ambassador
Sergeant Gorrec, Wasp, Pioneers
Icnumon, halfbreed, Pioneers
Jons Escarrabin, Beetle, Pioneers

Ceremon, Nethyen Mantis
Amalthae, mantis
Argastos, mystic

There is a full cast list in the glossary, at the back of the book, on page 655.

Stories so far

Stenwold Maker was once a lone voice of resistance to the Wasp Empire in his home city of Collegium. Now he is an elder statesman, the man who rallied the Lowlands against Imperial ambitions, and they give him the title 'War Master'. With the aid of Collegium's aviators and technological prowess he has driven the Empire back from his city's gates and smashed its air power, but the battle is a long way from won. The Eighth Army is still threatening Sarn to the north, and the Second Army, though thrown back, has not admitted defeat. Moreover, half the Lowlands remains in the possession of the Empire and its Spider allies. Stenwold has risked and lost a great deal to get to this point, compromising his morality and alienating his allies, and still the might of the Empire seems unstoppable.

General Tynan, commanding the Second Army, sees things very differently. Mauled by Collegium's air superiority, he is caught between the prospect of an advance into a fight that will butcher thousands of his soldiers and the immutability of his orders, which forbid a retreat. A decent man, a hero to his people, a loyal and obedient soldier, he has wished more than once that he had killed Stenwold Maker when the man was in his grasp. Twice now he has been at the gates of Collegium with his army, known as 'the Gears', and twice those gears have been thrown into reverse. Once, the death of the Emperor called him back, and perhaps there is no shame in that, but this second time he has been roundly beaten. His one compensation is that he can at least share the sting of it with his co-commander, the Spider-kinden Mycella of the Aldanrael, an uneasy ally now become Tynan's closest confidant.

Cheerwell Maker, known as 'Che' and niece to Stenwold, has not seen her home for a long time. During the last war with the Empire – the one that ended with the Emperor's death at the hands of the Mantis Tisamon – she was involved peripherally in a grand magical ritual that changed her. Once she was Apt, a child of the machine age who scoffed at magic. Now the workings of artifice are denied her, but in their place she has inherited a world of arcane wonder and terror. That path led her to the ancient, crumbling state of the Commonweal to rescue her foster-sister Tynisa from her father Tisamon's cruel ghost. With the ghost driven out, and Tynisa's duelling injuries healed, Che is coming home. She travels with Tynisa, the renegade Wasp Thalric, who was the Empress's lover before he became Che's, and a halfbreed necromancer named Maure.

Empress Seda is the first woman to rule the fiercely patriarchal Wasp Empire and temporally the most powerful individual in the known world. Seda has a secret, however: the world her fellow Wasps know is just a facade stretched over a magic-shadowed past of unknown depths. Instrumental in the same ritual that unmade Che Maker, she suffered the same curse, becoming a creature of the hidden world of the Inapt. Unlike Che, however, she seized her new nature and forced it to obey and serve her, just as she did with the Empire itself. Only too late did she discover that, linked inextricably to Che, in making herself the heir apparent to the magical world she was setting the Beetle girl on the same throne. Now, seeing Che as the one true threat to her power, she seeks a source of magical strength that she may claim alone in order to destroy her rival. Her first step was to take the ghost of Tisamon, freshly driven from Tynisa's mind, and raise it as her unliving bodyguard.

Straessa, called 'the Antspider' for her mixed blood, cares nothing for magic or for the designs of a distant Empress. Even the doings of closer generals and war masters concern her less than surviving the war with skin and friends intact. Not long ago she was just a student at Collegium's Great College, and her decision to enlist in the Coldstone Company is one that has engendered occasional second thoughts, not least when she was facing the Second Army in a disastrous land battle that only the Collegiate air power was able to turn around. Her relationship with the scholar Eujen Leadswell has suffered, as he disapproves of her military ambitions whilst simultaneously forming his own unauthorized 'Student Company' in an attempt, she suspects, to prove to her that he can be a soldier too. He should not be a soldier, in her assessment, and neither should their friends the artificer Gerethwy or the rogue Wasp Averic, but, with the Second Army still out there, soldiers are what Collegium needs.

Part One

Gates of the Green

'*We have fallen, we will rise again.*'
MOTTO OF THE FREE MYNAN RESISTANCE

Prologue

He had never seen the sea, but the vast expanse of green beneath him was what he imagined the sea to be like.

Back home in the Empire there were no forests like this. The Wasps had no use for them: such places were grown to harbour sedition and inferior kinden. Trees in the Empire behaved themselves, planted in neat rows ready for axe and saw.

For Hanto, this endless wind-rolled canopy reminded him only of the war in the Commonweal; he was just old enough to have seen the last years of it. There had been so much wasted land up in the north, untilled and uncut. There had been forests like this, where the Mantis-kinden lurked, against which the armies of the Emperor had broken when they first marched forth.

Only the first time, though. After that, they had destroyed each knot of stubborn resistance with fire and the sword, with the ingenuity of war machines and the cunning infiltration of the Pioneers. And that was where Hanto came in.

He had been barely more than a boy, in that war. Now, he was a veteran, and the army had called him up to take on this new challenge.

He had been flying for too long, letting that unrelieved green ocean pass beneath him, and now he let himself drop, coming down lightly in the top reaches of the canopy, still without any useful intelligence to bring back to his masters. Crouched in the branches, beneath the shadow of the leaves, he scanned the ground far below with his strung shortbow at the ready. Not a snapbow, not for Hanto: he was of that minority of Fly-kinden, the Inapt. Crossbows and all the other paraphernalia of the modern war were a closed book to him. His early life had been a hard one, all taunts and closed doors, but there were compensations. A place like this, an old place, an Inapt place that had preserved its secrets for centuries – his Apt comrades would never get this far, not for all their craft. Stealth here was a matter of blending in, and any of the Apt would stand out by a thousand years of hostile progress.

Not that Hanto was feeling particularly welcome right now. This was a bad place, he knew it in his bones. This was a magic place. All his life he had laughed at the idea, and always a little louder than his fellows, to cover the fact that he knew full well it was real. His mother had whispered it to him from his youngest days, to beware a place like this. He wished he had the option, but the Eighth Army desperately needed an eye within these trees.

The precise military situation was somewhat confused to Hanto – intelligence that a scout could never quite get hold of always concerned the doings of his own side. General Roder's proud Eighth had made fierce and fleet time on its westward march. Myna had been beaten into submission by superior technology, Helleron had opened its legs like a whore, and the Sarnesh fortress at Malkan's Stand had been reduced to rubble. Roder had fast been writing himself into the history books as one of the most successful generals the Empire had ever known.

And then . . . what? They had been skirting the southern edge of the forest, fending off constant angry attention from the Mantis-kinden who lurked there, but the army were making strong progress towards Sarn itself, one of the Lowlands' two key cities. And then they had stopped. And then they had actually retreated for a bit, as though some army was just past the horizon that even General Roder didn't fancy clashing with. And they had set up camp and sat around – had been doing so for some time now – and nobody knew why except, presumably, Roder himself.

Some said it was to do with the way things had gone to the south. Solid scuttlebutt claimed that the Second Army under General Tynan had been pushed back from Collegium with bad losses: the "Gears", as they were known, suddenly breaking their teeth against the hard walls of the Beetle city. What precisely had gone wrong was harder to pin down. Some said that Tynan's Spider-kinden allies had betrayed him and, though this would hardly be much of a surprise given the reputation of that race, other reports suggested that the Grand Army of the Aldanrael – or whatever they were called – was still beside the Second in the field, its treacheries undischarged as yet. Some aviators Hanto had overheard were saying instead that Collegium had won the air war, smashed Tynan's pilots over the city. That made halfway sense of Roder's halt, to Hanto. It seemed unlikely that a Collegiate column was about to come marching out of the south to take Roder in the flank, but the skies suddenly playing host to a mob of Beetle-kinden orthopters was entirely more probable.

So, there's a jolly thought, Hanto considered. Perhaps it was jollier than the other rumour, which was that Roder's suddenly arrested progress had been ordered: that the Empress herself had sent one of those new Red Watch types – cockier and far more dangerous than the old secret police of the Rekef had ever been – and just told the entire army to back up and then sit tight. For what reason? *Does the Empress need to explain herself to you, soldier? No? Didn't think so.*

Still, Roder was doing his best with the limited opportunities. They were going to make a fight of it soon enough and, although no doubt the general would have preferred that fight to be closer to Sarn's gates, he was going to be ready for it when it came. Hence Hanto's presence as a mote in the vast green eye of the forest.

Out there to the west the Ant-kinden of Sarn were mustering, no doubt, good soldiers but behind the Empire in artifice, mobility and imagination. Alone, Hanto would have bet two months' wages on the outcome and not sweated much over the chance of losing. Sarn had its allies, however, and here was where they dwelled.

The Mantis-kinden: savages, superstitious and barbaric, but nobody ever said they weren't dangerous. Hanto knew that Tynan's Second had clashed repeatedly with the Mantids of the southern coast, and destroyed swathes of their forest home, tree by tree. Well, here to the north of Roder's Eighth were far more trees and, presumably, far more Mantids – two entire communities of them – invisible beneath that green shade, organized and swift and deadly.

The Pioneers were out in force right now. It was plain that Roder was already bracing himself to send soldiers into that killing tangle of trees to suppress his unseen enemies. Every ragged fragment of information that men like Hanto could bring back would mean Wasp lives saved.

Except it wasn't as easy as that, and Hanto knew why. Most of the other Pioneers didn't. Most of them were Apt, or the Inapt who had fought their heritage so hard that they had learned not to listen to it. Hanto had seen a dozen Mantis holds in the Commonweal but nothing quite like this. He didn't like to think about the word 'evil', but this was no healthy place to be. This was a place that ate Pioneers, a place of more than just killer natives and killer beasts. Roder wanted maps, but Hanto knew in his heart you could not map a place like this any more than you could map the mind of a maniac.

It spoke to him.

When he heard that whispering voice, he wished he had not listened to his mother. He wished he did not believe in magic. It spoke to him and sometimes it spoke a name.

He was a veteran and he had a job to do. No Wasp, but he was a soldier of the Empire even so. He had come here, further than any other Pioneer, seeking signs of Mantis dwellings, of war-musters, of Sarnesh Ants already within the trees. He had ranged far, looking for landmarks and reference points for the cartographers of the Intelligence Corps. By now, he had a feeling that the topography of the forest was twisting and writhing every time he turned his back, like a nest of worms.

He wanted to go back, but he had spotted something on his last pass: something that looked like a building, perhaps. One little shard of intelligence and he could surely return to the Eighth: if he had something to show for himself then he could at least pretend to have done his duty.

The wind-tossed canopy was an exercise in misdirection, so now he descended, a branch at a time. He moved as the tree moved, arrow nocked and ready and his wings shimmering for balance. The forest beneath the branches was eerily quiet.

The trees were densely grown here, roots entangled, swollen trunks fighting each other for space. Hanto's eyes were good enough to cut through the gloom, but still he could see no more than a dozen yards before the forest closed him out.

Everything around him was *too* still, too silent. It was slowly winding the fear up tighter inside him. *Find it, get out,* but easier said than done. He flitted from tree to tree, trying to get his bearings, then hopping back up past the canopy for another look from on high. Back up there, battered by the wind, he felt he was in a different world.

Again there was that glimpse of something. Stone – natural or worked? Either way it would be something for the Empire's maps. He cast himself through the turbulent air towards it, but lost it almost immediately, passing over where he was sure he had seen something, seeing nothing but more of the same.

Cursing, he fell back into that green abyss, plunging past the surface to the stifling silence.

He saw it. For a moment, just as he broke through, there was something there, off between the trees. He saw a mound plated with a carapace of great stones. Did Mantids build like that? Not in the Commonweal, they hadn't. And old, it had looked old and cracked and moss-grown. A fort, perhaps: some ancient Mantis strongpoint. Now *that* was something to go back and tell his superiors.

He let himself drift forwards carefully, keeping an eye out for traps or webs or any movement that was not of the forest itself.

He kept catching glimpses of the place, and then losing it, and he was unhappily aware that the comings and goings of that mound were not particularly accounted for by his own movements or by the placement of the trees. *Magic*. But his superiors would not accept 'magic' as a reason for failure.

The utter stillness all around him was becoming a horror. He could not even hear the wind, that had been so insistent up above.

There: he had it. He froze, seeing it clearly for the first time, and only then realizing that the whisper, the little insidious voice that he had been trying to ignore, had been calling to him all that time, and calling from here.

It had a name, that voice. It called itself *Argastos*.

He saw the place now, that stone-clad barrow, and the sight sent a chill chasing through him, because he would swear this was no fort, no haunt of living men. It was a tomb.

That was it: he'd had enough. He'd report this *thing*, and his superiors would have to be happy with that, because there was no way that Hanto was staying a moment longer.

He turned, wings flurrying, and toothed, raptorial arms plucked him from the air in one swift motion. His last sight was of vast, coolly intelligent eyes and the blades of its mandibles as it brought him towards them.

One

To stare into the forest was to stare into the heart of time.

The darkness between those trees had not changed for centuries. Here had come no revolution, nor busy-handed Apt with their machines. The old ways still held sway in those green depths. The reclusive denizens lived by the bow and the spear, hunting and gathering what the forest gave up to them. Sometimes, in their season, they were hunted in turn by the great beasts they took their name from: Mantis-kinden, fierce and free.

And they fought. They honed their skills from the earliest age by practising against each other and against the world. Although the Apt kinden had shone their bright light across most of the Lowlands, here was a bastion of the old darkness that even the Ant-kinden had considered too costly to conquer. Generations of Sarnesh tacticians had turned their eyes to that brooding presence on their eastern horizon, then shaken their heads and turned away.

The forest itself was nameless, or else had a secret name as all the greatest of the Inapt things had secret names. The only labels the Apt ever recorded belonged to the two Mantis holds that held dominion within the trees: Etheryon to the west, Nethyon to the east.

They held to themselves, mostly, although a steady trickle of young Etheryen had broken tradition enough to take Sarnesh coin in exchange for the use of their skills. More recently they had gone to war, and the first tremor of change had disturbed the leaves of their forest. A conflict not of their own making: a war against the Wasp-kinden, because an Apt threat had finally arisen that would not just shake its head and go away.

If he stared into the trees long enough, Amnon felt that he could feel a faint connection, a path back to the same certainties he had once lived by, which had made him happy to serve, happy to lead, happy to know his place . . . His homeland was a city by a river a thousand years ago, the past held in gentle stasis as the seasons turned, all the sons and daughters of Khanaphes busy at their allotted tasks. He had lived most of his life with no question in his head that could not be answered by, *Because it is so.*

Then the Empire had come, the world he had been born to overwritten in just a pitiful few days: all the certainties crumbling to the touch. He had not missed it, not then. Instead, he had despised the old ways because they had failed his people. He had seen his exile from Khanaphes as a badge of honour.

He wished he could go back, now, but there was nowhere to return to. The Khanaphes that was marked as a protectorate on Imperial maps did not resemble the home of his younger days.

There had been a woman of Collegium, a machine-handed and clever beauty, and, as long as he had her, the past could blow away with the desert wind for all he cared. Praeda Rakespear, her name had been, and he had loved her, and she him. And the Wasps had killed her, and left him marooned in this island of the harsh present with no way back and nowhere to go.

When he stared into the Mantis forest, he almost felt that the dark past those trees harboured was somehow also the past of his youth, and that the bright sun of Khanaphes was what cast those deep shadows. Surely all pasts eventually converged on one another, if you walked far enough back down that river?

But now the drone of a Sarnesh spotter orthopter intruded,

boring into his ears and as impossible to ignore as a mosquito. The distant, certain past was wrenched away. At his back stood the Sarnesh camp – hundreds of those tan-skinned Ant-kinden bustling there, armoured in chainmail with their rectangular shields slung across their backs. They were all of them busy, the logistical weight of keeping an armed force in the field divided precisely across all their shoulders. They cooked, cleaned, sharpened, practised, patrolled, slept, relaxed, raised tents and stood watch, all with the exactness of clockwork, each in touch with the minds of their fellows, as content in their busy Aptitude as Amnon himself had ever felt back in Khanaphes. He envied them.

The Imperial Eighth under General Roder had already bested the Sarnesh once, toppling their fortress at Malkan's Folly and rebuffing their ground forces at the same time. After that, the Wasps had made swift progress until they began to pass south of this forest, where skirmishing raids from the Mantids had brought them to a halt.

Unlike most Ant city-states, Sarn knew the value of allies. Hence this camp at the edge of the forest. Hence Amnon, arrived here from Collegium as the bodyguard of a Beetle diplomat, because nobody there could think of much else to do with him. The Ants and their allies were planning their next move.

'Hey, big man!'

Thus warned, Amnon did not start as a small form dropped down beside him, the blurring wings fading away to nothing as the figure touched the ground.

'You coming back to us any time soon?' the diminutive newcomer asked him. Amnon was indeed a big man: the Fly-kinden barely came up to his waist.

'Back to you?' For a moment Amnon thought he meant something more, some meaning connected with the dark, unrippled past between the trees.

'Only, herself is starting to fret again. All these Mantids about: I don't know why she wanted to come, if she's so weird about them. Or maybe the weird is the why of it.' The Fly cast his eyes over the shadow-hung forest, the haunt of a thousand years of history.

'Spooky, isn't it,' was his verdict.

On the journey up from Collegium Amnon had found the man a troubling travelling companion, his abrasive good cheer matching poorly with Amnon's own thoughts. Troubling, mostly though, because remarks like that last one could still drag a smile onto Amnon's face, whether he wanted it or not. 'You have no heart, Laszlo. You're too Apt.'

'You're just as Apt as me,' the Fly countered. 'Now, seriously, Helma Bartrer is getting that look in her eye again, and there's that Moth-kinden about and, without your sober and overly serious gaze on her, she's likely to do something stupid.'

Amnon grunted, and turned away from the pensive regard of the dark trees. There was a core of lead within him since Praeda had died, and sometimes he felt that he should just cling to it and turn his back on the rest of the world. But Laszlo seemed an antidote to that, and the only way to shut off the little man's irrepressible talking would be to kill him. Or perhaps remind the Fly of his own troubles.

'Any luck?' he asked quietly, and for a moment the question did seem to decant some of his own seriousness into the Fly.

'Not yet, but the Sarnesh skipper hasn't shown yet, and I'm betting she's still with him. Hoping so, anyway.' Laszlo was part of the Collegiate delegation on utterly false pretences, as only Amnon knew. Not that he was a spy, or rather a spy for any party other than Collegium, but he had his own agenda.

They picked their way back into the camp, following a curious order of precedence. The Ants got out of their way smoothly, each tipped off by a dozen pairs of eyes in advance, and finding it simply more efficient to get clear of these clumsy, closed-minded foreigners. Laszlo and Amnon could have run straight at a dense mob of them and not jostled an elbow on the way through.

The Mantids were different. When their paths crossed, Amnon

and Laszlo stopped to let the locals stalk haughtily by. True, the Etheryen were at least somewhat used to outsiders, given Sarn's proximity, but this was their home and to cross them here was to challenge them. The formal alliance between the Inapt and Apt was very new; nobody wanted to test its limits.

They were tall and graceful, and every one of them armed, even the youngest and the oldest who had ventured from the forest. Pale and sharp-featured, most of them looked on all who were not their kin with arch condescension. They were the masters of battle whose steel had once ruled the Lowlands in the name of their Moth-kinden masters. That five centuries of progress had erased that world, beyond their borders, was not hinted at in their expressions.

As Laszlo had observed, Helma Bartrer, Collegiate Assembler and Master of the College, was constantly twitchy. A jumpy look came into her eye every time she caught sight of a Mantis or a Moth. Amnon had thought at first it was fear, curious in a woman who had volunteered herself for this duty. By now he had a sinking feeling that it might instead be academic curiosity, as if Bartrer was forcibly restraining herself from stuffing each Mantis-kinden in a pickling jar for further study. He understood she belonged to the College history faculty, which covered a multitude of sins.

'Ah, aha.' She offered them a vague wave as they approached. 'Good, in the nick of time. I think we're close to getting under way.' She was a broad, dark woman, solidly built as most Beetles were, with her hair drawn back into a bun and wearing formal College robes that somehow remained approximately white despite her living out of a tent. A delicate pair of spectacles sat on the bridge of her nose. Beside her was a man of around the same height, but of a slender build, grey of skin and with eyes of blank white: the ambassador from the Moths of Dorax. He had no name that Amnon had ever heard mentioned, and was dressed more like a scout than a diplomat, wearing a banded leather cuirass under his loose grey robe, and a bandolier of throwing knives over his narrow chest. Helma Bartrer became especially twitchy when Moths were about. If Amnon were to discover her dissecting the man for posterity, he would not be much surprised.

'Is the Sarnesh fellow here, then?' Laszlo asked eagerly,

'The tactician? Just arrived, I think,' Bartrer confirmed. 'And Master . . . tells me that the Nethyen delegates are expected any moment.'

The Moth, whom Bartrer consistently addressed as 'Master . . .', in a pointed attempt at fishing for a name, nodded smoothly.

'He says it's a sign of how grave matters have become that the Nethyen have actually agreed to send someone,' Bartrer went on, 'They're insular even for Mantids.'

'I'll be properly honoured, then,' Laszlo said. 'Look, I've got some official business to sort out for Sten Maker – you mind if I make myself scarce for a moment?'

Bartrer studied him narrowly through the lenses of her spectacles. 'You seem to have a lot of official business that nobody told me about,' she pointed out. 'I *am* the ambassador.'

'Mar'Maker's a busy man, Helma Bartrer,' Laszlo pointed out merrily, and with that he was off and winging on his way.

Bartrer made an undiplomatic grimace, then turned back to the Moth. While Amnon had a good idea why she always sought the man out when she could, why 'Master . . .' stood around for it was less clear. Perhaps, under the man's unflappable exterior, he was frantically trying to navigate an imagined maze of Collegiate etiquette. Perhaps the Moths were as frightened of alienating their allies as was everyone else?

He missed what Bartrer said next, though, because of a commotion starting up to the north of the camp, and because all the Ants around them had abruptly drawn their swords.

Balkus was not having a good time of it.

He was surrounded by his own people, and that was the problem. All those dun-coloured faces he could see were sufficiently like his own to have been sisters and brothers – indeed they *had* once been as close as sisters and brothers. Just like in any family, though, shared blood did not mean that you got on. Whilst most Ant-kinden knuckled down and let the mill of their peers grind all the awkward edges off them, a few found that what such a process would leave behind would no longer be *them*.

You did not abandon a city-state and then come back later. That decision was made once, and never revisited. To become renegade meant never going home.

Balkus liked life simple, and that had mostly involved going to the opposite end of the Lowlands to Sarn and selling his services as a fighter and nailbowman to anyone who had enough coin. Then he had gone into politics.

He hadn't realized that he was doing it, at the time. He had merely signed on with a Helleren crew that had turned out to be run by an agent of Stenwold Maker, the Collegiate spymaster. Then there had been a fight with the Wasps that had killed off several of Balkus's friends, and going along with Maker's plans to scupper the Empire had seemed the right and proper thing to do.

That had led to his becoming a sort of unofficial lieutenant to Maker, which had in turn led, somehow, to Balkus leading the Collegiate detachment at the Battle of Malkan's Folly – the first scrap there, where the Sarnesh and their allies had smashed the Imperial Seventh and won the war, rather than the more recent one where events had gone somewhat the other way.

Leading a group of non-Ants in an Ant-led battle had been hard, but not because of the hostility of his former kinsmen. In the heat of battle, Balkus had lost it. Instead of being the defiant renegade, he had been seamlessly taking mental orders from the Sarnesh tacticians and shouting them out to his Collegiate followers, never stopping to question them. He had become one of the colony again, for all that they said you could never go back. Memory of the experience still woke him up at night in a cold sweat, convinced he was losing himself in a great sea of everyone else.

He had left Maker's service for that reason, gone off with a friend to the new city of Princep Salma, which a rabble of idealistic refugees had been building west of Sarn. He should have known better. He should have gone far, far away.

Of course, he had turned out to be one of the most experienced fighting men that the young city possessed. Before he could really think about matters, he had ended up in charge of the defence of a part-built town with no borders and no real soldiers.

And when word came that the Wasps were coming again, and that the Sarnesh were gathering their allies, Balkus had found himself with a minuscule delegation sent to keep an eye on things. Princep had neither the capability nor the inclination to wage war, even on the Wasps, but Sarn was its shield, closest neighbour and greatest potential threat if things went wrong. It was imperative for Princep to know just what plans and promises were being made.

So here he was again – a big Ant, a head taller than most of his kin – had it been just that, in the end, that had marked him out as somehow wrong? – walking through an invisible sea of their comment and criticism, breathing in ill wishes while exhaling his own profound dislike of his native people. The pressure of them all around him kept him constantly on his guard – against the chance that they might decide that his being here was an insult demanding answer, against that small traitorous part of himself that wanted to give it all up and go home, even though he never could.

His delegation was all of two other people: his heliopter pilot and a Roach-kinden girl who was something approximating an agent of Princep's government, if the place could be said to have one. Her name was Syale, she was no more than twenty, and most of the time Balkus had no idea where she was or what she was doing. He would have worried, except that it turned out Roaches seemed to have some weird understanding with the Mantids. At least, if she was in their company, she was in no danger from anyone else.

Sperra, his friend from Maker's service, had not come, but Balkus reckoned that was mostly because the Sarnesh had tortured her last time she had been a guest of theirs, which tended to stick in the memory.

Balkus's own self-determined mission here was to not get into any trouble or come to anyone's attention, and he had just failed it.

He had been in the wrong place at the wrong time, basically. The Princep trio had set up their own little camp just beyond the outer ring of Sarnesh tents, and he had been crossing between them when he had seen the returning patrol: a dozen Ant-kinden cloaked and surcoated in grey-green over their mail, scouts out keeping watch for intruders. Now it looked as though they had caught someone.

Balkus had drifted closer, despite the immediate angry warnings he heard inside his skull. The prisoners seemed an odd lot to be Wasp spies, that was for sure.

The hammer-blow of recognition came a moment later.

There was a halfbreed woman there – some mangling of Moth and something else – whom he did not know; dressed like an itinerant beggar in a battered old Imperial long-coat, she seemed about as happy with the Sarnesh as Balkus himself was. He took her for old at first, for her hair was streaked with white and her oddly mottled skin and iris-less eyes misled him, but as he neared he saw that she was much younger than he was. A stranger, though – none of his business. The rest of them, however . . .

There was a Beetle girl there, a short, solid daughter of Collegium for all that she looked older than the mere passage of years could account for. Not really the awkward girl he recalled from Helleron and Collegium any more, but a serious-faced woman with enough of her uncle's authority about her that the Ants at her side seemed to be her escort and not her captors. She wore robes, but not Collegiate ones: layered garments of silks in green and black and dark blue.

There was a Spider, too, and it took Balkus a moment longer

to recognize her. She slowed the whole party by walking with an awkward limp, and her face – which he recalled as beautiful and mischievous – had been savaged by a scar running down one side of it, gashing the corner of her mouth and narrowly missing her eye. She was dressed after the Mantis fashion, arming jacket, breeches and boots and a Spider anywhere near this forest as much as promised bloodshed . . .

. . . If the last member of this little pack of spies didn't get them all executed first, of course. Balkus looked upon the man without love, although with a sort of wonder that *here he was again*, the man for whom one master was never enough, and yet somehow always one too many. Turning up now at a conference squarely aimed at exterminating his kind, the Wasp was a strong-framed man of middle years, with a bleak, hard look to him. He wore a breastplate, greaves and bracers of glittering grey chitin over clothes of dark silk – the garb of a Commonweal warrior noble – but Balkus found that nothing could surprise him where Major Thalric of the Rekef was concerned.

Thalric he would happily have left to rot, and the halfbreed was a stranger, but the other two were going to get him into trouble because they were former comrades in arms, and Ants, even renegades, all suffered from the curse of loyalty.

'What's going on, then? What's this?' He used words because he did not trust what thoughts he might reveal to the mindlink.

The voice of their officer was inside his head in an instant – *Nothing of yours* – with a dozen echoes as the thoughts of his men leaked out, in various degrees of hostility.

Balkus put himself squarely in their path, already kicking himself for the move, but life had a way of dropping these sorts of situations on him. 'Listen, I know them.'

That didn't go down quite as he hoped: no change of circumstances for the prisoners, but Balkus himself had become a focus for suspicion. The protection afforded by his status as ambassador abruptly looked vulnerable.

Clear out, if you know what's good for you. They're for the cells and the Wasp is for questioning, the officer sent to him. If you want to come along, you might find yourself part of the show, renegade.

'Balkus?' It was the Beetle girl, Che Maker, now recognizing him after a second look. 'It's all right. They're taking us to the tactician.'

'They're taking him to the torture machines, whatever they've told you.' He pointed at Thalric, almost enjoying the extra ripple of betrayal from the Sarnesh. 'Listen, you.' He jabbed a finger at the officer, aware that he now had the attention of the whole camp. 'I know them, and you don't want to mess with them. This one, she's Stenwold Maker's niece. You've heard of him.'

Abruptly there were at least another score of Ant soldiers all around him, their blades out.

Surrender your weapons, renegade. In covering for these spies you've crossed the line, came the thought of the officer, slightly blurred by all the simmering malice of the others. And, believe me, nobody's going to shed any tears if that rabble at Princep complain.

Balkus's weapon was his nailbow, a solid firepowder-charged repeater, loaded and primed. He had no intention of surrendering it. 'Listen, that's Sten Maker's niece. That Spider girl is his adopted daughter or something. I'm Princep's chief soldier and I came here because of some stuff about allies. Where'd that go all of a sudden?' He was listening out for the thoughts of the Sarnesh command, who surely had more sense than this, but although they were certainly hearing everything second-hand, they took no steps to stop it.

Then the Mantis-kinden was there.

He was a lean, weathered man, with his ragged beard irongrey, dressed in brown leathers and a cuirass of chitin scales, and he had a spear in his hand. His fierce gaze barely admitted to the presence of any of them there save the scarred Spider girl. Balkus had not even thought that complication through. Certainly the Ants were not a trusting breed, especially not in the wake of a military defeat, but the Mantis-kinden out-and-out *hated* Spiders, beyond any reason, and though Balkus knew the girl was half-Mantis by blood, that was just about the single piece of knowledge that would make matters even worse.

Still, the spearman's stare was narrowing to focus, not on her face, but on the badge she wore.

The Ants had gone quiet, watching intently as he levelled his spear towards the woman. 'To wear that badge undeservingly is to die,' he snapped.

'Are you challenging me?' The Spider girl, Tynisa, spoke sideways, her scar tugging at her mouth.

'You claim to have even the right to be challenged, rather than cut down where you stand?' the Mantis demanded.

'Enough,' Che Maker said, not even loudly, and Balkus fully expected nobody to pay her the blindest bit of notice. The Mantis started away from her, though, staring, and the half-dozen other Mantids close by were all staring too, even those surely out of earshot. That fierce regard caught the Ants' attention as well, so that everyone heard her next words.

'As I have told you, and as this man has confirmed, I am Cheerwell Maker of Collegium, and I'm no man's captive. You will not torture the Wasp-kinden, for he is mine and under my protection. You will not duel my sister, for she is mine and I forbid it. You understand me.' There was no question at the end of her words.

The spearman bared his teeth. 'This is not permitted!'

Balkus's immediate assumption was that Che must have said something as she stepped forwards, some word that silenced the man and staggered every Mantis-kinden in sight. Only in the confused mental babble that followed, from the Sarnesh comparing notes, did Balkus realize that no, she had not spoken: she had simply . . . It was as though there had been some sound, some great retort from that one footfall – one that only the Mantids had heard.

There was a flurry of motion from within the camp and the

Moth ambassador, whom Balkus had never seen without an expression of smug self-satisfaction, came pelting out from amidst the Ants, robe flying behind him, white eyes as wide as lamps. 'Who are you . . .?' he got out, before skidding to a halt. The Mantids had backed off, even the spearman: Tynisa was apparently off the menu. All those Inapt eyes were squarely fixed on Che, and Balkus had never seen such expressions on Mantid faces before.

There was an awkward moment as Sarnesh thoughts shuttled back and forth, trying to weave some sense out of it. 'I don't know what you just did,' the Sarnesh officer snapped at last, desperately trying to keep hold of the situation, 'but it won't wash with me.' His voice grew more strained as the hostility of the Mantids seemed to be turning on *him*, now it had been deflected from elsewhere, and the Moth was making some gesture as if to shut him up. 'It'll take more than the word of this renegade to vouch for you.'

'She is Cheerwell Maker,' a fresh voice boomed.

The officer rounded on the intruder to find himself face to face with the entire Collegiate delegation, and face to chest with the huge Beetle warrior who had just spoken.

'This is not your concern.' He was a dogged one, this officer. Balkus had to admire him for that.

'I know her. She is Maker's niece. I know the Wasp, too.' And if the big man's glance at Thalric was less fond, he was still plainly vouching for him.

'*Amnon?*' came Che's voice, more hesitant now, and stripped of its unaccountable power of moments before. 'What are you doing here?'

A change whipped through the Ants, all at once. Even Balkus felt the lash of it. Abruptly they had stepped away from Che's party, no longer guarding four people who were, therefore, no longer prisoners. The collective mind was now focused elsewhere, for a burly Ant-kinden was approaching with a half-dozen others dragged along in his wake. Balkus had never seen him before, but he knew who this man must be. The Sarnesh tactician, Milus, had just arrived.

Report, he gave out, and a concise and ordered account from the officer must have been served directly to his mind and for his consideration only. The tactician's iron-coloured eyes flicked across the newcomers – Che, Tynisa, Thalric and the halfbreed woman – then passed swiftly by Balkus to size up the Collegiates, Amnon in particular. With so much of their social interaction lived within the minds of their fellows, Ant-kinden seldom had the knack of impressing outsiders with the force of their personalities, but Milus had a weight to him, a tangible force of will. In Balkus's experience those who became tacticians were frequently those who tested the limits of public approval, their differences turned into virtues only when they were set above their fellows. That this man had been chosen to oversee the war against the Wasps argued that he was someone to be wary of.

Whatever this is about, it will wait, his thoughts told the Ants flatly, Balkus included. *Keep an eye on them, the Wasp especially, but I myself have seen Maker, and this girl does look a little like him. We have other concerns, though. We Apt must at least seem united.* His gaze swept over them: Balkus from Princep, the Collegiate woman Bartrer, Che Maker and the other newcomers. When he spoke, really spoke, his voice sounded gravelly and rough. 'The Nethyen ambassador is coming and we can get down to business.'

The Sarnesh, who had been quietly industrious ever since they had arrived, now abandoned their tasks, all at once and to a man, assembling instead in ruler-straight ranks facing the forest, wordless and vigilant with swords at their side and snapbows sloping against their shoulders. Their tactician wished to impress, that much was plain. To one side some Mantis-kinden – the locals, and yet less than a tenth of the Sarnesh's number – had formed a loose-knit mob, and Che found her gaze drawn to them. She had known very few of their kind, and none of them well, not even Tynisa's father. Beside the Ants' gleaming perfection, they looked scruffy, old-fashioned, provincial. She knew that they would each make deadly combatants, but how much did that truly count for in the age of the snapbow and the automotive? She herself, who had been robbed of her understanding of those technological wonders, found that she had more than a little sympathy for them.

'You'll stand with our delegation?' Helma Bartrer suggested to her. 'This is a historic moment. The Nethyen don't usually meet with strangers, Master . . . tells me.'

The Moth had kept pace with them, not quite close, yet always in earshot. It was hard to say what his blind-looking eyes were watching, but whenever Che moved, he moved. He had the manner of a man who wanted to ask questions, but whose dignity was getting the better of him.

'We've been on the road a long time,' Tynisa declared. 'And I'll likely be fighting a duel soon enough, whatever Che says. Let's leave politics to the statesmen.'

'We'll watch,' Che decided, and then, relenting, added, 'or I will. If you want to go and rest, then go and rest. I'm sure they can find a place for you here.'

Maure, the halfbreed magician they had brought from the Commonweal, was plainly about to do just that, but then Thalric spoke up: 'Che, it's clear that you're the reason we're still free right now. Let's stay in your shadow, until we know the ground.' His hand squeezed her shoulder, seeking reassurance under the pretence of providing it.

One of the Mantids was heading towards the forest now, a stern-looking woman with a green-brown cloak flowing behind her. Che's party and the Collegiates added a small huddle to one corner of the great Ant formation, close to where Balkus stood alone. Looking from Balkus to Amnon to her own party, Che could only think, *How we have all come up in the world.*

From the forest verge emerged another Mantis-kinden woman, a lean creature in chitin armour that was chased with silver. She met with her opposite number, and the two stared at one another for a long, slow moment, as though they shared some private linking of minds that even Ants were not privy to. There were a few words exchanged, but too low to carry. The Etheryen woman nodded once, curtly, as if agreeing some single point of business.

The blades flashed and clashed almost instantly. Of all the watchers, perhaps only Che and her fellows would admit that neither had actually bothered with anything so prosaic as *drawing* a sword – the rapiers had been in their hands in the moment of lunging, and a swift patter of a dozen scraping blows passed before the Ants even understood what was going on. She could guess at their shared question: *Is this a Mantis thing?* And it was, of course it was, but it was not done for mere play.

The Moth understood too. He was abruptly running forwards, arms out. 'No! Servants of the Green! I forbid it!' His voice was surprisingly loud and clear for such a slight-framed man.

In that moment the newcomer, the Nethyen woman, had won. Che had not followed the interchange of strikes but suddenly the Etheryen delegate was falling back, her throat opened by the other woman's rapier, and the Moth stumbled to a halt within inches of the sword's bloodied point.

'What have you done?' he demanded, shaken out of his composure before so many witnesses.

The Nethyen woman simply stared at him, undaunted, her sword level with his breast as though giving him the chance to take up the gauntlet. Then she turned, the blade vanished from her hands, as though dismissing the entire martial assembly from her mind. She stepped back into the forest, and was gone.

Two

Two tendays before.

Overlooking Collegium, and overlooking the sea, stood the old house on the cliffs.

It had been built two generations before as a retreat by a clique of philosophers, but its isolated location and the windswept nature of the surrounds had led to its abandonment a decade or so later, since when it had become the haunt of odd recluses, fugitives and perhaps spies. For the space of a few years, it had served as a wayhouse catering to just those sorts, and a few from Collegium who simply wished to get away from the crowd.

Some months ago, the Assembly had gifted the place to a new trading franchise, the Tidenfree Cartel, and placed a lamp atop its single tower. If ships' captains had complained that the new lighthouse served no useful purpose, well, they were seldom listened to in the Assembly. And those who muttered that sometimes the lamp blinked and flashed, as if sending out messages across the sea . . . well, seafarers were always telling tales.

Now Stenwold himself stood in the tower room below the lamp and stared out at the waves, the unquiet sea showing blue and grey in turns, cresting beneath a changing wind. He had taken refuge here many times since its most recent change of ownership. The Tidenfree Cartel were his creatures, in as much as they were anyone's, and he was their patron, their supporter, their conspirator in the great secret. Only he and Jodry Drillen, Speaker for the Assembly, knew that those miraculous metals and machine parts that the *Tidenfree* crew imported to the city did not come from some obscure city of Spiderlands artificers, as the cover story went, but instead from beneath the sea itself.

'They've cleared this place out good, now, haven't they?' A deep voice came from behind him. It was Tomasso, chief merchant of the Tidenfree Cartel and master of its single ship, of the same name. And a former pirate, of course, although to see him now, dressed respectably like a Collegiate citizen and wooed by a dozen mercantile concerns, one would never have known it. He was a burly Fly-kinden with a dark beard and a mischievous look to him, for all that he was close to Stenwold's age. His eyes roamed the walls, finding only absences there, for his crew had already passed through the lighthouse and stripped it of everything when the Wasps had got close to the city.

'The factora in the city is acceptable?' Stenwold asked him.

'Will do nicely until we chase the Jaspers away,' Tomasso agreed. 'This place started looking a bit exposed when their lads from the Second began setting up.' He grimaced. 'I'm no engineer, but you may have to pull the old place down. Gives too much of a vantage over the city.'

'Not that the Imperial artillery needs that, nowadays, but yes, it's been thought of. We've engines in the city that have calculated the range.' Stenwold was still staring out to sea as though trying to divine the future from the surging waves. 'She knows . . .?'

'. . . Not to come here,' Tomasso finished for him. 'Or anywhere, right now. I hear Despard's just back from down there, probably has letters for you even. But they know the score, the Sea-kinden. If the Wasps were coming by boat, your lad Aradocles would be sending up his monsters by the dozen, but I reckon the Spiders haven't forgotten the last time.'

Stenwold nodded. The Spider-kinden – many of whom were

now marching alongside the Wasp Second Army – had tried to send a fleet against Collegium, but Stenwold and Tomasso's newfound friends beneath the waves had dissuaded them. The tentative, secretive arrangements put in place between land and sea that rested so much on Tomasso and his opposite number below had been bearing fruit and working better than anyone had anticipated. If the Wasps had not revived the war, a whole new age of enlightenment might be dawning. Instead of which, Stenwold's city was scarred with bomb craters, his people turned into soldiers, and three dozen military decisions were currently prowling about the streets, waiting for him to return and put them out of their misery. Simply to avoid them, he had come out here, perhaps for the last time, to stare at the sea.

Paladrya, her name was. Every old man needed some romance in his life, and Stenwold's was separated from him by a barrier neither of them could cross for long. The land was too harsh and hostile for her, the sea a place of nightmares for him. Even their letters were cast in foreign alphabets.

'I hear the Wasp lads are keeping their distance, since you took the air from them,' Tomasso noted. As a Fly-kinden, control of the air was something he thoroughly approved of, and the Collegiate orthopters were currently the undisputed masters of the skies above the city.

'Still,' Stenwold observed, 'they're not going away.' At last he dragged his eyes away from the waves. 'What will you do, if it comes to that?'

Tomasso shrugged easily. 'The sea's an open road. We'll ship out when the time comes, and no hard feelings. You're welcome to take a berth with us. We've space for you.' Even as Stenwold opened his mouth, the Fly held his hands up. 'I know, I know, your place is here – noble War Master and all that. I'm just saying, though. The crew wouldn't begrudge the room if your Assembly decided to give you a kick.'

'It's kind of them,' Stenwold allowed, and then a scuffle sounded from somewhere below and a younger Fly burst into the room.

'Mar'Maker, there you are!'

'Laszlo,' Stenwold acknowledged him, abruptly tense. 'What news?'

'Oh, they need you right now back in the city, Mar'Maker. It's not the Wasps but, from the look on half the faces there, it might as well be.'

Stenwold nodded heavily, knowing immediately who the Fly meant. 'They've made good time then, but Ants always could march.'

'There's an automotive waiting to get you to the city, and I really think you should be there before this mob arrives. Otherwise someone's going to do something stupid.'

'Almost certainly right,' Stenwold agreed, and then he was clumping down the stairs, with Laszlo buzzing at his shoulder.

At the west wall of Collegium, Jodry Drillen watched the approaching force, and all around him were the city's Merchant Company soldiers, very pointedly not doing anything about it but plainly wishing that they could.

'Brings back memories,' someone could be heard to say, even as Stenwold stomped his way up the steps to the summit of the wall.

'Where's their representative?' he demanded.

Jodry turned and inclined his head to indicate a silent, dark figure standing at the battlements, given a wide berth by the locals.

'I hope you're sure of what you're doing, is all.' The Speaker for the Assembly was still a fat man, but the stresses of recent events had made all that weight hang on him as though it was sloughing off, from the pouchy bags under his eyes to the way his clothes all seemed ill-fitting. He and Stenwold had clashed a few times during the Wasps' last offensive, but now they were friends again, just about.

Stenwold made his way along the parapet to the Ant that stood alone there: short, ebony-skinned, and armoured against the world in a mail hauberk.

'Termes,' he named him, and the Ant nodded.

'War Master.'

Together they looked out at the Vekken army.

The last time a force from that Ant city had come to Collegium, it had been for conquest, and the time before that, as well. The Ants had been the city's enemies for most of Stenwold's life, certainly far longer than the Wasps had. It was a matter of scale, though. Vek was only one city, the Empire was many. Stenwold had worked extremely hard to bring the Vekken to a point where they might consider their Beetle neighbours as something other than a threat or a prize. He had worked even harder to convince his own people that such a change of heart in their old foes was even possible. Now here were the fruits.

'How many?' he asked.

'Eight hundred,' Termes told him. 'That was thought reasonable.'

Not enough for an invasion, but enough to be useful. The Vekken had considered their gesture seriously. They had no love for the Wasps and they knew that, if Collegium fell, the Empire would be outside their gates soon enough.

'They'll camp . . .?'

'Outside the city,' Termes confirmed. He did not say, *As we did last time*, but Stenwold almost heard the echo of the words.

'There are boats from Tsen on their way, I'm told.'

'We are aware of that.' Termes's face revealed nothing. Tsen was another Ant city, further west still, and no friend of Vek's save that both cities now found themselves friends of Collegium. 'We suggest they stay on the water. We will keep to the land.'

'It might be for the best.' Stenwold nodded and returned to Jodry's side. 'We'll need them, if the worst comes to the worst,' he pointed out, watching the immaculately disciplined Ants break their column and begin to pitch camp tactfully outside artillery range. But, then, the Vekken would have no fond memories of the effectiveness of Collegiate artillery.

'We've Sarnesh in the city also,' Jodry informed him. 'I thought it best not to invite them up onto the wall. More Ants around than we know what to do with, these days.'

'A messenger?'

'More than that – a full-blown tactician, as I understand it. I think our northern neighbours want to make a move. After this business at Malkan's Folly, I think the Sarnesh are starting to hate the Wasps more even than you do, Sten.'

There were still plenty of soldiers left on the walls as Jodry and Stenwold descended. They had not been posted there, and each would have given some humdrum excuse for his presence, but they were keeping an eye on the Vekken, and no mistake. It took no great leap of imagination to envisage those enemies of recent memory being in league with the Wasps, forming part of some grand betrayal. Stenwold could only hope that he had done his work well enough or, at worst, that the Vekken also hated the Wasps more than they hated their traditional foes.

The customary place to meet with foreign dignitaries was the Amphiophos, of course, but where those hallowed halls of white stone had once stood was now just one of the city's many new scars, bombarded by the Imperial air force into a warren of rubble and broken walls. Instead, a lecture hall at the College served, and it was there that Stenwold and Jodry, and a handful of other Beetle-kinden who had become Collegium's de facto high command, met with Milus of Sarn.

The Sarnesh tactician looked close to Stenwold's own years, belonging to that generation that, on all sides, was determining the course of the war. He had a small staff with him: three close-featured Ants of his own city and a pale Fly-kinden girl with gleaming red hair.

'You're making a mistake, of course,' Milus told the Beetles, even as they came in through the door.

'You mean the Vekken?' Stenwold looked him straight in the eye.

'I do, and you'll regret it in time. For now . . . who knows? The times are certainly unprecedented.' He made a grand gesture with his hands, just one shade from being spontaneous. Ants had little use for body language or expressions amongst themselves, which made them both hard to read and hard to relate to, but Milus had obviously learned a stock of conversational tools for occasions such as this. The fact that he was not making more capital out of the Vekken arrival was also telling. Here was a new sort of Sarnesh leader.

'Tactician,' Jodry addressed him, 'you have us here, the best of us. I assume you don't want the full Assembly convened? It's been a while since we last did that, and we're short of some-where to put them. It's just the War Council making most of the key decisions at the moment.'

Milus nodded approvingly. 'I have official business to discuss but, before that, I want to give you my personal congratulations. You'll be well aware that, while my people value our friends in Collegium for many reasons, your martial prowess has never been one of them. Yet you've scored more victories against the Empire than we have, of late, and I hear their Second Army is still hiding from your orthopters. Well done. Sarn takes great heart from your successes.' It was a prepared speech, but it was not what one expected, from Ant-kinden, and the Collegiates exchanged glances, reconsidering.

'You're kind,' Jodry spoke for them. 'We're left in the same position as you, though, with an army on our doorstep that is just not attacking *yet*. Do we take it that your presence here indicates a shift in Sarnesh tactics?'

'We're gathering our forces and we'll strike soon. Why the Eighth is just sitting there at the wrong end of the Nethyon, we don't know, but we intend to throw everything we have at them – our soldiers, our machines, our allies and all the tricks we can come up with,' Milus announced, raising a hand to forestall any comment. 'And I realize that you will not be able to lend substan-tial aid to us, just as we could not aid you. We each have our own worries, right now. However, I invite you to send some of your people to our councils, so that at least you know what we intend.'

'You will be directing this assault yourself, Tactician?' Stenwold asked him.

'I will.'

'You did not need to come in person simply to invite us to your conference.'

Milus smiled, with that same slight edge of formality. 'But I did to offer my plaudits, War Master. Some things can only be said in one's own voice.'

'So, aren't we the fast mover?'

The red-haired Fly-kinden woman froze in the midst of unpacking her satchel, kneeling on the bed the Collegiates had found for her at the College. For a second she was motionless, and Laszlo recognized that coiled-spring quality to her, ready for betrayal, for fight or flight.

Then she glanced up at the window where he was crouching. 'If the Sarnesh were to come in now, they'd shoot you. I don't care what you are in Collegium, to the Sarnesh an intruder's still an intruder.'

He swung his legs in and perched on the window sill. 'Te Liss,' he named her. 'Otherwise Lissart, or is there another name for you now?'

For a moment she just stared at him, acknowledging no past acquaintance, a hair's breadth away from violence – and he knew full well how dangerous she was. Then the very corner of her mouth twitched, and she said, 'Alisse, special adviser to Tactician Milus on matters of the Inapt. On account of how he doesn't trust Moths, and Mantids are rotten advisers. It's a long story.'

'It can't be that long. We were with the army only a month ago,' Laszlo pointed out. 'You must have already had a fallback in Sarn planned out somehow. But you never said.' He was aware how he was drinking her in but, then, she spent so little time staying in one place, acting civilly or even being trustworthy, that he wanted to make the most of her.

'I have lots of fallbacks. It's a spy thing. Stop staring at me

32

like that.' She was trying to be flippant, and Laszlo had certainly planned to appear cool and witty and blithely unconcerned. After she left him, with the Collegiate army just about to clash with the Wasp Second, he had gone a long way towards convincing himself that this little infatuation of his was done with. There had been work to do, after all, and he was not the kind of fool to waste time mooning over some girl. Especially when that girl had been a Wasp agent when he first met her, and something of a madwoman – and, beyond all of that, not a true Fly at all but someone who could shoot *fire* out of her *hands*. Best left well alone, best forgotten. He had worked hard to tell himself that.

And then, just today, she had come trotting back into his life, as bold as the sun, at the heels of Tactician Milus as though she had every reason to be attached to the Sarnesh command staff. And something within him, some dam, had cracked and now he was here and staring at her.

She stood carefully, and he saw in that movement the last traces of the wound she had taken in Solarno, the one that had severed her from Wasp service. 'Oh, Laszlo, don't be such a fool. The world turns, surely you know that?'

'Some of us are quick enough to keep up with it. And here you are.' Unable to read her expression, he pressed on. 'I killed the Wasp that was hunting you – their spy woman. And I looked for you, I did. Don't think you could just slip out of my mind. You're not as sneaky as all that. And here you are. And . . . with *Sarn*? Seriously?'

'Why not Sarn, when they pay their spies as well as anyone else?'

He thought there was a minute hesitation in there somewhere, and his stomach sank because abruptly he was convinced that simply being on the Ants' payroll was far too simple a web for her.

'And you're off back to Sarn with their tactician,' he prompted, feeling like a real spy for once, as he probed the edges of her infidelity.

'Or wherever Milus chooses. Or wherever I do, if I tire of him.'

Laszlo had seen Milus perform for the Collegiates, as smooth and dangerous as any Spider noble. 'He's a good man to tie your fortunes to, is he?'

'I'm not one to be tied, Laszlo . . .' Some mockery died on her lips. 'You've been thinking of me, truly?'

'Oh, well, sometimes. Once or twice when I wasn't busy.'

He thought she would come to him then – but a moment later he thought she would back away and be gone, feeling a cage closing about her. Then she found her equilibrium, and he had a glimpse of some inner layer of her – perhaps still not the true woman beneath, but something more closely overlying it than the face she showed the world most of the time. 'It won't work, Laszlo.'

'Try me.'

'I'm leaving with the Sarnesh.'

'You're off for some top-secret conference with the Mantis-kinden, which I've just so happened to get myself invited to as part of the Collegiate delegation.'

'Oh, really?' She folded her arms, but that unguarded look remained, of a woman caught between fight and flight, and not sure what to do about him. 'And, once again, you've no idea what you're getting into – the man who went to play spy in Solarno and used his real name, for the world's sake!'

'And got out of there with you after everything went wrong!' he reminded her.

'I recall getting out of there quite well enough, and being fool enough to drag you with me,' she scoffed. Her words wanted conviction, for she had been badly injured at the time. The plan had been hers, but he had carried it out. 'Go away, Laszlo.' The words were spoken fondly, but they still stung. 'I've made a living from moving on. The past's a thing to put behind you.'

And he was still perched at her window, despite that. 'Give me something, Liss,' he asked.

She waved a dismissive hand, and he saw her start to turn away, and yet not quite finish the movement, pulled back to face him as though drawn by a hook.

'You are a fine fool,' she told him. 'You scare me.' But at last she approached the window, until she stood within arm's reach of him. 'I don't worry about people. I don't care about people. That's not what I do. Don't try to change me. I've killed men for less.' But there was no sense of threat about her, and that look was still on her face, the masks held at bay for this one extended moment.

'I'll see you in Mantis-land,' he told her.

'You . . .' she began, putting her hands on his shoulders. Then there was a rattling at the door and she gave him a sudden shove, pitching him backwards and away, his wings catching him a storey further down.

He was grinning, though, as he flew off. Now he really would have to talk his way onto the Collegiate delegation, and all the while without anyone guessing that he had his own motives. Time to call on his old friend Stenwold Maker.

Laszlo skimmed off across the face of the College, wondering where Stenwold might have got to.

Three

The mid-morning calm was interrupted by the hammering of engines from nearby, while the ragged tree cover shook under the beating of wings as a dozen Spearflight orthopters scrambled into the air, clawing for height. The curved-bodied machines roared overhead, their wings a blur, rotary piercers already spinning up. A handful of the Light Airborne took wing after them, but only as observers, not as fighters. No general nor artificer had yet found any field of combat in which flying man and flying machine could realistically oppose one another.

General Tynan was not going to be that man, he knew. That aspect of warcraft had already moved beyond his experience. He did not have enough knowledge of the science or specifications of those machines to plan an air war.

Even he, though, knew that the Spearflights hurriedly flown to him from back home were yesterday's models, and no match for the Collegiate Stormreaders that would even now be speeding through the skies towards his forces. His Second Army had endured daily raids for a month now, and his Spearflights had done little but slow the enemy down. What sent the Beetle pilots home was not the terrible force of the Imperial Air Corps, but the simple fact that the Stormreaders had not been designed with ground attacks in mind, and they soon ran out of munitions.

The irony was that the last time he had been out this way,

Tynan had done his best to strip the place of any real cover. Only the coveted jewel that was Collegium had hauled him away before he had finished the job. He had not realized that he himself would need to hide here before the war was done. This was the Felyal, a former Mantis hold and thorn in the side of every Imperial advance up this coast. Tynan had beaten them twice, and had finally ousted them entirely from their forest haunts. Now a quarter of his Second Army was holed up in what dubious cover the forest could provide, with the remainder spread out in camps over several square miles, to deny the Stormreaders a satisfactory target. The forest itself hid the precise location of Tynan's surviving artillery, his paltry air defences, his supplies and the Sentinel automotives, although those last were probably sufficiently armoured to survive a direct bombing.

He had watchers out between here and Collegium, and if a large ground force marched out to attack, he was betting his life that he could regroup before they reached him. Thus far the Beetles had not tried it. Even though they had retained command of the skies, he had given their forces a bloody enough nose in the accompanying land battle that they were wary of another clash. Instead, their orthopters, smug and inviolate, coursed over his scattered army at any time of the day or night, trailing bombs and making his soldiers endure lives of constant uncertainty and fear.

Such fear was a weapon of war, he knew. He himself had deployed it against the people of Collegium, and there was a certain philosophical interest in being the recipient, now. *Go away*, the Collegiates were shouting at him, by means of their constant buzzing attacks. *Leave our lands. Go away.* His orders were to await resupply and then press on; despite the harrowing bombardment, the Second had no intention of retreating. They were the renowned Gears, and it was galling enough that they had been stopped in their tracks.

He heard the solid crump of the first bomb striking, not too far away. The Stormreaders were poor bombers, without the dedicated design needed to be accurate against ground targets, but they got lucky, and he had hundreds of dead to prove it. A moment later, one of the Collegiate machines passed swiftly overhead, and Tynan held himself still, waiting to see if this would be the day his own luck ran out. A second later, it was veering off after one of the Spearflights, which would do its best to lead the enemy on a dance all around the sky until it was shot down, or until the Collegiate broke off to go home or find another target.

Another flying machine passed overhead, this one even slower than the Spearflights: an antiquated four-winged orthopter with a broad, flat hull. It thundered low over the trees, spewing so much smoke that Tynan wondered if it had already been hit. This would be one of the machines found by his Spider-kinden allies, who had no air force of their own save for mercenary aviators. Like the Spearflights, the ragbag of machines the Spiders had come up with were doing nothing but delaying the inevitable.

An army under attack which cannot fight back is a miserable thing, and being on the sharp end of a technology gap for once was a bitter reversal. The soldiers of the Second were finding their morale eroded day by day. So far there had been no desertions, unless those had been covered up as deaths, but Tynan was expecting them. Even as this attack started he had been going through his sergeants' assessments of their subordinates' will to endure. There was plenty of angry talk amongst the rank and file, and Tynan could not blame them. They had done their duty, and this was none of their fault.

A bomb landed close to the glade in which he had been working, and he edged further under the cover of the trees – as though that would help should the Collegiates strike lucky. Across their widely separated camps, all his soldiers would be crouching under whatever defences they could find or dig out, and hoping that today was not their final day.

'General!' he heard, and he called out his location – a necessary risk, since the army still needed to communicate with itself. He, above all, must be findable, despite the threat of assassination that the Beetles had not quite got round to resorting to yet.

The messenger, half-running and half-flying, skidded to a halt before him. 'General, the supply flight's incoming.'

Tynan went cold, because his run of bad days had just got much worse. The Second Army was being supplied via the new Spider-kinden holdings in Tark and Kes, but the Spiders refused to use sea-power since their fleet had somehow been turned back from Collegium before. With that approach barred, and short of building a rail line from scratch, the only way to get sufficient food and materials to the beleaguered Second was by airship.

They had staggered the deliveries and mostly made them at night, playing a lethal guessing game with the Collegiates. The enemy knew full well that their orthopters would easily destroy the slow-moving airships, because neither Tynan's own fliers nor any escort the Spiders could put together had any chance of stopping them.

He stood there helplessly, a general without a plan, without any means of communicating with his army. 'Our machines—?'

'They're all moving to screen the airships, sir,' the messenger confirmed.

But that won't be enough. Now the Collegiates have smelt blood, they won't rest until they bring the ships down.

'Tell them . . .' His mind worked wildly. 'Get the fastest Fly-kinden we have – ours or the Spiders' – get them up to those airships. They need to put down now, I don't care how far off. We need those supplies safely on the ground. That way we can salvage something.' It was a wretched sort of a plan, but he had been forced to spin it from nothing,.

The messenger was off without even offering a salute, well aware of the urgency of his job.

'I want a detachment ready to get to the landing site!' Tynan snapped at the officers around him, very nearly saying *crash site*. 'Automotives, haulers, plenty of men ready to carry loads. Start moving now.' And all the while, in the back of his mind, *Too late, too late*.

'Get me . . .' But what he really wanted to say was, *Get me somewhere I can see what's going on.* He might exercise only a pitiful influence on the conflict, but it was his responsibility to watch it happening.

Quickly he made his way through the forest to the nearest tower: one of the makeshift wooden constructions engineered from sections of the travelling fort his men had brought with them, rising barely above tree level and dressed with deadwood to make it less of a visible target. He let his wings drag him up there despite the weight of his armour, though he felt every one of his nigh-on fifty years as he reached the top. The Fly-kinden lookout saluted briskly, making room as half of Tynan's body-guards made their laborious way up as well.

'Send word to the – the Spider colonel,' he ordered the Fly. He had almost referred to the woman by name, which always disconcerted his soldiers. 'Have her get ready any automotives she can. Tell her we're going to retrieve what we can from the airships.'

The Fly was off instantly, wings ablur.

Tynan looked out: the airships were plainly visible as little round shapes in the sky, approaching fast with a following wind and growing larger even as he watched. How much more obvious must they be to the Collegiate pilots whose eyes were trained to scan the sky, and everything in it?

Overhead, the aerial battle was moving away, heading east now towards the approaching supply ships. *At least we get spared a pummelling,* Tynan considered grimly. Suddenly the enemy had better things to do than scatter bombs randomly in the hope of killing Wasp soldiers.

Perhaps, after this, I can talk Mycella into sending our supplies by sea, although I suppose sea-ships would be just as vulnerable as airships. Mycella of the Aldanrael was rightly the joint commander of the Collegium campaign. Labelling her as a colonel had been the best way to keep Tynan's own people in line, though, for they had been trained rigorously to observe a rigid command structure: general to colonel to major in command, captains and lieutenants in the middle, sergeants and regular solders to fight and work and complain. An army had only one general. Two heads could not govern the same body, every Wasp knew.

Tynan knew better now, He had been initially surprised at how easy the Spider Arista was to work with. Then he had got to know her better, and to understand that she had been stripped of a great deal of her pomp and pride as a result of the failed armada attack on Collegium. After that, he had come to know her altogether too well by most standards. No doubt his intelligence officer, Colonel Cherten, had sent a few interesting reports back home, but no reprimand had come back to Tynan yet.

Still, amongst the Wasps she was a colonel and he supposed that it was a high honour: unprecedented for a woman, a non-Wasp and not even an Imperial citizen. He also suspected that she privately found this obsession with assigning ranks and titles deeply amusing.

The circular silhouettes presented by the airships against the sky began lengthening as they turned. Perhaps they had some broadsides of artillery ready to deal out, but in truth the Collegiate Stormreaders would be able to skip aside from anything the lumbering dirigibles might throw at them. Impatiently, Tynan flicked out his telescope and tried to make sense of what was going on.

Spying on an air battle was harder than the engineers made out. Tynan's circle of view wheeled constantly across the sky, catching the little insect shapes of the orthopters as they spun and danced against each other, the new way to fight a war that he was excluded from. The best he could gather was that his own side was putting up a spirited defence of their airships. His shaky viewpoint managed brief images of the Spearflights and the Spiders' motley collection of fliers throwing themselves against the nimble Stormreaders, clashing with them, loosing their weapons, executing turns that were too wide, too slow. He caught sight of one Spearflight in the very moment of its dissolution, falling away to the summons of the distant ground.

The airships were parting company, diverging enough to buy a few of them time to close another mile with the Second, perhaps. His own Fly messenger, be he ever so swift, would still be far from delivering Tynan's orders – he could not possibly have outstripped the orthopters in their chase towards the supply ships. *And I should have some small, fleet flying machine ready for that sort of messenger work – the old ways aren't good enough any more.*

Grinding his teeth with the impotent frustration of it, he wrestled with the telescope, desperate to see the end, no matter how disastrous.

He was rewarded by spotting the swift, hunched shape of a Stormreader go flitting across his view, another craft in hot pursuit, the two of them cornering agilely in the air and slipping out of his vision almost instantly, leaving his mind to interpret that brief glimpse. *What have I just seen?*

The aerial contest remained maddeningly opaque, his lens continually finding handfuls of empty sky wherever he took it. Then he found one of the airships – the only reference point that vast world had to offer – and was able to watch the swift darting of the orthopters all about it as its fate was decided.

He watched the Stormreaders dive in, bringing themselves into line to attack the gondola itself; and the defending fliers rise to meet them.

There was a moment of utter clarity, in which the hull shapes and wing patterns unshelled their secrets to him, as if he had been born an engineer, and he shouted out in a bark of triumph so violent that his bodyguards feared he had been shot.

After he had reassured them, he tried to focus again, but by that time the aerial tide had turned. The Stormreaders were already speeding off for home: not because they feared the fray – he had more than enough evidence of their fanatical tenacity when it was called for – but because Collegium would need to know that the Second Army had recovered some fragment of its air power.

Defending the airships had been a flight of the new Farsphex models that had come close to winning the air war once before. Tynan had no illusions that the fight was decided, but his army could at least put up a fight in the air. They were back in the war.

After the airships had set down safely, to the general enthusiasm of the Second Army, the flight of Farsphex made their landing – long, elegant machines, larger than the Spearflights and yet more agile in the air, representing a whole different generation of flying machine. Their four wings could be fixed for long-distance flight, they were designed to make use of the Empire's new and efficient mineral fuel and they were equally ready to duel in the air or to bombard a city.

Tynan saw only a dozen of them. The Stormreaders could probably have destroyed the lot, with losses, had they kept at it. The Collegiates valued knowledge over bloodshed, though, and Tynan suspected that they were right to do so.

Where are the rest? he asked himself, but he had a feeling this was all he was getting for now. No great strikes against the enemy, then. Perhaps just enough, with the Spearflights and the rest, to make taking to the skies over the Second costly for the Collegiate pilots.

'There will be new officers,' he told his staff. 'Some from the Air Corps at the least. Bring them to my tent. I want to know what's going on.'

The last batch of pilots he had worked with had proven a law unto themselves, clannish and close-mouthed, but of course he knew the reason for that now, although it had taken him a while to get his intelligence officer to reveal it.

The Empire keeping secrets from its own generals, but at least that's nothing new.

His tent, nothing grander than those of his subordinates since the Second's camp had been hit by the first Collegiate bombing, was a cramped place in which to hold a command conference, but Tynan wanted his own slice of secrecy this time. He felt a keen need to get to grips with this changing war before his soldiers were allowed time to speculate about it. *Old, I know – and getting older by the second, the way this war's going.* The future of the Empire was in the hands of cleverer men than he: artificers, pilots, diplomats, all innovating, changing the rules of his profession. Some days he felt surprised that the Empress had not replaced him.

He thought of sending for Mycella. Relations between her people and the Wasps had been fractious these last tendays, the enforced waiting and the bombing leading to much blame being cast about. Wasp soldiers were always ready to hold their allies of lesser kinden responsible when things went wrong. Usually, in Tynan's experience, they were right to do so, but in this case the assistance of the Spiders had proved invaluable in espionage and strategy, as well as in the actual fighting. Still, there had been skirmishes and brawls, and his sergeants were stretched to their limit in keeping discipline – those of them who were not themselves nursing a resentment against the Spider-kinden.

Having Mycella alongside him when he met the new arrivals would send a strong message of unity, but in the end he shied away from it. One never knew, after all, what orders might be coming from home. Instead he summoned Colonel Cherten of Army Intelligence, just in case he needed the man's sidelong perspective.

The two men who came to see Tynan and Cherten first were not pilots, nor even Wasps. In the lead was a bold little Fly-kinden man with a major's badge, wearing an outdoorsman's hard-wearing leathers with a striped tabard thrown over them. Studying him, Tynan would have taken him for an officer of scouts.

'Major Oski.' The salute was haphazard, but at least it was there. 'Engineers, and come with some fresh artillery for you.' He jerked a thumb at the larger man standing behind him. Tynan saw a stocky Bee-kinden, older than Oski, younger than Tynan himself, dark-skinned and flat-faced but with none of the sullen slave mindset that he was used to seeing in Bees. He wore a uniform of halved black and gold, but with an engineer's insignia at the chest.

'Captain-Auxillian Ernain,' Oski named him. 'He's my second.' He waited to see if Tynan would make something of that, because an Auxillian engineer holding that rank was a fair-sized stone likely to cause ripples.

'As long as he knows what he's doing,' Tynan remarked, because for him it was competence that was the paramount military virtue.

'That he does, sir. I've orders for you, also.' The little man handed over a sealed package. 'How do you like our entrance, by the way?' He seemed very pleased with himself.

'You must have been very sure of your escort, Major,' Tynan noted, breaking the seal. 'We were all set to pick over your corpses, since the Air Corps has failed me before.' He fixed the small major with a scowl before breaking the seal.

The orders were unambiguous: more space was devoted to the stamps, codes and signatures of authenticity than to the Empress's will.

'We're to march,' Tynan announced, his eyes seeking out Oski's. 'What the pits am I supposed to do about their air power, Major? I can assure you, unless those Farsphex have some new sky-clearing secret weapon, they'll not win the skies over Collegium. Perhaps Capitas underestimates just how tenacious the Beetles are, land or air.'

'I'm just artillery, sir,' Oski said with an easy shrug, an engineer passing up on another man's problem. 'I've been knocking walls down since the Twelve-year War and I'm looking forward to Collegium getting within greatshotter range.'

'So was your predecessor,' Tynan warned him. 'And the fact of your being here should tell you how *that* went. How many . . .' He stopped then, because a new voice was addressing his guards outside.

'Inside, now,' he snapped, and his new pilot officer ducked into the tent, shouldering Ernain the Bee aside.

Tynan registered the captain's insignia and the pilot's chitin helm and goggles dangling from the belt. In truth, he should have been ready for the rest of it, but still required a moment to recover his balance before he acknowledged the salute.

'Captain Bergild reporting for duty, sir,' said the Air Corps officer, a Wasp-kinden woman aged no more than twenty. But, of course, the older pilots had mostly died over Collegium in trying to break the Beetles' air defences. The supply of new pilots ready for combat was limited, and the Empire could not stand on ceremony when throwing them into the fray. But of course . . .

Of course the new pilots, that insular elite, were those possessing the Art that Ant-kinden took for granted, but which Wasps developed so rarely. They could speak mind to mind, these pilots, and that was the secret of their skill every bit as much as their improved machines and training. The mindlinking Art was hard to find, these days, after generations of it being rooted out. Anyone who possessed it – no matter who they were and despite centuries of Wasp traditions – was required to fly. There had been women in the last batch, and one of them had given her life trying to defend the Second when the Stormreaders came.

The newcomer was staring at him almost defiantly, and he guessed that she had endured her share of hostility in getting where she was and that, to be made leader of pilots over Wasp men, she must be very good at her job.

'Sir,' she repeated, waiting for his response, and he finally managed to remember his maxim – *competence above all* – and demanded of her, 'Where's the rest of you? What can I do with this handful, now that I've been ordered forwards?' A general berating a junior officer, nothing more.

'Not in my orders, sir. I'm here to provide you with air defence as you march. More Farsphex are on the way, but.' Her inflection closed the sentence firmly on that word.

'But?' Tynan pressed.

She exchanged a glance with Major Oski: this was something they had obviously discussed previously. 'Rumour, sir.'

Tynan's heavy gaze swung from face to face: the Bee, the woman, the little man who probably held the highest rank a Fly had ever attained in the Imperial army – assembled here as though someone had wanted to rub his nose in the changing times. 'Someone say something,' he growled.

'Rumour, sir,' Oski echoed, 'but there's something that's been brewed up at home to solve the air war problem. Search me for what, but the engineers are keeping some strange company these days. There's something planned, General, but it sounds as though you'll have to take it on faith, if they want you to march.'

Tynan was silent as the seconds ticked by, feeling his thoughts inexorably swing towards: *What option do I have?*

Four

'Your uncle's been going spare,' Balkus revealed to Che. 'About both of you,' he added, his nod picking out Tynisa as well. 'He thought you'd gone off the edge of the map.'

'Commonweal,' Che told him, 'so almost right.' She and her fellows had retreated to the Princep camp after the duel between the Mantids, because nobody seemed to know what was going on and the Ants were in a state of high tension that Balkus wanted to get well clear of. The Etheryen Mantis-kinden had done their best to deconstruct the duel for outsiders. The Nethyen woman, the visitor, had made some statement that had resulted in her counterpart challenging her – apparently a spontaneous matter of honour so critical that nothing short of instant bloodletting would do. As the challenger was dead and her opponent gone, nobody was supposedly any the wiser, but the Mantids had retreated into the trees shortly afterwards, leaving everyone with the feeling that they knew considerably more than they were saying.

The Collegiate ambassador was still trying to ask questions, of Ants and Mantids alike, which nobody was giving answers to. Helma Bartrer could be seen shuttling about the camp, increasingly frustrated with her own ignorance despite the fact that it was the common property of everyone there. Amnon was constantly looming behind her, and Che reflected that this was just as well, because the woman was plainly starting to get on people's nerves.

'And him,' Balkus was eyeing Thalric, who stared coldly back. 'Old Sten Maker heard how you were carrying on with him. He sent me a letter asking me to keep a watch out. He wasn't exactly keen.'

'Thalric is a reformed character,' Che replied. Her words should have sounded foolish, naive even, but she invested them with a certainty that warned Balkus off.

'All right. Good luck selling that to your uncle, though.' His gaze flicked to Tynisa, tracing the line of her scar. 'I can see *you've* been busy.'

She did not even look at him, her own attention focused entirely on the forest, as it had been since the duel took place.

In light of that silence, Balkus turned to the fourth member of their merry band. 'And where do you fit in?'

The halfbreed, Maure, blinked at him. Che knew the girl must make a strange figure and opened her mouth to excuse her, but Maure was already dissembling.

'A traveller from the Commonweal,' she said. 'I thought, "Why not see the Lowlands?" and with Che on her way home, when would I get a better chance?' She offered a bright smile to go with the words, quite out of character. Nothing was said about being a necromancer, making a living from dredging up ghosts and pieces of ghosts, counselling mourners and laying guilts to rest. Maure was a practical woman, for a magician, and Che guessed that she did not intend to practise her trade much, here in the Lowlands. Most likely, she was looking forward to spending time in some Apt city where nobody even believed in such skills.

'Che,' Tynisa murmured from the corner of her mouth. 'Trouble.'

A figure was storming towards them from the Ant camp, slender and almost rigid with suppressed emotion: the same Moth they had encountered earlier.

'You!' he called out, and there was no doubt who he meant. Che stood up, feeling surprisingly calm, because ever since Tynisa had been well enough to travel and they had made their plans to leave the Commonweal, she had anticipated this. The old Inapt powers of the Lowlands were jealous of their lore, and they had no love of Che's kinden at all. Of course the Moths would be shocked, when faced with what Che had become.

Whatever it is that I have become.

He had stitched together a little of his reserve, but the inscrutable Moth facade was still far from repaired. His hands clenched and unclenched as he stalked closer, and Che faced him squarely, hiding any uncertainties, because to a man of his kinden any weakness was exploitable.

And I may not be able to hide that well enough. In the Commonweal everyone believed in magic, and many practised it in a small and personal way, but they seemed to have no great magicians amongst them any more. Whether the Moths still did, she could not say, but they had whatever was left of magic in the Lowlands securely in their hands. Her odd and unasked-for status within the magical world might carry no weight with them. Or it might make them jealous to the point of telling their Mantis lackeys to cut Che's throat.

She was expecting a personal challenge, even an assault, but when the Moth spoke it was to jab a finger back towards the forest and demand, 'Is this your doing?'

She held his blank gaze, replying, 'The Mantis-kinden killing each other? No.' And then she continued to face him down, feeling his magic scrabble at her, feeling his Art trying to dominate her. He was no Skryre, though, no grand master of sorcery. She shrugged him off when he came with strength, and matched him move for move when he tried to creep past her guard. At last he took a step back, baffled and looking almost vulnerable.

'I am not your enemy,' Che assured him. 'I am a daughter of Collegium who has been given an unexpected gift, that is all.'

'That is *not* all,' he hissed, but more to himself than to her. 'You arrive here from – from where? – just in time for all my work to go suddenly awry.'

'I have been in the Commonweal, and if my time there taught

me anything it is that, amongst the Inapt, matters such as chance and coincidence are seldom entirely trustworthy,' Che declared. She was aware of the subtext within her words: this was not how the Apt spoke, certainly not how any Beetle-kinden he had met would speak. She was presenting her credentials and showing him she was part of his world.

His feet did not move, but she sensed a second mental step backwards, another concession granted her. She was sizing him up now, trying to place him and then – almost vertiginously – she thought she might even have met him before. She had once been in Sarn on her uncle's orders, contacting the Moth-kinden secret service known as the Arcanum, and there had been one brief meeting . . . She could not say, so long after, whether this man had been present, but she thought he might have been – and not as their leader. A magician, perhaps, but an intelligencer first, and from his presence at this meeting of powers it took no great leap of the imagination to see what his work here had been. He had been supporting the alliance of the Treaty of Gold, and now something had gone wrong amongst the Mantis-kinden.

'You are Cheerwell Maker, so they say,' he observed, and even this was him trying for power over her, the power of names that his people put such stock in.

'And you?' The unthinkable question, to a Moth, but she sensed that she had the authority to ask and she was damned if she would give him any more of her time if he would not expose himself to that small extent.

She saw his throat working, as though he were choking on something, and then he spat out, 'Terastos.'

It was a useful weather-gauge both of his low station and her apparent standing in the eyes of the Inapt. He did not like her but he could not deny her.

'So tell us what's going on,' she invited, sitting back down, cutting the tension from the moment by sidestepping it. 'We're none of us friends of the Empire here – no, not even Thalric. We know the Wasps are on the move again, and they must have taken control of the Alliance cities and Helleron fast, to get here so quickly. Perhaps we can even be of some help. So tell us.' Following her lead, her companions had also sat back down at the tent's mouth, and Terastos shifted from foot to foot, uncertain and ignorant, the worst thing for a Moth. At last the spy's practicality overcame the magician's pride, and he sat down.

'It is no secret that the Wasps are very near, their Eighth Army with all its machines. They have destroyed the Ant fortress that lay east of here, and beaten a field army too. The Sarnesh had hoped that speed would be their ally. Now they admit that they need real allies to carry the day. They have called on the Ancient League.'

'I remember when the Ancient League was formed. I spoke to your people in Sarn itself before the last war,' Che recalled.

Terastos blinked. 'That was not you.'

She gave him a small smile. 'Oh, it was. I was different then. I had not . . . lost touch. But it was me.'

'And here you are now.' He was shaken more than suspicious. She guessed that a very emphatic coded missive would soon be winging its way to the Skryres of Dorax, or perhaps he would send the news using his magic, if he was capable. No doubt the next Moth who came to confront her would be made of sterner stuff.

'The Ancient League . . .' he went on, glancing from her to her comrades and Balkus.

'Is not ancient,' Che finished for him. 'The Moths of Dorax and the Mantis-holds of this forest here might be united in their traditions, but there was never a league until the Wasps came last time. I can guess that, once the Wasps had gone, the League ceased to be, each of you back to your solitary pursuits?'

'And now the Sarnesh have called on us, whereupon we, being the masters of the League, have called upon our servants. And something has miscarried, yes. And you know *nothing* of this?'

'Not yet,' Che admitted. 'But we've only just arrived. What are the Wasps doing?'

'Waiting, no man knows for what.'

'What do you mean, *waiting*?' Thalric demanded, leaning into the conversation.

The Moth glowered at him. 'They were advancing, sweeping all before them. Then they stopped. They have been still some tendays now. They keep their scouts ready, and prevent any others coming close, but they just wait.'

'The cost of keeping an army in the field, at this distance from the nearest city, is enormous,' Thalric pointed out. 'Only orders from Capitas could allow it, unless someone's playing some very complex game with them.' His eyes slid aside from the Moth until they met Che's.

'Capitas,' she echoed: heart of Empire and domain of the Empress Seda. Seda, who had been touched by the same ritual that had stripped Che of her Aptitude, who shared that intangible mark that Terastos and the Mantis-kinden perceived on Che. Seda, who had added a swiftly burgeoning magical skill to the vast breadth of her temporal might.

Che stood up abruptly, tentatively reaching out. Seda scared her, and all Che's newfound power and knowledge did not help – it simply meant that she knew precisely why the woman was to be feared. Last time they clashed, only Maure's intervention had saved Che from being imprisoned forever within her own mind.

Another newcomer was approaching: a young Roach-kinden girl, slender and white-haired. She came hurrying up, stopping for a moment when she saw how many guests Balkus had.

'Syale, where have you been?' the Ant demanded, his companions forgotten. 'You're the ambassador, life's sake. You can't just up and vanish. I thought something had happened to you. What would I have told old Sfayot?'

The girl stood with arms folded, as if on the point of sulking. 'Firstly, don't you dare twit me with my father's name. If he had faith enough to send me, then that's all you need to know. Secondly, something very nearly did happen to me. I've news: the Mantis-kinden have gone mad.'

'Madd*er*,' Balkus responded sourly. 'Their Nethyen woman came out here and stabbed someone, in your absence, and now *nobody* knows what's going on.'

'*I* know,' Syale told him simply. 'Balkus, I was there *in* the forest when it happened. They're fighting.'

He opened his mouth, closed it, then said, 'You don't mean fighting the Wasps, do you?'

The girl shook her head and, in that wordless moment, Che saw just how shaken she was.

'The Mantis-kinden are fighting each other. Their two holds are at war.'

And Che, whose magical sense had been stretching itself towards distant Capitas, snapped back into herself with a hiss, flinching as though she had burned herself.

'What is it?' Thalric was at her shoulder.

'She's here.'

She heard questions, then: from the Moth, from Balkus, from Tynisa. Thalric had gone very still, though, because he understood all too well.

'The Empress, she's here now. She's with their army. She has done this.'

Five

'General, she's on her way in.'

General Roder glanced up, seeing one of the watch captains hovering at the door of his tent.

'Report,' he grunted.

'Airship and escort spotted by our scouts, General,' the officer informed him. 'Signals say it's her.'

Roder's expression still pinned him. He was famous for his hard stares, which owed a great deal to the paralysis that had locked half his face following a Spider assassin's poisoned strike. 'By airship? She must be mad,' the general muttered, half to himself. *One adventurous sortie by Sarnesh orthopters and the Empire's looking for a new ruler . . .*

'She's got some of the new fliers with her,' the captain added, as if reading his thoughts. 'Enough to throw back anything the Sarnesh could put in the air, sir. Maybe she'll hand them over to us.'

'Get the men turned out,' Roder snapped at a nearby lieutenant. 'If it is her, she'll see us at our best. And double our scouts, ground and air; this would be a very bad time for the enemy to find some gap in our perimeter. Oh, and get hold of that long streak of jerky she calls an adviser. She'll want him, I'd guess.'

'He's already out there,' the captain informed him. 'Even before our pilots reported back.'

Roder gave him a sour face. 'No mystery there: he knew when she'd be arriving all along, just decided that an Imperial general wasn't trustworthy enough to be told. Just goes to show, Captain, there are too many hands pulling in too many directions, back home, and precious few of them Wasp.' He stepped out of his tent and scowled at the daylight. 'Sends us headlong for Sarn, lets us smash them in the field, keep them off balance . . . and then what? Some ancient, dried-up freak turns up waving her writ and has us kicking our heels for tendays while the Sarnesh get their nerve back and build their strength. If you've some way to make sense of that, I'd welcome it. It makes none to me.'

The object of his ire was standing out in the centre of the camp, gazing up at the sky as though the sparse clouds held an inordinate fascination. The old creature was hunchbacked, though still absurdly tall, gaunt and withered and bald like an unearthed corpse. His grey skin was banded with white and he wore a shabby robe of halved black and gold. He was the Empress's slave, they said, and her adviser on unusual matters. He had been flown here by a Wasp belonging to something called the Red Watch – some new crowd of the Empress's favourites – and with enough seals and recommendations to set his word as law over even an Imperial general. That he had failed to make a friend of Roder was understandable.

His name was Gjegevey, which Roder seldom bothered to even attempt. Now the general stomped over to the man with a simple, 'Hey, you!'

The long face turned towards him, eyes glinting within their wrinkled sockets. 'General?'

'Your mistress is coming,' Roder told him. 'Now maybe we'll get to the bottom of this nonsense.' The placid gaze of the old slave made him angrier, and he had to bite off the other words that rose into his mouth. Even so – as always – Gjegevey seemed to hear them.

'Yes, General, if I have, hm, somehow misunderstood my orders, and held your Eighth here unnecessarily, I am sure that you'll have the pleasure of, ahm, stringing this old frame up on the crossed pikes. I would assure you that you were right in following my, mmn, advice, but you will have your confirmation soon enough.'

Even the slave's meandering speech was like nails on a chalkboard to Roder, but he gritted his teeth and bore it.

Another wing of Spearflights powered into the air, more security in case the Sarnesh got lucky, or in case Imperial intelligence had been compromised. The old Emperor – Seda's brother – had never left the capital and, for all that everyone admired this new girl's courage and enterprise, no general wanted the ruler of all the Empire actually looking over his shoulder, especially when faced with such nonsensical orders as had left the Eighth sitting idle for so long.

He spent some minutes inspecting his troops, stalking along the ranks and making his displeasure known if any officer's charges were found wanting. Save for those already out on patrol, here was the glorious Eighth, the Empress's Hammer: its legion of Light Airborne, the infantry, the Engineers, as well as a neat block of Auxillian Ants from Maille. They were a skilled and proven fighting force, and they were being wasted.

The Empress's airship was lowering itself, holding steady in the light breeze whilst its Farsphex escort flew in wide circles. The treasonous thought crossed Roder's mind that, were he an ambitious man, a little artillery accident might go a long way here. His current circumstances had bred a fair amount of resentment in him, but he had not been pushed anywhere near so far as treason, nor was he sure that his men would follow him. She put on a good show, did the Empress.

He waited impassively for her, standing at the head of his army. This would be his chance, he knew. Once away from the men he would be able to impress upon the girl just what the Eighth *should* have been doing these last tendays, and how it should be best used from now on. His experience and rank carried a great deal of weight in the Empire. She needed him. She would have to listen.

When she appeared at the top of the airship's ramp, after the ground crew had tied the lines off tight to hold it steady, she seemed no more than a slip of a girl, barely more than a child: slender and vulnerable before the might of the Eighth. Beautiful, too, and Roder could well appreciate it. He was sure that every man in the Empire holding a general's rank badge or the equivalent had entertained a thought that way before now. She had no husband, after all, and that no-pedigree outsider she had chosen as a regent had not been seen anywhere recently. Brugan of the Rekef was after her, Roder knew for a fact, but if she favoured the man, Seda had yet to recognize him formally.

Then she locked eyes with Roder, as she stepped down the ramp, and something jolted in his mind, his thoughts all abruptly thrown out of alignment. His eyes were hooked on her, unable to look away. He barely noted her bodyguards: the half-dozen Mantis women in black and gold mail, and the looming figure behind them in all-encompassing Mantis-wrought armour.

She wore the slight smile of a well-born girl out for a stroll and enjoying the air, but he was sure, beyond all logic, that she could read every one of his thoughts of the last half hour written plain on his face; all the trivial little treasons that an ambitious man gives wishful indulgence to. She saw them, and she knew him, and he felt the force of her – the sheer strength of her will and personality – drive him to one knee as she approached.

'General,' she greeted him, eyes drifting across the great mass of military drawn up for her approval. Roder heard the subtle but unmistakable sound of countless soldiers pulling themselves up that little bit straighter, chests thrust out an extra fraction of an inch. Even the Auxillians, who had far less reason to love her, were straining to be worthy of her nod. Kneeling at her feet, almost as though he was beneath the radiating beam of her regard, he nearly panicked, seeing the effect she had on them and knowing that he had no way to explain it. Then she said,

'Rise,' just for him, and he could do nothing but stand up into that irresistible flow of her personality, and be engulfed.

'Empress . . .' was all he managed.

'No doubt you have questions,' she observed wryly, but was walking away before he could ask any. In her wake stalked her Mantis-kinden, taut with suspicion and ready to take on the entire Eighth if needed. They might be elegant and poised, those women, but Roder had no doubts about their skill. To conquer nations, an army of the Apt was needed, but the old Inapt skills still had their place when things got personal.

The armoured form that came behind them was something Roder found himself averting his eyes from. That particular servant of the Empress had come to him before, arriving and leaving by its own means, hunting down the remnants of the Ant garrison at Malkan's Stand after they had gone to ground. Roder found that, rationalize as he might, he could not bring himself to think of that shape of Mantis-crafted mail as a *man* at all. Whatever walked there was something that hurt Roder's mind when he considered it too closely.

And there were others being disgorged by the airship, of course, for the Empress did not travel in a vacuum. There were air crew, servants, slaves, secretaries, a few of the new Red Watch and, no doubt, a Rekef agent or two here to check up on Roder's Eighth. All business as usual.

Then Gjegevey, who had stayed with him, was moving towards the ramp, and Roder saw two strangers bringing up the rear of the procession. Their grey robes identified them as Moth-kinden, who seemed to hold being drably dressed as a sacred charge. One was tall and willow-slim, the other shorter and decidedly more heavily built, and they faced off against Gjegevey with an initial wariness, before allowing themselves to step from the ramp and become guests of the Eighth.

Roder watched them approach, noting that the taller of the two was a woman: grey face and white eyes and high cheekbones, young seeming. She would have turned many heads, no doubt, but Roder had sworn off Inapt women since the poisoning that had frozen half his face. Now the Empress had moved on, his thoughts were free enough to assess these newcomers as a sign of the general rot back home that he had heard about – the lesser kinden, the Inapt creatures like Gjegevey, who seemed to have secured the Empress's ear so very easily.

Then the other figure turned his way, mid-word to Gjegevey, and Roder saw the flash of a pale face there – not a Moth after all, but a Wasp in their robes. A traitor, therefore, save that he had evidently bought the Empress's forbearance somehow.

And they call us off the Sarnesh, and have us sit here instead, in the shadow of this cursed forest, the Mantis heartland. His uneasiness was growing moment by moment. Was this *it*? Was he seeing here some great betrayal of the Empire, watching Seda led astray by the wicked old powers that had once owned the world before the rise of the Apt?

What can I do? And he knew that the moment the Empress called, or even turned her attention his way, he could do nothing. And no officer or agent or assassin he might draw on would be any more proof against her charms than he.

'Tonight,' Gjegevey declared, as the three of them neared the general.

Roder started from his inward-turning thoughts. 'What?' He tried to make it a demand, but it came out almost as a plea for help.

'She will make it clear to you tonight. All will be, mmn, understood.' Behind the tall, crooked slave, the Moth and the robed Wasp watched Roder thoughtfully.

Roder knew full well that Seda had not so much as exchanged a word with Gjegevey – had barely even glanced his way since her arrival – and yet here was the old man relaying her words. Worse, Roder found within himself no doubt at all that these *were* the Empress's intentions.

'And in the intervening time you should perhaps consider which of your soldiers are best placed for fighting within, ahm, challenging terrain,' Gjegevey suggested softly, his yellowed eyes flicking towards the forest. 'You have, hmm, Pioneers, are they? A list of suitable individuals and squads would impress her.'

Roder confined himself to a curt military nod.

'And you should withdraw your scouts from the forest edge all the, hm, way back to the camp.'

That was too much. 'That would leave us open to Mantis attack,' Roder snapped. *And is that the plan? Is that what happened to the Fourth Army when the Felyal Mantids wiped them out, betrayed from within before they could ever be destroyed from without?*

He thought he had broken away then – broken free of whatever madness had been quietly taking hold of the whole camp. He would call out for his men, and they would obey him. The traitors and lesser kinden surrounding the Empress he would put on crossed pikes, and she . . . she herself would listen to him. He would reclaim her from their evil influence and save the Empire . . .

Not for a moment did he think of actually turning on Seda herself. Later, thinking back, he wondered if that was what ultimately saved him.

There was a subtle shifting of the three of them, eyes focusing on something at his shoulder. Gjegevey himself just seemed resigned but the other two flinched away, and the woman – perhaps because she knew more than her Wasp convert – just kept backing off, as though the Eighth Army around her was safer company than what loomed behind the general.

Roder could not help himself. He turned to see.

It stood there, the Empress's own monster: the hulk of Mantis mail that had made the Sarnesh scream. It was tall, faceless within the darkness of its helm, each plate of its enamelled mail forged into elegant spines and curves. One gauntlet was just of leather, with a short, curved blade projecting from the fingers, the infamous Mantis fighting claw. Not long ago, a slave had killed the Emperor with just such a weapon, and now the Empress's very bodyguards carried them. For a moment Roder felt himself

61

teetering on the brink of some chasm of revelation, but his mind could not stretch so far – his Aptitude pulling him back from the brink.

'Tisamon,' Gjegevey addressed it, 'the general knows his duty.' And even the old man's voice, usually filled with mild assurance, sounded a little ragged.

There was no movement in the thing – it could have been a statue from some Mantis ruin – and yet every instinct in Roder's mind shrieked: *It's going to kill me!*

When he looked it in the visor and said, 'I do,' it was the hardest act in his career of war, but he was an Imperial general and he managed it. 'Until tonight, then.' And if his walk was brisk in departure, well, he was a busy man.

This could have been a fool's errand. Empress Seda the First almost wished it had been.

This had begun because she had been hungry for a sort of power that mere armies and conquest could not bring her. She had been adopted as a scion of the old times, gifted with a magical strength she could still only use haphazardly, and she had simultaneously been given a rival whose strength was as great and who would surely come to destroy Seda if the Empress did not overpower her first. *For the Beetle Cheerwell Maker is like me, at heart. The magic makes us so. If I cannot abide to see her face in the mirror, no more can she stand mine. Only one of us can prevail: the stronger sister shall live.*

But the secrets of the old days had been ebbing from the world for five centuries now, and she had ransacked all the crumbling histories she could find for some leftover worth the seizing. The one remnant she had found that had seemed promising was whatever had been locked away after the old powers' war with the Worm, whatever kinden that had truly been. The prospect had so alarmed Gjegevey that she had challenged him to find an alternative, whereupon he and the Tharen ambassador had cooked up this nonsense instead. Some fading shadow of old night locked up in the heart of these Mantis trees? A name: *Argastos*. And precious little more than the name.

She had humoured him because he had been her first friend, and this was his last chance to prove his usefulness before she cast him off. Besides, her brother had spent almost all his life inside the palace, and kept her there too, as his perennial victim. Now she could travel, and she did so. Let General Roder grumble: his soldiers saw her gracing their lives with her presence here, and they loved her for it.

When she had set off from Capitas, she had no great hopes regarding Gjegevey's find. Instead she had decided to make the best of it: to place some of her people close to Roder, to inspire the Eighth, weathering the queasy voyage inside the airship that all her Apt subjects would find smooth sailing.

But last night . . .

It was tempting to think of it as a dream, but that was her Apt past speaking. *Something* had come to her. Argastos? She could not know for sure, but *something*.

A shadow barely visible, but a shadow with nothing to cast it, standing in her bedchamber unsummoned. Tisamon had not reacted to it, but she had sensed its presence as a magical pressure as well as simply a trick of the light. A tall, straight shadow of a cloaked man, his silhouette bulked out by armour.

There you are.

The words had come unbidden to her mind, but that was a parlour trick that no longer impressed her.

'Give me your name,' she had challenged, and heard the ghost of faint laughter inside her head.

I have been calling for such a long time, and who could have thought that, when you finally came, you would be beautiful?

She had folded her arms. 'I have better flatterers at court. Give me your name.'

When we meet, you shall know me. When you come to me, I promise you such gifts as you cannot imagine, little Wasp girl. But you must make haste. I have been too long without company.

63

She had felt some faint glamour clutching at her, trying to hook her with an enchantment that would skew her judgement, compromise her defences, but she had shaken it off with contempt. Even as she did so, the shadow had faded, its presence waning into an absence. The visitation was gone.

She cared nothing for this clumsy attempt to ensnare her, robbed of any chance of success by distance and by her own strength of will. It was confirmation, though, that whatever relic of the old days lingered between Etheryon and Nethyon was worth her pursuit. There had been power there sufficient to reach out to her even though she was travelling by machine, and surrounded by the Apt.

Mine, she had decided, then and there. *Gjegevey proves his worth at last. And I will need to prove my strength if I am to master this thing on its own ground, Argastos or no.* But a woman who had made herself Empress of the Wasps was not one to shrink before a challenge.

She had sent one of her Red Watch to bring the last of the slaves to her chambers. The blood would help her think.

General Roder did as he was bidden, and even if thoughts of attacking this conspiracy of the Inapt crossed his mind twenty times before nightfall, he could never act on them. All too often he saw that armoured form when he glanced round, quite out of its expected place, until eventually he felt he was seeing it even when it was not there.

Then the old slave came for him, tracking him down amongst all the bustle of the camp, where Roder had tried to lose himself.

'It is time, General,' Gjegevey told him. 'You will understand, now.'

Roder wondered if he would survive that understanding but, by then, dying with that knowledge seemed almost preferable to living without it.

'Lead on, then.' He glowered into that kindly old face, whose wrinkles no doubt hid sins that the Wasps did not even have names for.

Gjegevey began shuffling away, poling himself along with a staff, his old man's pace unbearably slow to a man used to the fierce energy of a soldier's stride.

'You are, hm, suspicious, of course,' Gjegevey's voice drifted back to him. 'There have been many changes in the Empire of late, I know. New machines, new institutions, a shift in the balance of power, the Rekef perhaps not what it once was, the Engineers more . . .'

To hear that sort of sane and sensible talk, rather than a mystic's babble, was something of a surprise, but Roder reminded himself that this old man had been a slave to the late Emperor, and to the Emperor before that, a tool long kept in Imperial service. No doubt he had talk suitable for all markets.

'There were those in Capitas who doubted whose hand truly, hm, guided the Empire,' the slave continued, not looking back at Roder.

Were . . . ? And yet there had been odd news from the capital of late. A spate of disappearances, certainly – and with the Rekef about that was not surprising, save that half the names had been men high up in the Rekef itself.

They were nearing the camp's northern edge by now, and Roder keenly felt how exposed they were to anything that might have come creeping out of the forest that massed on the dark horizon.

'Believe me in this, General,' Gjegevey told him, slowing, 'it is all to do with *her*. All of it is her. She moves us all.' Almost a whisper, confidant to confidant.

There were figures up ahead, just a handful of them isolated beyond the bounds of the Eighth's camp. In the poor light he identified them: Seda, of course, and her bodyguards, including that armoured form that made his skin crawl. A couple of the Red Watch stood at the group's edge, and he saw the Moth woman was there too, and the traitor Wasp.

65

Is she mad? was all that Roder could think. That the Empress of all the Wasps, the most powerful, the most important woman in the world, was standing out here, prey for the first Mantis war band to come out of Nethyon, was inconceivable. Yet here she was, and he could not caution her or warn her, still less order her back to safety, as was surely his duty. A glance from her and his words of reproach were gone.

'General, thank you for joining us,' she acknowledged, a slight smile showing that she was well aware how little choice he had in the matter. 'You know Gjegevey, of course, and perhaps you know Tegrec, the Tharen ambassador?' This was the robed Wasp, once Imperial governor of Tharn and now employed as the Moth's turncoat ambassador to his own people.

'This is Yraea, also of Tharn.' Seda indicated the Moth woman. 'Gjegevey, perhaps some light?'

The old slave found an oil lamp on his person, and surprised Roder by flicking away at it with a steel lighter until the wick caught, rather than rubbing sticks together or however the Inapt might do it. The lamp itself, even just placed on the ground, was vastly reassuring. The darkness was still full of unseen assassins, but at least their imagined presence had been driven further away.

But then they arrived, stepping from that dark previously only peopled by Roder's fears. He started away with a curse, hand coming up ready to sting, but a single gesture by Seda stopped him.

He knew them, these newcomers. His soldiers had felt their depredations ever since they came close to the cursed forest. The Nethyen Mantids had not been slow in taking advantage of every weakness in the Eighth's security, so that Roder had been forced to make a new decision each day, weighing any progress against the lives he expected to lose. Their sporadic, savage raids on his forces had slowed him to a crawl, while all the scouts and Pioneers he could muster had netted but a fraction of the enemy. And here they were. *The enemy.*

66

He saw a half-dozen of them: Mantis men and women, tall and arrogant, with angular features and disdainful looks. They had come fully armed, with bows and spears, rapiers and claws, and they wore a mishmash of yesterday's armour: scaled cuirasses, plates of chitin, moth-fur and the odd piece of fantastically wrought metal that was a match for anything the Empress's mailed bodyguard wore.

Yraea the Moth went over to them straight away, and it was plain that she carried some weight with them. They at least paused to speak to her, though their arch expressions did not quite concede that she had power over them. Roder had heard how the Mantids used to be the Moths' slaves, back when the world was young, but he guessed that time had rubbed the shine off *that* arrangement, judging from the way these warriors shuffled and glowered and stared at the Empress's party.

Then the Moth woman was stepping aside – almost shouldered aside – and the Mantids were storming forwards. Roder tensed, and was not remotely reassured to find that the rest were bracing too – the Empress's women bodyguards and Tegrec, even Gjegevey. Only the mailed form remained still, and Roder felt that it harboured a constant tension anyway, always just on the verge of violence.

From Seda's manner, by contrast, she might be receiving a Beetle trade delegation in her throne room back at Capitas.

She opened her arms to the Mantids, displaying herself to them – and if her hands were spread to sting, well, amongst other kinden that was a gesture of friendship, was it not? If one of them jumped forwards with spear or rapier, then the Empire would be headless once again, and who knew what might follow?

Roder was almost physically holding himself back, ready at the first wrong move to leap forwards and fight for her, and well aware that he would be too slow, even so.

And they knelt. All six of them went down on one knee, heads bowed, weapons on the ground, the killing tension vanishing without any explanation. The Mantids abased themselves before the Empress of the Wasps, when they had barely spared a kind look for the Moth Yraea.

Roder stole a glance at the other faces gathered there. Surely they had all been expecting this? But he saw writ plain on that rabble of mystics' faces that they had not. They had expected terms, treaties, negotiations that they themselves could have meddled with – not this abject surrender.

'Rise,' the Empress said to them, just as she had to Roder earlier. 'Rise and speak.'

The foremost of the Mantids, a cord-lean woman, ageless and scarred, tried twice before she could utter a word. Her eyes were young, struck with a sort of adulation that Roder had never seen before, 'You will bring it back,' she whispered hoarsely.

'I will bring it all back, all that you once had,' Seda told her gently. 'Go and tell your people that their time is coming again. That *I* will do this thing, and none other, if they bind themselves to me.'

'We shall,' the Mantis woman whispered. 'Empress, we shall.'

And they were padding off, the six of them stepping swiftly into the darkness, eager to spread the word, and Seda turned her smiling face on Roder and trapped him in the radiance of her regard.

'You see, General? Even so simply does the Empire conquer. You understand all, now.'

'I understand nothing,' Roder frankly admitted, before he could stop himself. 'I understand enough,' he corrected himself.

'The Nethyen are with us, as is Tharn. The Inapt that formerly declared for Sarn and Collegium are divided. Now your work begins. The hold of Etheryon has always been close to Sarn, and likely they will hold to the Ants, as will the Moth-kinden at Dorax. There will be fighting amidst the trees even tonight. You must arrange for your very best, your scouts and Pioneers and wildsmen, to enter the forest and fight alongside our new allies. You can be sure the Sarnesh will be doing the same. Whoever controls this forest controls our road to Sarn.'

Roder considered the list that he had drawn up, at Gjegevey's urging. 'It shall be accomplished, Empress.'

'Of course it shall.' She was turning back to head for the camp, but more words forced themselves from Roder's lips.

'Empress . . . what you promised them . . .?'

Her smile was still as sweet. 'They feel betrayed, General. The Apt city-states of the Lowlands and their modern ways have made such inroads into the Mantis way of life, as the corruption of the Etheryen hold shows. Now the Nethyen will fight just for the right to be left to their own devices. Just as we do in the Empire, they value their traditions.'

Roder glanced at Seda's armoured shadow, to find that faceless helm looking right back at him. He had an unhappy feeling that he was somehow looking right into the heart of those old Mantis traditions, but he would never be able to put it into words.

He was about to hurry back to camp and surround himself with men whose company he understood, but Seda herself had paused, and for the first time that night Roder sensed that she was in less than complete control of the world.

The Empress was looking towards the hostile west, where the skies were still faintly grey with sunset. 'Gjegevey,' she murmured.

'Here, your, hm, Majesty.' The old slave was at her elbow immediately.

'Is it . . .?' A terrible, hard cast fell over the Empress's face. 'It's *her*.'

Roder had no idea who '*her*' might be, but whoever it was had better prepare herself for the end, for utter hatred was writ large in the Empress's expression.

'She's here, *here*!' Seda turned wild eyes on Gjegevey. 'She is here for your Argastos, just as I am. She seeks to keep it from me.'

The slave spread long-fingered hands in demurral, but Seda would not be forestalled. 'Then I cannot wait, nor will I be denied. General, have your soldiers ready to enter the forest tomorrow morning, in force. And have ready your very best Pioneers, your

69

most skilled trackers and hunters and woodsmen. I will have work for them all.'

'My Empress, no!' Gjegevey started, showing more courage in the face of her anger than Roder himself could have mustered.

'And wait for the leaden clash of armies while she steals what is mine?' Seda demanded. 'Only one of us can live, Gjegevey, the stronger of us. If she takes what is here, then it will be *her*. Is that what you *want*?'

'Empress, no, but—'

'Then prepare yourself, old man, for you're coming too.'

Six

'Look at this, though.'

Sartaea te Mosca glanced politely at the scroll Gerethwy had unrolled for her. 'Two matters, dear one,' she replied. 'Firstly, what in the world do you think that I would make of that, save for tinder? Secondly this would be considerably easier for me if you kept still. Consider that I am slightly smaller than your arm: every slightest twitch throws me about as though I'm in a hurricane.'

She exaggerated slightly, but he was an enormously tall, long-limbed man, a Woodlouse-kinden, perpetually hunched like an old man, but a young and sprightly student where the few others of his kinden that anyone had ever seen seemed to have been ancient forever, old as the stones of Collegium. He had come from the east with an esoteric but impressive understanding of machines that had won him a place at the Great College, and he had stayed on for the war.

Te Mosca herself was a Fly-kinden, and someone who had also turned up begging at the College gates, though in her case she had come from the Moth-kinden at Dorax, and had been looking for work. The old chair for Inapt studies – meaning those parts of the world that the Apt neither understood nor cared about – had been gathering dust, but even then they had not made her a full master, just had her marking out her time as though a replacement was expected at any moment. There had been votes in Assembly, she knew, to abolish the position entirely, but respect for tradition had thus far allowed her field of study to cling on by its fingernails.

She was small even for a Fly, delicate of frame and with a faint ashen tint to her skin, for her kinden often looked a little like those they grew up amongst. She taught the histories of the Inapt as they themselves would tell it, and she taught a little of the principles of magic, but her few students were mostly Apt and, however diligently they took notes, they could never grasp even the most basic tenets. It was a curiously futile existence, but she enlivened it by offering her skills as a doctor. Inapt kinden often fared far better under the care of an Inapt healer and, when it came to it, she could stitch a wound almost as well as any Collegiate surgeon.

She took Gerethwy's long hand in both of hers and inspected the stumps where an exploding weapon had torn off two fingers. 'Healing nicely,' she said, 'but it would heal far quicker if you'd not use the hand. It must hurt you, surely?'

He shrugged, something his bony hunchbacked frame was made for. 'But there's too much work. I'm due to drill with the Companies, and I need every moment I can get at the work-shops. Nobody else will.' He thrust the paper at her again, then dragged it back, recognizing the pointlessness of it. Gerethwy himself was a man who seemed to understand everything. He sat through her lectures as attentively as any Inapt scholar, seeming to take it all in, but then went off to the workshops to work on his devices. Her own masters had always muttered that the Woodlouse-kinden were a law unto themselves.

'Rational machinery,' Gerethwy insisted, and she recognized that doomed passion to explain from her own classes, in trying to hammer home some patently obvious point into skulls simply not designed for it. Now she was on the receiving end, and could only blink politely as his words gushed out – for he who had been so quiet and self-contained now had something he needed to speak of.

'It's the future,' he insisted. 'It's very simple.' His eyes were begging her to agree with him. 'It's all down to putting information in, and getting information out. It's all in the gear trains that convert one to the other. You can do *anything* with it, if you just work out the gearing. Machines that can do things for themselves in response to what you tell them.'

'As far as I'm aware, that works only indifferently with human beings,' she remarked, yanking on his arm to stop him gesturing with it, then immediately feeling guilty as he winced. She began to apply fresh bandages, not that the healing wound really needed them any longer, but more as a mnemonic so that Gerethwy would remember he was hurt, and therefore take more care.

'But, look . . . as a doctor, surely you can . . . It must look familiar?'

At last she squinted at the plans, seeing something resembling an explosion, a thousand little pieces scattered in random profusion.

She did not have to say it: he nodded resignedly. 'Ten years ago, before anyone in Collegium had even thought of the idea, someone in the Empire – some mad genius – was already building rational machines of a complexity that nobody has matched since. This work . . . it's beautiful, perfect. And I can learn from it, duplicate it even . . .'

'Well what is it, this glorious whatnot of yours?' Te Mosca was ready for it to be a weapon. Every artificer in the city was talking weapons just now and, given that they had only just beaten the Imperial Second Army back, she supposed that was entirely reasonable.

'It's an arm,' Gerethwy told her simply. 'He constructed a rational arm: a mechanical arm that would translate the motions of his stump.'

She looked at him, from his mangled hand to the frank, innocent and slightly off-balance look in his face, and felt very sad because, despite the long and learned pedigree of his kinden and the mystery of his origins, he was still little more than a boy, and

73

they had made him a soldier, and he still thought it could all be put right.

The tragedy was, she knew, that he was telling her precisely because she could not understand. Amongst his friends and his comrades, he would remain as taciturn as ever, unwilling to let them in on his secret projects for fear he would be told that none of them would work.

'Officer Antspider, orders for you.'

The Fly-kinden pressed the scroll into her hand and was off into the skies of Collegium before Straessa could object. She was left standing in the street, just twenty feet from the bookbinder's that Eujen lodged over. If she had been a little brisker on her way, then the missive might never have found her.

Straessa – called the Antspider because, whilst Collegiates might be fair to halfbreeds, they still tended to point at them in the street – had a strong urge to cast the scroll in a fire and deny it had ever found her, but she was not the feckless student she had once been. Putting on the uniform of the Merchant Companies had taken half her naivety from her, and going out to fight the Wasps had done the rest. Under the banner of the Coldstone Company she had shed blood for Collegium. Her commanding officer had been assassinated. Her maniple and its neighbours had been routed. Her friend Gerethwy had been maimed by his own weapon. She had rallied her troops and gone back, with the lunatics from Myna, to try and slow the Wasp advance, to attack their artillery, to do *something* other than simply wait for the end. Memories like that could be expected to leave their mark on a girl, she reckoned.

Since General Tynan's Second had been forced to retreat by Collegiate air-power, the soldiers of the Merchant Companies had been training and recruiting, or at least trying to recruit. Numbers were still down – hardly surprising after the beating they had taken at the hands of the more disciplined Wasp soldiers. Everyone was pulling double shifts: Straessa had little enough time to herself, and this should have been one of those times. She had wanted to take off the breastplate and the buff coat, just for a little while; to make it up with Eujen and pretend she was just a student again, with no more to worry about than the end-of-year exams and making a little money on the side as a sword instructor.

Orders were never a good thing. Orders meant that something had changed.

The Second is on the move again. That was the most obvious conclusion. For a moment, her mind's eye superimposed the battlefield over the tidy little Collegiate street, the shouting and the screams, the thunderous clatter of the monstrous Imperial automotives, the chaos of the retreat.

She steadied herself, by which time her hands had broken the seal. There was nothing for it now but to read.

That done, she read it all again, and even checked the signature for authenticity.

'Madness,' she murmured, and then hurried towards the book-binder's shop, opening the side-door and taking the stairs to Eujen's lodgings three at a time.

Eujen already had company, but she expected that. It was Averic the Wasp scholar – the Wasp *renegade,* she supposed he was now, for he wouldn't be going home any time soon – and the two of them were plainly midway through planning something, judging by the quantity of paper strewn about the small room.

'What's this? Plotting to overthrow the Assembly?' she observed, rather too heartily.

Eujen regarded her warily. 'Those plans were laid a long time ago,' he said, trying to match her jovial tone. 'Just training sched-ules for the Student Company.' Meaning his own project: that odd little band of amateur soldiers he had raised after she had persuaded him not to follow her into the regular military. Eujen Leadswell was a conflicted man: he had spent his life protesting against war – war with the Empire especially. He had debated constantly on the subject, accusing those who vilified the Wasps of bringing closer the very conflict claimed to be guarding against. Now that war was upon them, Eujen did not know whether he had been a prophet or a fool.

'That's going well?' She had always adopted an acerbic manner even amongst her friends, and normally it was accepted no more seriously than she meant it, but she and Eujen had not been seeing eye to eye recently.

'We're fine. We may not be your regulars, but we're making real progress.' His answer was too quick and too defensive. He was frightened for her, and resentful of the Companies that took her away from him, and so they argued, and were reconciled, and argued yet again. Averic was already looking ill at ease, and she guessed he might start making his excuses soon.

She wanted a fight with Eujen because at least she knew the rules to that game. She wanted to joke with him. The orders in her hand felt like they were burning her fingers.

'They were saying that, now you've got your Student Company, you'll be forming a Student Assembly next,' she put in. Anything to lighten the mood.

Eujen fixed her with a solemn stare. 'Were they?'

'You're not, are you?' Because that would be ridiculous. Because it would also be *just* like Eujen.

'Do you know it's more than a month since the Assembly last met properly?' Eujen asked her. 'The elected government of Collegium?'

'Yes, but—'

'Do you know who's now running the city? Making all the important decisions?' he pressed her. 'Because I can give you a handful of names – Maker, Drillen, Padstock – but of the rest? Nobody knows. It's whoever they call on, their friends and allies, and whoever the new chief officers are. The whole basis of our city-state just gone.'

'Since the Amphiophos was bombed—'

'Let them meet at the College. Let them meet in a marketplace,' Eujen contested hotly. 'The *place* wasn't important. The institution was. And now they've done away with it!'

'Only until the Wasps—' She was getting angry now at being talked over, but he had built his momentum and was running with it.

'And if we beat the Empire back, what then?. Some other threat? Some other excuse?'

'Eujen, we are at *war*! War needs swift decisions, firm leadership.' Even as she shouted the words at him, she realized that she did not necessarily believe them, but he was casting her as the establishment by virtue of her rank within the Companies. She had become an apologist for Stenwold Maker without ever being asked – and that, of course, just made her angrier.

'Right,' Averic stood up, as she had known he would, 'I'll just—'

'You stay right there.' Her mere glower halted him. 'I've got work to do.'

Eujen, who had a lot of argument in him yet and who had probably assumed that they would make peace later in the evening, went still. 'No you don't. You said that . . . wait, look . . .'

'No, really.' She attempted a smile, just about managed one. 'You think I'd back out of a fight with you just because I've been shouldering a snapbow all day? But it's orders, Eujen. New orders. They want me to go recruiting.'

'I thought they'd already done that to death,' Eujen replied, after a pause. 'I thought they'd pretty much squeezed out every volunteer the city had to offer.'

'Well, yes, and it looks like they – whoever, as you say, *they* are – have kind of come to the same conclusion.' She pitched him the incriminating scroll, because this news would be all over the city soon anyway, and because he would hear of it soon enough.

His eyes flicked over it, and the initial paragraphs had him so instantly exercised that she knew he would miss the other gems buried further in.

'They can't do this.'

'It's done.'

'And you agree with it? You'll do it?' he demanded of her.

'I'm going to do it.' She shrugged. 'Agree with it? Between orders like these and you deciding I'm Maker's lackey, I've lost track of what I agree with.'

'Conscription,' Eujen hissed. 'Not recruitment, *conscription*.'

Averic had taken the scroll and was reading assiduously. '"That all Collegiate citizens should play their part in the defence of their mother city,"' he quoted, '"whether by artifice, feat of arms or such other aid." And you get to go door to door, asking?'

'While the Wasps are licking their wounds, this looks like our main assignment,' the Antspider confirmed. The mood in the room had been calmed as if water had been thrown on a fire, the previous argument gone stone cold now that Eujen had something real to react against.

'Which means forced conscription into the Companies, for whoever they choose? Anyone they can point at and claim isn't pulling their weight,' he stated. 'Is this aimed at us?'

She had expected that. 'No, Eujen, it's not.'

'Disband the students, then parcel them out between the formal Companies?' he insisted.

'No, Eujen, it is not,' she repeated, more emphatically. 'Just read the thing properly, would you?'

He snatched the paper back from Averic, but Eujen was already so full of objections that his eyes simply slid off the relevant words, despite the Wasp trying to point them out to him.

'"All those of age not yet contributing to the defence shall be duly assigned between the Companies currently under arms,"' Straessa quoted from memory, '"namely the Coldstone Company, Outwright's Pike and Shot, Maker's Own, Fealty Street Company . . ."' She inserted the appropriate pause, enjoying making him wait. '". . . and the Student Company." Your people, Eujen.'

Eujen's eyes danced from the written words to Straessa's face, and back again. 'What is this supposed to mean?' he asked quietly.

'It means congratulations, Chief Officer Leadswell,' she told him. 'It means that the next time Stenwold Maker and his shadowy conspiracy meet to decide the fate of the city, you'll have a seat reserved for you. It also means, I'd guess, that those student citizens who haven't already signed will end up under your jurisdiction, which by my reckoning means you've inherited a tremendous bagful of problems to keep you busy.'

'They must be mad,' he murmured.

'There we agree, but it's done now. Maybe Sten Maker reckons he needs a conscience. After all, you did your bit during the last scrap.'

He was staring at her as though he had received a death sentence or a court summons; as if it were he who would now be called to go off and fight when the Wasps returned, rather than she. He had always been a statesman in training, she knew: a man of powerful ideals and few compromises who was itching to shake up the Collegiate establishment once he was old enough and influential enough to win a seat on the Assembly. Abruptly, at the age most students were securing an apprenticeship, he found himself at the heart of government.

'Well done, Eujen, you earned it – which is more than most Assemblers could say. Now you have to actually *do* it, rather than just talking a good fight.'

She had not meant the words to come out sounding like a jibe, but any antagonism washed over him without sticking.

'Yes,' he said, visibly shaken. 'I suppose I do.'

Collegium's pilots were led by a Solarnese Fly-kinden named te Schola Taki-Amre, a name that had been long forgotten by everyone else in favour of just 'Taki'. She was young, as most of them were. In fact, following the great cost with which the Collegiates had repulsed the Imperial air force the last time, it seemed to most people that the city's airmen and women were working to some bizarre backwards mathematics in which one could plot combat flight time against average age, and draw a line where one increased and the other only ever seemed to fall.

Taki had been flying against other pilots for years – over in now-occupied Solarno it had been a way of life – and she had become the leader of the pilots because they would accept nobody else. In their fast, fierce world, they had shaken off the steadying control of any land bound superiors. Stenwold Maker and his War Council might give them objectives and orders, but once in the air they recognized only their own. Taki was not the only one of them to consider that they had more in common with their airborne foes than with the people they left behind on the ground.

Now she was reporting to what passed for the Council – meaning whatever handful of luminaries could be convened at short notice to listen to her. In truth Eujen Leadswell did not know the half of it. Everyone in a position of importance was so busy actually fighting the war that citywide decisions were being made on the strength of whoever could find the time to turn up.

This time she found herself before Stenwold Maker himself, besides Remas Boltwright of the new-formed Fealty Street Company, some College woman she didn't know, and Willem Reader of the aviation department, who was co-creator of the Stormreader orthopters that most of her pilots flew. No Jodry Drillen, no Padstock of the Maker's Own, nor either of the two who had been promoted to fill dead men's shoes for the unrepresented Merchant Companies. The other absent faces that came to Taki's mind were of those already fallen in battle.

'So, they're back in business,' she finished, setting it out in terms a landsman could understand. 'We think there are around a dozen Farsphex with the Second now, which isn't enough to cause us problems, however good they are, but there'll be more.'

'Any chance of catching them on the ground?' Reader asked her.

'They've kept a solid air watch since we knocked them back,'

Taki informed him. 'My guess is that they won't restart the advance until they've got more air cover, but I could be wrong. They've got enough now to at least slow us down, make each raid more costly and, whilst I could harry them all day and night in my *Esca Magni*, many of the other Stormreaders don't have the same staying power. Any kind of serious resistance will cut down on our efficiency.'

'What about the new pilots?' the Beetle woman asked.

'Fit for defence, if we need them, but I wouldn't want to chance them against Farsphex unless I had to.' Taki and the best of her pilots had been training up newcomers as fast as they could, but there was a limit to the number of prospective pilots Collegium could produce.

'The Vekken have pilots they could lend us,' Willem Reader mused. All eyes turned to him and he shrugged. 'Desperate times?'

'Not that desperate,' Stenwold decided. 'I've worked harder than any to bring the Vekken into our alliance and, believe me, there are still a great many people who don't trust them even sitting outside our walls. Give them our best machines and there will be riots. And the first suggestion the Vekken get that we might turn on them . . . well, it'll confirm all their usual fears. So, no, not yet. We'll make do with what we have. Taki, anything more?'

'Not so's you'd notice.'

Stenwold nodded and, seeing that nobody else had any more questions for her, she ducked out of the room.

Stenwold himself spent an hour in debate with that husk of a council, concerning the best steps they could take next, before he tasked everyone there with some aspect of the resulting plan and sent them off. After that he settled down to read through the petitions – not the usual civilian business, but proposals from anyone in the city who thought they could help the war. There were hundreds of amateur inventors in Collegium, and most of them had nothing useful to offer and were offering it with great force. Yet there might be hidden gold amongst the dross, and they could not pass up on anything that would give them an advantage. Their last clash with the Wasps had made it plain that the Imperial artificers had not been idle.

Those proposals sorted through, he looked at his share of the endless supply of progress reports. All over the city there were men and women who had tasks allotted to them according to their talents. Builders carved trenches and earthworks; merchants stockpiled food and munitions; Company officers trained their recruits; smiths turned over their workshops to make snapbow bolts and clerks tallied how much of everyone else's industry the city might need. A legion of planners and doers greased the wheels of Collegium's amateur war machine, and when they had done their part, or when they encountered difficulties that blocked their way, they wrote it all down and it came to Stenwold or Jodry or a few others.

Stenwold sat patiently, leafing through them, eyes skipping over the words from long practice, pausing only where some problem had clearly identified itself, annotating and making recommendations, or passing the issue on to someone better suited. He seldom had to think much about each issue, but there was plenty to get through and, if he did not finish, there would be even more on the morrow.

He had lost track entirely of how much time had gone by, when there was a respectful cough from the doorway.

'It'll have to wait,' he said, without looking up. *Another half hour and I'll have this done, and then I can sleep. And then . . .*

'Master Maker, look at you,' came a familiar, gruff voice. 'Who'd have thought it: You, lord of all you survey, up to your nose in papers like some book-keeper's clerk.'

'Tomasso.' Stenwold looked up to see the black-bearded Fly-kinden grinning at him. At least the man's lightness of tone was guarantee that some other unlooked-for disaster was not about to come thundering down on him. 'What do you want?'

'Wys has been in with another shipment,' the Fly ex-pirate

explained. Wys was his opposite number beneath the waves, an enterprising Sea-kinden who was nominally Tomasso's wife, by some bizarre pirate custom.

'Have you . . .?'

'I've sent it on to the workshops, never you mind,' Tomasso assured him. The shipment would consist of machine parts and the superior almost-steel that the Sea-kinden produced.

'Then . . .?' Stenwold gestured at the paperwork. 'It's just, I have a lot to get through.'

For a painful moment he saw himself through Tomasso's eyes, the ex-pirate looking at him and seeing a man of action and adventure crippled and pared down to this thing of paper and sums. Tomasso's smile changed, less flippant, more calculating. 'Put it down, Master Maker, just for one evening.'

'It's not as easy as that—' Stenwold stopped talking immediately, because a woman was peering shyly around the doorframe, her expression equal parts trepidation and concern.

He almost kicked over his chair in getting to his feet, then stood there, feeling embarrassed by the vigour of his reaction, watching her even as she was watching him.

Her name was Paladrya, and she was Sea-kinden – although to the uninitiated she could pass as a Spider woman. When he had first met her they had both been prisoners, and torture and deprivation had left her bruised and gaunt. The marks of that ill-treatment were still there in the lines on her face, but she was now adviser to the new Sea-kinden ruler, and those days of incarceration and false accusations were behind her.

Tomasso slipped away while they were still gazing at each other, leaving Paladrya to walk carefully into the room, as though feeling out the borders of Stenwold's domain. He remembered their last parting, the mutual realization that they were creatures of different worlds. The crushing, lightless depths of the sea filled him with horror and despair, whilst the parched and barren land was utterly inhospitable to one of her people. And here she was.

'Wys said you were fighting,' she said, stopping out of arm's reach.

And in the end, being people of responsibilities and both well past the impetuous foolishness of youth, they had parted. She had sent letters, and so had he, but neither of them had made much headway with the alphabet of the other. What words they had exchanged that way had remained simplistic and unsatisfying. With a Beetle's Apt pragmatism, Stenwold had resigned himself to the task in hand – knowing that he would live with a little piece of himself forever out of balance, because of her, but aware that he *could* live that way for as long as was needed. He had assumed that she would have said the same.

'Not me personally. They wouldn't let me go. But fighting, yes.' The paperwork lurked at his elbow, waiting to drag him down once again. 'And soon to resume, I believe.'

'I just . . .' A pause. 'I forced Wys to bring me. She didn't want to – and Aradocles almost forbade me. But I had to come. Stenwold.'

'It's good to see you.' Weak words, he realized, but he did not know what to do with her, or where he was with her, and it was plain that she was caught in the same no-man's land. His mind sprang formal options at him: show her the College, the preparations, the soldiers drilling. Talk to her in bluff, unconcerned tones of the war to come, to lay her mind at rest. Draw her into discussions of politics, land and sea.

Instead, he found himself standing very close to her, his hand just brushing her pale cheek. Her expression held a great deal of fear but, in amongst her fear of the land and its dangers, there was fear for him.

'We will hold, don't worry,' he told her. 'I could show you a hundred things – inventions, fortifications, engines – that would convince you how we will hold. We have thrown them back twice before. We shall do so again.'

She was Inapt, of course, so all his inventions and engines

would mean nothing to her, but perhaps she had some touch of prophecy about her, because his words failed to reassure.

'I think of you a great deal in Hermatyre,' she whispered. 'Aradocles could use your counsel and your artifice, and I . . . Do you dream of the sea, Stenwold?' She must have seen it in his eyes: the nightmares he had still of chasmic depths, the churning tentacles of sea-monsters, drowning in the dark.

He saw, in her face, that she had faced just such fears in coming here, and only out of concern for him; a kind of selfish madness gripped him, and he said, 'When this is done, I will come to you.'

The words hung there between them, and he was shaken by his pledge, despite the vast weight of war that now stood between him and any chance of fulfilling the promise. He was shocked by the words, but he could not disown them. To his great surprise, they were sincere. To the pits with the city and its government and Jodry Drillen. When the Wasps were beaten back, he had earned himself a retirement. Thinking of those midnight waters was less terrible now, with Paladrya there beside him. He would adapt. Beetle-kinden always did.

The paperwork was abruptly an unbearable burden, and he found that he was no longer shackled to it. 'Let's leave here,' he decided. 'This is no place to be.' Collegium, even under threat of war, offered a hundred diversions and yet, just then, the only place he wanted to take her was home.

Seven

'Who's this headed over?'

Tynisa had been staring at the trees, trying to feel some sense of connection, to open up to her own Mantis-kinden blood, and now the unwelcome voice of Thalric pulled her from her reverie. She was supposed to be keeping watch, just as he was, but the great brooding expanse of the Etheryon–Nethyon forest had drawn her attention away. *In there are my people,* she had tried to tell herself, but she did not quite believe it. Her father, Tisamon, had been a poor adherent of the Mantis-kinden way – and the fact that her mother had been Spider-kinden, the Mantids' traditional enemies, was evidence of that. Tynisa herself could pass easily for one of her mother's kin, but the bloody-handed Mantis way of doing things had lived close to the surface in her for a long time. She had only recently reined it in and brought under control.

That combination within her – the Spider heritage, the Mantis miscegenation, the Weaponsmaster's badge that the Mantids put such store in – had surely earned her any number of challengers here, and she knew that Che could not hold them off forever. With her sister occupied, she had been expecting to be called out, but when Thalric dragged her back to the present moment, she recognized the approaching tread as being heavier than any Mantis: a man in armour, and in company.

It was the Ant tactician, the one who seemed to be in charge around here. Since the Mantis duel, the Ant camp had been in silent uproar as they tried to understand what was going on. Scouts and emissaries sent into the wood had been rebuffed: the Etheryen were not talking. Orthopters and Fly-kinden were already winging their way towards where the Imperial Eighth was camped to see what they were doing, and the usual Ant paranoia about outsiders was abruptly to the fore. The camp was a prickly place to be, all of a sudden; the delegations from Princep and Collegium were being carefully watched, and Che's party was practically under full-scale surveillance.

'He's come to see Che,' Thalric guessed.

Tynisa nodded without looking at him. The two of them made an uneasy pair of sentries. They had known each other for some years now, and had shared a variety of escapades, but they were not friends. Only their mutual care for Che kept them civil to each other.

Che herself was sitting closer to the trees than either of them would have liked, along with the halfbreed woman, Maure. The two of them had done precisely nothing for the past half hour, after Maure had scratched out some manner of circle in the ground and lit some candles to go around it, most of which had since blown out.

Magic – they're doing magic. Tynisa tested the words carefully. She had grown up in Collegium, where magic was a joke they made about the stupid things the Inapt believed and which, though Inapt herself, she had not credited. There was no magic, she had once been sure.

Now she was returned from the Commonweal, where everyone believed in it implicitly, and Tynisa herself had witnessed such things . . .

After that, Tynisa found that she could face the word *magic* and feel almost none of the old embarrassment. Instead, some deep-buried part of her, born of both her parents' kinden, rose eagerly for it, too long denied its proper place in her thoughts.

The real surprise had been Thalric, for he was as Apt as any Wasp. But when Che had declared that she and Maure would be undertaking a ritual to investigate just what was going on in the forest, he had merely nodded, jaw clenched a little, and said nothing.

Milus the tactician, however, was surely not going to be quite so accepting.

As he approached, Tynisa and Thalric drew closer together without intending to, making the space between them a barrier for the Ant. The threat was a weak one: the Tactician had a dozen men at his back, and there were hundreds of Ant-kinden just a thought away.

Still, as the Ants closed, Tynisa took another step forward, right into his path. The movement was awkward and stiff, thanks to the wound that had come close to finishing her, in that same fight which had mauled her face. In truth, Apt surgeons would probably have given up on her, or at the least confined her to a bed for months to come, but the Commonweal held other ideas about medicine, and those who wore the Weaponsmasters' badge could draw on unusual sources of strength. Tynisa's hand was closed about her rapier hilt, and she could feel the steel all the way down her spine, supporting her.

To his credit, Milus stopped deliberately before them, dispersing the threatened confrontation by pointed diplomacy. His eyes narrowed, fixing on Che and Maure inside their circle. 'What's she doing?' he asked.

Tynisa allowed herself to exchange a glance with Thalric. She had a choice, to obfuscate, or to simply baffle the man. She chose the latter.

'Magic.'

Tactician Milus nodded. 'She is Inapt, I'd guess. She must believe so.'

Tynisa blinked, trying to reassess him, but unable to quite pin him down.

'Do you think I'd come to treat with the Ancient League without some understanding of the Inapt?' Milus declared. 'I have a devious little adviser on such matters, who tells me all manner of lies about the business, but even so I cannot deny that many kinden believe in such things,' Milus frowned further. 'What's she hoping to achieve?'

'Divination,' Tynisa explained. 'Far-seeing.'

'She wants to spy on the enemy? Good, I need to talk to her.'

'She's busy,' Tynisa objected. Thalric was keeping his peace, she noted, and that was just as well. Even the most conciliatory words were unlikely to be received well from a Wasp.

Milus let two seconds' silence pass. 'I need to talk to her,' he repeated, slightly more forcefully. 'There is a Wasp army at hand. There is fighting in the Etheryon. I cannot afford to wait on her pleasure.'

There was iron in his glance, a seamless transition from friend to threat that nearly had Tynisa's rapier in her hand.

She opened her mouth to defy him, feeling a fighting calmness settle on her shoulders, all her thoughts and worries falling into the moment.

'Tynisa, it's all right.' Che's voice.

Tynisa did not look away from Milus. 'You're happy to talk?'

'I think I'd better,' Che confirmed. She started to get up, but the tactician strode between Tynisa and Thalric, near enough to touch either, and crouched down at her level.

'Tell me what's going on,' he said, back to being friendly and reassuring.

Tynisa saw Che take a deep breath. 'The Empress is here, with the Eighth,' she declared.

Milus gave a grunt of surprise. That was plainly not what he had expected to hear. Before he could question her, she added, 'Don't ask me how I know. I couldn't tell you in any way you'd understand. And I don't really expect you to believe me – but you did ask.'

After a moment of introspection, perhaps summing up the reactions and opinions of his advisers, or his whole army, he nodded. 'It seems unlikely,' was all he said.

'There is something in the forest she wants; that is all I am sure of. Maure and I have been trying to find out what it is, but . . . the magical landscape is much as you see the physical – tangled and knotted and dark, layer on layer. That there is something there at the heart of the wood, between the two holds, is plain. What it is . . . Tactician, permit me to suggest that you're taking this very well.'

Milus nodded. 'Some of what you say matches recent intelligence from my own sources, and from the Roach girl from Princep, who's been in and out of the green a few times. There's fighting going on in there, and the Etheryen think that there are Wasps under the trees already, helping out the Nethyen. The Empress? Who knows, but *something* has gone badly wrong. We've lost key allies, and if the forest is lost then we've lost our flank as well, and the next battlefield will probably be at the gates of Sarn. And still I don't know what's going on, which is the worst thing in the world for a tactician. The Mantis-kinden won't talk to me, so that's where you come in.'

Che's gaze remained level. 'What do you think I am, Tactician?' There was a keen tension between them, and Tynisa felt her instincts twitch and tighten as they sized each other up.

'I don't care what you are,' was Milus's answer. 'All I know is that I've never seen Mantids back down like they did when you confronted them. So: you're important. They will listen to you. You can find out what in the pits is going on. Possibly you can even put it right.'

'I need to go into the forest,' declared Che, and Tynisa frowned, trying to work out whether the Beetle girl was wrenching the conversation off on a new path, or whether it had always been heading there.

'That would seem sensible,' Milus agreed. 'You're Maker's niece, they say. You share his ideals, regarding the Empire?' If his eyes flicked towards Thalric it was only for a moment.

'These days I find myself opposed to the Empress most of all, and that of necessity,' Che murmured. 'For your purposes, though, the answer is yes.'

'Then I will give you whatever you might need, whether it's provisions or people.' He stood smoothly, for all that he was a man in middle years and wearing full armour. 'If there are Wasps in the forest, then I want to move my men in to counter them, and to aid our allies, but I need the Etheryen's nod for that. Too risky, otherwise. Before you go, see if you can secure their cooperation.'

'I'll do what I can,' Che agreed.

When the tactician had gone, Tynisa and Thalric both rounded on her.

'Are you mad? We're headed to Collegium,' the Wasp pointed out. 'Nobody goes into a Mantis forest – not without an army.'

'You don't have to come.'

He looked insulted. 'You know I do, but that doesn't matter. It's a mad plan. You're not doing it.'

Che glanced over at Maure, who was looking sorry for herself. 'You heard what I said: there is something in there that the Empress *wants*. We could feel that naked desire very plainly. You know the Empress, Thalric. Do you really think she would go to such lengths for no reason? And do you want her to secure what she's after? Whatever it is, whatever is at the heart of the wood, we need to get to it first.'

'Another Darakyon,' Tynisa found herself saying. The old dead forest west of Myna had once been a place avoided even by the most rational of the Apt. The histories of the Bad Old Days before the revolution were long and dark and bloody, and there was room for far more than one nest of atrocity there.

'Not quite,' Che said, after a moment's thought. 'Whatever is there has its own sense of . . . bitterness, pride . . . betrayal even, but power, too. Some knot of ancient power, the fulcrum between Etheryon and Nethyon. I must talk to the Moth, Terastos. There will be legends, even if they are not spoken of openly. I will make him tell me.'

'Che.' Thalric's face had become closed. 'When you say the

Empress is here, and there's something in the wood that she wants . . . do you mean *she*'s going in after it? In person?'

'Given what she is become, I do not think that whatever she seeks could just be retrieved by a squad of the Light Airborne,' Che agreed.

'Then she's mad, too,' Thalric decided, but his tone had changed. He did not add, *and we can kill her in there*, but Tynisa caught the thought from him like a disease. Yes, the Empress Seda would have soldiers and bodyguards but who could say what might happen in the heart of a Mantis forest?

It seemed irresistible to compare killing the Empress with Tynisa's father's fight before the previous Emperor. It would be as though she was continuing Tisamon's work.

She broke off from her thoughts to find Che already striding off towards the dark wall of the forest. 'Wait, you're going *now?*'

'I need to speak to the Etheryen, if I can find them, just as the tactician wanted.'

Tynisa hissed in frustration, limping awkwardly after her, pushing herself hard to catch up.

Close to the forest's edge, Laszlo waited. A single tree stood here, split by lightning years ago and long dead, yet retaining some faint ghost of menace for all that. The Sarnesh logging concerns had been operating here as part of their cautious and constantly renegotiated agreements with the Etheryen over the years, but this tree they had left, so Laszlo guessed it had some significance to the locals.

This was where Lissart had said for them to meet, when he had managed to catch a moment with her. Even with his credentials as part of the Collegiate delegation, he had been pushing the tolerance of her Ant guards in getting that close.

He had not yet seen her alone here and, although Tactician Milus might just be solicitous for Lissart's health, her position seemed to Laszlo more that of a prisoner than a trusted adviser. Of course, he knew better than most why that might be, since she had been working for the Wasps when he first met her. She had personally sabotaged Solarno's defences so that it could be taken by the Empire and its Spider allies and, had she not had some falling out with her superiors there, she might even now be sitting in that other armed camp on the far side of the forest.

She was not trustworthy, therefore.

He had not felt sure that she would come to meet him, but here she was. Her manner was furtive, flying low to the ground, halting abruptly, a pattern of stop and go that made her invisible each time she froze. Laszlo had better eyes than any Ant, but even he had trouble following her. When she reached him, she fell into his arms without warning, dragging him down into a crouch amongst twisted, dead roots.

For a long moment they were both silent, and he could feel the rapid beating of her heart. Ever the opportunist, Laszlo tried for a kiss, and she pushed him away angrily. A moment later, her expression was almost desperate, like a plea for help.

And she's unstable, he reminded himself, adding that thought to his earlier list of reasons for not being here. The only reason *to* be here, in fact, was currently holding herself at arm's length, trying to read his face through the lens of her own fractured expression. *I always did end up with the crazy ones.*

'Shall we skip the bit where you call me a fool for turning up, and talk about why you didn't jump ship in Collegium?'

'Why would I jump?' And a small smile from her.

'The Sarnesh seem like they're clipping your wings.'

'Am I not here?'

'Should I shout that information out and see what they think of it?' He was trying to be hard with her, but his voice caught on the last few words. 'Let me help you.'

'Why should I need help?' She half turned away from him, her eyes on the neat ranks of Sarnesh tents. 'It's just a little change in our deal. Tactician Milus is better informed than I thought.'

'You were trying to play him.'

'I had valuable information to provide. We had a deal. We still do.'

'Liss, who are you working for?'

'Sarn,' but she overplayed the innocence, a sign of her fraying confidence.

'Is it the Empire?'

'Is this your idea of an interrogation?' Mock flirting, perhaps, but his expression got to her and she added. 'I swear, not them. Not even after you killed Garvan for me, not them'

'Then who? No, fine, don't say.' For a moment he wondered if she was actually working for Collegium, for Sten Maker even, and it was just that nobody had mentioned it. 'Milus – he's clever, dangerous.'

And he saw she was scared, but she said, 'I'm on top of it. Like always.'

'Like in Solarno?' he tried.

'*Yes!* I was in control, in Solarno. You were just some glorified skivvy.'

'At least I was glorified.' But she would not smile at that, either. 'Tell me what's going on, why don't you'?'

'Tell you . . .?' Indignant at first, but then her gaze softened, and she continued, 'You are a truly awful spy. You are a disgrace to our profession, really you are.'

'Good enough to know you're in trouble,' he pointed out and, when she did not deny it, he added, 'So fly.'

'With you?'

'Right now,' he agreed, without hesitation.

Her expression seemed balanced on a knife edge. 'And the Collegiates – you'd abandon them, would you?'

'Bartrer and Amnon? Like a shot.'

'And Stenwold Maker?'

He made to speak, failed twice, then forced out the word, 'Yes.'

A flame kindled in the palm of her hand, her Art guttering and dancing there, lighting up her face so that his breath caught.

He was choked with memories of their time together travelling with the Spider-kinden baggage train, or trying to run for Collegium ahead of the advancing Wasps. 'You are a master's piece of work,' he murmured, even as he became aware she was sabotaging her own chances of escape, showing every Sarnesh sentry exactly where she was.

'And *you* are a fool, and you'd be as lost as I, with Sarn and Collegium both hunting us. And who would we sell ourselves to then? Who's left?' When he tried to speak her hand fell on his lips, the flame gone and her skin startlingly cool. 'I know what I'm doing. Milus isn't as smart as he thinks he is, and he won't pin me down. No ties, remember.' She was all confidence until her eyes left his to glance into the darkness. 'And I have work to do here, before I get clear. But I could use a lift, maybe, when you go to report to your man Maker about his niece. Just a lift, maybe. It's really not that important.'

'Why not now?' he demanded.

'Because I'm not ready to. Because Milus is almost where I want him, and then I'll know him, know the heart of him. And I'll have something to sell, then: something to put me back in the game. Because, as long as I can creep away like this, he hasn't won. And because it would hurt you.'

It was Laszlo's turn to be silent.

'I read you so well. I know every page. How you ever thought you'd be an agent for anyone taxes the mind.' But her tone was cautiously fond. 'I don't want you carrying the weight of betraying this Stenwold Maker of yours. I won't be struck with the blame for that. You promise too much in return for too little. I want you free of guilt.'

'And you're breaking with the Sarnesh?'

'If I do, your man Maker had better be able to protect me. Or I swear I'll go back to the Wasps. Just be ready for me, when the time comes for you to fly back to Collegium. Watch out for me.' She leant in to him abruptly, lips brushing his cheek light as air, and then she was off, with the same jerky, stop-start flight, for all that they must have detected her by now.

Tonight was one for farewells.

The Etheryen had not responded to Che's request to enter their domain. According to the Roach, Syale, the Loquae who led them were debating it even now, but the Mantids had only the loosest organization within the wood, and a response could come either tonight or in a tenday.

I would prefer not to go in uninvited. That would be classed as suicide by more resilient survivors than she, and she would be entrusting her life, and the lives of her fellows, to the nebulous strength of her own magical authority, a branch she did not want to put her full weight on just yet.

She would be walking in with the dawn, though, if the Mantids had sent no message meanwhile. The Empress would not hesitate, after all.

And what is it, that's in there? What is she after?

Che was uncomfortably aware that Empress Seda already knew of her presence. Each of them was like a needle in the mind of the other, impossible to ignore. Her best guess was that she had sensed the Empress first, or at worst they had recoiled from each other at the same moment. But, if Seda had become much more accomplished in her divinations, it was possible that she had set a trap for Che here.

In fact, it was possible that the entire business here was a trap. It sounded like hubris to think so, but Che remembered her last encounter with the woman, the unbridled hatred revealed just because Che found herself sharing in the woman's strange legacy.

Sharing was not something that the Empress was well suited for, Che had discovered. In that linked moment, Seda had nearly destroyed her mind out of reflexive fury, and that rage was still alive and well. Che could feel the heat of it.

But she could not afford to believe this was just a trap, because if the Empress unlocked some great power here, the entire world would suffer.

Thalric had laid a fire, and they were camping up near the trees, waiting for any word at all. The Sarnesh were keeping clear, but Balkus and his Roach girl had come to join them. Che had expected more remonstrations about her uncle, but the Ant stayed silent on that point. He himself was departing in the morning to take word to Princep.

'I remember you in Helleron,' she observed. 'You weren't half as serious, back then.'

His expression was a little hurt, a little sad. 'War does that,' he said solemnly, and then spoiled it by failing to suppress a smile. 'No, forget that. Finding somewhere you care enough to want to protect, that's what does it. I mean, anywhere that's mad enough to have me basically running its defence, that place deserves keeping around just for the laughs, doesn't it?' His sigh was wistful, a moment's requiem for the older, more carefree days. 'I'll pass word to Sperra for you: she always liked you. And Syale . . .?'

'I'm for the forest again,' the Roach girl replied.

Balkus grimaced, but made no attempt to talk her out of it.

'How?' Tynisa said, abruptly. 'I don't understand. You're . . . what are you, to the Mantids? Why don't they just kill you?' The words probably came out sounding more hostile than she intended.

'With the Mantis-kinden, there is only ever one reason,' Syale told her, rising to the challenge enough to look Tynisa in the eye. 'Why do they obey the Moths? Why do they hate your kinden so? History. Even if they don't remember the reason, they remember that it was thus in the Days of Lore, and so it cannot be any other way now. They have only their traditions left. Everything else has been stripped from them by time. If you don't understand that . . .' *'Then you'll die in there,'* was plainly on the tip of her tongue, but the words never came, the girl's eyes flicking to Tynisa's brooch: the sword and circle of the Weaponsmasters. 'You *do* understand that, even if you don't know it,' she said instead, frowning at Tynisa now. 'Enough to know that we were their friends and kin, long ago, and even if they've forgotten how or why, they have not forgotten that it was so.'

'We do not forget,' a new voice agreed, 'but nor do we submit. Even the Moths must learn that lesson sometimes.' A Mantis woman was suddenly there beside their fire, springing startled oaths from Balkus and Thalric. She studied them, the Ant's drawn sword and the Wasp's out-thrust palm, and dismissed them as irrelevant. She was a lean, hard figure clad in dun and russet leathers, with a cuirass of chitin scales. Her pale hair was bound back tautly against her skull, and her features could have been carved from white wood, so immobile were they even when she spoke. Her yellow eyes moved constantly between the people about her as though looking for a victim, and the intelligence burning there seemed to belong to something other than human. 'You would be wise, Roach girl, to remember that our history recounts its share of those outsiders who went too far.'

Syale shrugged, doing her best to seem calm, but Che noticed her swallow.

Time to see what their price is, I suppose. She hauled herself up to face the Mantis woman across the fire. 'You've been sent to me?'

That cold, yellow gaze flicked towards her, then away. 'No.' The slender length of a rapier blade gleamed in her hand, and Che could not have said whether it was there a moment before. 'To her.'

She did not even need to indicate whom she meant, for Tynisa was already levering herself to her feet.

'Your people sought this already,' Che insisted. 'I forbade it then and I forbid it now.'

The Mantis spared her barely a moment's regard. 'We do not

know what you are. We do not know from where your authority stems. I say to you what I said to the Roach. You, too, can go too far. Enter the woods with this one at your side, untested, and you will never be safe from us, nor will we ever be your allies. We call her out for bearing that badge and wearing that face.'

'Call me out for my father's blood as well as my mother's, then,' Tynisa told her flatly. 'I am ashamed of none of it.'

For a moment the Mantis's eyes finally stopped, narrowed as though she was trying to see into Tynisa's soul. At last she said, 'So,' a single word crammed with venom.

'Tynisa, this isn't necessary,' Che insisted, but her sister held up a hand to stop her.

'In this, Che, I know better than you, and it would happen sooner or later. Let it be now rather than when we've more important things to concern us.' Tynisa had not looked away from the Mantis woman, and those last words were pointed. 'Let's get it over with.'

Che opened her mouth a few times, as Tynisa limped away from their camp, moving closer to the trees. *I have magic*, she thought. *They have to listen to me!* But she was at the limits of her understanding, and whatever power had been invested in her, she was still growing into it. She only hoped the Empress found herself in the same position.

The others were watching her, but she could only shrug. Tynisa had taken up a stance, the elegant, Mantis-worked rapier in her hand levelled at her opponent. This would be the first time she had fought seriously, since taking her wounds. Another Mantis, another Weaponsmaster, had cut her up savagely in a duel in the Commonweal and, though she had won, the injuries had stayed with her, the scar-tissue stiffening her movements, making every day a trial of pain.

The Mantis woman had her own blade levelled, taking her place with an enviable, easy grace. For a moment the two of them stood motionless, the duel taking shape, silent and still, between them.

The Mantis struck first, darting in along the line of Tynisa's blade and thrusting for her heart. The lightest of parries knocked the strike away, nothing of Tynisa moving but the wrist, There was no riposte, and the Mantis ended up out of distance as she stepped back to avoid the counter-attack that never came. Another poised moment fell.

A few feints followed, the Mantis's sword flicking in from either side, testing her opponent's defences. Each time Tynisa turned her enemy's steel aside with a minimum of motion. Her arm did all. Her feet might as well have been nailed down.

Here it comes, Che thought, for the Mantis had got the measure of her opponent now and was gathering herself, the exploratory feints becoming more and more aggressive, her attacks fiercer and fiercer, and from more angles, stepping left and right to make her opponent move.

Tynisa moved. Abruptly she was dodging sideways to match the Mantis, and it was like a crippled beggar suddenly taking to his heels to avoid the guard. The limp, the stiffness, all were gone without trace, and Tynisa's old grace was back with her, born of her varied heritage and her long practice, of her own perfect affinity with the fight. The Mantis fell back, trying to open some space in which to adjust, but Tynisa flowed with her, sword dancing, clattering and scraping as it stooped and clashed with the other woman's blade.

What the others perceived, Che could not know, but her eyes saw the trick, the Weaponsmaster's discipline that Tynisa drew on. It was almost as if her rapier was fixed in the air, moving of its own accord and lending its wielder the strength to move with it. The sword led and Tynisa followed, an equal partnership of its strength and her direction. If she let go of the hilt, Che felt that her sister would collapse like a puppet.

The Mantis woman hissed in fury and tried to reclaim the

initiative, losing out to her emotions for only a moment: that this halfbreed, this abomination and trickster, was making a mockery of her people's ways. In that moment Tynisa had shrugged past her guard, rapier point dipping past the Mantis's quillons to gash her hand, to slice a thin line of red up her arm, to come to rest at the hollow of her throat. Now they were still again, just as they had started. For a long moment nobody spoke, nobody moved.

'Finish it,' the Mantis said quite calmly, as though the blade was pressed at someone else's neck.

'Cut your own throat, if you want,' Tynisa answered carelessly, and abruptly she stepped back, sword lowering, and turned her back on her opponent. The access to speed and poise that had possessed her drained away, and it was plain that her next few steps pained her. The sword had done its work, and now abandoned her to the aftermath.

'If you claim that badge, you claim our ways!' the Mantis shouted at her retreating back.

'I have lived by Mantis ways,' Tynisa said flatly, not looking at her. 'I have seen where they lead and I am amazed there are any of your kinden left alive. Save that I know that it is because *nobody* can live up to those iron rules you set yourselves. It is only by constant, concealed failures, day by day, that the Mantis-kinden can survive at all. I know this from my father and I know this from myself. And yet the badge is still with me, as is the sword, and I am worthy of both. Can you deny that?' At last she turned, inviting challenge.

The Mantis woman bared her teeth and braced herself, twice seeming on the very point of leaping at Tynisa and recommencing the duel. At the last, though, she could not.

'Che, we go into the wood tomorrow?' Tynisa asked.

'That's my plan.' Che did not even bother with the usual platitudes of, *You don't have to go with me*. 'The Sarnesh want to send soldiers in as well, so as to help the Etheryen counter the

Wasps. It'll make sense to travel with them at first, but we'll need to go faster, and deeper, soon enough.'

'Then tell them we are coming. Tell them a Weaponsmaster is coming. And tell them that all the rest, my blood, my face, none of it matters if I have earned this badge.' And Tynisa stared at the Mantis woman until she had retreated back into the woods, looking baffled and angry but unable to deny it.

Eight

His name was Esmail. His name was Ostrec. He had two faces and two lives, one lurking invisible beneath the other, like a fish hanging in dark waters with its eyes fixed on the surface.

The waters ran deeper still, for that outer shell of Ostrec was itself a many-layered thing. Lieutenant Ostrec of the Quartermasters Corps: ambitious young officer, pushy, arrogant, competitive, all the virtues the Wasps so loved. No doubt his outmanoeuvred or fallen rivals had all wondered what his secret was. It was that behind the outer face of Lieutenant Ostrec lurked Major Ostrec of the Rekef, hunter of traitors. He had been on close terms with great men until recently, had Major Ostrec, but then there had been a culling amongst those grandees of the secret police, a sudden dying off of the Rekef's leadership to isolate their General Brugan. His plots to control the Empress had gone awry, Brugan's allies were dead, and the Rekef itself was lessened. And Ostrec? Major Ostrec had seamlessly transferred his loyalty to the Empress, and nobody in the know had been much surprised. Who would not have done so, under the circumstances?

Now he was Major Ostrec of the Red Watch, a company of the elite created by the Empress herself. Most assumed that its members were all ex-Rekef spies and killers, or similar terrors, but there was a stranger secret at the heart of it as the man behind Ostrec's face knew only too well.

He knew the Empress was Inapt and a magician. She had hunted out Wasp-kinden with some faint touch of the old days in them – from mixed blood or some far-distant ancestor of power. These Wasps she had made her own, bound them to her by blood and named them her Red Watch. Each had a mere drop of magic in them, but together they fed their mistress by their deeds. Seda had come late to her power, by the slow decline of magic, but she was reinventing lost traditions at a frightening rate. She understood that darkness and fear and pain were not just tools of the arcane, they were weapons of statecraft.

So she had cast an eye over Ostrec, the duplicitous, and seen that spark strong within him, and made him hers, and never realized that here was a creature cunning enough to hide his true nature from her. She had never realized that Ostrec, the Quartermaster lieutenant and Rekef major, had been dead for tendays, and that the man she had taken into her closest circle was a spy and a killer of a very different kind.

His name was Ostrec. His name was Esmail. He was one of the very few left of his kinden, the Assassin Bugs who had fought and lost an ancient war against the Moth-kinden in ages forgotten to Apt history. He had been sent to the Empire by Moths of Tharn, but it was plain to him that those Tharen sages who had briefed him had lost out to bolder spirits, for Tharn was allied with the Empire now. He would be getting no further instructions.

They had briefed him to investigate the Empress, to find out what she was. More, they had briefed him to kill her.

He would be able to manufacture the opportunity, he knew, for Ostrec was trusted by the Empress. If he had been unconcerned with his own survival, then he could have done it already, but he had left family behind near Tharn, and he was not quite ready yet for the ultimate sacrifice.

More, he was not sure that he would do it, even if he could be sure to walk away from the deed. The frightening revelation was that the Empress *was* Inapt, and held a great deal of magical power, and if she was also capricious and wicked and ruthless, so what? These were not solely Wasp virtues, after all, and could be claimed by many of the great magicians of old. Looking on Seda, Esmail was only struck by how much the current crop had *lost* of their inheritance. For her part, she was young and vital and strong, and she did not hesitate to use her power. She had bound Mantis-kinden to her, destroyed her rivals and roused an Empire to war, and all this from being a timid girl living in the shadow of her brother's displeasure.

She claimed that she would bring back the old days. Esmail, whose heritage and training were sunk deep in those lost times, reckoned that, if anyone could do it, Seda could.

He was having a difficult time working out where his true loyalties should lie, and in the meantime the Empress was not standing still. Here they were at the gates of the Mantis dream, and tomorrow the Wasps would march in to support their Nethyen allies, and Seda would march along with them to secure . . .

He was not sure what, for she did not confide in anyone save the crooked Woodlouse-kinden Gjegevey. Power would be involved, though, that seemed beyond doubt. Something buried in the Mantis wood was calling to her. The thought of Seda with yet more power in her hands filled him with fear, and yet quickened his blood. *What might she not do? What might she not bring back from those dead ages?*

He would go with her into the trees tomorrow, he knew. He would go, and her Mantis bodyguards, and that creature Tisamon, which Esmail knew was no living man – another feat from the old stories that Seda had somehow recreated! With them would go the Empire's best, the most skilled Pioneers that General Roder could lay his hands on. Behind them would come the scouts and trackers and Light Airborne of the Eighth Army, those soldiers best suited to fighting in such a dark and twisted place.

I will bring it all back, she had said, and the prospect of killing her was receding, day by day. Even though she did not really know him, he was becoming her creature every bit as much as Tisamon was.

She will destroy us all, he warned himself, yet there was much of him that could not make himself regret it.

When Seda emerged from her tent, General Roder was waiting for her and had been for some time. She could read a great deal in his half-crippled face about just how well *that* sat with him.

She noticed his eyes register Tisamon, and saw him master an instinctual flinch away – such good instincts he had. Still, here he was, so plainly something important was gnawing at the general – or at least something that he considered important.

'Your Imperial Majesty.'

'Ah, General.' She favoured him with a smile. 'I hope you are not here hoping to dissuade me from my jaunt?' He had certainly tried to argue against her entering the Mantis wood, with fistfuls of reasons that to the Apt were entirely logical and persuasive. If that was his tune still this morning she would not be pleased, but she sensed something else had sunk its jaws into him.

'I have received word from the Second Army, Majesty,' Roder reported, holding out a scroll.

She waved it away. It would be in some Apt code, illegible to her even if she had been taught the cipher. But then, as Empress, she had people to read things for her. In such a fashion her Inapt nature went undiscovered even in the heart of the Empire. 'Tell me,' she instructed.

'General Tynan informs me he is on the move, as per orders. The Second has resumed its march on Collegium.'

She had not doubted it. Tynan was a solid, reliable officer, experienced enough to cope with his recent reversals against the Beetles. *Nobody ever said that conquering Collegium would be easy.* A lie: many back in Capitas had claimed the Beetles would fall before Tynan as swiftly as their kin in Helleron had capitulated, but they were fools who did not realize that a warrior spirit was not the sole route to determined resistance. The Beetles were tough and ingenious and, even though Seda could no longer understand all their clever Apt ways, she was well aware that they could still throw myriad problems at General Tynan's feet. His war would be fought by artificers just as much as by soldiers.

'He . . .' A moment's hesitation while Roder considered the words of a fellow general which had been meant only for him. 'He is concerned about his air strength against the Beetles. He has a great deal of respect for their pilots and machines.' Had Tynan's actual words expressed something stronger, something approaching criticism? No matter: Seda had looked into Tynan's face and soul. He would follow orders.

'The issue is in hand, General,' she told Roder, feeling a small degree of amusement that this part of Tynan's fight – a key element of the Second's strategy of which even Tynan was ignorant for now – was something that she could understand.

Still Roder stood there with the burden of something unsaid weighing him down. Seda sighed, feeling the pressure of her station and majesty: how to inspire awe in your underlings without all these awkward pauses while they searched their own words for treason? 'Just speak, General. The forest awaits me.'

The general nodded. 'It is a matter concerning the Second, Majesty.' His gaze flicked to Tisamon, and then back to her. She found it remarkable that the eye in the paralysed half of his face was perhaps his most expressive feature now. 'Tynan has the Spiders as his allies.'

Ah, there we are. 'General, we are confident in our strategies and in those we send to war,' she told him. 'You should concern yourself with your own campaign.' And she began to walk away.

'No, Majesty!' and he had put out a hand to physically stop her, whereupon Tisamon's gauntlet blade was at his throat, and it was only because Seda had a swift enough mind to rein her bodyguard in that she was not in need of a new general there and then.

'Explain yourself,' she snapped, staring at his frozen,

outstretched hand. *Perhaps I do need a new general, after all.* She had thought she had the measure of Roder's rebellious thoughts and insecurities, but this was new.

'Your Imperial Majesty,' Roder said carefully, the razor line of steel still touching his neck, 'do not trust the Spider-kinden. They *cannot* be trusted.' His eyes entreated her, afire with the need to communicate. 'I fought them in the last war, barely three years ago. They were our enemies then and they are our enemies now – save that they have a score to settle with Collegium. They were the Beetles' allies once, remember! When Tynan and his Second are at their most extended, when the fight balances on a knife-edge, they will betray him for the Beetles again. Or else, when he has won, his men depleted whilst the Spiders hold back, they will destroy him and claim the spoils that are ours. Majesty, Tynan has left a chain of such conquests in his wake – Tark, Merro, Kes – and they are all gone over to the Spiderlands, not to the Empire.'

Seda stared into that half-mask face. *What does he gain from this? This is because the Spiders poisoned him, is it? He hates them that much? Where has this come from?*

'Majesty,' Roder said again, and it was not the soldier that now spoke, but the plain man beneath. 'Heed me on this, I beg you. They are no fit allies for us, and Tynan is in danger every moment he marches alongside them. Ask *him*!' Incredibly, he was pointing at Tisamon, driven to calling upon the least likely aid in his attempt to persuade her. 'Ask your other bodyguards. Ask the Nethyen! The Mantids have known forever what the Eighth found out in the last war. I have seen my men poisoned and trapped, seduced from their duty, turned against their superiors. I have fought a war against them, and there is nothing of the soldier in them, no honour, no heart, just masks and more masks!' He was baring his soul now, and the bitter venom in there startled her. She recalled how he had asked to be given the southern front, before the Empire had allied itself with the Spiderlands Aristoi. *And that would have gone even more poorly than I thought, and we would even now be fighting around Solarno rather than most of the way to Collegium.* And yet, and yet . . .

The Spiders were an old Inapt power, and they had held onto that power when most of their peers from the Days of Lore had fallen into ruin. They controlled vast territories, cities of the Apt and the Inapt both, and just like Seda herself they made use of all the artificers' machines without needing to understand them. A jolt of uncertainty shot through her. *What have I overlooked?* Overconfidence was always the scourge of rulers. *Of course, the Spiders are clever – they have been playing for centuries the game I have invented for myself. So what is the true plan that the Aldanrael have hatched? Is Roder right?*

She could not say, and that gaping chasm in her knowledge came close to frightening her. But Roder *was* right in one thing: she could not be certain of the Spider-kinden as allies. They were treacherous, and she must remember that, and take steps to protect the Empire from them should they turn.

'General Roder,' she began, and her very tone was enough to retract Tisamon's blade and to dispel the tension that their little confrontation had been spreading throughout the camp. 'You are a good and loyal servant of the Empire,' she continued, 'and I hear your words. Our allies in the Spiderlands have been true to us so far, but there will come a time when we will not need them, or they will not need us. It is well to be watchful, and perhaps Tynan is indeed too trusting.'

She saw him relax, and at last glimpsed the spark of motive there. Yes, he hated the Spiders for the injuries of the last war – both to him and to his army – but there was more. His concern was for the Empire and for its greater war. True, if Tynan fell, then Roder would find himself caught between Sarn and the Collegiates, but it was more than that. Roder wanted the Empire to *win*. She realized, then, how close she had been to turning him away, how her own exalted station, her personal ambitions, could have compromised the war. *And they will do so, still, for I will brook no barriers, but I am Empress – as well as heiress to the*

Days of Lore. I must remember my people. She had a hollow, unhappy feeling that this would be harder and harder to achieve, in the days to come. *I will be Empress and magician-queen both. I will rule as the Spiders rule. And if the Spiders challenge me, then . . .*

'Captain Vrakir,' she snapped, and one of her Red Watch came rushing over to do her bidding. He had been listed to accompany her into the forest, but now she had another task for him. 'Commandeer an orthopter and fly to join the Second,' she told him. 'I will have sealed orders prepared for you. You are to act as adviser to General Tynan, with my full authority. Ostrec alone will suffice to represent the Red Watch in my escort.'

Vrakir saluted. He was a serious, intelligent man, formerly a lieutenant in the Fourth Army, one of the survivors of the Felyal massacre early in the last war. More, he was gifted: some great-grandparent had adulterated the Wasp blood within him, and she knew he had proved deficient with machines and maps, a poor representative of the Apt. He was no magician, of course – none of her Red Watch could have mastered the simplest magic – but he made a good vessel. There was just enough vestigial affinity within him that she could work through him, speak to him, even see through his eyes if she used all her strength. It would be like trying to force herself through the tiny holes of a sieve, but that was better than the solid wall presented by most Wasps.

'I will have orders drawn up by the time you are ready to leave,' she told him and, as Vrakir ran off, she turned her attention back to Roder. 'Now,' she said, 'show me my escorts, your picked men.'

Seda knew that Ant-kinden armies were built about their famed heavy infantry, blocks of supremely disciplined, mindlinked men and women who had mail and swords, shields and crossbows that made up the grand majority of every Ant army the Empire that ever faced – for all that the individual city-states were usually at each other's throats. They were slow to innovate, the Ants. All that intermingling of thoughts, which might have been a wellspring of invention, instead seemed to suppress any individuals with new ideas. Seda suspected that on the rare occasions an Ant with a different way of thinking was allowed any power, the world became aware of it rapidly. For that matter, she had been receiving some disturbing reports concerning the new Ant general opposing the Eighth.

Wasp armies, in contrast, had traditionally been built about the Light Airborne, soldiers armed with swords or spears and their stinging Art, and able to move swiftly about the battlefield, lacking the Ants' iron discipline but swifter and more flexible. Wasp heavy infantry could not stand toe to toe with the Ants for long – not even the old disbanded Sentinels could have done that, whatever retired veterans might tell each other – but the Wasps beat the Ants repeatedly by outmanoeuvring them and by out-thinking them, by using the strengths of their Auxillians – and by allowing individual talent to count for more.

The Pioneers were a good example of this. They had been created during the Twelve-year War against the Dragonflies of the Commonweal, a foe who at their best had been as mobile and unpredictable as the Wasps themselves. Often the Commonwealers had taken inaccessible spots as their strongholds – badlands, hill-forts, or the hearts of ancient forests just like this. Often, too, there had been Mantis-kinden fighting alongside them. The Pioneers had been some of the most skilled individuals that the Empire could draw upon, perhaps the first ever occasion when the usual considerations of purity of blood had been allowed to slacken, when sheer ability had become paramount. And they had died, of course. Fighting the enemy's war on the enemy's ground, they had suffered a rate of attrition worse than frontline battlefield units, but they had done their job. No Dragonfly fortress or holdout had survived the Empire's attentions, and in many cases it was the work of the Pioneers to bring in the rest of the army.

The war against the Lowlands had been a slow time for those veterans of the Commonweal, so far. The Lowlanders fought like the Apt should, with machines and with armies. The call had gone out though and, even as Roder's Eighth had crossed the Imperial border, the Pioneers had been strapping on their gear, taking up their weapons. Now Roder had brought before Seda the best of them that he could offer. His expression was pained, for they were hardly the immaculate paragons of Wasp soldiery that he might want, but they were good. They knew their craft and, if she was to break off from the main force within the forest and pursue her own aims, she would need them. The forest would be against her, and half the Mantis-kinden in it, together with whatever force the Sarnesh could commit. And *her* of course, the cursed Beetle girl, Seda's rival. Seda would need every advantage, including this ragged, disreputable trio.

There was one Wasp amongst them, and he was perhaps the biggest man Seda had ever seen, hulking head and shoulders over his peers as though he had some Mole Cricket blood in him. He was broad, too, bulked out with muscle, his bared arms massive, looking as though they could uproot every tree in the forest for her until she had what she wanted. Twin axes were sheathed across his back, each looking as though a normal man would need two hands to wield it, and he wore a long coat studded with chitin plates, with a dark metal breastplate beneath it, nothing of the black and gold about him. His name was Gorrec, Pioneer sergeant, and he was the closest to an Imperial soldier that she was looking at.

To his right stood Icnumon, who looked as though Gorrec could have crushed him in one hand. He was a slender, pale piece of work, his ash-fair hair worn long and tied back, his features sharp and slightly out of proportion, as so often with halfbreeds. He had Wasp blood in him but his father had been Mantis-kinden, which made for a very dangerous combination. He had his mother's sting, and the spines of his father's people speared out from his forearms. He was an assassin, Roder had explained, who had stalked the shadows of the Commonweal, playing hide and seek with Dragonfly scouts and executing enemy leaders within their own forest haunts. He wore no armour, just a loose, long tunic and cloak of mottled grey-brown. There was a short, recurved bow holstered at his back, and long knives at his belt, but Seda could tell far more than Roder could what the man's real advantage was. Through some teaching of his father or secrets learned in the Commonweal, Icnumon had a touch of the magician about him: a few incantations and half-understood tricks to complement his Art, to let him stalk unseen in the darkness.

To Gorrec's left was a shorter, squatter figure, and not what she would have expected among the Pioneers. Instead of a slender Inapt killer or a rugged Wasp, here was a solid, balding Beetle-kinden wearing a hauberk of reinforced leather that was one step removed from an artificer's protective overalls. He had a snapbow over his shoulder, not the standard infantry model but the shorter-barrelled pieces that she understood the Light Airborne preferred for speed and ease of movement. This man was Jons Escarrabin, who had been born in Collegium a very long time ago, and who had fought on both sides in the Twelve-year War, graduating from captive to Auxillian to Pioneer. He looked like a mild shop-keeper, and had been personally mentioned in reports as a crack shot, an expert wildsman and a halfway decent artificer. He fought for the Empire for the same reason that a surprising number of mercenary types did, because where else would they get such a rewarding opportunity to practise their trades?

'I shall take them,' she declared. 'General, begin moving your chosen forces into the forest. The Nethyen and their Moth-kinden masters are expecting you, and they shall serve your officers as guides and Auxillians, bringing you to the fray. No quarter for the Etheryen. No quarter for the Sarnesh. Drive them back wherever you meet them.' Roder would have some inkling of the magnitude of the task, the size of the forest, its beasts, its darkness, no fit terrain for the Wasp-kinden, and yet they would do their best, despite it all, for her glory and that of the Empire.

And if those two glories diverge slightly, who is to know?

'My retinue will be Gjegevey, Tisamon and my personal body-guards, Ostrec of the Red Watch and your three Pioneers. I shall commandeer such others as I see fit from the locals and your forces as I need them. For yourself, Roder, while the Mantis-kinden are at war, there will be no support from the woods for the Sarnesh. You have waited long enough. Ready your men to march.'

Nine

The drone of Imperial machines was all that was left in the sky now. The deceptively quiet Collegiate Stormreaders had been and gone and, from his position dug into a hollow alongside a handful of Spider mercenaries, Morkaris could not have said how much the new Farsphex had helped. He had heard a fair number of bombs going off, for all their efforts.

Cautiously he crept out of the hollow. Morkaris was a cadaverously thin Spider-kinden, seeming pale as the grave in his articulated black mail, with a double-handed axe across his back that looked too heavy for him to wield. He had been a mercenary all his adult life, though, fighting for every coin and at every station, from lone warrior to captain, from captain to captain of captains. Now he had signed on with the Aldanrael family as their adjutant, the man who kept all their varied mercenary forces in line – and damned if he wasn't regretting it.

I should have stayed in the Spiderlands.

The last few days had been a harsh lesson about how well the sort of war he was used to travelled. The Spiderlands Aristoi fought all the time, with various levels of deniability, and mercenaries were a common commodity over there, with a good company never short of work – sometimes taking the coin of three families in as many days – sometimes all on the same day, or even in the same battle. In the Spiderlands, war was something Morkaris understood. Here, though . . . between the

Collegiates' cursed flying machines and the Wasps' own murderous devices, he was feeling old and out of his depth.

'Chief,' one of his men said, and he looked up to see another Spider approaching, and not one he was pleased to see, either. There had just been an attack, with the Collegiates quartering the sky and dropping explosives on any target that presented itself, and here was Jadis of the Melisandyr, his full armour gleaming as though the man had sat polishing it throughout the bombardment.

Jadis was commander of the Aldanrael's regular forces, hence Morkaris's opposite number, chief rival and constant foil. Here was a man born with all the advantages Morkaris had been denied: good looks, good family, respect that didn't require the daily shedding of blood . . . Morkaris spat wearily as the man strode over.

'You're a hard man to find,' Jadis told him.

'I like to think the Collegiates say the same. What do you want?' Morkaris demanded. 'Worried about my health?'

The two men sized each other up, not for the first time, as the mercenaries moved out in a loose semicircle behind their leader. Jadis had come alone, but nothing in his pose or expression suggested that he was remotely worried about his safety.

If I thought that was just arrogance . . . Challenges between individuals of comparable rank was not uncommon in Spider armies. Just as Morkaris was here to keep the infighting of the mercenaries at an acceptable level, so he himself could kick up some trouble if he wished, and had Jadis been the powdered major-domo he would have expected, then perhaps a little accident might have been arranged. Jadis could *fight*, though. The Melisandyr trained their sons well. When the Felyen Mantis-kinden and their allies had attacked the camp, Morkaris had witnessed the man at work: sword and shield and mail, protecting his mistress. The sight had been an education.

'We're moving,' Jadis told him flatly. He was sharp enough to know just what Morkaris thought of him, and not to care overmuch. Being liked by mercenaries was plainly not an ambition of his.

'Who's we, and where to?'

'All of us. To Collegium.'

Not entirely unexpected, but no more welcome news for that. 'And once they pull the army together, what about the Collegiates? What do we give them, save for a target?' Morkaris pointed out. His hands itched for the haft of his axe, just on general principles.

'A moving target, at least,' Jadis replied. 'Those are your orders. Get your rabble together. What's left of it.'

Morkaris grimaced despite himself. It was no secret that, regardless of all he could do, more than a quarter of the mercenaries had deserted, companies and individuals deciding that living under daily bombardment had not been what they signed on for. To keep those who remained, he had personally fought four duels in the last few tendays. Whether going on the march under that continued aerial assault would help morale at all was an arguable point.

'The new machines will help, they say,' Jadis offered. 'They will keep off the worst of the attacks.'

'If they don't just explode, like the last lot,' the mercenary spat. The fate of the Second Army's last fliers was well known by now.

'This will not happen, they say,' Jadis continued implacably.

Morkaris scowled. 'I may not understand their machines, but I can still count. The new fliers are very few.'

'This is irrelevant. Gather your companies for the march, or be ready to explain your failure to the Aldanrael.' Not quite a challenge, not quite a personal insult and nothing that Morkaris could not ignore, but still . . . for just a moment the mercenary wondered about quitting, which would certainly mean taking on Jadis then and there. The odds were too wide open, though, and he was still owed pay.

Instead he decided to stick a knife in where he knew the man's mail didn't protect him. 'Oh, well, if the Wasps say to Herself that they've won the skies back, who am I to argue? If Herself's that won over by the Wasps, then tell her that her mercenaries will be ready for the march, no worries.' The barb went home and Morkaris saw the other man twitch a little. 'After all, no point arguing with you. You're not the one she listens to any more.'

Jadis's face remained very set, but he was a Spider Aristos and master of his own emotions. It was an open secret that his mistress, Mycella of the Aldanrael, was bedding the Wasp general, and it was similarly known that Jadis was eating himself with jealousy about it. There was barely a flicker, though, to betray the man's feelings. In spite of himself, Morkaris was impressed, for here was Aristoi reserve at its finest. Shame that it wouldn't save any lives when they got close to Collegium.

'Listen, Jadis,' he pointed out, feeling weary and old with the tedious predictability of the statement. 'The Wasps don't like us, and they can't be trusted, and they don't share power. Tell me she knows this. Tell me that her . . .' For a moment he nearly descended into an insult, an indelicate remark about Jadis's blessed mistress, and that would have meant a duel whether Morkaris felt ready for it or not. 'Tell me that her coming to an *accommodation* with the Wasp general is all about her twisting him around to do her bidding. Because my men have been talking.'

'Mercenaries.' One word to dismiss all that Morkaris and his followers were, but any mercenary captain learned to read his employers, and he could see the slightest flicker deep in Jadis's eyes.

'She had just better be in a position to sell him out before he does the same to us,' the mercenary adjutant muttered. 'And yes, we'll march. We're ready. As ready as we'll ever be.'

General Tynan had rough hands, not the hands of a man in command but those of a man who did things for himself. He had a soldier's scars, where a Spider in his position would have skin unblemished and smooth as silk. Spiders knew how to avoid fights they could not win, mostly, although her own family's great battle against the Empire had given the lie to that, as had her subsequent campaign against Collegium. Against the Wasps, she had lost countless soldiers. Against the Beetles she had lost family. The greatest loss had been the esteem of her peers. The Aldanrael family was not what it had been, which had led to Mycella being here at the head of an army in a last-ditch attempt to regain by brute war what they had lost.

Leading an armed force was not a position of great honour for the Spider-kinden, since they gave it over to their menfolk and their Hoipolloi. Great ladies of great families did not dirty their hands with such business unless they were as desperate as Mycella had become. It had been the only path left to her: to take up the mantle of Lady-Martial, to sail for Solarno with her force of loyal followers, allied minor families and a rabble of mercenaries, and it had almost destroyed her pride. On the ship, she had contemplated ending her own life, because that would at least have won a moment's approval of her peers.

To the Wasp-kinden, on the other hand, to lead an army was the highest accolade, the position that every man of them seemed to covet and work towards. She knew that they, too, had their greater and their lesser families, but success in battle could raise up even the lowliest of them. General Tynan himself had started life with a few advantages, but he had not been anything that Mycella might call nobility. His merit, his skill and judgement had effected a transformation in his status that would have been unthinkable in the Spiderlands. There, the best that a low-born could hope for was patronage by a greater family or to become a freelance for hire, like that oaf Morkaris.

She had sat up late with General Tynan for many nights, now, in her expansive tent, listening to him talk about war. He was not a bloodthirsty monster, the way his kinden were so often portrayed, but he loved warfare. It had been his life since he was a child of five, being taught the first principles of swordsmanship. War and the Empire to which he was so loyal. When he spoke of his passion he seemed fifteen years younger, filled with the burning zeal of the true adherent. He told her of his battles against the Lowlanders, against the Commonweal, against cities within the Empire. He spoke of men he had commanded – almost all of them dead by now – and of enemies he had met both on the field and off it. He showed her what a Wasp general's world looked like, and the values that he cherished – so alien, and yet how they had struck a chord in her!

She had set out to seduce him, succeeding despite his innate caution. He had known what she was about, she guessed, and yet he had given before her soon enough. The day she could not lure a Wasp-kinden soldier to her bed would be her last day . . . and yet . . . she had found something in General Tynan that made him far more valuable to her than a mere puppet to be manipulated. More, she had found emotions awoken in her that were unwise and unlooked for. Not just those rough hands and her explorations of the battle-map of scars he bore, for such physical pleasures were merely expedient and useful, nothing to truly move her. The true gift he had given her, all unknowing, was a return of her self-respect.

She was Lady-Martial of the war-host of the Aldanrael, but that was a mark of disgrace, as though the other families had branded their disdain onto her skin.

To General Tynan, however, for all that she was a woman who could never have attained such rank within the Empire, she counted as a peer, someone deserving admiration. Through his eyes she was a general, and that was a thing worth being.

She had chosen a robe of deep blue edged with gold, complementing the Imperial colours without matching them. Beneath, she wore a hauberk of delicate copperweave chain backed with felt, flashing in the sun when the wind caught at her gown and flurried it aside. As the Second and its allies prepared to move out, she sought out General Tynan, finding him already atop his personal automotive, scouts and messengers landing beside him for orders, then being sent off within seconds.

His eyes shone, alighting on her. *Still mine then, for now.* It was an uneasy relationship, though, for she shared him with an Empress.

He extended a hand to her, even as his driver made the engine roar. With a light step she vaulted atop the machine, a moment's climbing Art serving to keep her footing on the sloping armoured plates, and she took her place beside him.

She could feel the eyes of his army fixed on her, some of them doubtless bitter that she – a foreign woman after all – took such pride of place, whilst others would be making lewd jokes later on and drinking to the success of their general's love life. The Imperial reaction would pale in comparison to the net of gossip, scheming and speculation amongst her own followers.

Around them, much of the army was already on the move: scouts and Light Airborne taking wing and casting themselves forwards to hunt out traps and ambushes. The slower-moving infantry were marching, having lost much of their own mechanized transport in the retreat from Collegium a month before. The remaining troop automotives were being rotated through the squads of Tynan's army by some arcane logistical calculations performed by the quartermasters. Mycella's own forces had fewer machines, but some of them were cavalry, and on average they were faster than the Wasps, if more prone to spread out and lose cohesion.

'Now comes the test!' Tynan told her, over the engine's growl. 'They've seen us massing and, if I were them, I'd step up the air attacks now that we're giving them a better target. If they can take out our new artillery before we arrive, we'll look like fools in front of their gates.' A fresh consignment of the vaunted great-shotters had arrived straight from the foundries of the Iron Glove Cartel, but for now the devices lay disassembled on transport automotives, which had been split into groups and scattered throughout the army.

'And how are your new air machines?' she asked him. There were a few shapes in the sky overhead, but she knew they were the older vessels.

'Ready,' he told her briefly. 'They'll do their best to keep the enemy away from our transporters, but they'll have a fierce time of it, and it'll get worse the closer we get to Collegium. At which point we'll see if we still have artillery superiority.'

She frowned, because that was a new thought. She had a hard time keeping up with which machines were better, between the Wasps and their foes, but so much evidently turned on this that she was working very hard to understand, Inapt or not. 'Is there some doubt of that?' she demanded.

'Don't underestimate the Collegiates. They're very clever people, and they've seen what we can do. For all the Iron Glove assures us its advances can't be replicated just from watching the machines in use, or even examining the components, I have a great deal of respect for Beetle ingenuity.'

'And your grand plan for when we get to the walls—' she flashed him an almost exasperated grin – 'assuming we still have an army left by then? What about their air power?' She needed no Aptitude to envisage the long days of a siege under constant bombardment from the air.

Tynan scowled and leant in close to divulge news he was unwilling to share even by chance. 'There is a plan, but my own cursed intelligence officer insists he hasn't been told. Which means that it's something that the enemy could spike with ease, if they find out what it is. Which means it's a trick, and nobody in my position wants to rely on their very, very clever enemies not seeing right through some arse-backwards piece of misdirection, when the time comes. And, besides, tricks only work once.'

'I'm relying on you and your Empire a great deal,' she replied flatly. Seeing him unhappy with his own orders sent a chill down her spine. *Is he such a slave to what that woman in Capitas says? Or is it her plan, even? Some Wasp clerk with a grand opinion of his own wit may even now be dooming all of us.*

'I'll strive to be worthy of your trust,' he told her simply. The army was breaking out from the scorched remnants of the Felyal forest now and, as the ragged tree cover fell away, more and more soldiers were revealed. It was like some conjuror's trick, some play with mirrors: even though she could have had the precise numbers before her at a word, the sheer scale of the combined Spiderlands–Empire force humbled her. The fact that it was all moving in the same direction was a tribute to a great many hardworking people on both sides.

Their automotive jolted over the uneven, dusty ground, and then Tynan was pointing to the sky ahead. 'Here they come,' he said.

The few Imperial machines already in the air were changing course, moving to put themselves in the way – and there would be a few of her own motley flying machines up there too, whatever she had been able to scrounge from the Spiderlands' Apt satrapies. From surprisingly close behind, she heard the deep-throated thunder of the Farsphex, which were being carried, complete and ready for launch, on flatbed automotives that should ideally have been used for food and tents. She craned back to watch them rising, one by one, from within the vast expanse of the army, feeling that familiar disconnection she always did when faced with such ponderously heavy machines defying logic in order to throw themselves at the sky.

The army itself had orders, so the flanking detachments were already moving aside and making room, whilst those companies towards the army's centre were spreading out, no longer shoulder to shoulder but trying to adopt a looser formation to minimize potential losses. This inevitably slowed the army down, and different companies would get intermingled, sent into disarray, even scattered completely. She and Tynan had already weighed up the odds and decided they could not afford the casualties if every ill-aimed bomb could wipe out entire squads of close-packed men.

The Collegiate Stormreaders were skittering overhead even

now, and she knew that they would be making for the larger automotives. They could kill soldiers with ease, but the force set against them was so large that they might as well spit into a gale. Collegium's easiest victory would be to destroy the Empire's means to mount an attack when it arrived, or to cripple the army's ability to advance by destroying its supplies.

The Farsphex scattered across the sky in packs of two or three, feinting and threatening, and Mycella could see the patterns they made, even if she could not appreciate the machinery behind them. There was a collective grace to the Imperial pilots that their Beetle enemies lacked, for all their skill and the agility of their orthopters. And yet there were so many more Stormreaders clattering overhead.

Tynan had gripped her hand, still looking upwards. The game was joined, and for all he was a general and she a great lady of the Spiderlands, all they could do was watch.

The Collegiate fliers were coming in on three distinct fronts, and Bergild cross-referenced their attack pattern with the plan of the army's advance she had memorized, guessing at the most likely targets.

A thought from her and two Farsphex were peeling off on her right, gaining height to dive down on the enemy, with a third hanging back.

Another thought, and a further trio fell away to her left, to fend off what she guessed was probably a feint by the Collegiates, but which would no doubt turn into the real thing if she ignored it.

Her pilots spoke in her head, each in turn, confirming their assignments. There was no time for anything more. The men and women, Wasps and half-Wasps that she had trained with, were about to be put to the test.

Behind their words she could hear their confidence in her as a leader. Echoes of long tendays of training, when she and the other women, the halfbreeds too, had started off at the bottom:

despised and distrusted by men who had been taught since birth that they were *better*.

That mindlink, the fugitive Art that Wasps threw up so rarely, quickly changed all that. Speech mind to mind was shorn of masks, so that she could only wonder why the Ants had not conquered the world and made a perfect paradise of it for themselves. Ants had only their own minds, was her guess. Unlike Bergild and her fellows, they had never been hunted, therefore had never had to hide, never had to work to communicate with others whose minds were closed to them. Ants took for granted what Bergild and her kind were only now able to enjoy.

She was leader because she understood flying as none of the rest of them did, and that was it: a meritocracy at a stroke. The Engineer officers had tried to place a man over her, but their candidate had refused. In the end, Colonel Varsec, father of the new Air Corps, had pinned the captain's badge on her himself. Of all of them there, all those army officers and engineers and Consortium magnates, only Varsec had understood. When he had designed his Farsphex machines, he had specified who would be needed to fly them, focusing on that inviolable link from pilot to pilot that would make them the masters of the air. He had known what he was doing, even if his superiors had not appreciated it. He was changing the Empire in a small way, but at a fundamental level.

She veered left, cutting upwards in the air, seeing a knot of Stormreaders break apart, some heading for the artillery transports and others rising up to screen them. Two of her pilots were already stooping down out of the sky, rotary piercers blazing with spent firepowder, and she saw one of the Stormreaders rock and slide, recovering a moment later, but out of place as the Farsphex cut past, heading for the bombers.

The Stormreaders had never been designed for ground assault, she knew. They were made to fight other orthopters, and they were superb at it. They needed a good, unhindered run to drop an accurate bomb, though, and so the diving Farsphex scattered them, only one charge loosed, and falling wide of the automotives – to the detriment of a unit of infantry. But, then, everything down there was army, and there would always be a loser.

And away! And her pilots were already dragging out of their dive, not engaging the furiously circling enemy but locking their wings for extra speed and breaking away ready to swing back the moment they were not being chased.

She set her own course, seeing her targets fall into what must be their final approach. There was a wing of Stormreaders waiting above, she knew, which meant that she and her fellows would have company the moment they tried to intervene. *No choice, let's go.*

She had been a pilot's daughter. Her mother dead while bearing her, she had sat beside her father from a tender age, watching most of the Twelve-year War from a heliopter's cockpit. Two years before that war's end, her father had been killed in the air. A mad dragonfly-rider had actually put an arrow through his viewslit and through his eye as he sat right next to her. She had been fifteen. She had brought the heliopter down – not immediately, but where it had needed to go, perched on her dead father's lap to reach the controls. After that, a desperate quartermaster, who needed a pilot then and there, had written down the name 'Bergen' on his books, and she had been a man for the last two years of the war, drawing pay and flying supplies to the front.

In the Maynes rebellion that had brought the Commonweal war to a close, 'Sergeant Bergen' had dropped grenades on the insurrectionists and fought off their clumsy orthopters in the air.

They're right on you, came the thoughts of one of her spotters, packaged with a concise picture of how many and what trajectories, and she returned a response immediately, spreading her calculations to her flanking pilots so that they and she could split and rejoin in perfect coordination, throwing off the pursuing Collegiates, altering course and sheering through the air towards the bombing Stormreaders even as they made their approach.

Her weapons hammered away, the vibration of them felt through the stick, through the frame of the machine, entirely distinct from the rapid and regular beats of the engine.

After Maynes was subdued, she had been arrested, and for three tendays she had sat in a cell awaiting execution, with or without Rekef torture. She had seen it as her last victory then, for it had been a military prison, a man's place.

The man who came to let her out had been the same quartermaster who had invented poor Bergen, and later promoted the imaginary soldier to sergeant. She would learn later how hard he had fought to keep her alive, but he was a major by then, in recognition for his keeping his allotted part of the war effort in one piece, and he paid his debts.

'Go home, girl,' he had told her. For her, the war was now over.

But, of course, she had possessed two maverick gifts, not just the one.

Her shot raked the side of the lead Collegiate flier, and the Stormreader banked violently, almost into the path of one of its fellows. She ignored it, let her shot stray to the next, but its pilot had already realized the danger and was climbing so as not to be caught between the enemy and the ground. Another two had already broken off. That left . . .

There was one of them a little more dogged than the others, now alone as it streaked towards the transporters. There was a rapid shuttling of thoughts between Bergild and her companions, which she ended with, *Mine.*

The pursuing Stormreaders were right behind her, and her flankers split up to draw them away. Two remained with her, because the Collegiates weren't fools, and she let her Farsphex dance before them, denying them a clear shot whilst calculating her own. The Imperial machines were as fleet and nimble as could be – no bombs, no bombardiers, not a pound of spare weight that might mean the difference between life and death.

Stray shot sparked from her hull, one of her pursuers getting far too close, but then she was ready, falling into that moment when she would have to commit, and thus be at the mercy of her enemy.

Seconds only until the Stormreader would unleash its cargo. All those dumb minds down there watching that swift approach and desperate to live.

Now. And she was on her line, piercers opening up with their juddering roar, and she saw the constellation of sparks about the Stormreader's engine casing, punching a string of bolts towards the left wing.

Three hard strikes punched into her hull, but then one of her fellows was coming straight at her pursuers, shooting wildly and putting them off their aim.

For a moment, just one of those split seconds she was living between, she thought she had lost it and that the determination of the bomber would surpass the accuracy of her own flying, but then his wing splintered apart as her shot knifed into the joint, and the Stormreader was spinning away, end over end, ploughing into the ground behind its intended target. She saw a sudden plume of fire as his bomb detonated within the bay.

Then came the counter-attack, and she dragged her machine away, taking a half-dozen holes through the silk and wood of one wing. Her fellows were there to cover for her, but abruptly the fighting had become something new – not the fencing match of threat and counter-threat, but life and death as the Collegiates gave up on their ground targets to deal instead with their annoyances in the air. Her pilots had superior coherence and discipline, but the Stormreaders were arguably better machines for this duelling, and they had twice the numbers.

She took in her pilots' views of the air, formed them into a whole, found their best chance for survival, scattered her people across the sky without any of them ever being alone for a moment, all efforts now concentrated on evasion and yet refusing to be driven away, always there and never ceding the air to the enemy.

As one of her fellows died, she felt the stab of pain as if it was her own. His mind, within hers, was a briefly burning red-hot spark of pain and fear, snuffed out instantly as his Farsphex nosedived into the ground.

One less. And they could hardly spare it. Her thoughts rallied the others, spurred them on. *The Empire is counting on us.*

Her father had possessed the same poisoned gift: that mindlink Art whose known practitioners had been rounded up and executed just a generation before, by the Rekef secret police. *Never tell,* he had insisted. *You must never let them know.* But when she heard what the Empire wanted her kind for, she had turned herself in to the Engineers without a second thought.

Give me back the sky, had been her only desire,

The intervention of the other Imperial machines came as a surprise, not a part of her mental battle plan at all. They had most of them not been ready for immediate launch but, the moment the Stormreaders had been spotted, the ground crews would have been working towards it. Now that uneven clutter of old Spearflights and the flying rabble of the Spiderlands was all about, still not quite evening the numbers, but complicating matters for the Collegiates. The Stormreaders outmatched them badly, but there had been a clock ticking ever since the attack started. Most Stormreaders had a limited fighting range, and their forays over the Second Army were on a strict leash – and the more they had to fight, the more spring-stored power their clockwork hearts used up. The older Imperial machines could refuel when they needed it, and the Farsphex had been able to fly from the Empire to fight over Collegium itself, and then return in safety, so efficient was their fuel.

Her pilots called it in all at once, the moment the Stormreaders began flashing their signals to each other. *Fall back,* she instructed. *No heroics.* They could not risk losing another Farsphex to a sudden ambush. Defence of the army was all.

She pictured the pilot who had died, not so much the face as the feel of his mind. What they would do when they got closer to Collegium, when the Stormreaders would be able to fight for as long as they needed, she did not know.

So I hear that command has a plan: the thought of one of her fellows, filled with discontent.

We can only hope, came her reply.

Ten

'The problem, basically, is that the Mantis-kinden never fought a traditional battle in their lives. When we fight, we go in, we take and hold land, consolidate, press on. Them? They attack, kill, fade away. They don't stay where they were. Their only strongpoints are their actual holds, which are basically villages built into the trees, which you could pretty well miss if you walked right through them – until they killed you, anyway.'

Tynisa nodded, remembering her journey to the Felyal with her father. He had been bringing her there to see her people's way of life. Since then she felt she had run into more than her fair share of the Mantis way, and yet here she was again.

The speaker was an Ant-kinden named Sentius, placed in command of the Etheryen relief force by Tactician Milus. He was a lean, weathered Sarnesh with some grey in his dark hair, and he had ventured into the forest before to liaise with Sarn's allies.

'The Etheryen tell me that they won't attack holds, and the Nethyen won't either. Now, I reckon that's likely to change soon enough, either because someone starts losing or because your Wasps won't know the rules. For now it's a blood-pissing chaos in here. There's basically a whole third of the mid-forest that's full of war bands from either side all running about lying in wait and jumping out at each other, and both sides are striking out towards the other side of the wood – so we're only a hundred yards in and still I've got scouts out,' he went on. 'And then there's me with my men, and at least we can get as split up as you like and still know where we are, but I reckon that I'll be losing whole squads within a day or so, once the Nethyen get wind of us – and our friends will be doing the same for the Wasps, too. And then I have you lot to cope with as well. All of you.'

Overhead, the canopy was near full. The world beneath was cast in shades of dark green and pale grey, lanced by errant sunbeams. Just a hundred yards in, as Sentius had said, there was no mark of axe on any tree, but instead great bloated forest giants that three men could not have stretched their arms around, and growing far closer together than seemed reasonable, each one muscling up against its neighbours for room. The space between them was like some mad architect's fantasy, a vaulted, irregular colonnade that unravelled in every direction into the gloom. All around them were Sarnesh Ants, stepping carefully through the undergrowth that somehow clawed itself a hold here despite the poor light: great sprays of ferns, twisted nests of brambles, the jutting shelves of bracket fungus, and slender capped spires of mushrooms half the height of a man.

'Civilians,' Sentius pronounced, giving the word that special contempt unique to military men. His gaze raked the assembly, barely pausing on Che and her followers. Tynisa understood that they were already accepted, by order of Milus himself. The rest, however . . .

The Roach girl, Syale, was no surprise, and in truth she seemed to pass through these woods with an ease that surprised even the Mantis-kinden. Or perhaps she just had no common sense, of course, but it was plain that the Sarnesh were not going to keep her out. The ambassador from Princep Salma was here to stay.

The ambassador from Collegium was a more contentious figure, though. Helma Bartrer, Master of the Great College and representative of the Assembly, seemed oblivious to any hints.

Instead she had attached herself to Terastos, the Moth-kinden nominally representing Dorax, and she was not to be dislodged short of physical force. Any such attempt would be complicated by Amnon, her vast and unsubtle shadow.

'Listen to me,' Bartrer told Sentius sharply. 'I am an expert in the history of the Etheryen and their culture. I have studied these matters for longer than you've held a sword.'

'I've got experts, Mistress Bartrer,' Sentius told her with admirable mildness. 'I have him—' Terastos. 'And I have her—' Che, to her plain surprise. 'More to the point, I have every cursed Mantis who lives in this forest and isn't actively trying to kill me.'

'And you have me,' Bartrer finished, with great finality. 'Believe me, before this is done you'll be glad of me. Tell him, Mistress Maker.'

Che started in surprise, her thoughts obviously elsewhere. 'I . . . why?'

Helma Bartrer's eyes narrowed. 'Because I know what you're after here. And, believe me, you need me.'

There was some unheard signal from down the line, and Sentius abruptly blanked the entire conversation from his mind. The Sarnesh, who had been making a cautious advance, were instantly seeking cover, then freezing to stillness with crossbows and snap-bows at the ready.

Che and the other 'civilians' crouched together in the midst of an overarching stand of ferns. 'What are you talking about?' she hissed at Bartrer.

'Oh, I hear a lot.' The College woman seemed almost hostile. 'You reckon the Empress is coming here – or is here right now. You reckon she wants something in these woods, that's the word I hear, but you don't know what that something is. Even though you're *Inapt* now, I hear.' That last comment seemed the crux of the dislike in the woman's voice, and yet Tynisa could not see it as merely the Apt dismissing their forebears. Instead she read something like *envy* in Bartrer's tone. *Live long enough with history?*

133

she wondered. Like most Beetles, Bartrer would be Apt, making the study of the Inapt a maddeningly frustrating business.

Che looked from face to face. 'I assumed that if there's something here the Moths would know.' She cocked an eyebrow at Terastos.

The Moth grimaced. 'Some scraps perhaps. I am no Skryre, and my masters are jealous of their learning, And many of the texts in Collegium are lost to my folk, despite our demands for their return.'

Che looked into Bartrer's face again, and her eyes flicked to Amnon, who would presumably go where the academic went. Perhaps it was the thought of his able help that decided her.

'Then I need all the help I can get,' she admitted. Maure plucked at her sleeve, but she shook the halfbreed magician off.

By then the Sarnesh were moving again, some false alarm now dealt with. Squads were constantly moving off, to be rapidly lost in the darkness, guided only by the best-guess mental map they shared between them. Sentius reappeared with his repeating crossbow over his shoulder, and a Fly-kinden padding along almost under his armpit. This was Zerro, his chief of scouts, a gaunt and taciturn man who moved as silently in the forest as any Mantis.

'Bartrer's with me,' Che told him, pre-empting any argument.

Sentius nodded glumly. 'Fine. You get to tell your people when something happens to her. She's not my concern from this moment. And I gather that you'll all be out of my hair soon enough? Off on a jaunt into the depths?'

Che nodded.

'Zerro here will be with the vanguard. You break off from him at your discretion. 'I've been in here more than most. There's some bastard things in this wood that I only ever heard about from the locals. There are places the Mantids won't go. Wandering around with your mouth open's a fool's errand. But, like I say, we're up to our eyeballs in experts, and I reckon you've got your own, now.'

'Is that your way of wishing me good luck, Commander?' Che asked him drily, but he just shrugged.

Tynisa fell in alongside Maure. 'What is it?'

The magician glanced at her – obviously still a little uneasy in the Weaponsmaster's company after their jagged history in the Commonweal. 'The Beetle woman, Bartrer.'

'What about her?'

'I don't like her. There's something wrong with her: a ghost . . . or something like a ghost.'

Tynisa waved that away. 'You don't trust her, I don't trust her.' Thalric, the third member of their forced clique, had drifted in to eavesdrop, and she added, 'And you don't trust anyone, so that makes three of us.'

Thalric nodded curtly. 'Except Che, but yes, there's something eating that woman for sure.'

'The others?' Tynisa pressed.

'Amnon's straight up, from what I remember,' Thalric admitted. 'Moths are always trouble. For the rest, we'll all just keep our eyes a bit wider open.'

In his mind, Tynisa knew, everyone was an enemy, Sarnesh and Etheryen Mantids included. She found that she had begun to value his paranoia.

The Sarnesh camp at the edge of the forest was breaking up, its work accomplished. Those detachments chosen by Tactician Milus had entered the forest with the Etheryen blessing that Che Maker had negotiated. The balance, along with Milus himself, was readying itself to head for home.

Somewhat controversially, of course, both the Collegiate and Princep ambassadors had gone into Mantis territory. Balkus had already departed to report to his Monarch on the war's most recent twists. The Collegiate orthopter still stood, one of the last machines on the impromptu airfield. Its Beetle pilot was in her seat and ready to go, but the side-hatch was still open, with a small and lonely figure sitting there, staring out at the disintegrating camp. Laszlo was still waiting, and had been waiting since before dusk. Now the moon was high, the bulk of the Ants had left, with their trademark efficiency, and he refused to give up.

'Seriously.' The pilot's voice came from within. 'I don't know whether you noticed, but it's about an hour short of midnight by the clock. Can we go now?'

'She'll be here,' Laszlo declared, not for the first time.

'Well, then at least tell me who—'

'An agent. One with vital information for Collegium,' the Fly snapped back. That was his story, he had decided. Perhaps it was even true.

'She's stood you up,' the pilot's voice told him unhelpfully. 'Look—'

'Just – hold on.' For a moment, just a moment, hope flared inside him, but even he could not fool himself for more than a second. Yes, someone was approaching the orthopter, but it was not Lissart. This was an Ant and, as the figure neared, Laszlo with a sinking heart recognized Milus.

'Collegium is surely waiting for your word!' the tactician called out as he drew near. 'And yet here you are.' He must have had good night vision for an Ant, Laszlo considered, because he was able to look the Fly straight in the eye at that distance. His crisp little smile said a great deal. 'You're Laszlo, of course.'

Having his name known to the Sarnesh court was not a thing of joy to Laszlo. 'What of it?' he asked cautiously.

'She's not coming. I'd have let you exhaust your patience, but it's inefficient. Go home.'

For a moment Laszlo was frozen motionless, not a thought or quip or plan in his mind. 'What do you mean, she's not coming?' was all he could come up with in the end.

Milus's mind was unreadable from his face but, unlike with most Ants, it was not for want of an expression, just that the mild humour he posted up there was feigned entirely for Laszlo's benefit. 'My adviser, Alisse – or te Liss, as she called herself in Solarno – will not be joining you. You should go now.'

Laszlo had a knife, and he had a little cut-down snapbow known as a sleevebow, which could poke some nice holes in the Ant's mail, but there were a lot of Ants left about the place, and he was suddenly convinced, by his instincts and his Art, that there would be Ant marksmen with their weapons trained on him right now. 'What have you done?' he asked hoarsely.

'Taken her in for questioning,' Milus said, as if it were the most natural thing in the world. 'She was a Wasp agent, you know. Well, of course, you know.' That false smile broadened by the requisite amount.

'I . . .' Laszlo had always prided himself on his quick wits and ready tongue, but Milus was changing his ground faster than the Fly could keep up. 'What do you mean, I would know?'

'I read your report in Collegium, Laszlo.' The use of his name was pointed and deliberate.

'You've been spying on Collegium?'

A polite laugh. 'Collegium has been sharing its intelligence with its allies, the Sarnesh. Your report included.'

But I never . . . 'I didn't say anything in my report about—'

'A Wasp agent?' Milus's pale eyes flicked across his face as though Laszlo was a specimen in a jar. 'It was all there for an adequate intelligencer to read, in between the things you actually wrote. Without that one thing, none of your story really makes much sense. Her treachery completes the picture nicely. Although I am grateful to the look on your face for confirmation.'

Laszlo failed to say two or three separate things because his heart was hammering and he could not quite catch enough breath for them. He remembered Lissart telling him what a poor spy he was, over and over, and he had never realized how right she was, or that his failings would prove her undoing. His expression, whatever was left of it, prompted another careful widening of the tactician's smile.

'I know,' Milus admitted. 'We are Ants. We are terribly traditional. We make good soldiers and not much else. We do not understand you other kinden with your free-thinking minds: how very confusing and lonely you must all be, we think. We do not know how you think, and we cannot read your faces because we are ourselves so inscrutable. How our linked minds must cripple us, hm? How unfair, then, to discover at this late date that we can play the same games you can.'

What Laszlo finally got out, at that juncture, was, 'You can't take her.'

'She is taken. She is gone,' Milus assured him. 'You should also go.'

Piss on me, Laszlo found himself thinking. *And he's on* our *side!* 'I'll go to Mar'Maker about this.'

Milus regarded him with an expression now turning to pity. 'And he will be overjoyed that his *allies* are so committed to the war that he has lived for most of his life. I know Stenwold Maker well enough, from one meeting and three score reports. Stenwold Maker hates the Wasps. So do I, and therefore so do all who serve under my command. Stenwold Maker and I need each other, and we understand each other, and he will not care that an Imperial whore and spy is *assisting* me. Tell him I will let him have a report of what she knows. But go now. Your continued presence is inappropriate, and I am sure your pilot wants to see her home as soon as possible.'

Laszlo twitched twice, his impulse to attack the man being murdered before it could get him killed. He wanted to say something like, *This isn't over*, or warn Milus that if he harmed Lissart, then ... But he had no 'then'. He had no Lissart. He had precisely nothing.

Such oaths he swore only inside his head, where Milus could not tear them apart with his cold logic.

'Argastos.' Seda pronounced it with care, as she would any name of power. Thus far she had travelled within the general Wasp forces that were pushing into the Nethyon to support their Mantis allies – or that was the claim. Seda was unsure how much they could accomplish that the Nethyen would appreciate, but at least poor General Roder would get a clean battle with the Sarnesh, while the Lowlander Mantis-kinden writhed in their death throes. *Such a useful kinden. If only the Etheryen would bend the knee to me, then I could save them.* But she had not been able to approach them in person, and the Nethyen messenger bearing her offer reported that the Etheryen had taken it badly. Fatally, apparently, but perhaps there was only one sort of 'badly' that the Mantids knew.

When this is over, I will save some. I will transplant them to the Empire and make them mine. Did my people think they feared the Rekef? How much more would they tremble at the thought of Mantis-kinden secret police?

Seated at her fire were Gjegevey and the Tharen Wasp, Tegrec, serving as her chief advisers on this forest and its history. In this, Seda knew, the abominable Beetle girl would have an advantage, being leagued with the Doric Moths from whom Argastos surely sprang. For all that Seda's people might ransack the Empire's libraries for every mention of the name, the Maker girl would already know it all. *Curse her!*

A sudden savagery in her expression had apparently silenced the two of them, so she gestured irritably for them to continue.

Tegrec spoke first. 'This story goes back a long way, you understand, to the great wars of the Inapt world. And if you know Moth histories, you know that they aren't written as anything an Imperial historian would recognize. Almost no dates even in the Moth reckoning, place names given as metaphors, fact given as allegory, or the other way round. Any Apt reader would take it for some lurid fiction. Even we, with our . . . advantages, run into a cultural barrier. Even modern Moths—'

'Get to the point,' Seda ordered him flatly, and he swallowed nervously.

'There was a man named Argastos, and he was a Skryre, and he was a warrior, and he led a Mantis war-host and raised the greatest army the world had ever seen.' He said it as if he was reciting a text.

Seda stared at him. *So swift on my own thoughts comes this?* Some great magician, she had expected – for what else would make a Moth's name live on? – but a war leader? *I like him better already.*

And across the vast darkness of the forest, yet still intolerably under the same night sky, she knew that Che would be having the same guarded conversation with her no doubt far better informed advisers . . .

Terastos had prevaricated but now they had set up camp for the night, Che was not to be denied. 'She is after something,' she insisted, not needing to name the Empress for them. 'And Maure and I, we know that there is a knot of darkness in this forest, at the very heart of it. So tell me.'

The Moth started and stopped several times. 'My people fought many wars, long ago,' he would say. Or, 'It is written that a sole name once ruled all you can see.' And he was getting nowhere, to Che's increasing frustration. It was as though there was something he was trying to say, but a key word – a name – could not be forced through his teeth.

Until: 'Why, then, surely you are talking about Argastos,' Helma Bartrer declared, half putting him out of his misery, half archly establishing her credentials as expert.

Terastos reacted like a man released from a stranglehold, some spell broken by the simple mention of the name. 'There was a man named Argastos that made this place his own,' he admitted weakly. 'But we do not . . . we did not speak of him. Nobody has spoken of him for a very long time.'

Che glared in exasperation, then looked somewhat reluctantly to Bartrer. 'So speak,' she said.

Bartrer gave a smug little smile. 'There were wars, back then. It's as difficult as getting money out of a Helleren, to work out what they were about, but they had wars. This Argastos was a Moth, a magician, a warlord. This was early, too. He's named in a codex that lists the victorious war leaders of this particular scrap, and there are names from all over, and some that even read like Mosquito-kinden Blooded Ones – Sarcads as they called them. So if it's true that the Moths and Mosquitos actually did rip into each other, then this Argastos was before that. Really early, then. There were Woodlouse-kinden names, too, all given high honours, and that's about the last you hear of them in the histories as amounting to anything important. Spiders and Mantids side by side, Dragonfly noble families . . . Others I never could pin down. Basically, my reconstructions suggest that this Argastos was the brightest star in a gathering of war-leaders from pretty much everywhere the Moths could call on. And he lived right here in this forest. In fact he's described in two distinct ways: like a great Moth magician, and like one of the Mantis Loquae – their speakers and leaders – so he may have been a halfbreed, or he may have been just a Moth with an unusual talent for fighting. A Weaponsmaster, maybe.' Bartrer nodded familiarly at Tynisa's sword-and-circle brooch. 'But when they fought – whoever it was that all these people fought – he gets the most of the credit. He was a hero, a great man. At that time, anyway.'

'Those few mentions of him that we have, hm, found,' Gjegevey explained, 'seem to fall into two camps. He led the armies of the Inapt, and led them to victory, at great cost.'

He thought he was being clever, Seda considered, but she could read every wrinkle in his face. She let him speak because there was no point challenging him about it, not when the answers were written so plainly. 'So he was a great man, remembered in song and story,' she murmured.

'Hm, yes,' the old Woodlouse agreed, 'but other sources speak poorly of him. We, ahm, believe that relations between Argastos and the other Skryres deteriorated later . . . or that is our best, hm, reading.'

'Books that speak directly of him are simply not to be had,' Tegrec complained. 'Probably the Tharen Skryres keep them hidden. They do a lot of that. But some texts from – I don't know – generations after the man's time, perhaps? They mention him obliquely – he's used as a metaphor for pride and ambition, for turning on his betters. For . . . some sort of corruption – questionable magics, that sort of thing.'

'There is a play, even,' Gjegevey added, 'wherein it is, ahm, declaimed that, "Like Argastos, I have won for you the world, and gained but spite," or some such.'

But Seda was still considering what Tegrec had said. 'I was unaware that the Skryres considered any magics questionable.'

'I think . . .' Tegrec swallowed again. 'To read my own thoughts into what is left unsaid, I wonder if he was not held to blame for doing the Skryres' will. It would not be the only time they had made a terrible thing happen, and then found it convenient to hold their own agents accountable.'

'So –' *and enough meandering, old man* – 'this war, Gjegevey, that your ancient Argastos was so feted for. It was the war against the Worm, was it not?'

'We do *not* speak of such things,' Terastos hissed, cutting Bartrer off. Seeing the others' somewhat tired expressions he entreated them, 'Yes, so we are a secretive people. So we hold our knowledge close, and treasure it. But there are *names* that are not spoken. We damn them into obscurity, and in doing so we deny them power. If you are what you seem, you must *know* this, Beetle girl.'

Che met his gaze, her easy retort fading in her throat. *Yes, I do. Somehow I do. But times have changed.* 'The Empress will speak all the forbidden names there are, if it gives her even a thimbleful more power.'

The Moth actually shuddered. 'So I will speak of Argastos, but I will not speak of the war that he won.'

'The war against the Worm?' Bartrer said, obviously enjoying herself. 'And what was that, Moth-kinden? The great and terrible war, and yet only marginalia are left of it.'

'I warn you,' Terastos spat. 'Speak it again and I will abandon you all.' Incredibly, he turned his blank eyes on Che, entreating for her intervention.

Bartrer gave him a superior smile but, before she could speak, Maure stepped in.

'Enough,' the halfbreed stated. 'I know some little of that war. The Woodlouse-kinden that trained me taught me just so much. Argastos is one thing, whoever he was – or is – but we do not conjure *them* by naming them. Even the old insult for them, to call them "Worm", is too much. You are right, Mistress Bartrer, that a very many enemies joined together to defeat them. For ten generations after, there were nightmares of their return, for everyone knew that they were not so very finally defeated, and, even so, the means used to cast them down were enough to cripple half the powers of the world. Some never recovered their old strength. But we do not speak of them.'

Terastos nodded soberly. 'Suffice to say, Argastos was a hero, when he brought about their ruin, and after that he became something else.'

'A corpse, can we hope?' Thalric put in. 'Forgive me if I sound somewhat desperate, but the man is thousands of years dead. So what is *she* after and what are we expecting to find? And just tell me whatever you believe. Don't patronize me simply because I have the good fortune to be Apt.'

Che squeezed his hand. His answering smile was strained.

'There is something awake at the heart of the forest, this much we sensed,' Maure admitted.

'His memory must run long among the Mantis-kinden, if nothing else,' Bartrer mused. 'It's only after he comes and goes in the histories that you even get mention of the two holds here. Immediately before that they're calling the entire forest Argaryon – no prizes for guessing after who. So you're telling me that, throughout all those centuries, your "Servants of the Green" never told you they had a guest?'

Terastos shrugged. 'Our servants served under certain

conditions, and the sanctity of their places was one such. It was suspected that something of Argastos remained, but if so, the Mantids seemed a strong enough guard to keep him where he was. And until this cursed *Empress* decided to meddle, were we not right?'

How much does he honestly know, then? Che wondered, and she came to the depressing conclusion that Terastos was being particularly frank, for a Moth. The name of Argastos had been unpicked from their histories – the histories Terastos had access to at least – so that the man only knew something had been there, and that it was safely barred away from the world. The details of what had been there, and of what was to be feared, were lost.

She turned her gaze on Helma Bartrer, and decided that there were depths in the woman she could not decipher. *The driven academic on the edge of a breakthrough in her research? Or is there something else?*

'There is, hm, one more matter, of course. Once I had enough people searching for the name, ahm, Argastos, it was bound to come to light.' Gjegevey did not sound very happy about it.

'The report.' There was a similar reluctance in Tegrec's voice.

'So tell me and stop all this theatre,' Seda chided them both.

'During the last war, shortly before the, hm, battle known as Malkan's Stand, a reconnaissance airship from the Seventh went astray over this forest and was, hrm, brought down in a storm. A single survivor, one Sergeant Corver, made it out of the trees, but his sanity was, hrm, decidedly in question. His report is, ah, lurid, contradictory, lacking in internal logic. He speaks of a terrible place within the forest, of, ahm, dead men returning to life, of being drawn to a, hrm, hall of sorts, of great gates, and passing within them into a place of darkness where he met, hrm . . .' The old Woodlouse blinked several times. 'He met a Moth-kinden who named himself, hm, Argastos, who gave him a message. Despite the Rekef being most, ahm, *insistent* in questioning this sergeant, his story did not change.'

144

Seda's eyes gleamed. 'And the message?'

Gjegevey's face twisted. 'You understand we did not know this when we named Argastos for you back in Capitas.'

'*Tell* me.'

'The ahm, the message was thus: "Go to your Empress. Go to her and tell her: I am here, and ready for her. When she seeks me, she shall find me waiting."' Gjegevey sighed. 'At the time Corven first made his report, your, hm, brother still lived, Majesty. I do not know what to say.'

'Say that you were right, to bring this Argastos to my attention. Say that here is a power that has lasted a thousand years and more, and has still retained a modicum of wit. Most of all say that we will find Argastos before the Beetle girl, or else I will have everyone in this expedition on the crossed pikes.'

Part Two

Gates of Stone

'Outright Victory or Death'

— MOTTO OF OUTWRIGHT'S PIKE AND
SHOT MERCHANT COMPANY

Eleven

They were all waiting for Eujen when he walked in. He suspected that the lecture hall had never been so full as now, housing his new recruits.

Standing at the lectern, he did not feel the expected authority of a chief officer drop on his shoulders. He was still Eujen Leadswell, a mere student who had conceived the stupid idea of a Student Company, mostly because the girl he was sweet on had gone off and joined the Merchant Companies and then refused to allow him to do the same. *Stab me, but is this sort of rubbish what history is actually made of? Idiot people like me making bad decisions for all the wrong reasons?*

Oh, and sod Stenwold bloody Maker for taking me seriously, while I'm on the subject.

He had Averic standing beside him, and a stout Beetle girl who had been one of the first to sign up, so had de facto become a sort of officer. They all three wore the purple sashes that Eujen had adopted because he had known a clothier trying to shift an excess of that colour. The lectern bore a big pile of similar sashes, and a single snapbow.

His audience watched him as though expecting him to do tricks for their amusement. These were not his volunteers, who had rallied willingly to his banner out of a desire to protect their home. Before him instead were conscripts: those able-bodied individuals amongst the student population who had been forced to take up arms by Maker's Draft, and who had been assigned to him rather than to the Merchant Companies, because he was reckoned to be on their level or some such.

'Right,' he croaked, the acoustics of the room carrying his nervousness to the very back. 'You know why you're here, I suppose.'

He had a speech prepared, but one of the students was already standing. Eujen recognized him as Howell Graveller, a year older and one of Eujen's frequent detractors, who had mocked him when he tried to advocate peace with the Wasps, and yet had not come forward to volunteer for the Company when Eujen had started to talk about fighting. *And he's now going to walk out. And they're going to follow him, all of them. They don't take me seriously, and why would they? And what am I supposed to do then? Have them arrested or something? Go squeak to Stenwold Maker that my soldiers won't do what I tell them?*

But Graveller was still standing there, shuffling from foot to foot, glancing sidelong at his fellows. 'Look, Leadswell,' he said, after an awkward moment. 'I just wanted to say . . . this Student Company of yours, we're grateful for it, we really are.' His accompanying gesture defined the 'we' as those closest to him, his little clique of cronies. 'The conscription . . . we could have been stuck in Maker's Own or the Coldstone or something, right now. This . . . at least this isn't the front line.'

Eujen stared at him for a long moment, then took up the snapbow from the lectern, aimed at Graveller's chest and shot him.

The harsh *snap!* echoed about the lecture hall like the end of the world, along with Graveller's agonized gasp.

They had all frozen, and Eujen noted who had leapt up to act, who were still stupefied in their seat, finding himself already sorting them into grades and categories of soldier. 'The next one,' he said quietly into the utter silence that had gripped the room, 'will be loaded.'

Graveller looked as if he had pissed his robes. 'But why?' he got out.

'Because a Wasp will be holding it,' Eujen explained. *And now I have my audience, and they're taking me seriously, and none of them even glanced at my Wasp friend Averic when I said that. I would win golden honours in rhetoric from that sentence alone, were a Master here to mark me.*

'Listen to me,' he explained to them. 'This is not the alternative to fighting for real. You are all going to learn how to fight, to use one of these, and to work together. You're going to learn how to build barricades, how to shoot from cover, how to patch wounds, how to use artillery, and a whole lot more. And you're going to learn as much as you can as fast as you can, faster than any of us ever had to learn basic mechanics or the Collegium-Helleron social deficit, because the Imperial Second Army is on the move *right now*. And if you don't know what that means, then go to the library, get out a map and measure the distance between the Felyal and here, because that's how much time you have.'

They were still staring at him as though he was some horrible dream brought on by too much bad wine.

'Barricades and . . . what else?' someone asked, her voice petering out.

'Don't you understand what this is *for* – the Student Company?' Eujen spat out. 'The others, Outwright's, Maker's Own and the rest, may well go out to meet the Second in the field – wiser heads than mine decide that, and I'm glad of it – but we're the last line. When we commit to the fighting, we will be on the walls. If that's not enough, we will be on the streets, in the market-places, in the courtyards of the College itself. Because we are Collegium's final hope – and I'm cursed if I'm going to let that fail because you all thought this was the *easy* class to take.'

In their eyes he read their accusation of him, echoing Graveller and his friends' taunts of yesteryear. 'Oh, yes, I know I was always for reaching out to the Empire, and I will maintain unto death that we could have handled the Wasps better, and even avoided this war entirely had our elected masters possessed the will to do anything other than agitate. But the war is *here*, now. It takes two for peace, and so now we need to break the back of the Empire's advance to the point where peace becomes even a possibility, and to do that we need to stop them. We need to stop them out there, if we can. We need to stop them right here, if we cannot.' He looked at them and felt despair. *And where the plague were you lot, when I called for volunteers?* 'I'm not some Makerist firebrand frothing about a just war. I'm talking about the survival of all that we are. Your city, your history, casting Lots, classes in the College, drinks in the taverna: all those things that we all took for granted just a year ago.' He turned. 'Officer Averic.'

The Wasp stepped forward and Eujen noted, with almost scholarly interest, the ripple that went through them all as they tried to adjust.

'Tomorrow morning, one hour after dawn, you will assemble in the Briar Quad to commence training,' Averic told them. 'If you have access to weapons, bring them, please. Equipment is at a premium.' He glanced at Eujen for approval, got a brief nod. All words that Eujen himself could have said, but it was important for the new recruits to know which faces to take orders from, even when those faces bore pale Wasp features.

When they had filed out, with expressions ranging from stunned to incredulous to determined, Eujen sagged forward against the lectern.

'Well done, Chief Officer,' the Beetle girl commended him, laying a hand briefly on his shoulder. Her name was . . .? Not a good start for a chief officer, he realized, because he could not recall it.

'Now we have to work out how we're even going to train them,' he moaned.

'I, ah, took the liberty of finding some veterans – old fellows from the first war with the Vekken. They haven't used snapbows, but at least they've fought. And one of the artificing Masters can come and teach us about artillery. And . . . I thought we could improvise, after that.' She drew most of herself up, seeking for a military bearing. 'Is that all right?'

Ellery Heartwhill, that was her name. 'That's superb,' Eujen told her, and she beamed at him a little too eagerly.

'I can get someone from the Merchant Companies to train them with snapbows,' a new voice sounded from the door, making all three of them jump. Eujen twitched up to see none other than Stenwold Maker himself standing there.

'How much did you hear?' he demanded of the older man, as though he had been caught plotting some sort of sedition.

'Enough,' Stenwold confirmed. 'You did well.'

I didn't do it for you. But to Eujen's surprise, the words remained locked up in his mind. Now was not the time. 'Any help in getting them ready would be appreciated,' he managed.

'War Council will be meeting tomorrow . . .' A moment of calculation on Stenwold's part. 'Let's call it noon. You'll be ready for a break by then, though I'm not sure I can promise you one. I'd give you an agenda, except it would be out of date by dawn.'

Eujen nodded. *Surely there's an old Inapt saying, 'May you get what you ask for.'*

Taki brought her oft-repaired *Esca Magni* down messily on the airfield, the rest of her flight skewing their Stormreaders to a halt around her. She slapped up her cockpit lid and kicked herself out of her seat, her wings carrying her halfway across the field, battered by the wind of the landing orthopters.

A quick glance about located a familiar figure in Willem Reader, artificer and aviation scholar – and current object of her ire.

As she approached, she could see him counting the surviving sets of wings, and he met her grim expression with one of his own. He was a small-framed Beetle-kinden – though still bigger than herself – with a mild face set off by a small moustache. Perhaps no man's image of a great war hero, but his orthopter designs were all around them.

'We should have had them!' she exclaimed to him, as she

touched down. 'Even with the Farsphex screen, we had several clear runs at their supplies!'

'Then what went wrong, Taki?' came his measured response.

'What went wrong is that the Stormreaders can only carry a handful of underpowered explosives, and lining them up for the strike is painstaking fiddly work when you're being shot at. They may not have many Farsphex, but they know their business! When we were doing the same favour for them, not so long ago, they still got plenty of bombs on the ground – you know why?'

'Because they have a second crew member doing the aiming, Taki,' Willem broke in. 'And because the Empire built them with that in mind, and a cursed good job they did of it. Stormreaders are built to fight in the air. I *can't* make you good against the ground. We'd need a whole different type of orthopter – and you'd need to give me the time to work out the design. I won't say I haven't looked into it, but even if I'd started work straight after they left last time, we'd barely have a prototype when the Second arrive again. And as for reverse-engineering the Farsphex . . . we have a handful of their crashed vessels whole enough to study, and nobody around here seems to realize just how *complex* the things are – let alone their fuel, which we don't have, and which the chemical artifice department can't even guess at. Taki . . .'

She had been ready to shout at him for failing her, but she saw from his face that he had already spent nights and days trying to overcome mountains, and that nobody was more aware of the stakes than he was.

'I'm sorry, Willem,' she said. 'What can you give me?'

'There's a big consignment of the new steel just shipped in, and I can get another dozen or so Stormreaders fitted with replacement springs. About half your strike force, by then.'

She was shaking her head. 'No point having half our machines that can stay over the enemy for a day at a time, if we're still out of bombs in three passes.'

'I know, I know, but it's better than nothing. It's *something*.' Neither of them bothered to raise the obvious fact that, the closer the enemy came, the less important the simple staying power of the Stormreaders would prove. 'A lot of the city's resources are going elsewhere. They've new artillery on the walls, for example . . . and if it does come down to a siege, it shouldn't just be you standing between victory and defeat.'

'Let them keep telling themselves that,' Taki grumbled. 'I don't trust fancy new untested artillery, and those Wasp big leadshotters already have two cities to their tally is what I hear.' She waved over at one of the ground crew. 'Get them all re-tensioned, right away. Training flights in two hours!'

'You push yourself too hard,' Reader said softly.

'Me? I'm a Fly, Willem. We just keep buzzing.' She was aware that her grin was too bright and cheerful, to the point of cracking about the edges. 'Maker's Draft has given me three score Collegiates who think they can fly an orthopter. By the end of today I reckon at least a score of them will be wearing the sashes of the Merchant Companies and praying never to leave the ground again. The rest perhaps I can use.' *But they'll never have a chance to get good at it*, was another unspoken but shared thought. 'How's the family?' An awkward digression. Taki had lived in a world of feuding pilots most of her life and the small talk of other people baffled her. Only after coming to Collegium had she started to care about the earth-bound masses: men such as Willem Reader or Stenwold Maker. Only after running foul of the Empire had she started to appreciate the bigger issues and what they meant to the individuals around her.

'Jen's grumbling that they want to use her library as a hospital, if the worst comes to the worst. I swear she'd let the Empire in through the gates if they showed a thorough knowledge of indexing. Little Jen has been learning emergency drill at school, She always used to draw me pictures of orthopters, but now, when she does, they're fighting. Everything's gone mad.' He said it matter-of-factly, but there was a world of weariness there.

I'm not the only one pushing myself too hard, Taki decided. 'Come on, Willem, you don't need to oversee all this personally.'

'Better than the committees.' He shrugged. 'Which reminds me, the War Master wants a report from both of us. Now there's a man, I swear, who never sleeps.'

Outside Collegium's walls, another grand project was under way. The approach to the city was a broad and shallow slope of land that the river had ground out with its meanderings over thousands of years, the cliffs on either side dipping down gently towards the sea. This was the bowl that held Collegium, and it had been a coastal resort for the Moth-kinden once, but was now a seat of trade, rich farming and comfort for the Beetles. Defence had never been something the city had been sited for, and recent years had seen too many enemies simply come walking up to the city's gates. Now a great force of men and machines and animals was working on both sides of the river, and the rail line, to complicate the Second Army's last few hundred yards of advance.

Straessa was well aware that a battery of cartographers, architects, engineers and mathematicians had been up for nights working out the perfectly calibrated defence against the marching feet of the Wasps. Taking into account the arcs of the city's artillery, the strengths of the wall and the natural lie of the land, they had set out a complex maze of artificial topography to trip and slow, funnel and compress; to force the hand of the Imperial general and make his soldiers victims of Collegium's wall engines. The theory was all there and, as a student of the College, she could probably have done some of those calculations herself.

Standing with a spade in her hand, overlooking the toiling soldiers of the Coldstone Company working alongside the machines of a dozen professionals who had made moving earth their business, it all looked like a colossal mess to her. She could not shake off the feeling that this entire grandiose venture was simply to give the city's massed soldiery something to do.

'Water!' came a shout, and she turned gratefully. A draught beetle was dragging out what had been a fire engine until recently, but had now been pressed into service to quench the thirst of Collegium's defenders.

'Gorenn, get cups and buckets down the line,' she called, and a Dragonfly woman took off from a nearby mound of earth, glad to be out of it, and started to organize a bucket chain.

I should probably tell everyone how well they're doing, but for all I know we're going to have to shift everything ten feet to the left or something. Plans on paper were all very well, but putting them into action on the ground was another matter.

'Officer Antspider!' Another demand for her attention, but at least it gave her an excuse not to start shovelling again. All the privilege of rank had not stopped her underlings shaming her into doing her bit.

She had not recognized the voice but, turning, she knew the man. 'Gerethwy!' she cried, delighted. If her voice wavered very slightly over the last syllable of his name, well, he had changed somewhat since losing half a hand to an exploding snapbow. He had always been freakishly tall – long-limbed, long-faced, with that stooped hunch that all Woodlouse-kinden apparently had. Now his cheeks were hollow, and his grey skin seemed to show something beyond just his kinden's natural hue.

'Reporting for duty,' he told her, striding over the uneven ground. 'If you'll have me.'

'Te Mosca let you go, did she?'

'I need to *do* something.' And he was saying more than he used to, as well. Single words, nods and wry expressions had always seemed enough before. Now all those unspoken words were leaking out. 'What in the pits is this?' His eyes raked over all that grand effort of earth-moving.

'Second-to-last line of defence against the Wasps,' she told him. 'Get the ground all rucked up so that they can't just march over it without getting in the way of our artillery, and pack a load of the soil up against our walls to shield us from theirs.'

She thought he would go along with it, for a moment. She dearly wanted him to just nod along, as he always had done. That long face was swinging back and forth, though, the banded brow furrowing.

'All of this just for that?' he pressed her.

'It'll help: every little thing . . .' She should just be giving him orders, but he had been her friend longer than she had been his officer.

'Straessa,' he challenged her, still speaking in his quiet and gentle way, but now as if explaining something to a child, 'two-thirds of the Wasp army can *fly*. And their artillery can hit us from well beyond any of this stuff. And their orthopters . . .' He looked like a man trying to work out whether he was caught in a nightmare or not. 'We're fighting yesterday's war. What will all of this *achieve*?'

'I said that, too,' the Dragonfly woman, Gorenn, said, dropping down for more water. 'Would they listen? They would not.'

She wasn't the only one. Straessa had heard that Kymene, the leader of the Mynans in exile in Collegium, had got into a blazing row over that very same issue, having witnessed her own city fall to the Wasps, and of course half of Gorenn's homeland had been Wasp-occupied for years. It seemed their voices counted for little.

'They have ground troops,' she insisted, listening to herself defend a decision of her superiors that she had not really agreed with in the first place. 'You remember their infantry as well as I do.' *Better, probably, under the circumstances.* 'Their Spiderlands mob won't be in the air, either. So it'll help, and it's better than not having it.' There were a lot of soldiers listening in now, who had been slaving away in the sweat-harvesting sun for hours, and she was abruptly aware how tenuous the whole structure of Collegiate authority was, how much it relied on the consent of all concerned. 'Look, you said you were reporting for duty,' she pointed out, more harshly than she had intended.

He just looked at her, and she guessed he might walk away,

but then he had grabbed a spade, fumbling with it a little, and set to work, driving at the earth as though it was a surrogate for all the things he could not just bludgeon into place. He was half a hand short, but he was stronger than he looked, and soon everyone was back to following orders. *Thanks to me. Hooray for me.*

'Bookworm,' said Gorenn, drawing the final bucket of water, and Straessa looked up to see a wobbling figure weave unsteadily through the air until it had dropped down on the ground in front of her. This was Jodry Drillen's Fly-kinden secretary, who had taken to going about with a breastplate on, so heavy he made hard weather of even the short hop from the city walls. *Does he just want to look like a soldier, or does he know something about the range of the Wasp engines?*

'Where's your chief officer?' he demanded, not so much of the Antspider as of everyone.

'On the walls with the artillerists,' Straessa told him. 'You probably just passed him.'

The little man choked down his annoyance, smoothing his face over with his usual slightly superior expression. 'Well, kindly go and get him and send him on to the War Council. They need everyone.'

We're not even trying for a field battle, are we? Straessa wondered, but she remembered the last one quite well enough, most especially the way that all the courage, imagination, armament and righteousness of the Collegiate forces had been ground down and broken against the numbers and discipline of the Wasps. *And that discipline is something they learn from the womb, most likely. It's not something we can just work out from first principles.* And then there had been the Sentinels, the great armoured woodlouse-shaped machines armed with leadshotters and rotary piercers, proof against just about anything that the Collegiates had been able to throw at them, including aerial bombardment. *And has anyone got a clever plan for those, I wonder? Because, if so, nobody's said what it is.*

'I'll get him, don't worry,' she promised.

'To the Prowess Forum, that's where they're meeting. And now's not too soon,' the Fly snapped at her, and then he was clawing for the air again, touching down a couple of times as he built up speed, before lurching away back towards the city. *Easier for you to find him yourself, you overdressed little prig,* Straessa reflected, but no doubt the Speaker's vaunted secretary had better things to do. She glanced at Gerethwy, contemplating taking him along with her, but, looking at the fragile set of his face, she decided wretchedly that she couldn't cope with him just then, so she left him digging.

The new chief officer of the Coldstone Company was indeed up on the walls. Straessa uncharitably decided that he was playing with artillery rather than doing the job he had been elected to but, truth be told, Madagnus had come to Collegium ten years ago as a very skilled artillerist, and had only been honing his skills since. Now the College was installing its new toys on the walls, and wrestling him away was likely to be a full-time job.

Like his assassinated predecessor, Madagnus was an Ant, although from some Spiderlands city nobody had ever heard of. He was a gaunt man on the wrong side of middle years, his skin the colour of rusting iron, and he disdained armour save for the Company-issue buff coat, which he left open down the front. In a crowd of Beetle-kinden artillerists he was easy to spot.

She hung back to watch for a moment, seeing only a disappointingly small machine, something looking like a ballista with no arms mounted on a big wooden box. The elderly Beetle demonstrating it was saying something about building up a magnetic differential between the two ends of the device, therefore she gathered that the box contained something in the way of a dwarf lightning engine. *Which means I'm standing about three streets too close to it for comfort.* She was no artificer, though, and the details passed her by. By then the demonstrator had slipped an all-metal bolt into the thing, and declared it ready for a test.

The box beneath the machine began not making a noise. The Antspider could tell it was not making a noise because it was making the stones beneath her feet vibrate with all the silence it was putting out.

'Excuse me,' she put in, feeling a sudden stab of fear. 'Those are my soldiers out there beyond the walls.'

They all looked at her as though she was simple-minded, and the old man aiming the machine chuckled indulgently.

'This is intended to counter the Wasp *artillery*, girl. At this elevation nobody within a mile of the city's going to be in any danger.'

Straessa blinked at him, and at last the contraption began making an audible sound, a high whining just at the edge of hearing, which the old man clearly took as a good sign.

'And . . . loose!' He got it wrong, said it again, and then, a second later, the bolt was simply gone. Straessa had the faint sense of very swift motion, and no more. Of the missile's eventual impact there was no sign.

'Of course we'll tip the bolts with explosives when Wasps arrive,' the old artillerist said cheerily, 'but it's all about magnets and the new steel and good old College know-how.' And then the others were crowding in to study the device.

Straessa plucked at the sleeve of her chief officer's coat as he tried to elbow his way in. 'You're wanted, Chief.'

The Ant looked annoyed at that, but he glanced off over the walls – *east, towards the Wasps*, she thought – then nodded, and they descended together.

She accompanied him as far as the Prowess Forum, for fear that he would end up back on the walls again if she left his side. The College's old sparring ground had been decked out with banners, she saw, which meant that this gathering was not just another in the interminable series of committees that seemed to be Collegium's answer to everything. This was *it*. The great minds of the city had come together, and were about to impart their wisdom to their martial servants.

She saw Stenwold Maker within, sitting on the tiered seats as though waiting to watch a practice match. The sagging bulk of Jodry Drillen lurked in one doorway, speaking to another couple of Assemblers, and at least a score of others were already sitting in small cliques and factions, some there to speak and some to listen. She recognized the small form of Willem Reader, the aeronautics artificer, and a few others she could put a name to. One was Helmess Broiler, Collegium's least favourite son in many quarters, and a man often claimed to be on the Imperial payroll. The Prowess Forum was public, though, and many people had come to see the leaders of their city's armed might. *A morale exercise, then, more than anything. No state secrets here.*

She ticked off the banners, seeing the various chief officers and other military leaders arrive and assemble beneath them: five Companies and four others, nine men and women to direct the battle.

The Companies first. Red scarab was the badge of Maker's Own, and their chief officer, Elder Padstock, was the senior military figure there. *Through the Gate* was their motto, and Padstock was known to be a fervent, even fanatical supporter of Stenwold Maker.

Madagnus himself was standing beneath the banner depicting a white helm in profile – not the original Vekken design but an Imperial infantry helmet now, for reasons of politics. Their motto, and Straessa's own, was *In Our Enemy's Robes*, after the original inhabitants of Coldstone Street had taken arms and armour from Vekken dead to throw back the invaders.

Outwright's Pike and Shot had a wheel of pikes and snapbows as its device, whose intricacy must have left the embroiderers cursing. *Outright Victory or Death* went their words, and the original Outwright had indeed died defending Stenwold Maker from Imperial assassins. His nephew, someone-or-other Outwright, looked far too young for the job, but his soldiers had elected him out of fondness for his martyred uncle. Beside him stood sweating Remas Boltwright of the new Fealty Street

Company, his banner simple crossed crossbow bolts, his words *To End the Quarrel*. He was doing his best but, like Outwright Junior, he did not look the soldier.

Eujen Leadswell stood at his shoulder, beneath the purple banner displaying the open book. He and Averic had been devoting every waking moment to turning their rabble of malcontents into something approximating a fighting company, but some wit amongst the students had seen to it that the words *Learn to Live* had been added to their flag. In Straessa's experience it was entirely possible that Eujen, beneath them, had not even noticed. *So very focused, always.*

And curse me, but he looks the part. Eujen Leadswell, student of social history and outspoken detractor of no less a man than Stenwold Maker, stood straight-backed and proud in his breast-plate, and if any had been ready to mock the idea of the Student Company, or to slight him for his political beliefs, they held their tongues now.

I am not going to cry. But, looking at him, Straessa felt so very aware of how fragile he was, just as any man or woman was fragile. One bolt, one sword, and all that young promise would be gone.

The others came as no surprise, those defenders of the city who were not formally part of the Companies. She saw, standing beneath a sky-coloured banner without device or motto, the little Fly-kinden pilot who was everyone's darling after the Wasp Air Corps had been brought down last time.

Kymene the Mynan leader had her city's red arrows on black, one pointing up, one down, expounded by the words below them: *We Have Fallen. We Will Rise Again.* Straessa had a lot of time for Kymene save that she had always felt that the woman was so fiercely opposed to the Wasps that she might get a great many people killed for it one day.

Some close-faced, midnight-skinned Vekken stood, with no banner at all, representing that company of his kinsfolk who had come reluctantly to the aid of their new – and only – ally. Lastly, beneath a plain green flag, there was a Mantis-kinden woman Straessa did not know, standing for the Felyen exiles within Collegium, those last tatters of the Felyal hold destroyed by the Second Army on its last advance.

And that's it, thought the Antspider. *That's all of us, Beetle and non-Beetle, citizens and guests. These nine are the hope of the city in miniature.*

By that time the crowd was quite large, packing themselves in at every door, concerned men and women of Collegium who were ostensibly here to see history performed, but in reality just wanted to be told that everything would be all right.

Twelve

Sergeant Gorrec of the Pioneers was crouching low, his huge frame almost tucked into the tangled roots of one of the vast old trees, while all around him the Mantis-kinden were fighting.

It had come on very suddenly. The three Pioneers chosen to spearhead the Empress's expedition had been carefully breaking new ground, pressing deeper into the forest, and there had been some Nethyen Mantids with them, keeping pace. Gorrec hadn't liked that, but they weren't part of his chain of command, and he was cursed if he was going to go crying to the Empress about them. They had faded in and out: now gone from his sight, then a moment later there would be a full half-dozen just ghosting between the trees. *No friends of mine.* But friends weren't something that Gorrec was overly supplied with. A man didn't go into the Pioneers because he liked the company.

Then the other Mantids had turned up and everything had gone rapidly out of his control, if control was something he had ever actually had. There were Mantids everywhere, leaping out and trying to kill one another, and then instantly gone, sometimes leaving a body behind, sometimes not, as though their own irresistible momentum would not allow them to keep still long enough to finish the job. Gorrec saw the fight around him in frenzied slices, the dim air beneath the canopy briefly flaring into a vicious skirmish of blades and then falling still again, the combatants gone. He had his axes ready, those two huge Scorpion-made pieces with their curved hafts, which could be thrown some distance if the wielder was a man as big as Gorrec. So far he had not struck a blow: in the blur of those brief, deadly pairings he found he had no way to tell friend from foe. To him, the Etheryen and the Nethyen Mantids looked just about the same.

He would have followed Icnumon if he could. The halfbreed was Mantis as much as Wasp, and he seemed to have no difficulty knowing whom to kill – either that or he simply did not care. Keeping up with Icnumon was like chasing smoke, though, and Gorrec saw less of him than of the Mantids themselves.

Crouching in his hiding place, eyes almost useless in the gloom, with opponents that were here one moment and gone the next, he had been honing his other senses. When the sudden rush came at him out of nowhere, he was ready for it, kicking away from the tree with one axe arcing back to cleave the air between him and his attacker. *Thank you for letting me know which side you're on.* For all he knew, this could be a Nethyen Mantis who had turned coat, or maybe all the Mantids were his foes now, but for the moment being attacked was all the identification he needed.

His heels dug furrows into the forest floor as he changed direction, twisting suddenly to meet the oncoming Mantis. He had a fleeting image of a rangy man in greens and browns, trying to bring a spear down on him, but his own sudden reversal – and the sheer speed with which a man of his size had moved – gained him time enough to bat the needle point aside and bring his other axe about in an attempt at cutting the man in two. The Mantis leapt over the scything blade, dragging his spear up to skewer Gorrec like a fish, but the Wasp was still moving, letting his impetus carry him out of the spear's path and bringing both axes about so that they nearly crossed. There was a moment when the Mantis should have backed off, but the man's face was twisted with rage and loathing, finding this intruder in his people's hidden halls, and he just drove on forwards. The spearhead gouged a shallow line across the Wasp's shoulder, despite all Gorrec's

166

weavings, but then came the moment when the two axe-heads were just too large, too fast, to be avoided, taking up all available space about the Mantis warrior. Even then the man almost won free, diving through a gap that seemed too small to let a Fly through, but Gorrec and the twin axes went back a long way, and they knew each other well. Just as the Mantis was almost clear, there they were again, and this time their victim had nowhere to go.

Gorrec shook the blood from the blades, and the next Mantis was on him without warning, following the steel course of her rapier blade directed at his throat. He fell backwards – the only move that would keep him out of the weapon's path – and the woman had vaulted him, turned even as she landed, lunging back at his chest as he scrambled on his elbows to try and get out of the way.

Then she had pitched backwards, her deadly blade spinning from her hands, while Gorrec jumped to his feet, axes still in hand. Ten yards away, almost lost amidst the trees, the Beetle Jons Escarrabin was reloading his snapbow, hands working automatically as his eyes raked their surroundings.

Gorrec tensed, awaiting the next challenger, but there came nothing. Either the fight had moved on, or it had simply broken up. He and Escarrabin had the forest to themselves, save for the corpses.

Apparently satisfied, the Beetle Pioneer dropped to one knee by the closest body, essaying a quick search for anything of value. A moment later Icnumon sloped out of the shadows, sheathing his blades.

Just another day in the service, Gorrec considered, reaching into his pouch for his medicine kit, because he reckoned this was the sort of place wounds would turn bad fast, if you let them.

He put one axe down and issued his orders by way of hand gestures: *You two keep watch, advance slowly, I'm falling back to report. I'll catch up.* Pioneers weren't the talkative type.

I just hope Her Majesty has a free hand with the rewards, when we get back, was all he thought about it. Just because he had trained for this sort of work didn't mean he had to *like* heading into the darkest depths of a Mantis hold. Even amongst the Pioneers that approached as close to suicide as any of them cared to tread.

She waved away the big Pioneer's report as soon as he started to make it, simply saying, 'I *know*,' to his brutish, uncomprehending face. 'I know it all,' and she sent him back to his comrades, to continue breaking ground, to keep up with the rush of the Nethyen.

'Majesty . . .?' Gjegevey queried uncertainly. He did not feel it, she realized. Neither did Tegrec, the Wasp in Moth's clothing. They were both magicians in their way, but their power was wan and tepid, rusted from disuse in the one case, and newly minted and shallow in the other. Seda's speculative gaze moved on, past Tisamon and Ostrec, until she met the blank eyes of Yraea, the Moth ambassador, and in that featureless gaze she felt some kindred echo. Of course, the Moths had ruled over the Mantids for millennia, and now she, Seda, was treading where once they had held sole dominion.

And she does not like it. Seda found herself reading that much into those white eyes. *I wonder what orders she has been given by her Skryre masters? Find some way of taking my inheritance from me, and then down with the mistress of the Empire, no doubt.* She knew from her own researches that the Days of Lore had not been filled with peace and brotherhood between the Inapt powers. They had fought, jostled for dominance, destroyed one another. *By the time the Apt began to climb from the mud, their masters had already exhausted themselves.*

A failure I do not plan to repeat. I may have to destroy the Moths, if I cannot find a way to rule them. The same went for the others: she would brook no rivals. *Will I be safe only when I am the last magician left in the world?*

But let me start with the Beetle girl. Perhaps when she is gone the world will dance to my liking. I will brook no rivals, but especially not her.

And the girl was close, Seda was well aware. Closer and closer, weaving through the dense and haunted trees of this place, and seeking out Argastos for the power that the old shade held. More, she must feel just the same as Seda felt, as the forest spoke to her, as its convolutions and depths made themselves known.

Just as a map of a mountain range can only hint at the complex creases and folds the real earth is twisted into, so the visible forest was a mere gloss over a tightly knotted magical landscape centuries old. Here the Mantids had begun, here they had stretched out their mailed and spiny arm to overshadow the Lowlands, at the Moths' will. From here had sprung their poets and champions, Weaponsmasters, seers and heroes. Here they had shed blood, their own and that of others, offering by duel and feud so many delicious sacrifices to the wood's dark and rotten heart. Here their idols stood, drinking the lives of the fallen. And here they had retreated, once the world had turned. In the last days of their power, here they were to be found, in this place that had been theirs, and only theirs. This was the unconquered past, the last sanctuary of their histories, and it spoke to her. The forest was like a vast, malevolent mind dispersed and parcelled out between the trees, the beasts, even the people. She could sense it, this great and ancient thing that did not acknowledge the progressive world without. When the Pioneers and the Nethyen had fought, she had known of it. When blood was shed, she had rejoiced and grown stronger with it.

She stared into the face of Yraea, sounding out how far that kinship went, and found that she had outstripped the Moth already. Moth-kinden magic was different, more refined, more cautious, ever playing the long game: a thousand pieces on a board that reached to infinity. The Moths had mastered their Mantis servants, but they had left them their sacred places, their savagery and their bloody-handed pride. Wasps knew all about that. *We are the true inheritors of the Mantis-kinden, more than any other.*

And her spread senses resounded to the encroachment of the Etheryen, already flanking the Pioneers, and she called out 'To arms!' Her little band of magicians jumped, startled and unsure, but Tisamon was moving, as were her Mantis bodyguards in their black and gold mail. And there were Wasps beyond them, soldiers who knew what to do when an order came.

She levelled her hand, feeling the swift flurry through the dark that was the approaching enemy, knowing them as a part of her, tied by the same cords to the vast sounding board of the forest. When her sting spat, the gold fire searing into the chest of the leading Etheryen warrior, that death was her gift to the forest, and she and her victim were enacting a ritual as old as time.

The Mantis band was small, no more than half a dozen, but they were very swift, and she guessed they had been hunting for her, trying to hack the head from their enemy. Tisamon cut two arrows from the air that had been loosed at her, and then her soldiers were rushing forwards to interpose themselves, even as her bodyguards engaged. Mantis fought Mantis with all the grace and ferocity of their training, claw versus claw. Seda simply stood and waited, watching that handful of them eddy and sway, seeing Tisamon strike and strike again, swift and deadly, but meeting a skill that had the same roots as his own. A handful of Wasps had run in also, and two were dead already, but they had killed off the momentum of the Etheryen charge. For a moment it seemed that nothing was left except for the killing, but then a silver-haired Mantis man broke free of the melee, dancing aside from Tisamon's lunge with a young-man's nimble step, and he was driving at Seda the next moment.

And the forest did not care, of course. Blood was blood, and if she fell to this man's steel claw, that would also be fitting.

She exerted herself, however, focusing her attention on him in the brief second before he reached her. *Fear me, worship me, adore me.* Time slowed about her, and she wrestled with the arrowhead of his mind even as her palm spread, sting heating in her fingers.

Or am I too slow? As if in a dream, she saw him falter but not stop. The claw was drawn back, ready to drive itself down into her, and still she had no belief in it. *I am Seda, Empress of the Wasps. I cannot die.*

Then Ostrec was there, ducking in low under the Mantis's guard with shocking speed: no sting, not even a sword, but ramming a dagger home to the hilt, sending the Mantis staggering, keeping him just out of blade range of the Empress. The man refused to fall, but by then it was too late because Tisamon had caught him up, that one second making all the difference, and Seda let her sting cool again as her armoured ghost opened the silver-haired Mantis's throat with a hooking strike.

It was over by then. She had lost three soldiers and two of her six bodyguards, a steep price to pay. The small band of Etheryen had gambled all they had on killing her, on excising her from their world.

I am here to stay, and this is my world now. She hurled the thought out into the forest, and felt its answering response: approving, darkly amused and greedy for blood. She knew then that it would do its best to kill her, by the blades of its people, by the hooked arms of its monstrous beasts, by its sheer darkness – but it would do so with love. It would gather her to it, if she let it, and perhaps in a hundred years someone would come questing here to find *her* ghost.

But she was Seda the Empress, and she would master it, and make it hers, to enjoy or destroy as she saw fit. Here she had come at last into her true kingdom.

And, somewhere out there, Argastos.

There were few non-Ants in Sarnesh service, the lack of a mind-link proving an insurmountable failing for most. Ants could not fly, though, and whilst that link allowed them the coordination to move without error through the semi-dark of the Mantis forest, their vision could not pierce it the way those of the natives could. In their logical way, therefore, even the Ant-kinden kept a few outsiders on the payroll.

It must be hard, Che decided, as she stepped carefully through the tangled undergrowth. *There's nowhere in which to be an outsider quite like an Ant city-state.*

The chief scout's name was Zerro, and he must have lived amongst the Ants a long time, for he even had their look: that closed-mouthed, hard-eyed Ant expression that told of an untouchable internal world. No such world, of course, for a Fly-kinden like Zerro, but he almost acted as if there was, reading the thoughts of his comrades from their stance, from the minute traces of expression even Ants were prone to. As a scout, he led a weird backwards existence, creeping ahead of the line, but putting as much effort into remaining in sight of the Sarnesh as he did in keeping hidden from the enemy. If something happened to him, it was imperative that the Ants had warning, and being seen was the only way he could communicate that to them.

They had outstripped the main body of the Sarnesh – who were making a steady and careful advance behind them, meeting up with the Etheryen and skirting the locals' concealed tree-villages, trying to create an expanding frontier to force the Nethyen back. The Ant commander, Sentius, had been at absolute pains to work with the Mantis-kinden, to humour them and to respect their wishes. No Beetle diplomat could have done a better job, Che thought, and it was all just another facet of Ant-kinden efficiency, the easiest way for them to achieve their goal.

Zerro and his Sarnesh scouts were meanwhile already past all of that and into contested territory, though Che had witnessed no fighting yet. The Fly had not been at all happy about bringing her and her followers along with him, seeing them as a noisy, clumsy liability. She thought that his opinion might have changed by now. With the exception of Helma Bartrer, who was still stumbling along at the back even though she had changed her

Collegiate robes for a tunic and cloak of muted brown, the rest of them moved through the forest with surprising ease. Oh, no surprise that Tynisa was at home here, or even the Moth, Terastos; and Che supposed that Thalric had done enough sneaking about in his time, and Maure too. Even big Amnon had always had a smooth grace about him, whether hunting the Jamail delta of his homeland, or here so many miles away from it. *I suppose it is just me that actually surprises me*; Beetle stealth was the butt of a hundred Fly jokes. *How do you know a Beetle's breaking into your house? He knocks first.* Here, though . . .

The forest was a dark, cruel place, stained with old blood, but it knew her. 'Welcomed' would be a step too far, but the anointing she had received in Khanaphes was good currency here. The forest might kill her, in the end, but it would do so with respect, and she moved through the chest-high ferns and briars with a dancer's step, and her eyes knew no darkness.

The Sarnesh around them stopped, not a sudden jolt but a collective fading into stillness at some signal sent from ahead. Che closed her eyes and let herself take in the rhythms of the trees about her, the forest's slow old heartbeat. There were Nethyen hunting parties out there, she knew. She could not have told Zerro quite where they were, but she felt them impinge on her mind like tiny thorns. None so close as to be a threat, although there was already blood on the air from skirmishes and brief flashes of violence between the trees.

It had been a long time since there had been so much killing within this wood, she discerned, and she could feel the whole place *waking up* by increments, something primitive and sluggish gathering its wits.

For a moment her mind touched something else, and in a start of panic she thought it must be the Empress, but the texture of the mind that she sensed was not Seda the Wasp's. It lacked her fierce fire, but there was a great wellspring of power there nonetheless. Then it was gone in an instant, unlocatable, just a chance brushing of consciousness, but Che formed the name

Argastos in her mind. *And if I know your name, old Moth, does that give me power over you? Or have you transcended that?*

She had asked Maure what might be left of this ancient Moth hero-sorcerer by now. The halfbreed necromancer had just shaken her head. 'This whole place is just built of ghosts,' had been her response. 'I'd say "all of him" but I've a feeling that there might be more of him, now, than there ever was when he was alive. Just because we get to him first doesn't mean that we'll enjoy it a moment later. Maybe better to let the Wasp woman have that honour?'

But Che knew Seda's strength and indomitable will. *I cannot let her have Argastos – or whatever he left behind him. If that means I must take the risk myself, then so be it.* And, in the wake of that, she reflected: *I am thinking like a magician now. Where did all this ambition come from?*

They were moving again, heading off at an angle, very slowly, and she tried to work out what was going on. At first she used her mere eyes, as any slave of Aptitude might, and there was nothing. Then the Ants had frozen again, and she saw them readying their weapons, crossbows mostly because those were quieter than snapbows. *What is it? Tell me . . .*

Tynisa was moving forwards ahead of her, and already identifying the problem, but Che caught up effortlessly. *Now I see.* A strange, reckless feeling had overcome her, a need to discover what she could do in this new place. *There is magic concentrated here, layer on layer of old ritual and belief encrusted about the roots of every tree, far more than ever there was in the Commonweal.*

Zerro was right ahead, but he was not looking back at her. Instead, he had one hand out to the Ants, fingers moving in a slow, deliberate code. His eyes were fixed on the beast.

It stood one and a half times the height of a tall man. The tree cover here was dense, and yet a lush, strangely pallid undergrowth extended all about them, as though living on something other than sun and air. The mantis itself had an ivory sheen to it, and was near invisible in its perfect poise. Tynisa was already limping forwards, and Che recalled she had faced down just such a creature in the Commonweal, but she put a hand on her foster-sister's arm, stilling her.

'Che, don't play around,' Tynisa murmured from the corner of her mouth, eyes fixed firmly on the insect. Its killing arms were still drawn in tight, and its vast, pale eyes saw everything.

Che was acutely aware of all of them in that moment. The scout, Zerro, was signalling her, but she did not know his sign language, and she was not under his command. She could sense the sharp scrutiny of the Moth Terastos, his fear and uncertainty, and something like a bitter envy from Helma Bartrer, frustrated Apt scholar. Here was Maure, calm amidst the darkness because she understood what Che was about, and here she felt Thalric's concern, his slowly escalating tension that might lead him to do something rash . . .

She stepped forwards, one slow deliberate pace, and then another that put her closer to the mantis than either Tynisa or Zerro. She knew that the Ants all had their weapons levelled towards it, but the status of such creatures was uncertain. The locals held them in high esteem, so killing one might have reper-cussions. Or not: the Mantids never seemed to have the same attitudes towards death and killing as did civilized peoples.

From every facet of the creature's vast eyes, the forest watched her.

Go, she told it. *We are not your prey. You are not ours. We pass through like the wind. We leave not even footprints in our wake.* The forest wanted blood, she knew. Like a crowd at a Wasp arena, it wanted them to fight for its amusement, but she was Cheerwell Maker of Collegium, and nobody's pit-slave.

Its arms shifted, unclasping a little, reaching towards her in readiness for a strike, but she read the animal, and the immense semi-consciousness around her, as though they were a human face. *My time is not now, and this is not the agent of my death.* She stared into that compound gaze. *Enough hollow threats.* For a moment she actually felt a connection with the insect itself, a sharp and calculating mind with more understanding and contemplation than any simple animal should be able to own to.

'Pass on,' she told Zerro, just quiet words, but she could feel a faint shiver in the air and in the trees as she spoke, reacting to the authority she had taken on. Even the Fly and his Ants, the blind and deaf Apt, must have felt some change. From that moment on, she knew that they would look to her. She had taken command in a bloodless coup.

That distant presence, the eye of Argastos, had seen it all, she knew, and was evaluating her even now. *What is he like? Is there enough left to even be thought of as 'he'? Do we go to the man himself, or the ghost, or just his tomb?*

They were moving off again, and Che found herself keeping pace some half-dozen yards behind Zerro, Tynisa by her side. Her sister was eyeing her as though she had gone mad or turned into a stranger. Che smiled at her, but she had the feeling that her smiles were no longer the amiable and reassuring ones she had once worn.

Thirteen

There was a drug they called Chneuma, which had become a standard part of the Air Corps kit. It kept a pilot awake and alert for days, strung tight like a wire and ready for action. Too ready, perhaps. Bergild was pacing constantly, twitchy and unable to sit, making circuits of the crate-table where Major Oski and his Bee second, Ernain, were trying to play cards. They had hollowed out a nook amongst the disassembled artillery in the back of one of the transport automotives and, at every jolt and lurch, Bergild's wings would flower for a moment, ready to take to the air.

The Fly engineer cast her a baleful look. 'I am blaming you for losing the last three hands, you realize?'

For a moment she stopped, clenching and unclenching her fists, blinking at him as though she had never seen him before.

'Can't keep your mind in your head, these days?' was Oski's verdict, and when she opened her mouth he added, 'I know, I know, you've got worries. We've all got worries.'

Bergild's worries were her fellow pilots operating in shifts over the Second's advance, their minds touching hers moment to moment. They were overdue another visit from the Collegiate orthopters, so every Imperial pilot was on standby and plugged full of Chneuma. She did not want to think about coming down from the drug afterwards. Nightmares and shakes and dreadful cravings, they said, and none of the chemists really knew how long it was safe to keep using the cursed stuff. *But necessary. We are so few that we need all of us, every time.*

Then one of her pilots really *did* have something to report and, wings springing into being, she was at the back of the covered automotive immediately with Oski and Ernain leaping up behind her, for all the good they could do.

'It's . . . it's . . .' began her faltering response to their questions, and then, 'one orthopter. Farsphex. Ours.' But she was frowning because there was no mindlinked contact with the pilot. Not proper Air Corps, then. *A trick?* The incoming pilot was signalling with the heliograph codes that had been developed before the new breed of pilots had emerged, but Bergild and most of her people had never learned them. At last someone got hold of one of the older pilots who had, then interpreted an intent to land. Bergild instructed that the visitor be guided in far from anything critical.

So who's got one of my Farsphex?

She and Oski and Ernain skipped out of the automotive, their wings carrying them above the great marching mass of the Second and its Spider allies, over the labouring transports – wheeled, tracked and walkers – and the articulated forms of the Sentinel automotives. The Farsphex had come down, with one of her own machines still wheeling overhead, and some sergeant had detailed a few squads of Light Airborne to deal with whoever stepped out. By the time Bergild and the others had arrived, the orthopter's passenger had disembarked and presented his credentials – and was on his way to General Tynan post-haste.

The newly arrived pilot was still standing by his machine, and Bergild saw that his armour boasted a red insignia and pauldrons – nothing she recognized.

Ernain knew, though. The Bee-kinden was so well informed about goings on in the Empire that she would have taken him for Rekef if he wasn't so free with the information. *Although I wouldn't know what other information he's not being free with, I suppose.*

'Red Watch,' the Bee identified. 'Very new, the Empress's darlings. Looks like special orders for the general.'

A section of the army had halted for Tynan to receive the orthopter's passenger, and Major Oski was able to pull sufficient rank to get them within earshot as the man presented himself as one Captain Vrakir, also Red Watch. Looking up dourly after scanning through the newcomer's papers, Tynan did not appear delighted by this indication that the Empress had not forgotten him.

'So what does she want?' the general demanded. 'There are no orders here.' He did not suggest that Vrakir had been sent to spy on him, but that was hardly a wild leap of logic. *He should have had this meeting in private*, Bergild reckoned, but then General Tynan was a blunt-speaking man who did his best to live his life in the open. The Spider commander, the Aldanrael woman, was close by Tynan's side, though, and who knew what thoughts were passing behind her calm exterior?

'There will be orders, General, in due course,' Vrakir replied stoically. 'For now, I ask you to accept me as the Empress's voice here.'

For a moment Tynan looked as though he might argue, and surely everyone there was thinking, *This is not how you run an army*, but whatever the Empress had written on that paper in Tynan's hand, it was sufficient.

Then the word came, and Bergild called out, 'General, orthopters inbound!' because he was right there and it would save time. Everyone was looking at her instantly – perhaps all the more so in shock at a woman's voice daring to accost their leader – but she was already in the air and racing for the automotive that carried her machine ready for launch.

Behind her, Tynan was shouting out for everyone to get moving again – no stationary targets for the Collegiate bombs – and for the infantry to spread out as best they could. Everything fell into a well-rehearsed chaos, familiar from every previous day of this march. Bergild, herself, had thoughts only for the sky.

★

Taki had never flown a bombing run. She understood the necessity of the work, but it was not *her* work. She was a pilot of Solarno and she took her prey in the air. There was no glory in attacking an enemy that could not fight back. When she had explained that – the one time she had tried, anyway – to the Collegiate pilots, most of them had looked at her as if she was mad.

Beetle-kinden were a practical-minded lot. If they were forced to fight, then most of them would far rather build machines to do it for them, ideally in a way that precluded retaliation. That made Taki think of the Empire, the way it had brought Myna to its knees, with so little danger to its own side, by orthopter and artillery. Collegium would not be taken so readily, but the whole business brought a sour taste to the mouth. Where were those sunlit days in Solarno, when she would joust in the skies against her brothers, air-pirates, free pilots, Princep Exilla dragonfly-riders, and all bound by their common kinship? Here she was now at the cutting edge of Apt warfare and already mourning a lost way of life.

Mantis-kinden would understand, she thought, even as she adjusted her course to head against one of the Farsphex, as the Imperial machines rose out of the great marching host. *They wouldn't understand the machines, but the thoughts behind them. Oh, for an Apt Mantis to teach to fly . . .* Clouds of the Light Airborne were scattering upwards, wings aflare – not that they would be any real good in the fighting, but they would be out of the way of the bombs. The heavier infantry, the Spiderlands troops, and all the rest still shackled to the earth, they were dispersing as much as they could, losing cohesion and slowing their advance to do so. *Well, fine, we're not exactly here to bomb them to death, just to break their toys and kick over their larder.* For there was a multitude of automotives with the Imperial force, though not half as many as when they had come this way the first time. All the important loads that the Empire could not do without had been split up across the army – more good sense from the Wasps

– but it meant that any vehicle over a certain size became a target.

And this time they'll know it. The plan was typical committee-born Collegiate nonsense, and Taki had argued fiercely against it, but it was a good plan nonetheless. *Still doesn't mean I have to like it.*

Then the Farsphex was flashing into her sights, already turning aside as she began to shoot, obviously warned by some other Imperial pilot. Taki slung her *Esca Magni* into as tight a turn as she could, unhappily aware that she had managed it tighter in her time. Her prized craft had taken its share of knocks in the fighting over Collegium a month before and, although the mechanics had done their best, she was going to have to give up on it soon. Sentiment was something she had been indulging in, and could not truly afford. She needed a new orthopter.

The enemy pilot threw the Farsphex into a surprisingly nimble climb, but changed course suddenly, and Taki knew that the Imperial mind – the collected thoughts of its mindlinked pilots – had seen what new game Collegium had brought.

The Stormreaders were quartering the sky, seeking out the Imperial fighting craft and driving them mercilessly, but not one of them heading for the ground. They were making all-out war on the Farsphex, the Spearflights, the rabble of other machines the Empire had mustered, whilst at the same time the *rest* of Collegium's air force was hoping for a clear attack on the ground.

They had put a surprising amount of craft in the air, for such a grounded folk. The Collegiates had given Taki orthopters and fixed-wings and heliopters, and most of them were as lumbering and bulky as their owners – flying barrels, flying crates, all wood-hulled and unlovely things that had been drawn from a life of cargo-hauling or flying courier duty, or lugging complaining passengers from city to city in the Lowlands. There were more than two score of them, and most were loaded with bombs where the Stormreaders could only carry a handful. Each had a civilian pilot willing to make the run – no reluctant draftees here by

Taki's insistence – and another man or woman in the hold ready to rain fire and death on the Empire. Some of these craft had hastily fitted mechanisms to release their cargo, whilst others would rely on holes cut into the floor, or shoving bombs out of a side-hatch.

If the Farsphex got through to them – even if the older Spearflights did – then the result would be a massacre, but there were more Collegiate fighter craft in the air than Imperial, by some margin.

The Farsphex she was chasing twisted round and tried to double back, but another Stormreader was already there and arrowing in so sharply that Taki had to slacken her own pursuit or risk running into its bolts. She saw the Farsphex take a spray of hits, tilt a little in the air and then level out. By then she and her newfound wingman were both on its tail, harrying it away from the bombers and daring it to brave their shot.

Below them, the first bombs landed – delivered too hastily, with the rosy fire of their explosions cracking open ahead of the Imperial advance. But there were more where that came from, a great deal more.

Bergild's mind was full of the voices of her fellows, all of them trying to get past the Stormreaders in order to reach the bombers, and all of them being driven in every direction across the sky by the Collegiate fliers. They were doing their best to assist one another, to stay calm and coordinate their movements, but she could feel the desperation creeping in.

She corkscrewed her Farsphex groundwards, a dangerously steep descent at the best of times, bolts flashing past her from the craft following on her tail. Then another Stormreader was rushing at her, flat and low over the heads of the Second Army, its piercers stuttering. She had to jerk away: it was that or end up with shredded wings and unable to pull out of the dive she had been in. There was one of the clumsy Collegiate bombers in her eye, though, and she had pulled out not so far from it;

and so she feigned reaching for height, pulling her nose up, and then letting the Farsphex fall away to the right, towards her target, hoping against hope that her attackers would be fooled just long enough.

For a handful of seconds she was there, the two Stormreaders committing themselves to the false course she had abandoned, and she rattled the bombing fixed-wing with a score of bolts, punching into its solid hull. *Not enough.* But even as she thought that, the vessel lurched and pulled up, its pilot losing his nerve. Then her shadows were back with her and she threw the Farsphex up and away, giving up her target for the sake of saving her hide, but knowing that the cargo fixed-wing would circle back for another try, unmolested, unless she or another of her fellows could stop it.

One of her pilots shouted out a hit: a lumbering, bomb-heavy heliopter clipped out of the sky with broken rotors, tumbling end over end to plough into the earth, spilling crew and munitions. To her right a Spearflight, which had once been one of the fleetest craft in the air, was gutted by a Stormreader's bolts, the narrow metal needles cutting open its belly and smashing its motor, so that the Imperial aircraft slewed sideways in the air, wings stilled, and then fell, with the pilot struggling to get the cockpit open and bail out.

She was fighting to rejoin the battle, risking more and more to break through the cordon that the Stormreaders had thrown up, and dodging between the raking lines of their shot. There was another bomber now at the edge of her attention, as hard to reach as the centre of a maze. Bolts scattered across her hull, one smashing a cockpit pane. Bergild wrenched her goggles down as the wind roared about her.

Her target, an orthopter with something of the grace of a fighting craft, was lining itself up with one of the transport automotives, and she locked her wings, stilling their beat without engaging the propellers as the designer had intended. The Farsphex dropped as abruptly as though all Apt flight had been nothing but a tinker's dream. She took three hits to her under-side as she fell through the metal hail, one of which punched into the bombardier's compartment behind her and ricocheted wildly – *and how glad I am not to be carrying a passenger* – and then she was out of it, fighting to restart her wings as the ground yawned to receive her, coming down so swiftly, so true, that she almost collided with her target. The Stormreaders would already be stooping on her, hunched and deadly machines designed for just that, and she had seconds to strike before she would have to pull away, or die.

Her machine was sluggish in the air, the wings still finding their rhythm, but that only served to let her fall into line behind the bomber. She saw the first flash of its munitions, searing across whatever luckless segment of the Second was down below. The driver of its automotive target must have seen what was coming, but the machine lurched on over the uneven ground.

Her immaculately timed burst of shot chewed off the long vane of the orthopter's tail, butchering its smooth approach. Even then its pilot did not try to flee, and she could almost feel him fighting with suddenly unresponsive controls, determined to strike his mark. *A true pilot, then.* He was veering, though, unable to hold his place in the air with wings alone, as the killing rain of his bombs stamped blazing footprints across a scattering body of infantry, leaving the transporter untouched. Bergild was already pulling out, rising into a metal-filled sky, watching another Spearflight ripped apart even as she tried to come to its aid. Then the Stormreaders had her again.

Through the mind of another pilot she saw a bomber strike its target, a trundling automotive that must have been laden with ammunition. The bloom of fire and shrapnel scythed out on all sides, two score lives smashed beyond recovery, the flame gouting enough that the watching pilot felt the heat buffet his wings.

Another of her pilots shouted in her mind that he was on the cusp of a strike, and she could almost see him lined up behind the labouring bomber. Then he was gone, a storm of bolts cutting open the cockpit to rip him apart.

Major Oski spotted the plume of fire, and just kept shouting. He had long since run out of anything useful to say, but for a Fly-kinden officer, so easily overlooked, shouting had become his grease on the wheels of any interaction with Wasp soldiers. His current victims had a repeating ballista mounted on the back of little scouting automotive, and were frantically wheeling it round to face the onrushing fliers.

'The fixed wing there – the one like a barrel – that one, ready and aim!' He had his sleeves rolled up, his tunic grease-marked and sweaty from doing all a Fly could do to help get the artillery piece ready. His crew of three – Ernain and a couple of Light Airborne – were trying to line the piece up with his flying target, which was not a job the ballista had ever been meant for. 'Left three turns! Up two turns!' Oski's major's badge was hard-won, his gift for on-the-spot calculations earning him the grudging commendations of a string of superiors. 'Now! Get that bastard *shooting*, you morons!'

The repeating ballista began spitting out bolts randomly into the cluttered sky – none of them seeming to go near the approaching fixed-wing. They were explosive-tipped, fused to explode set seconds after launch, but he knew that some would end up dropping amidst the army – *just have to live with the complaints*. Then the flier was past, and they could not turn fast enough to follow it.

'Next target! Ugly bastard orthopter, there! *There!*'

All around him the bombs were landing, and they were all ruining *someone*'s day. He had no chance to assess how much real damage they were doing to the army's vital organs.

One landed close by, astray from its target but very nearly too close as far as Oski was concerned, their little automotive rocking with the blast.

'Should have put your *armour* on!' Ernain bellowed.

'No time!' Oski shot back, though Ernain himself had managed to don a mail hauberk. In truth it was that he just could not *fly* when loaded with an engineer's heavy mail, and he felt far less safe without his wings than with a steel skin. 'Two turns left – *two*! Ready – now! *Now!*'

The approaching orthopter was coming in lower than the last one, the pilot painstaking in lining up his unlikely bomber on some target behind Oski – *I bloody* hope *it's behind us anyway* – and the bolts that began bursting all around it rattled it visibly.

'Good! Keep at it! Good . . .' Then his makeshift anti-orthopter piece sent a bolt along the side of the approaching flier, impacting with a wing joint, and abruptly the target wasn't a flier any more, but was still coming their way.

Hoist with my own petard, seemed an appropriately engineer-worthy last thought. *So save it for later* . . . and he was shouting 'Pissing *move!*' even as his wings cast him away, sending him hurtling over the heads of the army as though he had been struck by a storm-wind.

Then the actual wind came. The orthopter, one wing still beating vainly, came down nose-first within yards of their little automotive, and its complement of explosives was ripped open, the hot air of the firestorm battering at him.

Ernain? 'Ernain!'

'Here.' Bee-kinden were not swift or agile in the air, but Ernain could get airborne even with all that metal on him.

'Stab me, man, I don't want to lose you. You're *important*, remember.' Oski stared at him, feeling shaken. 'See the quarter-master about new eyebrows after we're done.'

Ernain's slightly scorched face frowned at him, but then another explosion shook the ground beneath them.

'Let's go find more artillery.'

Taki chased off another Farsphex, noted that three more Stormreaders had followed her lead, and so she broke off to take stock of the situation. Her internal clock was telling her that the bombers would have done what they could, shed their loads, and the shorter-ranged craft would be running out of fuel or stored spring. The actual clock set into the *Esca*'s controls had been smashed by some stray bolt along with a window. *Shot through the clock? There's a new one.*

She saw several of the bombers already turned around, one still offloading a few late explosives randomly over the field, as though the pilot would be fined if he carried any home. Even as she watched, one fell prey to a Farsphex's sudden fly-by, and she realized that some of her pilots had lost focus, chasing the enemy too far, leaving the civilian craft vulnerable. She twitched the stick, letting the *Esca Magni* drop to a level where she could intercept, while still trying to work out what they had accomplished.

Do I count six – seven? – of their big transporters down? That probably means maybe ten total – there's bound to be a few I overlooked. Then a pause in calculations while she rose to loose a handful of bolts at a Spearflight, which jinked away from her, suitably chastened. *No idea how many of their actual people, but I reckon that was a grim business down there.* She still felt that they had not done all they could. *Air defence and ground defence have adapted too cursed well. They've not got that much, but they spread it around.* At least five of the bombers had been brought down, and far more had been put off their targets by the determined resistance of the Air Corps. At the same time the Imperial air casualties, especially amongst the non-Farsphex machines, had been far heavier than in their previous sorties. *We hurt them either way, but we'll never get as good a chance as now to make them smart. We need to make it count, more than we have.*

She was signalling *Home, home!* to anyone who could see her. The bulk of her pilots already knew it, and the rest would follow, in a fighting retreat against an enemy only too happy to see them gone.

And by now maybe the strike force will have done what it came for, for the Collegiate plan had other parts that she was not involved in, and there was no way to know how that had gone until she was back in the city and hearing the news in person. *Oh, to have that mental link the Farsphex pilots've got. If only I could get my people to drink a pint of Ant blood before each fight to acquire it – I'd wield the knife myself!*

In the end, it could have been worse, but it was bad, nevertheless. They had lost almost no artillery, according to the reports Oski had received, but their supplies and ammunition were seriously dented. He did not ask about lives, that not being engineer's prerogative, and he honestly did not want to know.

General Tynan had spoken to him – to him and Bergild and a selection of the other officers, delivering a brief, bleak little speech, its hollow commendations echoing with the knowledge that this was just the first, and that the Collegiates would keep at it. After that, the intelligence man, Colonel Cherten, had taken the stand and, once Tynan's back was turned, he had informed them briskly that what the general *meant* was that they should most definitely do *better* next time, that in fact they had failed the Empress, that they were all personally responsible for every loss, and that their names would reach Capitas the hard way if they did not start taking their jobs seriously. Oski could not remember seeing Cherten anywhere in evidence during the fight, but no doubt there had been vital intelligence work needing doing. *Who am I kidding? Call it Rekef work.* Ordinary intelligence men did not raise the spectre of Capitas. Plainly Cherten felt they needed motivating – and the Rekef only had one way of doing that.

At least Ernain survived. Oski had a great deal invested in Ernain. *And one day you'll get yours, Cherten, believe you me.* But that was a dangerous thing to even *think* just then. Plans and plans, yes, but the wheels turned slowly. Conspirators, like engineers, needed patience.

A day later, when the supply airship still had not come, everyone began to realize that it really had been worse all along. A scouting

Spearflight found the airships' wreckage – not just shot down but bombed into a charred mess. General Tynan ordered half rations, but Oski had a good head for maths, and began estimating their surviving stores and how many mouths.

The Collegiates may just have won the war. Another thought not safe to have, but he knew that he wasn't the only one harbouring it.

Fourteen

The attack came at night, heralded by the most appalling sounds Thalric had ever heard. Only in retrospect could he bring himself to believe they had issued from human throats.

Night in the forest was more than just darkness and the sounds of the wood creaking, or of the multitude of unseen things that made the place their home. Huddled down, fireless, with Che and the others and a handful of Zerro's scouts, the utter sightless blackness was like a solid thing, a weight pressing on his blindly open eyes. He could hear Che sleeping beside him, the rhythms of her breathing erratic enough that he knew she must be dreaming – and what dreams might come creeping in this place, he did not want to think. He was not sure how many others were even able to lay their heads down. The Sarnesh rose each morning looking as hollow-eyed as he himself felt, and Zerro let them rest out the first hour of dawn before having them move on. When they did sleep – when *he* slept – it was a troubled and intermittent business. He dreamt too, he knew, but he remembered none of it. *And for that I'm grateful.*

Worse was the fact that he had been in a place like this before, though only the unpleasant familiarity of the sensation had marked it for him: *Like being watched, but by something huge. Like being surrounded by enemies I can't see. Bloody Khanaphes all over again.*

Someone moved nearby and his heart leapt. *Within the camp.*

One of us. Surely it's one of us. I'm so pissing blind *here!* He had a hand directed out into the void, fingers crooked. 'Who?' he hissed.

'Amnon,' came the rumbling reply, and no mistaking that voice. *Why is it I end up travelling with so many people I don't like,* came another thought, although in truth Amnon had been a firm friend to him, historically, compared to Tynisa. *I suppose I shouldn't switch sides quite so often.* But on the tail of that thought came: *Better here than with Seda.* He had been consort and regent for Seda, at the start of her reign, a convenient man with no power of his own, set up to mollify those Wasps outraged by the idea of a woman ruling over them. *And if there are any such left, I'll bet they're shut up in Rekef cells.*

'Can't sleep either, hm?'

'This is a strange place,' Amnon's voice confirmed.

Reminds me of your home, and, even as he thought that, Thalric knew he could not voice it. When Amnon echoed, 'Reminds me of my home,' almost word for word, the mere coincidence seemed like evidence for some tightening supernatural noose.

'Your "Masters".' Thalric fought hard to make the word derisory, but the darkness sucked the contempt from it, and his low voice imparted a kind of unwilling reverence.

'There were no Masters. Or, if so, they were dead centuries before,' Amnon declared. 'It was all a trick, even if the Ministers came to believe their own lies at the last. It was simply a trick.'

For a long while Thalric said nothing, disentangling the conflicting tones within the big man's voice. Surely that was the sound of a man who was trying to believe, and could not quite throw off the shackles of his upbringing. But Apt Amnon had since seen the wider world, and had decided that the old superstitions of his own people were no more than that. This was an inspiring story that might be taught smugly in Collegium, save for one thing. *You poor bastard.*

'Che and I met your Masters,' Thalric declared. It was cruel, but he could be a cruel man sometimes. He was not sure if it was that quality within him prompting the words, or some rarely surfacing need for truth.

Now it was Amnon's turn for silence, until Thalric reckoned the man might never speak again without further prodding.

'We went below your city and we met your Masters. They're . . .' He had no clue as to Amnon's expression; the man might have cut his own throat by now. And what could Thalric say, now he had started on this course. 'They're really fat. They're fat, slimy, old, and they care piss-all for your people.' *I had forgotten till now that Che hadn't said anything to the Khanaphir, when we came up from the catacombs.* 'So, you know what? You're right. You're absolutely right. It was a trick, and you're better off without them.'

Still silence. Maybe Amnon had just walked away while Thalric was speaking. But then: 'I . . .' and, after another dragging pause, 'I must speak with Che on this.'

Sorry, Che. 'Probably for the best, as I can't claim to really understand it.' Thalric found himself grinning into the darkness, unhappily aware that it was probably just the mean satisfaction of having ruined someone else's night. *Oh, yes, and sleep well on that.* He had exceeded by some margin his actual antipathy to Amnon, now, and was left with the self-knowledge that all this needling was just because he himself felt so helpless.

Then the cacophony broke out: a hideous, confused yammering and screeching that seemed to come from all around them, sudden and shocking and close by. Thalric's involuntary yell was lost in it, but then he was scrambling for a sword he could not find. Those were seconds of utter confusion for him, but in which the Sarnesh had pulled themselves together and drawn blade, and then the night flashed with the brief sear of a Wasp sting – *not mine* – and someone triggered a chemical lamp, throwing out a bright, greenish light that the Sarnesh all closed their eyes against.

He was briefly blinded all over again, looking too closely towards the lamp when it flared, but then the camp was being overrun.

Wasps. A few Mantids too, possibly, but the bulk of the attackers were Wasps, somehow already penetrating this far into Etheryen territory. *Light Airborne make a better pace than plodding Ants, every time.* Thalric threw out his hand to direct a sting. In that moment he caught the expressions on the faces of the enemy, as blinded and surprised as he had been – and not running *to* but *from*. This was a clash of ill chance that there had been no need for, but no way to avoid it now, and there looked to be a fair number of them.

His sting flashed, striking one down – the Sarnesh were shooting, bolts punching running Wasps from their feet. The attackers were already in the camp, though, and it was down to swords almost instantly. Thalric saw Amnon – a huge dark shape of nightmare in the unhealthy light – discharge a snapbow virtually into one man's face and then club another down with the same weapon, before taking a sword from one of his victims to continue the fight.

Where's Che? But of course the Beetle girl was already up and utterly in control, standing in the centre of the camp with drawn blade, and not rushing off anywhere or doing anything stupid. *It's as if I don't know her any more.* Tynisa passed by in a blur of speed, clad only in her shift against the muggy night, but her blade already dissecting the air about her.

Thalric remained at a crouch, stinging at targets of opportunity, trusting that the Wasps would not be expecting such an attack from their enemies, and so might overlook him. The sword-to-sword fighting was furious, with the Wasps already in a frenzy, panicking and dangerous. The Sarnesh met them calmly, outnumbered but fighting as one. He could hear Zerro's high voice shouting orders, but could not make out what the Fly was saying.

Maure and Bartrer stayed with Che, practically hiding behind her, he saw, as though she was some sort of supernatural guardian. *Ludicrous thought.* And yet there was something there, a strength that had been growing in the girl, which made him think again.

Then a pair of Wasps tripped over him.

In that moment of confusion on their part – and because he *knew* all others of his kind were his enemies at this point – he killed one with a hand to the man's side, sting scorching where the light armour left off. The other man hacked at Thalric's head, so close that it was the crosspiece of his guard that gashed Thalric's temple and knocked him back to the forest floor. He was already stinging blindly in return with one hand, even as his head rattled, rolling over and feeling the enemy's stabbing blade pin his tunic rather than his chest. Then its wielder was gone, the sword left behind. He dragged it from the earth, seeing his attacker with a knife in his thigh, hands wide, looking around for his foes, utter despair on his face. Thalric killed him.

The Moth, Terastos, dropped to his knees by the corpse to retrieve his throwing blade. He looked a little scorched about his shoulder, which counted as a near miss for a stingshot wound. *Hope that wasn't me.*

There was a knot of Wasps still up, backs against a tree, sword and sting against Amnon and Tynisa and some of the Sarnesh. By this time Thalric had stopped fighting. The outcome was not in doubt and the expressions on his erstwhile countrymen left a sick taste in his mouth: *Men who do not want to be here.*

He saw behind them, looming around the trunk into the lamp's wan light, the pale shadow of the same mantis from before, its barbed arms reaching out, and then one of the Wasps was gone with a horrified cry, plucked from the midst of his fellows. That broke the rest and they tried to flee, but enough of the Sarnesh had crossbows reloaded to ensure that not one of them got away.

Thalric moved over to join Che, and indeed all of the non-Sarnesh were gathering there, their camp now split into two for no reason he could discern, save that the looming darkness seemed to work more towards division than unity.

'The mantis is back,' he murmured. 'The beast.'

'I know,' Che acknowledged calmly, and he had the imme-diate and unworthy thought, *And did she bring it here, after mastering it before?* Another in the growing line of questions he wanted no answer to.

'Zerro's dead,' announced one of the Sarnesh, and the rest were keeping their eyes on the trees. 'Two more of ours also, and the Moth's wounded.'

Thalric's eyes located the Fly's small corpse, sting-charred, with a short blade still clutched in each hand. He guessed the Fly had been done for by bad luck. The tide had turned against the Wasps quickly – they had not been ready for the fight, and the Sarnesh mindlink had given the Ants a cohesion that had proved fatal for the Imperial soldiers.

'We'll take stock in the morning,' the Sarnesh decided, and one of the others put the lamp out, relinquishing all to the darkness.

After dawn, they discovered the Imperial camp – so close to them amidst the trees that it seemed insane that they had not realized it was there, but the forest seemed to have its own laws governing such things.

There were another dozen dead Wasps at the camp itself, meaning that their force had been much larger than the Sarnesh band. Nocturnal scavengers had been busy with them, so that the precise story was hard to unpick. A small party of Etheryen Mantids stepped out of the trees shortly afterwards, with the Roach girl, Syale, at their head – they would have caught everyone by surprise had Che not looked up a moment before. For a while, they regarded the intruders into their realm stonily, apparently only belatedly remembering that they were all on the same side.

'The Mantids did this?' one of the Sarnesh demanded of them, indicating the Wasp camp.

'They slew some,' Syale agreed. What happened to the others, she did not say. Thalric's best guess – or at least the most palatable possibility – was that the Wasps had killed each other in the darkness after the Mantids loosed a few arrows at them. *The forest killed them,* was a thought he drove from his mind.

★

Argastos. There were good reasons he was chained where he was.

The Empress's party was at camp, having already outstripped the Imperial soldiers currently making their unhappy way through the trees. The Moth, Yraea, knew that their officers would be trying to treat the forest like a regular battlefield, to draw up their plans and maps, advance their troops to meet the Sarnesh, whilst the Mantids of both sides flowed about them like streams eroding sandbanks.

The Tharen Moth wondered if any of the military minds on either side had ever asked to see a map of the forest. Perhaps the Etheryen had even given one to the Sarnesh but, of course, the Ants would not be able to read it. The Inapt did not represent land and space in the way that simple Apt thinkers required. No measurements and topography, no precise relationships between landmarks: Inapt maps concerned themselves with paths, with significance, with the mapping of meaning rather than bland reality. There would be nothing in such a map that an Apt eye could recognize, just as Yraea herself would carry away little from the dry, annotated charts the Apt called maps.

She had in her mind a clear picture of the forest, though – not as a map but as a branching journey, spiralling inwards, station by station. And at its heart: Argastos.

And are you watching this, old man? Yraea knew he was. She could feel his stony presence observing her, his dead fingers brushing against her dreams. She knew all about him, far more than she would ever tell the Wasp girl. He had been laid down as a guardian, so long ago, as recognition of his achievements and in punishment for his hubris. Centuries had passed since the Skryres of the Moths had needed even to think of their errant son. But now the Empress had his name on her lips: it was evident Argastos had been stretching out his power, reminding the world of his presence. Whether the girl knew it or not, Yraea was sure that he had called the Empress to her – and probably this Beetle girl as well.

Time to go secure the cage, she knew. *He belongs where he was set. We do not want any once-Apt fool to carry Argastos away from here.* And for that she must now reach that hidden place that was Argastos's domain and also his prison.

It should not be so hard, for Argastos himself is working to ease the way. We might be able to just walk in. It has been known . . .

'But I do not believe it is wise for Her Majesty to just walk in,' she reflected aloud, letting her companion in on her thoughts. The woman was a Loquae of the Nethyen Mantids, a leathery old creature who was still a warrior despite her age, possessing a little of the seer's talents also. Yraea had crept away from the Empress's camp without difficulty – a combination of subtle magic and her dark-piercing eyes – to meet this woman out in the unpopulated night between the trees.

'My warriors say she is powerful, that she carries a great authority,' the Loquae mused. Her own eyes were nowhere near as keen, but she would be able to see the shadow that was Yraea.

'But she knows nothing,' the Moth insisted. 'That power she has stolen is put at the whim of a spoiled child. She has no history, no provenance. She has done nothing to earn what has been given to her. She is a danger to all of us.'

'She wishes to bring back the old days, she claims,' the old Mantis murmured.

'She lies. Her days are new and without honour. Her armies have destroyed your cousins of the Felyal, and signed treaties with the Spider-kinden. What she seeks here is power for herself. Most likely she will fail even in that, but cause great harm none-theless, both to your people and mine. What we have laid down in ages past is not to be meddled with by some Wasp girl who knows *nothing*.'

Yraea could see the Mantid's expression, unhappy and uncer-tain: a terrible look for one of her fierce kinden to wear. 'Servant of the Green,' the Moth hissed, using the old title that her people had given the Mantis-kinden, 'the Wasp *cannot* give you what she promises. She will only take and take. It is all she knows. She must not be allowed to enter within the heart of the wood.

She would defile all she found there. Instead, let her smooth my way, and thus she will be of use, but only for that. You must gather your warriors and bind them to this purpose. The Empress's companions will need to be dealt with as well. You understand?'

'And the Skryres of Tharn, this is their decree?'

'Yes.' *Some of them. Perhaps.* Tharen politics had always been fluid, and the Empress of the Wasps' new status as a magician of power had divided the Skryres all over again. A majority had agreed to join with the Empire – better that than another costly occupation like before – but how far to tread along the woman's path was another question. Out here, beyond the reach of her immediate superiors, Yraea had come to her own conclusions. *Stop Seda, secure Argastos in his chains. Maintain the status quo.*

'Well?' she pressed.

Again a long pause, the woman's expression of uncertainty only deepening. Yraea hissed with exasperation. 'Servant of the Green, do you turn against us now? Are you unfaithful after all this time? Is this what the Mantis-kinden have come to?'

In the darkness, the old woman's eyes flashed. 'Of course not, and you are right in all you say, and yet . . . my people hear her words. None has spoken of a return to the old ways for generations. We begin to despair. The Wasp's false hope is like a blade turning inside us. Yet it is better than your offer of no hope at all.'

The rebuke stung. 'If it could be done, do you not think we would do so? She lies. She cannot give you what she promises. Do not be misled by her,' Yraea repeated. 'Do not betray me, Servant of the Green. Your place is to obey.'

At last, the Loquae nodded. 'I will speak to my people,' she said, almost in a whisper, with more than a hint of defeat about it. She slunk off into the forest, leaving Yraea wondering just what was left of the Mantis-kinden at this frayed and Apt-ridden end of time.

Desperate, she decided. Whilst her own people had retreated to their mountain homes and learned patience, the Mantis-kinden had merely diminished as the years had gnawed away at what they had once been, and they knew it. The Wasp Empire's presence forcing them to resume dealings with the outside world served only as a jagged and unavoidable reminder that they had no real place in it any more. *As long as they obey me in this, they shall have served their purpose.*

That night, Seda saw the gates for the first time.

She dreamt, but ever since her conversion to the Inapt world, her dreams had become more than mere fancy. She had seen the depths beneath Khanaphes through Che Maker's eyes, in those dreams, just as Che had seen them through hers when Seda trod those buried paths herself. Now it seemed she woke from each night knowing some further scrap of information, some shred of lost lore or a new understanding of those around her.

In her latest dream she was in some part of the forest she had not seen – *yet!* – and in her mind arose the thought, *the Heart of the Green.* Here the land sloped up to a hill – a mound, rather, since it was the work of hands rather than nature. *A barrow,* some lost thought informed her: the resting place of the ancient, honoured dead. It had been surfaced with slabs of stone, but now with grass and ferns thrusting from between the cracks. It looked to her like the carapace of some long-dead armoured beast, or perhaps a vacant compound eye.

There were similar burial mounds in the North-Empire, in Hornet country, ancient relics of her own people's distant ancestors that the Apt tribesmen still avoided from long tradition. These days such tombs were prey to treasure hunters, those wily enough to evade the locals, but she was willing to bet that no daring thief had ever returned alive from the barrow she beheld in her dream.

Set into the mound's side was a gate, and this was what she was drawn to. The mound's own shape had been built out to accommodate this portal, which was nearly as tall as the mound's highest point. A trilithon of grey slabs formed its sides and lintel, but the twin gates themselves were layered with chipped scales of gilded wood that rustled faintly together, each one inscribed with elegant, potent sigils; as fine an entry way as any prince or emperor could command.

The name that came into her mind unbidden was *Argax*: signi-fying at once Argastos's hall and his tomb. *And perhaps more.* What she sought – that which she had come out and risked herself for – lay within, and all she had to do was open those gates.

Surely she must want to gaze upon the face of Argastos, after all this time.

The dream took her feet and tried to send her forwards to those gilded gates, but no magician of her skill was so careless as to let dreams get the better of her.

You mistake me. She formed the words. *I am not just some Apt peasant who has chanced upon power. I am the Empress of the Wasps.* And she slapped away the tendrils that had been attempting to drag her forwards. *Believe me, I shall come to you in my own time, and I shall come as Empress, not as servant. Others have made the same mistake, believing that I am here to learn, and to pay homage. I drank their blood. I can drink yours too, if you have any. And if you don't, I shall yet find some way to consume you if you will not serve me.*

She expected an instant response – almost certainly an angry one, but instead there was a cool measuring of her. She was not yet sure whether what she faced was a human mind or some echo of one, or just a facet of the forest itself, but it was old and cunning and patient, whatever it was. She could not provoke it so easily.

Come, then, she thought she heard it murmur. *Come conquer Argax for your Empire.* Mockery, but could she sense a sliver of respect there?

She forced herself to step back from the golden doors, and she became aware that she was not alone in her dream – or rather that this was the dream of Argastos and she was not the sole participant. Nearby she saw the Beetle girl, the Cheerwell Maker creature, but this time there was no immediate surge of hatred. Instead she saw that the girl had gone through the same experience, had shrugged off the obvious lure, and for a brief second the expression on the girl's dark face must have mirrored Seda's own.

I will destroy you, Seda declared, and the Beetle locked eyes with her, her gaze giving not an inch. The last time they had clashed, Seda had indeed nearly destroyed her, but they were both stronger and more skilled now. Any battle between them would not be decided so easily.

Looking into that hatefully familiar face, though, the expected rush of loathing or even of fear, did not come. In that dream of Argax, standing before the barrow of Argastos, Seda entertained the strange thought that, under other circumstances, here was the one creature in the world that might truly understand her. *A sister?* Save that all her siblings were dead, and the last practically by Seda's own hand.

Still there remained the uncharacteristic and melancholy thought: *I could have used a sister.*

Fifteen

The land lying south of the Etheryon–Nethyon forest, the great road that General Roder's Eighth Army would have to travel, had been turned into an invisible labyrinth.

Both sides were still awaiting the outcome of the clash within the forest – at the mercy of whoever became the winners there, who could then strike with impunity at either the Ants or the encroaching Wasps. Neither side was letting the dust settle, though. Roder had his orders, and Tactician Milus had sent his city's forces to meet him.

But not in pitched battle, because the Sarnesh had already suffered a costly defeat against the Eighth at Malkan's Folly. For now, they maintained faith in their forces and their allies within the forest, hoped for a better opportunity for their great stand, and held the bulk of their soldiers back at Sarn itself.

Imperial flying machines still made their forays that far – Spearflights and a handful of Farsphex making the Sarnesh nights a nerve-racking lottery of fire. The Sarnesh air force itself could coordinate impeccably in the air, but their machines were old: orthopters whose design had scarcely changed in eight years. They could have held their own against those bulky old heliopters the Empire had relied on at the Battle of the Rails, but even the benefit of their mindlink barely made them the equal of the fleeter Spearflights. Inevitably, the Farsphex smashed them from the air.

On the ground, Milus's tactic was to slow down the Empire as much as possible, hoping for a flanking attack from the Etheryen to the north, or even from a victorious Collegium to the south. He was no fool, Milus, and he could see that his people were right where the metal met. The future histories of the Lowlands were his either to write or be relegated to, depending on the decisions he now made.

Since the Imperial Eighth had begun its advance from Helleron, from before either the fortress fell at Malkan's Folly or the Nethyen Mantids turned on their own kind, the Ants had been at work on the overgrown, broken ground south of the forest. Wasp scouts would have spotted neither earth-moving machines nor large working parties, but instead there had been small bands of soldiers, camouflaged as best they could. Some had been engineers, others snipers picked for their skill with a snapbow. They had their own scouts as well, and a scattering of bold Fly-kinden for long flights and night work, but their most valued men and women had been the sapper-handlers.

Theirs was an ancient trade, and their tool was known as the First Art. Long, long ago, when the lives of men had been short and cheap, at constant hazard from the beasts they shared their world with, some few of them had found a way to reach across the chasm between man and insect, and so become the first kinden. At first they had only begged, but much later, there were negotiations, demands, orders. Nowadays that old Art was a rare thing, but ascendant mankind still lived alongside the beasts and drew inspiration from them in the form of Art. There had always been tunnels undermining Sarn, but not dug by the hands of men.

In that contested country east of Sarn, a band of Ants was crouching in a dugout, each of them touching the mind of their officer, whose periscope was even now spying out the Imperial advance.

Leading edge is composed of alternating blocks of infantry – close-packed, armed with spear and snapbow . . . and war automotives. I see several of the new design, those woodlouse-looking machines. *Artillery, supplies and non-combatants too far back to see.* The words were acknowledged by a Sarnesh relay post to the west and would be passed on, together with an approximation of what the officer saw, all the way back to the tacticians.

I see a skirmish along the line, seven hundred yards thereabouts. One of the others – Pallina's squad. The Ants reached out their minds to hear the distant echoes from their doomed comrades.

Light Airborne on their way, twenty seconds, concluded the officer, taking the periscope from his eye. *I trust we're all ready.* His face was without expression, but the others felt his humour. It was a good man to fight alongside, he who could look upon extremity and laugh.

They were going to die, to a man: all the little squads that Milus had posted out here were 'lorn detachments', suicide details. They would spend their lives in slowing down the Wasps.

For Sarn, came the answering thought, first from one, then from all of them. *Sarn the mother of us all!*

Scorvia. The officer focused his attention on their one sapper-handler. The woman looked at him for a moment, her mind else-where and tainted with the alien feel that always came with her particular Art.

Oh, ready, Officer, Scorvia confirmed. *For the mother of us all.*

The Light Airborne were coursing overhead, and the Ants huddled deeper in their dugout, almost holding their breaths in their wish to deny the Wasps any warning.

The waiting, after they had passed, strung them taut as wires, but the officer would not risk the lens of his periscope being spotted. They relied solely on sound and vibration – and on Scorvia, who had wider senses at her disposal.

The engines of the Wasp automotives could be heard now: a low grumbling as they idled at walking pace to keep alongside the squads of infantry. The skies overhead were busy with airborne and some few flying machines.

And Scorvia looked up and thought, *Now*.

One of the engineers lit the fuses for the mines, and seconds later the ground around them shook as the charges exploded beneath the approaching Wasps. There were shouts and cries, but the Ants were already on the move, piling out of the dugout with snapbows and grenades ready to hand.

They found a light automotive kicked wholly on to its side by the blast, its undercarriage blackened and cracked, and a squad of infantry still picking itself up, half a dozen of them dead on the ground. With brutal, desperate efficiency the Ants attacked, for all that there were only six of them against an army. Every dead Wasp meant one fewer to storm the gates of Sarn. Snapbows spat, and the officer and engineers threw grenades into the midst of the reforming enemy squad, stretching surprise as far as it would take them.

And further, too, for the ground all around the Wasps was rippling now, hard bodies thrusting their way clear of it, glistening black with serrated mandibles agape, crooked antennae tasting the scent of the enemy. The Sarnesh had brought their beasts to war.

A score of them only, but they were half the size of a man, dark-shelled ants tearing themselves from the ground in response to Scorvia's thought and hurling themselves at anything that was not their own. Their jaws clamped onto legs and arms, piercing and crushing, even severing hands and feet. Their abdomens stabbed in to sting, driving searing acid into the bodies of their foes. Ferocious, almost mindless, whipped to a rage by Scorvia's inciting commands, they tore the Wasp soldiers apart even at the cost of their own lives.

Another automotive was already coming close, and the soldier atop it let loose with a swivel-mounted rotary piercer, raking the mass of ants and not caring much if he hit his own allies. The weapon had been designed for a fixed position, though, and its firepowder charges rattled and bounced it around on its pivot, sending most of the bolts wide. Then the Sarnesh officer got his last grenade to drop neatly onto it, blowing apart weapon and crewman alike.

Snapbow shot was coming at them from both sides, more infantry squads now stopping to deal with them. The entire leading edge of the Eighth was falling out of step. It all meant delay, blessed delay, and more time for Sarn.

A bolt caught Scorvia in the chest, punching through her armour, but her scuttling charges were now unleashed, and they would fight until they were all slain, blindly attacking anything of the Empire's, whether men or machines.

There was another automotive approaching, and the officer saw that it was one of the new kind: those segmented, armoured killers with their single leadshotter eye. It had a pair of rotary piercers set low in front, just right for mowing down soldiers on the ground, and a double hail of bolts ripped into the ants, and into the remaining Sarnesh, too. The last engineer managed to lob a grenade that exploded perfectly against the machine's curved hull but barely scratched its plating. Then piercer-shot found the man and his mind winked out.

It was better that way, for they already knew that if the Wasps caught any enemies alive, their leader was having his captives impaled on the crossed pikes, a slow and agonizing death. General Roder had explained this to his first victims – the words linking their way back to the other Sarnesh, mind to mind. He wanted the broadcast pain of the few to erode the morale of the many.

Ignorant fool, the officer thought, even as he discharged his snapbow for the last time. *The strength of the many combats the pain of the few.* He dragged out his sword and ran towards the great armoured machine's side, keeping out of reach of the rotaries. *Perhaps there is a weak spot.*

He heard a rattle, as the snapbow barrels set between the plates were triggered, and a bolt tore through his leg, making him stumble. He looked at the nearly sheer side of the machine towering above him, seeing an injured ant trying to climb it, jaws scraping futilely at its metal flank.

He snatched up a Wasp snapbow from the ground, no time to check if it was loaded, and hauled himself to his feet, for a moment leaning against the very machine that had wounded him. He levelled his stolen weapon at the oncoming infantry. The trigger was loose, the air battery uncharged, but the threat had achieved its purpose. Five or six of them shot at the same time, at least two hitting their mark.

For the mother of us all, he thought, and died secure in the knowledge that he had done his best.

Balkus had made his report to the Monarch's advisers as soon as he got back to Princep Salma. Princep loved its Monarch, the Butterfly-kinden woman named Grief, but the half-built city-state was run by those beneath her, who ensured that the food came in, the waste went out, and who made all the little, vital decisions that would let Princep grow eventually into its full strength.

There had been a lot of frightened faces, as he made his report. Princep had been founded by refugees from the last war – the dispossessed, the impoverished, escaped slaves and reformed criminals. When the Dragonfly-kinden, Salma, had united them, he had given them hope and dreams. Even the presence of his lover, Grief, had sufficed to let those dreams flower. They were working on the perfect city, building by building, law by law. They had imported Collegiate thought and Commonweal aesthetics. Here, they had a place for all.

The one thing that they had not found a place for was war. They had more philosophers than soldiers, it seemed to Balkus, and those men of the sword who had come there did so mainly because they were tired of fighting. The fact that Balkus himself had been made their military commander – a renegade Sarnesh nailbowman whose chief credential was that he had once known Stenwold Maker – showed just how unfit they were for conflict.

He had his troops arrayed before him, and they were a ragged and sorry lot. He had a score of Dragonfly-kinden in their glittering mail that were his elite – a gift from the distant Monarch of the Commonweal to her perceived sister. Beyond that he had a couple of hundred volunteers who formed his militia, better suited to keeping a degree of order on the streets than actually fighting. About half were Roaches, the strong sons and daughters of the influx of that kinden that had come to Princep because it was one of the few places in the Lowlands that welcomed them. The rest were a ragbag drawn from the sweepings of every city from here to Capitas.

They were brave, he knew, and would do anything he asked of them. Really, for what they were, he could not have asked for more. They would perhaps have given an equal number of the Light Airborne a decent run, but Balkus somehow doubted the Empire would send its army out in such convenient pieces.

He felt that he should make some sort of inspiring speech, now that he had them all together in one place for once, but he was no good at that. Besides, he had a feeling that any speaking today was going to be left to others. The Sarnesh had come to talk to Princep.

When Milus had dropped from the sky with a handful of orthopters, Balkus had assumed he would speak to the Monarch and her council in private, but instead the Sarnesh tactician had declared that his words were for the whole city to hear. Nobody much liked that, but the Sarnesh were their allies and Milus was politely immovable on this point. So it was that Balkus had drawn up his fighting men for inspection, and a large crowd of Princep's residents had slowly gathered around them. They were in what would have been the square before the Monarch's palace, if only the place had been finished, but at least there were gates, and some steps before them from where the Monarch would address her people.

Even as he watched, the woman herself arrived, with a few of her advisers and some attendants in tow. She was still a striking woman, although after Salma's death her skin had lost its once-bright colours and faded to the drab grey of a Moth-kinden. She carried herself with an air of loss that was inviolable – Balkus had witnessed the demands of haughty diplomats crumble to ash before it. A figurehead, yes, but a useful one to have.

Many of her advisers were Roach-kinden, and chief amongst them the old white-bearded man who served as chancellor, but there was a new face there, too, that the Sarnesh would surely not like much. That Wasp-kinden man had been Imperial ambassador to Collegium until recently, Aagen by name, but he had deserted when the new war broke out and had come to Princep. Balkus had not seen much of him, but he seemed to have become a favourite of the Monarch.

A small hand tugged at his belt, and he looked down to see Sperra, the Fly-kinden woman who had come to Princep with him. Her face was solemn and drawn, and with good reason.

'You shouldn't be here,' he warned her.

She cocked her head to one side. When Sperra was last in Sarn she had been present for the assassination of the Ant queen, and they had not been slow to use their interrogation machines on her to prise out what they thought she knew of it. 'I don't trust the bastards,' was all she said – and that was something of an understatement.

'Well, you know *I* don't,' Balkus pointed out, 'but they are our allies, and they're better than the Empire, who they're fighting right now on our behalf. They're entitled to come and ask for help.'

'So you'll take your two hundred and twenty and go take on the Wasps, will you?'

He shrugged. 'Not for me to decide. The Monarch's people will make the call – anyway, here are the Sarnesh.'

Tactician Milus had only a small escort of a half-dozen Ants, but he strode into the square as though he owned it, and the crowd parted for him automatically. Many here had come to Princep from the foreigner's quarter in Sarn, and remembered what it was like there. Life for a foreigner in Sarn was quiet, ordered and peaceful, and there was an entire city-full of mindlinked Ants who made sure that anyone who might change that situation was swiftly dealt with.

Milus stopped in the square's centre and looked about at his audience, an amiable smile carefully poised on his face to suggest that he was encouraged by what he saw.

'Tactician,' the Monarch addressed him and, as always, Balkus was impressed by the power she could put into a simple word, the presence she could exude when she wished. Art, he guessed, filling out each sound to command the attention. Perhaps she did not even know she was doing it.

The Ant leader bowed, not really a natural motion for a man in armour, but he did his best with it. 'Great Monarch of Princep Salma,' he replied, pitching his voice so as to carry to everyone. Most Ants did not have a good-parade ground bellow, having no need of it amongst their own, but Milus had plainly practised. 'I am here to seek your help.'

Good start, that. But Balkus found himself out of step with everyone, already tense and sweating whilst the crowd all about the square nodded and murmured. He put a hand on Sperra's shoulder and she looked up warily, noting his expression.

What have I . . .? There had been nothing conscious received from the minds of the Sarnesh, but Balkus was picking up on *something*, some harsh undercurrent that belied Milus's mild expression and tone.

'We know we have Sarn to thank for many things, just as they themselves have much to thank our founder for,' Grief replied, august and dignified. Of course, Sarn had tolerated this new neighbour, and had sheltered many of the refugees during the last war, but likewise Salma and his warriors had died for them, striking a blow against the Imperial Seventh that had allowed the Sarnesh to defeat them at Malkan's Folly. The *first* Malkan's Folly, anyway. They were even, therefore, was what Grief was saying.

'The heroic acts of Prince Salme Dien are not forgotten,' Milus acknowledged. 'Believe me, I was present when our Royal

Court clasped hands with him, and were it not for his sacrifice we might all be wearing the black and yellow right now. But the Empire is tenacious, it seems. You know that they are on the march again, for the news has reached you even here.' And a slight edge, just for a moment, as Balkus tried to glean something from the Sarnesh minds, finding them all closed tight to him.

'The Eighth is already closing on my city,' Milus explained. 'Our soldiers do their best to slow it, but we cannot stop it. There will come a battle, and it may take place outside the very gates of Sarn.' His manner indicated frustration, a bold man with his hands shackled – a calculated performance, like the rest, Balkus knew. 'The Collegiates face the Imperial Second, and we cannot help them, nor they us. They have even taken on troops from *Vek*, their old enemies. Can you imagine that? And our Mantis allies are suddenly tearing into themselves, of no use to anyone. So Sarn calls upon Princep Salma. You must know we look upon you as our child, and every child must aid its parent in time of need.'

Oh, that's a good speech, Balkus acknowledged, and yet the feeling of dread would not go away.

The Monarch and her advisers had discussed matters, of course, and now she nodded graciously and said, 'We have little armed strength in Princep but, of course, we shall send our warriors to help you.' Her gesture took in Balkus and his few, as he had expected. 'For the rest, we can find some engineers, artisans, some scouts—'

'Forgive me, Monarch, but Sarn is already well supplied with those,' Milus broke in, and *now* his voice toughened up.

At Balkus's side, Sperra pushed closer, staring at the Sarnesh.

Grief did not flinch at being interrupted thus, but even as she opened her mouth to continue, Milus was speaking over her again.

'We need soldiers. We need bodies on the ground, spearmen, archers, swordsmen. They will not be Sarnesh, but even so they can hold ground, attack when ordered or man walls. I need men to carry stretchers and bring ammunition to our artillery. I need your surgeons and healers, even your cooks and cleaners. I'll take your whores, even.' And by now there was nothing amiable left in his face or voice, and he was staring straight at the Monarch as he uttered those last words.

A silence descended on the square, all eyes looking to Grief. When she finally spoke, her words were tight with outrage.

'This is not Sarn, and you are here as our guest, nor our master. Salma—'

'Is dead!' Milus broke in. 'And he died like a soldier. Did he do that so that you could all live like peasants? Well perhaps. I don't know Commonwealers. But listen to me. I am not here as your *guest*. I am here as your guardian. Sarn is fighting to keep the Empire from *your* doors, and, yes, you will send your soldiers.' *After all, they can stop snapbow bolts as well as anyone.*

And that last thought came straight from Milus's mind to Balkus.

'But I look around me and I see so many able bodies,' the tactician went on. 'And I will have them. Even the placid Beetles of Collegium have been conscripting their citizens into the military. How would I be serving my city if I overlooked this great resource at our very doorstep?'

He looked about him, before locking eyes with the Monarch again. 'Let me tell you what will happen. You will send me a minimum of fifteen hundred men and women, armed and armoured as best you can – and we'll make up the difference in equipment. We have the surplus. You'll send me a further five hundred, along with them, who have useful skills of some sort – craftsmen, doctors, engineers, as you say – *not* philosophers or musicians or any such nonsense. And, no, this is not a matter for your committees. I am *telling* you how it will be.'

There was an angry rumble amongst the crowd, but he quelled it with a glare.

'And if you do not,' he went on, 'then, if Sarn survives, you can be sure that we will remember that you held back on us in our time of need, and in the war's aftermath you will see us again, and we will not be coming as your *guests*. If you live safe in Sarn's shadow, then you will fight at our call. And, of course, if my city should fail for want of help, then you can preach your philosophy next to General Roder's Eighth Army and see how far it gets you.'

He waited for Grief to speak, but the Monarch's words had been blown away.

'And some specifics. Him.' He pointed at the Wasp, Aagen. 'He's an Imperial diplomat and officer' – and, as Grief rallied herself to speak, he hurried on – 'and, yes, he's a renegade. All the better. I want a full report on everything he knows about the Eighth and its capabilities. I want him sent with your people, too, to advise on Imperial procedures. And if I don't see him there. then my interrogators will come and *get* him. You don't know how much slack I'm giving you just by not taking him away with me right now.'

Balkus thought that a small, hard smile crossed Milus's face, but that was just within his mind.

'And I won't have a traitor to my city commanding your troops. You're to replace him. Of all your armed *might*, his is the one face I don't want to see. Traitor once is traitor ever.'

'*Bastard*,' whispered Sperra. 'Pox-ridden son of a whore. What the pits are we going to do?'

Balkus could already see it on the faces of the Monarch's advisers, even if the woman herself remained impassive. *We're going to do just what they ask, because they're right and we have no damn choice.* He wondered if they could even manage to scrape together fifteen hundred fighters from Princep's motley population.

'Well, seeing as I've just been relieved of command,' he whispered to her, making sure to keep his mind shut tight, 'I'm cursed well going to go tell Sten Maker what's just happened here, and I suggest you go with me.'

★

'Sir, this feels too much like a trap to me,' Colonel Cherten murmured, as they descended the uneven path towards the beach.

General Tynan frowned at his intelligence officer. 'You don't trust our allies? You've had some evidence that they're not sound?'

Cherten's eyes narrowed. 'No, General, but they're Spiders, and they are renowned for playing both sides. If something happens to you—'

'Then you or one of the other colonels will take over,' Tynan briskly finished for him. 'That's why we have a chain of command.' And, because Cherten was really starting to annoy him, he added, 'And it's not as if Mycella hasn't had plenty of chances to do me harm.'

He saw the colonel's face tighten immediately, and then the other man skidded on a loose stone so that Tynan had to catch his arm. Cherten was indeed very, very bitter about the fact that there was someone closer to his commanding officer than he was. *But, to be honest, if he got as close to me as Mycella is, he'd have to discipline himself for unsoldierly behaviour,* Tynan reflected with a spark of amusement. And, Empress knew, amusement was something in as short supply as rations right now.

Ahead of them, just moving out on to the crescent of stony beach, were Mycella and her people: her immaculately armoured bodyguard Jadis, a handful of her soldiers, and then a squad of burly Scorpions led by that emaciated mercenary adjutant of hers. Tynan himself had brought a half-dozen heavy infantry – who were finding the footing hard going – and there were a half-hundred of the Light Airborne atop the cliffs, ready to swoop down at need.

The Second had been making dragging progress since the loss of the supply airship. Such a huge assemblage of soldiers needed constant resupply to keep moving, and their previous advance on Collegium had stripped the land of any worthwhile forage. Food, clean water and wine had been rationed instantly, but they had also lost several supply automotives to the Collegiate bombers and, at the best of times, keeping much in reserve was logistically impossible. He had naturally sent one of their faster orthopters back east with an urgent request for aid, but how long that would take to arrange was a matter of guesswork.

And, of course, the Collegiates had not held off their attacks, although Major Oski had managed to get a creditable ground defence going, improvising all manner of artillery answers to the slow-flying bombers, so that further damage was at least being mitigated as much as possible.

Then Mycella had come to him and told him she had something to show him.

As always his thoughts, as he had looked on her, were mixed. Yes, she was beautiful. Yes, she was clever. Yes, the fact that they were lovers was by now common knowledge about the camp – though, to Tynan's surprise, his standing amongst his soldiers aside from Colonel Cherten had only gone up. They viewed Mycella of the Aldanrael as their general's conquest, for all that he suspected the Spider troops saw things quite the other way round.

But she was a Spider, and there was a grain of truth in Cherten's words. Could all this be an elaborate ploy? Yes. Could she be about to switch sides and declare for the Collegiates? Entirely possible. Could she lie to him with every word she spoke as they lay together? Of course.

But they were co-commanders of a force that would destroy itself in civil strife the moment its two leaders turned their backs on one another. Never before had an Imperial army worked in partnership with another power. *If sleeping with a beautiful woman is the price for that, I suppose I'll just have to pay it.* He gave another snort of stifled laughter, to more suspicious looks from Cherten. *And solid rumour names him as Rekef, but then Rekef writ doesn't run like it used to.* And Imperial generals had always been a little proof against the Rekef whilst actually commanding their armies.

His feet crunching on the gravel of the shore, he stared out at the grey breakers of the sea. 'So what's going on, Lady-Martial?'

'A gift for you, General,' she replied, flashing him a smile.

She was almost girlish when she did so, for all that she was probably ten years his senior, and he was no young man. *But the Inapt, they always seem able to stretch out their youth, whilst we spend ours all at once.*

Her Scorpion mercenaries had taken up station over to the left, the waves lapping their feet. Tynan sent his own infantry to the opposite side, so they could glower at each other.

'Sir, a sail.' Cherten pointed suddenly.

Tynan squinted at the horizon, unhappily aware that his eyes were not the equal of the colonel's. It took a count of ten before he could make out the little dark triangle, and by then Cherten was announcing more.

'What's going on?' the general demanded.

Mycella explained 'I made the decision when we nearly lost the supply airship previously – when it came in that time just as the Collegiates were attacking. It was plain that supply was going to prove a weak spot, so I sent some orders back to Kes and Merro, demanding boats.'

'I thought that you didn't want to use boats,' Tynan growled. After all, a grand Spider armada sent against Collegium had turned back because of some unspecified sea defences that had plainly shaken the Spiders very badly.

'Believe me, if we had sailed up the coast like last time, we'd all be on the sea bottom by now,' Mycella told him with some force. 'But the Collegiates aren't sinking every ship in the sea just for fear of us, and so . . .'

'That's a fishing boat,' Cherten declared disdainfully, as the closest vessel tacked for shore. The vessel did seem very small, Tynan had to agree.

'To avoid notice, and to make a landing at a place like this, compromises had to be made,' Mycella confirmed.

'Are you telling me that we can resupply by sea,' Tynan breathed.

'We are about to do just that,' she said. 'I have a dozen such vessels out there, loaded high with whatever would survive the trip, that are just waiting for my word before finding a cove to beach in. And they will keep coming like this until the Collegiates work out what we're up to and target them as enemies.'

'And then?'

'And then they will be sunk without trace, and we will only realize it when they fail to turn up,' she confirmed grimly.

There was a scraping sound as the first boat arrived, and the crew jumped overboard to drag it up the beach.

'Morkaris, get her unloaded,' Mycella's bodyguard snapped. The mercenary adjutant glared at him, but had his Scorpions move in the next moment, so Tynan signalled for the Light Airborne to come down and pitch in.

We eat for another day, and then another . . . and soon Collegium.

Sixteen

The Empress was unhappy, and that made her dangerous.

They were well and truly separated from the Wasp forces now. Whilst the Imperial soldiers were doing their best to make violent contact with the Sarnesh, in support of the Nethyen, Seda was following a different path altogether. By Apt maps, Yraea knew, they should have been travelling the same road – the soldiers heading west to fight, Seda bound westward for the forest's dark centre. *Such are the limits of an Apt mind.* For, of course, Seda's true direction was *inwards*, and nothing so prosaic as to be found on a compass rose.

In was not an easy direction to travel, though. *In* had its own defences.

Argastos was willing the way open, Yraea realized, just as she knew that there had been visitors into his domain in recent memory. The forest itself, though, was resisting him, and so was the collective will of the Mantis-kinden. Had Seda somehow slipped in here alone, then perhaps she could have navigated her way unimpeded to Argastos's very gate. Now the forest's temper was up, outsiders were roaming its halls with bared steel and the Mantids were fighting. All the old doors that might have hung open had been barred shut. Those who wished to pass on into the heart of the wood must either follow the correct path or be very lucky – or luckless, like those Imperial scouts from the last war she had heard mention of.

So far, luck had eluded the Empress. She had passed and re-passed, leading her followers over the same trails, seeking the invisible doorway into the deeper forest that she could plainly sense but yet not open. *Such power within her, and yet she is ignorant. She does not understand how things are done.*

Yraea, however, understood all too well, for she needed to make her way into the forest's heart, as well, to put Argastos back in his place. *Old shade, you are grown too strong and too unruly, to have dared call out to this stupid Wasp girl. Your masters must needs discipline you and remind you of your task.*

That carried with it an uncomfortable feeling, because Yraea had dreamt of Argastos only the night before – as a presence watching her, unseen, his mind like a thorn in her own. *So old was he, he should be nothing more than a purpose now, with barely a shred of personality left.* Yet what she had sensed had been all personality, something far more complete than any ghost had a right to be. Even the spectre of Tisamon, the Empress's ridiculous bodyguard construct, was less whole than what she had sensed Argastos to be.

I may have a fight on my hands, once I reach him. It was a daunting thought, for she would be on her own when she did so. The plan was swiftly falling away from anything envisaged by her masters back in Tharn.

The Empress had halted, staring angrily at the surrounding forest and trying to sense how it was denying her. Crippled by her lack of learning, she kept just bludgeoning about the trees with her will. Yraea watched her contemptuously, though none of that registered on her face. *Such a waste of strength, though! Well, all the more reason to deal with the woman soon.*

The others took this opportunity to rest their feet. The three Pioneers – big Wasp, Beetle and that dangerous-looking half-breed – took up watch, for this part of the forest was very much contested ground and there had been a few run-ins with the Etheryen. As for the rest, both the old Woodlouse and the Wasp magician Tegrec just collapsed, looking worn out. All this walking was not something they were used to, and the forest was heavy going. *Can I spare either of them?* Yraea considered. The old man was too loyal to Seda, surely, so he would definitely have to go. Tegrec was supposed to be of Tharn now, but he was still a Wasp. The whiff of the Empire still hung about him, and she found that she could not trust him, even though she quite liked him as a person. Of the rest, the Empress's bodyguards and that Ostrec character, with his Red Watch badge, all of them would have to die.

Especially Ostrec. Looking at him now, Yraea felt a strange shiver of uncertainty. She was well aware that Seda had sought out Wasps with some latent Inapt heritage as recruits for her Red Watch but, despite that, Ostrec seemed strange. Something about him did not quite match what Yraea thought she saw.

Dead, she decided. *I'm all for secrets, but let that one die with him.*

Tonight the Loquae and her Nethyen would come. They would even come as allies, so Seda would have no reason to suspect until it was too late. The forest would swallow Imperial ambitions, as it had swallowed so much else.

With Zerro dead and their numbers diminished, the remaining Sarnesh were uneasy about simply pressing on, but Syale had news for them on that front as well. The Roach-kinden girl obviously intended to travel with them for a while, though plainly not out of any concern for her own safety.

'There's a fair body of your lot that I can guide you to. Sentius is with them.' The direction she indicated seemed to be just about the same as they were already taking. To the unhappy Sarnesh this news was pure gold, though, and none of them was willing to question it, simply agreeing to accompany the girl and her Etheryen companions. Che, though, had misgivings, and made sure she was at Syale's side to voice them.

'I don't understand how Sentius can be ahead of us,' Che insisted. 'He sent Zerro and the rest forwards as scouts, and we've been making good time ever since.'

Syale's glance at her was simple amusement. 'Miss Maker, how far do you think you've come, exactly? And remember you let yourself follow the Ants' lead. I had Commander Sentius following mine, and he was glad to have it. In this place, you're better advised to walk round in circles than trust an Apt navigator.'

Che nodded, thinking, *Poor Zerro.* The Fly had done his best, but he had never been treading the right paths. Unlike Syale herself, who seemed to be able to go precisely where she wanted . . .

'We've had to fight to get this far,' she told the Roach. 'The Nethyen, then the Wasps . . . if not for their current strife, I think I'd be fighting the Etheryen Mantids as well. This forest is full of thorns for outsiders. A Mantis forest is a proverbially bad place to visit, and yet you . . . I'd give a great deal to learn that knack you have of walking free here.'

Syale flinched, disguising the moment with another smile, and Che realized that she had leant on the girl somehow – through some exercise of her power that she had not intended. She backed off a step, physically and symbolically, and sensed a degree of tension leach from the Roach-kinden.

'You could not learn it,' Syale declared simply. 'I have – what would you Collegiates say? – diplomatic immunity. So long as I comport myself as a guest, they will not touch me. It's a fragile thing, though. If I should lift a finger in this fight, my protection will evaporate like dew. I am like those little parasite animals that live in an ant's nest or a wasp hive. There is a scent about me that says "I am of you" and so they overlook me, and leave me to go my own ways. But the moment I truly come to their notice by some misstep or misguided action, then, believe me, I shall become as mortal as you.'

'And guiding the Sarnesh doesn't count as that?' Che pressed her.

The girl matched her gaze, or tried to. 'It hasn't yet. My city is Princep Salma, Miss Maker, and the Wasps will destroy it if they can, because it opposes everything in their ideology, and because it lies there in their path. So I do what I can for my home and my people.'

'As do I,' Che added, feeling herself deliberately steer the conversation along the precise path she wanted. 'But I must do more than simply aid the Sarnesh. The Empress is in these woods: you have heard me say it. She seeks . . . a power.'

'I know,' Syale said, her voice hushed. She was suddenly just a very young girl putting a brave face on for the adults all around her.

'Then you know I must get there first, and keep it from her. So with your "diplomatic immunity", can you guide me there?'

'The heart of the wood?' Syale whispered. 'That is a place I cannot go and still remain beneath the Mantids' notice.'

'Why?'

'Because it is not a place *they* go – or not willingly. None of them, Etheryen or Nethyen. It is the pit that divides them, the stain in their minds. They avoid that place, and yet still it takes some of them, one or two every few years. And yet others who would search for it cannot come to it, no matter how much they try.' She shook her head. 'You can walk from one end of these woods to the other and never find that centre. Or you can head outwards and outwards, and find nowhere else. And the moment I should step off the track and seek the heart, Miss Maker, I would become something alien to the Mantids, and they would deal with me in the same way they deal with all their problems.' She regarded Che for a long moment, as they proceeded carefully at the head of the column. 'Although you, whatever it is you have made yourself, maybe you're the one problem the Mantids have no idea how to deal with.'

An hour of marching later, with the forest opening up somewhat around them – trees further spaced and undergrowth easier to trudge through – the Etheryen Mantids that Syale had brought along were abruptly accelerating, rushing ahead through the grey

222

light that fought its way in from above, steel glinting in their hands. There was no mistaking that onrush: they were going into battle, without war cry or fanfare but no less determinedly for all that.

The handful of Sarnesh came to some group decision a second later, and then they were running ahead too, crossbows and swords out, but barely a rustle from their mail. And Che was keeping pace with them, her own blade to hand.

She could not have explained why. She had not quite formed the thought: *I go to fight.* Instead it was simply that those around her were speeding up, and some childish fear of being left behind whipped her on, hurrying her after those retreating backs.

Tynisa passed her on one side, rapier drawn and dashing in pursuit as easily as if she had never been wounded, and Che appreciated again how she borrowed strength from the blade, that Weaponsmaster's bond as plain to see as if it were a glowing web between them.

Thalric was shouting after her, but Che kept running, and ahead she heard the clatter of blades, and then the shadows of the forest resolved themselves into warriors of the Nethyen.

There were nearly twenty – more than the Etheryen and the Sarnesh together – but nobody was holding back because of the odds. Arrows whispered through the leaves and she heard the clacking of Sarnesh crossbows. The fight fragmented almost immediately, individual Mantids breaking off to duel one on one, others plunging past to find their own opponents. The arena was evidently wider and more scattered than Che could take in, and yet some part of her was tracking it all, somehow, mapping out a battlefield in the clashes of steel and pinpoints of shed blood.

Thalric arrived by her shoulder, and her hand shoved him hard, sending him against a tree with a yell, just as an arrow cut the air between them, urgent as a messenger. She caught a glimpse of his expression: angry, unnerved, shocked. Then she was moving again – not to bloody her blade but to remain at the heart of it.

She could not fathom her own impulses, but some inner magician had arisen there, some ancient instinct she must surely have borrowed from the trees themselves.

Ahead of her, two Mantis-kinden fought spear to spear, leaping and darting, still for a moment as they parted, then in again with their weapons spinning and lunging like living things, the wielders seeming almost an irrelevance. They looked interchangeable, but she could tell one for an Etheryen, the other for the enemy.

Amnon charged past behind them, putting on a burst of speed and taking an archer by surprise, gashing the woman's leg even as her wings ripped her out of his reach. Then a crossbow quarrel rammed itself into the Mantis woman's ribs and she fell at the Khanaphir's feet. A swift lunge finished her off, and the big man straightened, blade already up to guard himself and looking round for another target.

Che just stood still and let her consciousness wash over, sensing them all distantly in some wholly new manner, never granted to her before. It was as though their very feet on the forest floor announced their presence, like the vibrations a spider feels from its victims in the web. The Mantids were bright, and she could see others, too – Terastos the Moth running between the trees, busy hands casting daggers at opportunistic targets, and Tynisa like oiled silk as she drove a Nethyen swordsman back. She could even find Maure clearly, for all the halfbreed woman was hanging far back along with Syale, keeping well away from the bloodshed. The Apt were far fainter, harder to read, harder even to see. The Sarnesh were simply an absence, but there was a certain aura to Amnon, a man who had dwelt close to old magic all his life without ever understanding it. Thalric, too, had a feel to him, as if touched by some hand . . . *touched by my hand? No – touched by mine and the Empress's both.* He had been Seda's consort, after all, before he had abandoned the Empire forever.

And Helma Bartrer – likewise clear of the fight and with no intention of taking part – possessed some buried spark that made her flare brighter than the empty Sarnesh in Che's mind. *Why?*

Then the frenzy of the fighting had claimed her attention again, and she realized the conflict ranged far wider than she had thought. This pocket was just a skirmish, but there was a grander battle going on, split into little knots of combatants spread over nearly a square mile of woodland. *How can they coordinate?* she wondered, before recognizing that they could not. The Mantids would simply duel and die, seeking enemy after enemy until no foe could be found, and then their survivors would regroup as best they could. That was how they fought. They did not make elaborate plans: they were warriors alone, each and every one devoted to their independent skill.

And it was a shining, beautiful thing, which lit the forest all around her, and for a moment Che was lost in it: the dazzling silver fire that was the Mantis-kinden killing their own kin with their thousand-year-old fighting styles, spear and spine, claw and blade. For just a second she felt like one of them, experienced the exhilaration and the certainty, win or lose, the pride in their way of life, their joy in battle; heedless of victory, of pain, of death.

In that moment she also felt the wrong note, saw the hollowness, understood why they threw themselves into the fray to lose themselves: because they were not sure. These men and women had not chosen to fight their own kind, but wiser heads, leaders they trusted, had set them on this course. For one yawning moment Che sensed it all, their growing uneasiness with what was happening, their resentment of the outsiders within their domain – friends and foes both – and the doubts that no Mantis should entertain. So they fought because the fight itself was pure and, while they fought, the reasons for that fight did not need to trouble them.

Then they noticed her.

All at once at least half a dozen Nethyen were coming for her, their minds like barbed arrowheads. In their thoughts she could see their purpose clearly: *Kill the leader.* She was not sure how she had assumed that mantle, but it seemed inarguable.

One held a bow, but a flash of Thalric's sting took the archer down before he could draw the string. Che saw the Wasp step in front of her, one hand outstretched and a sword in the other. She could feel the Mantids approaching almost like a tide, a force of nature.

And I have to do something. And yet she remained quite still, passively observing all, incapable of breaking from her own spell. *They can't just . . . I was anointed in Khanaphes . . . I have authority* . . . And, of course, it was this authority that the Nethyen wanted to snuff out. *Should they not fear me?* And she realized, with a jolt, that they did. The very fact of her, unnatural hybrid as she was, terrified them, but they were facing their fear. They were coming to kill her.

Thalric's sting seared again and again, but the Mantids were moving too fast and never quite where he was aiming. He went for the leader with his sword, but had the blade parried away, and then another had rammed him with a spear, the point sliding off the Wasp's Commonweal armour but knocking him aside nonetheless.

Hear me!

And for a moment they paused, some backing off. She saw bared teeth, wide eyes. Some leaking edge of her untutored power had cut across them, but it had been wild, random. *There is something I can do, some way this is supposed to work.* But she could not adapt herself to the situation. Whatever magical tradition she was tapping, she could only fumble with it. It would not work for her.

Then Tynisa came to her aid yet again. Che sensed the rapier first, and her foster-sister second, but then the woman was in the midst of the Mantids, looking like a Spider but fighting like one of their own. They scattered, then came back for her, and Thalric's sting cut down another, striking from behind. Tynisa's blade flickered madly in Che's sight, never quite where she expected it to be – but her sister was being pressed back, giving ground step by grudging step. She could not hold off all four of them for long.

A hand tugged at Che's arm, hauling her round, and Che looked into the grey-mottled face of Maure.

Perhaps there was some magical way to break her from the trance, but the halfbreed merely slapped her hard. Instantly, Che was back in the world around her, her uselessly grand perceptions shrunk again to just what she could see and hear.

'Come on!' Maure shouted, trying to pull her away, but Che knew Tynisa was fighting right at her back, and losing ground. She turned, her own sword raised – as though that way she could accomplish anything at all.

She had a moment of utter clarity, falling back without warning into that dream-state for just a heartbeat, but now fully in control, letting her mind ripple out between the trees. She tried to hold herself there but, with Tynisa almost backing into her, with Maure trying to drag her away, she couldn't. But it was done: for a moment she had been a magician marshalling her troops.

Amnon came first, unaware that he had been summoned, but there he was, sword cleaving down, almost knocking a Mantis off her feet even though she got her own weapon in the way. Thalric's sting spoke again, dangerously close to Tynisa but driving a couple of attackers away from her. A Moth dagger spun into the back of one man's neck even as he made to lunge.

In the confusion, Tynisa struck, pushing past her enemies' disrupted guard, her rapier binding past an enemy spear to puncture chitin and leather and flesh. Another Mantis lashed out at her face with a claw, but then Amnon's opponent fell back and took Tynisa's adversary along with her, and when the two of them had gathered themselves together, they were practically surrounded, by Amnon, Thalric, Tynisa, Terastos the Moth, and Che of course. It was to Che the pair looked: the leader of all their enemies. The magician.

Maure relaxed, and Che could sense without looking that Helma Bartrer and Syale were approaching, falling into their predestined places. *My court*, she thought, with an arrogance that was not really hers. *But that is how magicians are supposed to be, and the forest has seen so many of them.*

'I challenge you,' the Nethyen woman said, her voice just a ragged whisper. 'Fight me.'

'I'll champion her,' Tynisa put in instantly.

'There's no need,' Che started. 'There must be some other way . . .' but her words tailed off because there were newcomers approaching, a score and more of them, armoured and making far heavier work of negotiating the forest than the locals who accompanied them. The Sarnesh, a sizeable group, with Sentius at their head just as Syale had promised.

Che saw immediately when the Sarnesh commander received a silent report from the scouts – the night attack, the death of Zerro – all of it writing itself on his face and being overwritten by the customary Sarnesh stoicism.

'Maker,' he called, approaching. Sentius looked haggard, not at all the almost cheerful man who had briefed her when they entered the forest, but someone older and more ill-used, someone who had fought hard and slept poorly since they had parted.

He stared at the two Mantids at bay, glancing from them to Che, and then to the Etheryen who had been fighting alongside him.

'Surprised to see you still alive,' he told Che. 'I've lost more than one in three to . . . to these.' *And some to other causes, I'm sure*, Che suspected, because it was there in the man's face once you saw him in the right light. The forest did not like the Sarnesh any more than it liked the Wasps.

'I challenge you,' the Nethyen woman announced to Sentius, almost spitting in his face. 'Fight me, coward.' It was all she had left.

Sentius stared at her bleakly and everyone was still waiting for him to utter some response when a handful of his men loosed their crossbows, cutting the Nethyen pair down where they stood.

The Ant gazed about, at his soldiers, at the Etheryen. 'This is war. We don't piss about,' he announced, almost to the forest itself as much as to anyone in particular.

Che held her breath, because surely this breached the iron-clad Mantis code. Surely the Etheryen would revolt, would turn on their allies with bloodied steel?

But the Mantids just looked at the bodies, and at the Ant-kinden, and shuffled silently, and she felt exactly what they felt, as much as if she had been one of them – standing there on ground they no longer recognized, their way of life suddenly brittle in their hands. *What is right?* It could hardly escape their notice that the bulk of the bodies all around them were of their own kind.

That night, the Nethyen came.

With her blank eyes, which knew no darkness, Yraea watched them arrive: a dozen, then a score, then two score, filing solemnly through the trees with the Loquae at their head. The halfbreed Pioneer gave a warning, and the Empress's camp was quickly up and ready, but the Mantis-kinden gave no sign that anything was amiss, save that they surrounded the little band, quietly and seemingly without threat.

The Moth watched the Imperials carefully – the Pioneers tense and unsure, with weapons to hand; the Red Watch man, Ostrec, taut as a wire, hands ready to sting or to strike. The Empress's bodyguard had already rallied round her, their steel claws extended, and at their head was Tisamon, the abomination of steel and spirit that the Empress was so proud of. *And I'm sure he scares those poor Apt generals and officers, but my people were playing with magic when yours were still trying to light fires.*

Closer by, the old man Gjegevey was watching her. *Does he suspect? What can he know?* She found that she, too, was on a knife-edge. *But it is too late for them to fight or flee. We have them.*

Tegrec appeared at her elbow then, anxious as usual. 'What's going on?'

For a moment she wanted to tell him, in the hope that his

loyalty really was to Tharn now, and not to the Empire he claimed to have turned his back on. But hope was not a luxury that circumstances allowed her. *I'm sorry, Tegrec.*

The Loquae stepped forward and bowed before Seda. 'Empress, you must come with us. Let these others stay here, but the forest calls for you.'

Yraea shifted uneasily, because that seemed too transparent, and she would prefer this moment to pass without an actual fight – the Empress's people would lose, but there was too much chance of Seda herself dying in some way that was no use to Yraea, or even of the Moth herself getting hurt. *Just do as I told you*, she thought, knowing that her words would echo in the old Mantis's head.

Seda was now speaking, as she glanced back at her followers.

'Tisamon, Ostrec, Gjegevey,' she decided. 'The rest of you stay here and await my return.'

The Loquae made no complaint, and the Mantis-kinden parted, opening a ragged path forwards. Yraea saw doubt and confusion on the faces of those about to be left behind – *and they will be waiting here until the forest claims them.* Then the Empress went striding through the Mantis throng as though they were indeed her subjects, and her select handful hurriedly followed.

Gjegevey came last, the old man shuffling slowly and leaning on his staff, as his wavering steps brought him close to the Moth.

'It is not too, hm, late,' he told her, in a hoarse whisper.

She blinked at him, momentarily fearful. *He knows? He can't, or he'd have said something, done something . . .* With no ready answer, she merely ignored him, and as the Mantis host began to filter off through the trees, she followed, slipping unseen from the camp, cloaked by magic and Art.

The old Mantis icons still stood in certain places of the forest, and Yraea knew that the Nethyen sometimes shed blood there after the fashion of the old ways. They had forgotten much of the rituals that would give true power to such sacrifices, but the Moths forgot nothing. Yraea had made a study of them before setting out. *For one might wander forever in trying to find the way to Argastos, even with his covert aid, but blood will open the gate.*

There it was ahead of them, the place that the Empress was being led to. The icon was composed of a patchwork of rotting wood, a great mantis sculpture eight feet tall, with its crooked arms outstretched for its next victim. The creatures of decay, and those that fed upon them, were busy about it, and the Nethyen would be constantly adding fresh wood to the feast. The idol lived through its own corruption, and in that it was part of the forest itself. *Mantis magic is such a crude and single-minded pursuit, but sometimes one gains a little satisfaction in descending to their level.*

Now the Empress stood directly before the icon, and still she did not fear. *Is that Wasp arrogance or Wasp ignorance, I wonder?* To Yraea, the mood of the Nethyen was quite plain. They were here for blood shed in the prescribed manner, and the forest had not seen a sacrifice such as this in a long time. *Let all your sweet power, Empress, become my weapon to put Argastos back in his place.*

'You know why you are here.' It was the voice of the Loquae.

'Of course.' Seda's prompt response.

Yraea gathered herself, took a deep breath, and cried out, 'Take them!'

There was a confusion of motion. Gjegevey was seized at once, incapable of offering harm even if he meant to. Two of the Nethyen staggered back from Ostrec, to Yraea's surprise – and she saw blood here, but none of it the Wasp's. A circle had formed about Tisamon and Seda, and she saw that the Mantids' old fear of magic – her own kinden's eternal hook in them – was working against her.

She spat out a word, fingers pointing towards the armoured form, and Tisamon fell still, shackled within his own steel. *Pathetic.*

Seda herself watched it all with an utter, regal calm, not even deigning to notice Ostrec when the Red Watch officer moved up to put his back to hers.

'Did you really think toys such as *this* were new?' Yraea asked the Empress, moving to touch Tisamon's breastplate. 'Did you think any true magician would fear them? Why do you think we had Mantis-kinden as our soldiers all those years, if such constructs of magic had been of use against our enemies?'

She knew that, magic aside, the Art contained within the Empress's very hands was dangerous enough, but she wanted the Wasp girl to recognize her own hubris before the end. She wanted to finally breach that reserve. *I want her to beg.*

'You have come far, for one of your kinden, but no further than this,' Yraea told her. 'You have discovered enough of the old ways to be useful to me, but no more.'

'Oh, quiet,' Seda told her. 'Do what you must.'

Yraea drew a sharp breath, but realized that the words had not been meant for her. Hands were laid on her before she could evade them: Mantis hands, wrenching her arms back, holding her tight. Her head whipped round to look for the Loquae. 'You!'

'I did all that was in my power to speak to my people,' the old Mantis woman said sadly. 'I told them to wait. I invoked the Masters of the Grey, our leaders since the dawn of time. I told them what they must do.'

Yraea was hauled forwards towards the icon, seeing Seda's slight smile pass her by. 'Release me! You traitors! Servants of the Green, release me!'

'They want more than you can offer,' Seda's light tones drifted over to her, whilst Tisamon stepped to her side, breaking Yraea's chains in the instant that he moved. 'And I have promised them so much more: Servants of the Green, Masters of the Black and Gold. This is a new world, Moth, and they do not understand it, and they do not like it. But one thing they do understand is that your people abandoned them long ago, after the revolution. You left them simply to fade away.'

'Lies!' Yraea shrieked, but the Mantids were ignoring her, and a moment later she was within the arc of those wooden limbs, and they were bringing forwards stakes and mallet to secure her.

'No,' she whispered. It had taken her that long for her to understand that the world had turned.

She looked round for the Loquae again, more than ready to beg, but the old Mantis herself had been seized by her own people.

'I gave all that I had for your words,' the Loquae stated flatly, without acrimony. 'I told them that they must follow me, or cast me down. They have made their choice. I have sought the future, seer, and I have found none. None for me, none for any of us. Let me die now.'

Yraea opened her mouth to call out, but then the first stake was rammed home into her palm and she screamed.

'The blood of a magician,' Seda pronounced. 'Not as valuable as the blood of an empress, but enough to open the door for me and mine.

Yraea barely heard her, as the world before her shuddered and swam. Seda's polite smile passed before her eyes; Gjegevey shaking his head miserably; Ostrec—

She saw Ostrec, but in that same moment she also saw beyond him. *Is that ...? Does Seda know what that is that wears her colours? Might I be avenged, still?*

And then pain, only pain.

Seventeen

To his credit, what with a hundred other pressing matters tugging at his elbow, Stenwold sat for twenty minutes and listened to the impassioned Fly's complaint. Laszlo told him everything, including many important facts about his Solarnese posting that Stenwold had only been able to infer from the Fly's official report – as, apparently, had Milus.

Stenwold had never met this Lissart girl back then, for she had fled the Collegiate army before its clash with the Wasps. He did, however, vaguely recall a Fly woman who had accompanied Tactician Milus when the Ant had come to Collegium, but no more than that.

And now Laszlo had finished his account, right down to Milus's parting words, and was waiting expectantly for Stenwold Maker, the War Master of Collegium, to jump into an orthopter and go and castigate the leader of the Sarnesh military. Because there was a girl that Laszlo was besotted with, who was now a Sarnesh prisoner.

The man's a pirate. How can he be so naive? But Stenwold had met the *Tidenfree* crew, after all, and realized that piracy was a great refuge of the innocent, in a curious sort of way. It was a simple way of life made entirely from ignoring other peoples' rules, and Laszlo's only idea of authority was the avuncular hand of Tomasso and the necessity of a ship's routines.

I should never have sent him to Solarno. But it had seemed harmless at the time – even a kind of reward. The proximity to the Spiderlands should have kept the Empire away. *Yet another thing I didn't see coming.*

He found it surprisingly hard to say: 'What do you expect me to do?'

'Tell him to let her go,' Laszlo replied earnestly.

'I cannot *tell* the tactician anything. And he's right – you know he's right, and you've admitted it yourself. She's an Imperial agent.'

'Was.' Laszlo scowled mutinously. 'She left them.'

'And then she left us and, again by your own admission, signed up with the Sarnesh under false pretences. And can you say with absolute certainty that the Empire did not send her there to inveigle her way into the Sarnesh councils?'

He could see that Laszlo wanted to swear to that, but the Fly could not quite look him in the eye.

'Mar'Maker, *please*,' he said quietly, 'I'm . . . afraid for her. That Milus, I don't like him. He doesn't care about anything except his own city.'

'Nor should he,' Stenwold stated shortly. 'Just as I must have the same single-minded devotion to mine. This war has become a chain of terrible things, Laszlo, and some of them have been my doing, and there will be more to come.' He took a deep breath. 'The most I can do is sent him a message politely asking that this woman of yours be kept in once piece. If she's sensible, and if she's clever, she can keep herself off the rack until the war's ended, and then the Sarnesh will have no more use for her, and probably they'll hand her over. I can do no more.'

'I'll take the message myself,' Laszlo declared.

'You will not. I don't need you stirring up trouble with our closest allies. I *need* the Sarnesh, and it doesn't matter how unpleasant their leader may be. ' Stenwold stood up laboriously. 'The war comes first, Laszlo, and what we ourselves want comes a distant second. You know that I've more cause to say it than most.'

The Fly nodded unhappily. 'You're for the docks now, are you?'

Stenwold mentally reviewed the many tasks that awaited him, and made exactly the sort of decision he had just advised against. *But they will not wait forever, and what would I seem, if I did not say goodbye?*

'Coming with me?' he asked.

'Don't know.' But when Stenwold strode from his office, the Fly went tagging along behind, still sulking a little, addressing the back of Stenwold's belt. 'Tomasso will just find something for me to do.'

'What if *I* found something for you to do?' Stenwold offered. 'If you're interested, that is? I need a liaison with the Tseni, for when their ships arrive.'

'Would it help?' Laszlo demanded, meaning, shamelessly, *Would it help me?*

'It might,' Stenwold cast back. 'If you're part of the Collegium military in some way, doing your bit for the defence of the city, that's likely to make you more of a consideration in Milus's eyes, anyway.'

'Then I'll do it.'

Oh, to be so young that you can make decisions just like that – with not a committee in sight. Stenwold sighed.

They made for the docks, near empty of ships, with only Tomasso's *Tidenfree* and a couple of others rocking at anchor. *The old pirate's clinging on, then.* The old wayhouse that had been Tomasso's base of operations this last half-year had been pulled down within the last tenday, another page of Collegium's history overwritten to deny the Empire cover for its artillery. Tomasso had taken it philosophically.

But he will not stay when the Empire gets closer, and I don't blame him.

Tomasso and half his crew were meanwhile infesting the Port Authority, occupying a set of rooms given over to them partly because they had Stenwold's favour and partly because the dock clerks were afraid of them. They had become considerably more respectable since Stenwold had first seen them, transforming themselves into citizens and merchants, yet never quite losing their piratical edge. Their new domain was cluttered with crates and sacks and boxes, the salvage from their clifftop retreat, and Tomasso was sitting on one pile as though it was a makeshift throne.

Fly-kinden, all of them there, save one.

She rose when Stenwold ducked into the room. He had spent as much time as he could with her, and she had stayed far longer than he had hoped, but now it seemed to him as though she had arrived only yesterday, and he had barely managed to spare her a moment.

'Paladrya.'

She went to him and clasped his hands. The sun had burned her pale skin in some places, and her eyes were very red with drying out, and most of the food that land-kinden took for granted remained anathema to her, and yet she had dragged out her stay this long, and in the end he had been forced to set the date of her repatriation.

Out there to the east, the Second Army was growing close. Taki's pilots had done their level best to slow them down, striking blow after blow against them, killing their soldiers, smashing their machines, and yet still they came, and soon there would be a reckoning. Stenwold did not want Paladrya to be in the city when that day came.

She saw it in his face. 'It's time, then?'

'Wys is waiting.' Tomasso spoke for him. 'I mean, she'll wait but . . .'

'Your enemies . . .?' Her eyes would not leave Stenwold's.

'We've beaten them back twice before. We'll do so again, and maybe this time they'll get the message,' Stenwold told her. It was the same bluff sort of speech he had been using to assure Assemblers and magnates for the last couple of tendays. 'But you've seen what they do, the damage they can cause.' The city bore plenty of scars from the Imperial bombing raids. 'I don't want you here where you could get hurt.' *I don't want to have to worry about you.*

She nodded, ever the practical one. That was one more thing about her that tugged at his feelings.

She went with him to the docks, and stepped along one particular rickety pier that they both remembered from past adventures.

'I know your first duty is to your city,' she said, standing there and looking out across the limitless sea. 'I know that if I place an obligation on you, to keep yourself safe, then that will come second. But even so . . .' Her smile was hesitant. 'And when your people are safe, will you still . . .?'

'I will.' With that dark, fathomless sea so plainly in evidence he had not thought he would have the courage to affirm his promise, but he found a curious weight was gone from him. All the crushing waters of the deep seemed a small thing, and he could picture the radiant light that was her home of Hermatyre. *And simply the relief of not having every cursed man and woman in the city thinking I'm personally responsible to them for every little thing. No more committees. No Assembly.* Seen like that, he was amazed he hadn't already jumped into the water and started swimming.

Something was hanging there in the dark water, just visible as a great shape of coiled segments, large enough to scrape at the bottom, and with its rounded bulk almost breaking the waves. It was the Sea-kinden submersible run by Wys, Tomasso's wife: their vital link between land and sea.

Paladrya leant towards Stenwold and kissed him almost chastely. 'Cast off your enemies soon,' she whispered, hanging there close to his ear for a moment longer, which told him she wanted to say more. He clasped her to him, suddenly aware of how delicate she was, feeling her wince as he touched her sunburned shoulders.

Then she stepped back and off the pier, plunging straight into the water like a knife, her Collegiate robes swirling about her. Anyone watching must think this some bizarre suicide, but of course her Art could draw life from the water as easily as from the air.

He watched the Sea-kinden vessel manoeuvring clumsily about, and then coast out into deeper water, sinking away until he could not make out any trace of it.

Then he turned back to the city, to *his* city, with its myriad demands.

There was a fair crowd of people waiting to see him when he arrived at the College. Some would have vital business about the war, others would have petty personal issues that were not worth his time, and often there was no way of telling between the two in advance. He noted a few faces that he knew he needed to speak to, made a mental list with them at the top, knowing that there would always be time-wasters who got through his guard and important people too modest to get themselves noticed. *Shouldn't Jodry be dealing with most of these?* But that was unfair. The Speaker for the Assembly would have just as many suitors at his door. It was a by-product of Collegium's participative government that everyone expected their voice to be heard. *I'll bet the Empress doesn't get this.*

He pushed through them, fending them off, telling them all in good time, asking for their patience; and they allowed him sufficient space to shoulder into the small study room he had commandeered. His careful list went to pieces then. Someone was already inside.

He noticed the woman only as he was sitting down. She had been standing very still, Art-shadowed: if she had been an assassin he would be a dead man. As it was, he froze halfway onto the chair seat, heart abruptly lurching as she made herself apparent to him.

He knew her, he realized. Her name was Akkestrae and she was one of the Felyal Mantids, their official spokesperson – *Loquae* as they called it. She wore an arming jacket and breeches, but they had been machine-made in the city, and the savagery in her had a near-transparent veneer of Collegiate urbanity, for all that she had come close to killing Stenwold once, under other circumstances. She was not one of the many refugees from the coastal hold that the Empire had destroyed, but had lived in Collegium for years, as leader of the little colony of expatriates that the city had accumulated. Now, though, she found herself responsible for a swollen community of angry, bitter exiles. She had stood alongside the Mynans and the Merchant Companies and the Vekken – *the Vekken, for the world's sake!* – before Collegium's concerned citizens, to demonstrate that the Felyen were committed to the defence of the city that had taken them in, but Stenwold was well aware that the Mantids in his city were an unhappy, unruly lot. He had been expecting something like this.

'Come on, then, out with it,' he invited, sitting down at last. It was hardly a diplomatic opening but these days he was too tired for pleasantries, and she would not have appreciated it anyway.

'The Empire is nearing the city,' she told him, which was nothing he did not already know. At his nod, she continued, 'My people are going to attack them.'

No surprises there. 'I know it's hard for you to be patient, but you've seen the work we've put into fortifying this city, making the approach hazardous for them—'

'War Master, we are not asking your permission. We are informing you.'

He nodded more slowly. 'What will you achieve, precisely?'

'We will shed the blood of our enemies,' she explained simply. 'We will kill Wasps and Spiders.'

'And your people have tried to attack the Second Army twice, and each time—'

'War Master.' The words fell from her mouth like lead weights: just his title, but enough to silence him. She paused for a count of three, but he found nothing to say that would brave that quiet.

'War Master,' she said again, more gently, 'we are not fit for fighting behind walls. It is not our way. It is without honour. We do not *defend*. We attack. We bring the fight to the foe. And if we die, then that is also our way. There is no better ending for my people than in blood, and with the blood of enemies on our blades. Your people have your patience and your preparations, your walls and excavations and engines. I respect all you have. I do not belittle it. I have seen your city and its marvels. You are building a future here that will be the envy of the world.' He had not heard such words from her kinden ever before. There was a surprising passion in her voice, a bitterness that made a mockery of her words. 'But it is not *our* future,' she continued. 'If my people, in pursuit of our own ways, can rid you of some of your enemies, then that is good. But we *will* attack. We will not die behind walls.'

'When do you intend to—?'

'Soon, very soon. Perhaps today we will march.'

'Will you wait just a day?' His mind was working very fast now. 'I need to speak to Jodry. If you're set on this course, then . . . Will you wait?'

'One day,' she confirmed.

He came out of his office with her, to the perplexity of his suitors, and found a messenger to take word to Jodry, top priority. In the intervening time he began filleting through the mob, trying to separate wheat from chaff before the return message arrived.

These days a War Council was whenever Stenwold, Jodry or both of them could round up a few other people from a changing list to validate their decisions. Or that was what it felt like, much of the time.

On this occasion, once Stenwold had prised the Speaker away from his own responsibilities, he was able to get hold of the Mynan leader, Kymene, and Chief Officer Elder Padstock of the

Maker's Own Company. Padstock looked attentive, as she always did when Stenwold was present, an idolizing that he was always uncomfortable with. And yet it was so convenient to have someone he *knew* would vote with him whenever he and Jodry quarrelled, and so where did that leave him, when he did nothing to discourage her? Kymene looked as though she had better things to do than sit through yet another committee – the Mynans not being great respecters of the Collegiate way of doing things. Like the Mantids, they wanted to kill Wasps.

Twenty words later, after Stenwold had explained the situation, she was all ears.

'No, no, no,' Jodry was saying immediately. 'We can't just let our defenders sally off on their own recognizance! We *need* them here for when the Wasps come. It's not . . . it's not as though they'll have long to wait.'

'Jodry—' Stenwold started, and the Speaker stared him down.

'You're considering it,' he accused.

'Jodry, listen to me. Akkestrae is right: the Felyen aren't exactly at their best fighting against a mechanized enemy from behind walls. Or even a running battle in the streets, if things get to that.' Unlike Jodry, he did not stumble when he said the words, for all that he felt a lurch in his stomach on uttering them. 'After all,' he added drily, 'they wouldn't run, and then they'd die. Mantis-kinden, Jodry: one on one the best killers the Lowlands has, and they would be wasted, diluted by fighting a war our way. I've been looking into the siege at the end of the last war – and we had a fair number of Felyen with us then. By all accounts they accomplished little – shot some arrows, killed Wasps on the battlements – but the real war was being fought all around them with orthopters and airships and snapbows and artillery.'

'We're talking about hundreds of swords just taken out of the city – a *pointless* waste of life!' Jodry exclaimed.

'Who are we to—?'

'You will *not* say, "Who are we to judge"!' Jodry snapped. 'We are Collegium. We value life even if the Mantids don't. Even if nobody else in this pox-ridden world seems to!' He looked about the table, feeling himself one man alone. Padstock, of course, was taking Stenwold's line, and Kymene . . .

'We support them,' she said, quite simply.

That was more than Stenwold had expected, and for a moment he sat silent while Jodry goggled. Of the four of them, Kymene had the best mind for strategy, by his reckoning, and that included the sort of hard-edged strategy that came with casualties already worked into the maths.

'You fight a good defensive war, you Collegiates. You fight a thinking man's war. But I've seen what happens when they get to your walls and start work on a city.'

'Different city, different walls,' Jodry said. 'Even you'll allow our engines are better than—'

'Than ours? Yes. Than the Wasps'? You can't know that, and you're a fool if you'll stake all on testing it in the field.' She spoke with fire but without anger, the same woman Stenwold remembered rousing up the resistance in Myna years before. 'The air attacks are all very well, but I talk to my pilots and their gains are limited – too few machines, too many Wasps, and the Gears don't slow. They keep on coming. But you know this.'

Jodry glowered at her, but said nothing.

'And now the Mantids are set on marching out and striking at the enemy,' Kymene declared. 'Do you really think you'll stop them going? Do you think they'd thank you, if you tried? I know their mind on this, for my own people come to me every day complaining that they want to fight *now*.'

'You'd go with them?' Stenwold broke in.

'Gladly.' Her answering gaze was calm and sane.

'The Mantids will want to launch a night attack. Your people can't see in the dark like they can.'

'The Mantids can't set explosives like we can,' she countered.

The other three digested this silently.

There is precedent, Stenwold reflected. *Salma's Landsarmy against the Seventh, in the last war. But the cost . . .*

Elder Padstock cleared her throat, watching Stenwold carefully for his reaction. 'There are those among the Companies who *can* see in the dark, War Master. Spiders, Flies, halfbreeds . . .'

'Now wait,' interrupted Jodry, 'even if they can, and even if your Mynans could keep up, I might just about believe that a few hundred Mantis warriors could bring the fight all the way to the Wasp perimeter after dark. But the rest of you . . . Come on, *think*, will you?'

'I'm not even convinced the Mantids could manage it,' Kymene allowed. 'The Wasps will keep a good watch, and their Spider-kinden allies see well in the dark.'

'Well, what then . . .?' Jodry put in uncertainly.

'So we bring them in supported by our troops, and we provide a distraction so that they're on the Wasps before the Second even knows it. And we let them run wild, as they will – for there'll be no controlling them – while our people strike at those same targets that the Stormreaders have been trying to get their bombs to. And then perhaps we get out again. Anything's possible.'

Jodry opened his mouth again, but the cast of his expression had changed. He had been a man vociferous in opposition, now he was on the edge of a chasm, staring fearfully into it but becoming resigned to the drop.

Before he could voice the question, Kymene answered it. 'By air. We do it by air. The Mantids won't like that but, if it gets them to the Wasps faster, and means they can shed more blood, then they'll live with it.'

'We need more than the four of us, to make this decision.' Jodry's voice was hollow. 'The Assembly—'

'Hasn't met since this action started, not in any real sense,' Stenwold told him. 'And if we're to make this happen, we need to start now. You're the Speaker, I'm the War Master, and we have the authority. Or if we don't, who's going to tell us so?'

Jodry was still shaking his head, holding on by his fingertips to the trailing edge of his lost argument, but his words had run dry.

'I'll speak with Akkestrae,' Kymene announced. 'Chief Officer Padstock, would you ask for volunteers from the Company soldiers for a night attack? No more information than that, at this point. Master Maker, Master Drillen, perhaps you would see what airships you can commandeer.'

'Brace yourself,' Averic advised, hand extended.

The Beetle girl behind the shield looked scared to death, cringing away, so that, when the Wasp student's hand flashed fire, the impact nearly took her off her feet. The watching members of the Student Company recoiled collectively – not at the light or the crackling sound, but at the very concept. This, *this* was the symbol of the Wasp Empire, if anything was: their killing Art.

Straessa and Gerethwy, off duty this morning, had come out early to watch the students train. The Antspider tried to see how Averic took it: the way they looked at him as though he ate children. That old familiar closed expression held sway on the Wasp's face, though, the same that had got him through a year's study at the College before the war broke out.

'Every one of my people can do this,' the Wasp explained. 'Some are stronger at it, but every single Wasp becomes armed from the moment this Art begins to show. But I have to concentrate – even a soldier with a score of battles under his belt must concentrate – and so it's not ideal for close-in fighting much of the time. Unless, of course, your enemy falls back from you, like you're falling back from me right now. Give me room, and you give me the advantage.'

Quick and easy lessons on how to kill your own kin, Straessa thought. But, if he thought about it that way, Averic was letting nothing out.

'And the range is nowhere near that of a crossbow or a snapbow,' Averic went on, stalking about in front of them. 'And you see – it's scorched the wood and you must have felt how

245

it's not just flame but a real physical force there. Nevertheless, the shield has held, and good armour such as we're issued with will hold as well, most of the time. That's the sting of my people, and don't forget it. But don't forget that Aptitude has given you better weapons.'

'He's good at this,' the Antspider admitted.

'He hates it.' Eujen was standing beside her in his purple sash, as chief officer of the Student Company. She had barely seen him these last few days, what with her shifts and his meetings, and now, having sought him out, she found instead someone she did not quite know.

Averic was going on to explain about the composition of an Imperial army, the likely tactics of the Light Airborne and infantry. Straessa shook her head.

'It doesn't feel right somehow,' she said.

'He told me that he's made his stand now,' Eujen murmured. 'I think he wants to prove himself to . . . to them. To show them he's on their side.'

'I think that's a losing battle.'

'Oi, Antspider!'

A loud, slightly slurred voice had cut across Averic's patient lecturing, drawing all eyes. A gaunt Ant-kinden was striding over to them, seemingly on the point of lurching off balance at every step, and yet making swift progress despite it. Chief Officer Madagnus of the Coldstone Company was paying a visit.

Straessa shot an apologetic look at Eujen.

'Whose eyes did you inherit, halfbreed?' Madagnus demanded.

Straessa found herself stiffening in outrage, biting back hasty, angry words. Oh, surely she had come in for that sort of abuse before, and worse, and told herself none of it mattered, but she had been in Collegium for over a year now, and if people looked down their noses at miscegenation, still they practised what they preached enough not to give rein to their inner bigots. Madagnus was drunk, though, and more so than usual.

With an exercise of will she restricted her response to, 'Chief?'

He stopped in front of her. 'See in the dark much, Antspider?'

'Some, Chief.'

'Madagnus, what do you want?' Eujen demanded and Straessa flinched inwardly, waiting for an explosion. But she was thinking of her friend as being no more than he had been when a vociferous student. Of course, now, Eujen ranked alongside the man, one chief officer to another, and a shifty, shamefaced look came over the Ant's face.

'Looking for my officer here, Leadswell,' he explained, a little steadier. 'Got some work for her.'

'I'm off duty, Chief,' Straessa put in, but he spoke over her.

'Nobody's off duty, right now – not even me. Ma Padstock herself slapped me awake and hauled me out of bed to tell me that. You see in the dark? Good for you. They're wanting volunteers like you from all Companies. Going to make a go of it by night, Padstock says. She'll come for you, too, Leadswell, you just mark me.' He found a crate of armour that Eujen had wheedled out of the armouries and sat down on it in a mess of angular shoulders, knees and elbows. 'Go find the Company, Antspider. Go fish for volunteers who can see in the dark. Have them ready by the third hour after noon, urgent as urgent. You see in the dark, Leadswell?'

Eujen shook his head wordlessly.

'Me neither.' Madagnus levered himself upright and turned about, before striding off with as much dignity as he could muster.

'How did your lot ever come to choose him?' Eujen wondered aloud, even as Averic came over to join them.

'He's a good artificer even when drunk. A really good one if you can get him sober. And brave, too. Besides he was one of the few who would stand.' Straessa felt abruptly angry with herself for defending the man. 'Anyway, I didn't cast my lot for him, but he's the one we've got.'

'A night attack?' Averic pondered, and then, 'Will you . . .?'

'I can't . . .' She felt Eujen's hand on her shoulder, and leant herself against him despite all the Student Company gawking. 'I

247

can't ask people to volunteer if I won't go myself. I just can't.'
She managed a weak smile. 'How about you, Gereth? *You* see
in the dark.'

'Better than a Moth,' the Woodlouse replied.

'And you can spare time from your whatever that you're
working on?'

'The rational bow?' He shrugged his hunched shoulders. 'You
think I'd let you go off and get yourself lost in the dark?'

She reached out and squeezed his arm. 'Thought not. So, let's
go and find the troops and see who's up for it.' She kept her
voice deliberately light, but it was a long moment before she
would shrug off Eujen's hand.

The darkening sky was crowded with slow-moving, rounded
shadows, as though all the Masters of the College had come
together to construct the world's grandest orrery. Watching those
vast shapes circle and glide lazily was a curiously awe-inspiring
sight, even for Collegium. Straessa had never before seen so
many airships together.

'Of course, they've rather overdone it,' she pointed out. 'Unless
we get one each or something.'

She exaggerated but, even so, the Company volunteers would
have fitted easily aboard one of the larger dirigibles. The great
passenger liner the *Sky Without*, for example, could have held
every one of them in high style until it was time to fight.

'Forty-three Mynans, all explosives-trained I think,' Gerethwy
confirmed. 'And I make it two hundred and forty-seven Company
soldiers.'

'The Empire must be shaking in its sandals,' the Antspider
remarked, desperately trying to be droll. They had gathered in
the broad square that had once fronted the Amphiophos,
Collegium's seat of government, before the Imperial bombs had
turned the place into a sea of rubble, toppled columns and walls
rising like broken teeth.

A strange cross-section of the city's defenders, this. It was the requirement to be able to fight at night that had winnowed them down to this few, rather than any lack of courage. Here was a good number of Fly-kinden, who made small targets but could pull a trigger as well as anyone. Here were Spider-kinden renegades and the odd urbanized Mantis. Here were Moths who had evidently turned their backs on their heritage; two Roaches, three Scorpion-kinden, the Dragonfly Castre Gorenn. The rest were Beetles, the lucky or unlucky few, who had manifested the rare Art of shrugging off darkness entirely to see the midnight world in shades of grey.

They were all armed and armoured as best their city could equip them: buff coats stuffed with rags to slow a spinning snapbow bolt, overlain with breastplates and lobster-tail helms now being enthusiastically blacked up to stop the wan moon-light glinting on them. The Apt amongst them carried snapbows, the more skilled amongst the Inapt bore bows, and the rest made do with spear and sword.

'Here you are.' Suddenly, from nowhere, a small figure tugged at Straessa's belt, making her twitch: Sartaea te Mosca, Fly-kinden lecturer in Inapt studies, possible magician, and healer. 'How did I know I'd find you here?'

'Eujen told you?' Straessa suggested. She had a momentary surfacing of unbidden memories: nights spent in Sartaea's rooms, their diminutive hostess filling each glass as it was emptied; evenings at Raullo Mummers's studio – burned out now – back when the war was just a thing that people talked about; te Mosca, after the battle, frantically trying to save as much as possible of Gerethwy's maimed hand.

'What's going on?' Gerethwy asked. 'Or is this it? Are we so desperate that we're going to send a handful of soldiers off against the Second, travelling in technology that the *last* war showed us was useless?'

'Oh, more than that,' te Mosca stated. 'They've roused every Inapt healer they can get their hands on, so it'd *better* be more than that . . . See there.' She pointed to where the reinforce-ments were arriving.

Mantis-kinden of the Felyal, they saw: the refugees that had started to take up residence after the Second Army ousted them in the first war, and had only grown more numerous as the Empire trampled over their forest home, tore up their trees and burned their holds. Here they came, tall and lean and sour-faced, with bow and spear, rapier and metal claw. Some had beautifully crafted carapace mail, and others wore chitin or leather, or just an arming jacket. Many had no armour at all. And they were many, a column snaking right back into the city, marching soft-footed to stand before the corpse of the Amphiophos, as though they were about to storm it.

'Oh,' said Straessa quietly, as they kept coming – and 'Oh,' again, realizing slightly before the rest just what was going on. 'No . . .'

And the Felyen continued to arrive, every single one of them.

Stenwold had already taken his stand where the steps ascended to the churned debris that had been the Amphiophos's main entrance, with Akkestrae beside him. Seeing the Mantids arrive in such numbers, and with so little sound, he could not suppress a shiver. They were so grave, so solemn, a sight out of another time. *And like nothing Collegium has known since the Bad Old Days, and perhaps not even then.*

So many warriors, he thought. *Every Felyen who can bear a sword must be gathering for their piece of the Empire.*

And then he saw it, too, and his breath stilled as the Felyen continued to march in and assemble. He looked from face to face, those stern and unforgiving masks – but such faces. He had not known, before this. He had not understood.

The tail end of their procession was now trailing in, and he took them in by the lamplight and by the moon: the Mantids of the Felyal – their surviving warriors, yes, but more. He saw old men and women who must have seven decades to their names, grown thin and haggard with age even for a long-lived kinden. He saw children – fourteen years, twelve . . . And the more he looked, the younger they seemed to be: a boy of ten with a short spear in his hands, a girl of eight clutching a little hunting bow, a child of five with a dagger, her expression just a clouded mirror of the adults'. He saw women with babies in arms, or slung across their backs, and those women were armed as warriors.

He saw the Felyen, all of them, and the sorrow of it was laid out plain. The very young, the very old, they were in the majority. Those men and women of true fighting age were barely two or three in ten, such had been their losses to the Wasps.

'This was not what we spoke about,' he told Akkestrae, hearing his voice shake slightly.

'This was what *I* spoke about,' she told him impassively. 'What you chose to hear is your own business.'

'No, wait . . . you're mad,' he insisted. 'You can't send *this* against the Empire! What can you possibly hope to accomplish?'

Her face, that glass-calm Mantis facade, regarding him coolly. 'You know exactly what.'

'But we've made you welcome here – don't you trust us to look after them? Why . . .?' Stenwold was aware that his voice was carrying across the square, but he decided he did not care.

For a moment, Akkestrae's expression remained fixed, but then he saw the cracks appear, fractures widening and widening until something raw gaped at him, like an unhealable wound. 'Because there is no *place* for us in your cursed city!' she yelled, screaming the words into his face. 'Because you have taken our *time* from us! Because your Apt world has written itself over ours, as if we had never been! And there is nowhere left under the sun that your kind, you Apt, have not corrupted with your *industry*.' That last word she spat out like an insult, leaving her drained and swaying. 'And we have come to the end,' she said more quietly, 'and we seek only that end, which is to fight and die as we were meant to do – *all* of us. All my people, Maker. If your people may derive some *profit* from it, then so be it, but know that you have already won. You have made a world we cannot live in. You have made a memory of us, at last. And soon not even that.'

'But I . . . the Wasps . . .' Stenwold stammered. 'We didn't burn your forests—'

'I would rather face the blades of the Empire than Collegium's good intentions,' she replied flatly. 'At least the Wasps understand that *their* progress destroys. Now bring down your *machines*, and take us to the fight.'

Eighteen

Tynisa was almost running, weaving her way through the dense trees. She could smell smoke from ahead, although the fighting that Che had somehow divined must be over, for there was no sound of it now. That said *ambush* to her, and she felt the forest all around her, reaching her by channels other than mere eyes and ears. Something in this place had accepted her, tasting the blood in her that came from her father Tisamon. She was going native.

None of the others could move as she could through this place – certainly not the Sarnesh, and not her companions either. The Bartrer woman was hopeless, Thalric barely better, and Che, though she had an ease here that surprised Tynisa, was yet no scout. This was why the Sarnesh employed men like Zerro, and now she had taken on his mantle.

She would not let herself be yoked to the Ants, though, for all that they kept insisting she stay in sight. How could she scout the way ahead with them dragging virtually at her heels? Instead, she had chosen her deputies, the two of her companions least clumsy and most at home here, and let them trail her, ready to send word back if the worst came to the worst.

When she stopped to listen, as she did now, she felt the taut pain of her ravaged hip settle back on to her like stiff clothes, enough to nearly cripple her. When she gave in to sleep, the pain was a deep throb in her side, chastising her for having treated it as though it was not there. But whenever she moved through the trees, or drew blade to fight, it was gone. The mystery of her discipline sustained her, just as she had witnessed her father receive wounds enough for a half-dozen men and still hunt down his victim.

And then he died, and I may die, too, if I keep pushing my limits. But feeling alive and free like this was addictive, while being trapped in her wounded body was unbearable. *Better life like this, for whatever time I have, than a long death.*

She glanced back to seek out her shadows. After a moment she located Terastos, ten yards back, kneeling with his shoulder against a tree. The Moth had a surprising tenacity about him, bearing his stingshot wound without complaint, and he had shown an aptitude for the wilds that Tynisa would not have guessed at. He was quiet, too, and not averse to hard work – quite different to the charlatan stereotype the Collegiates were fond of.

Further back – somewhere within Terastos's sight – would be the halfbreed Maure, a woman more than used to roughing it in the Commonweal, and Tynisa's next best choice as least useless scout.

With rapier in hand, she scanned the close-grown forest ahead. She could see smoke hazing the air, and yet still no sign of an enemy. They had been lost in this forest for days now. Lost, because wherever Che was trying to reach seemed utterly myth-ical, to the extent that Tynisa sometimes wondered if they were moving in circles. And yet, for all that they seemed to just turn left and left and left again, the forest never looked quite the same. It was as though they were staying still while their surroundings flowed and transformed around them. And still Che was searching, but not finding.

Syale had gone ahead, yet another thing Tynisa was not happy with, but Che seemed to trust her to find whatever she was looking for. The rest had just kept plodding on, Tynisa and her deputies ahead, a block of Sarnesh loaned by Sentius bringing up the rear. Then Che had suddenly broken out of some reverie and announced that there was fighting, and that they had to get there.

So where is everyone? Tynisa was more than conscious that there might be thirty Nethyen ahead, hidden on their home ground and watching this Spider-looking girl intrude. No sign, though, and she could hardly stay here forever. The rest would probably have caught up with Maure already, and be closing on Terastos's position.

Forward. If there was an ambush, let her flush it out. With sword in hand, she was ready for anything.

In her final dash forwards she realized that she was rushing straight into a Mantis hold: faint glimpses of round-walled, organic buildings on all sides, but woven in between the trees so that no line could be drawn between *within* and *without*. Except the Mantids *would* draw just such a line. To be in their home uninvited would be to draw sufficient ire that even Tynisa and her blade might not be able to fend it off.

She was part way through glancing back to signal Terastos, still moving forwards as she did so, when the rest of the scene around her began to register on her senses. She stuttered to a stop, hopelessly exposed to any archer who wanted her, while trying to match up expectation and discovery.

The smoke in her nose, the greedy buzz of flies, the smell of death, the corpses.

She had her blade ready, as though this sight itself was an enemy. There had been fighting here, surely, but not recently enough for Che to have heard any of it. The nearest buildings were charred; she saw the blackened foundations of the smithy – the only stonework the Mantids would have needed – and guessed that the fire had leapt from there, chewed through a handful of the nearest wooden homes and then wasted its guttering strength against the indomitable trees themselves. The true destruction had been in lives, not architecture.

Just as the inhabitants had not lived in a close-knit Apt village, so they had not fought an Apt battle. Instead, everywhere she looked there were Mantis dead, and when she looked beyond them, between the trees further away, more dead still. They were scattered as they had died, weapons mostly still to hand, strewn disjointedly in knots of four and five, the ragdolls of history. They bore their wounds with pride, she reckoned. *Live by the sword.*

At a movement behind her, she turned, already registering Terastos before her sword could threaten him. The Moth's blank eyes were wide, head twitching from side to side as he took it all in.

'Oh, this is wrong,' he murmured, just loud enough for her to hear.

'It's war.' Tynisa tried to sound hardened to it all.

'No.' The Moth shook his head. 'No, this is not the way. Mantis-kinden, they don't . . . they wouldn't . . .'

Tynisa shrugged, still holding tenuously on to her composure. 'The Wasps did it, then?' *Maybe the Sarnesh,* but that was a thought she did not voice aloud.

Terastos stalked past her, looking from body to body. 'I see arrows, blade wounds . . . no stingshot burns, nothing from a snapbow bolt. They died fighting each other.' As he looked back at her, centuries of hidden history were hiding behind those white eyes. 'What have they been driven to?' he whispered. 'Between the Sarnesh and the Empire, they are going mad. This kinslaying . . . Mantis has always shed the blood of Mantis, it is their way, but with respect and by consent.'

'Consent . . .?' Tynisa stopped, because some pieces of the picture that she had been keeping at arm's length were coming to her now, and refusing to be denied. She was standing by one of the larger sprawls of Mantis dead, and she could see now that more than warriors had died here. Many of the bodies were so small, thin limbs and faces surely too young to display such expressions of determination and defiance. Whoever had swept through here had been as mad as Terastos said. They had given no quarter.

'Whose was this, Etheryen or Nethyen?' she asked.

'Does it matter?' Terastos spread his hands. 'I can't say.'

Maure was approaching them now, and Tynisa thought for a moment that the sight would be too much for the other woman. She had forgotten the magician's calling, though. The necromancer slowed as she neared them, and what her eyes registered there, in the heart of that dead hold, Tynisa did not want to know. *Enough ghosts for a dozen lifetimes.*

'Tell me,' Terastos said, and Tynisa realized with surprise that he was deferring to the halfbreed like a student seeking the advice of the learned.

'Despair, nothing but despair.' Maure's eyes were closed, her voice was barely audible. 'Those who attacked here, they had been broken in the hands of the outsiders, sick of fighting the wars of others, sick of promises of a better future, sick of hearing the justifications of the Apt for why they must kill their own kin, sick of the doubt of their leaders. All they had left was their honour. Mantis honour, which always has one last resort left to it. And so they came home.'

Terastos and Tynisa were both staring at her. 'Home?' the Moth echoed.

'To salvage what they could of their way of life. To protect their people from the outside world that had changed them.' Maure's voice was precise and calm. 'To save their children from the future they had seen.'

Then the others began turning up, stepping cautiously through the trees and each one slowing as they realized where they were. Che was the only one to step past Tynisa, Amnon and Thalric trailing to a halt in her wake.

'Che . . .?'

But the Beetle girl was staring out into the trees, as if she had not seen any of it, as though her sight was focused entirely elsewhere.

The Sarnesh were now spreading out, searching for . . . survivors? Clues? Tynisa could not guess.

They came home. Maure's words kept going round and round inside her skull. Not a clash between Etheryen and Nethyen, but . . .

'Miss Maker!' It came from one of the Sarnesh, rousing Che from her introspection, and Tynisa actually *saw* her glance about, clearly bewildered at where she was, and then seeing it as if for the first time.

The Sarnesh were clustered about one of the burned-out and broken huts, and Tynisa approached with trepidation, dragged unwillingly along at Che's heels. There had been another faceless act of extinction here, she discovered. The victims who had holed up in that cramped space had been children, for all that they had plainly fought to the last with knives and teeth. One body stood out: the only non-Mantis there, lying convulsed across the threshold, pinned by the spear that had killed both her and the infant she held.

Syale had forfeited her neutrality.

Che stared at the corpse for a long time, and Tynisa was becoming more and more unsettled by just how *little* emotion was evident on her foster-sister's face. The Che of old, that soft and insecure child of Collegium, would fly into fits of passion at just about anything. Now . . . there was more expression on even Thalric's face than on Che's.

'We need to move on,' was all the Beetle woman said. Even the Sarnesh were looking uncertain now.

'Che . . .' Tynisa gestured at the scene. 'We can't . . .'

'They made their choice. What do you think we can do?'

Tynisa flinched away, because there was something in Che now that frightened her badly, that had hold of her sister's face and throat and made her say words that just did not belong to her. The worst was that Tynisa's own ready and angry answer just died in her throat. She felt some clawing thing deep within her, closing off her voice. *Fear.* That same old Mantis fear of magic that had kept them as the Moths' lackeys in the Days of Lore. *But I can't be scared of Che . . .* And in that moment she

258

saw just how far her sister had travelled from their childhood. *I thought I'd changed, but she is something different now. A magician of the Bad Old Days?*

Then Maure hooked a hand about Che's arm. 'We cannot go yet. I have work to do.'

Che turned on her, and Tynisa could clearly see the balance of power – how the Beetle had become a vessel overflowing with it, ready to rain thunder on this halfbreed upstart – and how Maure, who had known magic all her life, was just a leaf on the wind before her.

I am thinking like the Inapt, Tynisa realized.

Yet the hand remained on Che's arm, the channel for some revelation that Maure was willing Che to listen to, and a moment later the Beetle's face practically disintegrated, all that fierce resolve falling away, and Che sagged, letting out a single ragged breath, and became the girl Tynisa recognized once again.

'Of course. Do what you must. Do what you can.' Che put a hand to her temple. Thalric stepped in, and for a moment she gestured him off as though she did not want to corrupt him with her touch. Then she was in his arms – and Tynisa turned away, supplanted and resentful, and mean-spirited for feeling so.

For more than an hour, Maure sat amongst the ruins in the centre of a circle she had made from the weapons of the fallen, her head bowed and unmoving, and doing who knew what. Tynisa, who could no longer deny that fragments of the dead might be pinned to the world – things of raw emotion, anger and loss – hoped that the woman could accomplish something here, and did not envy her the task.

She tried to approach Che, meanwhile, but the Beetle girl would barely speak to her, fighting battles inside her head, mumbling to herself in a rambling monologue that abruptly stilled whenever Tynisa approached.

At last Maure was done, standing up smoothly and kicking at the ring of swords and spears to disperse it. The Sarnesh gathered themselves and, one by one, their expedition reassembled.

Che was the last, and something of that proud, hard look was back on her face, despite her best efforts.

'We must move now,' she told them. 'I can feel her.' Seeing their blank looks she elaborated. 'The Empress – she's close.'

Argastos had come to Seda last night, walking in past the vigilant Pioneer sentry to stand before her fire.

She had not seen him, quite – no more than a troubling of the darkness – but she had known him as that same shade that had reached out to her aboard the airship.

Oh, bravely done, had come a voice formed from the sounds of the forest itself. *You have pierced the walls they built about me. You are truly the one.*

She had taken this in her stride. 'So walk out and greet me, old man.'

Surely he must have been off balance after that, but the roiling shadow had communicated nothing save its continued presence.

'You are a prisoner, or whatever's left of you,' she had told him. 'Play the great lord all you like. There is power where you are now, but you are not its master. You need me to come and rescue you.'

Again just silence from the spectre. A faint grate of metal indicated Tisamon moving, and she knew his helm would be turned towards this intruder.

Then: *Please* . . . faint as a breeze.

'Does the great Argastos beg?' she had demanded.

It has been so long. And, with that distant utterance, a wave of emotion had passed over her, far more eloquent than mere words: abandonment, loneliness, frustration, injustice. For a moment she had been rocked, the feelings riding on her own emotions to strike behind her defences. Then she had shaken them off.

'Oh I am coming to you, never fear,' she had replied sharply, 'but how I deal with *you*, once I have emptied your treasury, will depend on how you approach me. Keep begging, old Moth. Get used to being on your knees. I may find a use for you but, if you try to manipulate me, to pry at my mind with such weak games, I will leave behind not even memories of you.'

He had vanished then, snapped back to the inner forest where he was penned, and she had found herself gazing about the fire at her companions, meeting their uneasy eyes and forcing them to look away. They had heard every word she had said.

Only old Gjegevey understood, she decided, but his expression was anything but reassuring.

However, she had opened the way, now. After battering so long at the forest's defences, the blood sacrifice had unbarred the door. The day after, and they were at last on their way inwards, and all she had to worry about was . . .

A thorn pricked in her mind, even as she thought it, and her eyes flicked wide.

Her!

'Faster!' she snapped. 'Move faster!' For her twin was approaching, that hateful Beetle girl. For a moment, even as the Pioneers ahead picked up their pace, Seda was torn: *Turn back and catch them, ambush them between the trees? One shot, one sting, to rid me of my rival?* But the girl had grown in power since Seda had cast her down in Khanaphes, and this time she had strong allies with her – a Weaponsmaster, magicians, not to mention whatever mundane warriors she had mustered, Sarnesh or Etheryen or both. And there was always the chance that, during the fighting the Beetle girl herself might just . . . slip away.

She hears the call as I do, and if she gets there first, she might . . .

'Major Ostrec, rearguard with the Nethyen!' Seda yelled. 'Hurry, they are almost upon us!'

The Red Watch officer snapped out orders, falling back. The handful of Nethyen Mantids who had been ever more unwillingly accompanying her went with him gladly. *Something their small minds understand at last.* At a thought, Tisamon dropped behind as well to shield her.

The Beetle-kinden Pioneer dashed past her, snapbow halfway to his shoulder and face weirdly peaceful as he sought a target.

At Seda's side, Gjegevey was laboriously poling himself along with his staff.

'Come on, old man,' she urged, but she could see that he was doing his best. She grasped the haggard slave's arm to encourage him. *A curse on propriety. I am the Empress and I shall do as I like.* 'You've come with me this far,' she told him. 'You'll see it through.'

He nodded raggedly, leaning on her as he let her drag him along.

Behind she heard the unmistakable sound of a snapbow, followed by the war cries of the Mantids.

One of the Sarnesh went down immediately, a bolt tearing through his mail. Tynisa doubled her speed, spotting shapes ahead. *This time Che's got it right.* Rushing into a fight like this, with no clear picture of whom she fought or even where they were, reminded her of the Commonweal, when she still had been in thrall to her father's ghost.

Oh, but those were fights, though. Before she had broken away from him, the pair of them had been something superhuman and undefeatable. And uncontrollable, too, possessed of a terrible, callous bloodlust, which was why she had declined that gift in the end. *I will have to be enough on my own.*

There were Mantis-kinden coming against her, she saw, and already the Sarnesh crossbows were loosing, their bolts springing between the trees. There was another crack – Amnon or someone shooting. She began hearing the sizzle of stingshot from both sides.

A fierce-faced woman of about her own age was suddenly lunging for her with a metal claw, spinning away from Tynisa's instant parry to come back at her from the other side, twisting from her riposte at the same time. Tynisa conceded three steps, the very forest keeping her footing for her, even as it urged the Mantis on. *Old bastard only wants its blood, doesn't care whose.* She snapped her arm out, drew a red line across the Mantis's hip, then swayed back as the clawed gauntlet sliced past her eyes. The woman's other arm came driving in, trying to jab her with those vicious forearm spines, but Tynisa batted it away with her off hand, then stepped past her assailant and tried to cut her throat on the way. She caught only air, and then they had parted, turning back against one another, the Mantis already trying to close the gap.

Another Mantis was coming in, spear in hand, but Amnon cannoned into him, both of them going down and then scrabbling to regain their feet. Beyond her opponent, Tynisa could see others retreating – a flash of pale hair – *the Empress?*

The distraction nearly killed her, as the Mantis's blade darted towards her stomach, but her own sword knew its work and slipped in the way just in time, letting her dance backwards – *losing ground again.* And she knew that right now she was losing their best chance to win the war, to defeat the Empire in one stroke.

So go. And she went, whipping her opponent's steel aside, cutting just enough of an opening to get past her, kicking into a full run even as she did so, and be damned to the price that her hip would exact later.

A snapbow bolt spat past behind her, its author not adjusting for just how fast Tynisa was suddenly moving. Then there was a Wasp in the way, raising his hand to sting, but her blade was already in motion.

He was a dead man – just some Wasp soldier with red insignia – but somehow he put his raised hand in the way of her stroke. From the shock of impact, it seemed as though she had struck metal, yet when he fell out of her path, there was no blood, no sense that she had wounded him. *And no time to wonder about it.*

She had already realized that she was following the Mantis path to its logical conclusion. It was hard to see how she would survive this, success or failure, but she had to *try.*

She saw the Empress in front of her, with an old man who looked like a malformed corpse in tow. Just twenty yards – fifteen – then the Wasp woman was shouting out a word – a name – and someone else stood in the way.

Tynisa saw a man armoured head to foot in a style she knew

only from old books and museums, armour as fine and elegant as ever a Commonweal noble wore, but crafted to an entirely darker, sharper aesthetic. She had never seen a full suit of Mantis-kinden carapace armour before.

It gave her pause, despite her entire attack plan being built on going *forwards*, and then the man was coming for her, his clawed gauntlet stooping like a hunting dragonfly – barely turned by her own sword – then back to guard, without leaving room for a counter-attack.

She froze. She could not help it. Her mind had choked on the utter certainty that had come to her, even as her sword parried three more strokes and her feet carried her backwards.

Around her, the Empress's followers were falling back after their mistress. The Wasp with the red badge and a Beetle snap-bowman passed her, retreating with professional care.

She took three more blows numbly, the last scratching her shoulder before she was able to turn it.

The name the Empress had shouted had been *Tisamon*. And even had the name been unspoken, she would still have known. She had fought her father before, and she had lived with his barbed ghost in her mind, and she knew him, and here he was.

Then Amnon was there, lashing a blade out at the armoured form, and the claw that had been stooping towards her veered aside to block his stroke. With a shriek of nameless emotion Tynisa lunged for him, for his very throat, but he had fallen back a step, her lunge failing to reach him, even as he nicked Amnon's arm and deflected the big Beetle's next blow.

Then there was some summons – Tynisa did not hear it, but it was plain from the armoured man's – *Tisamon's* – stance, and he was turning and sprinting away, in full mail but fast enough that neither she nor Amnon had the chance to strike at him. She was after him a moment later, barely enough of a delay to slide a knife blade into, but the forest around seemed suddenly very dark, shadows hung on every bough, and she was blundering into the gloom. And where was the Empress?

And . . .?

She stopped, hearing the others catching up with her, Amnon almost at her elbow, staring about in confusion.

Where is she?

Of the Empress and her entire retinue there was neither track nor trace.

Nineteen

'This is such a stupid idea,' was Gerethwy's informed opinion.

The night was unseasonably chill, or perhaps it was just due to the altitude. There were no clouds above, the stars clear as cut glass, and only the faintest sliver of moon to detract from them.

'Wasn't my first choice either,' the airship's master grunted. 'Beats training on those deathtrap Stormreaders, though.' His name was Jons Allanbridge and he seemed to be some kind of associate of Stenwold Maker, although he didn't exactly speak of the War Master fondly. His vessel, the *Windlass*, was carrying the two Company volunteer officers and a fair number of their soldiers. Nobody had explained to Straessa that she would be one half of the Collegiate command team on this mission, and she had the unhappy feeling that possibly nobody had really thought about it either. Apparently the non-Mantis side of the operation would be spearheaded by the Mynans, and she and her people would just have to try and keep up. Although the overall plan might not be as foolish as Gerethwy claimed, the details really did seem to be lacking.

They put this one together in a hurry, and surely the Wasps'll see us coming, and then . . . But if the Imperial Air Force caught them aloft in these big, slow airships, that would be a death sentence for anyone who couldn't take wing and fly. Gerethwy was right in that – all the artificers were in agreement that airships as a tool of war had had their day.

Until now, apparently, because heavier-than-air fliers just could not have carried this many people to the enemy.

There were a dozen other dirigibles blotting out the night sky around them, which were doing their best to be stealthy. They kept no lights, and were coasting on a westerly wind so that the nocturnal quiet was not defiled by the sound of engines. Even the enormous *Sky Without*, its elegant staterooms now the squatting ground of the Mantis warriors, was coursing through the upper air like a great, bloated ghost.

'You're sure you can even *find* the enemy? I never really appreciated just how much land there is until I saw it from up here,' Straessa put in.

'They're coming along the coast, so it won't be hard,' Allanbridge told her. 'More important for us not to overshoot.' He checked his instruments. 'Not much further, if reports can be believed.'

'We're going to get shot down. This is ridiculous,' Gerethwy complained, from his post at the bow, but then a Fly-kinden messenger spiralled out of the sky to land at Allanbridge's left side, making the man curse furiously.

'Time,' the small woman announced. 'Down, now.' Then she was off for the next ship: an old fashioned way of passing the word, but lamp signals had been judged too risky.

The other Company officer, a Fly-kinden named Serena from the Fealty Street Company, had come up on deck. 'We're going down?'

'The easy way,' Allanbridge confirmed. All around them, the airship fleet was descending, and there was still no sense that the Empire had noticed their coming.

'Let's go and get the troops,' Serena suggested. 'I'll go over to the *Sky* and make some order there.' At the end of those words, she was already standing on the *Windlass*'s rail, and kicked off with her wings flashing from her shoulders, catching the air and arrowing off towards the larger vessel.

'They can't not have seen us,' Gerethwy muttered, as though bitter about Imperial failings.

'Plan is to give them other things to worry about, lad, never you mind,' Allanbridge replied, then added awkwardly, 'And you try to get your hide and your mob back to us intact, right? Now get ready to jump off and secure us, why don't you?'

Straessa went below decks to find the soldiers there mostly ready, strung out on that combination of tension, excitement and fear that she knew so well herself. Before they felt the *Windlass*'s keel scraping and bumping at the ground, they were out on deck and casting rope ladders over the side, even as Gerethwy fought with the anchor. The airship was emptied of troops with more efficiency than the Antspider would have bet on and, looking about, she could see other craft bobbing low, with swarms of Mantis-kinden flying or climbing from them, forming up into one turbulent, angry mob that was plainly itching to get at the enemy.

'Over there, quickly,' she ordered her people, and set a fast pace, well aware how the entire Felyen force might just vanish off into the night, leaving their allies too far behind to support them.

By the time she arrived, so had everyone else. She picked out the Mynans because their leader was already stalling the Mantis-kinden.

'Kymene?'

The Mynan leader glanced towards her. 'Your people are ready?'

Serena had made herself known by then, and Straessa nodded, shouldering her snapbow. 'I hadn't thought you'd be here yourself, Commander.'

'Neither did Sten Maker,' Kymene acknowledged. 'Too late for him to do anything about it now, though, isn't it? We're waiting a signal . . .' And then, with a fierce look at the woman who led the Felyen, '*Yes*, we are.'

'Your signal is late,' the Mantis spat.

'No, it's not. Just listen,' Kymene shot back. 'Everyone, quiet and *listen!*'

Straessa shook her head, hearing nothing at all but not wanting to state the obvious, but Gerethwy squeezed her shoulder, cocking his head.

He was smiling – a little thinly perhaps but she was glad of any smile from him just the same.

And then she heard it, though scarcely a moment before the Stormreaders started passing overhead. The clatter of their clock-work engines was so much quieter than the noisy oil-driven motors favoured by the Empire.

They circled almost invisibly save where they occasionally blotted out the stars, and Straessa heard one coming in to land, the thunder of wind thrown up by its wings hitting them with shocking suddenness as the nimble machine cornered and hovered for a moment, before choosing its spot.

Kymene went running over and, without much thought, Straessa ran after her, Serena and the Mantis leader following on her heels.

The cockpit was hinged open by the time they got there, and the Antspider recognized the Fly-kinden pilot seated inside as the Solarnese, Taki, who seemed to be in charge of Collegium's air defences.

'You've about a mile of ground to cover still to reach their pickets,' the pilot told them as they approached, and Straessa could hear the clockwork still ticking over, ready to take off again the moment the wings were engaged. 'We'll allow you a decent countdown and then move in to give them something to think about. But you're going to have to make good time.'

'We'll be there,' Kymene told her. 'Just make sure *you're* not late.'

The Fly grinned at her, then waved them away, and even though they were running back to the massed strike force, the downbeat of the Stormreader's wings almost knocked them off their feet.

'We run!' the Mantis leader was shouting at her followers, and Straessa expected a great roar of approval that would probably be heard over in Capitas. Instead, the Mantis-kinden just moved off silently, the entire pack breaking into a ground-eating lope, leaving the others to catch up.

General Tynan made do with very little sleep, so he was still awake and poring over quartermasters' reports when the camp around him suddenly exploded into life. He heard the Farsphex engines start up, and knew that the engineers would be dragging the cloaking tarpaulins off them even as the pilots crawled into their seats. *A night attack.* With the continued valiant resistance put up by the Imperial pilots and artillery, he had expected such a move. It was exactly the pattern that the Second's own fliers had fallen into when dropping their bombs, denied free rein over Collegium during daytime.

Of course, the Beetles won't have the same night vision as our Fly bombardiers had. And, of course, he had kept his camp without lights, despite the chill, to deny them any clear targets, but even a random bombardment would do its inevitable damage.

From the back of his tent, he heard Mycella stir, and she joined him moments later, swathed in a silk robe, even as the first watch officers rushed in to report. The first man had just time to salute before Tynan himself could hear the clatter of the enemy orthopters.

'Our pilots?' he snapped out.

'Taking to the air, sir. Artillery as well, but we—'

The first dull boom signified that one of the Collegiates had been a little too enthusiastic, unloading surely somewhere far short of the confines of the camp. The soldiers of the Second and their allies would be rushing from their tents, scattering and spreading.

'No dedicated bombers seen amongst them,' the watch officer continued. 'Just their Stormreaders, like before.'

The Air Corps will have to do its best, Tynan decided.

'Sir, there was a report of airships, too, but—'

Just then the real bombardment started, a half-dozen explosions, and one close enough to punch in the wall of the tent, leaving the poles leaning at drunken angles, pulling the ropes from the ground. There were cries of pain on the air, and a secondary retort as something caught fire and went up. Tynan looked skywards, gritting his teeth. *Luck's the emperor of this battlefield.* He knew the Airborne would be taking wing, but much of the army did not have that luxury.

'What do airships signify?' Mycella pressed him. Another explosion sounded further off, and he knew that the Stormreaders would be turning to make another approach, despite the best efforts of the Farsphex pilots.

'If they start to position airships over the camp, we'll give the order to scatter. They can carry more bombs than any number of orthopters. Slow, though, so we'll have warning. And perhaps the Farsphex will manage to bring some down.'

'Yes, sir, but I don't think . . .' The watch officer flinched as another bomb landed somewhere off towards the coast. 'They've not been seen again . . . I'd thought' – flinch – 'our scouts must be mistaken.'

'Then go and get me better intelligence!' Tynan snapped, and the man backed out hurriedly. The Wasp general sighed and buckled on his swordbelt, more for the comfort it would give him than anything else.

'Tynan, these ships . . .' Mycella began said pensively.

'If there were any.' But he found himself believing that there were. It would have to have been a very curious trick of the moonlight, otherwise . . .

'They can carry more than bombs,' she pointed out.

Their eyes locked, communication passing between them as

efficiently as through an Ant's Art. In the next moment they were both shouting for their underlings.

'Duty officer! Reinforce the perimeter. I want the reserve watch mustered now!' *And what a gamble – because if there's a force coming for us, we must huddle close so as to repel it – and make ourselves easy meat for their bombs. And if we don't . . .* But he found that he accepted Mycella's intuition without question.

Meanwhile the Spider Arista had called in her man Jadis. 'Have all our people to arms and ready to fight!' she ordered. 'Get the mercenaries up and ready. We're under attack.'

Even as she said it, a Fly messenger fought her way into the tent and dropped down by Mycella's feet.

'Mantis-kinden!' she got out.

Before they reached the camp, the Fly-kinden returned in her Stormreader, wheeling wildly over the Mantis onrush before setting down practically on top of Kymene's people, the cockpit already open.

'Here!' she called, pitching her voice high over the crump of explosives beyond. 'Map!'

Straessa struggled over, her chest heaving and already envying the solid endurance of the Beetle-kinden. The Fly proffered a tattered piece of paper, on which she had drawn a rough sketch of the camp's layout – something she must have done while in the air – marking out whatever looked as if it needed blowing up. 'Remember, strike fast, then pull out!' she shouted to Kymene. 'The airships will be coming in, and we'll cover them while you get away!'

The Mynan woman took a second to stare at the scribbled map, committing it to memory. She made no promises about the retreat, Straessa noted. Then the Antspider found the map in her own hands, and Kymene and her squad were off again, and so must she be if she did not want to get left behind.

She picked up speed, an extra burst to try and make up lost ground. Ahead, the bright flare of a bomb going off revealed the great Mantis host as stark silhouettes. Beyond them, some of the Second's camp was on fire, and there was a brief impression of a great many Wasps rushing about, in the air and on the ground, without having a clear idea of what was going on. Then . . .

Straessa would remember this moment. She would dream of it: the Mantis-kinden of the Felyal hitting the Second Army's camp. Not just as a mob of warriors and old men and children, not the last dregs of a culture casting themselves into the fire. In her memories they would be like a tide, a great cresting wave and, although the Wasps put a fair few soldiers in their way, nothing could stop them. They had come to finish their long history with the Second Army, one way or another.

They let nothing stop them. The Wasp sentries were hacked down within seconds, and even though the flashes of stings and the deadly needles of snapbow bolts kept darting out from amidst the camp, there was no suggestion of strategy from the Mantids, nothing so human as a fear of death, or even an acknowledgement of it. They ran and they flew as a great barbed host, and killed everyone they encountered, even as the Wasps pulled back to form up again deeper within their camp.

The air was alive with their arrows, and the night's darkness to them was merely dusk. As the first reordered force of Wasps advanced to try and hold them, the wave broke, the Mantid onslaught fragmenting into war bands of a dozen or a score, each hunting its own bloody end in the streets of the tent city that the Second had built.

'What's first on the shopping list?' Gerethwy shouted in Straessa's ear. The bombing had stopped – *and just as well!* – but the camp was reduced to a chaos of random clashes of arms, with Mantids and Wasps hurling themselves at each other, neither quarter nor hesitation from either side. When Straessa's squad halted at a crouch, quiet and still, they might as well have been invisible. The Imperials had other problems right then.

'Fordyke, take a dozen and head left, that way. Velme, you cut left of centre, down that way. And you' – *and I have no idea who you are* – 'you've got straight on.' And she parcelled out her command into tiny vulnerable pieces, just as the plan had called for, so that they could inflict the most damage for the least cost, for if the Wasps caught them all together, they would be butchered to a man. 'I'm heading deeper in. Looks like something's there needs setting on fire.' She squinted again at the pilot's map and hoped it wasn't just an inopportune twitch of the pencil. 'Use your grenades, but make sure you lob them *away* from your friends. Shoot every damn Imperial you see, and anyone else who isn't a Mantis and doesn't wear a sash. Blow things up. Questions? No? Get going.'

All said far too fast to allow objections, of course, and just as well because Straessa herself could feel fear gripping her by the throat, trying to throttle her words, and only by rattling them off that quickly could she get them out at all. The expressions of those Merchant and Student Company soldiers fool enough to volunteer were wide-eyed and horrified, and if she left them a moment they would just lock up, the reality of their situation clenching like a paralysis about them. But she shouted 'Move!' for her own benefit as much as theirs, and then they were all going, peeling off on their separate assignments, running as if all the ghosts of the Bad Old Days were after them.

She herself had the Dragonfly Castre Gorenn, who had brought a longbow that even the Mantids might envy. She had Gerethwy, who was holding his snapbow off-handed because he had lost his usual trigger finger in the last big fight. She had another half-dozen Beetles and Fly-kinden, and they were all waiting to follow her lead.

She went, feeling as though she had to put a shoulder to her fear and shove it out of the way by brute force, but she went anyway. There were Mantis-kinden fighting ahead, a handful of them cutting and leaping at Wasps who were trying hard to stay out of reach until reinforcements arrived. Straessa levelled her snapbow even as she ran, her aim shaking and bouncing as she tried to steady the barrel long enough for a shot. She loosed – but her target was already out of her sights, the bolt flying wildly off into the night. Then the man was dead, just pitching over without a Mantis anywhere near him, and she only heard the thrum of Gorenn's bowstring as the woman's second shot took an unarmoured Wasp in the small of the back. Straessa herself was trying to reload and recharge without slowing her pace, but the Dragonfly was already ahead of her, plucking another arrow from one of her two quivers, nocking and drawing, then letting her wings lift her from the ground, steady in the air for a heartbeat as she shot, then down and running again without missing a step.

As the Antspider's little band passed the melee, Gorenn put five arrows into it, each one claiming a Wasp, and two of those victims picked out of the close fighting with the Mantids. The Dragonfly's face was serene. The Commonweal Retaliatory Army, she had named herself, but Straessa had never taken her seriously before now.

'Behind us!' someone shouted, and she risked a glance over her shoulder to see a good score and a half of Wasps bearing down behind them – more intent on wiping out the Mantids than Straessa's people, but that would only be a matter of time. Then one of her Fly-kinden had kicked off into the air, his wings propelling him back towards the enemy. The Antspider saw a flare as he dragged the fuse of a grenade over the rough catch-strip tab on his belt and, as he swung out of his dive, he left the grenade behind, arcing its way into the Wasps with the momentum of his flight. He timed it perfectly – the bright lash of it hurled the front dozen Wasps in all directions, with only some of them staggering to their feet afterwards. And then the Mantids had rushed them, just four now against so many, but Straessa had no chance to see how they fared. She had her own mission.

She heard the first explosion, one of the sabotage teams either being creditably fast or horribly premature. 'Gereth, start the clock!' she ordered. Now the sands were running, and she hoped that all her other teams were counting as well.

★

The seer said there would be fire and blood.

Mycella regularly had her fortune cast, and seldom paid much heed to it. 'Fire and blood' could mean just about anything – the daily Collegiate fly-overs, the continual just-controlled friction between the Empire and its Spider allies . . . But this morning her seer had been insistent – not specific but very, very emphatic.

She had listened, this once, and given orders for more of her people than usual to be in readiness at all times, doubling watches, overlapping shifts. She had reckoned it nonsense at the time, but some deep instinct had compelled her.

Seeing what she saw here, she was not sure that she had done the right thing.

Hatred had a face, and that face was Mantis-kinden. She had always known that their people hated hers from time out of mind, and with a fervour that defied logic and offered no reasons. Back in the Spiderlands it had been a joke, those ravaging rustics in their primitive longships and shabby tree-houses. Whatever the Mantis-kinden had once been, they were that no longer – just an atavistic pack of malcontents squatting in their coastal forest between Kes and Collegium, menacing the nearby shipping and brooding over their obsolescence.

Now they had come in all their fury, and she saw that, just for this one night, they had recaptured the days of their old glory.

They came in a ravening wave, killing everything in their path, slaughtering the Wasp sentries who tried to deter them, killing unarmoured, just-woken Imperial soldiers scrabbling desperately from their tents, putting their hungry blades into every living thing in their path, combatant or not, Wasp or Auxillian or mercenary. Or Spider. Most especially Spider.

They were wild and fierce and had no plan, no strategy that she might have misdirected. All she was faced with was their hate.

Her soldiers, those brave men and women loyal to the Aldanrael and its tributaries, were flooding past her, clad in their armour of leather and chitin and silk, throwing themselves into the maw

of that bloody melee, killing Mantids and being killed in turn –
losing two for one at best, perhaps more. They were gallant and
skilled, her soldiers, and they loved her and were loyal to her
every inch as much as Tynan's people obeyed him and revered
their Empress. They knew, too, that they were not the born and
honed killers the Mantids were, and yet they rushed in and
fought, and they held the line even as their very presence – the
hated Spider-kinden – drew more and more of the Felyen into
the fight. Her people held out because more of them were still
coming, rushing past her into the fray with grim desperation,
decanting out their lives like spilt wine, just to keep the Felyen
assault at bay.

'Mistress.' She heard Jadis urging at her side. 'You must fall
back. They cannot keep the Mantids back long.'

She shook him off, feeling his fear for her – not ever for
himself – and drinking in the strength which that love and fealty
gave her. She summoned up all her reserves of Art.

'Servants of the Aldanrael!' she called out, and her voice thun-
dered over them all, friend and enemy alike. 'Hold fast, Aldanrael!
Be not afraid! I am with you! I shall take not one step back!
Hold fast and make them pay in blood for every inch of ground!
Aldanrael! Aldanrael and the Spiderlands!'

Her Art, the hidden strength of the Aristoi, washed over her
soldiers, firing them with courage and giving them heart, quickening their limbs and staving off pain, so that for a moment the
Mantids began actually losing ground. Then the arrows came
in, feathering through the air towards her, and she stepped left
and right in a graceful dance, and let Jadis's shield take the rest
– nimble as a young girl until one found her shoulder.

The silk and mail she had donned took the brunt, but it drew
blood nonetheless, and Jadis was practically dragging at her arm,
but Mycella stood her ground, just as she had exhorted her
servants to do. 'Hold!' she called again, aware that the Mantids
were trying to flank her forces; aware that the battle-lines were
getting thinner and thinner. 'For the Aldanrael, hold!'

Fire and blood, she remembered suddenly. *And we have had the blood but was that little bombing really the fire?* 'Bring me Morkaris,' she demanded. 'Where is he?'

The mercenary adjutant was fighting at one end of the line, with a pack of his unruly Scorpion-kinden, but at Jadis's shout he dropped back to join Mycella, still keeping half an eye on the conflict. His black armour was battered and scratched and he had a jagged, bloody gash across one cheek, but his eyes widened when he saw the arrow still standing proud of her shoulder.

'There will be others,' she informed him, calm and clear despite it all. 'Beetles, Ants, the Apt – they will send artificers against the same targets their flying machines have been trying to destroy.' Now she had thought of it, it seemed obvious. 'Take your Scorpions and any other of the mercenaries you can gather. Spread them out. Send them to check the provisions, and the siege machines. Drive off any enemies you find there.'

Morkaris glanced from her to Jadis, and from Jadis to the ongoing battle, to the line that was being pushed closer and closer.

'Obey the Lady-Martial!' Jadis snapped at him, and the mercenary scowled and went to drag his Scorpions out of the fray.

Jadis of the Melisandyr had moved closer to her now, arrows rattling off his shield. 'Lady . . .' she heard him start, but he added nothing, for to say more would be to question her.

'We are buying time, Jadis,' she told him gently, drawing her rapier with her uninjured arm. 'We must hope that Tynan can order and rally his men in the space of time that we are buying him, because soon enough we will need him to return the favour.'

Ahead Straessa saw several automotives burdened with some bulky load. She was not at all sure she knew where she was on Taki's map, and she was keenly aware that shortly the only relevant direction would be 'out', in any event.

'There!' she directed. 'Set your bombs there!'

The two chosen artificers hurried forwards, and Straessa began looking round for the enemy, snapbow raised to her shoulder. Beside her, Castre Gorenn loosed a shaft that caught a half-armoured Wasp in the throat even as he stepped out from around the automotive, killing the man before he knew what was going on.

A skirmishing knot of Mantids passed by, briefly visible between the tents, Wasps converging on them on the ground and from the air. Straessa crouched low, Gerethwy beside her.

'Come on, come on,' she murmured impatiently, but she knew the bomb-setters would be working as quickly as possible, securing their explosives to the automotives at their most vulnerable points, setting their clockwork timers carefully.

'Inbound,' Gerethwy said flatly. 'They see us.'

She saw just huge shapes moving in the dark, at first – far bigger than Wasps had any right to be. Then they resolved into Scorpion-kinden, a dozen at least, bearing down on them at a full charge.

Her snapbow jumped in her grasp and one of them stumbled and fell, while an arrow from Gorenn wounded a second. She saw Gerethwy fumbling with his weapon, teeth bared. Another two shots sounded from nearby, claiming one victim between them.

The Scorpions let out a hoarse roar of fury, almost upon them now. Straessa saw Gerethwy drag his snapbow up, missing his target at close range, then just swinging the weapon into the face of the leader, whipping his helmed head to one side. The Scorpion was already bringing down a halberd at him, too close, and he caught at the shaft desperately. His long-boned frame was surprisingly strong, Straessa knew, and for a moment he held the weapon off, and she leapt in with her rapier and found the thin mail under the big man's arm, lancing through the links and provoking an agonized yell.

Another huge warrior loomed before her as she hauled on her blade to free it. She looked up to see a greatsword drawn back, and then the Scorpion's head snapped sideways, an arrow standing out from the visor of his helmet.

'Come on, Antspider!' Gorenn was shouting. 'More on the way!'

Straessa finally got her blade clear, and immediately lunged at another enemy, even as Gerethwy liberated the halberd and began laying about himself, sacrificing finesse for sheer force and speed.

'Officer, we're done!' She heard the words but made nothing of them as she twisted aside away from an axe-stroke, her own thrust scraping off mail. Gerethwy's halberd blade bounced off her opponent's shoulderguard, and sent the man staggering.

'Seriously, Antspider! Time to go!' the Dragonfly yelled, while someone else shouted, 'Clock!' as though they were still at the Prowess Forum.

Belatedly the understanding stumbled into her mind that all this chatter meant that the bombs would shortly explode.

She measured her sword against the axe of her opponent, let his stroke fall short and then lunged, throwing her shoulder forward the way she always employed to out-strike her fencing opponents, this time gashing the Scorpion across the side of his neck and sending him staggering away.

'Clear! Go!' she cried, and did her best to obey her own order. *Clock* meant that it was time they were gone for good – too much time having elapsed since the first explosion. Time to try and extricate their fingers from the trap, or the airships would leave them behind.

Another enemy was upon her, though, before she could get more than three steps away – a cadaverous Spider in dark mail, whipping an axe at her double-handed. She tried to dodge back, fell over instead, so that the crescent blade scythed just over-head. Her reflexive stab caught him at the knee, but his armour turned the blow. He had his axe upraised again in one smooth motion, and she rolled aside frantically, but then he had turned, shoulder coming up, and Gorenn's arrow struck the high neck-guard of his pauldrons, sending the Spider reeling but otherwise unharmed. Straessa seized her moment and scrambled away, but gained only another foot of ground before a Scorpion blade sliced down in front of her.

Gerethwy barged into the newcomer, knocking him aside, and the two of them went down in a tangle of flailing limbs. Straessa forced herself to her feet even as the Spider came back for her.

Then the explosives blew.

The artificers had done well, for the automotives were gutted in an instant. The force of the blast was mostly directed in and up, so that one machine's entire weight of iron and brass and wood jumped five feet before coming down on its side, a second explosion slewing its back end towards the fighting. The rush of displaced air knocked the Spider over, and Straessa as well, slapping her to the ground with casual force and leaving her weak and dizzy with the impact. A moment later, though, long, lean arms had hauled her up, and she was in Gerethwy's grip, being hurried away, as Gorenn's arrows darted past, swift as angry thoughts, to discourage pursuit.

'Put me down, you bastard, I can run as good as anyone.' But she said it so quietly, mumbling through a mouthful of blood, that he didn't hear her.

'General, we've got them on the run!'

Tynan regarded Colonel Cherten narrowly. 'Don't give me that nonsense. They're *Mantis*-kinden.' *The problem with the Intelligence Corps is that they underestimate everyone else's.* 'What's the situation?'

'The saboteurs have fled, at least,' Cherten amended. 'All key resources are now under our control.' Just then, another explosion retorted like thunder from somewhere in the camp and, under other circumstances, Tynan would have laughed at the timing. Instead he forcibly restrained himself from punching the colonel.

Hurriedly, Cherten went on. 'The Mantids are still in the camp. Most of them are gathered up now, and the Spider-kinden are holding them. We're mopping them up right now – infantry and airborne squads have surrounded them. They're fighting to the last, of course, but with snapbows and stings we have them outmatched.'

And what bloody cost has this night brought us? 'I want a full report of the damage: lost men, supplies and siege—'

Just then a sergeant landed nearby, stumbling slightly as he saluted. His armour was streaked with blood. 'General, sight of airships coming in.'

And their damned orthopters too, of course. And we've formed up in nice big groups and there are fires all over camp to light their way. 'Send out the order: break up every unit into skirmish spread, if they're not actively fighting. And get me – Major Oski!'

The Fly had been skulking about a moment before and now he appeared at Tynan's elbow as though brought into being simply by the use of his name. 'Sir?'

'I want everything you have aimed at the sky – I *know* their Stormreaders are too fast for you, but just make the air as busy as you can. Make their lives difficult.'

The Fly saluted, wings flashing from his shoulders to carry him away.

'Now—' Tynan started, and an arrow struck Cherten in the chest, bouncing off his armour but knocking him down. Tynan's blade cleared its sheath, without need for thought, and his left hand jabbed out at a target he had not even consciously seen as the Mantids arrived.

'Defend the general!' someone shouted, but Tynan was too busy defending himself. His sting crackled, catching the onrushing woman a glancing blow that barely slowed her, and then he had caught her spear with his sword, beating it away as she raked him with her arm-spines, which squealed across his mail. One of his aides got a sword into her then – too close to risk a sting – but the Mantis woman seemed barely discouraged. There was clear knowledge in her eyes that she was fighting the Wasps' leader.

She struck him in the chest with the shaft of the spear, trying to knock him back far enough for her to ram the point into him, but he flailed out and somehow seized her by the wrist. Furious, she pulled back, but a tug of war was not what he intended. The fierce heat of his sting charred her flesh to the bone and she hissed – such a small sound – and rammed the spines of her other arm at his neck, abandoning the spear altogether.

His aide got his sword into her back then, and practically levered her off his superior, while all about there was fighting. Surely there were no more than eight or nine Mantids broken from their main force, but they had struck the mother-lode of enemy officers to kill. Cherten was on the ground, one arm running with blood but still lashing out with his sting at any target that presented itself, and Tynan saw the Red Watch captain, Vrakir, fighting savagely with a Mantis swordsman, matching his enemy for three fierce exchanges of blows before getting a sting in that sent the man reeling back with his chest on fire.

Another Mantis came for Tynan with one of those bladed gauntlets, but by that time his staff had rallied, and a snapbow bolt cut the enemy down before he got close. In another moment the Spider-kinden were there, striking from the same direction the Mantids had issued from. Tynan saw Mycella's bodyguard literally hurl himself into a pair of them, slender sword flashing, his shield and mail warding off their return strikes, and yet he moved nearly as fast as they did, for all the weight of metal he carried.

Then he saw her, striding through the fighting like a queen, the rapier in her hand stained with blood. Despite the attack, and despite the losses he knew his army must have suffered, the sight of her brought a smile to his lips.

The airships were coming for them. Straessa could see them descending, so silent and peaceful, as if they belonged to another world entirely, while behind her the Wasp camp burned and the fighting continued. One of the Stormreader pilots must have been watching for the first bombs exploding, then gone to fetch the transport straight away.

'Let me down!' she insisted, somewhat louder and clearer now. She was aware that some of her people were turning to shooting behind them. 'Curse you, Gereth, put me down. I need to fight!'

'With what?' he asked. There was a flash and a boom from ahead, and she realized that some of the airship crew had brought smallshotters up to the rails and were now loosing, randomly into the enemy camp to discourage pursuit.

With supreme effort she wrestled herself out of Gerethwy's grip, then had to lean on him when the ground proved unexpectedly uncooperative beneath her feet.

'Wounded this way!' called a shrill voice – te Mosca's surely. 'Wounded to me!'

'Wounded here!' Gerethwy shouted, and tugged at Straessa's arm.

'I'm not wounded!' she snapped. 'Just bit my tongue and a bit dizzy,' but he was dragging her onwards anyway, and he was stronger than she was.

She tried to form a picture of the retreat – there was a scatter of Collegiates all over, on the ground and some in the air, making for the airships with all the speed they could muster, and some pausing to help those who really had been cut up. The numbers looked surprisingly hopeful. *Did we actually get away with it?*

'Here with the wounded!' Sartaea te Mosca called again, and then Gerethwy was hustling Straessa towards the curving hull of the self-same *Windlass* that she had arrived on – apparently someone had decided its hold would make a good infirmary.

She refused to end up in the hoist they had rigged up, instead climbing with fierce determination up the rope ladder, which made her head swim. *Never stand near explosives again. Good rule to live by.*

'Is this all of you?' Jons Allanbridge demanded, and she caught a brief glimpse of surprise on his solid, serious features. 'Where's the rest?'

The Mantids, she realized. *The Felyen, they're not coming back. They never were.* A brief image, from the muster, of all those

284

lean, grim men and women – the old, the young, children and babes in arms, all of them. *All of them. The Felyal ends here. What have we done?*

She staggered over to the rail, where one of Allanbridge's people was hastily reloading the breach of his smallshotter. There were still a few trying to flee the camp, but she could see Wasps approaching, now, and she had the feeling that anyone who had left it this long had left it too late.

Stormreaders streaked over the Second's camp, lashing down trails of piercer bolts and releasing the occasional bomb

'Going up!' Allanbridge shouted.

'Wait!' Three running figures below were just closing with the rope ladder.

The airship began to rise, but Gerethwy kept paying out the ladder to keep it within reach of them until all three had hold of it and were climbing.

She stretched out a hand and hauled up the first to reach the rail. Smoke-blackened beneath the ruined visor of a battered helm, it took her a moment to recognize Kymene. The two behind her were a pair of her Mynan saboteurs.

The two women just stared at one another, then the Mynan leader clasped Straessa's shoulder in wordless solidarity.

'The sky!' someone was shouting. 'The sky!'

The Antspider looked up, but saw nothing but the underside of the *Windlass*'s balloon. Then understanding came to her: the *Sky*.

The *Sky Without* was too late in departing, or perhaps it was just such a grand target that the Wasps had sought it out first. The immense airship still hung low to the ground, and Straessa could see Wasp airborne swarming over it, fighting on its decks, mad for revenge.

'Hammer and tongs,' whispered Allanbridge, next to her.

A moment later they saw a flash, something exploding below decks, towards the stern. Abruptly there was smoke pouring from the *Sky*'s hatches, and then Straessa could see fire glaring from the rearmost windows, working its way forward a cabin at a time. Soon there would be cinders alighting on the envelope, shrivelling the silk.

She sagged to the deck. *Let it all be worth it. What are we, if none of this was worth it?*

'How bad?' Tynan asked.

Mycella's face remained calm, even as one of her healers attended to the arrow in her shoulder. They both knew that the wound was not what the general was referring to.

'Almost half of my people, mercenaries and my own troops equally,' she said softly. Tynan had heard how the fight had gone – how the Spider-kinden had simply not stopped throwing themselves into the fray, into that whirl of blades that the Mantis-kinden had put up – and how the Mantids had been happy to welcome them, given an opportunity to spill the blood of their oldest enemy. That sacrifice had saved countless Wasp lives and perhaps held the whole camp together.

'The Empire will remember,' he assured her.

'Don't make promises that you can't keep,' she replied wryly. 'It's enough that you yourself remember.'

Tynan turned to the Fly engineer. 'Major Oski.' All around them he could hear the sound of the Second Army counting over the cost, removing bodies and tending wounds, putting out fires. *This* was the crucial report, though.

Oski would not meet his gaze, which was a bad sign right now. 'General, supplies are mostly intact. Splitting them up as much as possible, well, there was nothing there that made a decent target for them. Artillery . . . sir, they took out most of our larger engines, and blew a couple of the firepowder stores, too. We have two greatshotters still in working order, one other that could be repaired if I've got two days. Of the rest, we lost seventeen of the ballistae we've been using against the enemy fliers, and Captain Bergild reports two Farsphex down as well.'

'In summary?' Tynan kept his voice level.

'We're going to take far more of a pounding from their air – our ability to keep them at bay has taken a serious beating. And, General – when we get there, we don't have the engines to take down their walls. We'd have to assault with just the Light Airborne, and they'd have their orthopters harrying us all the time . . . Sir, when you pulled back from Collegium the last time, well . . . it's not much different to that. I don't see how we can take the city.'

Tynan felt a sick clenching within him. *Not again!* But they had been marching towards this moment ever since the order came. *Where is that air support I was promised?* His eyes met Mycella's, and he saw her reading these conclusions from his face. She might not know the artifice involved, but she knew him.

'The attack will proceed.'

Tynan started, suddenly aware of Vrakir standing beside him. There was a strange look to the Red Watch officer, a sheen of sweat on his brow.

'Captain Vrakir . . .' Tynan started, but the man looked at him with such an expression that the general found himself unexpectedly silenced.

'I speak with the Empress's voice,' Vrakir declared. 'New weapons, new troops are coming. You will continue the march. Collegium will fall.'

In the resulting silence, Tynan merely stared at the man. It was as though a flash-fever had descended on Vrakir; as though . . .

As though someone was speaking through him, something long-hidden rising to the surface at this time of need. He had the inexplicable feeling that, had he only asked an hour before, Vrakir would have known nothing about these new orders.

'Sir.' Colonel Cherten was now at his other side, one arm in a sling still spotted with blood. 'You saw his papers. He carries the Empress's authority.'

'I will not waste the lives of my soldiers,' Tynan said quietly.

Vrakir's stare seemed to be fixed on something beyond him.

'General, the Empress has full confidence in your loyalty and obedience.'

Something cold traced its way down Tynan's spine – caused by the words and the weirdly distant voice combined. He was suddenly aware of Cherten being a Rekef man, almost certainly . . . and how many others here? Who amongst his officers would oppose him, if he tried to steer them against this supposed word of the Empress.

And worse, he *did* believe it was the word of the Empress. He found within himself no doubt at all, and that scared him more than anything else.

'Do not fear, General. You shall have your victory,' Vrakir insisted. 'Collegium shall fall to you.'

There were a lot of unhappy looks around then – not least Major Oski and Mycella herself – but Tynan had built himself a career based on loyalty first and foremost.

'We march on,' he confirmed. 'Do what you can for the wounded, and get the army ready to move.'

Twenty

It had taken Che a day to exhaust the patience of the Sarnesh. While she had been heading forwards, they had been happy to follow her. When she had led them to the Empress herself they had been exultant. It had not mattered that Seda had then vanished into the forest, that the woman and her fellows had somehow left no tracks, or that the Nethyen might happen on them at any time. Che had led them so far, and Che would lead them to the Empress again. A decisive victory for Sarn was imminent, and that was all that mattered.

A full day later, however, and it had become clear to them that Che was leading them nowhere. Not that they stayed still, but the Beetle girl's path wound round and circled, doubling back and trailing off, so that by evening it was apparent that they had crossed and recrossed only a small patch of forest, and ended up where they had started.

They were going to report back, they explained the next morning, but it was obvious that their confidence in her had evaporated. For a moment the old Inapt mysteries had carried them along, but no further. They were rationalists and it was plain that Che was mad.

The others, Che's own retinue, had stayed with her, but she could feel that their confidence was slipping, too, watching her through the hours of morning and then on past noon, and the day creeping away – and still no progress and no explanation.

Tynisa particularly . . . Che was worried about Tynisa. 'That was my father,' she had said, and Che had stared at her and tried to convince her that she was wrong, but the girl had become more and more insistent. Her father had been there with the Empress, guarding her. *How can that be, Che?* And Che's denials had fallen on deaf ears.

Then Maure herself had come and stepped between them and said, *Che, she's right.* Simple words, but Che already knew inside that they were true. For, of course, the Empress had been present there when Tisamon died. Of course the Empress could call up Tisamon's shade, especially since Tynisa had rejected it and cast it out.

One more thing to put right when we find Seda, Che had vowed. But they could not find Seda. The Empress had taken a path that they could not follow.

'I don't understand it,' Che confided to Maure. 'I can feel her still. She's *there*. She's not even far away. It's just . . . every direction I choose takes me further away from her.'

'She has gone *inwards*,' Maure confirmed. 'I think . . . she has paid some price or enacted some ritual that has let her through. I can feel the ghosts of this place all around, angry and confused. If we had come here alone, then we might have just walked in – assuming the Mantids didn't kill us. Now, though, the division of the locals has tangled the way. The Empress has been able to buy or force her way through, but we cannot follow.'

'Why not?' Che demanded. 'Doesn't this place . . .' *know who I am?* But that would be a foolish line to take. 'Then find me the price, and it will be paid.'

Maure just stared at her, and after a moment Che reconsidered what she had said, and sighed. 'I mean, *we* will have to find a way in. We have to stop her, Maure. Last night I dreamt that . . . this Argastos was calling to me. I could sense that Seda was nearing him.'

'Che, this is a Mantis place.'

'I know that, and I . . . you mean the price?'

Maure nodded.

'But blood? Hasn't there been enough?'

'Blood to the Mantis-kinden is like machines to the Apt,' the halfbreed observed philosophically. 'They see so many distinctions and divisions, where to us it is all just . . .'

'But I thought blood rituals were . . . for the Mosquito-kinden?'

Maure closed her eyes for a moment, as though pained. 'Blood is a symbol, Che – a symbol of power, violence, identity. Mosquito-kinden might have made it an art form, but blood was always the Mantis way. Be thankful it was the Moths that got to them first.'

Che blinked. 'You're talking about a sacrifice. I don't think I can do that.'

Maure just shrugged. 'It's no magic that I was ever tutored in. It's not the Woodlouse way, nor that of the Moths, for they have other ways of exerting power. But I have been trying to find the path *in*, and it is as barred to me as it is to you. If Terastos was a greater magician, perhaps he would have some way of circumventing it, but he admits that he's out of his depth.'

'There must be some other way.'

The necromancer shrugged again.

'Che,' came Tynisa's soft call. 'We're not alone.'

The Beetle girl's eyes opened wide, and she reached out, seeking . . .

Fool, to become too focused on this. 'Nethyen,' she managed to warn them. 'Everyone, ready to move.'

'Where?' Thalric hissed.

'Away.' But he was right. Even as they were moving off, Tynisa leading the way with drawn blade, every step took them further from their destination – that destination that could only be reached by travelling in some direction off the compass, off all maps.

And without that destination, that star to steer by, where could they go? They were deep in the forest of the Mantis-kinden, and they could not run forever.

Nonetheless, run they did. In Che's mind appeared the

Nethyen, a score of them spread out between the trees and closing fast – some of them already running alongside the stragglers, racing to get ahead of the fugitive band. She heard Thalric's sting crackle and spit, but knew that he had hit nothing, merely making himself a target. Ahead, Tynisa stopped and turned, waiting only for a second to ensure that Che and the others were still behind her before springing into motion again.

Helma Bartrer was falling behind. The Collegiate woman was not used to such a chase – *and since when was I?* – and was making too much heavy going amidst the undergrowth, virtually bouncing off the trees. Che felt Terastos's exasperation as he dropped back himself, to drag her onwards.

Thalric was ahead of her now, looking over to their left, and Che knew he could see the shadows of Mantis-kinden there. Maure was beyond him, almost catching up with Tynisa – a surprising turn of speed from her, but then she had been many years taking care of her own skin, and perhaps the Mantids would even spare her out of respect for her skills.

Amnon was just behind her, slowing himself to keep pace, ready to protect her from . . . Che did not think he would have the chance to protect her from anything.

And I am not thinking! Was I not crowned by the Masters of Khanaphir? Do I have no authority? I should not have to run like a roach.

'There's something ahead!' Thalric called out. 'I see walls!'

She risked a glance, expecting the half-seen rounded structures of a Mantis hold, but instead caught a glimpse of a timbered frame ahead, curved, but no Mantis work. Nor any sort of building she knew except . . .

Is that a boat?

Focus. And she tried to project her mind out, to thrust her authority and importance into the faces of the pursuing Mantis-kinden. The running made it harder, constantly stumbling and staggering, and then an arrow skipped past her, making her heart leap and throwing her off stride again.

Focus! There was a feeling within her, encapsulating all that had changed since she had lost her Aptitude, all that she had instead been gifted with beneath Khanaphes, and she threw it outwards, a wordless demand for recognition from the Mantids, from the forest, from the Empress herself had the woman not been so maddeningly *elsewhere.*

She had it. She felt their minds, felt them shudder as she reached for them. *You will know me!*

It was Amnon who broke it, ramming out a straightened arm and knocking her from her feet with a scream, all her efforts in vain.

What is he . . .? Why did he . . .? Betrayer! Her fury was something beyond her, a magician's self-obsessed rage at being thwarted, and she twisted on the ground to reach for him, intending to do she knew not what, hands out and fingers crooked like a stage actor hamming a witch.

She saw the stroke that came for him, that might have been coming for her. It unfolded from the trees, but he was closing with it, blade out, and had got closer than the attacker had intended. Instead of meeting the razor-spined inner edges of those terrible weapons, Amnon was simply struck by the hard backs as the twin arms lashed out. He was thrown clear over Che, sword spinning from his hand, and she heard him land behind her.

The mantis loomed over her, arms folding back with an air of disappointment. It was a drab green mottled with black, save where its underbelly was paler, and its eyes were the colour of old gold.

She heard Thalric's yell, but she could spare him no attention. Those vast orbs were now her whole world.

The mantis twitched back, and the bright flash of the Wasp's sting glittered across its carapace, to no visible effect. It went for Thalric with one arm, an elegant feint of a blow that sent him reeling away from its unexpected reach. Che could feel the creature as a knot in the weave of the forest, just as she could feel

the Mantis-kinden themselves. And one in particular. She realized that the beast before her had a . . . not a master but a
companion, another mind, another pair of eyes, adding up to
one formidable opponent, Mantis and mantis united.

It struck and, though she was watching, it moved faster than
she could follow. The arms scything down and raking her up
into their jagged embrace.

Thalric turned to see Amnon struggling to his feet, and Che –
gone, no sign of her, just movement in the trees.

He turned, boots digging into the dirt, and let his wings carry
him back the way he had come. 'Amnon!'

The big Khanaphir threw himself forwards, but a Mantis-
kinden woman leapt on him even as he did so, bladed gauntlet
upraised. The two of them went down, and then Amnon had
backhanded the woman off him. She turned, quick as a coiling
centipede, driving for him again, but Thalric's sting took her in
the throat, snapping her backwards almost head over heels.

An arrow spun from between the trees and struck the Wasp
full in the chest, and he himself went over, feet skidding out from
under him. The force was like a strong man's punch and his
chitin breastplate cracked slightly under the force, but his mail
kept his hide intact.

'Where is she?' he yelled at Amnon.

The big Beetle was looking about him wildly. 'They took her!
She's . . .' He made an abortive little run into the trees, then
backed off. 'I don't see tracks. No tracks at all.'

Like the Empress? Or perhaps they just flew, or . . .

'What happened?' Thalric shouted.

Tynisa passed him, darting in between the trees and then skidding to a stop. 'They're coming for us!' she shouted at him.

'We have to go after Che!' he insisted.

Her face, as it turned to him, was devoid of expression. 'Where
is she?'

Another arrow lanced towards them, and she turned it away

with a lightning flicker of her rapier, without even looking. Thalric's quick glance around detected plenty of movement coming their way, just as Tynisa said.

'They know she's special,' he stated. 'They wouldn't . . .'

'They're *Mantis*-kinden, Thalric. Of course they would.' Only at these last words did her voice shake, a brief window on the fear and rage inside her.

Amnon had his snapbow out, a bolt chambered and the battery charged. 'We fight?'

'A sacrifice,' Tynisa breathed.

Thalric stared at her, but he had no need to ask what she meant. Outside Khanaphes, other Mantis-kinden had very nearly done for *him* at one of their nasty little shrines. And of course, as he said, Che was *special*. She was owed a special death.

'I've an idea, but it means we need to speak to them. So we need to be able to hold them off,' Tynisa was dancing quickly backwards, heading in the direction where Maure had gone. 'Come on, quickly.'

'But . . .!'

'Thalric, die here and what have you accomplished?' Whatever she saw in his face prompted her to add, 'The Commonweal trick, Thalric. Remember?'

They were all of them backing off now, because the Mantids were so close. Thalric let his sting speak three times in the hope that it would deter them. *The Commonweal trick* . . . 'Didn't work so cursed well last time.' Her ravaged face, and the limp that seized on her the moment she wasn't fighting or running, those were her rewards from the Commonweal trick.

And who's to say it'll work again? Another arrow glanced from his pauldron – uncomfortably close to his face – and abruptly he was running, and cursing himself for it. The other two followed right behind him.

Ahead of them rose those wooden walls, and he had already identified exactly what they had once been. He had seen vessels like this often enough during his time in the army. *Imperial scout airship, old model – but there were still enough of them around by the end of the last war.* Even before he saw it, he had been expecting the Seventh Army insignia he saw there: the badge of General Malkan's Winged Furies that had been destroyed by the Sarnesh and their allies at the place still known as Malkan's Folly.

The vessel's hull lay at an odd angle within the clearing it had carved as it came down. There was little sign of a balloon or rigging, and the hull was mossy and probably part rotten from a few years in a place unfit for human craftsmanship, but it offered cover at least. The only problem was that it might become a tomb as easily as a hiding place.

Maure appeared at the open hatch, and then ducked back inside almost immediately, as an arrow thudded deep into the wood right beside her hand. Thalric let his wings bloom, kicking into an extended dive that pitched him neatly through the square opening, and then he was turning back, hauling Tynisa inside and putting out a hand for Amnon. The Khanaphir leapt to the hatch in one clear bound, paused there for a moment to discharge his snapbow – Thalric heard a cry as the hasty shot nonetheless hit home – and then dropped in, already fumbling for another bolt.

Thalric took up station with him at the hatch, one hand poised to sting as he waited for the Nethyen to make an appearance. There was plenty of movement between the trees, but nothing that made a good target. The corpse of the man that Amnon shot lay in a crumpled heap just inside the clearing. *Too keen by half.*

'We're not the first to end up hiding here,' Maure observed softly, in the silence that descended. Thalric risked a glance backwards, and saw her kneeling by a skeleton still attired in Imperial armour, picked clean by busy scavengers long since.

'Probably died in the crash,' he decided.

'He didn't,' the necromancer corrected him, and he felt disinclined to press the matter.

'Where the hell are the Moth and that Collegiate woman anyway?'

Amnon shook his head. 'They fell behind.' There was a finality to his tone.

Behind them, Tynisa swore, but with a hint of awe in her tone. 'Thalric . . .'

Leaving Amnon watching, Thalric navigated the sloped interior to see what Tynisa had found. He expected another body, or some further evidence of Mantis atrocity. He had not expected to find a fortune, but there was a chest there – Quartermaster Corps heavy-duty issue – which was still nearly full of Imperial mint gold coins.

'Some deal they were brokering with the Mantids?' Tynisa suggested.

He shrugged. 'Maybe. Not a currency that's any good around here though, certainly not at the time this boat must have come down. Your plan, Tynisa – it's a fool's plan.'

'We're all fools anyway, so that works out well,' she retorted, 'but I'll make Che the stakes of the wager.' Her eyes shifted over to the hatch, past Amnon's shoulder. The sky was darkening already. 'Mantis honour. Let's hope *that* currency's still good around here.'

She made as if to go, but Thalric caught her arm. For a moment he held her, just looking into her eyes, words rising in him and being thrust back down again. In the end, he could not bring himself to thank her for what she was about to try, although it was a debt that weighed on him heavily. *After all, it doesn't matter that we don't like each other, so long as we both love Che.*

She nodded, and in that brief motion he saw that she understood. Then she was stepping carefully over to Amnon, the only one of them who did not know what the Commonweal gambit actually entailed.

He knew Mantis-kinden, though, and after a few brief words she had him nodding agreement. '*I* will go, though,' he put in.

Tynisa jabbed a thumb at the sword-and-circle brooch she wore. 'This badge says *I* go.' She stepped past him and hauled herself out into the square stretch of greying sky that the hatch delineated, holding her sword high.

One arrow, right now, and the Commonweal trick hits the dirt, thought Thalric. But perhaps that raised weapon signalled Tynisa's intent, for no shaft feathered from the trees to seek her out.

And the problem with the Commonweal trick is that it isn't a trick at all. And surely those Mantids out there will have a few of those badges between them.

And, of course, you couldn't solve all the world's problems just by fighting a duel of champions. Not even the Mantis-kinden world worked like that. So Tynisa could buy Che a slightly longer life, but they were all still intruders in the Mantis heartland. There was only so much some Mantis swordsman's death could buy for them.

Or Tynisa's life. And Thalric was surprised to find that the prospect of Tisamon's daughter getting her surely justified come-uppance did not delight him the way it once had. *I am running out of peers. I shouldn't squander the few I have left.*

'Hear me!' Tynisa called out. 'Know me by the badge I wear. Are any of you bold enough to meet me?'

Thalric waited, still half-expecting that arrow, but then Amnon grunted, 'Someone comes.'

A lone, lean figure stepped out into the clearing, and Thalric wondered if that same wariness – of a sudden and treacherous shot – had affected their enemy as well. *Even Mantis-kinden must fear a bad death.* The woman who stepped forwards had a bow in one hand, but no arrow to it, and she looked up at Che curiously.

'For entering our forests, you will die,' the Nethyon declared, her voice clear and sharp. 'And for being of our enemy's kinden, you must die. For being of that kinden, and *worse*, death is better than you deserve.' She looked up at Tynisa fiercely. 'And yet you bear the badge . . . I see Parosyal on you, halfbreed.'

'I earned this on the island,' Tynisa agreed. 'I was accepted there. No words of yours can strip me of my right to bear the sword and circle.'

Thalric expected an angry response, but the Mantis woman's shoulders sagged, and he could almost put the words into her mouth: *What is the world coming to?* For a long time she just stood there, looking up at Tynisa, at the unforgivable adulteration of Mantis ways that she represented, and at the badge she also bore.

She would rather we had just shot her, Thalric guessed.

'Let it be at dawn,' Tynisa declared, when it was plain that the woman was not going to say anything. 'And I claim as trophy the Beetle woman your people have taken, she is the victor's prize. Not one drop of her blood must be shed, until we have fought.' She said the words boldly, but Thalric was already trying to plan for her failure: *How can I get Che out of this mess?* And, furthermore, he knew that Tynisa was fully aware he would be thinking just that. *So Mantis honour is a blade that only cuts one way, is it?*

'You speak of the great magician?' the Mantis woman asked.

Tynisa hesitated, but Maure spoke up: 'Yes! That is who we mean!'

'We don't have her,' the Nethyen said slowly. 'We are hunting her, and she may be killed, once she is found. If she is taken alive, we will kill her after we have killed you, but I cannot guarantee that she is not already dead – or that she will not die soon. We know better than to take risks when hunting a magician.'

Tynisa remained very still, but Thalric could see the fingers of her off-hand clawing at the rotting wood of the hatch's edge.

'Let it be dawn, though,' the Mantis woman finished. 'Why not?'

Terastos let his attention flow out between the trees, trying to project all his senses, into hunting out his enemies. Night was drawing in – his advantage, for his eyes were better than any Mantis-kinden's – and he neither could see nor hear any suggestion that the Nethyen were close by. Nor did his paltry magic suggest it

'Gone,' he whispered for Helma Bartrer's benefit. 'Gone off after the Maker girl and the others.'

The Beetle woman shifted, in a single motion making a remarkable amount of noise. They were almost completely buried amid a stand of bracken, its fronds curling almost to man-height above them, but every time Bartrer moved their entire hiding place shuddered as if the wind was at it.

'Oh, they clearly know who's important,' the woman said acidly. 'The Maker girl and her newfound heritage, yes. Not us.'

'Thankfully,' Terastos added. 'Come full night, I'll see what trail I can find. We can catch up with them . . . if they got away, that is.'

'I have a feeling that Che Maker is quite safe. There was a purpose in her coming here. Not necessarily the purpose she assumed,' Bartrer put in.

The Moth turned to her. 'You're well read, for a Collegiate.'

'I've been studying the old ways since before you were born,' Bartrer boasted. 'And I might not understand what the Maker girl *is* now, or how she does it, but I can read between the lines.'

'And what is your scholarly conclusion?' Terastos enquired somewhat archly.

'Argastos *wants* her here.'

He turned to her, wide-eyed. 'You think?'

'I told you, I've read enough to know some scraps of history about this place. I only wish I'd got to visit here when there wasn't a *war* going on to complicate things. History books, yes, but a scholar can't live off books forever. There was an Argastos once, and I believe that there is an Argastos still, somehow, some shadow of him.'

'You're a remarkable Beetle,' he conceded.

'Not as remarkable as Che Maker, it's true,' she allowed bitterly, 'but I do my best.' She rammed her dagger up under his ribcage with all the force she could muster, right up to the hilt, so that what emerged from his lips was not a cry but only blood.

She struck two, three more times, and made a sorry mess of the task, too. She was, after all, an academic and not a habitual killer.

Then she wanted to retch, to cast aside the knife and retreat from her horrible handiwork, but she knew that time was of the essence.

'Argastos,' she said, for even though she possessed no power, she had still learned that names were power among the Inapt. *If I go through the motions well enough . . .?* 'Argastos, this is yours, this blood. I have no altar, no icon. Take his life, though. It is my gift to you. Argastos, I am weak. I am the last of my line, the dregs of a once proud lineage. In times long past my family were loyal followers of your kinden. We were your servants and your slaves, Argastos, and that was our purpose and our place in the world. But we have lost our meaning, generation on generation, and now I *know* I am just a weak and empty vessel, but *please*, there must be enough – some last spark of the old ways in me – that you can hear my words. Argastos, I shed his blood, a *magician*'s blood, for you. Please, please, please let me in.'

Her head jerked up. *Was that . . .?* Had she heard some faint voice on the wind, something distant as a dream?

The night was coming on, though. It was time for dreams.

She stood up, hands still dripping with Terastos's blood, and walked out from among the ferns.

And into another forest, another place.

Twenty-One

I've had this conversation before, on a smaller scale. Not a reference to Laszlo's size, but here were Balkus and Sperra, freshly arrived from Princep Salma, both complaining about exactly the same man.

'What do you expect me to do?' Stenwold asked them.

Balkus folded his arms. 'I don't know. Something. Thinking of what to do is supposed to be your strong point.'

Stenwold crossed to the window of his current office, staring out over his city, with special reference to the scars of the bombing, the conscripted soldiers below being taught battle formation, the factories turning out Stormreader parts and new artillery for the walls. *This is what my home has become.*

'Seriously, Master Maker,' Balkus persevered from behind him, 'it's an attack on Princep's sovereignty, is what it is. He just about annexed us on behalf of Sarn. You've got to *do* something.'

'Why me?'

'I can't think who else that man might listen to,' Sperra put in, speaking from around Balkus's waist level.

Stenwold took a deep breath. 'He is the military leader of my city's foremost ally. He is dedicated to fighting the Wasps. What am I supposed to say? Do I tell him we're not his friends any more because of one girl?'

'One what?' Sperra and Balkus exclaimed almost together, high and low like two-part harmony.

For a moment Stenwold lost track of the present conversation. He had been making do with perilously little sleep this last tenday. *Not the girl this time, that was Laszlo.* 'For just one city. Princep Salma. Do I call off the alliance?'

'Threaten to do it,' Sperra insisted.

'And he'll know I'm bluffing, and all I'll achieve is to alienate the Sarnesh.'

'Then *don't* bluff!' Balkus had his turn now.

At that, Stenwold turned round, sitting back on the windowsill. Something in his expression tapped the big Ant's anger and drained it, leaving the man almost fearful.

'It would be a bluff, because we cannot afford to do without Sarn,' Stenwold said simply. 'They cannot do without us, it's true, but our need is mutual. It's an alliance, after all.'

'But it's wrong,' Sperra said, sounding almost childlike.

'We *need* to win this war, Sperra. We need to defeat the Empire, or what has it all been for? We need to . . . somehow we need to bring this to a close. I'm being frank with you. Believe me, Sarn could go much further down that path, and I'd still back them. I have to.' And good sense told him to stop there, but his mouth continued speaking. 'And a lot of people would ask whether Princep should not be expected to fight to defend its freedom.'

Balkus stared at him. 'They came to my city and they turned my people into their soldiers, under their orders, at their command. How is that different from the Auxillians of the Empire?' And then, before Stenwold could riposte: 'Maker, I thought we were friends. Is this it, then? Were we only ever just hirelings of yours? To be cast off when you don't need us?'

Of course not.

It's not like that.

You're not seeing the whole picture.

Balkus, just see sense for once. This is bigger than . . .

But Stenwold said none of those things; he just looked at Balkus and Sperra and said nothing at all, with no real idea of how cold and hostile his expression might have become. He saw

Balkus balling his fists, Balkus the Ant mercenary, with a sword at his belt and a nailbow slung over his shoulder.

But he knew Balkus. The Ant was no danger to him. They were friends, after all.

The Sarnesh renegade's face twisted in some strangled expression obviously taught to him by living amongst other kinden. Then Sperra was tugging gently at his arm, her eyes regarding Stenwold sadly.

'Bye, War Master,' she said. 'We'll leave you to your war.' She did not even remind him of the time the Sarnesh had tortured her on his account. Not a word, not a facial tic to recall it, and yet the thought might almost have leapt straight from her mind to his. And as for Balkus: the Ant had led Collegium's own forces in the last war, had been a hero to the people of Stenwold's city.

But I don't need them now. I need Tactician Milus and the Sarnesh. So he simply watched them go, the two of them, and knew that he had betrayed them utterly, unreservedly.

Tactician, we have each considered your plans.

Milus waited, standing on the battlements of Sarn, whilst all about him a city was preparing for war. Not an army but a city. Every Ant-kinden became a warrior in time of need, and now the artisans, the labourers, the merchants among his people were being kitted out with hauberk, crossbow and shortsword, forming a citizen militia to hold the walls and support the main army.

His mind was linked with the Royal Court, the King and the other tacticians, those who had given him oversight of the campaign against the Empire. That they were not instantly agreeing with him was a point of concern, but he allowed them time. They had shown their faith in him when they appointed him. His was a rare mind for an Ant, able to chew over many problems at once, able to see unusual solutions to difficult problems – and often to simplify those problems by tearing right through them where a lesser man might get mired in detail.

We could have done with the Collegiates pressing their advantage after they drove the Second off, one of Milus's peers mused. *A relief column from the Beetles would be very welcome now.*

For the record, the Collegiates have done their best with what is available to them: superior artifice and inferior warriors, Milus stated firmly. It was not his place to speak thus, but he had little care for propriety now. It was all part of that same eccentricity of mind that saw some Ants exiled and a very few raised high. He had made few friends and yet, to date, nobody could disagree with his methods or his results.

Within the mental space between him and the Court hovered a dream of their forces, represented simply and surely: the Sarnesh main army, the citizen militia, the auxiliary militia from the Foreigners' Quarter, the makeshift warriors from Princep – present but palpably unhappy to be so – and several hundred Mynan warriors who had fled the fall of their city – basically the great majority of their remaining land army. Of the non-Sarnesh forces, it was only those same Mynans that Milus had any great faith in, and even then they were an expendable resource. They would fight well, but their long-term aims did not necessarily chime with those of Sarn. Best therefore to spend them now.

We cannot see that there is anything more that can be done. We have gathered all we can, made every preparation. That was the voice of the King himself. All about Milus, the wall was crowded with engines, every piece of artillery mounted and ready to strike at the enemy as they approached. Much of it was antiquated, but Milus was bleakly aware that this would not matter, because even the most modern Sarnesh engines possessed only a fraction of the range of the new Imperial machines, if the Mynans could be believed.

So, therefore, attack. A bitter but inescapable conclusion, the same decision that had won the last war, and then cost them so dearly at Malkan's Folly.

Beneath the ground stretching before Sarn, the ant-nest was digging at the behest of its Art-gifted handlers: creating a network of reinforced tunnels with sally points ready for Sarnesh troops

305

to spring out of, into the midst of the enemy, and some of those tunnels ran for miles. Explosive mines had been set, as well, and a large force of Sarnesh scouts and wildsmen was already lying in wait, hidden as best they could in the hope of catching the enemy in the flank once battle was joined. The Imperial advantage in technology would have to be matched by Sarnesh superiority in discipline and organization.

I have done my best, he reflected, in that quiet corner of his mind fenced off from all others. *Circumstances have been inopportune, but I have played the hand I was dealt as well as anyone could.*

If the Mantis-kinden had only held firm, if the Moths had not lost control of their Nethyen lackeys, then this would all be very different. Burdened with a hostile northern front, the Wasps would be far slower to advance; and the Ancient League and Sarn together could have taken them, just as they had at Malkan's Folly the first time. But the Nethyen had turned, and now Milus was having to expend Sarnesh blood in the forest just to make sure that the Wasps did not gain control of it. He had read Sentius's reports, that it was becoming a bloody business in there – for the Wasps and for Milus's soldiers, but most of all for the locals. They were falling on one another as though they had been waiting five hundred years for this opportunity. *Could they not have waited one year more?*

And yet even there he had done his best. He had reinforced the Etheryen and there was still some chance that battle would be won, although by that time there might not be enough Mantis survivors to make useful allies. He had even sent that deranged Beetle girl in, Maker's niece. The Mantids obviously respected her somehow, and surely that had been the right thing to do for she could hardly make matters worse.

And of course there was his own 'special adviser' regarding the Inapt: the Fly halfbreed Lissart, as her real name was. Milus spared her a thought, incarcerated now in the secure cells beneath the Court. She was an intriguing, damaged creature. The interrogator's art had yielded a surprising bounty of Imperial practice and information from her but, being an erratic little monster, there were still secrets to plumb there, especially as to who might have sent her to spy on him in the first place. However, if this battle could be won, there would be both the time and the machines to fillet out what she knew. She could be a valuable asset indeed if the war could be carried further east.

If he could defeat the Empire in front of Sarn.

I have done all within my power.

And still the Eighth Army was drawing closer, although constant Sarnesh ambushes had slowed its advance to a crawl. It was Milus's faint hope that Collegium might manage a decisive strike against the Second, and be able to send a force north just in time – perhaps some of their new orthopters to counter the crushing air power that the Empire was able to field.

And still final confirmation from the Court did not come. He badly wanted it to approve. He wanted his city's full confidence.

In the end, he realized that such total confidence simply did not exist. There was doubt and fear rooted deep in the Court. Not doubt in him, Milus – for he had truly done all that was possible to give his city every chance of survival. No, it was doubt in the odds, doubt that even all this mustered strength, all this strategy, could win the day. *They have taken Tark. They have taken Kes.* Those cities were the traditional enemies of Sarn, their peers who had for centuries held the balance of power in the Lowlands. Now the hungry Empire had swept the map clean.

Within the privacy of his own head, Milus considered the future. This was his hour, he knew, and he was history's man. In his own mind there could be no room for doubt. What was the use of it? The King and his Court wasted their thoughts on the possibility, or even the probability of defeat. To resist was all: to resist and to triumph, odds be damned. *I would rather see my city in ruins and every one of my people dead than for us to lose. If the Mynans thought like me, perhaps they would never have lost their city to the Empire. Or they would be dead, with their honour and pride still intact.*

We will win. Milus could countenance no other choice, if only because he would be dead himself before the Empire claimed his home. *And when we have won, when I have brought about that future, then Sarn will recognize me.* The current King had not been in office long, but he was no young man. Milus, strange and slightly disaffected Milus, had never been a contender for the throne but, with a victory over the Empire under his belt, who would say no?

I am only glad that I have lived to see times such as these. How I might have been wasted otherwise!

The Second Army's new arrivals very nearly failed to arrive entirely. A Farsphex and two Spearflights, they appeared at the tail end of a Collegiate air attack, in danger not so much from the retreating Stormreaders as from their fellow Imperials, who simply saw them as *enemy*. Only a rapid reassessment by the first attacking pilot, *after* his initial run, managed to call the rest off. Long before she landed, Bergild had already begun cursing the fools who let non-mindlinked aviators blunder about the sky.

The Collegiate air attacks had grown more and more frequent as the Second neared the city. They appeared twice, sometimes three times a day at random intervals, and occasionally at night, although the Beetles were plainly not keen on flying after dark if they did not have to. The link shared by the Farsphex pilots gave them a far better mental map of a dark sky. In response to this escalation, Tynan had his army march and camp in dispersed formations as much as possible, individual elements of it operating almost independently. The entire force covered square miles of countryside, with supplies being spread out across each individual infantryman, leaving only the remaining artillery pieces as tempting targets. Fly-kinden messengers shuttled constantly between the army's constituent parts, carrying orders to pick up the pace, to slow down, to pull in or fall back. Thankfully, the

Beetles had shown no signs of wanting to risk another field battle after the last one went so badly for them.

This new marching order slowed them a little, but they managed it, despite nobody having ever tried such an advance before in recorded history. *There are few forces in the world that could achieve this without simply disintegrating,* Tynan considered with a spark of pride. *Stab me, but I'm not sure which other* Imperial *armies could manage it, for that matter.*

He had an automotive available, but for the moment he was marching alongside his men – it was good for morale and it stopped him becoming a target. The illusion of being just another soldier was somewhat tarnished by the constant stream of Flies and Wasps who dropped down around him to report or to receive orders, but he did his best to pretend. *I remember when I used to do this for real.* And he did remember, but only just.

In the aftermath of the Collegiate attack, he saw the new arrivals being escorted down by Bergild's pilots, in slow looping circles over the far-spread army until they found a suitable landing site. Tynan eyed them: *News from home?* A mixed blessing normally, but right now he was desperate for some kind of explanation, some magic reversal of the picture that would present him with the tools for a successful siege of Collegium. He had insufficient air support, precious little artillery, and supplies by air and sea were easy targets for the Collegiate orthopters.

This must be it, he decided. 'Find me Cherten, Oski – and get me Captain Bergild, if she's down yet.'

Captain Vrakir of the Red Watch had a way of staring at Tynan that made the general's scalp itch. He had no need to present himself and salute, for the fact of his presence imposed itself gradually until it was impossible to ignore.

Tynan sighed. 'Sound a general halt and let the trailing companies catch up. Double watch for the Collegiates coming back.' And his messengers sprang away to pass on the word. Stopping an army so spread out was the hardest part. It was easy for hundreds of men to simply march off without realizing that they were inadvertently deserting.

He considered sending for Mycella, but he wanted to hear this for himself first. Under her scrutiny, he found his own ignorance of the Empire's wider plan a hard thing to bear.

He had his little court of officers assembled soon enough: all those he had called for save Bergild – and with Vrakir as well, unsummoned and unwanted but impossible to get rid of. The captain of aviators appeared at the last moment with the new guests in tow, and at first glance they did not seem to be the answer to Tynan's hopes. One was a young lieutenant with Red Watch mail, who sought out Vrakir and started murmuring to him without even acknowledging the general's presence. The other . . .

He was a tall, broad-shouldered man, but there his resemblance to a soldier of the Empire stopped. He had a sash dyed black and gold about his waist, but no other nod to the uniform. Instead he had a long leather coat, patched more than once, and a cuirass of chitin scales, as though the armourer's craft had not intruded these last few centuries on wherever he came from. A cord about his neck was strung with a selection of barbs and spines and shards that Tynan recognized as being trophies from dead animals. The man himself, though he might have passed for a civilized Wasp if he had been cleaned up and dressed properly, must be from the northern hill-tribes, the half-savages who still eked out a barbarous living in the way that Tynan's own great-grandfather might have done. He had a gaunt, unshaven face, and his pale hair was long and ragged and filthy.

He was not Tynan's idea of the man who might drive the enemy from the skies, nor was he the obvious solution to any other problem currently facing the Second Army.

'What is this?' the general demanded.

The newcomer managed an approximate salute. 'Captain Nistic, sir.' His voice was hoarse and scratchy, as though from disuse.

'*Captain?*' Tynan reined himself in before he said something unwise, but if this man had earned a captain's badge, then something had gone badly wrong back home.

'It should have been major, sir, but they wouldn't have it,' this Nistic agreed. Now he had spoken more than a couple of words, there was something definitely odd about him, something unhealthy that made Tynan uncomfortable. He made no eye contact, and it almost seemed that he was carrying on some other conversation inside his head. *And this was a captain!*

'General.' Vrakir broke away from his conference to step over to Nistic's side. 'Captain Nistic here is in charge of the force that Capitas is sending to defeat the Collegiate fliers.'

'Is he now?' Tynan stared at the two of them. 'Perhaps you could explain to us just how that's to be accomplished.'

'No, sir,' Vrakir said smartly. 'The captain's mission is one of utmost secrecy. Orders are that you simply meet Nistic and be informed that his troops are on their way. Estimated arrival is in a tenday, by which time I would think the Second will be outside Collegium's gates.'

With no air support or artillery and precious little capability of maintaining a siege. Tynan locked eyes with Vrakir. 'These are the Empress's orders?'

'I speak with her voice, sir,' the Red Watch captain declared, not forcibly but firmly. 'You are to bring the assault against Collegium, and their air forces will be dealt with.'

I should demand to see those orders, Tynan considered, but he knew there would be nothing written down. Perhaps the newly arrived lieutenant had not even brought any orders, but they had come to Vrakir from the same place all the rest of the Empress's words seemed to emerge from – some space within his own mind.

And yet when Tynan had complained to Colonel Cherten about the maddening influence of the Red Watch his intelligence officer had become very solemn very quickly. 'Don't cross them, sir,' had been his hushed advice. 'I hear word from Capitas –

they really are the Empress's voice there, now that she's off with the Eighth. You remember how it was with the Rekef at the end of the last war – men being arrested for treason, from soldier up to general, and most of them never to be seen again? And you remember how it was always the Rekef man you *didn't* see who was the dangerous one, how the open Rekef officers at least trod carefully? Well, the Red Watch are all out in the open, and even the Rekef's scared of them now – and, believe me, there's a whole mess of high-ranking Rekef who haven't been seen recently.' Cherten's eyes had been wide. 'A general's rank badge won't save you, Tynan, if you go against them. For me, I intend to do exactly as they say, just as if they were the Empress herself.'

But Tynan was still a soldier, an officer, a man with thousands of subordinates depending on him. 'Unacceptable,' he stated softly, feeling Cherten twitch beside him at the word. 'I cannot go into battle blind.'

There was a physical force in Vrakir's stare that was now wrestling with his own, trying to get him to look away. But Tynan was an old campaigner, with the force of will to bend an army to his purpose, and he held firm. 'Once he has carried out his orders here, Captain Nistic is no doubt returning to his "troops", who are somehow approaching us without being spotted by either our own scouts or the Collegiates. Well, then: Captain Bergild, can your pilots spare you a day's absence?'

The woman tensed immediately on being drawn into the confrontation, but she managed a 'Yes, sir,' because there was plainly no other suitable answer as far as Tynan was concerned.

'Good,' the general pronounced, still matching Vrakir stare for stare. 'Then you will take Major Oski and escort Nistic back to wherever he happens to be going. Our major of Engineers will take a look at whatever reinforcements we can expect, and report back to me. This is my order as a general, and if the Empress herself were here I'd tell her the same. I will win this war for her, if it can be won. I will take Collegium, if it can be taken. But I will *not* be crippled by my own side.'

He felt his palms itch for stinging, so kept his hands clenched into fists, noting how Vrakir was doing just the same. *And what a web of mutiny that would be, if we just killed each other stone dead.* He well knew he was sowing a great deal of trouble to harvest later, just as if he had gone about tweaking the nose of the Rekef back when they were at the height of their power and paranoia. But here and now, he could stand on one unshakable fact: he was the general of the Second. The Empire *needed* him more than it needed this cold-eyed man with his red badge. Let Vrakir nurse his grievances in silence and look to tomorrow. Today's victory was Tynan's.

'Very well, sir,' the Red Watch captain said softly, and finally blinked.

For a moment Tynan thought he saw uncertainty in the other man – a second of wondering, *Where did I get all that from?* But then his mask was back in place and Vrakir was taking a step back. 'Captain Nistic,' he stated. 'Make what preparations you need.'

'I'll have orders for the quartermasters right enough, and the engineers,' the Hornet-kinden officer pronounced. His expression was still weirdly distant, as if the sparring match between Vrakir and the general had passed him by.

'And, Major Oski, before you leave, I want to have your brightest artillerist brief me on our best approach to damage Collegium's walls and engines,' Tynan instructed, mentally adding, *what little we have left.* 'Get me one of the Sentinel handlers, too. It's about time they started to earn their keep.'

'So,' Oski ventured, as the group of officers set about their individual orders, 'your 'thopter's bomb hold, or whatever, can it fit me and a Bee-kinden?'

'Your captain?' Bergild asked, a little amused. 'It'd be cosy. You'd not keep many secrets from each other, but yes.' As they headed off towards the nearest band of engineers, who had gathered to inspect some damage to one of the remaining greatshotters, she levelled a shrewd stare down upon him. 'Are you and he . . . Ant-lovers?'

Oski stopped and stared up at her. 'It's nothing like that,' he snapped. 'We've just been through a lot and, the way things are going around here, I don't want to get back and find something's happened to him.'

She spread her hands. 'It's no big deal to me, Major. I know they're meant to whip you for it, the rules say, but I grew up amongst soldiers and I know it goes on.'

'Well, you think whatever you want, *Captain*,' Oski replied pointedly, before hailing one of the engineers. 'Lieutenant Brant, compile a report on precisely what engines we can still field for the general, will you? With special reference to the fact that we won't stand a hope against Collegium's bloody walls.'

The man he had singled out looked mutinous, but saluted, and Oski spared no more time on him, already setting off on his next errand. Bergild saw the way the other engineers stared at his departing back, then hurried to catch up.

'Always angling for the love of your subordinates?'

'I'm a Fly-kinden and a major, and they're never going to swallow that one easily. If I was regular army, I'd have been stabbed in the back during action by now. But it's different in the Engineers: if you're good at your job, then they have to respect you. A strong grasp of artifice is too precious to waste. How'd you think the old Colonel-Auxillian got away with it?' Oski grinned. 'Curse me, but he was a fine man to learn the trade under. A real bastard, but you could pick up more just by walking in his shadow than sitting in any classroom back in Capitas. And now he turns up again on the Exalsee, Lord of the Iron Glove, eh?' He chuckled. 'I like that. Man's done well for himself.'

Bergild made a noncommittal noise, but by then they had reached two of the great articulated shells belonging to the Sentinels – the new war-automotives built for the Empire by that same Iron Glove Cartel. Even at rest they looked imposing, segment after overlapping segment of formidably durable armour making that high-prowed woodlouse shape with its single blank eye that served as the cover for a leadshotter barrel. Twin piercers, mounted low at the front, gave the impression of blunt and vicious mandibles, and the whole was mounted on ten jointed legs controlled by a ratiocinator that translated the driver's controls into smooth, almost organic motion.

Though not 'driver', for the term used was handler, as if the Sentinels had crossed some fine line from mere metal into something that lived and thought.

'Hoi, you two!' Oski called. The handlers turned to him in unison: a pair of Bee-kinden from some lengthily named city on the Exalsee, with closed, dark faces. Unsurprisingly, they did not mix with the Imperial forces, and the Wasps did not come near them out of respect for the murderous devices they commanded. The distance that surrounded them was more than that, though, for they almost never spoke even amongst themselves. They had no dealings with anyone save to draw rations, and seemed barely more approachable than the machines that they tended.

'General wants to see one of you, don't care which,' Oski told them. 'I reckon he's going to put you through your paces, so maybe you'd better think about what your toys can do when we reach the Beetle city, hm?'

The two men gave him identical stares, then one of them nodded and marched off without a word.

Oski shrugged. 'I'll go get Ernain.'

Bergild nodded; the flat regard of the remaining Sentinel handler did not encourage her to linger. 'I'll come with you,' she decided. 'They're already refuelling my 'Sphex, so I'm just baggage until we set off.'

As they left the shadow of the Sentinels, Oski jerked a thumb backwards. 'You've worked it out, surely – what's up with them?'

She nodded soberly. 'I've heard that mindlinking turns up in Bees about as often as with Wasps – which is to say, not often. The Iron Glove was obviously thinking along the same lines.'

'And if we managed to spot it, then it'll be common knowledge back at Severn Hill,' Oski agreed, naming the headquarters of the Engineering Corps. 'The Colonel-Auxillian's name is on more than a few people's lips since he came back from the dead, and not in a good way, either. I hope he knows what he's doing . . . Hoi, Ernain!'

Midway into a hand of cards with some of the Quartermaster Corps, the Bee-kinden looked up.

'Finish up,' Oski told him. 'We've got a flight to make.'

Twenty-Two

'She's alive.'

The silence within the ruined airship had grown and grown, as the light outside waned, and Maure's words, quiet as they were, made everyone start. For some time the halfbreed woman had been sitting cross-legged, eyes closed and oblivious, whilst the other three took wordless watches at the hatch in case the Nethyen decided that waiting until morning was not the Mantis way.

Thalric's immediate reaction was to demand how she knew, but fighting that sort of question back was almost automatic now: he had gone off the edge of his map a long time before. Instead he just waited, leaving it to Tynisa to ask, 'Where?' From her sharp tone, Che's foster-sister was plainly ready to mount a rescue attempt the moment she knew where to go.

'Not that, not yet.' Maure shook her head. 'But she is out there, alive . . . not in pain, I think, or great fear.'

Tynisa stared at her angrily. 'Then magic *harder*!' she got out, before rounding furiously on Thalric when he snorted. 'You think this is *funny*?'

He met her stare levelly. 'I think it's completely nonsensical, but telling someone to "magic harder" is surely not going to help.'

Amnon, standing at the hatch, shifted a little, and for a moment they thought he had something to add. Then he just shook his head and concentrated again on his watch. No doubt things had been done differently in Khanaphes.

'Is there anything more?' Thalric asked carefully. Questioning a magician was not unlike dealing with a particularly secretive agent, he decided: you didn't know where they got their information from, nor would you ever understand their networks or their sources, but that did not mean that they could not tell you things. After that it was just a matter of weighing the information and sifting it for truth.

'I . . .' Maure's eyes remained closed, her entire body very still, but her tone was conversational. 'I am not a great seer: my training lies elsewhere. Still, I have some of the craft and I am trying to find where the web centres . . .'

'Surely you can just cast about until you find her – or a trail leading to her, or something?' Tynisa complained.

'It's not like that. Tracking someone, from their past steps to their present location, well, there are trades to help you there, but magic is by no means a good one. From the present to the future, though, where Che is going to be . . .'

Thalric found himself sharing a glance with Tynisa. 'Explain, if you can,' he prompted.

'I never thought I'd be having this conversation with one of the Apt,' Maure remarked drily. 'But you've been in Che's shadow long enough, and over in Khanaphes I think that not understanding and not believing are still two different things. Also . . .' But whatever she was about to say about Tynisa – Inapt but raised by the Apt – went unspoken. 'I have a rock, say, and you know that I will throw it. Can you tell me where it will land? No. But you know it will come from my hand, so you could try predicting its future. But the further the rock travels away from me, the further from your prediction of its landing it is likely to end up. Well, then, try to turn that inside out and you have a magician predicting the future.' At the pointed silence that followed she sighed again and went on, 'I can find where Che is going to be – she is significant, and her actions will be significant. When she exerts her power the world bends around her, and I can pare down the future to that moment – where the likelihood is that

Che will be, and where she will act. But I cannot tell you the path that will bring her there, so it is like the rock in reverse – I know where it will land, but not from where it is thrown. Perhaps on my best day I could track it back a little, but here . . . the landscape is too heavily folded and twisted. More, whoever she is with has some magic and Art of their own that conceals them, and her. But I can see where they will take her in the end . . . Soon, tonight.'

'Where?' Tynisa demanded, and it was plain that ideas of ambush were already in her mind.

There came a sound from Amnon, merely a wordless indication that he had seen something. Immediately afterwards, Maure pointed. 'There.'

'What is it?' Thalric demanded, ducking over to stand at the man's shoulder.

'Fire,' Amnon said flatly, his snapbow resting on the hatch rim.

Thalric peered out into the darkness, where a burgeoning red glow was immediately evident, some distance away through the trees.

'They're burning the forest down?' he suggested. *Must be the Empire, surely.*

'Burning something,' Amnon confirmed. 'I don't see it spreading.'

'There,' Maure said again, and Tynisa glanced back to her.

'That's where . . .?'

'It is a Mantis hold,' Maure said firmly. 'That is where Che will be.'

'They're going to burn her?' Tynisa hissed.

'They would not. She is not fit for that,' Maure told her. Then added hurriedly, 'It is the Mantis way. Fire is the warrior, destroyer and purifier. A fire such as that is meant only for their honoured dead. The Nethyen are holding a wake.'

'A little premature when we're not done fighting,' Thalric suggested.

'The Mantis-kinden are never done with fighting,' she told him bluntly.

'Of course, I forgot. If it involves Mantis-kinden, it's all about death,' he spat tiredly. Tynisa shot him an angry look, but he weathered it, unrepentant.

'There was more to their ways, in the past. In the Commonweal there still is. But when they are faced with doubt, with change, or with loss, it is the old certainties that they fall back on, and none more so than death,' Maure pronounced. 'They mourn a thousand years of decline. They have given up looking to the future, for they cannot find their way towards it. The coming of the Empire has only brought them sooner to a destination they have been approaching for centuries. So they burn their dead and sing their songs for the last time.' Her voice had grown ragged and distant, and Thalric saw that she was shaking slightly.

'Maure!' he snapped, in his best officer's voice, and she twitched and opened her eyes.

'Thank you,' she whispered. 'The forest reeks of their despair. It can be . . . hard to stay clear of it.'

Thalric wanted to say something like 'I can imagine', but it was so abundantly plain he could not, that any consolation would be absurd. 'Well, we know something now that we didn't before,' he concluded brightly. 'We know where they'll bring Che tonight – guest of honour at a mass funeral.'

'Fine,' Tynisa agreed. 'So that's where we'll go.'

The other three regarded her doubtfully, and she faced them down as though they were the enemy.

'I am to fight their champion tomorrow. This badge and my sword have won that for us. Tonight, Che will be taken to their hold. Tonight we will meet her there, to get her out if we can, or to show her that we are there for her if we cannot. I will not sit out the night in this rotting coffin if we know where Che will be.'

'They'll kill us,' Thalric insisted.

'They will – *tomorrow*. After the duel they'll kill us. Probably they'll find some reason to try even if I win. So I'm going to walk into their hold and wait for Che, because I don't see that there's much to lose in doing so. You stay here if you want.'

'Maure?' Thalric pressed, because the magician seemed to have the best-honed survival instincts of anyone there, save for himself.

'They will not kill us out of hand, I think. The duel is too important to them. But their despair is very heavy. It may make them act in strange ways. Mantis honour has not fitted in with the world well in living memory, and now they have to twist and strain it to breaking point to adapt to the events around them. It is hard to say what they might consider the honourable course of action.'

'So you're staying?' Thalric confirmed.

'I'm going,' Maure said. 'Because, once Tynisa leaves here, there is nothing stopping the Nethyen from killing the rest of us. She is our champion. They don't need the rest of us.'

Tynisa's expression was openly defiant. 'Stand aside, Amnon. I'm going.'

'We all are,' the Khanaphir replied heavily, slinging his snapbow.

'She is Amalthae,' the Mantis-kinden answered.

Che nodded cautiously. It was not quite true to say that the great insect was looking at her – for its attention seemed entirely devoted to cleaning the razor-sharp barbs on its forelimbs, one by one. But its eyes were vast, all-seeing. There were few places in this little clearing where Che would not become an object of that peripheral scrutiny.

'And who are you?' she asked him. The Mantis frowned, as though surprised that anyone should wish to know. He was a long-boned man, perhaps ten years Che's senior, or perhaps not even that. His face was as expressionless as an Ant's, and for the same reason. He wore no armour, only loose garments dyed in forest colours, while a bladed gauntlet was folded into his belt.

'Ceremon, I was called,' he said, pausing over the name so that she wondered just how long it had been since someone had actually called him anything at all save for Amalthae's . . . what?

'Her companion?' she ventured.

'Her consort,' he corrected.

'You have the Art of Speech?' As well as being constantly under that faceted sight, there was no place in this clearing that would not be within the lightning reach of the creature's arms. When those limbs had snatched her up from the ground and drawn her close to the mantis's scissoring mandibles she had believed it was the end. Something other than hunger had been behind the strike, however – something other even than Mantis-kinden hatred of intruders, it seemed, for here she was, still alive.

Ceremon just nodded. Like Amalthae, he did not look at her directly much, yet was always aware of where she was and what she did. Every small move of hers froze the pair of them for the briefest moment as they recalculated the quickest way to catch or kill her if that proved necessary. So far, Che had given them no excuse.

'So . . . when do the rest get here?' she tried.

'No others. Just us.' Amalthae went entirely still, even her antennae barely swaying, and Ceremon was suddenly motion-less too, fading deeper into himself so that Che's sense of his *presence* – for all that he stood right before her – almost vanished. Had she come walking into the clearing just then, she would have noticed neither man nor insect.

And died, probably. She tried to project her own mind. *What is it they've heard? Tynisa? Thalric?* But she found no resonance of her friends, no minds at all nearby, only the convoluted density of the forest itself.

Something moved, beside and behind her. *Another mantis?* But she had a feeling she would not have heard it, if it was. Despite herself, she flinched, retreating towards the known killer and away from the unknown.

She saw something glitter, a black carapace and busy legs, as a beetle pushed itself between the close-grown trees, half scuttling, half climbing. It had large, round eyes and jaws like twin blades, a world away from those patient draught animals she had seen working on Collegiate farms as a child. Longer than she herself was, and a hunter in its own right, it regarded her fiercely, working through the small number of choices its mind allowed it.

Had she the Speech-Art she could have calmed it and turned it aside. As it was, she thought she might find some way to accomplish the same result through magic, but she knew that she had no need. She was watched over by something more terrible than this armoured beast.

It went for her, breaking into a run that would have covered the ground in seconds save that, barely halfway towards her, it was gone. Che, who had been expecting the move, was still surprised by it, the beetle barely seeming to exist in the space between the ground and the mantis's closed arms, before Amalthae's mouthparts sawed neatly into the insect's head and stilled its frantic struggles with surgical grace.

Ceremon took a deep breath, releasing his Art and returning to the foreground of her attention. Che had formerly understood that the Speech Art fell mostly one way: commands issued and very little save for basic impulses communicated in return. She felt that between this man and his consort there existed a more profound connection.

'You haven't killed me yet,' Che observed, as calmly as she could after that predatory display.

'No.' Ceremon stared into the forest. 'But you are right to think it. My people would have killed you if they had caught you. Either your blood on the forest floor there and then, or a proper bloodletting to strengthen the forest, at one of our places.'

'But not you? Are you waiting till your consort gets hungry enough?'

'Amalthae . . .?' Ceremon frowned for the first time. 'Because of her, I am not as my people are. It is difficult to . . .' He cocked his head, so plainly listening to the beast beside him that Che looked up, expecting to meet a sentient gaze, but Amalthae continued to eat daintily, and spared her no direct attention.

Ceremon nodded as if conceding some unheard point. 'All kinden derive from their totem,' he explained. 'Each has its mystery, some easy to follow, some not.' He glanced up at the feeding beast again, then down at the ground. 'To the Beetle: endure. To the Ants: hold to one another. To the Moths: mastery of the mysteries of the dark. And so . . . our own path . . . To the Mantids: fight. It sounds simple, surely?' He spread his hands. 'And yet we have fought and fought since the very first of us, unyielding – proud and bloody – and where are we? It would have served us better if our mandate had been to *win*.'

'I've never heard a Mantis speak like this,' Che admitted.

'Nor will you. These are *her* thoughts,' he said sadly. 'I only couch them in a way you may understand. We have fallen short, always, of our ideals, and now time has become an enemy we cannot fight, and in their desperation my people have come to the last twist on the Mantis path.'

'Becoming allies of the Wasps,' Che observed.

Ceremon shrugged. 'The Lady of the Wasps came to my people and promised a return to the old dark times, the simple times when what we were was sufficient; when what we were meant something. Some of my people believed her, or at least held to some small hope that she spoke true. And others . . . more knew that we would never receive our birthright from the hands of the Wasps, but that the simple fact of her standing there and making such an offer showed how the world had truly turned, once and for all, and that we had outlived our time in it. These, too, counselled that we should join with the Wasps, but not for any silver future. We should join with the Wasps so that we might make the world run red – or some small part of it – a final battle, a struggle to the death. And afterwards . . . for us? Nothing afterwards. No Nethyen, no Etheryen . . . Even as the Felyen to the south have passed from this world, so we would follow—'

'The Felyen?' Che demanded. 'They fought . . .?'

'They are gone,' Ceremon confirmed softly. 'No blood of theirs remains unshed. They have carved their own gate and stepped through it, and no more shall they be known. There are many of my people who would see that as a good thing, something to be desired.'

'But not you?'

He met her eyes briefly. 'If not for Amalthae, I might think it, but she . . . she shows me that we have strayed from our path – no, that the path is too hard, and the ways we have fallen into are because we have strived and failed. That so many of us now see extinction as preferable to finding a new way is proof of that, she says.'

Che nodded carefully. 'And where do I come in?'

'You are able to speak with the same authority as the Lady of the Wasps. We know this, for Amalthae can see the brand upon you, even now. If you demand it, my people will listen.'

'Your people will kill me.'

'Perhaps, but first they will listen. Amalthae says speak with them. Guide them.'

'To what end?' This time Che was addressing the great mantis directly, and it paused in its devouring, only the abdomen of the beetle left intact.

'She says . . . she says she wishes you to save us. She says you are the only one whose words might be heard. She says . . . she has lived long and I am her third consort. Her kind . . . we are her children, and she fears for us.' The man's soft voice began to quaver. 'She does not want us to go.'

Sergeant Gorrec of the Pioneers watched the Empress as she spoke with Tegrec the Turncoat and with that gangly old Woodlouse, noting all the signs – ones he was more than familiar with, of superiors in disagreement. *Of all possible places, this is not the one for argument.* Not that anyone would openly defy the

Empress, of course, but she was asking questions they could not answer – or maybe she did not like the answers they gave her.

The other two Pioneers huddled close, Icnumon and Jons Escarrabin. The Beetle looked just about how Gorrec felt – namely miserable and lost and worried. He clutched his snapbow to him like a talisman. The halfbreed, though: Icnumon had changed when they . . . well, Gorrec couldn't say precisely what they had done, but things were definitely different.

They had passed through into what seemed somehow a different forest. The trees grew closer, were more gnarled, their branches a solid interlacing canopy ahead, whilst the undergrowth was now shot through with briars, making progress tiring and painful. There was almost no sign of animal life – Gorrec and his fellows were tried woodsmen and knew what to look for. They spotted only the occasional mark or track that Icnumon identified as the killer mantids. The air was dim and curiously obscuring as though some shreds of fog remained even at noon, and the colours . . . nothing here was bright. Sounds were muted and, in the long silences, it seemed as if there were other noises just at the edge of hearing, a whispering and a murmuring.

Only one of the Empress's female bodyguards had made it this far, the Sarnesh and the Etheryen having accounted for the rest. The woman sat by herself, withdrawn and wordless; the Wasp soldier, Ostrec, seemed little better. Even the armoured man that Seda called Tisamon seemed changed here, a troubled introspection evident in his immobile stance.

Gorrec shifted closer to Icnumon, meaning to question him, but the halfbreed's look warned him off.

'If I could tell you, I would,' the man said, 'but there are no words.'

Then there was a sharp sound – a *real* sound – and the three Pioneers leapt to their feet, weapons to hand. Tegrec was sitting down, one hand clamped to his face, Seda standing over him.

'No more discussion,' the Empress declared. 'You will follow my lead or you will die here.'

'Your Majesty,' came Tegrec's thin voice, 'Gjegevey and myself, we have both sought for the path, and in doing so we have seen where it leads. Majesty, this is not . . . this is what we wished to *avoid*! The Seal . . . it is *here*. No records, no stories even, but—'

'You pair of blind fools,' Seda snapped back. 'Of course there is a seal here. Which war did Argastos win? Which enemy was he victorious over, except the Worm? And you thought that they would just set him as a guard in the wilderness? Oh, there are seals in many places, but Argastos guards the greatest.'

Gorrec would not have credited the paunchy Wasp turncoat with much courage, but holding his argument against the Empress must have required all of it. 'But we brought you here . . .'

She planted a booted foot on his chest, her hand out with palm directed towards his face. The old Woodlouse made a convulsive, aborted movement as though about to intervene, then stepped back.

'I know you sought to divert me from the Worm by dangling Argastos before me. I sought advice, and this was yours. And you were right, for Argastos *is* power, and a power I had best claim before my sis— before that damned Beetle can do so. But if I cannot do so – if I must destroy Argastos, or if his power is truly nothing more than a shadow – then how convenient that I shall be in place to follow my original plan, hmm?'

Tegrec goggled up at her, but he had run out of words.

'And what about you?' she demanded of the old slave. 'Anything to say?'

Gjegevey shook his head and looked away.

Gorrec had been convinced that the robed Wasp was already a dead man, but Seda turned away from him, letting him stand up. 'This place still resists us,' she snapped. 'Even though Argastos himself tries to smooth the way, there is a will here that contrives a maze for us. Go find me the path, the two of you. Prove to me that you have value yet. Lead me to Argastos.'

Icnumon straightened suddenly, starting a pace forwards, then stopping.

'What?' Gorrec demanded. Not that any of them exactly liked it here, but the halfbreed was taut as a bowstring and jumping at shadows. Or at things that were very real but that Gorrec and Jons were unable to see. *Nasty thought.*

'Thought I saw . . .' Icnumon grimaced. 'A person. A Beetle woman.' He spoke the words quietly but Seda – a good fifteen feet away – whirled round instantly.

'You saw *what?*' she exclaimed, storming over. Behind her, Gorrec saw Tegrec get well out of the way, no more willing to help the Pioneers than they were to assist him.

Icnumon tried to mumble something and dismiss the matter, but Seda was staring at him and, whilst Gorrec was quite scared enough of the woman, his comrade plainly knew enough to be fully terrified.

'I thought I saw a Beetle, Majesty . . . a Beetle woman, just for a moment.'

'The girl is here *already?*' Seda demanded. Again, Gorrec thought she would lose hold of her temper and just kill the nearest target, but again she reined it in – an admirable trait in a commander, he had to admit.

'Wouldn't call her a girl, Majesty,' Icnumon said hoarsely. 'Older . . . going grey. Old as Jons's mother might be.'

Seda frowned. 'Then she's not . . .' It was plain that she made no sense of it. 'No matter,' she decided. 'We press on. If you see such a woman again, bring her down if you can. Kill her if you must.'

The Mantis-kinden were silent killers, of course, and there would be no warning when they struck. That was plainly what Thalric and Amnon were thinking, anyway, for Tynisa could read the tension in every move they made.

When the drum started beating, they jumped, poised to take

on the wave of killers that must surely be about to descend from the darkness.

She realized she had been expecting it. It was not loud, a soft, slow rhythm like a heart, and it spoke to her at a deep and primal level.

Thalric started speaking, some suspicious, nasty-minded comment no doubt, but she hissed him into silence. The glower of the fire lit up the woods ahead, yet always further through the trees as they approached, until it was revealed as a far greater blaze than they had expected. *But, then, they have many dead.*

When the singing started, she felt her own throat tighten with it, moments from joining in. There was no hint of words to it, and it felt older than speech to her: something preserved by the Mantis-kinden from the depths of time, and not heard by any outsider since the revolution. The last ebb tide of the old ways.

The voices, three of them, climbed like vines about each other, each with its own song, each complementing the others without seeming to intend it, as though three independent singers had somehow come together by impossibly prolonged coincidence. The voices soared, but never joyously, and the depths of their grief and loss stuck daggers into Tynisa, because she could share it. She had been born to it, and no amount of Collegium years could rid her of that burden, and that birthright.

She felt a hand on her arm: Maure, regarding her solemnly. *She understands. She has Mantis blood too.*

And Tynisa strode onward towards the blaze, drawing the rest in her wake. And they were already amongst the Nethyen, spread out amongst the trees with blades to hand, staring at these intruders, these unthinkable trespassers on their rites.

'No weapons,' Tynisa murmured, because her own rapier was clinging to its scabbard and showing no signs of leaping to her hand. 'Fists closed, Thalric.'

'These are Mantis-kinden,' he argued. 'Weapons and fighting are the only things they respect.'

'Then I'll let them kill you. Here and now, I say no weapons. There is more to my . . . to their kinden than you know.'

'Not *much* more,' he muttered, yet his sword stayed sheathed.

The Nethyen were approaching cautiously, from behind and on either side, but ahead there was only the fire. She could now see the singers, three women, old and young and middle-aged, their voices drifting into silence as the intruders stepped out into the clearing surrounding the blaze.

Bodies on the fire, of course, and Tynisa counted one short of a dozen corpses, and beyond the flames stood one of their idols, this one a ten-foot giant whose rotting wood was enlivened with bone, clusters of skulls giving it makeshift compound eyes.

She was aware of many eyes fixed on them, tens of Nethyen, seen and unseen, staring silently. She felt their despair – not outrage but *despair* – at this intrusion. The presence of the enemy here in their heartland confirmed to them what they had feared for some time now. She could read it fluently on each face. *The future is here for us. What else was ours alone, save the fire, save the blade's point? Are even these things robbed of their power and sanctity?*

They could not kill these outsiders, not yet, for they were bound by the duel, bound by their own agreement to stay their hands. And, despite Maure's fears, that code still held them. Instead they just stared, and Tynisa felt suddenly mean and guilty. This ceremony, this wake, it was all they had, more important to them than she could appreciate, and she had pushed in and denied them even that.

Then Maure knelt down by the fire, not far from the three singers, and drew a deep breath. And Tynisa reminded herself just what sort of magic the woman was skilled in.

She began to sing, not quite after the style that the Nethyen had given voice to, but something akin to it, and with words that Tynisa could now follow. Maure sang with her eyes closed, her frame as still as when she had been seeking out Che.

'Take wing, take wing,
Between the trees the horn is calling
It summons you
It summons you to your great battle
Look not back
For we shall come to you
And we shall bear your name
Until the day we meet once more
Take wing, take wing
The gates of night are open
And we shall bear your deeds
That they shall be known evermore
Go, warrior,
Go, great hunter,
Take wing, take wing.'

Maure paused, opening those strange, iris-less eyes. Other than the crackling of the flames, the forest was utterly stilled. Tynisa saw the necromancer's gaze shift, focusing on something that she herself could not discern, or perhaps just the smoke that shrouded the fire and twisted upwards towards the night sky.

A Mantis woman approached Maure, and Thalric and Amnon were both instantly on edge once more, but Tynisa put a hand up to calm them. What was offered was not sharp steel, but a cup.

Then the Mantis singers started up again, their song subtly different but still wordless, and something invisible that was all around them had been inverted like a coat, so that the strangers – the trespassers – were somehow *in* now, their passage bought by Maure's song, or by Tynisa's badge, or *something*.

When the chitin cup came to Tynisa, she drank deeply, and knew it for mead mixed with blood and bitter herbs – something distantly akin to the draught they had offered her when she earned her Weaponsmaster's brooch. It did not come to the two Apt men, and she sensed that was for the best. She could already feel her awareness shifting – in some ways sharpening, in others blurring – but who knew how Thalric and Amnon might take that? She glanced back towards them, seeing that the Wasp was plainly ill at ease, still suspecting a trap, a betrayal. *But why not, for that is the meat he has served others with for so long. Now he is slower to trust than the Nethyen themselves.* Amnon had sat down before the fire, though, and she saw tears glinting on his cheeks. Maure's song had included them all in this wake, and so it had included their dead also. Amnon stared into the flames and mourned his lost Praeda, as perhaps he had never been able to, before now.

And I? She had done her mourning back in the Commonweal. No weeping left for her now. The lack of it felt hollow within her, and worse was that she shared her dry eyes with Thalric. *If he ever had any tears, they were burned out of him long before we first met.*

Then the Wasp had twitched back, a movement sharp enough for half the Mantids near him to be instantly on their guard. His cry was lost amid the song but Tynisa read it on his lips.

'Che!'

Twenty-Three

'Do you see it?' Bergild demanded, the first words spoken in some time. Oski and Ernain, cramped together in a space not intended for two, had been bearing their discomfort stoically as the pilot followed the Red Watch machine towards wherever it was that they were going. Now, apparently, they had arrived.

Oski tried to crane past Ernain's shoulder to look down the length of the crawlspace leading to the cockpit, but could make out nothing, and said so loudly.

'I'll fly past,' Bergild called back. 'Get the side hatch open.'

'Seriously?'

'You've both got your wings, haven't you? Just open the cursed thing. You're going to want to see this!'

'Don't be so pissing cryptic, woman,' the Fly snapped, but Ernain was already fumbling at the catch, bracing himself against the walls to resist the sudden rush of wind trying to drag them both out.

For a moment Oski could see nothing but sky – then Bergild banked, and something incredible slid into view.

It was an airship, and the base model was one he knew well. This was a big cargo-hauler that had already seen service for twenty years and more, not unlike the vessels that were now attempting to keep the Second supplied. When the original had been constructed, its designers had cared for little save storage

space and not having it fall out of the air: certainly a more innocent age of warfare.

Some fool had been busy with this one, though. The broad
and rounded boat-like hull had been attacked savagely, and now
there were rows and rows of circular hatches studding the vessel's
exterior so densely that the entire ship looked as though it had
been hobnailed. Bergild let their craft drift closer, and Oski had
a fine view of them, hundreds of sealed ports each perhaps three
feet across. The effect was ugly and warlike and dangerous. And
useless.

'Oh, balls,' the Fly engineer cursed. 'Oh, piss on it. General
Tynan's going to have a fit.'

'It's a city-breaker, it must be.' Bergild had plainly been thinking
along the same lines. 'Bomb-chutes . . . or modified leadshotters, maybe. You could pulverize whole districts with the thing.'

'If you got it to fly over them,' said Oski in a horrified whisper.
'Oh, sod me, some bright spark's spent fifty thousand in gold
solving the wrong problem!'

'One look at that thing and the Collegiate fliers'll be all over
it. Or they'll be above it, rather, shredding the airbag and loosing
bombs,' the pilot agreed. 'I don't see any of those hatches pointing
up, after all. And there's no *way* my people can protect this thing.
It's huge, and the Collegiates'll see it just like we do. Nothing
we can do will pull them off it until they've dropped the cursed
thing right in Tynan's lap.'

'The stupid bastards,' Oski swore. 'Is that . . . Where's our
boy gone? Is that his craft landed on their top deck there?'

'It is.'

'Well we better go down after him, and see if someone can
tell us just what the hell they're playing at.'

Landing on the gondola of an airship was tricky, but nothing
to tax Bergild's skills, and she soon had them down neatly, facing
the Red Watch Farsphex in a somewhat confrontational way. The
three of them extricated themselves from their vessel and took
a moment to look about the deck.

Oski noted three distinct divisions of crew, none of which brought him much joy. There were a half-dozen Beetle-kinden who looked like Consortium aviators, men more used to cargo runs than any sort of fighting. Overseeing them were a trio of Wasps with Red Watch badges, all of whom were regarding the newcomers coldly. Lastly, Captain Nistic had gone to join a gang of men who looked every bit as wild as he did. Their gaze was scarcely more friendly than that of the Red Watch men, and the amused comments they muttered to one another were plainly at the expense of their visitors.

Oski found the other two instinctively drawing close to him, because this flying monstrosity did not seem like a healthy place to be. *Still, I'm the chief of Engineers for the Second Army and I don't care how big a secret this idiocy is supposed to be. I'm betting they can't afford to just do away with me.* He was not a gambling man by nature, but it was time to start measuring rank badges with these men, and to make them forget that he was only half their size.

'Who's in charge here?' he demanded.

Nistic took a few steps forward, looking down at the Fly-kinden as though he was some species of prey not usually worth the hunting, but it was the Red Watch lieutenant who spoke.

'Your general has forced us to allow your presence here, Major, but this is a classified matter. All you need to do is to go back and report to him that help is on its way.'

'Help?' demanded Oski. 'Lieutenant, this is . . . what is this? It's a bad joke. The Second has been attacked for tendays now, day in, day out, by a foe with superior air power, and one which'll make short work of our entire army once a siege begins. We've been promised some means of defending ourselves, of taking back the air!'

'And you shall have it, Major,' the lieutenant told him grandly. 'Tell your general so.'

Oski glanced up at his companions, feeling as if he and the

Red Watch man were simply having two quite separate conversations. 'I'm headed below decks,' he announced. 'I'm going to see how far this stupidity goes.'

'I'll show you myself, Major,' the lieutenant offered, with mocking smile. 'Please follow me, *sir*.'

'You keep your stinging hands ready,' Oski murmured back to Bergild. 'This reeks. First sign that it's a set-up, we're out of the nearest bomb-hatch, or whatever they are, and we'll take our chances.'

'My flier—'

'Your life, Captain. You can't requisition a new one of *those* from stores.'

'Yes, sir.'

Under Nistic's barbed gaze, they descended into the interior of the vessel, which turned out to be minute.

The entire innards had been reworked. Oski knew what he had expected from this pattern of vessel, but he found almost none of it. It was as though the interior of a far smaller gondola had been transplanted inside, offering narrow corridors and cabins, a galley and the engine room, all cramped enough to make a Fly-kinden feel at home. And no windows, save for portholes at the very rear, where the engines were. Everything else was as closed in as a cave.

'How do we get to the bomb deck?' Oski demanded, once they had traversed the entire little warren twice.

'There is no bomb deck,' the lieutenant told him smoothly. 'Have you seen enough, sir?'

'Enough is just what I haven't seen,' Oski insisted. 'There must be a way. How do we get the other side of this?' And he banged on the curve of the wall.

The gesture had just been to make a point: he had not expected anything to come of it. A moment after his small fist thudded against the wood, though, there was a sound. It froze them in their tracks, a deep rumble growling out from behind the wall, like the muted roar of some manner of engine which Oski had never encountered before. There was something about the pitch of sound, too – something that affected him at a deep and primal level. It spoke only one word to him: *fear*. Abruptly he was sweating in those claustrophobic quarters – afraid without understanding why – as that deep throbbing sound built and built . . .

And it multiplied. All around them, through that false wall, they heard a legion of voices, soft at first, but rising to an air-trembling thunder that shook the very substance of the ship.

Not leadshots, not bombs . . . Oski tried to think. *Machines? Some manner of machines designed to fight orthopters?* His head swam with half-formed ideas. *Can you make a flying machine without a pilot? Can they do that with ratiocinators, now? Or is the sound itself the weapon? Will this drive them mad, or shake their machines apart? What have we created here?* He found he did not know. His own trade had outstripped him.

By then he had his hands clamped to his ears, because the sound was virtually shaking the very air around them. But then someone was shaking his shoulder hard enough almost to batter him against the wall.

Ernain: he saw Ernain. The Bee-kinden looked ashen, his eyes as wide with fear as Oski had ever seen on any man – not just the instinctive reaction which this resonating pitch had struck in all of them, but more. Ernain plainly *knew* what was going on, and it terrified him beyond all reason.

Oski could see his mouth working and, although the words went unheard, he read: 'We have to get out of here! *Now!*'

Moments later the three of them were stumbling out on deck again, that terrible sound following them – and, at its heart, the laughter of the Red Watch lieutenant.

When the Second Army was approaching along the sea road, where its path curved south about the bay on its final leg to Collegium, it met the Vekken.

Repeated air attack meant that the army was still scattered, but Tynan had men watching out for a sortie from the city. The

Ant-kinden had been in place for days, though, concealing themselves in dugouts and holes and waiting with the silent patience of their kind, unsuspected until it was too late.

They let the airborne scouts pass over them, each hiding Ant almost blind, but together combining hundreds of little scraps and pinholes of sight to put together a picture of the world outside. When the main body of the Wasp force got close, the entire Vekken force, a good eight hundred Ant-kinden soldiers, attacked as one, springing out with crossbows and Collegiate snapbows and butchering every Wasp within reach.

The loose marching order of the Second Army meant that the casualties were lighter than might have been expected, but the Wasps could not bring their forces together to bottle up the Ants, not in the time they had. Though the Light Airborne did their best, they took heavy losses from the Vekken marksmanship, and were unable to contain the more heavily armoured Ants on the ground. Wasp orders were reaching parts of the Second Army piecemeal, and for over an hour this solid block of Ants effectively held off an army many times its own size.

By then someone had sent for the Sentinels, and the Vekken were well enough briefed to know that they had outstayed their welcome. Their formation disintegrated, spreading out into a far-flung net of Ants more efficiently than the Wasps had managed, but grouping in squads of twenty and fifty when threatened. They made short work of the miles to Collegium, and made the vanguard of the pursuing Light Airborne regret their diligence. Ant casualties totalled just under one hundred.

To the Beetle-kinden this was an education. Stenwold stood on the walls with the Vekken commander, Termes, knowing that two thoughts would dominate every Collegiate mind at that moment. Firstly, *Isn't it a good thing that the Vekken are on our side just now?* and secondly, *When did they learn to do that?* It seemed that defeat at the hands of mere Beetles could spur even the most insular of Ants to innovate.

The Second was bloodied. The Second was slowed. The army

was named 'the Gears', though, and it ground on, visible from the walls, marching south towards the great maze of earthworks that defended the city from its enemies.

Everything we have thrown at them – burning their orthopters over the city, all those air assaults, destroying their supply airships, the Felyen, the Vekken, and yet here they are.

Madagnus of the Coldstone Company had readied the wall artillery – the new magnetic bows with a range to match the greatshotters of the Empire – save that the Empire seemed not to have any left. The Collegiate attacks had devastated the enemy siege engines, and those losses did not seem to have been replaced. Stenwold was left to scan his telescope over the arriving enemy and think, *What do they know that we do not? Because, if I were in the position I see them in, I would not have come. Or is that because I am a Beetle, and sane, and these Wasps are so mad for battle they would throw themselves into a fire for it? Are they worse even than the Mantids?*

He heard Madagnus make a disgusted sound nearby, and glanced up. The cadaverous Ant had his own glass out and trained on the enemy.

'Far enough away that we'd fall short, by my calculation,' the man declared. 'I was hoping to give them a bit of fun, after they'd set camp.'

'And their own range?' Stenwold called over to him.

'They were a good two hundred yards closer when they set up their artillery last time,' Madagnus told him. 'They were hurrying, back then, so we reckoned they'd put the shotters at their extreme range – which is comparable to ours. If they do manage to hit us from right out there, though . . .?' He shrugged. 'Then the aviators get to take them. Either way, anything as big and stationary as those artillery pieces of theirs isn't going to last long.'

'Scouts!' someone called, and Stenwold watched a haze of Light Airborne rising up from the Second Army, which was still deployed in a somewhat dispersed formation. A scattering of flying Wasps darted through the air – too few for an assault – and spent twenty minutes overflying the earthworks, but none of them getting close enough to the walls to become a target. As they returned home, Stenwold fancied they had something of a downtrodden air.

'We going out there to poke them?' Madagnus asked.

'You're keen?'

'Not me. Give me walls and artillery any day.'

Stenwold nodded. 'Eminently sensible. We've no plans for a serious sortie, now that the Vekken are back. The Stormreaders will keep on at them, though.'

'Scouts!' someone called out again, and then, 'Just the one!'

Stenwold frowned quartering the sky to try and find the errant enemy but, before he did, the original spotter had added, 'Carrying a flag – black and gold.'

'Going to stick it on the College and then tell us we're conquered?' Madagnus suggested.

'They want to talk.'

'Don't blame them. I don't see they've got any other way in but sweet-talking.'

'Keep the artillery in readiness. It could just as easily be a trick,' Stenwold warned the Ant. 'Someone bring the messenger to me! I want to hear this.'

Collegium's full Assembly had not been brought together in any one place since the start of hostilities, Stenwold recalled. Certainly not since Imperial bombs had destroyed much of the Amphiophos, formerly the heart of government in the Beetle city.

They had returned to old haunts, though, despite the devastation. Jodry Drillen had summoned them, and here they were, at least two-thirds of the Assemblers who had been present there to hear the declaration of war. This part of the ruin was partially cleared, creating an uneven floor to speak from, and the gathered Masters of the College and merchant magnates, the townsmen and gownsmen of Collegium, now sat on broken stone and tumbled walls, finding a place for themselves wherever the devastation allowed it. It was a melancholy sight.

Jodry stood before them, a great, sagging hulk of a man, his formal robes creased and stained, having been stored uncleaned by a man who had not thought to need them, and whose servants had mostly gone to serve their city instead.

'You have heard,' he addressed them. Without walls, his voice was a lost thing denied its customary authority. 'I have given you the best picture I can of our circumstances.' Indeed he had already trotted before them a whole string of experts to report on the city's fortunes. Madagnus had discoursed on the wall engines, barely a slur to his words. Elder Padstock had reported, in a smart military manner, on the troops of the Merchant Companies. Willem Reader had spoken of Collegium's air strength and successes. There had been others, too: the city's stores, its walls, the latest noncommittal word from Sarn. Stenwold gazed all about him at faces he had not seen for some time. They looked worn: older and more haggard, testimony to sleepless nights and days of unaccustomed strain and labour.

'They have offered to meet with a delegation from the city,' Jodry explained. 'You'll have heard that, and I'll call for a vote in a moment. I don't honestly imagine we'll refuse, though. Collegiate citizens not fond of the sounds of their own voices? Of course we'll talk. The reason we're here, after all this time, is to do a little cribbing and prepare some answers ahead of the moment. There aren't many topics likely to come up, after all. We can second-guess most of them.'

Stenwold let him talk, eyes still moving from face to face. Some met his gaze with a nod or a wan smile, while others avoided it, or simply did not look at him at all.

One man locked stares with him, frankly hostile, and the expression on his solid, sour face suggested, *How did you let it come to this?* Hardly a fair question when Stenwold might ask, in return, *How much of this did you help bring about?* The man was Helmess Broiler, long a political adversary of both Stenwold and Jodry, but more than that. Stenwold knew well enough that the man had been in the Empire's pocket, and possessed other transient

341

loyalties that were not in the city's best interests. He had kept mainly to his townhouse until now, for word had filtered among the Companies of what sort of man he was, and they had made their feelings plain on several occasions. But here he was, like a cursed object in an old story, always turning up when least wanted.

Stenwold tried to read in his expression just what Helmess might know of the Empire's prospects, but either the man was as clueless as everyone else or he could hide his knowledge all too well.

After the gathering, Stenwold retired to converse with Jodry, as the two of them had so often before. Their appropriated study now was a wall short of the set, and roofless to boot, but beggars must take what they were given.

'You'll go, of course,' Jodry pressed him.

'It's about time I renewed my acquaintance with General Tynan, yes,' Stenwold agreed.

'I'd like to lay eyes on the man myself. After all, there's supposed to be some benefit in knowing your enemy.'

'You're not going,' Stenwold said firmly. Seeing Jodry's outrage begin to bloom, he raised a conciliatory hand. 'This could easily be a trap, and eliminating the two of us together would be too tempting. I would greatly *prefer* it, let's say, if you stayed on the walls and watched the general through a glass.'

Jodry summoned all his authority, jowls quivering, but then he subsided. 'Well, perhaps you're right at that. Eight, though? You've some names in mind?'

The War Master nodded. 'Enough.'

There was a pause, then: 'Look, if it's worrying you, why don't you stay home and I'll go for once.'

That brought a faint smile to Stenwold. 'No. Tynan and I . . . when we spoke at the end of the last war, we understood each other. If anyone can get through to him, it's me.' *It's just that . . .* Stenwold had been at war with the Wasps for almost two decades more than anyone else in Collegium, but these last years spent facing the Empire's actual assaults, its repeated attempts to devour the Lowlands entire, which could be repulsed but seemingly never ended . . . And here they were, full circle, as the blind determination of the Second Army, the Gears, came grinding towards their gates yet again. *I just want it over with.* More and more, in those few moments of private time that life allowed him, he was thinking of the sea – of Paladrya and the sea. *To escape from all this. To be free . . .*

The votes been had passed without difficulty, motion after motion, so that Jodry had seemed less a statesman and more a ringmaster, trotting out each proposal to do its trick and then pass on. Still, there had been a surprising number of abstentions, and Stenwold could see his own tiredness in those faces – not of people who objected or opposed, but those for whom simply getting here had removed their last drachm of public spirit; who had been hammered by war and loss until they could not bring themselves to fight any further, not for any cause.

A hasty exchange of Fly messengers hammered out a location that resulted in one solitary soldier of the Light Airborne planting a flag out there amongst the earthworks, on a patch of cleared ground that would be in plain sight to both sides.

Stenwold flew out by orthopter, so as not to give the Second any assistance in navigating Collegium's end of the earthworks. Crouching in the belly of a cargo flier that nonetheless looked fleet enough for a quick getaway, he fought off the tides of weariness that were already threatening to sap his concentration. Around him, his picked team were restless and tense – and armed, of course. Wasps never went unarmed, so bringing snapbows and swords had been non-negotiable.

The last time he had left Collegium to parlay with General Tynan had been in markedly different circumstances, and he had then done his best to divest himself of the honour guard that had attached itself to him. That time, as now, Elder Padstock had refused to be shaken off, and it was only fitting that she follow him into this particular piece of folly as well.

He had a second chief officer with him, which was probably

343

not in the city's interests, but Stenwold had wanted Eujen Leadswell of the Student Company along, because the man was intelligent and was almost certainly going to end up a player in the Assembly soon enough. He should be here, if only to hear what was said.

And perhaps also because of his ongoing and dogged refusal to accept that Stenwold was *right* about everything. There used to be plenty of other people like that. It had been the majority view in the Assembly for years. Now even Helmess Broiler kept his mouth shut, and everyone else just nodded, every time the War Master opened his mouth. *War Master? I almost feel that the War Master is my real enemy: the man who stands between me and what I want. And is that how Leadswell sees things?* Stenwold knew he was unlikely ever to win Eujen over, but something in him kept trying, and until then it was good to have someone who would protest, if the War Master went too far.

Choices beyond that had proved harder. He had Laszlo – a strong and resourceful flier, if getting swift word back to Collegium became vital. Not Jodry. Not Kymene, for the same reasons. Not Balkus, either, because the man had not so much as spoken to Stenwold since their last argument. The remaining three places were two soldiers of the Maker's Own, and the Coldstone officer known as the Antspider, included at Leadswell's request. Eujen had wanted to bring along that gangling Woodlouse friend of his, but the man lacked half a hand and, although by all accounts this had only spurred on his artificing, he could not shoot straight. Stenwold, conversely, had wanted to bring Eujen's Wasp friend Averic, as an object lesson, but the man had been so manifestly unwilling that he had relented.

'They're coming by automotive,' the pilot announced, and Stenwold hung halfway out of the hatch to look. True enough, the Imperial delegation was taking this opportunity to test out the ground, as their eight-legged machine slowly navigated the uneven terrain. General Tynan was clearly going to wring every drop of advantage out of this meeting.

And on that subject . . . Holding on with one hand, Stenwold thrust the other towards Padstock, who snapped out a telescope and passed it to him. As steadily as he could, Stenwold trained it on the approaching machine, which was obligingly open-topped.

He counted eight passengers plus a driver: six Wasps and two Spiders. He could still his view enough to see the bald crown of General Tynan himself, which he recognized well enough. He knew the woman beside the general, too: Mycella of the Aldanrael – whom he had last seen on the deck of her flagship, watching her fleet start to sink.

Troubles are like feckless children, went the saying. *Send them into the world, they'll be back at your door soon enough – and they'll bring friends.*

The Collegiates had settled down by the time the Imperial automotive finally found its way, with their orthopter close enough to take cover inside it, and angled so as not to block any line of sight from the city walls. Its wings were folded vertically upwards, and it would need only the throw of a single lever to engage the gear train, and have the machine thundering upwards.

But, despite all that and despite planning against one, Stenwold did not expect a trap. He remembered General Tynan, and had a good idea of the Empire's position, and he knew that killing the Collegiate War Master would not take Collegium, any more than killing Tynan would change the Second Army's orders. And he'd thought of it, of course, because this was war, after all, but it seemed plain to him that having a living Tynan he could talk to was better than a dead Tynan, and some newly vengeful colonel sitting across the table. That was the problem with the Imperial chain of command. You couldn't kill it with a beheading.

The enemy formed up opposite him, their positioning and deployment as careful as any strategist's. The general took the centre, and there was a colonel to his right – intelligence officer probably – and a captain, with some red badge Stenwold didn't recognize on his left. Mycella demurely took the general's far left flank, backed by a solidly built man in immaculately shining

345

mail, and there were three heavy infantry on the right – not the sort of men to cut and run, but to hold the enemy while more important lives than theirs were saved. Tynan mopped his brow briefly – the sun was past its zenith but there was no cover out there, and Stenwold was hoping that the general was thinking about *that* discomfort as well.

'General.'

'War Master. I'm glad it's you speaking for your city. I wasn't sure who I'd get.' Tynan was sizing him up, even as he himself was sized up in turn. 'You've not brought your Spider girl?'

For a moment Stenwold thought that was deliberate, like a bully's kick, but there was no suggestion of such in Tynan's face. 'She's dead,' he answered bluntly.

'I'm sorry.' And the Wasp was, just in that moment, but in the next it was all wiped away. 'Business, then.'

'You asked to talk. So talk,' Stenwold invited.

'My orders are to take your city, War Master,' Tynan told him. 'No surprise for you, I'm sure, but non-negotiable. However . . .' He took a deep breath. 'Nobody in the Empire would ever have thought that Collegium could fight as it has done, Maker. After all, look how we took Tark, look how Helleron practically begged us to take the city over. The Exalsee is in awe of us, and we've whipped the Mynans and their friends back into the fold. And Sarn will fall, and we both know it. And we expect a tough fight, when it's with Ants – after all, we've been winning wars against Ants for generations. But you people . . . There are a lot of gambling officers in Capitas who've lost their fortunes on Collegium. Who could have thought that Beetle-kinden had it in them to fight so!' He shook his head wonderingly. 'My people respect that, War Master. We respect a valiant adversary, even if their cause is hopeless in the long run. Collegium will fly the Black and Gold sooner or later.'

Stenwold was about to make some bravado comment then, some 'Then let it be later,' or, 'Not while I live', but Tynan forestalled him.

'I will offer terms for Collegium's surrender, War Master, and they are terms that will see me brought before the throne to explain myself, but I am a general, and my word will hold.' At this mention of the throne, the captain with the red badge twitched, staring pointedly at Tynan, who ignored him. Stenwold read that exchange easily enough: *Rekef or something like it, whatever that badge means.*

'Maker,' Tynan went on, 'let Collegium lay down its arms with no further bloodshed and I will grant an amnesty to all its citizens, its fighting men, its pilots – all those who have opposed us. I will give orders that my soldiers must not harm its populace – no nights of rape and plunder – and believe me I will have to promise them gold from my own coffers, for they will want their reward, after what you've put them through, every step and every mile. When the new governor arrives, he will rule with the advice of your Assembly, just as our man in Helleron does with the Council there. Your merchants will have their chance to join the Consortium and profit thereby. Collegium shall become the new jewel of the Empire, valued and made to shine.'

From the expressions of Tynan's Wasp subordinates – however they fought to hide them – Stenwold could see that these terms were beyond reason as far as they were concerned, which convinced him of the general's intentions. There was something unsaid, though, and he could divine well enough what it was.

'And Collegium's leaders?' he asked.

'Taken to Capitas in chains,' Tynan confirmed. 'But who knows who your city's leaders are, War Master? You govern in such an upside-down way that it could be anyone. Except that one name is of course known even in the Imperial court.'

Stenwold nodded. *No need to ask whose.* 'I expected that.'

'You'll put this to your Assembly?'

'No need.' Stenwold managed a tight smile. 'We covered this possibility when we met earlier today. Even on the generous terms you propose, General, we will not yield our freedom to the Empire.'

Tynan had not expected his request to have been rejected even before it was made, and into that gap Stenwold pressed determinedly on.

'Instead I have an offer for you, General Tynan, and I will ground it in facts, show my reasoning just as you did. You say you are surprised at our success in resisting the Empire? We are, after all, a city of thinkers and builders, not warriors such as yourself. You say you respect our new-found martial prowess? Well, then, know this: we do not respect you as an enemy.' He watched a ripple of anger pass through the Wasps gathered there, though Tynan himself remained unmoved. 'We do not respect our enemies; we despair of them. Your struggle, your fierce will to prevail in spite of all, we do not admire this. We see only a terrible, senseless waste of life – both ours and yours. We see murdered potential, young men and women who might have become anything becoming only corpses through one woman's dreams of conquering a city she has not even *seen*. Because we will not be owned or dictated to. Because we will not be slaves and bare our backs to the lash. And all because your Empress cannot bear there to be some empty name on a map somewhere that is not *hers*. She must be insane.'

That certainly struck fire in the Wasp faces there, the red-badge man especially, and still Tynan remained calm.

'All emperors and empresses must be insane,' Stenwold explained to them. 'Anyone who looks out towards the horizons and says, 'All this must be mine – and more, until there is no more.' What sort of overweening arrogance is it, to have thousands and tens of thousands of her own people march and die, to destroy the cities and cultures and ways of life of dozens of other kinden, to trample and to pillage, sack and rape, butcher and enslave all within reach, just to indulge some inner weakness that fears whatever it cannot control? Look at what has brought us to this!' These words were not the ones that Stenwold had planned. He was off his script, now, and travelling through the wilds of his own mind. 'Look at what your own people have endured and inflicted, Tynan! From the deaths at Helleron, when they tried to take the *Pride*, the losses at Tark, the Fourth Army obliterated by the Felyen, all the dead at the Battle of the Rails, Malkan's Seventh smashed by the Sarnesh – and now you're back, and the Eighth is probably locked in a death struggle with Sarn even now, and we have destroyed your Air Corps and bludgeoned you and bombed you and strewn your path with thorns all the way from the Felyal to here. And here we are. Chief Officer Leadswell, forward, please.'

Eujen started in surprise, then took a small step forward.

'This man has suggested that we might have made some lasting peace with the Empire, after the last war – that we might have found enough common ground to prevent this new conflict coming to pass. I admit I was too busy preparing for this day to even consider it, but he's right. A lasting and honest peace between our people could accomplish great things, and the world would be so much the richer. Leadswell has overlooked one thing, however. He believes that your people are men as deserving as any to enjoy life and happiness, but he forgets that your own leaders do not share that belief. If they did, none of this could come about. To your Empress and her court, you and all your soldiers are nothing more than a sword to strike out at the world with, and keep striking until either the world or the sword breaks. Until your Empire is ruled with some acceptance that human life has a *value* – irrespective of whether that life is Imperial or Collegiate or your poor bloody Auxillians – then all this man's good intentions will go to naught, and we will continue to resist you. We cannot be slaves, and under Imperial rule, everyone is a slave, bar one.'

Mycella of the Aldanrael was smiling slightly, and the Wasps were clearly at the very limits of their patience, but Tynan still regarded the War Master without obvious emotion. Stenwold thought, *He knows. I tell him the Empress is insane, and it's no news to him.*

'We should destroy the Second,' Stenwold declared, 'to the

last man, if we can. We should take away the Empress's sword, because at least there will be a pause before she forges a new one. Nevertheless, I am authorized by the Assembly to make *you* an offer, General. Walk away. We both know the losses your army has suffered in getting here, and now we are in the same position as we were when you fell back the last time. We have the advantage in the air and in artillery, and we still have our walls. You cannot sustain a siege long, and we can prevent supplies coming to you by air or sea – whilst the Tseni navy will ensure that food and ammunition keep coming in for us. Go now and, so long as you keep retreating, Collegium shall not harass your forces. But keep on retreating, for we are coming to liberate Tark and Myna and those other places that you have shackled. Go now, for if you try to take our city, you can be sure that the skies will never be clear for whatever is left of your army, all the way back to Capitas.'

Tynan nodded slightly, and for a long moment there was quiet. Reading the expressions of the other Wasps, it was plain that they were concerned what Tynan's response might be. The man with the red badge kept shifting restlessly, as though reminding the general of his presence, and of his invisible authority. *Typical Rekef – or whatever he is.*

'This will not seem a compliment, to you,' Tynan said at last, 'but the Empire has never had a Beetle-kinden general – not artificer, diplomat, merchant or soldier. If you had been born under the Black and Gold, I think that things might have been different. I think that matters might have fallen out in very different way, had you been in a position to advise the Empress, or advise the Emperor before her. The world might be a better place.'

All eyes were fixed on him, and the convulsive jerk that ran through the man with the red badge almost seemed like a spasm. It was, Stenwold realized a moment later, a man at the extremes of self-restraint, fighting down the impulse to sting his own general. *Treason,* he thought. *Was that treason we heard, from General Tynan?*

Does he doubt his Empress? And it was plain that he did, and that Tynan knew that everything Stenwold said was true, yet . . .

'I have my orders,' the Wasp stated. 'I have never disobeyed an order from the crown. That same quality took my Second away from your gates the first time. It will keep me here now. I thank you for your offer, but I cannot accept.'

Twenty-Four

She had sold him her story, just as she had sold it to the Nethyen, and for a while she had convinced him, even though she must have been unaware just who it was she was convincing.

Esmail had been sent by the Tharen to the Empress's court as a spy and assassin, the one by training, the other supposedly an inalienable quality of his blood.

Kill her, they had told him. There had been more in terms of qualifiers and conditions, but it all boiled down to that. They had loosed him from the string, and, curve as he might, his course was intended to bring him point-first to the Empress.

Even when he read his orders, he had guessed that Tharn was riven with factions – and how true that had turned out to be – what with two Tharen emissaries actually accompanying the Wasp woman, and even those two splitting from each other, so that only one remained and the other had been sacrificed to aid their progress. He had no idea if the splinter faction that had given him his original orders still existed.

Since he had followed the Empress into the forest, he had thought a lot on his family: his Dragonfly wife, his pureblood children. He had thought about them deliberately, so that events could not push them from his mind. He was now in the rush of the game, after so long – and how the game had broadened. They had sent him to kill an Empress, and instead he had bent the knee. He had helped her against her enemies. He had been given the chance, more than once, to drive an Art-deadly hand straight into her heart, and he had failed.

She had not given him her speech about the renewed glories of the old days, nor had she needed to. Back in Capitas he had discerned it in her: the Inapt and sorcerous Empress of a great Apt nation. He had hidden long amongst the Moths, and his main impression was that they lived only in the past tense and that, protest as they may, some part of them had already given up the fight. They lived in their own shadows, fought their empty factional games, and did their best to pretend that the world beyond their grey halls did not exist. If anything of the gloried past was to return – or even survive – they would not be responsible. Empress Seda the First, however . . .

That was the promise she had made by her mere presence, and he had drunk blood for her, and sworn allegiance to her, not from any compulsions she had laid on him – his kinden and his profession alike were skilled in slipping such chains – but because he had *believed*.

But he had forgotten that the past was not just the glories of Inapt rule – the age of magicians, wisdom and great deeds – and now, after hearing those words, he could not banish them from his mind.

The Seal of the Worm.

He could claim no great knowledge of his people's lore, for the Assassin-kinden were scattered, their ways lost. He had lived and studied amongst Moths, though. That the Empress should seek the power hoarded by Argastos was no surprise. Esmail was no seer but his senses were ever honed for the moment, and he could feel that dark, bloated knot of power ahead. If it was corrupt and decayed, well, find any great node of the old power that was not. The Moths had always loved darkness, and used fear as their weapon, and time would have rotted that into something worse. It was *power*, though, and he could not fault Seda for seeking it.

He could feel the Seal, however, and that was a different

matter. The Seal, whose stony grey *absence* was pinned down by Argastos's decomposing weight, and, beyond it . . .

In truth, Esmail could not say what lay beyond it, but he knew the tales. That great war which had encompassed all the known world, just as the Empire's current conflict seemed to . . . That great foe which had united the powers of the day against it, so that deadly enemies could clasp hands and put aside their enmities in order to defeat this common adversary: the Worm. Call them that, and not by their true name, for names are power.

They had sought to make all other races the same as them, said the stories. Meaning conquest? Meaning the extermination of all other kinden until only they themselves remained? Not even that, the stories insisted: they sought to make all the same as them, and it was such a perversion of the fundamentals of nature that in the end all were united against them, and there followed a war the like of which the world would never see again.

And when they were defeated but not destroyed, when they were cast down into their subterranean lairs, the cost was so great that the Moths – the leaders of this great host, for even then the Khanaphir Masters were already in decline – knew that no repeat of this war could be allowed. The Worm must not be permitted to regain its strength and bring such horrors again. But the Moths and their allies could not purge that underground realm of them, though armies of thousands were sent down, never to return. So there had been a ritual, the Moths' ultimate sanction, one of a power and a cost unprecedented. In its wake the ancient world was forever changed, some powers exhausted and near destroyed by the cost of the war. And it was a shameful victory, too – as Esmail had read in secret tomes the Moths had never intended him to find. The Moths had banished the Worm, and sealed the path of its return, but not only the Worm, Esmail discovered. The Moths had failed, in the end, and that ritual had been nobody's first choice.

Save one, perhaps.

Esmail had fallen a long way short of his purpose, and even

that purpose had been someone else's. He himself possessed nothing but that fragile family – no kinden, no agenda. He had almost forgotten that he was not truly one of the Empress's Red Watch. That was an inherent peril of taking another's face and voice: it was easy to become too engrossed in the role.

And the Empress was here for Argastos, and not the Worm. Not the Worm *yet*.

For he felt he knew the Empress now, and even if she consumed Argastos entirely she would still be hungry. It was in her nature – perhaps in the nature of all absolute tyrants – to want more.

Do I turn on her? But, despite his years, she frightened Esmail, with her power and her ruthlessness, and there was still that dream, that impossible promise of a return of the old ways. If those days could return, then perhaps even the Assassin-kinden might walk the world again as they once had.

It was when his thoughts were so thoroughly caught in such a vice, unable to claw their way to any action, that he considered the *other*. The Empress, she who could consider breaking the Seal of the Worm with equanimity, was still frightened by one thing.

Esmail had felt her presence, and hidden from it, just as he hid from Seda and from the trailing tendrils of Argastos himself. Like Seda, the *other* had a strength that lacked subtlety, allowing Esmail to spy on her, sensing a power that was sister to the Empress's own, but with a very different mind behind it.

However, she was distant now, almost untraceable, and perhaps that was the end of it. Perhaps nothing could stand between the Seal and the Empress, if she chose to undo the work of all those past ages. But Esmail found that he had not entirely given up hope. Beetles had surprised a lot of people, over the years. Just ask the Moths.

How the Nethyen might have taken it, had Maure's song not changed their mood, Tynisa could not say. But, of course, the halfbreed claimed to have seen this moment coming, and perhaps the woman had genuinely been working towards preparing Che's entrance.

The Beetle girl stood at the clearing's edge, her dark skin rubied under the leaping firelight, and she had seized the attention of every Mantis-kinden there. A Nethyen man stood beside her, unkempt and long-haired, and looking over her other shoulder was surely the very mantis that had abducted her in the first place, the largest of its kind Tynisa had ever seen.

The Mantids were gathering close together, many with weapons in hand, and she could see Thalric trying to move towards Che and being excluded again and again, walled away from her by the bodies of the Nethyen. Amnon stood back and watched, snapbow in hand.

'Wait,' Tynisa instructed them both. Thalric threw her a desperate glance, but something in her expression must have got through to him. Whether it was because of Maure's song or Che's newfound presence, for once the Mantids had something on their minds other than blood.

'I understand now,' said Che. The moment she opened her mouth, the only competition for their ears was the cracking of wood on the fire.

'My sister has spoken to you,' the Beetle girl declared, at which Tynisa twitched but, of course, Che did not mean *her*. She meant that other sister, Seda. 'Will you let me speak now as well?' It seemed unnecessary to ask, as everyone was already hanging on her every word, but Tynisa sensed some additional significance to the question – *a magician asking permission?* She glanced at Maure, and saw a profoundly serious expression on the necromancer's face. Whatever Che was doing, there was more to it than Tynisa either saw or could understand.

No word was spoken, but Che plainly took that silence as assent. 'She has promised you, I don't know what: power, the redress of old grievances. I suppose it's the way of things that I should make promises as well.' There was a calm assurance to Che standing before that armed host, something that Collegiate

Assemblers would envy. 'But I have spoken to Amalthae.' Here she made a brief gesture towards the insect towering beside her, and Tynisa saw its huge-eyed head cock minutely as it followed the movement.

'Of course, I want you to stop fighting the Empress's war,' Che addressed them. 'And I should be standing here like a daughter of Collegium, and telling you about our cause and how right we are, and all the same things she has told you, whatever they were. I should bully and taunt and bribe you into becoming my foot-soldiers instead of hers. Sorry, but can I have some water or something?'

Tynisa snorted with laughter, horribly loud in that silent clearing, but *that* was more like the Che she knew. *That* was her sister, sure enough.

There was an awkward pause, until one of the Nethyen cautiously approached her and proffered a cup. It was not water, Tynisa knew, but Che took a gulp without hesitating, and in doing so she sealed her safe conduct for that night, or at least for the length of her speech. *More invisible walls and customs.*

'I'm not going to tell you to march out and fight alongside the Sarnesh,' Che explained to them. 'It's something much more important than that.' She held up a hand quickly, though nobody had spoken. 'And it's not about Argastos.' At the name, a ripple of disquiet ran through them. 'The Empress seeks Argastos for his power, but that's between me and her, and not your problem. But you do have a problem.' She was looking about at them, peering amidst the trees as though trying to estimate just how many Mantis-kinden were listening, and Tynisa saw her bracing her shoulders. 'Change,' she announced. 'You won't change, yet the world must. Your nature is to fight, so you've tried to fight time just as you'd fight any other enemy. And you've lost, and been reduced to this – to this forest, these holds.' The intensity of their regard was frightening, all those sharp eyes lancing into her, but Che took it in her stride.

'We've come to the last sand in the hourglass, I think,' she told them. 'That's what I have to tell you. Whether you fight for the Empress because she's promised you your old glories back again, or because you agree with Imperial aims, or for any other reason, it doesn't really matter. You already know her promises can't be trusted, as much as I do. In your hearts, you do. And if you had subjugated yourselves to the Sarnesh, or even still obeyed the Tharen, it would make no real difference. You'd still be serving someone. Servants of the Green, that's how the Moths used to put it. And maybe, in those days, doing what the Moths wanted was a good thing. They were great magicians and wise, after all. But it seems to me that ever since those days, you've just been waiting for them to return and tell you how to get it all back. And they haven't, because they don't know.'

Thalric had managed to find his way through to her by then, and when he rested a hand on her shoulder she squeezed it gratefully.

'Then the Empress came instead, and I can understand why you've ended up fighting for her – because fighting is what you do, and because nobody had a better offer. Until now, I hope.' She was speeding up a little, sensing that her claim on their attention might be shorter than she thought. 'But I think that you never did quite believe her. Instead, she came as a sign – the sort of sign the Moths once prophesied of – a sign of the end. I have walked through your forest, and witnessed you and the Etheryen tearing one another apart. I have seen an entire hold slaughtered by its own kin, and I have felt the horror and despair that you all feel. The whole forest is rank with it. The Empress's very arrival made you face the world, *her* world. She was something new that you couldn't ignore. She gave you an excuse to die, and you jumped at it – for, in your deepest selves, you saw this as an escape from a world that had gone so far wrong as to create *her*. And me, too, I suppose. I'm certainly not something that the great magicians of old might have envisaged or approved of.'

She let the silence linger, and the Mantids were still angry and resentful but it was that sort of anger that only truth can provoke. Che's words had sunk barbed hooks in them.

'No matter what the Empress promises, the Days of Lore will never come again,' said Che, in that silent glade. 'And now that past is sufficiently far gone that it's a *Wasp* who comes to broker deals with you as though she was one of your old masters – and a Beetle-kinden stands here to lecture you about what you should and shouldn't do.' She shrugged. 'If you want to pass on, if the world's so intolerable to you now, then that's your right. The great Mantis tradition of the Lowlands could be snuffed out quite easily, if that's what you want. All those centuries of history just gone, and by your own hands. If you want to make a start by cutting my throat, I can hardly stop you.

'Because otherwise you have to change as the world has changed. Yes, it's an Apt world, but it still recognizes Mantis-kinden fighting skill. There is a place for you in it, yet, if you'll take it. Wait another generation, and maybe there won't be. Maybe then a good death will be all you can hope for.

'You must decide, all of you, whether you want to live. I won't insult you by telling you that living is harder than dying, that continuing to fight is more worthy than a good end. I'm not Mantis, I can't weigh these things for you.'

She took a deep breath. 'But know that, if you pass from this world, you will be remembered. But it will not be in your old songs. Gone will be the stories you tell of your heroes, gone the legends of the Days of Lore. None will be left to tell the histories as you once told them. Instead, you'll be remembered by *my* people. Can you imagine what Beetle-kinden stories of your people are like? Can you conceive just how wrong we get it all? How we turn all your glories and your tragedies into farce and bathos? And yet, if you are gone, nobody will ever know any better. Our clumsy Apt retellings will be all anyone ever knows of the Mantis-kinden.'

She seemed to shrink, then, before the gaze of her audience, discarding some invisible mantle of authority that she had donned simply to hold their interest. 'I've said my piece,' she finished. Then she reached out and hugged Thalric to her, plainly more glad than she could say to have him there. The others made their way over, too: Tynisa, Amnon, Maure. None dared break the silence, but she hugged each in turn.

There was a stir amongst the Nethyen. One of the older women was picking her way through them, her eyes fixed on the Beetle girl. Her hair was silver-white, but she stood straight and there was a rapier at her hip and spines jutting from her forearms.

'Loquae,' Che addressed her, for this must be one of the leaders of the Mantids.

The old woman regarded her with a mixture of hostility, respect and that fear of the magical that the Moths had taken pains to instil in their servants. 'You, too, may as well style yourself Loquae here, although you have nothing but harsh words for us.'

'True words,' Che corrected.

'Those are often the harshest. What do you *want*, child of Collegium? What is it you want from us?'

Che glanced back towards Ceremon and Amalthae. 'When I came to your forest, it was for two reasons. I needed to stop the Empress finding Argastos and assuming his power, and that's my personal goal still. I also came to help the Sarnesh and the Etheryen fight off the Empire. If the Sarnesh leader was here he'd tell me to try and persuade you to fight the Empire too – as you did under the Ancient League. But I won't.'

The Loquae cocked an eyebrow, waiting.

'I'm not going to tell you what to do. Being told what to do has already done too much damage to your kinden, whether it's by heeding the Moths or the Empire. I'm *asking* you to consider your options while you still have them, but I won't beg on behalf of the Sarnesh. I won't even beg for Collegium. I am not a child of Collegium any more.' It seemed only as she said it that she realized it was true. 'I am here as the inheritrix of the old ways, for all that I never chose to be. Amalthae has asked me to inter-cede, to try and help *you*, not Sarn, and not myself. I want you to live. I want there to be Mantis-kinden in the Lowlands in a generation's time.'

'Why do you care?' It was an accusation, the way the woman said it.

'Because what I have become carries a responsibility. Because it was Mantis magic as much as anything that made me this way. Because it's *right*.'

The woman's hand rested on her sword hilt, but there was no suggestion that she meant to draw the blade. Despite her age and her warrior's bearing she seemed lost, almost bewildered. 'We must speak about what you have said, and we are only one hold here.'

'Then I ask that you pass my words on, to all the others, Nethyen and Etheryen alike. And maybe some will choose to live and some prefer to die. Or all to die. I don't know.' She tried a brittle smile. 'And what do you yourself intend, now I've said my words?'

The old Loquae looked about the firelit clearing as though seeking volunteers, but there seemed no will for violence amongst the Mantids, for once.

'We will talk,' she said. 'And *you* should go. Your presence is like salt on a wound. Perhaps that is what we need, but I am not sure.'

Che glanced at her fellows briefly, as though canvassing their unspoken thoughts. 'You know where I must go.'

The Loquae nodded unhappily. 'You go to Argastos.'

'Not for myself but only because the Empress must not have him.'

For a long while the Loquae's eyes searched Che's expression over and over. Tynisa was waiting for Che to give some reassurance, to draw out some proof of her virtuous intent, and yet the Beetle girl seemed momentarily frightened that she could find no such evidence within herself. *Magicians and power*, came the unwelcome thought. *Can she be so sure she will not use it?*

The Loquae plainly saw the same, but merely shrugged. 'You go wherever you must. The Nethyen will not stop you.'

'Will they open the way for me?' Che pressed.

The old woman's eyes widened. 'The way is open for you, Beetle Skryre. How can you not know that? The blood price has already been paid, for you and yours.'

Che mastered her expression quickly, perhaps with a queasy twitch over just whose blood that might have been, which had opened the gate.

'Your followers, though, have further business with us.' And was that the sharp edge of a smile on the Loquae's lean face? Tynisa sensed the lurching moment that Che stumbled over her own ignorance.

'Explain,' the Beetle got out.

'The duel,' Amnon stated flatly, and Tynisa echoed him a moment later.

'What have you done?' Che demanded of them.

'Bought time by issuing a challenge,' Thalric drawled. 'The Commonweal trick.'

And now we come to pay for the Commonweal trick, Tynisa decided. 'Well that's fine,' she declared, loud enough to draw all eyes. 'So let's get it over with now, and we can be on our way. Which of you is champion?'

'Tynisa . . .' Che started, but this was Mantis business, and she could not prevent it.

'Amalthae stands for us,' the Loquae stated, and Che froze.

Tynisa had heard the name, and not quite connected it with a face. 'Fine, so which of you is she? Let's see her.' She looked from face to pale Mantis face, as they shuffled aside, expecting to see a human opponent revealed by their eddying movement. Instead . . .

'Ah.'

The cleared fighting ground stretched from her to the trees, and she saw the great mottled shape that swayed there, glittering eyes casting back the firelight.

362

Tynisa felt her bravado dry up. She would face any human opponent without flinching, but she knew full well the creature's sheer speed and strength. She was Mantis enough to know the creature at once as something not merely physically powerful, but supernatural as well, an incarnation of her father's kinden made armoured flesh.

But she stood, blade outstretched, and in a quiet, calm voice got out, 'Well come on, then, for my sister would be gone.'

The long-haired Mantis beside the creature cleared his throat. 'Amalthae bids you: go with your sister, for she will need you. A duel pledged cannot be taken back, and she and you shall meet. But not now, nor at dawn. Go, for she knows you will return to honour your word.'

Tynisa lowered her blade slowly, and the very character of the air seemed to change around her, the Mantids reacting to this validation of her badge and her blood. They might still hate her, but never again could they deny her.

Che glanced about, testing the quality of the silence. 'Then there is one thing I will ask, then, if you can grant it.'

The Loquae's eyes narrowed and she waited.

Che drew herself up as tall as she could – not physically, but gathering together the trailing folds of a power that, here at this pyre, Tynisa could almost see. 'Give me your blessing on my journey,' the Beetle asked. 'Let my steps be light until I find the Empress, for if I catch her before she catches Argastos, then we need never know what I might do with him.'

'Our blessing?'

'These are your lands,' and it was a recognition of sovereignty the Empress had surely never granted them. 'I walk here as your guest now. Give me your blessing, wish me well, speed me on my way.'

And Tynisa saw, at last, something like approval in the old Mantis woman's face, because Che had said the right thing. *Just words, but words have power.* Ancient compacts had been brought to light, a respect for the Mantis-kinden that the ages had not shown them – and so elegantly expressed.

'I give you our blessing,' the Loquae breathed, and the forest breathed with her. 'Now go on your way.'

Twenty-Five

That morning, Major Oski turned up before his general. He was out of uniform, wearing dark, baggy clothes and with his face blacked like a comic artificer in a play.

'General.' The little man saluted. 'Apologies, I've not had time to change.'

A horn sounded – in the last few days it had become a familiar and miserable call. It meant the Collegiate orthopters had been sighted on their way for another bombing run, under skies still grey with dawn. The Farsphex pilots and ground artillerists would be scrabbling to ready themselves, but those repeating ballistae with which the Empire had been threatening the slower enemy bombers had themselves become the prime targets, and each time the Collegiate machines flew over once again – several times a day now – the resistance offered was that much less.

Tynan kept an eye on the sky. 'Explain.'

'I've been over to look at the walls, sir,' Oski told him. 'Trick I learned from the Colonel-Auxillian – he always went for a look in the dark in person. Anyway, I thought I'd take a look at the closest gate, shooting arcs and the like. I've got a plan of attack now, if you'll have it.'

Tynan gestured for him to continue. The first bomb fell, released too soon and impacting out in the earthworks. There was always someone too keen or too nervous, amongst the enemy. The growl of the Farsphex engines was all around them, too:

Bergild's pilots lifting into the air to do what they could. The numbers were stacked against them, though, and if they tried too hard they would find themselves shot down. Their game of feint and threat was growing more and more difficult, and most of the time Collegium could spare a score of Stormreaders to ward them off, whilst the rest got to work on the army.

And the Second Army was still spreading itself thin, but when the order came to press the actual attack, the Wasps would have to gather their soldiers, and then the bombing would begin in earnest. At this rate it seemed touch and go whether they could get close to the walls at all, given all the Collegiate artillery out there. And when they did, how long would they have to sit under bombardment before the ramparts could be taken or the wall breached?

Too long, was the thought nobody dared voice, for Captain Vrakir and his Red Watch constantly stalked through the army with their Imperial writ, just waiting for someone to express doubts about the Empress's plans.

'This airship,' Tynan spat out, over the sound of the bombs.

'Bergild and I, we calculate it'll be in sight by late dawn tomorrow – and believe me, the Collegiates won't miss it. That's the other thing: Vrakir's ordered all our fliers made ready for it – our artificers have been busy brewing up that muck that their Captain Nistic gave them the recipe for – and it's nothing I recognize, I can tell you. Stinks, though, sir. Nobody wants a bed near where they're boiling it.'

'And you're confident this will work, this scheme of theirs?'

'No, sir.' Oski looked profoundly unhappy, enough so that the bomb that now impacted close enough to shake the ground beneath them barely made him flinch. 'Sir, this is outside my profession, and I have no idea at all. But we all know we've got nothing else.'

'Too true,' Tynan agreed moodily. 'So, tell me about the walls. What have we got left that will put a dent in them?'

'The walls themselves? Nothing reliable unless we can undermine then and pack the tunnel with explosive. And I reckon those walls go down a way, too. The gate, I think we have a chance against if we're left free to work. I can adapt some lead-shotters as ramming engines, and they should get through it if we can bring them to bear. Other than that . . . well, the Sentinel handlers reckon that their machines might be up to it, but I'm not convinced. It's not what they're built for, and I just don't know their specifications well enough.'

'Get the ramming engines ready,' Tynan told him. 'Do what you can.' Another explosion nearby left a fine mist of dirt sifting down on them.

'I reckon we'll receive at least one attack from their fliers overnight, if they've any sense,' Oski ventured. 'I'll have the ground crew ready to refuel and patch up the Farsphex, once they're down from that. Then it's down to the chemical artificers and that stink of theirs.'

Tynan was not looking at him, nor at the wheeling orthopters, but instead somewhere off and away, towards the walls of Collegium, so that eventually Oski had to prompt him, 'Sir?'

'Do what you can,' the general repeated. He looked as if he was trying on the face of his own corpse: a general faced with the choice of sending thousands of his soldiers into a catastrophic attack, or else disobeying an order. Then he gestured for one of his officers. 'Send out messengers. The advance commences at dawn, battle order unchanged.' Then, more thoughts spoken aloud. 'If their fliers are likely to be occupied with this airship, even for a moment, we'll make use of that time.'

Awkwardly, Oski backed away, and turned at a respectful distance to fly off and get his hands dirty, because some hard and absorbing engineering was just what he needed to chase the image of General Tynan's face from his mind.

The Vekken were all within Collegiate walls now, and nobody had complained about it. That seven hundred of the city's oldest enemy were suddenly being welcomed with open arms, and nobody – not *anybody* – had stood up and remarked on the fact, was perhaps the most telling sign of how the world had changed.

There had been word from Sarn, too, but nothing good. The Eighth Army was not as far advanced as the Second, but there was only so much the Sarnesh could do to slow it, and they would inevitably clash soon. With the Mantis question still unanswered, who would prevail remained anybody's guess.

And then there's the other aspect of the Sarnesh. Both Laszlo and Balkus had tried to corner him on the subject of Tactician Milus and the liberties he took, but Stenwold had waved them both away. After all, there was nothing he could do.

Laszlo was kicking about the city, sulking, but he would get over it. He was probably commiserating with the rest of the *Tidenfree* crew even now. The ship itself remained in harbour, given that the Empire had precious little way to strike at it, but the former pirates would be taking their leave soon, Stenwold knew. As for Balkus and Sperra, for all he knew, they were forming a Princep government in exile or something similarly impolitic.

Or they don't have anywhere else to turn but to call on me. An unhappy thought, given that he had nothing for them. *After the war, we can sort it all out.* Although Stenwold had an uncomfortable feeling that, if Sarn decided to take control of Princep now, the Ants would not be so easily dislodged later.

The Second Army had held off, still spread out and hard to damage with bombs; also still just outside artillery range – a distance established after a few incautious Imperials came too close and Madagnus showed them the new teeth the city had. *Waiting for something* . . . Or perhaps Tynan was just frozen with indecision, knowing how bad his position was. But Stenwold did not believe that.

'Maker.'

It was after dark now, but he had plenty of paperwork to keep him up, enough to fill the time until this diminutive figure slouched into his current office, still wearing grease-dirty pilot's leathers, with a chitin helm and goggles hanging from her belt.

'Taki,' he nodded.

The Solarnese woman looked worn out, but then she was well known for pushing herself far further than any of the pilots who served under her. She found a footstool and sat down on it, and Stenwold poured her a bowl of wine.

She took it in both hands and sipped, wrinkling up her face. 'Maker, back home the only way you'd find wine this bad is by pissing it out after a heavy night.'

'It's all I've got left. There's a city-wide shortage. We've asked the Tseni if they could ship some in, but apparently they don't drink it off the Atoll Coast.' He shrugged apologetically. 'We've had some interrupted harvests, what with . . . everything, you know. A few years that won't have a vintage. What did you find?'

'Nothing,' she told him tiredly. 'I went up the coast, halfway to Tark, I swear. No reinforcements, nothing coming in by sea, no automotives . . . not even a supply airship. The only thing is if maybe they've got another twenty Farsphex coming from somewhere – and they could get here overnight. We've got the Great Ear listening out for their engines, if they do. But nothing yet, Stenwold.'

She tried the wine again, and forced down a throat-full. 'Not got anything to eat, have you? I came straight here.'

'I appreciate it.' Stenwold had some bread and goat's cheese left, and shoved it across his desk towards her. 'What about their army?'

'They'll come for you tomorrow, I reckon,' Taki confirmed. 'They're still all over the place, but by evening we could see how each detachment of them was pulling itself together, forming up. Maybe they'll try a night attack, but I know that the Companies and the artillery are ready for that. We've got lights all along the wall and people watching the air, I think – and an extra guard on the gatehouse just in case. And it's not as if they could really sneak up on us.'

'You should get some sleep,' Stenwold advised.

'I should have *got* some sleep last night,' she corrected. 'Tonight we're going to stop the Wasps getting any sleep instead.'

'Let someone else lead the flight.'

'I see better in the dark.' She sagged, looking very small, almost flimsy enough to blow away. 'Pits, maybe you're right, at that. When I came here, you remember what the deal was? You made me a new flier, I taught at your College – Associate Mastership or whatever. Didn't say anything about commanding your air defences and fighting wars for you.'

'I know, we owe you a great deal and we take you for granted,' Stenwold confirmed. 'At the moment I can't afford not to take for granted those people I know can be relied on.'

'Pisspoor compliment that is,' she muttered. 'Anyway, not as if I can exactly go home any time soon.' Solarno, her home city, was held between the Wasps and their Spider allies: one of the first conquests of the war. 'Might as well be here. At least I get to fly.'

'Seriously, though, get some sleep. Those are War Master's orders,' he told her gently. 'If they're going to march tomorrow, we'll need you fresh.'

She was cramming bread into her mouth and just nodded vaguely, dipping it into the wine to soften it, seeming almost too tired to chew. When she found him staring at her, she met his gaze with raised eyebrows, and that irreverence, at least, was something of her usual manner.

Then there was another Fly-kinden appearing at his door, with a brisk knock. Jodry's secretary come to fetch him to deal with some new disaster of bureaucracy. Stenwold shrugged at Taki. 'Finish the wine, if you can stomach it,' he suggested, and then bustled out, only hoping that Taki would actually take his advice and get some sleep.

'What's this?' Bergild demanded. She had been kicked out of fitful sleep by the complaints of her pilots that the engineers were tampering with their Farsphex. Most of her team slept beside or even inside their craft these days, what with the alarm ready to be sounded night or day. Also, many were so strung out on Chneuma that they barely slept at all. Any long period of inactivity just resulted in a sort of slack-jawed trance plagued by horrible, nightmarish daydreams, breaking into instant wakefulness the moment the call to arms went up.

Now the engineers appeared to be set on making even their waking hours as unreal and unpleasant as possible.

'What are you doing?' she shouted. She had been in Oski's tent, having been left there after nodding off in the small hours. The anticipated Collegium night attack had come and gone, but casualties had been lighter than expected. Although the Second was mustering for their attack, the enemy pilots had been put off their aim by the thick dark of cloud cover, and had wasted most of their cargo.

'Orders,' one of the engineers yelled over his shoulder. He was only a lieutenant and so there should have been a "sir", but she was used to not receiving it. What she was not used to was the smell.

The engineers wore masks to exclude the worst of it, but a wide berth was already being given to her craft – *and all the others, her mindlink confirmed* – as a reeking mixture was slopped over every surface of the flier. It was . . . she found it hard to say just what it was like: acrid and sharp, bringing tears to the eyes, and biting at the inside of her nose.

'Whose orders?' she wanted to know.

'Captain Vrakir's,' and then, because the lieutenant registered how close she was, and that she had her hands open and slightly directed towards him, he added, 'Sir.'

'It's the new plan, sir. Captain Nistic, that came a couple days ago, he gave us the recipe for this,' another engineer explained. 'We're to paint it onto every flier we've got. And no, we don't know why, sir, or what it's for. But you've seen how the Red Watch faces up to the general. Empress's own words, that's what they say.'

And what makes you think the Empress knows the first thing about air combat? Bergild reflected. *What makes you think she knows the first thing about what Captain Vrakir's doing in her name, either?* But this last observation sounded hollow even in her own mind. Whenever Vrakir spoke, there was some authority leaking out in his words that she could not account for. Certainly it was true that Tynan himself listened to him, even if he was plainly unhappy about it.

'No problems, I'm sure, Captain?'

She jumped. The man was right behind her and she was unused to being surprised.

'Captain Vrakir,' she addressed him coldly, 'what's the meaning of this? Is this . . . *reek* supposed to keep the Collegiates away?'

'It's a necessary precaution, that's all. More than that, you—'

'Don't need to know,' she finished for him, and had the pleasure of seeing his lips tighten in annoyance. 'This plan of yours . . .?'

He held a finger up. 'Is not to be spoken of. You, Major Oski and his slave have been circumspect so far, and tomorrow – almost today, now – all will become clear to everyone, most especially to the Empress's enemies. But don't abandon your discretion. There could be Collegiate spies listening even now.'

The engineers, who had most surely been eavesdropping, resumed their foul task with exaggerated dedication.

Vrakir moved very close, but Bergild would not give ground before him. She found she regretted that when he spoke virtually into her ear, 'You have seen, though. You know what we will do to them.'

'I don't think *anyone* knows what will happen once that surprise gets here,' she replied, fighting down her instinct to squirm away from him. 'Not you, and not Captain Nistic either. And you've seen him. He's mad.'

'A little savage, perhaps,' Vrakir allowed, and she could almost mime his next words, they were so predictable: 'but these are savage times. Believe me, Captain Nistic is devoted to the Empire. He and his fellows have waited a long time to bring their particular talents to bear.'

At last she stepped back, because that red badge of his, pressing almost against her shoulder, felt as though it might burn or bite her at any moment.

Then the alarm came instantly into her mind: *Captain – enemy orthopters.* She kicked off immediately and was halfway into her craft's side-hatch, about to wriggle down the crawlspace for the cockpit, when she heard; *Three – no, four only. Not stopping and keeping well north of us,* and she decided, *Scouts.*

Not overflying the army, Captain. Pursue?

She had a mental image of their direction now, as though revealed on a map. 'They've found your new toy, Vrakir,' she told the man, who had caught up with her. 'The Collegiates know it's there, somehow. Four orthopters are off to look at it right now.'

For a moment his face froze, as if left unattended at the front of his head, while thoughts meshed behind it. 'The escort can fend off four,' he decided.

She nodded, 'But your secret's out.'

'How much longer was it ever going to stay a secret?' he pointed out. Whatever his source of inspiration, which seemed to recite the Empress's plans seemingly without his knowing them before he spoke, it had obviously found him a new groove to run in. 'Let them see. Let them run back to their city with the news. And you – every one of our pilots, whether Farsphex, Spearflight or even the Spider rabble – you're to get into the air once you hear those orthopters heading back home. You're to go and meet our airship and defend it from all comers.'

'The army . . .' she said uncertainly, because the Second was so much more vulnerable now, as it gathered itself to take the ground between here and Collegium's walls.

'Not your concern,' Vrakir told her flatly. 'And you!' He rounded on the engineers. 'Double pace! I want all the machines fully slopped over with this filth before then! Or I'll have every tenth man on crossed pikes, by the Empress's own word!'

They woke her close on dawn, and every other sleeping pilot too, banging on the door of the airfield barracks as if they were trying to beat it down.

Taki leapt awake, kicking into the air with wings a-blur, and with no clear sense of who she was or what was going on. *Must be an emergency – Exalsee pilots never get up at this hour.* But of course she was a long way from the Exalsee – from what in retrospect had been a comfortable and pampered life. Now Collegium was her surrogate city, and it was at war.

And, with that thought, the urgency of the banging and kicking and shouting jolted her alert. One of the Beetle pilots had opened the door by then, and another couple of her aviators almost fell into the room.

'All right, all right!' Taki shouted at them. 'We're all awake, so tell me what the picture is.'

'Chief,' one of them acknowledged her. She had not really earned the Company title, but everyone seemed to take her for the Chief Officer of pilots these days. 'The Ear went off a couple of hours ago now. It's picked up more Farsphex on their way.'

'A couple of *hours*?' Taki demanded instantly. 'Why wasn't I—'

'Chief, they said we should let you sleep,' the other put in. *Bloody Maker sticking his nose in.* 'What's the situation?'

'They reckoned four or six, from the Ear – not enough to tip the balance – so four of us went out to take a look. The Wasps've got something mad coming our way – an airship, more than sixty yards long, bow to stern – and . . .' His language apparently failed him, but the other pilot took it up.

'The whole hull's covered with bomb-hatches or something – hundreds of them,' she put in. 'And the Farsphex were flying escort. It's coming close, Chief. By now maybe they could spot it from the walls with a telescope, it's that big.'

Taki frowned. *This makes no sense.* But then it would take a heavy airship some time to reach Collegium from the Empire, and maybe this plan had made sense when the thing set off. Or maybe . . .

'Let me see it,' she decided. 'Get me a glass and . . . wait.' She had slept in her tunic, and it was the work of a moment to struggle into her stained, rank-smelling flying leathers. *Ah for the Exalsee, where we had servants for everything.* 'Everyone else, get dressed and to your machines!' she directed. 'I reckon we've just had some work handed to us.'

She was on the wall within minutes and, from the stir amongst the lookouts there, she guessed that the aerial behemoth had already been spotted. The chill, grey half-light from the east served to silhouette it: still too far to make out any details even through a glass, but its size was undeniable, and . . .

'Will you look at that,' Taki murmured, because there was definite movement from the Second. She was not so much interested to see that the might of the Imperial army and its Spider allies had actually drawn itself up into a conveniently bombable battle order. What had caught her eye were the enemy fliers. Even as she watched, she could see them lifting off in ones and twos, both the Farsphex that she had come to respect, and what remained of the rest, the outdated and the makeshift. They were all of them reaching for the air, and heading not towards Collegium but away. Heading for the same approaching airship.

That's how you're playing it, is it? But still she did not understand. Even with a handful of extra Farsphex, the Empire did not have enough fighting craft to keep that airship intact and aloft. But it looked as though they were going to try.

Maybe if they care enough about the cursed thing, we'll be able to pin them down at last – clear the entire sky of them. She had a great deal of respect for the Farsphex pilots, at least, who had made the very best of a bad job in complicating the bombing of the Second, but it would serve Taki well if the Empire's tenuous grasp on the sky was finally prised off. If the Wasps were committing themselves to defending this monstrosity, then this might be the opportunity they were waiting for.

'Every Stormreader that's ready to fly, get a pilot to it quickly, and let's get into the air,' she decided. *Too big a target, too good an opportunity to pass up.* And still the whole business nagged at her. *So what do they hope to achieve? Are they really so desperate, or such fools?*

At the very prow of his airship's gondola, Captain Nistic stood waiting. His moment was near at hand. His fellows, those who shared his mystery, were scattered about the deck, each concentrating on his own private preparation, letting their minds fall into that requisite void.

Below their feet, in the dark hold: their massed soldiers.

The sky about the airship was criss-crossed with orthopters, their scant escort reinforced with the air power of the Second – or what it could muster. Nistic did not care. Oh, surely it was part of the plan, to focus the minds of the Collegiates, but it meant nothing to him.

He took a deep breath. *Awake, now.*

Some of the troops below were awake already, because his anticipation had been bleeding out into their minds since before dawn. Ahead, the sky was only just shaking off its shroud of darkness, the fateful day cresting over Collegium. If he leant forwards, he could see the Second Army just beginning to move: not as individual soldiers but a composite mass.

His warriors were stirring themselves below, rousing drowsily from their slumber, then springing to alertness. And with their wakefulness he felt their rage.

Such rage: he thrilled to it. He shared it. He heard gasps and sharp grunts as his fellows were caught up in it, like loops in the same chain when the anchor is dropped.

My soldiers! he projected his thoughts down. *Your time is come! Rejoice, for all that you wish for shall be yours!*

There was a call from one of the aircrew – he was pointing,

and Nistic knew this meant the Collegiate fliers were on their way.

Tell me what you wish for! he exhorted his followers, and their words came back to him like swelling, angry tide.

Killkillkillkillkillkillkillkill . . .

He held fast to the rail, because his troops would enter the battle soon and, unless he kept a tight grip, he would be tempted to join them, swept up in their murder-lust. They knew nothing but anger and battle, and he stirred them further, he roused them, he reached into their minds and stoked the fires until the whole airship was heaving with their savagery.

See, the enemy comes! And he lent them his eyes, aware that the furthest out of the Imperial machines were already clawing for height, desperate to defend the airship just as they had been ordered.

But we *need no defending. My soldiers! My faithful! The time has come to kill!*

And from below, from all around, doubling and redoubling, it echoed back from the minds of his fellows: *Killkillkillkillkill kill* . . .

They were Apt, Nistic and his fellows, but the mystery of their calling had not changed since the old days. They were among the last remaining, but they had no doubt that this day was what everything had been leading up to. Today they would vindicate their ancestors. Today the ancient traditions of the Hornet-kinden – which the more civilized Wasp folk had long abandoned – would change the world.

He tilted back his head and screamed out his joy and rage, but the sound was almost lost amidst the roar from below.

Taki slid her *Esca Magni* into a smooth curve that took her up against the flank of a passing Farsphex. As expected, the Imperial craft pulled aside, coursing across the great canvas of the airship's balloon and leading her away. But she lazily broke away and crested the rounded summit of the dirigible, as if to loose a bomb, and sure enough the enemy came back, unable to lead her off on a chase, forced to put itself in harm's way to protect this lumbering offence to aeronautics. She hauled sharply on the stick, stopping her wings dead for a second despite her gear trains' complaints, switching from flying machine to hurtling dead weight for an eye blink, until she set one wing beating to sling her about. Flying backwards, both wings fighting with gravity and her own thwarted momentum, she let loose at the returning Farsphex with a full burst from her rotaries, catching it about the cockpit and wings. It jinked sideways with impressive agility, but she moved along with it, making minute, unconscious adjustments to the stick. A moment later, one of the Farsphex's wings was simply gone, and it was fast parting company with the sky. Taki pulled away, no need to see the end result.

A Spearflight tried to get in her way, with desperate courage, and she chewed its tail off, effortlessly twitching aside from its own shot. Then somehow a pair of Farsphex had joined together to hunt her, and she led them off down the length of the balloon, putting a few bolts in for good measure. If she'd come loaded with bombs she would have dropped one right then, to see if it would take hold on the envelope, but Collegium used its bigger, slower orthopters for bombing work these days, and a good half of the Stormreader pilots had followed her lead in refusing the extra weight.

She dropped out into the vast and busy sky ahead of the airship, and immediately a quartet of Stormreaders were onto her pursuers. With deft practice she reversed her direction again – something this current rebuild of the *Esca* was very suited for, for some reason – and took a more careful look at the airship itself. It was still wallowing through the air at its sedate pace, as though heedless of the air-duelling that went on all around it. She could see the gondola's upper deck passing almost close enough for the crew to loose a sting at her – a handful of airmen crouched low for cover, and some weirdly dressed Wasps standing near the front.

What's that noise?

Over the wind, over the clatter of her wings, reaching her as a tremor in her bones more than through her ears: a deep, pulsating thunder.

From the airship?

No engine, though. Nothing she had ever heard before, except . . . fear. It struck fear into her, at a base and childish level. She had to fight herself to keep the *Esca* level for a second. *What? There's nothing. There's nothing. Only . . .*

A heliopter looking like something put together by a clumsy child tried to challenge her with a repeating ballista, barely fitter for the air than the airship itself, and she sliced off its rotors almost contemptuously. *Please, we were building better than that machine on the Exalsee thirty years back.*

She let the *Esca* circle the stern of the airship, and a Stormreader rose up and crossed her path, signalling furiously with its lamp. She tried to decipher the message, but the pilot was hammering the shutters so fast that whatever signals were intended just ran together and got lost. That insistent vibration was still assaulting her insides, an unreasoning unease encroaching on her despite all rational thought, and she dropped down to see where the Stormreader had come from, to see what it had seen.

She swung a wide course about the belly of the airship.

The hatches had opened, all of them.

But they're two miles short of the city. Are they going to bomb their own army now? A mad thought: what if they had all somehow misunderstood? What if this was a friendly airship under attack from the Empire, and she was supposed to be protecting it? She had gone short on sleep recently, but it hardly seemed possible that she could get it *that* wrong . . .

The sound was so much louder now.

Another Farsphex flashed by, under pursuit, but she let it go, drawing further away from the airship's port-riddled underside. *And they couldn't have got more hatches there if they'd tried. Looks like the whole hull's been attacked by giant woodworm . . .*

Oh.

Oh, mother help me.

There was a head pushing out of one of the holes. It was triangular, dominated by two oval eyes and a set of saw-edged mandibles. Segmented antennae sprang forward as soon as they were free, and then it had forced its hunching thorax clear of the hole and began flexing its wings.

She was bringing the *Esca* back in the tightest turn she could manage, so she could draw a line on the thing and kill it before it could drag that curved black and yellow abdomen from its resting place. But by then there were heads pushing out from every hole across the breadth of the airship's underside: tens of them, hundreds of them, emerging in a second hatching and tasting the air. Tasting the enemy.

Each was not so much smaller than the *Esca* – from its serrated jaws to the barbed sting on its tail. When they stirred their wings into life together, the thunderous buzz rattled every part of Taki and her orthopter, and spoke terror to her in a language she had obviously been born with, all unknowing.

She had her line, and her piercers raked across the airship's hull, and a handful of the host just exploded into wet shards of chitin and wing fragments at the touch of her bolts. But then they were airborne. They were coming for her.

Nistic's body jerked with exaltation as his soldiers took wing and filled the air, mad with rage, desperate to drive their stings into the enemy that was all around them. The scent that the Imperial vessels had been daubed with reeked with sheer incitement, the concentrated musk of alarm and retribution that the hornets themselves would respond to in the wild. Perhaps it would keep the Empire's orthopters safe, perhaps not. It only helped lash the swarm into a berserk frenzy.

Killkillkillkillkillkillkill . . .

'Kill!' Nistic screamed, and all of his fellows screamed in unison:

no mindlink here, but their Art made them part of the swarm and that was as good – indeed was better.

He took a hand from the rail – the other was white-knuckled in its efforts to keep him still on deck – and drew his blade. The old ways knew: a price must be paid to buy the service of the swarm, a price and a reward. In Nistic's mind the host's hundreds raged, waiting only for him to become a true part of them.

At last he let go of the rail, hanging suspended between the deck beneath his feet and the murder-storm of the swarm's collective mind. One hand found where his corselet of chitin scales left off, and he wrenched it up to expose the hollow beneath his ribs.

The swarm was strong and mad, but he would give it direction. For as long as it raged, it would share some fragment of his human mind, and fall upon the enemies of the Empire in blood and fury.

He poised his knife, letting its point hover over his flesh like a stinger.

With a great shout he drove it home, and let his mind fly free.

Taki spun frantically out of the way, but the sky was already full of them – everywhere she turned there were frantic, insanely angry insects battering and stooping and attacking everything in sight, and her mind was running over and over with the mantra: *You can't do this. Everyone knows this isn't how it's done.* Insect against orthopter never worked – the insects were too nimble to be shot, the orthopters proof against the arrows and spears of their riders. But that was wisdom from flying against the dragonfly cavalry of Princep Exilla, over the Exalsee, and these hornets didn't even *have* riders to control them.

In these moments – in these last moments, she reckoned – the Empire had taught her something new about fighting in the air.

A Stormreader wheeled past, spinning out of control with its wings still powering, a hornet clinging to its underside, mindlessly jamming its sting into the machine's guts. A second

Collegiate machine, cutting ahead of her, simply crashed into another insect, the orthopter's blurred wings cutting the creature in two but faltering a moment later, one vane half smashed by the collision.

Taki tried for height, catching a brief glimpse of an Imperial Spearflight weaving desperately through the host – not being attacked but still barely able to navigate the thronging sky.

Got to get clear. She knew she could outrun these creatures with ease, but she was boxed in, insects diving on her from every side, almost brushing wingtips with her as the *Esca* slipped by them. She had given up trying for targets. Her world had condensed into trying to survive the next half-minute intact.

Bergild kept trying to get above, into clear air, but there were just too many insects clogging the heavens, more appearing everywhere she tried to fly. The sky about her became a chaos of horrific sights: everywhere she tried to fly she saw Collegiate machines locked in combat with the hornets – sometimes two or three of the creatures clinging to a single flier, chewing, grappling, stabbing, heedless that their simple weight was dragging the machines out of the sky.

We can't fight in this – get on the ground. But her crystal-clear link with the other pilots was cluttered by that surrounding buzz, the deep fear it provoked coming back to her from every one of her pilots. They were losing their coordinated picture of the battle, and losing control.

Then one of her own pilots was screaming, because a hornet had slammed into his Farsphex and had thrust its jagged mandibles through the glass of the cockpit, and perhaps the engineers had stinted on the foul-smelling paint or perhaps the hornets were just mad now, and jealous of anything else in the sky.

Down! she cried out mind to mind, and just hoped the Spearflight pilots and the others would register her intentions. *Down, all!* Then she followed her own advice, dropping as fast as she could and hoping nothing would get in her way.

She had already lost perhaps one in three of her pilots to the superior numbers of the Stormreaders, and who knew how many she would now lose to the Empire's own secret weapon. *Was this the plan? Whose stupid plan was this?*

Then she had broken through into a clear sky, and was dropping, for once in her aviator's career wanting nothing more than the safety of the ground.

In the moment before impact, Taki had simply lost track of everything, her concentration funnelling down to encompass only the sky directly ahead, trying to turn back for Collegium and hoping that her comrades would reach the same conclusion. *This is not a fight we can win. This is barely even a fight.*

Then something slammed into her, skewing the *Esca* sideways in the air, its weight suddenly monstrously loaded to the right, and she realized that one of them had her.

Two hooked claws scratched across the cockpit, and she was limping sideways across the sky, still somehow keeping height and her aircraft's wings working freely. But then the hornet must have rammed its sting home, because something slapped the *Esca* hard enough to make Taki's teeth rattle, and in the wake of that she had no steering at all and the *Esca* was making a grand slow circle that was going to bring it round into . . .

Into the side of the airship. She had come all the way back.

She wrestled with the stick, but it was loose, all control severed. Then there was a splintering, grinding sound from behind her, and she knew that the beast had started chewing away with its jaws, blindly tearing through wood and metal to get at whatever was inside.

She was inside.

Despite all of this, and her very rational realization that she was dead in any number of ways if she stayed put, it still took supreme willpower to reach for the cockpit release. Even then she had to fight: the single barbed foot the insect had grappled to it was keeping it closed, and she had to put both hands up and push with all her strength to prise it open far enough to let her out.

Out into that busy, hungry sky, and whilst the swarm should not have been able to take on orthopters the way it was doing, it was most certainly well suited for taking living things on the wing.

The side of the airship's gondola was coming up fast.

With a cry of despair over the loss of her flier, the loss of the battle and her fellows, but most of all out of sheer terror, she squeezed out of the cockpit and abandoned her machine, tumbling over and over into that terrible sky.

Twenty-Six

Esmail had already worked out that they would have been having a very different time of it here without *her*. These grey woods, the inner forest, this was not abandoned empty ground. Things dwelt here. Or perhaps it was more accurate to say that things were *remembered* here. The landscape was composed of knots and snarls of memory – particularly the memory of Argastos that slowly decayed year to year, like one of the Mantids' idols, and yet never went away.

The three Pioneers, who should have been breaking new ground ahead of the rest, had seen it too. They clung close to the Empress, divining correctly that if they strayed from her notice, they might never get the chance to stray back.

Esmail had seen a great mantis stalking between the trees, its carapace scarred and battered, its eyes like intricate stained glass. He had seen the rushing shadows of Mantis-kinden all clad in ancient armour – war bands of centuries past, perhaps Argastos's own followers from when he drew breath and knew the sun. There were others, too, barely glimpsed, and Esmail knew that they must be those unfortunates who had found their way here in more recent times – who had slipped in so easily, without needing even a blood sacrifice to open the way, back before the Mantis-kinden were riled up and the forest suddenly bristled with hostility. He had seen Moths and Ants, Collegiate Beetles, Imperial soldiers: the forest's many victims, still caught in image, here in the web of Argastos's thoughts. Perhaps being killed by the Nethyen without would have been a mercy.

And will they see us here, too, those who come after us? If the Empress fails, I am afraid they will.

And that was another reason to stay his hand, should he ever find that combination of courage and motivation to carry out his Tharen orders. For, if he killed her here, there was no guarantee that he was magician enough to find his own way out.

Gjegevey had been leading the way. Seda had more raw power in one fingertip than the old slave had in his whole weary body, but he was wise. He had a skill and application that only years of experience could bring, and he had been guiding them through this tormented forest with patience and care, step by step. Now he leant on his staff, looking well past his time to die, plainly exhausted beyond all measure. Seda's hands twitched angrily, and Esmail thought she would berate the haggard old man, but she visibly restrained herself, and something unfamiliar and awkward touched her expression. Seen on the face of the Empress of the Wasps, it was hard to recognize anything approaching compassion.

'Rest now,' she ordered, and Gjegevey sank down gratefully. Esmail knew he would need help getting up, too. Since entering the forest they had been travelling for so long that it seemed they should have passed every tree within it at least twice. Here, in this bleak place, where the sun never quite rose, the air was chill enough to leach away a body's warmth and Gjegevey had been funnelling all his fading strength into finding a path for his mistress. He was indeed old, but *old* was a feeble word compared to just how many years the man must have resting on his shoulders. Esmail knew little of the Woodlouse-kinden save that they had been a Power once, and had declined irrevocably centuries before ever a Beetle thought of revolution. With a jolt, some more of the old histories came to him: had it been the war with the Worm that had done for Gjegevey's people, left them the hermits and recluses that they now were? And did that mean the ancient magician had his own reasons for being here?

To a mind used to intrigue it was an attractive thought, yet Esmail found that he did not believe it. Perhaps the old man had once pursued double purposes, served more than one master, but, at this faded, trailing end of his life, he was Seda's creature, and perhaps he was the one man she would actually pause pursuit of her ambitions for. He had, after all, turned her away from the Worm once, if only to seek that self-same Seal again here with Argastos.

Thunder rumbled from the sky above them. That sky was mostly hidden behind the vault of the forest roof and, when it could be seen, coursed with clouds that seemed ragged and decomposing even as they seeped overhead.

Abruptly Gjegevey began scrabbling for his staff, and big Gorrec hauled him to his feet without being asked to. Everyone was now looking up at the sky, and the Wasp magician Tegrec cried out, holding his hands up as though to fend something off.

Something's coming. Argastos? But Esmail could sense that whatever was on its way now was as alien to this place as they were.

'We must move!' the hunched Woodlouse cried. He was trembling all over, and Seda took his arm.

'Eyes out, lads!' Gorrec shouted. The Pioneers already had weapons to hand, as did Seda's remaining bodyguard. Tisamon's right hand was his clawed gauntlet, of course, and he never took it off. *Or can't, more like.*

Gjegevey had doubled his speed, even though he stumbled and skidded over the uneven ground, and around them all the ghosts of the forest flickered and danced, appearing almost too briefly to be registered, then gone in the next blink. A wind had struck up, fierce and unheralded, which clawed at the branches overhead, as if trying to find a way in.

Is this what it was like here when we forced our own way in?

There was something ahead . . . a mound, was it? And, on sight of it, Seda had cried out in triumph—

Then that thunder sounded again, so close, so apocalyptically loud, that Esmail found himself thrown to the ground, stunned by the sheer savagery of the air that shook and jumped with the impact of it.

And, in its wake, everything had changed.

The thunder itself was a poor accompaniment for the soundless shudder of force that rushed through that other forest, and Seda understood that *she* was following at last. Whilst Seda had been battling her way towards Argastos, *she* had somehow simply stepped here – had bided her time on the outside, had . . .

Seda tasted the sour triumph of the *other*'s arrival. Yes, *she* had won over the Nethyen; she had severed them from Seda's own purpose.

But my purpose was only to get here – to get to Argastos – and I'm almost there. So close!

And she felt the mind of her enemy like a hot ball of iron, and knew that the Beetle had found her in turn.

'They come!' she called. Gjegevey was standing still, looking back. 'Move, old man!' she spat at him. He sensed only enough to know everything was now going wrong.

'Soldiers, destroy them,' she snapped at Gorrec and the pioneers, while she hauled on Gjegevey's arm. 'Come, slave.' And she found the stab of fear she felt was not for herself but for him. *She* could defend herself, and he . . . he was withered and frail and, despite her many threats, he was *hers*, and he had been her friend once. 'Ostrec – see them destroyed, every one of them,' for the Maker girl had her own soldiers, she could detect them. Each new set of feet set this unnatural terrain dancing like a spider web, telling her – telling both of them – exactly where the fighters were, marking out the woodland between them like a chessboard. 'Tegrec, help me with him.'

But she saw now that her intervention was required, or else her troops would have no chance of victory. She saw how it must be done. 'No, lead him away, take him some place safe, Tegrec,' she spat the words at the turncoat Wasp, 'or I swear I will have your very spirit on crossed pikes for all eternity. Tisamon, guard me.'

Gorrec glanced at the Red Watch officer, Ostrec, but the man seemed disinclined to give any orders, just staring off into the grey mist of the trees as though he saw some great truth there. *Up to me as usual.* The Mantis woman who was Seda's remaining bodyguard loped past him, the claw of her gauntlet jutting downwards like a dagger blade.

He was no great strategist, but he had led men in a fight before, and this cluttered and gloomy forest was as much ideal Pioneer territory as anywhere.

'I'll hold the centre,' he announced, because it was what he was better fitted for than the other two. 'Jons, left. Ic, right – flank, strike, fade. Once you've engaged I'm pulling back.'

'She's not left you many places to pull back *to*,' Jons Escarrabin pointed out, hands busy working the winch handle to charge his cut-down snapbow.

Gorrec shrugged. He had a broad-headed axe in each hand and a heavy feeling in his stomach. *How many enemy? How well armed? Nothing but 'They come!' from Herself.* Still, he had known before now that he and his fellows were reckoned expendable. The Empress had not brought them here because she enjoyed their scintillating conversation.

Icnumon the halfbreed had his shortbow out, an arrow to the string, and he slunk off between the trees without a word, reliable as ever.

'Good luck, Sergeant.' Jons threw Gorrec an abbreviated salute and was gone, too, stepping away with stealth rare for a Beetle. The Empress was still in sight, behind, with that armoured – whatever it was – standing before her. *Not my problem, not right now. Right now,* I'm *my problem.* He crouched down, taking cover leaning against a tree, ready to throw himself at an enemy or out of the way, as circumstances recommended. Many thoughts rose to mind, but he let them pass.

When she passed beyond, through that gate opened by blood – *whose blood?* – Che realized that she had wooed the Nethyen too well. She was here at the very heart, within reach of Argastos's barrow – and so was *she*.

'The Empress is here! Ready yourselves!' she managed to gasp. 'They're coming!' Because, of course, Seda would sense Che just as easily and, of course, she would send her followers. No, more than that. Che *knew* they were coming, as if she could see the forest from above and track each man's progress by the ripple of undergrowth. 'There, that way!' She dragged her sword out, and instantly her three protectors – the Wasp, the Mantis halfbreed, the Beetle – were moving as directed, whilst Maure hung back, with a shortsword in her hand and absolutely no intention of using it.

The woods here were less overgrown, but there was a misty gloom over everything that even Che's eyes made little headway with. Still, she saw Tynisa clearly, as she rushed forwards, leading the way with her blade – saw Amnon peeling off to the right, moving to intercept some enemy that he must have seen or heard, but that Che could not know about – save that she *did*. She could feel that dagger-like mind drawing near, drenched in thoughts of blood and honour.

She stood stock still, trembling, having stepped into a world that was crowding in on her with knowledge.

Thalric she had already lost track of, somewhere off in the trees and acting on his own recognizance. She reached for him but felt only a shadow, an echo of him that she could not pin down.

Then the killing began, as swiftly as that. A Mantis woman was abruptly rushing Amnon, breaking from the greying ferns too rapidly for him to bring his snapbow to bear. He caught her blade-arm with one hand and her off-hand spines raked down his breastplate before he cast her aside. His snapbow swung back on its strap and, when she leapt for him again, he had his sword out, fending off two jabbing lunges. Che felt the woman's astonishment at finding a Beetle so swift, and yet still strong enough to snap her in half. The Mantis fell back a pace, daring Amnon to follow her, darting in again as he tried to make more distance between them. Che found herself almost rehearsing Amnon's moves as he made them, even though he was out of her sight, even though she had none of his skill and experience.

Her own hands twitched as the big Beetle twisted at the woman's next lunge, letting the metal claw gouge a furrow in his backplate. When his sword came in, the Mantis was ready for it, her free hand slapping his strong, lumbering stroke aside – just the sort of artless stabbing she expected from a Beetle – *and Che saw the thought as if it had been her own* – but then a solid blow from Amnon's left hand thundered into the juncture of neck and shoulder, sending the woman staggering to one knee.

He did not hesitate, kicking her in the chest with all his strength, enough to send her sprawling six feet away. She was on her feet in moments, but he had his snapbow aimed and the trigger pulled in the same space of time, and the bolt snapped her head back before she knew it.

Che's attention jumped elsewhere, because Tynisa had found an enemy that she herself had almost missed. To her, he seemed barely there, just as Thalric had become a thing of glass and shadows. This man came to her only through Tynisa's focus on him: a big, burly Wasp-kinden, almost a match for Amnon, and more than happy to meet Tynisa one on one. He had a pair of huge axes and he danced with them, never letting them fall still, so their whistling passage made a steel maze for Tynisa to step through. She was faster, but the man was an old hand, and Che could read in his defences a long experience of fighting against swift Inapt blades, Mantis and Dragonfly both. Tynisa was forcing him back, evading his explosive counter-attacks, but he turned any retreat in a circle, losing individual steps but never giving any real ground.

And elsewhere: here was a stealthy half-Mantis killer stalking her . . . here was another Wasp – *no, what was he—?* – watching Tynisa's fight without stepping in . . . there was the Empress, with Tisamon the revenant as her shield. And behind her, some others, making a crippled escape – but who was so important that the Empress herself would cover their escape?

How do I know all this . . .?

Then came to her a sublime understanding that allowed her to master all this mental clamour. She was in a place of magic, as perhaps so much more of the Lowlands had been once upon a time. She was a magician facing another magician, each with their cadre of loyal followers. She was waging a war the likes of which this land had not seen, perhaps, since the Revolution. She was fighting as a wizard fought.

Chess, she realized. This was where chess came from, and the Tactician piece – or Arista, or Emperor, whatever name was given to it – so vulnerable and powerless, *that* was her. But of course the Tactician was not powerless, because she governed and controlled the other pieces.

And the implication was plain: magicians did not care about the deaths of their pieces so long as they *won*; but the only pieces Che could advance were her friends.

For a moment she fought against it, ready to let them act according to their own direction. But, of course, the Empress would not hesitate, and surely Che understood this, or must soon grasp it.

And the halfbreed killer was getting close now.

Che reached out and made her move.

Amnon, stalking forwards, suddenly changed his course, coming upon Tynisa's battle with the Wasp. Too close together for a snapbow shot, he broke in with his sword, no doubt assuming that the two of them could take the man, but Tynisa was already falling back, knowing only that she had to, until Che had drawn her to confront the halfbreed – *Icnumon. His name is Icnumon.*

The man abandoned his bow in an instant, the paired blades sliding silent from their sheaths to meet Tynisa's rapier. *Now I leave her and must trust to her skill.* Amnon and the big Wasp were circling, both slightly wounded, the big Beetle's direct style a better match than Tynisa's for the Wasp's two gleaming axes. But that other man, the officer . . .

Still watching, and his mind –

Che touched his mind, and for a moment could name him Ostrec, Rekef man. And she would have passed on, save that . . . *how is it that I can touch him at all?* The axeman and Thalric were transparent to her; even Amnon was a shadow barely illuminated by the distant, fading glories of Khanaphes that had shaped him. Tynisa and Icnumon were both fierce fires: Inapt and therefore fitting tools for a magician. But this Ostrec . . .

And she pressed, and Ostrec broke like an eggshell beneath her touch. Then she and the man behind that mask were standing looking at one another. He drew new veils, too swiftly and skilfully for her to find out who he was, but he was no Wasp. He was Inapt, he was an *impostor*, and she knew beyond question that Seda was not aware of it.

If you are an enemy of the Empress, now is your moment. Her own voice sounded weak and timid in her mind, but he trembled when he heard it, as though some great warlord had spoken.

She had a momentary awareness of Thalric, full of purpose, skirting the flanks of the battle. *Seda, he is hunting Seda,* but Che couldn't be sure, and then he was gone.

In her absence, Amnon had hacked the big Wasp across one hand, shattering bones and leaving an axe buried in the forest floor. Now the man was falling back, and Che could sense the Empress and her guardian waiting there. Amnon was faster, though. He hurled himself forwards, getting an elbow across the man's jaw, and then the two of them had toppled over, crashing into the briars. The finish was brutal artistry, with Amnon pinning the man's good arm, his own sword drawn back. Its descent was clean and final.

The officer, the impostor, the not-Ostrec, just stared at him, then a moment later he had vanished into the woods, absenting himself from the skirmish entirely.

Tynisa kept pressing Icnumon hard, keeping clear of those shorter blades that Che could virtually taste the poison on, but denying herself an opportunity for a telling blow. The man was good, but he was no great duellist, better suited to striking from the shadows and in the back. Che reached for his mind, but it was slippery and venomous, and she could not get a hold on it.

Then he broke through Tynisa's guard, sending her hopping back a handful of steps – *Surely a feint?* – but no, she was off-balance; one honed edge sliced a shallow line across her arming jacket as she dodged away. Che witnessed the Weaponsmaster's mystery then, that perfect unison of sword and wielder. Even as Tynisa fought for balance, her arm was coming about, knocking her opponent's lunge aside with her rapier's curved guard and, though her quillons kept winding round, her weapon's point was just hanging there between them, the long blade angling and angling to keep itself there so that Icnumon almost ran on to it, trying to follow her up. In that moment, when he had skidded and twisted to a halt to avoid being impaled, and both of his weapons were coming together to bind her sword aside, she lunged, arm snapping out straight to ram the point into his stomach, razoring through him halfway to the hilt and then out again in another smooth motion that left her well beyond his reach.

Icnumon collapsed, shuddering but still silent, and Tynisa was already running back to support Amnon.

Che sensed the very moment that Seda understood what was happening. Perhaps because she exercised such autocratic control over her subordinates in the world outside, the woman had come to this new form of battle moments too late. And now her forces were in disarray and fallen, and here came Amnon, led to her by Che's firm governance, and only Tisamon stood between him and the end of an Imperial rule.

Only Tisamon.

Jons Escarrabin had been a Pioneer for many long years. He had cast in his lot with the Empire during the Twelve-year War, after a stint of fighting against it, because he recognized what winners looked like. He had not looked back since. A loner and an opportunist by nature, the life of a Pioneer suited him well, and being a servant of the Empire provided him with the latest toys – like his snapbow – and the opportunity to use them.

But he had never been anywhere like this, even in the Commonweal. The forest around seemed bizarrely inconstant, nothing ever quite where it should be when he took a second look, and since they arrived they had been stalked by fleeting enemies, never quite seen but always sensed.

Now those enemies had become a reality, though, and he was inching forwards with his snapbow levelled, trying to flank a skirmish that he could hear far too distantly and not pin down. *I hope you're doing your job, Gorrec.* But he had a cold feeling that this clash was not one that could ever go well – not in this place.

He was trying to follow a curving course so as to take the notional enemy in the back or the side, as Icnumon should be doing opposite him, but still he had encountered nobody, and the actual fighting seemed to have drifted away, leaving him seemingly the last man alive in this forest.

This is ridiculous; pull yourself together. Just another Mantis forest. But he could not quite make himself believe it.

He pushed onwards, because even the illusion of progress was better than nothing, his eyes scanning the dingy greyness of his surroundings for . . . anything, any sign of life. Show him a Sarnesh soldier right now, and he would be glad of it.

And then there was a shadowy figure in the drifting fog that seemed to hang in rotting sheets in front of his eyes. Surely, there was someone there – or, no, perhaps two of them? His eyes ached from squinting, and he had a terror that, if he just loosed now at those nebulous forms, they would be gone and he would have no evidence that they had ever been.

Keeping his eyes fixed firmly on them, and hardly daring to blink, he inched forwards, straining for any detail. For all he could be sure, he might have simply trodden in a grand circle. He could even now have a snapbow levelled on the Empress himself.

No, too short and stocky for the Empress. He wasn't sure about one of them, but the other was more like a woman of his own kinden . . .

A Beetle girl? Hadn't the Empress been cursing some Beetle girl?

Jons swallowed, and crept still closer, step by careful step, stalking the two women as painstakingly as he would hunt an animal.

Tisamon was faster than Che could follow, each movement appreciable only in its aftermath. Amnon had discharged his snapbow even as he ran forwards, aiming straight at the ornate Mantis breastplate, but Tisamon was already moving, the bolt vanishing between the trees Che was thinking, *No, the Empress! Shoot the Empress!* But too late, for Tisamon had closed the gap between them, his bladed gauntlet lashing out with blurred speed – and it was over.

She was so convinced of it, of the inevitability, that she could not even watch. She missed Amnon's skidding to a stop, his sword catching the darting metal claw and knocking it aside, even managing a weak riposte that Tisamon swayed aside from. For a moment the two were poised, drawn back to just outside each other's reach: the living Beetle – former First Soldier of Khanaphes – against the risen Mantis Weaponsmaster.

Tisamon struck out, making nothing of the distance, his crooked blade driving down like an axe, but Amnon had read the move somehow – not Che's doing, since she was neither fast nor fighter enough to help him – and twitched to one side, the weapon slicing at the sleeve of his buff coat but not quite drawing blood. His answering lunge met only air. They circled.

Che saw the Empress, then. The woman had sidestepped the duel neatly, her eyes fixed on Amnon and her hand outstretched. Empress and magician, yes, but she was still a Wasp, and she could sting.

Amnon had not noticed her, but with Che watching over him he did not need to. Without knowing why, he had ducked aside, breaking away from Tisamon and drawing the revenant almost into the bolt of gold fire the Empress had loosed He let the Mantis come to him, staying on the defensive, sacrificing his attack to keep Tisamon between him and Seda.

And even as the Empress tried to find a clear line towards Amnon, Tynisa came rushing between the trees. Che sensed her sister's loathing and rage that this *thing* was what the Empress had made of her father – nothing but a fighting puppet of blood and old armour. There were no words: the anticipated oaths and threats never came. Instead the girl drove straight for Seda.

Tisamon was faster, taking a blow of Amnon's blade that dented his mail, but placing himself between Tynisa and his mistress. Then the battle was truly joined and, incredibly, the risen Weaponsmaster was on the defensive, unable to press his advantage lest he let one or other of his enemies past him, dancing and whirling with inhuman speed, and yet giving ground an inch at a time, contending all at once with Amnon's strength and long-honed experience, and with Tynisa's speed and skill.

The interplay of blades had been too fast for Che to follow from the first, and she knew Seda was experiencing the same. It was down to the skill of the three combatants now, as to who lived and who died.

For a moment, she felt herself face Seda directly, each looking into the mind's eye of the other. The bitter loathing there did not surprise her, but there was fear, too. In her innermost heart the Empress of all the Wasps feared this implacable girl from Collegium.

Then Seda was backing off through the trees, retreating behind Tisamon's fierce defence – but not yet defeated, for she had worked out some use for her magic that Che could not follow, some target . . .

Then Che was dragged back to herself, the world wheeling around her, and Maure had crashed into her, knocking her to the ground.

Che shook her head, unable to work out what was going on. The halfbreed was standing over her, blade extended, directed at . . .

There was a man there, another Beetle-kinden, a stranger. She almost took him for some ghost of this place, but he had a snapbow and it was levelled at the two of them. It was plain that he would prefer to shoot her, but that he would take Maure if need be, and trust to his speed in reloading.

Che tried to twist him, to deflect him, but she was rattled, and he was Apt. He had managed to walk like a ghost through her battle without her ever realizing he was there. *A little magic will destroy him*, she thought, for being Apt he would have no defence against it. Surely here, where the land was so fit for it, she could drive this man mad, force him to flee in fear, control his muscles, stop his heart?

But she was frightened now, and the sudden disconnection had scattered her concentration. Maure was already trying something, she knew, but the other woman's skills were with the dead, not the living. Even so, the snapbowman hesitated, as if for a moment he saw some familiar face before him, or perhaps nothing at all.

The stingshot that struck him had been aimed hurriedly, catching him across one arm and spinning him about, but not knocking him down. The second came even as he tried to swing his weapon about, seeking this new adversary. Then Thalric had him – the searing bolt smashed the snapbow's air battery and punched into the man's chest, hurling him, already dead, from his feet.

But he was hunting the Empress. She could not know whether Thalric had come back for her, or just become lost in the greyness, but she had a task for him now. 'Thalric, follow me! The Empress, she's . . .' *But what is she doing?* Che cast her mind out again, fighting for a clear picture of what was going on. There was the furious mêlée between Amnon, Tynisa and Tisamon. There was the Empress, now barely in sight of it. There . . .

The killer, Icnumon, that Tynisa had run through, had been bleeding his last out into the thirsty forest floor, but was not dead, not quite. A spark had remained in him, guttering and flickering with every moment.

Seda had fanned it.

Even as she watched the man haul himself unsteadily to his feet, Che was thinking wildly, *Can that be done?* as though the evidence of her own scrying was not enough. Blood still pumped from the wound Tynisa had given him, even more now than before, but there seemed an inexhaustible supply. And then Che understood: this was Mosquito-kinden magic run backwards, something that had surely not been achieved since before the Revolution, but more likely had never been done at all. If blood was power, so too power was blood. Seda was clawing up handfuls of the cold energy of this place and channelling it through the wretched Icnumon, her last remaining soldier still clinging to life. Now she had him on his feet, blades to hand . . . and a moment later he was running.

For me? But, no, Seda was looking to her own defence. Tisamon was hard-pressed, and she was sending the revived assassin to settle matters there.

'We have to go!' Che could not just pick up Thalric like a game piece and move him towards the fight. She would have to lead him there. She dashed off into the forest, half running, half flying, without another word, knowing that he would follow, with Maure trailing behind them both.

The skirmish ahead was as bright as a lantern in her mind compared to the ghostly trees which loomed and lurched suddenly out of the mist, so that she was constantly moments from running into them or being tripped by their roots. She could see the battle, feel each move of it: Tynisa's straight-arm lunge that Tisamon stepped aside from, even as he caught Amnon's descending blade with his claw and bound it aside, almost wrenching it from the Beetle's grip. The answering sweep of the revenant's blade sent both of his opponents a step back, and he whipped it up and lashed at Tynisa's face, Che choked, already seeing the attack carving another brutal mark there, but Tynisa had fallen back before it, ducking so far that one knee was level with her chin. The seeking steel fell short, then was dragged back sharply to deflect Amnon's next lunge, giving Tynisa a chance to find her balance again.

But the other dead man, the tortured form of Icnumon, would be there at any moment. And beyond, Seda was out there but further and further away, joined by two more allies and shepherding them towards Argastos, and there . . .

There was the spy, the impostor, and Che sensed a sour reek of doubt arising from him: a man who did not know what to do. Even as she pelted through the forest, she was crying out to him, *Do what is right! This is your one chance!*

She was moving as fast as she could, but not fast enough, caught out by Seda's vicious use of blood magic. Even so, the fighting ahead must have been visible to the mere eye, for Thalric had abruptly taken wing, hurling himself forwards far faster than she could.

Icnumon was weaving his way through the trees, leaving a trail of impossibly still-gouting blood behind him, the poisoned blades in his hands just moments from striking. And Che had no choice. She reached out to grab Tynisa's attention, showing her the threat, knowing that this distraction itself might be fatal.

Tisamon's scything blade cut at her neck but her rapier was there to catch it, and Tynisa pushed against it hard, sending the revenant a pace off his mark, and using the resistance provided to throw herself out of his reach . . . already turning as the ghastly near-corpse of Icnumon leapt towards her.

Amnon did not hesitate, driving his blade in but reaching for Tisamon's weapon arm as well. Briefly he had it, and tried to bear the slighter man down, but that slender armoured form was like iron, just as strong as Amnon was. For a moment they were locked together, and then Thalric dropped in, hand extended but denied a clear target.

Tisamon spotted him, and that the dark helm snapped about in clear and murderous recognition, and he cast Amnon aside almost contemptuously. Thalric got one sting off, which vanished past the revenant's mailed shoulder, and then the dead Mantis was rushing him. Plainly there were some enmities that had carried over quite readily into this new incarnation.

Icnumon moved like a spider on its web, all sudden jerks and stops, nothing so predictable as a living opponent. He lunged and cut with the same speed and skill, but made no attempt to defend himself, and Tynisa had holed him three more times, each one running red, before she realized that she was getting nowhere. The man's face was twisted in terror and agony, the lips twitching, eyes rolling madly in their sockets.

And Che was there, pausing in horror, in time to see Thalric suddenly backing up, wings flowering from his back, then a second stingshot striking Tisamon in the chest but barely staggering him, boiling off that old Mantis plate.

The clawed gauntlet stabbed out. Thalric's sword was out of line and too slow to parry, and yet the killing stroke never reached him. Amnon had lunged and hooked a hand about Tisamon's pauldron, dragging him back, his sword stabbing down.

The point scraped off Tisamon's mail, the dead man twisting in time to shrug off the force of it, and backhanding Amnon with a faceful of spines, sending the Beetle staggering away, clutching at his eye. Thalric struck again, only to have his sword slapped aside, and then Tisamon kicked him solidly in the chest, pitching him over backwards – and took Amnon's lunging sword on his forearm, the edge savaging his gauntlet, the blade of his claw drawn back along the line of his arm, inside Amnon's guard.

It flicked out with a spasm of Tisamon's fingers, the point resting for a second on the rim of Amnon's breastplate, before he drove it in with one sure, sudden motion, its keen edge cleaving halfway into the big Beetle's neck.

Che cried out in horror, and for a second she was fumbling at the last traces of Amnon's life, fully intent on turning the man into an abomination akin to the thing that Tynisa was battling. But she did not know how, and she could not replicate the magic – and a moment later she was glad of that.

Tisamon paused a moment, whether in respect or simply receiving new instructions, and Che reached out to Icnumon – all power and no subtlety, just like the Empress herself – and unravelled him, pulling apart the knot of blood and magic that was keeping him in motion, so that his body collapsed with a final gasp of relief, and he was allowed to die.

By then Tisamon was on the move again, and coming straight at her, but Tynisa was there to defend her, and Thalric as well . . . and Che cast her mind out towards that errant false Wasp whom she could still sense out there and gave him an ultimatum.

Act now, she ordered him, allowing no room for negotiation. And he did.

Twenty-Seven

'What just happened to the orthopters?' Straessa demanded. She had no telescope, and the only glass within reach was at the eye of Madagnus, her commanding officer. There was a sort of a cloud that had suddenly sprung up around that looming airship, though, now dispersing into . . . were those other flying machines? There was some sort of ferocious air battle going on, which hadn't been the plan explained to the ground forces.

And speaking of ground forces . . .

The Second Army was making its advance, too far away for her to see anything more than solid blocks of black and gold broaching the uneven, churned-up ground that would funnel them into the hammer of Collegium's artillery.

Madagnus swore and rammed the telescope into her hands. 'Get the magnets ready! Loose as fast as you can – put as much shot into them as you're able.'

The magnetic ballistae were already charged, so the first volley went off in glorious unison, explosive bolts breaking into bright flashes of fire across the Imperial front lines. There were only a dozen of these weapons along Collegium's wall, all the artificers had been able to build, and they had been intended for destroying the Empire's greatshotter artillery, which had been mostly lost on the road to Collegium. All their range and accuracy meant little against the great mass of the Second Army.

Then they were recharging from their lightning engines, and

that meant just dead time in which the Empire's soldiers crept closer and closer. The earthworks were slowing them down, but not as much as they should have done: most of the Imperial army could fly, after all, and even armoured men could manage a brief hop over obstructions. Straessa could see knots of soldiers struggling with siege engines, though, carrying ramps to ease them up the jumbled path the Collegiates had dug for them. She remembered how much sweating, back-breaking work all that digging had entailed. *And now we see if it was worth the effort.*

Judging that the Empire was still a way off from reaching snapbow range, she lifted the glass to view the aerial battle, steadying it as best she could to try and make out something of what was going on.

By that time it was mostly over. The great Imperial airship hung there, listing slightly, its hull seemingly peppered with holes, but the skies around it were almost clear of orthopters, for those winged forms madly circling the vessel didn't look like . . . Straessa blinked, lowering the glass when at last she understood what she was looking at. *But that wouldn't work, surely?* But even now there were Stormreaders overhead, yet so very few of them, and many virtually limping through the air with wings battered and torn. And the Imperial Air Corps? The only blessing was that it seemed to have gone to ground as well, and Straessa wondered just how discriminating those infuriated insects had been.

The flying elite that had dominated the battlefield up until now had been abruptly swept away. The war had been reclaimed for the ordinary soldiers, such as the thousands of Wasps presently toiling towards them, heedless of the magnetic ballistae, and now getting within range of the other wall engines.

They're certainly keeping up a pace, Straessa thought, slightly nervously.

Someone dumped a crate full of what looked like random pieces of metal beside her, and she looked round, into the face of Gerethwy.

'Where have you been?' she demanded.

'It's finished,' he declared. His eyes were red-rimmed and wide, the look of a man with too many ideas and not enough sleep. 'My rational snapbow, Antspider. I just need space to set it up.'

'What the pits are you doing?' Madagnus demanded. He had been sighting up at the Wasp vanguard, calculating ranges, and nearly fell over Gerethwy's apparatus on his way to the nearest leadshotter crew. 'Get that out of here.'

'Chief, this is my new weapon,' the Woodlouse student objected. 'You won't believe it, I've rigged a repeating snapbow to a ratiocinator and—'

'Son, this is not the time for experiment,' his chief officer interrupted him flatly. For once, Madagnus looked scowling sober. 'Get that out of here, I said.'

Gerethwy frowned. 'Chief, you don't understand.' It seemed as if he was about to deliver a lecture to enlighten the man.

'I don't have time for you,' Madagnus told him. 'Get this junk off the wall. Get yourself off it, too. You can't even shoot straight. You're no use to me.'

The Woodlouse gaped at him, mouth forming unspoken words of protest.

Straessa took his arm. 'Gereth, just go. Get yourself some-where safe,' she said softly.

He stared at her in a look of utter betrayal, his maimed hand twitching towards the crate, and then he was dragging it back down the steps.

A street further back from the wall, in the incongruous surround-ings of a rooftop garden, Eujen Leadswell was trying to stay calm. He had a maniple of his Student Company surrounding him, armed with pike and snapbow, while, to left and right, every rooftop that would take them had another. In the end the Assembly had not trusted his latecomer soldiers with manning the wall or the gate, but this line of defence had been judged within their capability. Now he could see the new wall engines – the long-range ones – loosing at targets somewhere beyond the wall, and the other engines were being readied and aimed.

'Nobody here can fly?' he demanded. Nobody could, as he had known already. The troops stationed on the wall – Coldstone Company and Outwright's Pike and Shot – were supposed to send messengers back to keep him informed, but that appeared to have been overlooked. *Let's face it, they don't think we're up to much as soldiers. 'Learn to Live' indeed, and starting with trying to learn our own battle plan.* He tried to spot Straessa but there were too many soldiers there, at this distance seemingly crammed elbow to elbow. She would be just one more helm and backplate amongst many.

In the streets below was gathered the strength of Maker's Own Company, maniples spread out in case of enemy artillery, but ready to hold the gate or sally forth as needed, with the heavy armour of the Vekken to back them up. Kymene's Mynans, a notably smaller contingent, had a mobile brief to reinforce the wall or the gate as required. Eujen could only take comfort in the fact that Remas Boltwright's Fealty Street Company was even further from the fighting, held in reserve to deal with possible incursions by the Airborne. *We rate higher than that, anyway.*

There was a twitch of alarm amongst his troops as Averic dropped down at the roof's edge, fending off an over-eager pike-head.

'Everyone's in place, Chief,' he told Eujen. 'We're on pretty much every roof within bowshot of the walls.'

Eujen nodded, on the point of saying, *Go and find Straessa, Make sure she's all right,* even though the real fighting had not even started yet. But that would not be a responsible course of action. He was going to live up to the rank the Assembly had bestowed on him. He was going to do the Right Thing.

There was a hollow boom, then he saw smoke rising from the wall. The tense glance he shared with Averic spoke volumes. *That was the first leadshotter. How fast are they coming? And what happened to the Stormreaders?*

406

'Averic, go and poach a Fly-kinden from one of our maniples. No, make it two: I need messengers or I'll never find out anything,' he decided. The Wasp student's hand moved, a gesture hastily suppressed, and Eujen realized that his friend had been about to salute him.

'And Averic?' he added, as the Wasp's wings flashed from his shoulders. 'Go check on . . . Officer Straessa, if you get the chance.'

'Will do.' With a brief, wan smile, Averic stepped off the rooftop and swerved away over the city. Another half-dozen leadshotters spoke, then, a hollow percussion that rolled back and forth along the wall.

Down at ground level, Stenwold heard out the hurried, somewhat garbled report of the air battle impatiently. Before the messenger had finished, he had already considered a half-dozen plans and eventualities. He had seen the Wasp army in action many times before, but they did not stand still, and each engagement had brought some manner of new artifice to change the nature of the battlefield. *So what comes now?* The remaining Imperial air power was an unknown question, but for the moment it seemed that the field had been abandoned to more traditional tactics: the mass movement of fighting men.

'Commander Termes, Chief Officer Padstock,' he began formally, regarding his two subordinates. The Vekken Ant was expressionless as ever, but there was a hard anticipation on Elder Padstock's face. She wanted to kill Wasps in the name of her city, Stenwold knew. 'I'm heading up the wall to get a first-hand view,' he told them. 'I'll send orders down, to brace the gate in the worst case, to sally out in the best. Until then, eyes on the sky. I'm expecting company soon.'

'War Master,' Padstock acknowledged. Termes just nodded wordlessly.

Stenwold climbed the steps at speed, because, if he slowed, then he might just grind to a halt altogether. The weight of his breastplate and helm combined with score of aches, pains and old wounds to nag at him, and he consoled himself with thoughts of the magical time of *after this* . . .

Chief Officer Outwright, of the Pike and Shot, was young enough to be Stenwold's son, and looked young enough to be his grandson. His armour shone like the best silverware, but his face was ashen and frightened when Stenwold reached him. His attention had been focused across the wall, of course, where the Wasps were navigating the complex earth-works with steady determination, closing and closing even as more and more wall engines began bedevilling them. Stenwold saw that they had chosen a mixed marching order: there were solid blocks of their heavier infantry out there, but they were surrounded by a looser-knit shifting mass of soldiers that must be the Light Airborne, and whose open order denied the Collegiate artillery good targets. There were plenty of small siege engines amongst the Wasps, though, making heavier work of the terrain and attracting much shot from the walls. Even as Stenwold watched, a lucky leadshot impacted near one, the missile exploding into shrapnel as its internal charge went off. The distance was too great to count casualties, but the Imperial engine – some sort of modified leadshotter – seemed to have ended up on its side.

'Be ready, Outwright,' Stenwold told the young chief officer. 'They're taking a lot of damage from our engines. They'll try to do something about that soon, when they're close enough to make a swift rush of it. Just remember your briefing.'

'Yes, War Master,' Outwright gasped. Thankfully his company had experienced officers who were already relaying the order: *Ready snapbows, ready pikes.* Stenwold clapped the man on the shoulder, a public gesture to boost his morale and his soldiers' confidence, and carried on along the wall, looking for Madagnus,

The Ant artillerist was sighting up one of the magnetic bows, and Stenwold could feel, as much as hear, the crackle from its charged lightning engine. A moment later the air relaxed as the machine discharged, its explosive-tipped bolt vanished from its groove, and Madagnus was obviously cheered by the result, because he was cackling to himself even as he dragged at a lever to recharge the device. Down the wall from him, a pneumatic repeating ballista was just starting to loose, its pistons banging out a solid rhythm as it began throwing bolts into the front line of the enemy.

Stenwold looked out at the Second. They were just about close enough, he reckoned. A lot depended on the speed and stamina of their Airborne, but there seemed to be a distinct order now imposed over the somewhat unruly ranks. He took out his glass and extended it, scanning the lines, seeing definite preparation, the magnification enough to see individual faces, to spot sergeants passing amongst their men, mouths opening to shout silent orders. More than Airborne, too: as well as the Wasp heavies, he saw a good number of Spider troops, also in loose skirmish order, and starting to move ahead of their Imperial colleagues. *But they don't fly, and so they don't bother me as much.*

It was back to basics for the Wasp army, at least for now. The Light Airborne, their traditional strength, was about to test itself against Collegium marksmanship.

'There!' Madagnus barked out. 'Let's take a crack at that monster.'

He was indicating a Sentinel, the armoured, woodlouse-like form humping and scrabbling over the broken terrain without obvious difficulty. Stenwold had seen the automotives in action first-hand at Myna and, once the wall had come down, they had been a terror in the street-to-street fighting, but he did not see them as a priority. *Because it won't come to that. Because we will hold the gate, and they do not have the means to break the wall.*

The Sentinel was making quick work of the earthworks, its multiple legs scrabbling and pulling it over anything it encountered, and the magnetic ballistae had not been intended for such a mobile target, but Madagnus apparently took this as some sort of a challenge. His lips moved, counting to himself, and he wound the engine degree after degree until he was leading the galloping Sentinel by the required distance.

Then he loosed, soundlessly, only a shudder in the air to indicate it, and cried out with triumph as he scored a hit. Stenwold looked out at the stricken machine – close enough to need no glass now – and saw it shake itself just like an animal, as though getting its armour plating to fall back into place again. A moment later it was moving on again, not even a serious dent to show for the impact.

'Right.' The set of Madagnus's jaw presaged dangerous risk-taking, and Stenwold grabbed his arm.

'Go for the threats to our gate, Chief. Priorities, remember.'

The Ant stared at him blankly for a second, then nodded briefly. 'Ramming engines,' he confirmed.

There was a series of shouts and snapbow shot from down the wall, and for a moment Stenwold thought he had missed the Second's attack, but it was one of the great hornets, far from the Imperial airship and still mad for blood, that had come droning over the wall. The snapbowmen were far better suited to destroying such creatures than were the pilots who had shared the air with them but there were still some scores of the beasts circling out there.

He had just turned again to look out at the enemy when the Wasps made their move, and the entire front seven ranks of the Second Army exploded, thousands of soldiers taking to the air in a vast cloud, and he felt a ripple of shock pass through the entire Collegiate wall detachment. Then the Airborne were coming for them like a storm, and he heard the cries of officers on both sides: 'Pikes out and hold! Snapbows ready!'

The Airborne had taken dozens of cities like this, making a mockery of traditional fortifications, but, back during their heyday, there had been nothing as accurate as a snapbow in their enemies' hands. Even the Sarnesh crossbowmen at the Battle of the Rails had inflicted savage casualties on them. Stenwold did not envy those attackers their duty, even as he prepared himself to kill as many of them as he could. He had his little pocket snapbow already out, and two score bolts he did not intend to waste.

On the ground, the Imperial ramming engines were grinding on towards the gate, with the heavy infantry to back them up. The Airborne alone would not be able to engage the wall for long, and the Empire would need to get its better-armoured troops inside the city soon. Without serious artillery to break down the walls, without the provisions for a long siege, that meant that they would have to force the gate and hope to hold it somehow.

The shock of seeing the Imperials suddenly in flight was still evident in the faces of many of the Company soldiers about him, but enough of them had their snapbows levelled even as the artillerists bent to their task of singling out the ramming engines as they advanced.

'Ready!' called out a young officer nearby – that Antspider woman, Stenwold recognized; Eujen Leadswell's friend. 'And loose!'

The stuttering racket of hundreds of snapbows exploded from around him, rippling along the wall as the other maniples took their cue. Stenwold saw soldiers falling from the sky, here and there, but the great mass of oncoming enemy seemed undiminished. All around him the Company soldiers were recharging and reloading their bows and, although they had trained and trained again, and although many of them had actively fought before, now their hands shook and he saw plenty of faces taut with fear. *Because this is our home and they've come this far.*

'And loose! Pikes brace!' the Antspider shouted. When she had discharged her own snapbow she slung it over her shoulder and drew a rapier from her belt. Beside her, Madagnus focused on targeting another ramming engine, muttering calculations to himself with utter absorption, as though nothing else in the world mattered.

Then the Airborne were on them. All along the wall, the Inapt soldiers of the Companies had levelled their pikes so as to make a mass onslaught by air as costly as possible, and nobody had actually imagined that the Empire's soldiers would just blunder right in, but that was exactly what happened. Whether it was bravery or stupidity or merely momentum, Stenwold never knew, but he had a chance to get off one shot with his little snapbow – too close to miss, right into a man's face – and then he was almost thrown off the wall altogether, with a Wasp solder scrabbling on top of him, his sting-warm hand finding Stenwold's face. A moment later a Company soldier had put a bolt into the assailant, the impact sending the Wasp convulsing off Stenwold, and down, down towards the streets of Collegium. Stenwold sat up and dragged his sword from its sheath.

All around him was a bitter, frantic melee. The men of the Airborne were trying to get to the wall engines, and in that same moment Stenwold saw the fighting wash over a leadshotter along the line, the artillerists cut down by sting even as they were sighting up, and then a handful of Wasps trying to lever the weight of the machine off the wall entirely, before the Company soldiers could get to them. Interspersed with the human soldiers had come a handful of their insects, not acting to any battle plan but just mad for killing, their sheer carapaced bulk slamming into the Collegiate soldiers, stings and jaws jerking convulsively even as they died. Most of the pikes had been abandoned by now – many with luckless Wasps still impaled on them – and the Company soldiers were switching from sword to snapbow as chance allowed them. Stenwold saw the Antspider, standing practically back to back with Madagnus, as she lunged forwards an impossible distance to pierce a Wasp's throat, then drew back to parry a sword blow aimed at her chief – whilst a pair of Fly snapbowmen crouched in her shadow and shot at whatever presented itself.

Overhead, the air was full of shot. More and more airborne were arriving every moment, but the Student Company archers positioned a street back – unengaged so far – were sniping at every safe target, meaning every Wasp still in the air. The Imperial death toll was horrific in those first moments, and there was a terrible expression to be seen on the faces of the Wasps. These were the men who had marched here under constant attack from the Stormreaders, and had then faced the last of the Felyen. They had already paid in friends and blood to get this far, and, if they failed now, it would all have been for nothing.

Straessa took down another soldier as he landed – ramming in between his ribs even before he had a chance to see her. Everywhere there were knots of fighting Wasps – her own maniple had been broken apart as the Imperials simply dropped in amongst them, stinging and stabbing indiscriminately. Her only point of stability was Madagnus and his magnetic ballista – and the sound of her own voice, constantly rallying anyone nearby to stand firm with her.

Another soldier stooped on her, but he was dead even as he dropped, taken by one of Eujen's sharpshooters, and the next flier wore Collegium colours and she still came within an inch of skewering him.

Averic wore a buff coat and a Collegiate lobster-tail helm, and that was just enough to overcome the reality of his kinden.

'What the pissing pits are *you* doing here?' she demanded, jabbing her blade straight over his shoulder at another of the Airborne as the man landed, but this time beyond even her longest reach. 'And *don't* say Eujen was worried about me, or I really will kill you.'

His conflicted expression confirmed the truth of that, or maybe the world didn't just revolve around her and it was the mass death of his own kin that was torturing him. Even so, when another wave of Airborne was abruptly on them, she saw his hands flashing with his own sting, standing shoulder to shoulder with her.

She saw an opening, and fumbled for her snapbow, the sword tucked awkwardly under one arm. Behind her, Madagnus gave out another shout of joy as he crippled one of the ramming engines.

She had her snapbow to her shoulder, trying to sight along it, when a newly arrived Wasp came up from below the level of the wall and rammed himself into her, the two of them going down in a tangle of limbs. Averic was beside her instantly, hauling the man off. Straessa saw the Airborne instinctively reach out with an open hand, and she yanked at the man's arm even as Averic's own sting hammered into the soldier's chest, melting the armour there but not piercing through. Then the soldier had backhanded the Wasp student, kicking to his feet with a flare of wings, and Straessa stabbed him clumsily through the unprotected leg.

He fell away, and she lost track of him a moment later, because she saw Madagnus get shot. A snapbow bolt came skimming along the line of the crenellations and struck him under the arm even as he aimed, and he pitched sideways with an outraged expression.

'Chief!' But by the time she got to him, he was almost all gone. He had a moment to clutch at her arm, no recognition in his eyes, and his last words became just a spray of bloody mist.

She saw Stenwold Maker himself close by, discharging a Wasp snapbow at one of the Airborne, and then lurching over to the wall to measure the rate of Imperial progress down on the ground. She shouted to him that her superior was down, but he heard none of it.

Then he was shouting back at her and pointing down, but she could not make it out, not a word, and then he was drawing back from the wall, still shouting, bellowing even – something about an attack? But surely that was old news: the Wasps were already here . . .

They were not alone. She saw the first arm hook over the top of the wall, and Stenwold lunged forwards to hack at it – no finesse, but then none was needed. A moment later the Spider-kinden appeared all along the wall top, because there were other ways to deal with fortifications than with wings.

Straessa cursed, darting forwards to run her sword through

a lithe, lightly armoured figure even as the man dragged himself up over the wall. 'Averic, get reinforcements up here! Get the Mynans, or Eujen, or *someone*!'

And he was gone, wings a-blur, and she turned to see the Spider-kinden already making a stand atop the wall. Just a score of them so far, but more were on their way, hundreds more.

There was a ferocious hammering, louder than all the other sounds of war except the leadshotters, and one face of the mustering Spider front caved in. She saw a big Sarnesh Ant in a mail hauberk shouldering forwards with a nailbow, knocking Sten Maker aside whilst fitting another magazine to it. Straessa darted in on Maker's other side, crossing blades briefly with a Spider soldier, letting him get the measure of her before rolling her shoulder forwards to jab at him, even as he tried to pull back out of her reach. Then the Collegiate lines went shuddering back, another flood of Spider-kinden cresting the wall even as the Airborne renewed their attack, and she saw ahead of her, clambering over, a man she recognized from the night fight.

He wore his black armour, still, and he must have been a strong climber to make it up in all that weight, but now that he was here he was laying about himself with that double-handed axe – just the right weapon to carve a space amid the close-quarters fighting. The nailbow hammered again, but the big Ant was shooting up at the Airborne now, while the armoured Spider officer was pressing ever forwards, keeping close to the Collegiates he was fighting to deny anyone a clear shot at him.

Mine, she decided, and was cutting a course to meet the axe-wielder, stabbing out at any Wasp or Spider in the way, but stepping onwards to meet the man as neatly as if they had made arrangements beforehand.

She thought she had him – lancing for his face below the rim of his open helm – but he got that axe of his in the way far faster than she anticipated, and turned his parry into a hasty swipe at her head that she swayed aside from. They were jostled by a dozen other skirmishes all around them, hardly ideal space for either weapon now, but they made do and, if he could not get his blade to her, he beat at her with the haft or the butt, and she punched him in the face with her guard.

Then a shudder went through the melee, and she saw that the Mynans had arrived at the far side of the Spider incursion, recognizing the flash of their black and red colours. They had shortswords and daggers to back up their snapbows, and most of them had cut their teeth in the resistance: vicious, dirty fighting on the streets of their occupied city. Abruptly the Spiders were no longer pressing forwards, but just trying to hold whatever ground they had, and the axeman thrust the haft of his weapon before him and pushed hard, hurling her back into the press of her fellows even as her rapier point scraped off the mail over his groin. Then the axe was swinging freely, and she had to drop almost to her knees to get out of its way. He was shouting something, some encouragement to his fellows, and she struck upwards, aiming for the thin mail under his arm. He twisted at the last moment, and her blade caught on the lip of his breastplate and bowed alarmingly. Then a flagging snapbow bolt ricocheted from his helm and he lurched backwards, his pale face clenching in pain, He was still whirling his axe about him, but the tide had turned, carrying him further away from her, and she was not sure that was a bad thing.

The Spiders were retreating over the wall now, leaving plenty of their dead behind them, and the attack of the Airborne slackened off as the Wasps tried to regroup. Straessa found Stenwold Maker at the wall, looking outwards. The balance of the Second had made good time, but where was there for them to go? The gate was still closed, and where were their rams?

'The engines?' she shouted.

'Gone!' he called back. 'I don't see any that made it to the gate!' Although there were still plenty of Airborne out there, some of the soldiers on the wall were starting to shoot down at the Imperial infantry. 'I need a messenger for Maker's Own Company. They should be ready for a sally once the Empire starts its retreat.

'They're going to retreat, then?' Straessa asked him.

'What else is left to them?' he demanded.

The big Sarnesh turned up just then. 'Maker.'

Stenwold's glance at him was evasive, 'Balkus? You didn't have to come.' A Fly-kinden passed by, distributing ammunition, and Stenwold grabbed the small woman and sent her down to Elder Padstock with new orders.

'I need your help for my city, Maker,' the man called Balkus explained. 'That means I need you alive.'

Stenwold opened his mouth, but the next voice to be heard came from somewhere along the wall: 'They're going for the gate! Artillery!'

Many of the soldiers up on the wall were shooting straight down now, and Straessa saw several artillery pieces testing the limits of their aim, declining as far as they could go.

'Hammer and tongs,' Stenwold spat. 'They're trying the Sentinels. They must be desperate.'

Then the Airborne were coming back, trying to keep the increasingly punishing snapbow shot off the infantry by offering themselves up instead as fleeter, harder targets, and Straessa could spare the gate no more thought.

Stenwold, though, was still watching. So far, there were a good half-dozen Sentinels ranged before the gate, with others still crawling about the field before the walls. They were not troubled by the wall engines, for those few able to angle low enough to shoot at them saw their leadshot and bolts just scarring and denting that armour, without seeming to touch the workings or the crew within. Stenwold was forced to fight down an uneasy thought. *There is someone within, is there not?* The sure and fluid movements of the Sentinels had always seemed more like those of things alive in their own right than something piloted by the hands of man. Then the first of them was backing up, legs moving in an intricate dance as it prepared to charge the gate.

This is ludicrous, he found himself thinking. *These aren't ramming engines.* But even as he thought it, he saw that, below the blind and covered eye that was its leadshotter barrel, someone had mounted a blunt, square-sectioned point, like an ugly little horn just at the right level for the centre of the gates.

Stenwold felt cold within himself, and looked about for a messenger, but the Wasp Airborne was on the attack all around, and he had nobody available but himself. With sword drawn, he found the steps and half-ran, half-skidded down them towards ground level and the gate.

He found some preparation there: three lines of Vekken soldiers stood before the gates, in the shadow of the wall's arched tunnel, and someone had already mounted a set of metal braces to reinforce the great bronze shutters that had been lowered into place to back up the gate. Here would always be the weakest point of a wall, but Collegium made solid gates even so.

'We need more bracing!' he was shouting, as he reached the ground and started running in earnest. 'Padstock! Termes! More bracing!'

Then he felt the impact through his feet even as he heard it, realizing that the Sentinel had scrabbled its way forwards, visualizing the great weight of articulated metal rushing on with that horrifyingly sudden speed. Ahead of him, he saw the gate shutters bow, the inner wood of the doors crunching under the tremendous impact, the five bars straining in their sockets, and the metal shutters themselves – all that Stenwold could actually see – warping visibly. One of the braces – a girder of solid steel angling out from the gate's centre to the ground – buckled all at once, and instantly Vekken soldiers went rushing forwards, manhandling its redundant weight out of the way so that a new one could be put in place.

The next impact came even as they were at it, and Stenwold had only a moment to think, *Impossible! There can't have been time for it to back up!* But of course there had been more than one Sentinel out there, and a new one had come thundering in even whilst the first rammer was backing away. The gates groaned like a wounded giant, and abruptly the Vekken had dispersed, splitting into neat units to fetch more bracing forwards, abandoning any idea of a quick sally out to rout the enemy.

Then the Airborne came.

This was their plan, he understood: they must have abandoned the wall top altogether, for suddenly the air and ground on this side of the gates was full of them, Wasp soldiers came shooting and stinging and stabbing – and dying from the very moment they arrived, but fighting to keep the gate from being reinforced. In their midst, the crazed insects brought by their airship still blundered and savaged, men and beasts alike in their utter carelessness for their own lives. For that first brief moment, the Vekken and the soldiers of Maker's Own were caught unawares, ceding the Wasps a tenuous foothold before the gates, but then the Ants had adjusted to circumstances, descending on their enemies with silent determination, swords out and wreaking a terrible carnage in that enclosed space. Stenwold saw the Mynans hurrying down the nearest steps to provide reinforcement, and the Student Company archers on the overlooking rooftops were taking advantage of every clear shot they could. But the Wasps would not be driven back – the Airborne and their insects driving themselves into a killing frenzy to hold their ground – and all the time the rhythm of the Sentinels pounding against the gate was quickening, each driving in at top speed, with a force that seemed to rock the very foundations of the wall, before rattling smoothly back even as the next one charged.

Twenty-Eight

His was a kinden steeped in treachery and cunning from the very dawn of history. To those Inapt scholars who knew of the Assassin Bug-kinden legacy, his kin were a byword for duplicity – and they had paid the price, but the Moths still shuddered to think how *close* they had come to ruling the world. His Art made even his hands into killing weapons that could shear through steel.

He was of a profession, an old and honoured profession, that made deception its watchword, that wore the faces – the *minds* even – of others as easily as another might put on a coat. And he was a veteran who had honed his magical and his physical skills over decades.

And, beyond that, he was learned. He had been a parasite within the archives of the Moth-kinden, who had kept him half prisoner and half guest, as a tool to be used in dire need only. More recently, he had worn an Imperial rank badge and seen how the gears of the Empire turned.

All Esmail knew now was that he was woefully out of his depth, meddling in – no, not even meddling but being dragged into – matters that no sane man would ever want anything to do with.

He should have backed out when he first met the Empress . . . or perhaps followed his orders and tried to kill her – *tried*, he suspected, being the relevant word. Instead he had listened to her golden words, her promises; he had studied her and seen the bewildering potential that chance and fate had somehow hatched within her. A queen amongst magicians, the inheritrix of the ancient world: what could such a woman not achieve?

And he had been a fool, an overawed fool.

And too late the Worm had been mentioned, and he had understood the flaw in that plan, just as had old Gjegevey. He had previously counted himself lucky that Seda was power without finesse – for how else could he have hidden from her, after all? But that same power, yoked to the driving acquisitiveness of an Empress, lacked the discernment to know what to reach for, and what to hold back from. And she knew about the Worm, and she saw there just *power*, because they had been powerful.

And it was here her feet had led her – or the idiot *Gjegevey* had led her – to the Master Seal, the keystone in the edifice that had rid the world of the Worm.

And still he had held back because of that promise, that potential . . . for when would the world see such a chance to restore the balance of history, but in her?

He could still hear the conflict as he moved through the mist-shrouded forest, and a little focus sufficed to gain a hazy picture of it. He sensed Tisamon hard pressed, being forced to give ground to keep between his increasingly mobile enemies and his mistress.

Everything had changed.

He was keeping his mind tight shut now. It had been a shock when that other voice had bludgeoned its way in, with the same raw, clumsy power as the Empress. More of a shock had been the understanding behind it, which had caught him unprepared and *seen* what he was – cracking Ostrec's stolen shell by elegant and unconscious intuition. As she did so, he had seen small shards of her, too: yes, she knew of his profession and had faced such spies before. Yes, she knew of his kin, even. That same power as Seda's, but yoked to a very different and more contemplative mind.

The Empress had spoken about her, the hated Beetle girl, who had somehow assumed the same mantle: her sister, her joint heir. Esmail had not understood until now.

And he had a terrible, seductive thought, *Perhaps something may be saved? Perhaps this girl, this Cheerwell Maker, might be manipulated. Surely easier than trying to steer the Empress?*

And another thought – one that no man in his position ought to allow himself: *Perhaps she would not even need manipulating.*

And she had survived. The Empress's minions had gone for her, and had fallen one after the other, until now only Tisamon barred the way.

And here stood Esmail, between them and the Empress, using all his craft to cloak himself from *anyone*'s attention.

If he returned to Tharn right now, or somehow found a way to share thoughts with one of their Skryres, what orders might he be given? *Depends on which Skryre*, arose the depressing thought. He was on his own now, as a spy always was in the end: cut off from his masters and with only his faltering judgement to rely on.

And here was the Empress herself, just ahead, with that fool old Woodlouse and the turncoat Wasp in Moth's robes, brought to bay at last. Any moment now, Tisamon must surely give way, and then the Beetle girl's followers would break through and kill the Empress themselves, and what would Esmail have gained?

He found inside himself an unending supply of fear. The Empress terrified him. To take action and lose his cover terrified him. To do nothing terrified him even more. He stepped forwards.

Seda's head swung towards him almost blindly, and he braced himself for an assault, magical or physical. He underestimated his spycraft and her own distraction, because her expression revealed only relief.

'Ostrec, get over here!' she snapped. 'Tisamon can't hold them off for long.'

And indeed he could hear the clatter of steel, and imagined

the followers of the Beetle girl twisting and turning, and Tisamon giving ground step after step.

'Majesty,' he said heavily.

'Draw your sword,' she instructed him, and he did so, to allay her suspicions. He was more dangerous without it, with both hands free. He closed the distance between them in three easy strides.

'This way.' And she was off, and now he felt that pulling point, the centre of this place, so that Seda trod a spiral path towards it like a moth to a candle. *Argastos.* Of course, because if she could subvert and appropriate that power, she might still win,

Unless I stop her.

Gjegevey went labouring after her – she had surely stopped only to give the old man time to catch his breath – and his face wore the set and despairing expression of a teacher whose student had gone beyond him without learning important truths. *Well, your fault, Woodlouse, if that is so.* Tegrec had been helping him along, but now he was running after Seda too, and Esmail read in him the nervous gait of a man close to breaking. *All the better.*

'Ostrec!' Gjegevey wailed and, despite himself, he turned back, virtually hauling the old man's arm up about his shoulders and hustling this wheezing, hunched encumbrance along. *To get me closer to the Empress,* he reassured himself, but just then his motives were so muddled as to be beyond divination.

Ahead . . .

They were running short of trees, ahead, which meant he was running out of time. The ground suddenly rose there, forming a hill too rounded to be natural, faced and plated with slabs of grey stone: a piecemeal carapace whose gaping cracks sprouted weeds and briars and even stunted trees. There was a gate there, too, set into an outcrop of the hill and framed in stone, the doors themselves made of thousands of little flakes of wood, suspended off a frame, like the scales of a moth's wing, wormy and blackened by age.

They had been gilded once, he understood. *For this is Argax, seat*

of Argastos, greatest war leader of the ancient world. The knowledge came unbidden and unwanted. *Not a barrow, but a hall once. Nobody builds doors into a barrow.*

Gjegevey broke from him and actually outstripped him, hobbling frantically with his staff, 'Majesty!' he called out, and Esmail knew this was his moment – if moments existed for misbegotten creatures such as himself.

Seda turned, and on her face there was a strange mixture of elation and desperation. She had found Argastos's lair and yet, at the same time, she had only moments left to discover how to draw power from it, and even Esmail himself could sense no obvious breach in the place's armour. The undoubted magic was not simply for the taking.

Because it's in someone's hands already? But he was speeding up now, hard on Gjegevey's heels, and cast that thought aside.

'Help me, Gjegevey,' the Empress commanded. 'Quickly – they're coming.'

And Esmail found it in his heart to pity her then, just a young Wasp girl risen higher than ever a woman of her kinden had before, but frightened, at the end of her resources. Who would not have done the same as she had, in her position.

Perhaps it was that pity that gave him away, for Ostrec had never allowed any for anyone save himself.

He was almost in reach of her when he saw her eyes widen . . . and abruptly Ostrec was in tatters, the falseness of his guise showing through at every edge. Seda cried out in shock and Esmail lunged forwards – one Art-edged hand extended to cut her heart out.

It was the old man that got in the way. He had that much idiocy left in him, or perhaps it was courage. Whatever the Empress had been to him, he threw his tired bones before the Assassin's stroke, so that Esmail's hand cut his staff in two, and then sawed into his ribs, shearing them apart, opening his chest in a sudden rush of ruptured blood. Gjegevey collapsed like a bundle of sticks, and Seda screamed in rage and grief. Esmail, trying to close those last paces of distance, was braced for the magical lash of her temper, but the flash of light he saw was something far more prosaic than that. Her sting struck him about the shoulder and side, with a searing blow that staggered and stopped him, slapping him to the ground, and he knew he had failed.

Not dead, though – not dead yet. And he was lurching up on one elbow, knowing another sting must come, and desperate to live despite it all, even as Ostrec was sloughing off him like moulting chitin. And then he opened his eyes to see her standing there, a hand thrust out to kill him, but her temper restrained by reins of iron. Her eyes were the coldest things Esmail had ever seen.

'Show me your true face, spy,' she spat. 'Before you die, let me see my enemy, I *command* it.'

And he felt her magic take hold of him with clumsy fingers, prising and straining, so that he screamed with the pain of violation that was worse even than the burning of her sting. But in the midst of it, a little jewel of calm remained, because resisting pain, staving off torture, was part of his training, and Seda was not skilled enough to break his mask with mere force alone.

But if he did not give her something, she would simply kill him, destroy his mind by trying to unlock it. He must choose a face for her.

He almost showed her the grey skin and white eyes of a Moth. It would have been appropriate, for it would have placed blame where it was due. He had no love for the people who had been his jailers for all those years, in all but name.

But his family, his wife, his children, they were still under the shadow of the Moths. Whatever else he might wish, whatever vengeance might be his due, he could not endanger them further.

When he gave her a face, just another face that was not his own, he saw Seda recoil, but she accepted it. It was one of the few options he had that would be believed implicitly, and he put all his skill into it, presenting such a perfect and polished likeness that it would have been accepted over the real thing. He gave her the lean and elegant features of a Spider-kinden.

Tegrec was kneeling by Gjegevey's side, but his expression showed Seda plainly that the ancient man was past any help that magic or surgery might offer. When the turncoat Wasp stood up, he was backing away, retreating from her, fear and misery running rampant across his face.

Seda stared at the assassin now revealed to her: 'Ostrec' had been a Spider all this time, and it made sense. It made far too much sense. Oh, she had read about the old Inapt spies and their face-changing magic, although she had never thought to encounter one. Whilst they were not an exclusively Spider elite, it was from that kinden that most of them derived. And here she was, with her armies marching alongside the Spiders, and surely she had known there would be a betrayal, a reckoning at some time. And, of course, General Roder had warned her: never trust a Spider. Everyone *knew* they were treacherous.

And so, after Roder's advice, she had made provision for that. She had given special orders to Captain Vrakir, sending the man off to keep an eye on General Tynan and the Second, had she not? And, with that, a thought went out to the Red Watch, who were bound to her in blood. Vrakir would know what to do.

But as for this traitor before her, who had killed her beloved slave and who had come so close to killing her—

And Tisamon came bursting backwards into the clearing, and she realized that she had allowed herself to be distracted, perhaps fatally, for here were her other enemies.

It was a Spider girl that the revenant Mantis was duelling with, and Seda saw, with a lurch of her heart, that she was somehow managing to hold Tisamon off, landing no blows but keeping him at bay with the blurring passes of her rapier, and there, breaking away from the fight in a brief flurry of wings, to drop down ten feet behind Tisamon, was—

She froze. She had not known.

'*Thalric?*'

Of course she knew that he had not died in Khanaphes, as General Brugan had tried to claim, but she had not tried to find him. She had thought that he would come back to her of his own accord. He had been her consort, after all, when she had needed one. He had shared her bed . . .

And he had a hand out towards her, palm open, and she looked him in the eye and waited, but his sting never came. He was just staring at her, and she wondered how he might remember those nights spent together. She saw his jaw clench.

Somewhere beyond their collective notice, Tegrec found the very limit of his courage, and a moment later he was running for the trees, and nobody even spared him a glance.

Then *she* was there, the loathsome Beetle girl, dark and squat and ugly, blundering out from the trees with some ragged half-breed as her handmaiden. And, at Seda's merest thought, Tisamon had broken from his opponent and gone for her, in a frantic attempt to rid the Empress of her most pressing problem.

Thalric kicked back into the air immediately, and his sting-shot punched the armoured revenant in the side, sending Tisamon off balance for two seconds. Long enough for the Spider woman to catch him and force him to face her. Long enough for Thalric to drop between him and his prize, defending the Beetle girl with his own life.

'Thalric!' Seda shouted in rage and despair, seeking out the magic with which the Beetle had bound him to herself, but unable to grasp it. *How has she done this?*

In a lightning rush, Tisamon disengaged and fell back towards her, putting himself between her and her enemies. Seda's eyes found the Beetle girl's – Cheerwell Maker's – and the hate crackled and spat between them. And yet only one way: her own spite breaking against the girl's placid resistance. Beetles endured, was that not what they said? Oh, she could sense that the girl had grown as a magician, just as much as she herself had, but in different directions: less suited to attack, more to defence.

427

And still an impasse, but Seda already knew what she could do about that. Right here, within that mound, there was as much power as she could ever want, ready for her to overwhelm the Beetle girl entirely, destroy her, destroy her followers, destroy Thalric if she so chose.

She reached out and began gathering that power, dipping into that well beneath them, drawing it out to herself as though she was hauling up an endless bolt of cloth. As Tisamon turned and readied himself, as Thalric and the Spider girl spread out, slowly stalking in, Seda stood quite still and drew it all to herself, pulling and pulling and . . .

And she met resistance, and in a fury she dragged harder and harder at it, aware only that at any moment the Beetle girl would realize what she was about and step in to stop her, and so she hauled and hauled, with all the might the Khanaphir had endowed her with, and then, abruptly, there was no more resistance and, had it been a physical struggle, she would have fallen backwards like a fool. As it was, she found herself reeling, unsure what had happened, until she realized there was someone new amongst them, someone who demanded the attention of everyone. A dark figure with pale eyes and a thin smile like a razor blade.

Argastos.

And all the power she had thought she was gathering to herself was still attached to *him* and under his firm command, far stronger than she had thought. This was no treasure to be pillaged, but a weapon in hands that still knew how to use it, no matter how many centuries had gone by since they had possessed life.

And Argastos laughed, and the world fell away.

Twenty-Nine

The wall top was still firmly in Collegiate hands when Laszlo arrived, lurching through the air as he towed a heavy sack behind him. The Airborne kept striking, fighting to keep the attention of the defenders off the infantry below, but the Coldstone Company and the Mynans were holding them at bay. A scattering of surviving hornets was visible in the sky, but the bloodlust that had motivated them seemed to be waning, and more and more were simply departing, or swinging off over the city. Outside, the Sentinels continued their inexorable ramming, four of them taking it in turns, and loosing leadshot whenever they had a clear shot. That the gate had stood firm even this long was a tribute to Collegiate engineering.

Laszlo dropped down and started asking where Stenwold Maker was, but nobody seemed to know, so he worked his way along the wall, ducking away from any skirmishes, putting a knife into any Wasp that he managed a clear stab at, and occasionally loosing his cut-down snapbow or his shortbow at targets of opportunity, depending on range and inclination. The world of the wall top was an alien one to him. Not that he was a stranger to a fight: he had killed men from a ship's rigging during a storm, and still this random, brutal chaos of a battle was enough to make him wish himself elsewhere. *And where the pits has Maker got himself to?*

He made a quick hop over to the next maniple of Collegiates, nearly getting himself impaled for his pains.

'Easy! Easy! I'm just looking for Mar'Maker!' he shouted.

'What?' The Spider halfbreed woman with the quick sword frowned.

Laszlo was about to clarify, when a particularly savage crashing from below stopped his words in mid-flow. He scrambled to the crenellations, looking down to see those gleaming, segmented bulks as they took rapid turn at the gate. When he looked up, something had drained from his face. 'Oh, piss,' he said. 'That looks ugly.'

'Who are you and what do you want?' the swordswoman demanded. They were unengaged for the moment, and half of her maniple was standing at the wall's edge, shooting down futilely at the plated machines, whilst the rest watched the skies.

'Name's Laszlo, M– Stenwold Maker's friend.'

'Antspider, officer,' the woman introduced herself. 'Maker went below.' She was pointing down at the arch of the gateway. Laszlo had seen a real festering fight going on there, and Wasp soldiers were still darting down to join the fray, risking the raking shot of the Collegiates up on the rooftops. *So, of course that's where he is.* Laszlo crouched for a moment: he had not imagined it would be like this. When Tomasso had sent him to find Maker with that pointless, idiotic offer, he had envisaged soldiers in neat rows and the Wasps still on the far side of the wall; a nice, orderly defence befitting Collegium sensibilities.

'What do you want?' the Antspider demanded of him.

'That's another leadshotter crew down,' one of her people said expressionlessly.

'Anyone got spare bolts?' from another.

'I came . . .' *I came because Tomasso's about to cast off and there's a berth for Stenwold Maker if he wants it, but what a stupid thing that would be to say right now. I told* the skipper Sten Maker's no runner, *but he wouldn't listen, oh no . . .* 'I've got something for the defence, from ship's stores. I thought . . .' and it had seemed a grand idea, a present for the gallant defenders. Now, though . . . He tugged open the sack, revealing the grenades he had taken from the *Tidenfree*, dated weapons from Spiderlands artificers that the ship's crew had used when boarding actions went bad, inferior to Beetle make in all ways save that they were made for Fly-kinden hands. 'I thought . . .' he managed, looking the Antspider in the eye and unable to articulate just what he might have thought. With desperate courage, Laszlo grabbed one and threw the little munition over the wall, aiming for the jostling Sentinels. His aim was perfect, taking it just where one plate slid over another, and at the sharp impact the weapon detonated instantly, a bright flash of fire leaving not even a fresh mark on that scarred carapace.

'No more useless than our snapbows,' the Antspider told him, and from below there came a catastrophic cracking sound, enough to shiver the stones beneath their feet. Then a storm of Wasp Airborne were all about them – but these had come up from below, where they had ceased disputing the ground inside the gate. Snapbow bolts darted through their number, picking some off, but they were keeping low to the wall – close enough for the Antspider to have stabbed one if she had been quick enough – denying the Student Company snapbowmen across the street an easy target.

Laszlo and most of the others risked a glimpse over the parapet, despite the sporadic snapbow shot sleeting up towards them. The Sentinels were still in motion, the barrels of those single eyes flashing fire as they cast leadshot at the gate, whilst one was now stepping backwards, almost dainty despite its size, lining itself up for what looked like a final charge.

Laszlo stared at them, watching ballista bolts and shot rock the heavy machines without harming them, seeing those lead-shotter eyes blaze. His career had been a varied one, with all the resourcefulness of a pirate who has to make do with whatever's to hand. He had seen a great many tricks tried, during his young life, and heard of many more. Most of all, he had never given up. Even as a prisoner at the bottom of the sea, surrounded by the killing ocean on all sides, he had not lost heart. It would take more than the Wasp Empire to break him.

'Antspider, you've got archers? Real bowmen?'

Stenwold was out of bolts, but there were handfuls for the taking wherever he looked, in the quivers of the fallen, or just spilled onto the ground. He dropped down beside a dead Wasp soldier and, as his hands worked to strip the man of his ammunition, he considered the convenience of Collegium having inherited this weapon from the Empire in the first place. The standard for snapbow ammunition was more universal than the Helleren mint.

Elder Padstock's voice came to him from close by – she was trying to shout her soldiers into some sort of order, but the Wasps were not cooperating. They were everywhere – each man operating on his own, striking and flying, keeping on the move, refusing to stand and fight. A couple of their giant insects remained, too, wings shattered and their chitin cracked by shot, but still scissoring their mandibles at every enemy within reach. Enough of the Imperials were getting in the way of the Vekken to ensure that the gates had barely been reinforced, just a few more girders fitted in place before the Ant-kinden had turned to defending themselves. In the close confines of the gateway, their shortswords claimed more of the enemy than the Collegiate snapbows, while the Maker's Own soldiers resorted to swords of their own, trusting to their heavier armour to counterbalance their lesser skill.

The gates were crashing and shuddering under a solid rhythm now, like a bar of metal being hammered into shape by three smiths all at once. Ordinary rams would not have achieved so much, with their slow, patient battering. Of all the malevolent wonders of artifice this war had brought with it, only the Sentinels had endured to this bitter end.

We should have a gatehouse here, not just a square and a broad avenue, was Stenwold's desperate thought. *Even with soldiers on every rooftop, it should not be so easy to break into our city.* But, of course, Collegium's gates were primarily built to welcome in trade, with defence a distant second. *Did we have time to change that, since the Vekken first attacked?*

'Through the Gate!' Padstock was bellowing, sounding ludicrous really, but it was the war cry of Maker's Own, and her men took it as the inspiration it was meant to be. Stenwold emptied his borrowed snapbow into the first Wasp he saw – missing even at this range, shooting too high in his fear of hitting his allies. Then another dozen Airborne had crashed into the group of soldiers beside him, and someone kicked him in the chest as he crouched there, bowling him over. He lost hold of the snapbow again and simply picked up a discarded sword, seeing Elder Padstock hack her blade into the neck of a Wasp, bludgeoning him down by main force rather than any attempt at fencing.

The next impact on the gates thundered through the enclosed space like a grenade explosion, carrying with it the snapping of wood and the shrieking of metal wrenched beyond its capability to resist. Stenwold stood there, unused sword in hand, and his eyes registered what the gates had become. The bracing had been uprooted by the impact, a mess of jagged-ended metal that had torn into attackers and defenders alike, and the heavy shutters backing the gate had been twisted apart, revealing the abused and splintered timber beneath, with a dozen gashes of daylight already ripped in them.

The Airborne were instantly departing, and it seemed a victory, a momentary, ridiculous victory, because it would have made more sense for them to stay and try to hold the breach so that their infantry comrades could break through. But their losses, and the anticipation that the gates were about to give way, triggered something in them that had them funnelling back into the open, braving the Collegiate shot to flee back to their own lines. The Vekken and Maker's Own were left in sole possession of the gateway.

The ravaged gates shuddered and spasmed like dying things under the Sentinels' leadshot barrage, but still they held, doing generations of Collegiate engineers proud. The Vekken – those that were left – formed a solid shield wall backed by crossbowmen, a tight-packed formation five men deep, and Stenwold was shouting for them to back off, because that was the previous generation's war, which Vek – and the Ant-kinden in general – should have discarded by now. He saw a dark face look back at him – perhaps it was even Termes – but they did not shift, instead just bracing themselves and leaving space before the gate for the ram to come through.

But when it did come through, it was far more than a ram of course. The blunt prow of the Sentinel hammered home, and this time the gates parted, wood and twisted metal slamming back against the walls and the voracious machine shouldering through, its front a map of dents and scars, but its armour intact despite that. Its eye opened and the leadshotter spoke, mounted too high for the enemy facing it, but the sheer explosive sound of it staggered them all, and the ball whistled overhead to smash into the front of a building directly across the square, punching out an extra, rough-edged window.

Then the twin rotary piercers, set lower down, opened up – or at least one of them did, the other failing to spin into life at all, a casualty of the ramming. Stenwold watched half the Vekken formation falling, the enemy's bolts punching through shields and mail and men, chewing through their close-knit ranks like a scythe through corn. The Ants were on the move immediately, though, rushing at the machine, more of them falling to its built-in snapbows, and more still to the Wasp infantry who were pushing in at either side of the Sentinel, desperate to force the breach. Then the Sentinel itself was stepping forwards, unstoppable, inexorable, becoming both shield and hammer of the Imperial army. Snapbow bolts rattled and danced off its carapace, and the Vekken soldiers, trying to climb it and lever apart its plates with all the strength their Art gave them, were picked off without accomplishing anything, until even they were falling back, those of them that could.

Elder Padstock was calling for her soldiers to hold firm, and they held, but all Stenwold could wonder, as he chambered another bolt, was, *For how long?*

'We used to do this going ship to ship, you know?' Laszlo had explained. 'Inapt archers, Apt toys, you see? Our artificer, Despard, she came up with a plan for putting these fellows just where we wanted them – get a bowman in the rigging and you can shoot the things onto the enemy's deck or at his mast or whatever.'

As she listened to him, Castre Gorenn heard the usual sort of nonsense babble that people in Collegium spoke, most of which made no sense to her whatsoever. She had seen how the little artificer's stones in his bag blazed into fire when they struck things, and then he had shown her how, with a little application, they could be tied to an arrow. She would not have listened even that far, save that the little man actually possessed a bow of his own, for all that it was a pitiful piece of work compared to hers.

'Now, I'm going to prime this for you, so you be careful: put the arrow to the string, and don't, whatever you do, knock it against anything. We want it to go bang at their end, not ours.'

Laszlo did something to the unwieldy weight that was encumbering the end of her arrow, and then something similar to his own.

'Now we go hunting, right?' He grinned at her, and she returned the smile, because hunting was something she did understand.

The Fly-kinden's wings flashed, and he dropped off the wall on the city side, and she followed suit, taking exaggerated care with the deadly burden she had nocked.

Above them, the Light Airborne were beginning to return to the wall-top, not rushing it now, but shooting down with sting and snapbow, trading shot with the Company soldiers. Gorenn twitched to go back and kill more of them, but the Antspider had told her to help Laszlo and, although she resented the order, she did as she was told.

And then they dropped into the shadow of the gateway and saw the monster that was advancing through it, segment by segment, clambering over the uneven wreckage of the gate braces, and with Imperial soldiers on either side. The defenders – Maker's Own Company and a ragged ghost of the Vekken detachment – were gradually giving ground, shooting at the soldiers but powerless to halt the terrible machine.

For a moment, Laszlo hesitated, but then he went diving in, skimming the arched ceiling of the gateway, darting close even as the Wasps realized he was there. She saw his arrow leave the string, shooting back towards the front of the Sentinel, aiming between its armour plates, and the flash and bang of the grenade fooled her into thinking he had accomplished something. The machine still ground on, though, and she tried her own shot, striking the Sentinel low down, cutting the feet from a Wasp soldier and flaring bright about the front leg of the advancing automotive. But that armour, too, seemed to be proof against Laszlo's weaponry, and she saw nothing worse than some charring and scratches. The missile had flown like a bloated autumn beetle, almost dropping from the string, and achieving a range of a few yards at best with no real accuracy.

The two of them dropped back behind the defenders, and a moment later she saw the circular hatch in the machine's front sliding open. A colossal gout of flame and noise belched forth from it, hurling some projectile faster than her eye could follow. It smashed against the already battered front wall of a house across the way, bringing the entire building down, including with it the soldiers who had been stationed on its roof.

Laszlo had fitted another bulbous weapon to one of his stubby little shafts, but she had seen how close he had gone to get his arrow off, and how only the surprise of the Wasps had kept them from simply shooting him dead as he hovered to make the first shot.

436

He glanced at her, trying to mask his frustration with a weak smile. 'This isn't going to work, is it?'

The Sentinel lurched forwards another few feet, freeing itself entirely from the entangling wreckage of the gate. To Gorenn it was not a machine, for she knew machines. The Wasps had subjugated half her homeland with them, the noisy, stinking, clumsy things. This was something new, because no machine ever moved like that. To her, it was a living monster out of the worst of the old stories.

The Collegiates were now using the edges of the gateway for cover, driven back that far. It was all going to end soon. She had come here as the Commonweal Retaliatory Army, to fight the Wasps that had slaughtered her people in the Twelve-year War, but what had she accomplished?

'Give it to me. Make it ready to catch fire,' she told Laszlo.

'Honestly, I don't think it's going to work—'

'Just do it.'

The pair of them ducked out of the way as one of the Sentinel's weapons struck stone chips from the nearby flagstones.

'I have to get back to my ship,' Laszlo was saying. 'I have to find Mar'Maker . . . I don't know what I have to do.' But he was binding another of the little fire-stones to her arrowhead. 'Seriously, this—'

She brushed him off and, before her, its rounded prow almost fully out into the Collegium street, the great machine flexed and shook itself, settling the plates of its carapace and preparing itself for one last push.

She stepped into the air, arrow to the string, drawing back slowly, almost walking on nothing, so smooth was her ascent. Snapbow bolts spat past her, but only a few. She was nobody's priority just then, compared to all the Apt soldiers with modern weapons that Collegium was fielding.

The monster looked at her as if it recognized the challenge. She hung in the air before its great blind face and heard the roar of its innards, felt the warmth of its engine breath wash over her.

437

It opened its great eye, which glared death, just like in the old stories but, knowing those stories as she did, she knew how heroes slew such monsters.

The arrow left the string without conscious thought or aim, and a thousand-year-old tradition met the most sophisticated artifice of the Iron Glove Cartel and the Wasp Empire, with a detour via the piecemeal arsenal of the *Tidenfree*, as she sent the grenade straight down the barrel of the Sentinel's leadshotter.

She should have ducked away, then, but in her head she was the hero of myth, and such heroes did not shoot and run. They stood and watched the monster fall, or else they died. She was exactly in line with that killer eye, and if it spoke again, then there would not be enough left of Castre Gorenn to identify her kinden.

The grenade went off. She saw the flare and, for a moment, could not say whether this meant her triumph or her death. A moment later there was a hollow, muted thunder, and the Sentinel leapt a foot backwards, clawed metal feet skidding on the flag-stones, and smoke was forcing its way out between its segments, and it was dead.

Then the Wasps began shooting at her in earnest, and Laszlo nipped past and caught hold of her ankle and hauled her out of the way, or she would surely have been killed.

'Now! Charge them!' came Padstock's call. 'Forward for Collegium! Through the Gate!'

The Wasps either side of the Sentinel braced themselves, with spears jutting forwards and snapbowmen behind, but they were packed together too closely to fight easily, and yet in a column too narrow for many of them to attack. They had been trading shot with the Collegiate archers, but as the Beetles and their allies surged forwards, Balkus pushed to the front and unloaded his nailbow into the closest batch, killing the spearmen in the front and clearing the way for the Vekken, who descended upon them with brutal efficiency. On the far side, a pair of Company soldiers followed his example with a repeating snapbow that miraculously failed to jam. Then the Maker's Own Company rushed forwards, claiming either side of the smoking Sentinel and holding the gate.

Out there, beyond the wreckage of gate and machine, waited the Second Army in all its strength, yet still being picked apart piecemeal by the soldiers on the wall.

Stenwold claimed yet another abandoned snapbow and joined the other defenders. He could see a great many infantry out there, and now there came a brutal squad of Scorpion-kinden, the Aldanrael's no doubt, armed with greatswords and already running full-speed as they rounded the gateway. There were pikemen amongst the Collegiate soldiers, but few of them, and it fell to the Vekken to shoulder forwards and hold the gap, shields locked and staving the huge warriors off, so that the Collegiate snapbowmen could bring them down one by one.

'Maker!' Balkus was shouting, pointing. Stenwold tried to peer beyond the fighting at what had caught the man's eye. There was activity at the rear of the ruined Sentinel, but for a blurred moment he could not discern what it was.

'They're going to haul it out!' Balkus yelled over the fighting. 'We're dead if they do!'

The engineers working there were shielded by the bulk of their dead machine. Stenwold backed off and round looked for a messenger. 'Laszlo?'

'Here, Mar'Maker!' The little man presented himself smartly. 'Got a message from the—'

'No time,' Stenwold snapped back. Right now it didn't matter *what* the man was here for. 'Get up to the wall, tell them to shoot anyone trying to get this wreck out of the gateway.'

Laszlo hesitated for a moment, caught in mid-errand, and then nodded and was gone, speeding out of the gateway and then straight up the wall.

The Imperial infantry was coming in again, as the last of the Scorpions fell, and now the Collegiates had the same difficulties, with those at the back unable to find a target. The Vekken shields held, though, and it was the Empire's own hunger to take the gate that betrayed it. Had the Wasps stood off and kept shooting, the Ants would have been cut down in short order, but instead they threw themselves physically into the gap, and met the iron discipline of Vek and the marksmanship of the Merchant Companies.

Stenwold craned sideways, trying to mark the progress of the towing crew. He caught glimpses that showed him that Laszlo had passed on his orders – there was definitely shot coming from above – but flights of the Light Airborne were taking off as well, and he knew that they would tie up the soldiers on the wall.

He was so concerned with this that he missed what the other Sentinels were doing. Nobody noticed, until the Wasps on the right-hand side of the gateway fell back and scattered – by all appearances, a victory for the defenders. What was revealed, however, was the plated countenance of another of the armoured automotives, weirdly hunched so as to lower the aim of its lead-shotter eye. There was barely a moment even to shout a warning before the thunderstroke of the weapon eclipsed all else, hammering into that narrow, packed corridor, obliterating the Vekken shield wall and killing a score and more of Company soldiers ranged behind them. Then the Imperial infantry were back, leading with their spears, trampling the wounded and the dying in order to claim that side of the broken Sentinel, just as the fallen machine began to scrape backwards, hauled by the efforts of its brethren.

Padstock was calling for her soldiers to hold fast, encouraging them, almost threatening them, but they were giving ground on both sides now, and soon there would not be two sides at all, but just a great gaping wound in the city's defences. Stenwold heard Balkus's nailbow sound off again, another magazine emptied, and then, stripped of ammunition, the big Ant had his sword out.

Stenwold discharged the snapbow over the heads of his fellows, hitting nothing, and then he drew his sword.

'Collegium!' he cried. 'Collegium and liberty!'

Soldiers were crowding past him, pushing in to hold the gap, their faces taut with desperation. The air was thick with snapbow bolts, like little hornets.

Stenwold stepped forwards, at that moment no more than an extra defender against the tide, and a bolt ripped into him, cutting through his armour and between his ribs and exiting almost in the same instant, puncturing a clean hole all the way through, marked with a spray of blood.

He sat down, more surprised than anything. There was pain, but it came only when he breathed in. When he let the breath go there was just coughing, and blood on his hand when he took it away from his mouth.

He found he could not stand up. The strength that had carried him this far in his fight against the Empire had abruptly deserted him.

Someone was shaking him, which wasn't helping. He saw Elder Padstock loom over him, her face aghast as it had never been during the fighting. Stenwold tried to reach up to comfort her, but his arm seemed far, far away.

'Get him out of here!' she was saying. 'Get him to the surgeons!'

They must be talking about me, he realized. He tried to tell her that she had more important things to do, but he could only cough.

Beyond her, the Wasps were breaking through, He could only watch, see the last moments of the battle for the gateway, the bloody-minded determination on both sides, no quarter given, not an inch of ground won save in blood and bodies.

Then he was being lifted, a heavy old Beetle man cradled in the arms of a broad-shouldered Ant. Balkus.

Padstock turned back for the fight, chambering another bolt in her snapbow, and Stenwold saw her stagger, struck in the gut by one shot that punched its way out through her backplate. The next bolt snapped her head back, as though she was suddenly looking for the enemy amid the stones of the gateway above her. He saw her fall.

Then Balkus was lurching away, and Stenwold was denied the last moments of the city's defence, the unspoken heroism of the end, such as never finds its way into the histories.

He felt Balkus stumble to one knee with a gasp, but then the man was up again, shambling and staggering, but putting distance between them and the gate.

A moment later there was a man buzzing about them, a high-pitched voice demanding to know what had happened: Laszlo.

'Where's the nearest surgeon?' Balkus demanded, his voice strained, and then, 'Piss on your cursed *boat*, we can't make it all the way to the docks! Where's a surgeon, *please!*'

'I'll get one, I'll get one!' Laszlo promised, and he was off, with Balkus yelling, 'And a stretcher!' after him,

They were three streets away from the gate now, and Stenwold found himself being lowered into a sitting position, his back against the wall of someone's house. There were soldiers running past them, in both directions. Nobody seemed to be in charge but at least none of them was a Wasp, not yet.

Balkus sat down beside him. 'Maker . . .'

Stenwold managed to turn his head. There was a terrible pallor to the Ant's skin, and where he had slid down the wall Stenwold could see a red smear. He tried to speak, but the words collapsed into little more than a grunt.

Balkus took a deep breath. 'If you make it. When this is over. If you win.' He grimaced. 'Don't let Sarn have Princep. You owe me that, now. Do something. Don't let them ruin everything.'

A long pause.

'And look after Sperra.' The Ant gave long sigh. 'This is a pisspoor way to go. I don't like it.'

'Not gone yet,' it was just a whisper that Stenwold managed, but Balkus seemed to hear it. He did not answer, though.

Then people were crowding him, and he recognized the purple sashes of the Student Company. 'It's the War Master!' And someone saying to get him to the College, where a lot of the healers and stitchers had been stationed.

'Take him,' he hacked out the words, jabbing a weak finger at Balkus, not knowing if the Ant lived or not.

The Light Airborne were persistent, but Straessa's remaining command were allowing them nothing. Atop the wall, they had formed a tight cluster bristling with pikes, and with enough snap-bows to make the Wasps hurt every time they came close. One flank had already gone – she saw Wasps all over the wall there – but Kymene's Mynans were holding firm on the far side, not so many of them as before, but they were solid, not giving an inch. And it seemed to the Antspider that the Airborne's fervour was now slackening off. *Are we beating them back? Surely we are.*

Beside her, Castre Gorenn loosed her last shaft, slung her bow carefully on her shoulder, and then took up a pike that a fallen soldier had dropped, Straessa speculated grimly how many snapbow bolts her followers had left between them. She wondered how the rest of the Companies were faring, and what Eujen was doing. In that fraught time, as she loosed shot after shot, dragging her increasingly heavy sword free whenever the enemy got too close, she had time to wonder about a lot of things.

Then she heard her name called, and a moment later Averic almost bounced off the wall. He was looking pale, and with one sleeve slashed open and bloody. Someone hauled him upright and he clutched at Straessa, gasping 'Get off the wall!'

'We can't. The defence—' she started.

'The gate's lost!' Averic managed to say. 'Get down now or they'll be coming up the stairs for you.'

'Averic, seriously, we can't just—'

'Outwright's is already going, those of his that can. The Spider-kinden are at them already. You've got to move,' he insisted. He put a hand absently to his slashed sleeve and seemed surprised to see the blood there.

Straessa cursed and peered beyond the Mynans, to where Outwright's Pike and Shot should be holding their space of wall. To her lurching horror she saw that, yes, they were fighting fiercely, sword to sword, but getting off the wall as well in a desperate rearguard action that looked just one death from a rout.

She had a moment to think about the right thing to do, but she had already made that decision when the Companies had marched against the Second in the field, the last time they came. She had chosen to save the lives of her people then, and she would do so now.

'Gorenn, get over to Kymene and tell her what Av's just told us.'

The Dragonfly nodded and launched herself along the wall, her wings a skittering blur, dodging aside from one of the Airborne who tried to sting her.

'Down the steps! Back into the city!' Straessa cried out. 'Keep it ordered, keep the pikes up, and shoot any bastard who tries it on with us! Come on, we're moving!'

She helped Averic to his feet. 'What's Eujen doing?'

'Sending me to help you, last time I saw him,' the Wasp student replied with a bleak, brief smile. 'The Student Company is the front line now. No idea what Fealty Street are doing, but Maker's Own and the Vekken took the worst of it. I need to get back to Eujen.'

'If I know him, he's watching us right now,' Straessa remarked. 'And you need a surgeon.' She sounded so very calm, and inside her something was yammering, *We've lost the gate, we've lost the wall!*

Down at the foot of the wall, her soldiers broke quickly across the open ground, before reforming between the buildings across the square. Straessa was one of the last down, running alongside Kymene and her Mynans, as snapbow bolts lanced past them. Once in cover, they could look back and see the Wasps and their Spider allies claiming the wall a slice at a time, descending on any remaining defenders and routing or killing them. Four Sentinels stalked in through the gateway and created a cordon between them that no Collegiate felt ready to brave, whilst behind

444

them soldiers fortified their position, erecting temporary barricades out of the material of the gates themselves.

Straessa and the others waited and watched, and above them Eujen's Student Company watched too, waiting for the inevitable moment when the Wasp tide rolled forwards and swept into the streets, and the real battle for Collegium would begin. But the Second Army simply secured its entry to the city, thronged the wall-top with its soldiers, and waited, too.

Then, with evening beginning to veil the sky in the west, a lone Fly-kinden in Imperial uniform stepped forth, somewhat hesitantly, from the newly established Imperial lines and walked out, closed fists held up, with a message for the Assembly.

They convened in the ruins of the Amphiophos, as before, but in sparser ranks. Some had fallen on the wall or at the gate, no doubt. Others perhaps did not want to be noted as a member of that august body, in case there should be some Imperial scrutiny of the minutes of this latest gathering.

Jodry Drillen, a great, baggy weight of a man, robes awry and dirty, eyes shadowed by lack of sleep, stood up before them, a neat little slip of paper in his hand, barely large enough to be called a scroll. He was scanning the faces of the attendees, as if seeking allies.

Eujen Leadswell watched him. Unlike the elected representatives of the city, who had mostly bowed to protocol sufficiently to make some attempt at robing up, he remained in his armour, buff coat and breastplate, with his helm tucked beneath his arm. Beside him was Remas Boltwright of the Fealty Street Company, who had somehow failed to lead his soldiers into battle at all, waiting in reserve all that time for a call to arms that, he said, had never come. The two of them – and neither of them exactly veterans – were here representing the armed might of Collegium. Kymene had refused to attend; Taki, spokeswoman for the pilots, was in the infirmary; and the rest of the Company chief officers were dead, as was Termes of Vek.

Eujen saw Jodry's lips move, as though the man was rehearsing, but someone shouted out, 'Can't hear you!' – an echo of the old Assembly, if there ever was one – and the Speaker's head snapped up. For a moment his eyes darted about, and Eujen knew exactly who he was looking for, and which notable absence was weighing on everyone's minds. But finally he spoke.

'General Tynan of the Second has sent us an ultimatum,' he explained. 'We are to surrender, he demands.'

He did not seem inclined to elaborate, but his eyes kept sliding off to one figure out of many, a man Eujen recognized as Helmess Broiler, ever Jodry's political opponent. Broiler was sitting quite peaceably, however, making no attempt to leap up and rouse the rabble.

'Terms, Drillen!' someone else called from the back. 'What terms?'

'Does it matter?' Drillen challenged the questioner. 'Surrender our city, really? Are we countenancing such a thing?'

'Speaker, at least tell us what the Wasp wrote,' said a woman Eujen recognized from the Artificing faculty of the College.

Jodry nodded tiredly. 'If we surrender now, then our soldiers will be allowed to lay down their arms and return to their trades without sanction, nor will there be repercussions against ourselves – us Assemblers – save for some small list of names who are counted enemies of the Empire.' He smiled weakly. 'I am proud to find my own name there. My mother once said I would amount to nothing.'

Some three or four raised a smirk at that. No more.

'Added to this, the Assembly will be permitted to advise the new governor . . . the usual assurances that Collegium will become a valued part of their Empire, and . . . that Imperial rule will be imposed on our streets with no more force than proves necessary.' As he uttered the words, his voice shrank until it seemed just a ghost of itself, but his gaze, shifting about him at his peers, was firm. 'Do I need to recount to you what they say will happen

446

if we resist? I'm sure you can imagine their threats – to our soldiers and our citizens and ourselves.'

Several Assemblers had stood, wishing to speak, and Jodry's thick finger had picked out one – one of his allies perhaps – but two or three others were already speaking over the top of each other, demanding that Jodry tell them everything, demanding that the Empire come and speak in person, one even swearing defiance. Eujen looked from face to face, and abruptly it seemed that everyone there was talking together – trying to hush each other or shouting at each other, or most of them shouting at Jodry. Suddenly they all seemed to be on their feet – with even a scuffle between two elderly Assemblers on the far side of the ruin. There was a kind of chorus, amidst the chaos, that came to Eujen's ears. It was a tally of grief and human cost. He heard people demanding if Jodry knew how many had died, how much had been destroyed – their levelled surroundings were suddenly no longer a warning to *never forget*, but a reminder of just how much the Empire had made them pay already. Jodry had his hands extended for calm and his lips moved, but not a word reached Eujen's ears intact.

And then, finally, he could be heard. 'Please, Masters, please!' A ripple of silence passed over the face of the ruin, touching each in turn, until only Jodry's voice troubled the quiet.

Stenwold Maker had arrived.

He was supported by two members of Eujen's own Student Company, and they were making a crippled snail's pace of it. He looked as ghastly as an exhumed corpse – not just from the mass of bandage swathing his chest and shoulder, but there were livid, angry spots like plague-marks blotching his skin. The Faculty of Medicine had been working on him as recently as an hour ago, and Eujen knew they had been trying all manner of serums and alchemy on the worst injured, where experimental failure would be unlikely to make things worse. Eujen had heard of a few notable successes out of their treatments, and the fact that

Stenwold Maker was here, however close to death he looked, seemed proof of that.

All eyes were on him as he shuffled forwards and was lowered onto a tumbled stone, where he sat like a dead weight, staring at the ground. A Fly-kinden man – Eujen recognized Laszlo, whom he had encountered briefly during the battle – dropped down to stand beside him, looking the worse for wear himself, bruised and dirty and deathly weary.

'We cannot give up our independence,' the Fly spoke into the silence, and Eujen could just see Stenwold's lips moving and prompting him. 'Mar'Maker says – listen to me! – what you've lost up till now is nothing . . . Yes, they have killed your people and destroyed your homes but, if you let them, they will destroy your freedom. Collegium was a slave city once, he says . . . slaves of the Moths, before the revolution. For five centuries this city's been free, the jewel of the world . . . in trade, in learning, in the philosophy of its government,' he stumbled a little over the words, but his voice sounded strong and clear. 'Give in to the Wasps, he says, and you will end that era. You will close that book of history, and you'll let the Wasps write the next.'

Stenwold lifted his head with visible effort, and a shudder went through him, a sign of the physicians' serums still at work within his body, either to mend or to ruin him.

Jodry's eyes flicked to Helmess Broiler once more. The man was keeping a keen eye on proceedings, but still he made no sign that he intended to speak. Instead another man stood up, across the gathering, some merchant magnate from the look of him, and he was speaking before Jodry could invite him to.

'Speaker, War Master.' No ranting agitator this, just a sad, worn-down man on the wrong side of middle age. 'We know this. We all know the stakes. You put this war before us, and we went into it with our eyes open. I voted for it myself. And we've accomplished so much. We broke their air power, and we cast them back the first time. We fought them on the field, and we've made their lives miserable all the way back here. And yet they're here. We've done everything, and they're still here.'

He had the whole Assembly listening, and Eujen wondered whether this man had ever before enjoyed such a rapt audience.

'I lost a warehouse to their bombs,' the Assembler continued. 'Others lost their homes, their workplaces. Many lost their lives. And when we went out to meet them on the field . . . well, there were plenty who didn't come back. And how many young men and women have gone up in one of those Stormreaders, never to land safely?' The tremble in his voice, valiantly fought down, spoke of some personal loss. 'There are no Felyen left. *None.* An entire culture, yet they broke against the Second Army, and now they're no more – not their home, nor any of them, not a one. And the killing at the wall just today, my friends, my children . . .' For a moment he did lose control, his voice cracking and the raw, molten grief glaring out from within it. But then he paused for breath and was his own man again, forcing all that terrible depth of loss away, holding it at arm's length. 'And, yes, we can make them pay for every street. We can fight them for each house. But they will destroy those streets and those houses, just to take them from us. They will destroy the whole city, if they must, if we will not give it to them. Look at what they have done so far, and look at everything they have taken from us. Masters, we do not have so much to lose, now. The men and women whose lives we would throw at them, there are not so very many of them left. Please . . .'

'What are you saying?' Jodry demanded, but the man was already breaking down, sitting with his face in his hands, no more words left in him. The Speaker looked about, trying to assess the mood of his fellows. 'Listen to me. Listen!'

'A vote!' A new voice, crisp and clear and hard-edged.

Jodry turned to face his old enemy. Helmess Broiler had chosen his moment.

'A vote!' the man repeated, now standing. 'Come, you've had your say, Jodry, and the War Master has had his, by surrogate.

And we've all heard what Master Wisden has had to say. Furthermore, we've all been out there! We're seen it, the war and its leavings. So let's bring this to a close and vote. Do we take what mercy General Tynan has offered us? Choose wisely, or you may not get another chance to wear these robes.'

There were many there who looked to Stenwold, but the War Master just stared at the ground, and the Fly-kinden beside him stood mute, and at the last Jodry could put it off no longer.

Before nightfall the Assembly of Collegium, by a reasonable majority, had agreed to accept what terms the Empire might offer, word to be sent to General Tynan at first light. The war was over.

Part Three

Gates of Dusk

'Through the Gate'

— MOTTO OF MAKER'S OWN MERCHANT COMPANY

Thirty

In the air hung curtains of dawn mist and Che could hear, all around, an army standing quietly, so absurdly quietly. She heard the creak of leather and the scrape of metal, the stamp and snort of horses and the click of chitin. Such small noises, and yet she knew that there were thousands assembled here, a great war-host gathered on a strange, sparsely wooded hillside in the half-light, waiting to fight the greatest battle of their lives. They had come here to save the world.

'History will sing of this day for all the centuries to come,' said a voice from beside her, almost conversationally. 'We will be heroes, every one of us.'

'Let us hope history has the chance,' from another voice, but receding, and she hurried after it, into the mist that was even now beginning to thin. The shadows of the soldiers all around her were filling out with details. Mantis-kinden, she saw, rank on rank of them, and all clad in intricately crafted mail of chitin and steel. She cowered before their massed regard, expecting any moment for one of them to call her out. She did not belong here, that much was plain, and Mantis-kinden were notorious for their intolerance of intruders.

But they ignored her, as if beneath their notice, and yet, as she stepped amongst them, she felt there were memories submerged somewhere in her mind . . . Had she not had dealings with the Mantids only recently, and from a position of strength?

The realization that she was dreaming came creeping on her, not quite confirmed yet but well on its way. She had been through too many visions and wonders to be held in ignorance for too long. For now, though, she followed the two speakers through the Mantids' silent ranks, because they were her only point of reference.

'We have driven them this far,' said that the first voice, so rich and smooth, a voice of character and power. 'Across the world, we have driven them. They have brought all their armies together to face us, in their last stand. When we break them now, they must come to terms. Even a hate as mad as theirs must know limits.'

'Must it?' The other voice was female, older and more melancholy, and Che had caught up with them now, stepping absurdly close because now she had understood that nobody here would notice her. She was inviolate because she was only an afterthought, a spectator to someone else's thoughts.

When she saw him, that first speaker, she knew whose thoughts they were. He was a Moth-kinden, but nothing like the breed she knew from Tharn or Dorax. Tall and broad-shouldered from a life of action, with a long sword hanging low and horizontal behind him, everything about him spoke *warrior*. His white stare was fierce and proud, and when it turned on her she felt a jolt of contact even though he was gazing straight through her. His features sent a shiver through her, too: something in them of Achaeos, her dead lover. Here were the grey skin and blank eyes of his kinden, yes, but more than that. Here was the face of a man who had lived and fought, known triumph and defeat, and had conquered both. Infinitely human, fallible and yet a man who had faced his own failings.

He was one of the most handsome men she had ever seen. Perhaps only Salme Dien had been a more beautiful specimen of humanity.

He wore a hauberk of chitin scales that fell to his knees, with a loose, open robe slung over it, and in the crook of his arm rested a high, crested helm set with glittering iridescent wings, the very picture of a warrior prince from the distant past, back when even the Days of Lore were young. And he was a magician, too, for she could smell it on him.

Argastos in life, seen through his own recollections.

The woman beside him was taller, hunched and bald, her pasty skin banded with grey: a Woodlouse-kinden but a warrior as well. Che had never seen the like, for she was encased in great articulated lames of bronze, a metal carapace that must weigh two hundred pounds or more, and yet the woman moved easily inside it, for all her apparent years.

And now the mist was blowing away.

'We must triumph today,' Argastos declared. 'There must be an end to it.'

The army took shape about them, in between the scattered trees, and Che caught her breath. She had never seen such a sight, nor had anyone else for a thousand years.

The Mantis-kinden were all around them, and she realized that these were Argastos's personal guard, all five hundred of them; and beyond them were ranged the other war bands, together making up a host of the Inapt such as she had never seen. She saw more Mantids, and groups of Moth-kinden in leather and chitin mail, with arrows to their bows. There was the glittering finery of Dragonfly nobles on horseback, lifting their long swords towards the ascending dawn and shouting out their battle cries. She saw whole blocks of armoured Woodlouse-kinden bristling with pikes and halberds, and knots of large-framed Scorpions trailed by packs of their beasts, claws agape. Haughty Spider-kinden in bright silks stalked forwards with bow and spear, giving the Mantids a wide berth. And there were more, too: here was a score of lean, lightly armoured men and women she knew for Assassin Bugs, and there – she shuddered to see them out in the morning light, but there was no mistaking those red eyes set in pallid faces – Mosquito-kinden, armed and armoured for battle, standing almost shoulder to shoulder with a dozen kinden who hated them with a passion.

455

And, as she kept looking, she saw the others as well: less bright, less magical, less prominent, but gathered in numbers nonetheless. Ant-kinden with wooden shields and leather armour; Beetles – her own ancestors – in bronze mail of a style that recalled Khanaphes; Great Mole Crickets; the darting forms of Flies. Here was the whole world, and it had come to do battle.

And now there was a great woman striding between those war bands, tall as a Mole Cricket but of a less massive build, robed and partly armoured in chitin plate, pointing a staff down the hillside and calling out to Argastos, 'War Master! They come!'

The huge woman's helm was open, and Che looked upon her face and knew her name. *Elysiath Neptellian, Lady of the Bright Water, She whose Word Breaks all Bonds, Princess of the Thousand.* Last seen by Che in the catacombs beneath Khanaphes, a millennium later, but here she was young and far from the great city of her people – a people who must already be in decline – and she had come to fight. They had all come to fight.

And Che could see, further down the hill, another host that seemed to be forming out of the very earth itself: a vast horde of armoured figures. A fear arose at the sight of them – the fear of all about her regarding that terrible enemy. She understood – because Argastos understood – that many of those out there had been their kin, somehow, before falling into darkness. For this was the army of the Worm that sought to make everything like itself.

'Their seers block ours,' the Woodlouse woman announced. 'We cannot know their full strength.'

'They are many, what else do we need to know?' Argastos asked her. 'We have forced them to this battle. We can hardly leave them hungry now, can we?'

The host of the Worm was beginning to move, though Che could make out scant detail of them. She saw the war bands jostle amongst themselves, archers moving forwards and readying their arrows, and the others forming no real line, nothing like a modern battle order, each war band to its own. But she understood, having been in those same shoes, that there were magicians here – many, many magicians of all kinden. Each would direct a band, and speak to his or her fellows, for thus were the wars of the Inapt conducted back in the days of great magics.

And Argastos turned to her and smiled, lifting his helm to his head. 'You do not want to see this,' he told her. 'What is a battle, after all? And this battle, above all others, with no quarter given, no mercy, no call to hold until we had driven the Worm entirely from the land. And even then, even then they would not yield, but massed in their underground fastnesses and swore vengeance. And try as we might . . . what could we do, other than what we did?'

She found him again, seated on a fallen tree and staring at a hole in the ground.

A change had come over him in however long the battle had lasted. His armour was battered, scales cracked and lost, and his helm had lost its crest. His robe was torn, and she saw a wound in his shoulder, now patched over with a poultice in the style of Moth medicine. The real change was in his face, though, and she wondered how many years the battle could have taken, to leave him looking so drawn and lined.

But his pale eyes discerned her, despite the fact that she was not there. 'What else can we do?' he asked. 'Even now, my fellow war leaders consider my proposal. But we must win. We must have outright victory, or what was it all for?'

The hole was ten feet across and rimmed with stone, she saw, and there were soldiers there – the mixture of kinden that she had seen before. Even as she watched, some were descending – flying or climbing as their Art permitted – and others were emerging. She knew, by that same dream logic by which all knowledge came to her here, that there was still fighting taking place below, that the Worm was holding out, just as Argastos had said, and planning its return.

'They would make us all like them,' Argastos explained. 'That is what they want, just segment after identical segment of a single whole, until they become the entire world.'

A small group was approaching him now, and Che studied them. Leaders, warlords and great magicians, surely: a Moth woman in a silver skullcap who must have been a Skryre; a Dragonfly prince; a Spider Arista; a Mosquito with a fluid red birthmark blemishing his pallid forehead; a Mantis Weapons-master, with a brooch that would hardly have changed by Tisamon's day, though everything else about them was made unfamiliar by all the years that stood between their time and hers. At the back, poling himself along with a staff, another of the ponderous Masters of Khanaphes, this one a stranger to her. The mighty and powerful of this early age, and yet their attitude to Argastos was one of wary deference.

'War Master,' said the Moth, 'we have thought on what you say.' Her face was twisted with uncertainty, doubts bubbling to the surface and about to be raised, but a hand raised by Argastos brought silence.

'Give me another option,' he challenged them. 'Show me another way that does not leave the Worm free to return. I will *not* repeat the slaughter of this war, nor would I wish it on the future.'

'The cost,' the Dragonfly observed. 'You do not just condemn the Worm. Think of their slaves – and those of our own people trapped below . . .'

'And yet the more we send to rescue them, the more we lose in trying to fight the Worm on its own ground,' Argastos replied flatly. 'I know. Nethonwy is down there, my closest counsellor, lost trying to free her kin from the yoke of the Worm. Do not think that I don't know, but there is no other way – and now, whilst the magicians of the Worm are weak, and cannot prevent us.' He stood up suddenly. 'And they gain in strength even now. We all realize this.'

They were all of them unhappy, but Che could feel them

yielding to his logic. *In war, sometimes one must do terrible things,* but she knew that what they would enact now would be the most terrible thing of all: a magical violation of the world never before seen, never attempted since, that would make the harrowing of the Darakyon seem like a handful of dust in comparison. In this age, with magic waxing at its highest and these great practitioners banded together – at no other time in history could such a thing have been done.

And, hearing her thoughts, Argastos looked from his allies back to her and said, 'Be grateful, then, for that.'

The world around them was fading out, as though a curtain had been drawn over the sun. The others – those magicians of the elder days – withdrew into the gathering shadows, falling back into a history that had forgotten them, until she stood alone before Argastos in utter darkness, and her night-seeing Art could find nothing to relieve it.

'You sealed them off,' she accused him. 'You stopped up their tunnels and buried them, is that it?'

He regarded her, at once imperious and tragic and damned. 'Bury the Worm? Bury those that live in the earth? And how would that have helped? They were sovereign lords of their realm, as we discovered when we tried to bring the war to them. They knew that, even if we had defeated them beneath the sun, we could not hope to triumph below. They knew that all they had to do was wait. There would always be another chance.'

Che searched his face, trying to elicit some truth from it – from that image of himself that he chose to show her. Had he been a good man? He had been courageous and strong, she guessed, but those qualities were independent of vice or virtue. *What alternatives did they actually try, before resorting to their ultimate sanction?*

'Oh, you censure me, Cheerwell Maker,' he said softly. 'You pass judgement on the victories that made your whole world possible. You cannot imagine the hate, though. You cannot know how they hated us – all of us, every kinden other than their own.

Your Wasp Empire would seem a kindness compared to the Worm.'

'And yet they were human, a whole kinden, men, women and children – and slaves, too. And you killed them all.'

His face was a cipher. 'But we did not kill them, Cheerwell Maker. We rid the world of them, but we did not kill them. They are still there – or whatever they have become in their long centuries of exile. You cannot bury the Worm, so we enacted our ritual of last resort. We took their domain and everything in it – the Worm and their slaves and all those we had sent down and who could not return – and we excised them from the world entirely. We folded the weave of the cosmos around them and seared the join shut. And, as they had always wanted to be sole masters of creation, we gave them what they wished. We made their realm its own separate and sealed creation. We removed them from the world.'

Che felt that she should make some remark about how impossible that surely must be, but instead she found herself understanding the principle. The strength required to accomplish it, she could not guess at, but the magician in her recognized the theory behind it to be sound.

'Such power it demanded, and the war itself had already cost so many lives, and our guilt regarding so many lost beneath the earth – lost through our own ritual . . . Perhaps that was when the world began to turn, the magic to fade from it. The grand alliance between the great powers broke up almost immediately. Some never recovered: the Woodlouse-kinden abandoned their domains and retreated to their rotting heartland. The Khanaphir were already failing. There was civil war amongst the Spider-kinden. My people's doom came slower, for they had taken upon themselves the mantle of protector of the world, and in that cause they would fight slow-burning wars against many of their erstwhile allies, confident in their vision of a better future. Except it was not their future they were fighting to bring about – it was yours.' And he said this with no rancour, without any bitterness at all.

'And you?' she asked him. 'Where were you in all this?'

He laughed, without much humour. 'Watch.'

She was further off now, watching the next proceedings from the trees – not quite the tangled, knotted old woodland that the Nethyen and their neighbours called home in her time, but a younger, greener place, more innocent to her eyes. She wondered if all the world had been that way once, before the Inapt and later the Apt had come, to corrupt and to despoil it.

In front of her was a clearing, and she saw quite a crowd gathered about a mound. Ant-kinden workers were busy laying stone slabs over it, as though trying to armour the earth itself. She saw a gaping mouth there, a gap that was being turned into a door.

'They tore down Argax, my beloved hall.' The voice of Argastos sounded clearly in her mind, though he was nowhere near her. 'They broke it apart, timber by timber, and they brought its golden gates here, where they had raised this abomination of a barrow over the Great Seal – the key Seal that kept the Worm forever elsewhere. It was necessary, they claimed. After all that had been lost, after all we had done, they could not risk some fool breaking the Seal and letting them out.' His voice had changed, grown older, bitter and angry.

She saw them there: a score or more of Moths in their grey robes, and at least twice that number of Mantis-kinden. The latter were armed and armoured, just as they had been on the battlefield, and yet there was a terrible air of defeat hanging about them, also dread. Even as she watched, they were filing into the mound, one by one.

'My people, my followers,' Argastos whispered. 'Betrayed, as I was betrayed, sacrificed to keep me company in my vigil. So necessary, they insisted, and all the while I looked into their minds and saw how they simply wanted rid of me, because of what we had done. I was too great a reminder of the lengths we had gone to, in order to win the war.'

And Che watched Argastos, in bright, unblemished mail, turn to face those other Moths, and she watched as his shoulders slumped, and then he turned and stepped into darkness.

'They left me no choice,' continued the voice in her mind.

She watched the great gates being raised, with their scales of gilded wood gleaming in the sun, and she knew that Argastos and his followers had been bound, within the heart of the hill, bound over the Seal of the Worm for all time. After that, the Moths had gone some way towards removing his name from any histories the outside world might uncover. And he was still there – still *here* – even in this late age when hardly anyone even remembered his name.

And the vision faded once more, leaving her again in that vacant blackness with Argastos.

'And here you are,' he remarked and, knowing what she did, she could read any amount of terrible intentions in those elegant features.

'Do you mean to break the Seal, after all this time?' she asked. It seemed the natural way for him to punish those that had turned on him.

'No!' He raised his eyebrows. 'Of all things not that – not after the cost that we all paid. Not after the friends I lost – the friends I had to abandon because they had gone below and never returned. But I will escape this place, believe me. I will be avenged.'

A sudden thought occurred to her. 'And you're showing all of this to *her* as well, aren't you?' There was no need to specify whom she spoke of.

Argastos's smile should have pleasant, but it sent a shudder down Che's spine.

'Of course,' he said. 'When wooing two sisters, it is not gallant to show a preference, after all.'

'When *what*?' she demanded, but he was already walking away, and she had no way of following him into the void.

'We will speak again, in the flesh. You have seen what you

must, in order to know the justice of my cause. Now I shall show you what they left me with!'

Then he was gone: a sudden flurry of robes and he had become part of the darkness. And, with a sudden start, Che awoke.

Thirty-One

She woke with a start just as someone virtually kicked in the door of the infirmary. All around her people were jolting awake, and those that could do so were already reaching for weapons that weren't there.

'Taki!' Her name. There were other names, too – at least half a dozen Company soldiers had burst in, each seeking someone else, and she recognized most of those names because they were pilots – the ones who had escaped the swarm, either with their Stormreaders or without.

'Here.' She had been almost dead from exhaustion by the time she regained the city – her Art had not proved strong enough to carry her the whole distance and she had dropped to the ground virtually within arm's reach of the walls. They had carried her in, and the time from then until now was a haze of half-waking, of doctors, of nightmares of tearing mandibles and thrusting stings.

The soldier before her looked about sixteen and bore the sash of the Students. 'Can you fly?' he demanded, without introduction.

The impact of her ordeal showed in her initial assumption that he was referring to her Art, but who would be asking after that? 'I can pilot a Stormreader, if that's what you mean.' She got her legs over the side of the bed, feeling each muscle and joint resist her, and hoped her words were true.

'Then you're needed,' the boy continued, and she was struck by the discontinuity of him speaking to her as if he was a blunt veteran.

'The Farsphex are back? They're bombing the city? What's the situation there?'

Something in his face caved then, under the weight of everything she did not know. He had not expected to be the one to tell her.

He told her it all, and she just sat there, aghast. All around her, the news was spreading through the infirmary – and through the city, no doubt. How many would refuse to believe it? How many would be secretly relieved?

'So what the piss do you want from me?' she spat bitterly. 'You want me flying loop-the-loops over the Second Army's triumphant entry into the city?'

'We want you out of the city, because your name is included on their list as an enemy of the Empire,' the student told her flatly. 'And we want you flying escort for if they come after.'

'After? Look, did nobody tell you how to put your thoughts in order over at the College?' But she was already scrabbling for her clothes and not finding them, standing wearing nothing but a shift before this adolescent, and she did not care, and he did not even blink at it. 'Piss on it, get me some artificer's overalls, at least. And some sort of goggles. What time is it?'

'Three past midnight, and a half. There are Farsphex over the city, but we've a flight of Stormreaders ready to go up, enough to shield an airship. Everyone who we reckon's on the Empire's list, we're trying to get them to Sarn.'

'One airship?'

'We have eleven Stormreaders able to fly, all with the new clockwork so they can last to Sarn,' he told her. She did the calculations herself and nodded. Touch and go, if the Farsphex were up for it. Two airships would be indefensible, just handing the Empire an easy kill.

'I'll fly,' she told him. 'Get me something to wear and get me to an orthopter.'

Space aboard the *Windlass* had already run out. Jons Allanbridge had emptied his hold of everything but the water barrels in order to stuff people in, calculating weights and flight tolerances with each new passenger. His vessel was larger than its predecessor, but even so it had never been intended for bulk. He traded in small-volume valuable goods.

He had some of the Assemblers on board – a fraction of the number who had actually *wanted* to come, and only those who had played a significant part in the city's defence. He had a similar slice of the College's staff, mostly those who possessed artificing knowledge that nobody wanted the Empire getting hold of. The number turned away by the Company soldiers was large, so there was still an angry, frustrated crowd of the great and the good and the learned milling around the airfield, getting in everyone's way.

The next figure was ascending, just as Jons guessed he had got as many down below as he could. The woman clambering up the rope ladder now – rather than waiting for the airfield's hoist crane to swing up its platform – was well known to him.

'Commander Kymene,' he noted.

The Mynan leader did not refuse his hand, once she got to the rail, although he had thought she might. Now he saw her close up, she appeared as though she had already been under the Wasp interrogators for a week, bruised and tired and drawn.

'My people.' Her voice came in a rasp.

'All on board, those who've come to me.' There had been an outcry amongst those denied passage when they found that every surviving Mynan was getting out of Collegium on the *Windlass*, a substantial proportion of Allanbridge's living cargo, standing virtually shoulder to shoulder below and a good dozen above decks still. It had been the whispered words of Stenwold Maker, Jons had heard, that had settled the matter. He had observed

466

that, to the Wasps, Mynans were rebellious slaves, and that meant the crossed pikes for every single one – and probably worse for Kymene herself. Had anyone else advanced this argument, Jons guessed the Mynans would have been told to take their chances, but Maker's will still bore just enough weight to carry the vote.

And where the pits is the man himself? For the War Master's name most certainly headed up the list of passengers, but still he stayed away. *False heroics, or . . .?* Not something Jons wanted to think about, but he'd heard how Maker was playing cards with death just about now, winning some hands and losing others.

Kymene stomped past him, then halted. 'How long?' she demanded.

'Ask the Empire,' Jons replied shortly. 'Once they start paying notice, then we get the Stormreaders in the air and get moving. Or a single incendiary could end all our plans, right off.'

Her curt nod told him that she understood him perfectly.

And here was another row erupting on the approaching hoist platform – someone trying to bully their way on to the ship, no doubt, with their money or their College accredits or . . .

The crane swung the hoist round, with them still arguing loudly, and Jons saw it was a small Beetle man in artificer's canvas that looked as though he had been toiling in it for two days straight, and a woman with him holding a girl of no more than ten in her arms.

Willem Reader, Jons identified the man as the aviation artificer. *How tired must I be that it even took me that long?*

Reader had been arguing, but not on his own behalf, for he was very plainly marked as a man to be kept out of the Empire's hands. Instead, he had been trying to get away from the *Windlass*, and indeed the two Company soldiers on the hoist alongside him seemed more a guard than an escort.

It was the woman's voice that Jons heard most clearly, as the hoist reached the deck.

'You'll go,' she told him. 'Will, it's not me the Engineering

Corps will be hunting, to get at what's in your head. It's not me that the Sarnesh will need to modernize their air power. We'll stay here, and we won't even look the Wasps in the eye, and I'll tell her every night that you're coming back, and bringing an army with you. Look at me, Will!'

The *Windlass* was already groaning at the seams with its cargo, and all the Collegiates below decks had loved ones that they had been forced to part from. *No exceptions,* Jons knew, and he shook his head shortly when Reader looked to him.

'Jen . . .' Reader managed.

'Go,' she told him, clasping him tightly, and then giving him a shove that propelled him onto the deck of the *Windlass.*

'Get below, Reader,' Jons snapped at the artificer, wondering if even one more man would fit. But then Kymene was shouting a warning, just as the hoist platform began to swing away.

Jons's head snapped up. Engines – orthopter engines, but the Stormreaders' clockwork didn't make anything like so much noise.

'Empire!' Kymene was now yelling.

Oh, hammer and tongs. Jons found he could not move, hearing only the diving descent of the Farsphex, hearing the sudden panic in the crowd, waiting for the bombs.

The roaring sound peaked, and he saw sparks fly, heard screams from the crowd, the angry stammer that was a rotary piercer spun up to full speed. Then splinters flew from the deck, and one of the Mynans jerked and pitched over the rail.

'Jen!' Reader was shouting, and Jons bellowed at him to get below, He was calling to cast off before feeling the lurch of the deck beneath his feet – comforting even as it sent him staggering – knowing that someone on the ground had had the sense to cut the mooring ties. He had a brief glimpse of the hoist platform as it slipped past, Jen Reader standing there with the two Company soldiers flanking her, her daughter in her arms, watching the airship swiftly ascend.

The first Stormreader skittered past, looping about the *Windlass*'s envelope to engage the Farsphex – *And how many holes did they punch in the canvas, eh?* He thrust the thought away and bent to his task, gauging the wind and bringing his ship around on a course that would take them to Sarn. More of the orthopter escort were lifting past him now, and he could see flashes out in the night as they threw themselves at the handful of Farsphex that had located them. Kymene and a few of her Mynans had even taken to the *Windlass*'s rails with snapbows, providing a desperate last line of defence if it was needed.

Jons looked back, and down, seeing his city diminishing and becoming something less, until the night had swallowed it entirely.

Three streets away stood the wall, where the black and gold flag was already raised, indicating that segment of Collegium's shell that was already claimed by the Empire. The nearest buildings had rapidly been abandoned by their owners: the merchants, artisans and their families fleeing the reach of the Wasps. Now only soldiers of the Fealty Street Company kept watch, awaiting dawn and the formal surrender.

And there remained one other man, on the roof of this one townhouse: a poor and ill-kept building, the shame of the neighbourhood, the dilapidated exterior of which bomb scars had barely managed to disfigure.

The battered little automotive pulling up outside it had a clockwork engine badly in need of maintenance, the gear trains clattering and ratcheting against one another, sounding on the point of working loose. The driver in his open cab was a Sarnesh in a Student Company sash. Behind him was a tailgated flatbed, hooded with canvas stretched over a looped metal frame.

As the engine was hacking to a halt, Laszlo put his head out and glanced around. There had been a rumour of Wasp deathsquads stalking the streets, winged soldiers creeping into the city to kill anyone they found. Or else Spiders with their stealthy blades, come to exact a final price before the surrender. The city was alive with fear tonight.

He hopped over towards the peeling door and hammered on

it, keeping one eye still on the sky. On the second repetition another Fly appeared in the doorway, brandishing an uncocked crossbow and looking furious. 'What is this riot? Are we come to this already? Be off with you!' His clothes were plain but impeccably neat, his face blotchy and red-eyed.

'Where's Drillen?' demanded Laszlo. 'We've got an airship to catch, and he's supposed to be on it.'

The Fly at the door stared at him for a moment. 'You're Maker's man? Laszlo?' His eyes flicked towards the automotive. 'Oh, no . . .' In a moment he was out into the street, wings taking him to the covered rear of the automotive, peering into the gloom until he locked eyes with the half-supine form of Stenwold Maker.

'War Master? You must get yourself to the *Windlass!*' he exclaimed.

Stenwold hissed in frustration and rasped out. 'And so must your master, Arvi. Where the pits is he?'

Jodry Drillen's secretary shook his head. 'You can't be here! I sent the message myself! Please, just go!'

'I've had no message. I've been to every place Jodry owns in the city, save this,' Stenwold rasped. 'He's here, isn't he? Then go and get him. We can still get aloft.'

'War Master,' Arvi told him solemnly, 'he's not going.'

There was a ghastly, strained silence, and then a sudden clang as, with one convulsive movement, Stenwold kicked the tailgate open.

'Mar'Maker, no. He's right, we've got to go,' Laszlo insisted, but Stenwold heaved and dragged himself to the edge. His Ant-kinden driver had dashed round the side by then to support his weight, so that he ended up on his feet at the back of the auto-motive, gasping, clutching at a stout stick to steady himself but plainly only held up by the Art of his helper.

'If he won't come . . . to me,' he wheezed out, 'then I will . . . go . . . to him.'

Arvi watched him, aghast, as he lurched through the door and inside, leaning on stick and driver at every heavy step.

'Where?' came the War Master's whisper, with a frustrated sigh when Arvi indicated the stairs. Before Stenwold could brace himself for the climb, though, the ponderous figure of Jodry Drillen began descending, regarding his old friend and ally with inordinate sadness.

'Stenwold, get to the airship.'

Stenwold's reply was lost, but Laszlo translated: 'Soon as you get in the automotive, he says.'

Halfway down the stairs, Drillen sat. 'I've given it some thought, Sten. It's not going to happen. I'm Speaker, after all. I brought us all to this, as much as anyone did . . . yes, don't flatter yourself, just as much as you. When the word of our surrender goes out to the Wasps at dawn, I'll take it myself.'

Stenwold's spitting remonstrance was all but inaudible, but it needed no translation.

'Oh, maybe, maybe,' the Speaker for the Assembly confirmed tiredly. 'But maybe not, after all. And if I go myself, and give myself into their hands, then perhaps it will soften the blow for the rest of the city. Perhaps I'll be able to achieve something that way.' He shook his head, his jowls quivering. 'There's always a first time.'

Stenwold looked up at him, fighting for breath. 'You utter fool,' he got out.

'That's just the standard of debate I should expect from a firebrand like you.' Jodry forced a smile. 'Now get gone. We don't know what they'll do with me, but you've been on the Rekef's list since before the first war. Get out of my house, Sten. Get out of my city, for that matter. Piss off to Sarn, why don't you?'

'Come on, Mar'Maker,' Laszlo insisted. 'You know he's right.'

Stenwold's face twisted for a moment, but it was not clear whether it was sentiment or the continuing effects of the physicians' alchemy that was responsible. 'See you again, Jodry,' he managed, as the Ant-kinden began to manhandle him back towards the door.

'Of course you will,' Jodry agreed hollowly. 'Go carefully, Sten.'

471

They were halfway to the airfield when they heard the Farsphex engines, but none of them drew the right conclusion until the driver ground the automotive to a skidding halt. There, lifting from the city ahead, was the grey shadow of the *Windlass*, the fleeter shapes of the Stormreaders wheeling all around it. Gone, and already drawing the notice of the Empire with its departure.

Stenwold drew a ragged breath when the driver told him. Other than that, the news seemed unable to injure him more than he was damaged already.

Laszlo, ever resourceful, was leaning over beside their driver, giving urgent directions.

'We're getting clear, Mar'Maker!' he shouted. 'Never you worry.'

They rattled through the dark streets of Collegium, away from the Empire-held gate, for the harbour, with Laszlo all the while flitting from Stenwold back to the driver, babbling reassuring optimism whilst trying to calculate just what decisions might have been made in his absence, especially once the Farsphex started flying.

And when they reached the docks, and when the driver had brought them to a stop, Laszlo dropped out from the automotive and simply stood there, looking out to sea. Not a ship was in, not a single one. Most certainly not the *Tidenfree*.

For once in his life, Laszlo had no words, and he felt tears welling up – not adult tears but those of a child abandoned. He folded slowly to his knees, fighting to keep a hold on himself. *The orthopters* . . . He had known that attack from the air was what Tomasso had feared most, and that the *Tidenfree* would be easy prey for incendiaries from above. He had known all that and, when he had gone to help Stenwold, he had been warned of just that. And he had ignored it because, of course, they would not go without *him*.

If he squinted, he could make out a sail far out on the waves. Maybe he could fly the distance, if they were making poor headway. Maybe he could chase after them and call them back. Maybe he could make everything right again. Even as he had the thought, the *Tidenfree* slipped further and further away.

He knew the other gates to the city were already blockaded by Imperial and Spider troops, and anyone trying to escape the city would get a snapbow bolt for his pains – as some had already found out.

Laszlo slumped into the automotive as the driver called, 'Where next?'

Where indeed? He met Stenwold's eyes, hearing his short, painful words.

'Get us back to the College,' Laszlo translated. Where else was there?

He had kept watch through the last hour of the night from the roof of this rundown little house. Not his own grand townhouse, close to the College, which everyone knew as the home of Jodry Drillen. This ramshackle place, kept in careful disorder, which he disappeared to when he was ducking official business or keeping clandestine assignments. Or he had done, when he was younger, and less a prisoner of his own sagging flesh.

Now he stood up and went downstairs into the house itself, calling for his secretary.

Arvi appeared, looking as though he was already attending Jodry's funeral, and the Speaker for the Assembly scowled at him. 'Nobody has any faith,' he muttered. 'Get my Assembly robes, will you? Might as well make a good impression.' And that was not just provincial Lowlander thinking, either. The robes of an Imperial diplomat might be edged in black and gold, but even they were modelled on the Collegiate Assembly's particular style. *We have led the world in times of peace,* he reflected. *Could we have done more with that influence?* He thought of Eujen Leadswell, unregarded demagogue and chief officer of the Student Company. *He would say yes to that, and perhaps he was right, after all. Our chosen path doesn't seem to have brought us anywhere useful.*

By that time, Arvi had attired him as a man worthy of his

position, every fold and drape immaculate, Jodry was embarrassed to hear the normally unflappable little man snivelling as he did so.

'Now get off to your family,' he directed.

'My mother died two years ago, Master,' Arvi reminded him in a shaky voice.

'Of course she did, I'm sorry. Get to . . .' Jodry found that the world had become a place short of safe harbours. 'I don't know. You'll be all right. Even the Wasps value a good secretary.'

'I wouldn't,' the Fly-kinden hissed, horrified.

Jodry didn't have the energy to argue with him. 'I'd write you a reference, but I don't imagine that would do much good. For what it's worth, you've been a useful fellow to have around.'

Arvi had stepped back, and was staring at his feet, as if not trusting himself to reply, whereupon Jodry gave a great sigh and stepped out of the house, into the grey dawn air.

The walk, the few streets to the gate, seemed the longest of his life. Emerging from the buildings out onto that square was almost too much for him. The bodies of the previous day's fighting had been taken away, but three Sentinels kept silent watch, like monumental effigies in steel. Above them, the top of the wall was now lined with Wasp-kinden soldiers, snapbows at the ready, hundreds of them, and all with their eyes fixed on him. There were more at ground level, men in heavier armour, with spears shouldered, stepping out from the gate's shadow cautiously, to watch this one fat old Beetle-kinden man approach them.

Jodry fought to retain his dignity, that smooth progress that was the mark of a confident, self-contained man. He kept his head high, meeting their massed gaze as best he could. For all that his feet wanted to slow down as he neared the Sentinels, he kept up a steady but unhurried pace.

Then the leftmost Sentinel moved, just a fluid, irritable shifting of its legs. He jumped back with a brief cry of alarm, and a ripple of derisive jeering coursed across the wall top.

The armoured infantry had meanwhile formed two lines, an

honour guard of sorts, funnelling him into the gatehouse. With a deep breath, Jodry approached them, feeling his heart knocking harder and harder in his chest, his guts turning to water. They had such hard, pale faces! Surely even the Felyen had been gentler of aspect when they marched off to their deaths.

He halted. He could not help himself. He could see through the gate now to the far side, to the camp of the Second Army, the thousands that backed up the hundreds already on the wall. His eyes sought some sign from the soldiers beside him, but they seemed to be staring past him, waiting for him to step within.

I could just walk away. But he felt they would shoot him for cowardice if he did.

Mustering his courage, gathering great handfuls of it and clutching it to him, Jodry walked through the gate of his own city, and into the enemy's camp.

Some manner of officer approached him, and he called out, 'I bring the word of the Assembly!' The Wasps all around him seemed so different from his own people, such a fierce warrior breed, that he almost felt that they would not understand human speech.

'With me,' the officer said. 'You're expected.' And he was already marching off at a pace that made Jodry hustle to keep up, out of breath after only half a dozen steps.

General Tynan met him in a tent, perhaps the finest that Jodry had ever seen, multi-roomed, its heavy fabric woven with gold thread. It seemed more opulent by far than the house he himself had spent a sleepless night in. Possibly it was worth more, too.

The Wasp general wore armour, and presented a surprisingly down-to-earth figure: just a bald, ageing soldier after all, with a few scars and a steady gaze, sitting on a camp stool. Before him was a folding table on which paperwork sat half completed, reservoir pen only now laid down, as though the master of the Gears was just some quartermaster's clerk. Or, perhaps, the Speaker for the Assembly.

The woman beside him provided all the glamour he lacked, elegantly beautiful in armour of white-dyed leather ornamented with gold arabesques, and Jodry knew that this must be Mycella of the Aldanrael, the Spiderlands Arista. A heavily armoured Spider man stood at her shoulder, staring at Jodry as though his bulk hid a team of assassins. At Tynan's shoulder was another Wasp officer, a colonel but with some corps insignia that Jodry could not place.

'My name is Jodry Drillen,' he began, keeping his voice admirably calm. 'I am the Speaker of the Assembly, duly elected by the will of the people of Collegium, and come here to answer your demands.'

'Of course you are.' Tynan did not seem surprised. 'No War Master Maker this time?'

Jodry shrugged. 'The Assembly has voted to accept your generous offer, General. With no war, why would we need a War Master?' He held his breath at his own flippancy, but Tynan grudged him a small smile.

'We will begin moving our troops in to secure the city immediately, then. I trust that the Assembly's decision has been fully communicated to your citizens? Anyone who decides that their personal war is still ongoing will find the repercussions wide-ranging. I'm glad,' he added quietly. 'I would rather lives had been spared by your accepting my offer before the walls, but this is better than nothing. You have spared your city a great deal.'

And your army, too, Jodry thought but did not say. *Does he know how I argued against it?* He had a bleak certainty that the name of every speaker at that ragged Assembly was in the books of the Rekef already. 'If I may speak, General . . .'

Tynan's eyes slid over to the Aldanrael woman, and they obviously shared some understanding denied to him, before the general nodded for him to continue.

'I thought,' he said, irritated by the nervousness in his voice, which had never let him down before, 'that I would offer myself as a go-between. Now you are masters of Collegium, after all, you will want someone . . . who knows how it all works.' His voice trailed off on seeing Tynan's expression, and mostly because there was more pity in it than anything else. The general leant back to make some murmured enquiry of the colonel at his shoulder, but the Spider Arista was still studying Jodry carefully.

'My son mentioned you in his last report, Master Drillen,' she said briskly, and it took Jodry an unaccustomed moment to work out what she meant. But, of course, she was here to avenge both the turning back of her armada and the death of her child Teornis, whom Stenwold had killed in Princep.

Jodry made himself lift a polite eyebrow. 'And what did he write, my lady?'

'He recommended keeping you alive, Master Drillen,' Mycella explained. 'I think he liked you. He was terribly sentimental, I'm afraid.' She sighed. 'The innocence of those days, had we only known.'

Tynan had now heard his colonel's reply and turned back, face expressionless. 'Your services will not be required. The Empire has appointed a new officer to command your Assembly, to better advise and assist our governance of the city in line with Imperial policy.' He stood up, and Jodry took an involuntary step back, as though the general himself was going to put a sword in him. His back struck against the unyielding chill of armour, and he whirled round to find that there were a half-dozen soldiers inside the tent now, whom he had not even noticed entering.

He fought to recover his composure, but the same fear that had assailed him before the gatehouse was back with reinforcements. The faces of the soldiers, of the general and the Lady-Martial all seemed mere masks of human skin over something murderous. *Or is it we in Collegium who have gone against human nature. Is their warlike drive the true humanity?* Right now a single friendly Beetle face would be a blessedly welcome sight.

'Cherten, let's get this over with. Bring in the major,' Tynan directed, and the colonel bowed and stepped past Jodry, heading out of the tent.

What are you going to do with me? But to ask that question would be to invite the answer, and Jodry had no wish to hear it. Instead, he just stood there and fought to keep back the terror that was stealing over him.

In almost no time, Colonel Cherten was back, followed by a man wearing the robes of the Empire's Diplomatic Corps, that misleadingly Collegiate style recast in black and gold.

'Why, hello, Jodry,' said Helmess Broiler, with a smile that could cut glass.

Jodry nodded to him, managing that same cordial coldness with which he would have greeted the man in the Assembly. 'Broiler.'

'Who would have thought it,' Helmess mused. 'The votes are in and I was made Speaker, after all. Fancy that, eh?'

Tynan shifted slightly, and Jodry saw a moment of quickly stifled fright in Helmess's eyes, before the man said, 'Yes, General, you wished to see me?'

'Major Broiler, a matter involving the Collegiate Assembly has come up,' Tynan told him. To Jodry's ear there was absolutely no liking for the turncoat Beetle in the general's voice, but he knew that would not change anything. 'Perhaps you have a solution?'

Helmess smiled – not even an unctuous, favour-currying smile but his usual avuncular beam, which had served him so well in Collegiate politics. 'Why, certainly, sir. As you know, Master Drillen is near the top of the list of the Empire's enemies. Under other circumstances I would expect him to be passed over to the interrogators to be examined on the wider capabilities of Collegium's allies, news from Sarn and all the rest. However . . .' He turned that smile now on Jodry, who remained very still and did not look him in the eye. 'In all honesty the man's little more than a figurehead, and there are wiser men who know far more and who are already on our list.'

For a hollow moment Jodry found he had been given the unasked-for gift of hope. It was a poisoned gift, he knew, and yet he could not stop his heart leaping at it, just as Helmess must have expected.

'I would suggest that Colonel Cherten's staff turn their attention instead to his knowledge of those on our list whose whereabouts are unknown – a detailed and systematic inquiry as to who remains within the city, who has fled, and who was killed in the fighting. These details he will know, sir.'

Tynan stepped forwards, close enough for Jodry to reach out and touch him if he dared. His eyes flicked sideways at Cherten, who nodded minutely.

'And then?' the general asked.

Helmess's face emptied of anything approaching common humanity. 'Collegium needs to be sent a clear message, sir. I believe crossed pikes are traditional.'

Tynan studied him for a long while, and Jodry had every chance to decipher the minutiae of the man's expression, to see just how much loathing the soldier felt for this traitor, however useful that betrayal had been. If Helmess had not been Cherten's man, then Jodry would not have given a stripped gear for his chances.

At last: 'Although their use has become somewhat widespread in recent years,' the general declared, 'the pikes are properly a punishment for those of the Empire who have turned against their masters: escaped slaves and rebellious generals alike.' He looked Jodry in the eye. 'But you're right about sending a message. Some other means, then, quick but public.'

Helmess kept his face carefully empty of disappointment. 'The Lady-Martial's people use just such a method to dispose of their criminals,' he observed.

Tynan nodded, still staring into Jodry's face. His thoughts were plain: he respected Jodry's coming in person to deliver the surrender, but he would do nothing to stop his people torturing and killing him. Indeed he would applaud it, because to him it was the right and necessary thing to do. Here was the Empire in miniature.

'You'll get nothing from me!' Jodry bellowed, finding his voice at last as the soldiers took hold of him. Nobody was listening, though, as they hauled him out of the tent. Or perhaps only Helmess heard, as he followed the knot of men outside to watch Jodry depart, and stood grinning from ear to ear.

And, towards evening the same day, Helmess stood on the wall above the north gate, watching the tail end of the Second Army march into the city. There were soldiers on every rooftop now, watching out for trouble, whilst elsewhere the Company soldiers were surrendering their arms, no doubt desperately hoping that the Empire would keep its word. While Cherten's interrogators had put Jodry on the rack, Helmess had stood here and watched the Empire's vanguard entering the city. There had been quite a few there to watch, displaying the traditional Collegiate inability to stay away from anything that was happening, however appalling. The silence of that crowd had been deafening, and Helmess had made quite a study of their expressions as his people had witnessed the boots of the Empire march over their much-cherished freedoms.

He was glad to have Jodry beside him now, for one last put-down, before his work began.

'"You'll get nothing from me",' he mimicked. 'Oh, I'll wager they'd never heard that one before. And you squealed, you fat bastard. You broke and blubbered and told them everything they wanted. Of course you did.'

He took a deep breath, savouring the air. Tomorrow the Assembly would meet – *his* Assembly – and he would tell them how it was going to be. And there would be other duties, happy ones. He had some old friends to go and look in on, thanks to what Jodry had revealed.

Tonight, though, he would spend in the Empire's camp, because the Wasp soldiers had fought *hard* to capture this city, and this was their night. Woe betide the taverner who tried to charge them for their wine. Woe to any woman who wanted to say no. Woe to Collegium, really, but hadn't Helmess been warning them not to fight, all this time?

'Just think if I had won at Lots and been made Speaker, how much of this could have been avoided?' he asked Jodry aloud. 'Just think how many of our people you got killed – you and Maker between you – just to bring us to this point after all.'

Beside him, with a tortured creaking, the massive corpse of Jodry Drillen revolved and swayed on the gibbet.

Thirty-Two

Tegrec had been running for longer than was good for him. He had never been a man who had taken to exercise, the prestige of his family propelling him just far enough up the ranks that he could delegate the running around to others. Now he ran as he had never run before, and at the same time he was drawing on all the magic he had ever learned, with just one end in mind:

Find a way out of this place.

The domain of Argastos pressed all around him, that grey, gnarled shadow of the forest without, but its master's attention was most decidedly elsewhere. Tegrec, a minor distraction at the most, had some small space of time to get clear before the place noticed him again and made him pay.

He could sense all around him the spirits of the imprisoned dead. Argastos' home was like a pitcher plant, and all those who ever entered had neither left nor truly died. The agonized remnants of them were impaled on the trees surrounding him, writhing and screaming. If he came to their attention, he would join them in short order.

And not just death but a living death, as a slave of Argastos. He saw it all so clearly now.

He had not wanted things to turn out like this, but that was hardly worth saying. Born a Wasp without Aptitude, he had lived his whole life as an impostor amongst his own people. He had learned magic in scraps and tatters, leaching what little could be had from the spoils of the Twelve-year War and carefully playing his political games until a golden opportunity had come his way: when the Empire took Tharn, home of the Moth-kinden. He had been sent there as governor, and he had sold out his own people in return for knowledge and power, and he had given himself over to the Moths.

And they had given him back, in a way, so that he had ended up at the Imperial court as Tharen ambassador, brokering an alliance between his surrogate and his birth kinden that the Moths would never have considered had the Empress not been who – or what – she was.

So far, so good, but then everything had fallen apart. He had never wanted to come to this terrible place, in the Empress's entourage; to see the murder of his fellow Moth ambassador; to see that other impostor, the assassin, suddenly spring out from behind the guise of dull Major Ostrec . . .

He was not a man temperamentally suited to such events, and so he ran, hoping that he could outdistance the reach of both Argastos and Seda before he was noticed again.

All around him he could feel this horribly dead place waking up. Its attention had contracted towards its centre, dragging in its chosen victims – the Empress and her opposite – but now the tendrils of its thought were flexing and twitching, its trap was setting itself again, and he was still within its range; he could not find the way out.

Fear endowed him with a sudden surge of strength, increasing his stumbling pace as he battered at the fabric of Argastos's realm like a man clawing through cobwebs.

And it gave way, and the forest he found himself staggering through was no less dark and grim of aspect, but at least it was real and physical.

He paused, and leant against a tree, fighting to get his breath back. *Clear, I'm clear!* Even the murky forest air seemed sweet to him.

483

Something moved close by, and he felt a chill pass through him. *Did something else come with me?*

He looked about and realized that he was surrounded. There was a score of Mantis-kinden shifting in and out of sight amid the trees, with bows and spears. Nethyen or Etheryen? He could not tell.

'Servants of the Green,' he croaked, using the ancient Moth greeting to their followers.

For a long moment those words hung in the air, testing their power against the Mantids, while the world itself seemed to hold its breath.

Then one of them shook her head. 'No masters,' she said. 'Not any more. Seize the trespasser.'

'No!' Tegrec gasped. *Not after all I've been through.* And he began backing away, seeing some of them drawing back their bowstrings, others spreading out. They were not moving towards him, though, even as he took step after step away. Their attention, hungry for blood, was focused elsewhere.

And at last he turned to see another Mantis behind him, a weathered-looking man with his long hair unbound.

'What do you want?' Tegrec gasped.

'No masters,' the man echoed. 'Amalthae?' Something in the way he stood led Tegrec's gaze sideways and upwards, until at last he saw the colossal beast towering by the Mantis's side.

Tegrec lashed out with all the force of his magic, but the mind he encountered was more than his equal. Then those dread killing arms were reaching for him.

Che awoke into darkness, but this was no new thing for her. She found herself standing, with walls pressing close on three sides.

Argastos's domain.

And she was a daughter of Collegium, whether Apt or Inapt, and she had been raised to question. First she called on her Art, and found that the gloom about her was not dispelled, but hung

484

before her eyes all the more. *So, nothing as mundane as mere darkness, then. This is what Argastos wants me to see.*

Not utterly dark, either – because Argastos wanted her to see just enough and no further. Enough to see that the indistinct walls around her comprised a dead end in what must be a maze. She remembered reading about Moths and mazes in a book, while she had been looting the College library for anything that might help her with her newly imposed Inaptitude. It had been a favourite pastime of Moth Skryres to trap their enemies in mazes of the mind. Che herself had nearly become lost in one through Seda's doing, snared in her own memories. *Until Maure walked into my mind to rescue me.*

And did that mean Maure was just as capable of rescuing herself, or was she also a prisoner elsewhere in this labyrinth, or in some other cell altogether?

What does Argastos want? Is this a test? She stepped forwards and began to try a handful of turns, leftwards always. Her hand found the wall's surface weirdly discontinuous, metallic and lanced with spines, nothing that matched what the eye could make out.

She had every expectation of the maze's configuration shifting around her, because why should Argastos play fair? If there was a test here, it was not of her ability to solve a physical maze, after all.

She closed her eyes, seeking strength within her, before applying it carefully to the walls all around her, and making them creak. It seemed possible that sheer force might suffice, to break this place asunder, but what if that was something Argastos had foreseen? Would it leave her in an even worse position?

Instead, she let her mind flow out from her, twisting and turning over the contours of the maze, appreciating its nuances all at once and giving it no chance to change behind her back. She had not realized that she was capable of such concentration, and perhaps it was only here, in this pit of old magic, that she could have done it, but soon she had the entire maze in mind, and still her senses drifted outwards, calm and curious, until she found Maure.

Che?

Are you well?

I'm surrounded by the dead. There came sense of Maure's bleak amusement. *I won't say it's pleasant but it is what I trained for.*

Is Argastos dead? Che asked her.

Interesting question. He's not merely a ghost, anyway. There's no cast-off image of him here, because the core of him never moved on. It was bound here, trapped in this place over the centuries.

So what does that make him, and what can we do about him?

There was an almost academic quality to Maure's response. *He is a man, still, but one who has been held in a place of great magic – dark Moth magic – for a very long time. Is he dead? Probably. Does he know it? Possibly. Is he powerful? Certainly. He's been steeped in power for centuries.*

More powerful than me?

A long pause before Maure answered that. *Perhaps not, but more skilled. He was a strong and experienced magician before this happened to him, and he won't have grown rusty.*

Che nodded to herself, and stepped out of the maze. It only needed that one step, now that she had plumbed its every twist and turn. A moment later there was no maze, and she was in a cavern, its ceiling dimly knotted with roots, the air hazy with half-glimpsed forms. *More games?*

Then another real mind, for a moment, and the touch of it startled her. *A trick, a deception? I must be mistaken,* but she had the sense of someone staring right back at her. *Hello, Cheerwell Maker.* And a most uncharacteristic malice: *Enjoying yourself?*

Che recoiled, and then the fleeting touch was gone, as if it had never been. *But was that really . . .?* She could not bring herself to believe that it had actually been the Collegiate scholar Helma Bartrer . . .

Using her power as a light that burned the darkness like cheap oil, she came upon Maure, finding her surrounded by nebulous phantoms that fled at Che's approach.

'Real ghosts?'

The woman started at finding Che before her in the flesh. 'This place is clogged with ghosts,' she remarked quietly. 'Argastos did not come here alone when he was imprisoned here, and he has gained plenty of company since, I think.'

'We need to find the others.'

Maure nodded, 'I've been trying to—'

But Che held a hand up to cut her off.

There was a new voice.

Cheerwell Maker.

Che froze, knowing immediately who had spoken, and that knowledge sent a sudden stab of fear through her – far more than Argastos's voice might have done. Immediately she was raising defences, filling her mind with thought of armour and shield, walls, fortifications. In that moment, the encroaching dark of this subterranean domain was nothing compared to her fear of her rival, her jagged memories of the last time.

And at last, she replied, *Seda.*

She sensed a hint of amusement at all her preparations. *Well, sister, how very far you have come from the little girl you once were. You have grown into your power. I'll not catch you unawares again.* Possibly there was a trace of respect there, or Seda might be trying to inveigle her way through Che's defences by instilling some false confidence.

What do you want, Seda? Che demanded. Using the woman's given name represented a calculated insult. Under no circumstances would she use the title 'Empress' and, of course, to show someone that you held their name was to have a hook in them from the start.

You have spoken with Argastos, of course?

'Any sign of the others?' Che murmured sidelong to Maure, and thought, *So?*

Even as Maure answered in the negative, Che heard Seda

487

sigh. *We will fight, you and I, over his power. We are opposites, and I will destroy you if I can, just as you would destroy me. We are two people standing in the same place, and neither of us can tolerate that. This rivalry is the last joke of the Masters of Khanaphes. But, for now, Argastos's power is firmly bound within Argastos himself, and he has brought us both here for his own purposes.*

I came here only to stop you, Che growled at her.

Tell yourself that if you wish, but I know the truth. If you had discovered Argastos first, then it would be I chasing at your heels to keep him from you. We are sisters, you and I. We are not so different. You feel the pull of power just as I do.

Che's instant response died within her mind, leaving her wondering if Seda was right after all. And surely she would have justified it to herself, how she needed his strength to hold off Seda later on, or to deal with some other threat . . . or just because if was safer in her hands than any other's . . .

What do you want? Che repeated.

A truce, for now, until Argastos has played his hand. We are stronger than he is, but not if we fight each other. Let us recommence our feud over his body.

You're supposing that I want to fight him, Che shot back, but the disdain with which that remark was greeted was withering.

Do you honestly think he means you any good? Seda demanded. *Or either of us?*

Well, no doubt he'll tell us soon enough, Che snapped irritably, then calmed herself, feeling her defences grow shakier as she gave in to anger. *But, for now, you want a truce?*

Until Argastos's intentions become clear, I will harm neither you nor your companions.

Maure tugged at her sleeve, demanding to know what was going on, and Che explained in as few words as possible.

'What do you think?'

The necromancer frowned. 'All I know is that this is just the sort of place that gives my profession a bad name. Moth magic is bad enough most of the time, with all that Path of Shadows business, and Mantis magic is all about death, and this place reeks of both of them in the worst possible way. Whatever is left of the man that was, whatever Argastos has become, it can't intend any good to us – or to anyone. And I get the impression that the original man himself wasn't exactly a paragon of virtue.'

'He was a hero,' Che responded automatically, and then stopped, surprised at herself.

'He saw himself as a hero,' Maure corrected her carefully. 'So do many others, who do the most appalling things. By believing yourself a hero, all your actions become heroic, no matter what they are.'

Che closed her eyes again, feeling exactly the opposite – that no course of action open to her now was in any way desirable. *Very well, let us have our truce, Seda,* whilst privately adding, *but I'm not lowering my defences or trusting you an inch.*

Good. The response was brisk and pragmatic. *As a token of goodwill, I have located your companions.*

Che froze, fighting down the whirl of thoughts that statement prompted.

They are unharmed, although I need your help with the halfbreed girl.

And . . . Thalric? It had been Che's terrible fear that Thalric might simply be gone, his Aptitude untraceable in this maze of the Inapt.

Here with me, Seda informed her, with a proprietorial air that made Che bristle.

Let me see him. Let me see you.

Again that arch amusement: *Very well.* And abruptly Che found the path between them laid out plainly, skirting all of Argastos's tricks and sleights of hand.

The landscape around them remained uncertain of precisely what it was supposed to be, from blurred impressions of forest to caverns to occasional suggestions of the metal-walled maze, but Che found she could ignore it, simple force of will driving it away from her. Maure walked almost in her shadow, one hand resting on her shoulder.

And, in so few steps, she found herself face to face with Seda.

In her mind the Empress of the Wasps had become a monster, ten feet tall and dripping with blood, inhuman and ravening, evil written in every feature of her. It was hard, then, to remember that here was the outward truth: this slender Wasp girl, younger even than Che, with her pale skin and golden hair. The power that stirred within her was the sibling to Che's own and, when they met there – their first physical meeting, and in such a place – the world around them seemed to shudder for a moment, as at the tolling of a huge but silent bell.

Che heard Maure's sucked-in breath, and she wondered if, all over the Lowlands, magicians were twitching awake with a start, or crying out in their dreams. *But surely we are not so important, she and I? How much does the mark of Khanaphes count for?*

'Che!'

Then Thalric was there, coming close but stopping out of reach, his eyes flicking between Che and Seda. And Che began to go to him, to throw her arms about him for the simple joy of seeing him alive, but there was an abrupt crackling sense of chill from Seda, and she held back.

But of course. She had forgotten that Thalric had been Seda's once. Che had pushed that knowledge right out of her mind. It hurt a great deal, she discovered, to be reminded.

And if I press matters now . . . if I call Thalric and demand that he comes to me? Then, she guessed, her truce with Seda might be broken sooner than either of them was ready for, because she could sense it there – the tie between the Empress and her former consort – not a bond of love, she told herself, but one of presumed ownership.

'Where is Tynisa?' she asked, because she had to say *some-thing* to kill the tension. Her eyes sought Thalric's and found his gaze evasive. *What were they doing together, before I arrived? How long . . . ?* She repressed the thought.

'With Tisamon,' Seda declared.

Che's stomach lurched. 'Then—'

'Yes. And I can stop him, but not her. Between us we must separate them. We may need them against Argastos and his minions.'

Tynisa fought, and the fight had no beginning and no end.

She fought in the sewers beneath Myna. She fought in the Prowess Forum of Collegium. She fought in the Commonweal. She fought in the forest of the Nethyen. One fight spread over the years, as she tried to escape from the shadow of her father.

He was faster than her, but not by so much as he once had been. Death had dulled him a little, whilst her life had only sharpened her. She had learned new tricks that he had not taught her: every fight that she had entered into since his death had honed her, whilst he had remained the same broken thing he had always been.

In this dim no-place they dodged and cut, rapier against claw, a constant negotiation of reach and distance. She danced with him, Weaponsmaster to Weaponsmaster. Part of her mind was roiling with the need to destroy him, for the abomination he was; to strike down the insult to the man he had been, but there was more than that. No matter what he had become, what manner of revenant the Empress had raised from his memory, her blade and the mystery of her order knew that the fight itself was pure. This was the fight her life had been leading up to – and the fact that she and Tisamon had been allies, before the man's death, had been only a temporary diversion.

No matter that she hated what he was, part of her exulted in fighting him again at last.

And sometimes he struck the death blow, and sometimes, less frequently, she did, but those strikes never landed, and they found themselves apart again, blade-tip to blade-tip . . . and then began again. Over and over, they began.

How long they had been fighting, Tynisa could not know. She

was living in the eternal present, moment by moment ticking by and yet the clock standing still.

When something changed, and when the voice came, she resisted hearing it, so perfect was this instant she was living in. She stepped through her paces, her rapier a blur as it fended off Tisamon's strikes and made its own inroads into his defence. But, at last, the demands became too insistent to ignore.

Tynisa! Che's voice was an unwelcome reminder that there was more to life than this.

Stop this! You have to stop fighting!

The concept seemed utterly alien to her, and she shrugged it off, but Che was insistent.

Tynisa, Seda is going to rein in Tisamon, but only if you yourself stop. This is pointless. We have more important problems right now.

For a moment, Tynisa lost her rhythm, and a scything sweep of Tisamon's claw nearly killed her, but she ceded three paces and repaired her defence.

Tynisa—

Go away, Che. And Tynisa applied herself utterly to the duel.

She sensed her foster-sister's abrupt frustration with her, which might once have been a source only of amusement, but now there was a great power building behind it, a wave of influence that increased and increased until all that Tynisa represented, her badge, her sword, her whole being, was tiny in comparison.

'No!' she cried out, and heard, *I'm sorry*, in reply. And then the great fist of Che's strength descended and clasped itself about her, locking her rigid, every limb frozen.

She had a moment of staring into Tisamon's helm, that dark, half-seen face that was so familiar, and she tried to brace herself for the death strike . . . but she could not even do that.

Then he had frozen as well, his blade already halfway towards her, and a moment later they were not alone: Che, Thalric, Maure . . . and there too was Seda, whom Tynisa had seen in Capitas only the once, on the day that her father had died.

The grip left her, and she dropped to her knees with a curse.

492

'I'm sorry,' Che repeated, as Tisamon stalked stiffly over to Seda's side.

Tynisa glowered up at Che. 'If you *ever* do that to me again, I swear . . .' But she was not sure what she could swear to, considering the sheer strength of the girl, the utter reversal of their roles. For the first time in her life, Tynisa suddenly felt ignorant and useless compared to whatever it was that Che had access to. *And is that the way that she had always felt, before?*

She got to her feet, sword already home in its sheath. 'What now?'

'Now?' And they all spun about at this unexpected intrusion. He stood there in his chitin scale mail, shoulders broad beneath his open grey robe, and his winged helm under his arm: Argastos the warlord, the Moth who went to war. 'Now you shall come with me as my guests,' his rich voice resonated. 'We have much to talk about.'

Thirty-Three

That next morning, word had been sent to every Assembler remaining in Collegium. College Masters, merchant magnates, the great and the good who had not left the city or died in the fighting were all visited at the stroke of dawn. To avoid any unfortunate shooting of messengers, Helmess had used the Collegiate Guild to carry his instructions, demonstrating that business as usual, in some small way, was still the order of the day.

The message itself was simple. The Collegiate Assembly was still very much in existence, and a full gathering of its members would be held later that morning. Attendance was mandatory. Collegium had passed through a time of turmoil and needed the help of all of its leaders to regain its feet, and anyone who felt that they had better things to do would be noted in their absence.

Turnout was impressive, certainly more so than the last two emergency Assemblies presided over by the late Jodry Drillen.

They met in the same ruins as before, in the harsh light of the early morning, and Helmess marvelled at the discipline of it – all those men and women, brought here by their learning, their wealth, their power, and where were the divisions, where the mutterings, the heckling, the unseemly jokes? Where were those who merely came to snore through the speeches, or to conduct private business while matters of state were discussed? Every eye was upon him, rapt with attention.

Although, he had to admit, most eyes did tend to twitch to the three score Wasp soldiers that had dropped down to form a loose perimeter about the proceedings.

'My friends,' he addressed their silence. 'Thank you for answering the call of your city in its time of need.' He had a scroll in one hand, which was unfurled almost down to his knees, and, as he spoke, his eyes flicked over the Assemblers and he marked off name after name. 'I had thought of taking roll call, as they do in the College,' he explained with a self-deprecating smile, 'but that would not be becoming of the dignity of our body. Still, no hiding at the back, there. It would be tragic if I was to overlook any of you, after all.' He permitted himself a little frown, knowing that his audience was hanging on the very minutiae of his expression. 'Still a few absentees, I see. Ah well.'

There was a slow building of murmured discontent, as he had expected. 'Masters, the world around us has changed, but this our city – and our Assembly – do not need to change so much as you might think. The Empire, whose borders now encompass Collegium, need not be such a harsh master as you might imagine. After all, we have resisted them, fought them with all our misguided strength, and still they have agreed that our Assembly shall remain – properly supervised of course – and I think you will find that, with a little adjustment, our citizens will hardly notice that there is a black and gold flag where once there was none. I . . . yes?'

For someone had stood up, a burly, heavy-set man that it took Helmess a moment to identify as one of the airship magnates. Helmess ticked his name off meticulously as the man clenched his fists and took a deep breath.

'I don't know where you yourself spent the evening, Master Broiler, but I think our citizens are well bloody aware that your Wasp friends are here, because they were surely helping themselves to every cursed thing in the city last night. Two of my clerks are gone this morning: one because the fool went out after this "curfew" and the other because she . . . because one of your *friends* decided that she was . . . that she was worth a moment

495

of his time, and no more. And you say that everything's just rolling along like normal, do you? You think our folk will just play along? If this Assembly still exists, then what is it going to *do* about it, eh?'

'Why, Master Parrymill,' Helmess snapped back, with a sideways glance towards the soldiers that nobody missed – and abruptly the airship magnate's voice stuttered to a halt. Helmess smiled. 'What a pertinent question,' he added cordially. The soldiers did not descend on Parrymill and bundle him away there and then, but suddenly their loosely spaced cordon seemed like the walls of a prison, and the outspoken Assembler sat down heavily, his face turning grey.

'I should take steps right now to correct what may be a fundamental misapprehension,' Helmess went on. 'This Assembly is convened not to *complain* or *object*. We are not here to plot against the Empire, or to work against its laws. We have a simple function, Masters. We are here to make the Empress's will a reality as simply as possible. Because what the Empire wishes *will* happen, make no mistake, and how much better for Collegium that it happens through our own mediation? The Empire will have its commands carried out in the most efficient way, Masters, and if you wish to spare our citizens the rod, then you must ensure that any leniency also serves that same efficiency. I know that all of us will have to make adjustments. Some of you may find it difficult to grasp your new role. You may find it harsh, restricting, even oppressive.' He gave them a moment to decide that this was indeed so. 'But I put to you one inarguable point: last night was *nothing*. Last night was the soldiers of the Second and their allies being given their just rewards for all we put them through on the way to our city. Did you think we could kill their friends, bomb them, starve them, and they would act like genial College tutors once they closed our gates behind them? No, Masters, they are soldiers, and they were owed their due reward. But believe me, General Tynan has kept them on a tight rein. The sergeants of the Second have been on watch to ensure that indulgence has not become excess. Consider how few buildings burned, how few deaths there actually were, and even rape in moderation. Believe me, Masters, it could all have been so much *worse*. We truly are blessed in the enlightened attitudes of our conquerors.'

They stared at him, some still defiant, others simply appalled, or else bewildered as though they could not have heard him correctly. A fair proportion, though, would not meet his eyes, and he counted them as the ones who had already accepted the logic of his words.

'And there will be benefits. We all recall the endless infighting, the factions, the timewasting speeches of our august body here. Yes, you all complained about it, just as much as you contributed to it. It's amazing we accomplished anything at all. But now, Masters, if we want a crime punished, a law made iron, we need only submit our request to the Imperial governor, and it shall happen. Our government will be given the firm hand it has always lacked. We shall go forward in partnership with the Wasp-kinden, and they shall profit from our wisdom, we from their strength.'

And he gave them his best smile, and knew that some, at least, would already be thinking about how this situation could be used to personal advantage. And it would be they who prospered, whilst anyone trying to hold on to what the Assembly had once represented would fall, and probably sooner rather than later.

'But to business,' he urged them brightly. 'The clerks have given you each a list of names, and I'm sure you all recognize them. These are those individuals who have proved such intractable enemies to the Empire that they cannot be allowed to retain their liberty within our new city. Masters, the Empire is currently considering our methods of selecting Assemblers. It goes without saying that anyone assisting the Empire at this crucial time will help to demonstrate to the Wasps the usefulness of our traditional institutions, as well as preserving their own position within our body.' *Unless they're a halfbreed, of course, or a woman.* 'Conversely, if any citizens are found to be sheltering

497

someone on this list, then not only shall they find themselves a guest of the Empire's interrogators, but that invitation will be extended to their family, friends and associates, because the Empire is *very* concerned that such dissent not be allowed to spread.'

He scanned the mass of them and made some more notes on his scroll, this time underlining the names – Parrymill's amongst them – of those he believed would simply not fit in with the new times. *If the gears are to mesh smoothly, we must remove any defective components.* Also a few individuals that he simply did not like, but then that was a privilege of rank.

'The curfew meanwhile remains in place, no movement out of doors after dark, until further notice. After all, who, save for dissidents and criminals, would be skulking about at such times anyway? Over the next few tendays, the Empire will be introducing its own overseers into various concerns – factories, the College and the like. I would suggest you avoid unofficial gatherings, as well, since it will take the Wasps a while to learn our ways, and they are likely to misinterpret such events. For now, as we are the leaders of our people, I suggest you use what influence you have to promote order and cooperation. And those who do not will be noted.'

The following day, the names had already started to trickle in.

It was inevitable, Helmess knew, and those few of the Assembly sufficiently idealistic to abstain were already mostly on his list. The rest would bow before the tide of circumstance, as pragmatic Beetle-kinden were renowned for doing. The majority would do so not out of treachery, nor through a wish for advancement, nor even through fear for their own lives. Instead, they would betray their fellows to protect their families, to soften the blow of the Empire's domination. From such small stones would Helmess build an Imperial city here in the heart of the Lowlands.

He was discharging his duties well, he reckoned. General

Tynan would have no complaints. Helmess was determined to prove himself irreplaceable, for there was always the danger that the future governor of Collegium, whenever appointed, might be tempted to dispense with his services. What Helmess wanted was a man with sufficient ambitions for advancement back in Capitas that governing a well-run, profitable Beetle city would prove enough, without needing to meddle in the workings himself. Thus, Helmess should become the sole channel by which the Empire communicated with its vassal state, ruler in all but name.

Unless the Spiders decide to take an interest.

That was always a cause for concern, both because they played the political game better than the Wasps, and because Helmess was honestly not sure what records they might have kept from their previous run-in with Collegium, when he himself had nominally been one of their agents. He had a suspicion that the Aldanrael might be keenly interested in his involvement in that debacle, so he was keeping well out of the way of their Lady-Martial whenever possible.

Yesterday had been given over to the business of telling the Assembly how the world now worked, using words simple enough that even the dullest or most resistant of them could understand. That same evening, Helmess had taken a sumptuous dinner with Colonel Cherten, who seemed to appreciate what Broiler was doing for the Empire. Today he had no formal appointments lined up, therefore it was time for him to indulge himself.

There had already been a few reports regarding those the Empire wanted to arrest, but of course there was one in particular that Helmess wanted to see crossed off his list. He had bitterly assumed that the man had already fled, but recent news had come in to suggest otherwise. Helmess was now going to hunt down Stenwold Maker himself, and the knowledge made him feel as giddy as a child.

There was still a handful of Spiderlands agents within the city, seeded there long ago and now well established, who had avoided every investigation that Maker and his allies had set in motion.

It was their reports that had first reached Helmess, mentioning a few possible hiding places for the War Master. Finally, a public-spirited Assembler had provided more definite confirmation, and Helmess knew that he must act quickly before the Empire became involved and took the credit.

It was lucky that Collegium was such a large and complex city. Tynan's troops might be inventorying everything, workshops and businesses and cartels surrendering their accounts and manifests for the Empire, but there were whole swathes of the city yet unexamined. Imperial priority would not be to check the College first. So far it had remained inviolate – and within its vaults hid a prize.

Stenwold Maker never left the city. He retired, ailing, to the College infirmary. And he is there right now.

Waving his newly awarded major's badge had earned Helmess the services of a dozen Wasp infantry, although he could see that they were not exactly keen to be at his beck and call. They would share in his reflected glory, though, so he expected their attitude to improve markedly once Maker was firmly in their custody.

The looks that he received, as he marched his troops through Collegium, were priceless. He had always known the envy of lesser folk – the scowls of those whose inadequate enterprise had guaranteed them a place as his inferiors – but now the masks were off. There were definite winners and losers in Collegium, and every stare, every fearful averted face, each half-hidden glare spoke only of validation.

And then he was standing before the College itself.

Not the whole College, of course, because the institution was spread in separate buildings across in the city, and this was not even the largest section of it. It was the oldest, though, and had been old before Collegium's new masters decided to adopt the College as the basis of their city's new name. Here were located the library and the infirmary, some of the social history departments, and a network of cellars housing laboratories, study rooms and a rather fine collection of wine. *A collection wasted here now, of course. I shall have to remove it to somewhere more practical.*

The academic edifice was somewhat more self-contained than most, with a walled courtyard, high walls and remarkably small windows – all the columns, statues and adornment of Beetle hands had done little to disguise the original architecture of the Moth-kinden, who had little use for the sun. *Ridiculous place to house a library, after all.* Helmess recalled years of straining his eyes in that dimness within. *Perhaps I should remove the library while I'm at it.*

There was a pair of Wasp soldiers outside, who saluted Helmess without hesitation, because a major's rank badge was a good thing to have.

'Arrest anyone that I indicate to you, and don't hesitate to get rough with them,' Helmess instructed his sergeant. 'There may be a few idealists amongst the students who need to learn that scholarly debate is no longer the fashion.'

There were about a dozen students loitering in the courtyard, and a couple slipped away almost immediately. The rest looked alarmed, but nowhere near as much as they should be. Their education had hardly prepared them for the sort of world that they would now be living in.

'Good day to you,' he declared grandly. 'Perhaps you'd be so good as to summon any of the College Masters who are currently in the building. I've a few words for them.'

A few others sidled out, whether to obey him or to hide themselves away, he couldn't say. Perhaps the latter would be wiser. It seemed likely that he would have to have someone shot at some point, just to ram his point home.

But now others were emerging, so that was good. He recognized a few of them as Masters: that tall fellow was Berjek Gripshod, the historian, and Helmess recalled that the man had been somewhat pally with Maker recently, so perhaps it would be best to haul him in now. The woman beside him was some manner of artificer, he recalled, or maybe a naturalist. And there, too, was that Fly woman who had taken on teaching Inapt studies. He couldn't remember her name, therefore she wasn't really important.

More students came filing out, and he was amused to see that a surprising number of them still wore their Company sashes – even a few buff coats and breastplates. *Oh the poor fools, they have no idea.*

The courtyard was becoming full, and mostly of young, worried faces. He cast his eyes over them, these Beetle-kinden boys and girls who had abandoned their studies in engineering or political theory to come out and hear the most valuable lecture of their lives. The other faces, the outsiders, leapt out at him: a couple of Ants, a Spider or two, a band-skinned Woodlouse-kinden in a Coldstone Company sash, a Dragonfly, some half-breeds. *They'll have to go, for a start.*

'Now, then.' Helmess raised his hands to quieten the incessant muttering that students were so prone to. 'No doubt you're all desperate to get back to your studies, and—'

'You strung up the Speaker!'

Broiler choked on his words. 'Who said that?' He found the culprit almost immediately: a man who looked too old to be a student, in a wine-stained and filthy tunic and standing at the sort of angle that made it plain that more wine had recently gone in than out. He was pointing a finger in Helmess's general direction, and those nearest were trying to restrain him as he blurted out, 'He did, he did!'

The soldiers nearest to Helmess had their snapbows levelled, and he recalled that thrusting out a hand at someone was tantamount to an assassination attempt where they came from. 'Enough!' he boomed out, in his best public-speaking voice, and gestured the soldiers' weapons down. 'Who is this sot?'

'He's Raullo Mummers. He's an artist, Master Broiler,' said a student from the front of the crowd. 'Forgive him. He's drunk.'

'Shut him up, then, or he'll be the worse for drink.' Helmess realized that he recognized the speaker. 'Hold on, aren't you Leadswell?'

The chief officer of the ridiculous Student Company nodded. Like many there, he still bore his sash, but he had stripped off his armour.

'Why that's marvellous,' Helmess beamed. 'Sergeant, grab this one for a start. Master Leadswell, you must know that the Empire wishes a word with you.'

'I'd guessed as much.' Leadswell replied calmly. There was a surprising upsurge of discontent amongst the surrounding students, but when the sergeant and a couple of other soldiers stepped forwards to lay hands on him, he did not resist. *And as well for everyone else here that he didn't. Sensible lad . . . But then the Leadswell boy always had a good mind and a gift for speeches, didn't he?* Helmess's eyes narrowed as he studied him. Hadn't Leadswell been the one to go on about coming to an accommodation with the Empire, and avoiding war? *Maybe he and the Wasps really* would *have something to talk about, after all.* An image was quick to find a place in Helmess's mind: Eujen Leadswell leaving General Tynan's presence with a rank badge and a mandate to bring Collegium and its conquerors closer together. *A rival, in other words.*

He stared at Leadswell in a colder light. *Make an example of him, maybe?* But the crowd was still unruly, if not quite rebellious, and there was such a thing as pushing your luck.

'Eujen!' A halfbreed woman from the crowd came shouldering forwards, almost barging into the sergeant. She was still in uniform, Coldstone Company again, and for a moment Helmess thought that everything might ignite there and then, as the sergeant shoved her backwards.

'Straessa, peace,' Leadswell was saying, even though Helmess was willing for him to incite his own execution. 'It's going to be fine.'

There was a garbled exclamation to the contrary from the reeling artist Mummers, and the halfbreed woman – *the Antspider, is it?* – looked as though she was going to attempt something unwise. Then Leadswell said something more, and she backed off reluctantly.

Ah, shame.

'Now, Master Gripshod, I see there.' Helmess mentally washed his hands of the altercation and turned to more important matters. 'I take you for the senior hand here, so why don't you arrange to go and bring me out Stenwold Maker.'

The old historian Gripshod retained a creditable card-player's face, but the ripple of anger and shock passing among the rest of the students betrayed him. Yes, Maker was here. Yes, they all knew it.

Even so, Gripshod raised his head and declared, bold-facedly, 'The War Master has surely fled the city, Master Broiler.'

'Master *Speaker*, you'll address me as,' Helmess replied venomously. 'Or Major Broiler if you prefer, *Master* Gripshod. And I know full well that Maker's here and, given that you're already marked as his accomplice, I'll ask again that you have him brought out. Or else I'll have you executed right here and now for resisting the Empire's authority.'

There were two snapbows already levelled at Gripshod, and those closest to the old man began shuffling aside, staring at him, staring at the Wasps.

'It's true, Maker's not here,' Leadswell protested, whereupon the sergeant backhanded him across the face, viciously hard yet utterly impersonally, as though this was some habitual gesture of his that he had no real control over. Helmess noticed the sudden surge of students towards their captive leader – just a minor ripple in the crowd, but the situation was clearly becoming undisciplined.

'Very well,' he proceeded. 'Master Gripshod, *kindly* fetch me my old friend Stenwold Maker at once, or I'll have Leadswell here executed. How about that? I'll give you a slow count of ten to allow you to make your choice.' *And either way I win, I think. And if I do get Maker now, Leadswell can have a tragic accident at some other time.* And then occurred a blink: a sudden disconnection between the world as Helmess knew it to be and what his eyes were seeing. *Why does that student have a snapbow?*

There was a general motion now in the crowd, and it was not the vacillating of a confused and unhappy mob. It was military.

His eyes kept alighting on the glint of steel: barrels, air-batteries, swords.

'Sergeant,' he hissed. 'The Student Company was disarmed along with the rest, wasn't it?'

The sergeant's head snapped round to reveal an expression entirely blank. 'What's a Student Company, sir?'

In Helmess's mind there rapidly coalesced a possible train of events, a series of communications between agents and the army, detailing Collegium's strength, and then the order coming back to disarm the Companies. Which Companies? The Merchant Companies, of course.

Because students were students, and soldiers were soldiers, and really, with their entire male population pressed into the army, what an ironic slip it was for some Wasp to make.

That was a broken second's worth of thought, as the soldiers around him caught sight the same weapons, but they were not sure what his orders were. The sergeant was staring at him, perhaps coming to the same abysmal conclusion, and—

Half the sergeant's head was suddenly gone, a fist of blood and broken bone leaping from the cavity that was left, and the shooting started. Helmess dropped to his knees, hands over his head, hearing shouts and screams – but all of it so brief, so brief. The dozen men he had brought along were horribly outmatched from the start, and by mere *students*! Even as they tried to discharge their own snapbows they were cut down, and then the Dragonfly vaulted straight over him, ending up on the wall and shooting down at the two sentries even as they burst in to see what was going on, one arrow piercing straight down alongside the collar of each man's armour, loosed almost faster than Helmess could register.

In moments, only moments, Helmess was cowering alone before that great angry host of the young.

'Who shot?' Eujen demanded. And then, because the question was plainly twenty snapbow bolts too late, he amended it to, 'Who loosed first?'

A terrible silence had otherwise fallen now that the Wasps were dead. The mood of the mob tilted between feeling aghast at what they had done to being fully determined to do more.

One man pushed his way forwards, his eyes locked on Eujen. Pale among the Beetle majority, he was an alien that fate had surely never intended to be standing there, not in that uniform and with a Collegiate snapbow in his hand.

'Averic,' Eujen identified him.

'I couldn't let them take you,' the Wasp said flatly. There was a great deal of emotion in his voice, but none of it suggested regret. 'I *know* what they'd do to you.'

'You couldn't—' Eujen started, but Mummers broke in.

'They'd have picked you apart, man! And what about the War Master?' the artist slurred.

'Since when were you such an admirer of Stenwold Maker?' Eujen demanded of him.

'But he's right,' old Berjek Gripshod put in. 'So what now?'

Why are they all staring at me? was Eujen's only thought. But he wore the sash still, chief officer's badge and all, and something iron and businesslike descended like a gate inside his mind. 'How many hurt on our side?'

'Peddic Gorseway and Laina Mowwell are dead,' reported Sartaea te Mosca promptly. 'Four injured beyond that – one seriously.'

'Get them to the infirmary,' Eujen ordered. *Yes, ordered. That was the word for it.* 'Get . . . there's a Student Company armoury in the blue dormitory. Anyone who's with us, wherever the pits we're going, and wants a snapbow and bolts, go get them.' Then:

'Straessa?' For of course, the Coldstone Company had been dis-armed just like all the regulars.

'Oh, count on me, Chief,' the Antspider told him, already turning to go. Gerethwy threw Eujen a nod of affirmation as he followed at her heels.

'Anyone who wants to have not been here can go now,' Eujen told the assembly. 'And I mean that. We've a short breathing space before the Wasps come to investigate.' He gave a nod of acknowledgement towards Castre Gorenn, who had been quick to cut off any chance of the alarm getting out. 'But they'll be here soon enough, and this could go any number of ways. None of you asked to be party to this, so go now, and I only ask you keep your mouths shut.'

And some went, only a handful, with averted eyes and muttered apologies, but he would remember just how few they were, remember this with bafflement and pride for the rest of his life.

'Get the Wasp dead taken away . . . one of the cold rooms in the cellars should do. Officers, I want people stationed at every window.' The old Moth architecture rose above them, built at the command of a race who thought in terms of entry by air, and therefore how best to deny it. There were a handful of balconies and windows big enough to be forced by determined opposition, but not so many, and not so hard to hold. 'I want a few fast fliers up on the courtyard wall, to keep watch and let us know the moment things turn bad.' Castre Gorenn, already in position, signalled her approval, and a couple of Fly-kinden were already winging up to join her.

'And as for me,' Eujen finished, 'I need to speak to Stenwold Maker.'

'And what about this turncoat here?' Raullo Mummers demanded, and Eujen followed the direction of his finger to see Helmess Broiler slowly uncurling, his eyes on the weapons of the students around him.

'Now listen,' the new Speaker of the Assembly said. 'You've all just signed your death warrants, you must know that – *unless*

I somehow plead mitigation to the general on your behalf. If you want to get out of this with *anything*, then you have to listen to me very carefully and do everything I say.'

He was standing up, hands held out for calm, and that damnable smile creeping back on to his face, not a sign that he saw the bodies around him, the soldiers who had died in his defence. Eujen, mildest of men, who had spent the last however many years preaching peace to a world on the brink of war, felt that gate in his mind lock tight. *If I had to choose between you and the Empress, to speak on my behalf, then I'd place my faith in her before I'd trust it to you.*

'Averic,' he said. 'We have all seen just how Speakers of the Assembly are served by the new administration.' He could not believe it was his voice, saying such things, but the words came out regardless. 'Find some room with a sufficiently robust ceiling, and serve Master Broiler just the same.'

Thirty-Four

'We're at the crossroads of history, you know?' Tactician Milus remarked softly. It was dark here, in the cell, but he knew her eyes were better than his for such gloom, just like the Fly she resembled. 'The Empire . . . it's like some new treatment for a formerly incurable disease. Either it kills us, or . . . or our future becomes something . . . different.'

There was a single high window, just a handful of inches across and set at what was ground level outside. The grey light filtering through it was continually crossed and recrossed by shadows as people moved past, all of them at a smart pace. Sarn was mobilizing, and if Milus let his mind out, he would feel it, the immaculate perfection that was an Ant city-state going to war. But he chose not to. His plans made, his orders given, he permitted himself to sit down here with his prisoner, only to be disturbed if some lightning move of the Empire broke through the confines of his expectations.

He could feel the woman who called herself Lissart staring at him and, if he deigned to glance her way, perhaps he would see the light glinting in her eyes. She was well secured – a dangerous creature, for sure, because of the Art she could call upon. Valuable, though. Precious, even.

'But your city is strength eternal, surely,' she whispered. 'What possible disease could the Wasps be coming to cure?'

He chuckled indulgently. Because here he could *talk* rather than just share thoughts that ceased to be his in the moment of their thinking. Here he could say words and get a reaction, and hear words that originated from outside, from another, separate mind. And if the result of those words was that she was sent back to the questioners, to be reminded of their deal, then so be it. They both knew the game by now.

'Stagnation is the disease that kills cities. It's killed Tark and Kes, and came close to killing Vek. Collegium saved us once, although they hardly meant to, by teaching us their ways: no slaves, tolerance of foreigners, and of course the tide of trade and technology that comes *gushing* in once you open your doors to Beetles. There must have been a lot of resistance at the time, but the queen back then was truly a visionary. Change and growth: just what the Ant-kinden city-states of the Lowlands haven't experienced for centuries. We've sat and fought each other, without any great gain or loss, and we've been in a rut, ground deeper and deeper year to year. And now the Empire. Thanks to Collegium enlivening us a generation ago, we have a chance. And if we can beat the Eighth back, then . . .'

'Then what? What do you imagine you'll achieve, even if you can? Which you won't,' she hissed, but he let her have her little tantrums: it made her easier to work for information. These days she hardly needed encouragement.

Once the interrogators had confirmed that there seemed to be no practical upper limit to her tolerance for heat, it would have been down to the knives and the rack, under normal circumstances. A shame, Milus had thought. Ruin someone irrevocably and you start the sands running on their usefulness as a resource,

Collegium had come to the rescue once again, though. Their clever academics had long before devised a way to make things cold, so as to assist them in their researches, and Sarnesh artificers had been able to apply this to the case in hand. Milus supposed that what they had ended up with was the reverse of a branding iron, but with the additional advantage that, no matter how excruciating the pain it inflicted, the icy blue-white marks it traced about the woman's body faded after a tenday or so, leaving a blank slate for further inscription.

He had not been given much time, what with his principal work devoted to slowing the Eighth Army's advance as much as possible, but he had been present when they had first broken her, searing coldly through her remarkable reserves of strength and leaving her twitching and sobbing, begging for release.

Then had come the questions, with the machine ever on hand to remind her to tell the truth. But then again, how else were Ant-kinden to have any chance of believing a hostile outsider?

'I'll have to leave you,' he told her. 'It won't be for long.'

'I'll be waiting for you.' He liked the fact that at least a ghost of her defiance came back to her so readily. It was the reason he came down here to talk to her on the rare occasions the war could spare him. And he knew he could crack her wide open just by bringing the machine back, just by letting her look at it. Such was the game they played.

She had not known much about the Eighth Army itself, but there was no reason why she should. He already knew she had been stationed in Solarno, a different operation altogether. In fact she turned out to know relatively little even about the Second Army that had set off from there – and only from her time spent hiding amongst them.

But she had been questioned for hour after long hour about Imperial Intelligence: everything she knew about their methods, their agents, their means of communication. She had not understood at first, because – like so many – she had not realized the scope of Milus's ambitions, which were the ambitions of Sarn itself.

Milus was planning for the battle against the Eighth, certainly, but more than that he was planning for a war against the Empire, and he intended to take that all way to the gates of Capitas itself.

If Thalric had been plunged into this place during the last war, as the man he had then been – the hard-minded Rekef killer –

he would surely have broken before now. It was the greatest expression of his not being the same man, that he could be surrounded by so much smoke and shadow, so little that made sense, and retain his mind intact. Not *easy*, no, but his world had been sliding away from the rational and the sane for long enough that he could keep his balance on the slope. Seda and her unwholesome appetites; the catacombs beneath Khanaphes; the Commonweal; Che.

That had been his first glimpse of Argastos but he had not doubted for a moment who the man was. The warlike Moth-kinden had appeared there without warning; just as suddenly he was gone, and where the gloom-hung wall had stood behind him, now there was a ragged, shroud-hung corridor that they were plainly intended to walk along. Thalric's disbelief was in suspension, awaiting some more stable time when he might make use of it to begin covering over these memories and restoring his world view, but for now he was deep in the nightmare and clinging on.

And Seda. *There* had been a shock he was not prepared for. The woman he had fought so hard to get clear of, and who he had irrevocably made his enemy when he threw his lot in with Che, and yet he had not been able to kill her when given the chance, and now here she was again.

When she had found him, in this dark, shifting place. When *she* had found him, not Che, he had been ready for the explosion, the lash of vengeance. In the time since he had left her, surely the rapacious Empress would have driven out any sign of the girl he once knew, that fading spark in Seda's eyes that had spoken of when she had been vulnerable, merely a pawn of her brother.

But she was still there, that girl. Her expression, when she found him, had been fond. There had been no recriminations, and for a moment he had been about to go to her as though he had never left, as though she had never become the creature she now was. The traitor thought had been there in his mind: *How simple life would have been if only . . .*

For all that he had bitten it back, fought it down, it was there still. He had lived a long time as a servant of the Empire, and here was the Empire itself in human form.

He was therefore very glad when Che had turned up soon afterwards. Seeing the Beetle girl, almost absurd in her lack of the majesty and threat that practically radiated from Seda, grounded him back in reality, reminded him where his loyalties – and his affection – now lay.

'Who's that?' Seda demanded sharply, and Thalric snapped back to the here and now. They had been making a cautious progress through the tunnel that Argastos had revealed, but now there was someone ahead of them, plainly visible despite the darkness, as though a lamp were shining only on her.

'Is that . . .?' Tynisa murmured.

'Mistress Bartrer?' Che exclaimed.

Thalric looked again. Was it? He realized he had not paid much attention to the academic, but this apparition did seem to bear her face. She had shed her Collegiate robes, though, and was wearing something simpler but of an antique cut, a long sleeveless brown tunic, ornamented with delicate black stitching at every edge. There was also some lavish piece of gold at her throat, perhaps a torc.

Not a torc: a collar.

'I've seen depictions of clothes like that in old books,' Che said softly. 'Slaves' garments, from long before the Revolution. Maure, what are we looking at?'

'Some trick,' Thalric tried, but not sure whether he believed it.

'No image, no ghost, just the living woman,' Maure confirmed.

'But how can she be here? How can you . . .?' Che walked forward to stand before the other woman. 'Helma, can you hear me?'

The eyes swivelled to follow her, and abruptly Helma Bartrer's face assumed an unexpected expression: pure spite. 'Oh, I hear you, Maker,' she acknowledged. 'The master has sent me to bring you to his table.'

'But I don't understand,' Che insisted. 'Why are you here? How did you even get here?'

'By hard work, by guessing, by faith in my master,' Bartrer hissed. 'By knowing my place and staying true to our betters.'

'The Moth-kinden?'

'Do you deny it now that you are here?' Barter challenged her.

'She's Arcanum,' Thalric guessed, speaking of the Moth intelligence service. 'She has been all this time.'

'More than that.' Seda spoke from right beside him. 'Your people were slaves once, Maker. Small wonder, then, if there's some remnant cult who want those days back. Never underestimate how much some people want to be led.'

Helma Bartrer stared at the Empress. 'Your kinden were slaves, too, Wasp girl, and they still are. It's just that their taste in masters has deteriorated.'

'Wait, you came all this way . . . how could you even know this was going to happen?' Che demanded of her.

'Oh, I hoped.' Again that ugly look. 'Everything to do with the Moths, I tried to associate myself with. We have been faithful, generation on generation, waiting for this day when we could present ourselves to our masters. Perhaps all but I had given up any hope. But *you*!' And the sudden venom was startling. 'You had it all given to you, by mere chance! You've become something special, something that *he*'s interested in . . . and how is that just, that you could blunder into such a thing when I've been loyal in my heart all my life?' She would have gone on but something stayed her, a reprimand audible to her only snapping her head back. 'Come with me,' she muttered, and hurried off into the darkness, with that reflected light never quite leaving her, making the woman a beacon for them to navigate by.

It lit up nothing else, though, so they had arrived before they realized it. When the green-white lanterns sprang up around them, they all froze. Thalric felt meanly glad to see the same startled, fearful look on Che's and Maure's faces as he knew must have appeared on his own.

'Please be seated,' Helma Bartrer declared flatly.

There was a table there, its top a single slab of black-varnished wood, its edges uneven and ragged with the contours of the tree it had been hacked from. The chairs were little better, just slats and wands of wood twisted and grown together as though their maker, in striving to ape the natural, had finished up with something utterly unearthly. The walls pressed in on all sides, allowing barely room to drag the chairs back. Thalric could see them only dimly and, when he brushed one with his elbow, he felt angled metal there, and he shivered without quite knowing why.

It did not help that those corpse-light lanterns lacked sconces: just fitful, pallid flames guttering in the air.

At the head of the table, he saw one seat they were plainly not being invited to sit in. It was more a throne, intricately carved with intertwining briars, beetles and grubs, centipedes and woodlice and all things associated with decay, while its arms resembled the crooked claws of a mantis. As if that was not grand enough for their host, suspended behind it was the complete, hollow exoskeleton of just such a beast, battle-scarred and one-eyed, and long enough dead for the light to lend it a translucent glow.

Barbaric trophies, Thalric decided, and the gaudy ostentation gave him back some of his lost control, because here, at least, was a human thing, if only a desire to show off. Whatever Argastos now was, this was a part of him Thalric could relate to. He had seen similar trophies even in the possession of Imperial officers, and they had been mere bragging boasts of their owner's self-importance.

Che's hand found his arm and squeezed it slightly, and then she was sitting down, calmly and confidently, the first of them to do so. Seda followed suit a second behind, choosing a seat across the table from her, with Tisamon inevitably taking station at her

515

shoulder. With that, there was nothing else but for Tynisa to do likewise, but Thalric was cursed if he was going to hover on his feet like a house-slave. Maure had already slipped in beside Che, and so he ended up at the end of the table facing that throne.

Their host arrived, just not all at once. Thalric had the best view of its progress, which he regretted. There was a scuttling and a massing within the intricate carving of the throne, and the things previously only represented there were now springing from the wood, a dusty swarm of empty shells, wing-cases, sightless eyes and hollow mandibles, the tiny bloodless cadavers of a thousand crawling things amalgamating and writhing, and growing ever greater until they had transformed into the slouching shape of a seated man. Thalric just stared, tightly motionless but unable to tear his eyes from the sight.

Then the scuttling dead things began disintegrating, a shedding rain of chitin flakes and segments drifting away, and revealed was Argastos, clad in his mail, with his easy, empty smile and those blank white eyes.

From somewhere inside him, a part of Thalric rose up and gave himself a slap, because he had been staring like some superstitious Commonwealer peasant at this show. And it *was* a show. *What was the point of this, if not to play to the crowd? We've seen him pop in and out like a sergeant in a brothel. Why the grand entrance, if not to awe the newcomers?* And with that thought he managed to muster a reasonable head of contempt sufficient to take the edge off his fear. *Well, maybe you can still be taken down a step, Argastos.*

There was a bowl in front of him. He assured himself it had always been there. In this bad light, who knew? Now Helma Bartrer, Mistress of the Great College, was fetching some sort of cauldron, and Thalric realized that, of all things, she was about to serve them.

But, of course, that's her place in Argastos's world.

What she decanted into his bowl looked, in the unhealthy light, like greasy grey dishwater tinted with rot.

'You have no idea,' Argastos stated, 'how long I have been waiting for you. Long enough that I ceased searching the future for some hope of deliverance, centuries ago.'

Che and Seda exchanged glances and the Beetle inquired, 'And who did you think you were waiting for?'

The Moth smiled easily. He possessed the sort of confident, self-satisfied manner and elegant good looks that made Thalric's palms itch. 'You, exactly you. A new kind of magician, not tied to the old and yet with power, true power. I see the mark of the old Masters on the two of you, clear as day, and yet just look at you! Are you Skryres of my kinden? Are you Manipuli of the Spiders or Mosquito Sarcads? You are not.'

He did not sound damning about that, either. Thalric might have expected contempt, but Argastos was playing a deeper game.

'Beetles, Wasps, Ants – the inheritors of the world,' the Moth continued admiringly. 'Look at you. Look at *him*, a typical specimen.' He jabbed his finger at Thalric himself, who twitched in response, and had to press his hands down against the table to keep his Art in check.

'Not a grain of magic in him,' Argastos went on, 'and yet his kind, your kin – the Apt – are the great masters of today, swarming over the earth, lords and ladies of the new world. Don't think I have not witnessed it, even locked away in here. Between then and now, I have had visitors whose minds have shown me all.'

There's a pleasant thought, Thalric reflected unhappily, as he cast a glance around at the oppressively confining walls. They only rose to around head-height, with the cave-like ceiling arching high above, and they seemed . . . less than solid, as though there were gaps and holes in them, or shapes . . . His skin crawled.

'You don't resent us for taking away the world you knew, then?' Seda asked the Moth haughtily. 'Or the diminishing of your people?'

'You overestimate how much I care about my kinden,' Argastos replied sharply, making Helma Bartrer twitch. 'I owe them a great deal, yes indeed, and it will be paid back, every drop. I do not begrudge you, Empress of the Wasps. Your kind and her kind, all the Apt, you have built well. You have built more than we ever did, perhaps. And, believe me, I am the only man in the world who can say this, for I remember my own time clearly – no false nostalgia for me. I am a thousand years of watching the world turn, and everything you have built is built on my triumphs. If not for me, there would be nothing but the Worm.'

'That's a grand claim,' Che observed cautiously.

'Is it?' Argastos still sounded very pleasant, very well-mannered, but Thalric kept hearing something hollow resonating in the man's words, some agenda prowling behind them as if trying to fight its way clear. He tried to catch Maure's eye, in the hope that the woman had some insight, but the halfbreed was staring down at her bowl and keeping her eyes well away from Argastos.

'That was their sole intent, to cover the world with their kind, to leave nothing else under the sun or beneath the earth but themselves – not even their slaves once they had no more use for them,' Argastos explained. 'The long wars of the Inapt kinden led them to that. In the end they could not feel safe while any other kinden shared their world. And I stopped them. I was War Master of the great host, I won the battles, I drove them back into their holes. And, when the time came, it was I who made the decision to rid the world of them entirely, no matter the cost, so that we could have a future secure from their resurgence.'

The hard tone creeping into that rich voice was exactly what Thalric had been expecting.

'Are we supposed to applaud you?' Seda enquired.

'Why not? Is what I accomplished to be considered nothing? To have been the saviour of the whole world? Who else could say that, before or after me? You must see this – especially you two, the magician-queens of this latter age. You must understand me. I have brought you here so that you can know me.'

'You did not bring us here,' Che said, almost half-heartedly. Seda was merely looking thoughtful.

'I have brought you here,' Argastos repeated, 'and I appeal to you both. To the Beetle, for justice; to the Wasp, for revenge. Is it just that I should be trapped here for all eternity, become a martyr to my own life's work? Should I not plot my vengeance?'

And something must have happened to the light, then, though it hardly seemed brighter, because now Thalric could see the walls around them in detail, and saw that they were not walls at all, and that the maze had not been a maze. The great mantis shell strung behind Argastos's throne was only one trophy amongst hundreds.

Armour, ranks and ranks of it, stretching back into the gloom on every side, hanging empty and hollow like the insect carapace suspended above. Thalric's eyes flicked from suit to suit. The vast majority of it was Mantis-kinden work, that ornate and intricately worked mail and plate that collectors paid ridiculous sums for, but here was a collection that all Helleron would have beggared itself to acquire, each suit unique, yet each following the same aesthetic. *How many Mantis dreams lie buried here?* And his eyes moved on from helm to faceless helm, over glittering gold, enamel in green and black, spines and blades and elegantly shaped curves, that no smith now living could perhaps have wrought.

And there was more, alongside that antique host. He saw plenty in amongst them that seemed to be relics of a more recent time: the same chitin and leather as had been worn by the Nethyen still living outside, back where the world was at least nominally sane. They hung from their stands right alongside their elder cousins and, if he had been minded, he could have traced the evolution: the decline of Mantis culture from its glory days to the remnants of the present.

Black and gold caught his eye, and he realized that Argastos had welcomed more visitors than just the locals.

There was the dark chainmail of Sarnesh Ants, too, a variety of designs as though this was some armourer's museum. He saw Collegiate robes draped slack and empty, now they were gutted of their Beetle owner, and aviator's canvas, helm and goggles and all. And of course there were the Wasps, for the Seventh Army had been this way in recent memory. A handful of the Light Airborne, some heavier infantry plate, the light mail they had distributed to Imperial pilots during the last war, so that he thought of that downed airship they had taken refuge in.

Che gave a shuddering breath, and he spotted it just as she did. Here was a Collegiate Company soldier's armour built for a massive frame, and around it the others: the loose, discarded gear of Seda's Pioneers. The Empress's eyes were fixed on a ragged old robe, scarcely worthy of a stand of its own.

'I have had many visitors over the years,' Argastos intoned. 'They are no more than memories now, my trophies. But you! You are special. You have come to bring me my revenge, the two of you. Such strength you possess, and yet so little idea how to use it, and here I am, with a millennium's experience, just waiting for that burst of power to set me free.'

He was standing now, leaning forward over the table.

'And, believe me, when I am free the world shall know it. Between us, we three shall shake it to its foundations. We shall cast down my kin, and right all wrongs, and all things that displease us shall be banished from this world, even as the Worm was. No mercy! You, the inheritors of the old days, you shall be my brides, my lovers, and we shall use your power to remake the world in our image.'

And surely Che or Seda were bound to laugh at him then, or at least slap him down somehow, and yet the two of them seemed to be paying Argastos far too much heed. And so Thalric decided to play to his own strengths and puncture the man's expanding self-esteem.

'Revenge on the Moths? A bit late, no? And if anything you Inapt were capable of could achieve anything, why wouldn't they have done it already? It's not for want of trying that they're next to extinct.'

He succeeded in getting Argastos's attention then, which was the most he could claim. The Moth was suddenly staring at him as though one of the chairs had piped up of its own accord. And . . .

With a single crash, in perfect unison, every suit of armour, every set of garments there had taken a step forward, raising dust from the floor which had gone undisturbed since the start of time, and they were now all occupied, every one. Thalric froze in place, his further words dying inside his mouth. A grey face in every helm, curdled eyes staring out at him. Lean, sharp Mantis faces, the brown of Beetles' skins now charred to coal, the brother-sister likenesses of Ants and the death-pallor of his own kinden, and all staring out at him with expressions of such hopeless, terrifying misery that it shook him, it shook everything he called his own.

He met the gaze of the nearest Wasp, a man in the armour of the Airborne, and saw the man's lips moving over and over: *Help me, help me, help me . . .*

And Thalric felt his innards turn to water, a fear twisting inside him that was as old as his kinden, as old as the darkness itself, and he said no more.

Che could not bring herself to look at Amnon's armour, not now that he would be occupying it once again. *Trapped here like all of them, so many, I had not thought* . . . Was this what the ancient Skryres had intended, when they had devised this place? That it should be a pitcher plant trap for the ghosts of all who came here during the years to come?

She decided that they had. She knew that much at least about the Moth-kinden. And she could even appreciate why, for below her, directly below her, was the Great Seal, the capstone of Argastos's grand plan, which kept the Worm trapped in whatever half-world had been curled about it. Argastos had wrought it, using all the might of the Inapt, and then his own people had doomed him to guard it forever, and she did not know whether that was justice or not. His followers had come, too, in their loyal, unthinking ranks, his Mantis war band taking their place for all eternity at their master's side, likewise everyone else who had been drawn here, and died here . . .

She looked at Maure, and found the woman staring out over that dead host, the tears running down her face, and she understood. Not just cast-off shells, not just left-over cocoons where the real occupant had fled. Like Argastos himself, these were the true minds and essences of the dead.

And his fate was not just. He was right about that. But surely he was part of this injustice, the disease and not the remedy.

But he was staring at her and at Seda, and his attention, his strength of personality, was all around her, and she found she could not venture to speak.

'Your slave thinks I am deluded,' he said, in almost a whisper. It was not clear to which of them he was attributing Thalric's servitude. 'But I am no fool, and I know the world has moved on. I have my army here, my legion of the undying, but what would that count for against the wide Apt world?' He really did have a very compelling smile. 'But I will not have to rely on anything so antiquated. You yourselves have shown me that.' And he nodded companionably at Seda, who was staring at him with the same unwilling fixation as Che herself. 'For I will have myself an Empire,' Argastos breathed. 'And I will have a city of the Apt to serve my will. And I do not *need* to understand it, so long as my slaves know their trades – and so long as I have you as my consorts.'

Che tried to open her mouth to respond, but there was an invisible hand laid on her that stopped her words, censoring her very thoughts. She reached out for her power, but Argastos stood firmly between her will and her ability. She was stronger than him, she knew, for she had been crowned in Khanaphes, and Seda too. But they were in Argastos's realm now, and he had been working on them, unthought-of and unsuspected, ever since they had come there.

And he really did have a presence about him, a strong, smooth confidence. She found herself staring into his face, marking those elegant Moth lines. Had Achaeos ever looked like that? She did not think so. And Thalric? Thalric was some ugly Apt creature, a servant, a slave. *Not like us.* For of course the world was divided into Apt and Inapt for a reason, and she should simply be grateful that she had somehow crossed onto the right side.

So when he said, 'With your aid, I shall regain my proper place in the world,' she found herself nodding along with it, even though a panicking undercurrent in her mind was desperately trying to fight him off. He must have known that he had her in thrall, then, for his smile broadened as he declared, 'All shall know that the War Master is returned.'

And Thalric snickered.

The world seemed to stop around them, and in this single moment Argastos's self-control fractured. The one thing he had never been anticipating was mockery.

Then his minions came marching forwards, and they had blades in their hands, and Thalric was pinned to his seat by Argastos's mere stare as they closed in. But Che felt that hand being lifted from her, its grip broken during that one brief moment when someone had looked on Argastos and found him not terrible, but ridiculous. With enormous effort she clawed for her strength as the blades went up . . . but it was Seda who got there first, casting enough raw, untutored force out to send the dead Mantis-kinden staggering.

Thalric's eyes sought out Che's. 'Sorry,' he managed. 'I'm afraid the only War Master I know is your uncle, and I can't quite see him saying any of that stuff to the Assembly.'

It was not funny. Nothing about their situation was funny, but Che felt a near-hysterical laugh build up inside her nonetheless.

Argastos's face was set in stone. No, it was as though he had simply abandoned it, its last expression just sitting there like a slack-stringed puppet, because whatever was behind it had no further use for it. 'You dare,' he hissed, 'to mock the War Master?'

It was the worst thing he could possibly have said, for Che burst out with a horrified whoop of laughter despite herself, despite everything. She caught a glimpse of Seda's face, too, bewildered but no longer bewitched.

And only then could she see, beyond that smoothly handsome exterior, that warrior's frame in its archaic armour. Just for a second she saw the dried-stick thing that was Argastos, the corpse a thousand years in the ground, decaying and renewed like one of those Mantis icons, until only some hideous stub of a man endured, leathery and preserved and barely larger than a child, its face locked into the same expression of dismay that it must have worn as they sealed the man in his tomb, so very long ago.

And he shrieked, a high, inhuman sound, knowing that she had seen. Although she tried to muster her power to resist him, he was correct about his superior skill, for he cast her down with ease and banished her into the far reaches of his nightmare.

Thirty-Five

That morning Captain Vrakir of the Red Watch awoke and finally understood the meaning of the insistent dreams he had been having.

With trembling hands he went and opened the orders that his Empress had given him before he set off to find General Tynan.

'So you see, Master Maker, matters have advanced somewhat,' Eujen finished.

Stenwold regarded him calmly, whilst all about them the business of the College infirmary carried on, just as it had to. The beds were close-packed here – a room designed to deal with a handful of ill students now catering to some thirty injured soldiers, and even to the city's War Master.

He was sitting up, at least, though he still felt leaden and tired. If he tried to do anything active, he ran out of strength pitifully fast, but he was alive and getting stronger. They called the stuff they had pumped into him 'Instar', something concocted by the College chemists. They would not have dared trying it on humans save for the war, and even then it was administered to those who would have died anyway, in the surgeons' opinion. *Kill or cure* it most certainly was. They had even branded Stenwold on the shoulder, adding further injury to injury, as the mark of someone who had received a dose of this Instar, to warn off future doctors. All indications suggested that two doses would be painfully fatal.

Two doses in how long? Stenwold had asked them. Tests on animals had not shown an upper limit, he was told. Two doses in a man's lifetime was one too many.

Eujen stepped back to let the Fly-kinden nurse take a reading of Stenwold's pulse. As she did so, her hard, accusing eyes lanced into her patient. Balkus lay in the next bed, sometimes conscious, sometimes not, and Sperra plainly blamed Stenwold for his condition, perhaps not unjustly. The War Master was perhaps the only man who could now help Princep Salma, though, so she was bitterly and ruthlessly doing her bit to keep him alive. Much more of that guilt-laden care, and Stenwold would force himself to get out of bed, even if it killed him.

'Do you have anything resembling a plan?' he wheezed at Eujen, already trying to think of how to salvage the current situation. *Was this why Jodry brought the war to a close, just so some pack of students could go and poke the Wasps' nest? And for what?*

'I do,' Eujen confirmed, plainly nettled by Stenwold's tone. 'I have sent messengers to some of the major magnates and artisans of the neighbouring districts – community leaders that my own people believe are loyal to the city. Some are here already, but they want to talk to *you* of course, not to me. The Wasps went on the rampage last night, and there have been arrests all through today. Whole areas of the city are just off boiling point. They *hanged* Jodry Drillen, Master Maker. I wouldn't have believed that his death would spark such fires, but everywhere people are talking about it.'

Stenwold stared at him, thinking, *You bloody fool, Jodry*, and wanting to say something disdainful, to knock this arrogant young man back down. *He's, what, eighteen years, nineteen, and what does he think he knows? I remember him when he was saying we should be avoiding a war, and now look at him trying to start . . .*

'Revolt,' he said, and then one of those irresistible spasms went through him and he wasted a valuable half-minute coughing up what felt like a whole lung. His eyes never left Eujen Leadswell's face, though, and this latest attack gave his thoughts the chance to turn the wheel once more.

Like: *What might have happened, if we had worked harder to avoid this war? Because it surely doesn't seem to have turned out well for any of us.* And: *If any man should be saying, 'I told you so,' it's him.* But there was nothing but earnestness on Eujen's face, a man determined to meet the challenge the world has burdened him with.

'What news from Sarn, anyone?' He tried to look around. 'Laszlo?'

The Fly-kinden glanced up from his hushed conversation with Sperra. 'Nothing, Mar'Maker. But I reckon they're fighting about now, must be. Or maybe the Mantids have seen sense and pitched in at last.'

'If we can hold out until Sarn relieves us . . .' Stenwold murmured, almost too quietly to be heard. 'If the city is still up in arms, then Sarn *must* come to our aid. Or even Vek. *Someone.*' He was aware that his gaze fixed on Eujen was almost beseeching, but the student was nodding agreement.

'We need the city, though. Not just us,' he replied. 'We need the whole city to rise. And the city needs the War Master.'

Stenwold took a deep breath. 'Where the pits is my stick?' he demanded.

Laszlo passed it over: a heavy length of wood bound in brass with a hooked head, as warlike a support as any War Master could require.

With a great effort, Stenwold levered himself to his feet, expecting Sperra to protest and try to stop him. She just stared, though, as if she would not be entirely unhappy to see him spilling onto his backside. He managed to get upright, despite some trembling, and took another breath, conscious of its shallowness. The Instar was still working, but he was not sure that he would be the same again, not ever.

At last one of the medical staff was bustling over to protest – Sartaea te Mosca, and why so many of the healers were Flies he had no idea – with her hands extended, insisting that he at least sat back down. The resistance she provided was gratifying. It gave him something to lean against.

'Chief Officer Leadswell,' he snapped, 'who do we have here?'

'Master Vendall of the Vendall Balkhead workshops. Storvus the machinist from Faculty Row. Someone from Grounder Imports. A couple from the Messengers' Guild. Possibly more by now.' Eujen shrugged.

'You've been busy,' Stenwold remarked.

'We have very little time.'

'Then let me speak to them.'

'Hard to think that from this dismal ruin ruled the power that might once have challenged the Empire,' General Tynan observed. Around them extended the broken teeth of the Amphiophos: half-crumbled walls, caved-in domes, a maze of back rooms mostly roofless, everywhere tumbled, fire-blackened stones.

'They probably think it still is,' Mycella remarked, standing at his elbow. There was a cordon of Wasp soldiers strung about the place, looking out for any Collegiate citizen showing an unhealthy amount of civic pride, but Tynan had little fear of that.

He was here, at last, in the heart of the enemy's city. After so long, he had broken them.

'I know you were here before, with your fleet – sorry, your *armada* is the term in the Spiderlands, isn't it? I know that they've wounded you – and I can't even guess at the situation back home that forces you to be here. Even though you've told me about it, I still can't really guess.' He smiled at her, and some of her Fly servants appeared with a decanter and small glasses and set them up on one of the toppled stones, casting a cloth down first so as not to contaminate the vintage with the dust of Collegium's fall. 'What you may not understand, though, is what this means to me to be here at last. Three times, I've marched against this city. Three times I've taken the road from Tark, fought the bloody

Felyen, got right to their walls, and . . . the Emperor dies, or we lose our Air Corps and I give the order to fall back, because maintaining a siege in such conditions would be suicide. And then the Empress tells me, no, straight back in you go. And we rewrote the textbooks when we took that gate: Light Airborne and the Sentinels and no real artillery? They'll be saying we set the science of war back twenty years. But we did it, my boys and your followers.' He chose a piece of overturned Collegiate government to sit on and received his tiny glass with its oil-black contents. 'Here we are,' he concluded.

Mycella was regarding him with a curious expression, but it was mostly fond. *Of course*, he had to remind himself, *what are such expressions worth?* But that was only form, for he had relaxed with her in slow stages, and now he wanted to interpret the outer show for the inner thought.

'Is Aldanrael honour now avenged?' he asked her.

At that, her face lifted slightly. 'Thank you for believing that we have any. The Mantids would tell you we've none – the Collegiates too, most likely. Treachery and deceit are bred into our bones, they say. But, yes, here I stand, joint mistress of all I survey, and the voices of my slain son and niece are quieted for me. And when I return home again it shall be as a conqueror, with my power and influence restored. I shall have redeemed my family with a currency my people *must* recognize: success.'

'And the alliance with the Empire?'

'That also. Given the mess that came out of our states actually locking swords last time, I think it's in everyone's interest, except the rest of the world's.' And she raised her glass and rolled the contents over her tongue, savouring the liquid. Tynan did likewise – finding it was something like sweet vinegar, far beyond his normal taste and yet he knew it was a vastly expensive delicacy for her people.

An acquired taste, but I am fast acquiring it.

'There is an occupation force mustering – perhaps already

on its way,' he remarked. 'Then some lucky colonel will be made governor of this place. And the Second will resupply and reinforce and set off towards Vek, assuming Roder can do his job up north. And you?'

She gave a delicate little one-shouldered shrug. 'If you'd asked me that a month ago, I'd have said the Spiderlands for sure, but who knows . . . it would be stretching credibility to say that I'd heard Vek was lovely at this time of year, or at any time, but perhaps I'll see its walls with you, nonetheless.'

When he placed a hand to her chin, the better to admire her, he heard the slight shift of her bodyguard, Jadis. But the man was not close by, and Tynan could virtually plot the intimacy of his relationship with Mycella on a graph by assessing the distance off that Jadis stood over time, each day a little further away.

Then there was a new Fly-kinden at her elbow, slipping in so swiftly and suddenly that half the Airborne there were still trying to take aim at him even as he got too close for them to do so. He was dressed in a tunic of Collegiate fashion, but he knelt before Mycella nevertheless.

'General, one moment.' There was a shadow of worry on her face as she stepped aside.

The report her agent made to her was brief and to the point, murmured low enough that Tynan caught none of it. But the moment the man had finished, she returned to his side.

'We may be a little premature, it seems. My man has received details of some considerable unrest near the College. He thinks that your soldiers might have some work to do there yet.'

Tynan wanted to scoff, because the city was his, and in his hands, and he had *known* himself to be the master of it. He had not come this far, though, without discovering that her sources of intelligence – and her instincts – were superior to his own. A gesture, and he had a soldier before him, ready for orders.

'Get me Colonel Cherten, and I don't care what he's doing,' he commanded. 'He needs to hear this.'

★

Castre Gorenn, Commonweal Retaliatory Army and currently feeling every inch of it, crouched atop the courtyard wall, keeping an eye on the street below. To her left was Officer Serena, formerly of the Fealty Street Company before it was disbanded, with another Fly-kinden to her right. Both had snapbows, held out of sight, and both were out of uniform and doing their level best to appear simply interested in the view. Gorenn herself was sufficiently foreign that, though she kept her bow below the level of the wall top – with a half-dozen arrows lying ready on the stonework for swiftness – she had kept her buff coat and sash on, because it hardly seemed that they would make much of a difference.

And still the Wasps did not arrive. She had assumed that there would be a patrol, or a fly-over, or even just someone putting their Wasp-kinden head around the corner, but her sharp eyes had seen none of that, though by now everyone in the district must be aware that *something* had happened. After all, there had been a lot of shouting and dying only two hours ago, and even these lumpen Beetle-kinden had ears.

But nothing, and she began to wonder about the turncoat Beetle nobleman – or however the hierarchy worked here – who had turned up with those soldiers in tow. Could it be that he hadn't *told* anyone he was coming here?

The Wasps wouldn't just overlook a dozen missing soldiers when they were tallying up their troops – she knew enough about how they did things – but what if they had no clues, what if . . .?

Then some Wasps arrived just as she was pondering this, a little squad of five, and she froze, one unseen hand reaching deftly for her first arrow. But the Wasps were approaching without any overt caution, so maybe in their minds *missing* had not yet become *dead*. Even so, the moment they drew near, surely everything was going to go to the black pit, because none of these Beetle-kinden could dissemble worth a damn.

'Good day, soldier . . . Sergeant?' Serena's high, clear voice sang out, and she projected just the right combination of nervous good humour and concern. 'Can we . . . can we help you?'

The lead soldier stared up at her, and then made a short, ugly gesture to beckon her down. For a second Serena hesitated, hands still on her snapbow below the wall's lip, but then she silently set it down and hopped over the edge, drifting down on her Art wings.

Gorenn crouched even lower and listened intently.

'I'm looking for your chief, Boiler the Speaker,' the sergeant stated. 'He's somewhere around here with a dozen soldiers he's not entitled to. You seen him?'

'Helmess Broiler?' Serena appeared all bafflement. 'Why would he be here?'

'Why the piss would I know?' the sergeant demanded. 'Have you seen him or haven't you? He came this way, for sure.'

'Not a sight of him,' Serena insisted and, at the man's suspicious look, added, 'What?'

He moved in closer, forcing her to skitter back a couple of paces. 'You're lucky one of yours is being trusted like he is. If he's been cooking up some business with you here, then you'll be having a Wasp as the Speaker of your whatever-it-is, and no mistake.'

Serena's incredulity was unfeigned. 'Believe me, we're not *covering up* for Helmess Broiler. He's not popular around here.'

That last sounded altogether too heartfelt for Gorenn's liking, especially given that Broiler's mortal remains were still suspended from a beam inside, but the sergeant seemed to take it in good humour.

'Sounds as it should be. You see him, tell his sergeant to get the man straight back to command. I imagine you'll be glad to be rid of him, to hear you.'

Serena nodded. 'You know how it is, Sergeant,' and he certainly seemed to, and Gorenn saw Serena's wings flicker into being to carry her back to the wall. But there were more Wasps suddenly, a half-dozen running out of the machine shops down Faculty Row, and Gorenn could hear a noise – a sort of liquid, rumbling sound – that at first she did not realize emerged from human throats.

'Sergeant, trouble!'

'Report like a soldier!' the sergeant snapped back. He had forgotten Serena but she lingered down there beside him, because this was obviously news.

'Looks like some of the locals are having a go, Sergeant. There's a mob – maybe two score – and it's all artificers' workshops down there, so who knows what they've got.'

The sergeant swore. 'Go, contain the situation if you can, pull back to here if you can't. I'll fetch more some men.' At his brief gesture, the soldiers were hurrying back the way they had come, the sergeant's four alongside them. Left alone, the Wasp's own wings flicked out and . . .

Gorenn shot him. Coming up from behind the cover of the wall in one smooth motion, she lanced an arrow straight through his open mouth, then dropped back on one knee to fit another shaft to the string.

'You . . . what . . .?' Serena turned a pale face up towards her, showing a spatter of blood across one cheek. 'We were just—'

'Go tell the War Master they've started without him,' Gorenn ordered her, even though the diminutive woman had been an officer not long before. 'They're all still inside there. Beetles, always talking at the wrong times. Go tell them it's started.'

'You think Helmess Broiler has started a rebellion?' Tynan demanded.

Colonel Cherten shook his head hastily. 'It's the last thing I'd believe . . . but the fact remains that we can't find him, and our men have just been thrown out of everywhere within three streets from the College library – with casualties. There are Beetles out in force, and most of them armed – not with snapbows, mostly, but they don't lack for crossbows, and some have worse.'

'You've sent in enough men to form a perimeter?'

'General, yes, but it may not be enough. We've seen this sort of thing before in cities throughout the Empire. The next insurgence could come anywhere across the city.'

Tynan considered this information. 'Around the College, you say?'

'From the Airborne reports, some of the College buildings are at the heart of it. They are at least passably defensible.'

'Get some artillery in, including some of the wall engines we took from the Collegiates. Push in and break it open.'

'General, we can't,' Cherten protested.

Tynan fixed him with a cold stare. 'Justify yourself, Colonel.'

'We have orders to retrieve certain texts from the library. The Empress herself has given me a list of topics . . . It'll mean a month's work or more for the new governor, but it's imperative that—'

Cherten was babbling too quickly, too nervously, and Tynan silenced him with a look.

'Cherten, we were *bombing* this place from the air not so long ago. What would have happened if the College had caught a charge and burned to the ground?'

The intelligence officer swallowed. 'Then perhaps we'd have found ourselves on crossed pikes. I don't *know*, General, but these orders came via Captain Vrakir, after you were ordered to press forwards. The Empress . . .' He glanced around, but the two of them had Tynan's recently appropriated quarters to themselves. 'Her orders are . . . difficult, inexplicable sometimes. The privilege of her exalted position, no doubt. But they're clear, in the main. Even if we can contain the fighting to the College, if we can disperse the troublemakers on the streets, then we will have to storm the place in the old way, with soldiers forcing the entrances.'

Tynan growled, deep in his throat, but nodded. 'Mycella has gone to mobilize her people. She reckons they might be better at street-to-street skirmishing than ours – certainly come nightfall I reckon they'll play all sorts of games with the locals. But for our initial response . . . Collegium has such good wide-open streets.'

534

Cherten regarded him steadily. 'I see, General. How many?'

'Three Sentinels should make them think again. I heard good reports of their effectiveness in Myna, when the Eighth was pushing into the city. Get me grenadiers and nailbowmen as well, and we can make best use of our snapbows if they're short of them. Men on roofs, men in windows – make every street a killing ground. Anyone who isn't fleeing when they see the black and gold, they've earned themselves a death. Who's this?'

'General.' Captain Vrakir pushed inside, looking pale enough that Tynan fully expected the news that half Collegium was up in arms with a Sarnesh relief force coming over the horizon.

'Speak, man.'

'Orders from the Empress, sir.' Vrakir thrust a folded scroll forwards, its seal broken.

'Just in?'

'No, sir, I've had them with me since I first came to you, but not to be delivered to you unless . . .' And there Vrakir faltered for a moment before regaining his composure. 'They are relevant *now*, sir.'

Tynan looked ready to question that, but Cherten cleared his throat to forestall him. 'General, he is Red Watch. He is the mouthpiece of the Empress.'

The general frowned. 'I know that, but—'

'General, these things happen now. Check the seals on the orders if you doubt them, but this isn't the first time the Red Watch have suddenly brought new orders despite . . . Despite.'

Vrakir was still proffering his scroll, and Tynan snatched it from him irritably, opening it and carefully checking the seals and signatures. True enough, it had all the marks of the Empress's own hand, and from the look of it, it must have been drafted when she was still with the Eighth Army.

He read the contents.

Cold silence followed.

Cherten was watching him, he knew. Vrakir's eyes were practically lancing into his face, but then the man already knew what these orders were. Beyond them both waited the Second Army, Tynan's people, thousands of loyal servants of the Empire. Of the Empress.

He could decode the tension in Vrakir now: not at the orders themselves, or however they had come to him, but waiting for Tynan's reaction. And the general wondered idly what precautions the man had taken, for surely he must have taken them.

Who has he turned against me?

He re-read the orders carefully, even though their wording was brief and plain and clear, admirably so given their sudden and inexplicable appearance.

'The Empress orders . . .' And there he stopped. *Am I not permitted to ask why? Can I not question this? It is madness. It is insane.*

But of course it made perfect sense, even the timing, save for their current complication involving the Collegiates. There were wider currents of Imperial foreign policy than he was aware of, after all. And if he had been thinking more clearly before now, he might even have expected something like this.

Still, he let his eyes move over the document, until the symbols there, the words and their component letters, became drained of all meaning, just scribbles on a page.

I cannot give this order.

He was finding it hard to draw breath.

I will kill Vrakir. The Second will follow my lead. Anyone who doesn't . . . and when they hear of it, back in Capitas . . . I will . . . I will . . .

It felt like a blow, deep inside him, to know that he would do none of that. He was General Tynan, and he had ended wars and begun them at his Empire's behest, and now he would do worse. He would do just as he had been ordered.

'Cherten.' He shoved the paper towards his colonel, heard the choked exclamation as the man read it. 'This calls . . .' Tynan's voice shook, and he took a deep breath and started again. 'This calls for a redeployment. We will need all able-bodied men

536

mobilized immediately, and we will have very little time before they realize what we're about. Have the Sentinels move against the Collegiate-held streets as planned, backed by your current forces there and by a further five hundred Light Airborne. Use the Air Corps as well. If we can't bomb the library we can still bomb the rest. Everyone else . . .'

'I understand, General.' There was relief in Cherten's voice, and it told Tynan two things: firstly that, having seen the orders, he had obviously considered Tynan's response to them in doubt, and secondly, that his own loyalty to Tynan was plainly not strong enough to survive such a shift. 'Shall I take command of . . .?' he held up the scroll with its broken seal.

Tynan took it back from him. 'No, it's my responsibility. You're in command of putting down the insurgents – or at least containing them until this other business is done. Vrakir, with me.'

And Tynan stormed out, and the orders clutched in his hand seemed to burn his skin: *Destroy the Spider-kinden forces of the Aldanrael, their mercenaries, their Auxillians and allies, to the very last. Eliminate all Spider-kinden from Collegium. Do not spare a single one.*

At the College, matters were now moving sufficiently fast that Stenwold felt his ailing body could not keep up with them. Up on the wall overlooking the street, he just sat and let the tide of news wash over him.

'They've got Shod Street and Marley Row,' Serena was reporting, breathless but still forcing the words out. Sartaea te Mosca was bandaging a gash across the woman's arm even as she spoke, a close encounter with a snapbow bolt.

'What about beyond?' Eujen demanded. Stenwold let him take the lead – partly because these were his people, partly because Stenwold himself was still suffering moments when his strength would just evaporate – and other moments when he would be suddenly filled with an angry, burning energy that he could not dissipate.

'Some sign of something off towards the manufactories, or maybe those fancy townhouses on the other side.'

Eujen looked out from the courtyard wall, as if he could somehow comprehend all of Collegium at once. The sound of fighting was not close, but it was there – most of the Student Company was out on the streets, adding their discipline and armament to the local resistance, but there were houses within a hundred yards that had changed hands two or three times already, and the Wasps would bring in more men, hour by hour. The rest of the city was key, and he had hoped that revolt would spread like a flame across the city once the streets beside the College went up in arms, but so far a lot of people were keeping their heads down.

'Eujen, hoi!'

Leadswell's head snapped down, and Stenwold craned over to see the ragged band of re-armed Coldstone Company soldiers that Serena had nominally been spotting for. The Antspider was waving up at him, looking exasperated at having to shout her report. She had her one-handed Woodlouse and that Dragonfly woman and a couple of others with her, none of them particularly recovered from losing the gate, and yet all of them running to Eujen's orders.

'Come on up,' Leadswell called down, then glanced at Stenwold.

'You're doing well,' the War Master wheezed.

'I'm doing all I can,' Eujen said shortly. 'I don't need you—'

'Then why look at me as if you expect me to grade you?' Stenwold snarled back.

For a moment Eujen's expression was caught between a number of conflicting emotions, and Stenwold was reminded just how young he was – and how young were most of the Collegiate soldiers who had been left under arms. Then the Antspider woman came pounding up the steps.

'Good news and bad!' she announced. 'Don't know what the Jaspers are doing, but they're not reinforcing properly. We've won back Marley Row already, and we're still pushing. Gereth wants to get hold of something heavier to have a go at them. Gorenn needs more arrows.'

'Arrows? Do we even have arrows?'

'Apparently we do,' Straessa confirmed. 'But, look, they've one of those big bastard machines coming in there as well – and that's going to be as good as a whole load of actual soldiers, unless we can stop it. We need some grenades, little ones preferably.' She was talking very fast, obviously fighting to seem offhand about the whole business, but there was an unhealthy tremble about her eyes, like a woman holding her composure together with both hands. 'Eujen, I don't know what they're doing. Makes no sense to me. You need to look out for—'

'In case they come from elsewhere, yes,' Eujen finished up, plainly trying to sound businesslike.

Stenwold shied away from the weight of unsaid words between the two of them. *I should have some counsel to offer. I should tell them to speak to each other now, because later may be too late. But that's hardly advice I ever heeded myself.*

'Chief!' A student came bursting out of the building behind them with a box under her arm. Wearing an ink-smudged smock, she virtually vaulted the stairs up towards them, slamming her burden down on the wall's edge with pride. It contained a stack of papers, the sort of polemic familiar to Collegiate citizens from a score of Assembly elections. The text was bold, simple: *RISE UP, CHILDREN OF COLLEGIUM! NOW IS YOUR CHANCE! LIBERTY TODAY, OR SLAVERY FOREVER!* Then there was an image, simply delineated, yet with a kind of dynamic power to it: a Beetle man brandishing a hammer out towards the reader, his face a picture of grim determination – and not entirely dissimilar to Stenwold's own.

'Raullo did this?' Eujen asked, and Stenwold recalled the artist who had surely been too inebriated to achieve any such thing. The printer was nodding enthusiastically, though, and Eujen locked eyes with Stenwold, who had the grace to shrug.

'It will serve. He's done us proud.' Eujen thrust the box at Serena. 'Can you fly with this?'

She weighed it up, winced at her newly bandaged arm, then nodded.

'Good. Get out past their blockade. Drop these on the far side, those districts that haven't risen yet.'

'I went to the same classes as you, Chief. I know what we're about,' she confirmed.

Then Laszlo dropped down on the very brink of the wall, feet skidding for a moment before he righted himself.

'They're fighting!' he announced.

'That's hardly news,' Eujen objected, but Laszlo gave him the cold shoulder and addressed Stenwold directly.

'Mar'Maker, they're fighting *each other*!'

There was a heartbeat of stunned silence, and then Stenwold nodded stiffly to Eujen. 'Report to the chief officer.'

The Fly looked put out, but complied. 'Over that way, you've got a row of big warehouses or factories or something, where we thought they were mustering . . . well they're not. They're in and out of every building there, and they're killing each other.'

'The Wasps?' Eujen demanded.

'The Wasps are fighting their Spiders,' Laszlo explained, as though it was obvious. 'They've actually done it: they've gone after each other. There's hundreds and hundreds scrapping all over – and you know the Spiders aren't just sitting still and taking it. They've got archers at every window, and the Wasps are bringing their engines in, and . . . it's a mess, a real mess.'

Eujen and Stenwold's glances met sharply.

'Stab me, that changes everything,' the Antspider murmured.

'Push them,' Eujen decided. 'All along their line. They have no reinforcements now. Keep their machines busy and push them back, and . . . the city must learn of it. Print me more leaflets, and call up every Fly-kinden who can get out there – just to spread the word. This is our chance. This is our *chance*!'

Thirty-Six

'So, what now?' Che demanded. 'Come on, Argastos. What's your next sally?'

Another dark place, and she received a sudden insight that there might be nothing else left in the man's withered mind. He had lain bound in the earth for so long that he could not remember the sun. Here was some gloomy cavern, with her placed on a ledge beside a drop that fell in folds of rock for three hundred feet. Down there, she could see faint signs of fire, in pinpoints like stars.

'This is the place of my enemy,' came his voice, and he faded into existence almost within arm's reach, and with none of the excessive drama he had used at the table. What illuminated him, she could not say, but he cut a stark figure of grey and black and white, the scales of his mail glinting like moonlight, his skin like stone, his cloak merging seamlessly into the darkness.

'Some might say you're too obsessed with them,' Che pointed out, 'given they're a thousand years gone.'

'But they're not gone. They endure, on the far side of the Seal. And I was sacrificed to a living death to keep them there – not because it was needful, for in a thousand years the Worm have never tried to break through, nor could they ever. I was buried and forgotten because they thought they could bury their own guilt along with me.' He eyed her bitterly. 'Do you not agree, just for one moment, that I have been treated poorly? Am I not deserving of some sympathy, Beetle girl?'

Che folded her arms, trying to stretch out her power as subtly as she could in order to find the edges of this charade he had woven about her, and so tear it down, but he was always ahead of her, dancing where she must lumber, forever extending the world beyond her reach. 'And for this I become your whore, do I? And relinquish all I have to you?'

'You will be my concubine, valued and treasured,' he told her. 'And as for "all you have", if you will only use your power as I direct, what might you then learn about how to control it? See: you are the stronger, I freely admit, and yet you are like your kinden's namesake, a beetle blundering blindly about while I lead you one way and another. You have so much to learn, and do you think that there is anyone left in the world to teach you, save me? And you know I am no mean power myself, for why else did you and the Wasp girl come here, save to steal what is mine? With our strengths combined, what might we not accomplish?'

'Nothing good,' she decided, and, when he just stared at her, she went on, 'Argastos, yes, you are hard done by. What a terrible thing they did to you, all those years ago. And had you not spent all the years in-between in dooming everyone who came here to that exact same fate, then you might be able to presume on my sympathies. But I have seen your collection of victims, and I am not at all sure that your solution for dealing with the Worm does not deserve some guilt and expiation. And I still do not believe that anything you intend is for the good. For anyone's good – least of all mine.'

She felt strong, while saying that, and for a moment the shadowy world around her seemed to waver.

Then he was on his feet, glowering at her. 'You self-righteous child! How can you know how it was? How can you know what I thought, or what might have been! I was *there*! Someone had to make the choice, and I was the only one strong enough to do it! And you stand here, with your unearned inheritance, your life of freedom that *I* bought for you with my everlasting torment, and you dare to *judge*? You should come to me on your knees in gratitude for what I have done for the world!'

Che sighed. 'So, you have tried to draw on my better nature, and now you try to threaten me. What next, Argastos? For if you could simply take what you wanted from me, then you would have done so without hesitation. I am just a slave girl who has stolen something that's of value, to you. If you must woo me, it is for that reason only.'

For a long moment their gazes locked, and she felt relieved at the honesty visible there, the open acknowledgement that everything she had said was true. And then he nodded, and the hardedged expression that came across his face almost made her want to withdraw her words.

'Perhaps you think I will beg?' he suggested. 'No, I will wait for you to beg me. You are right. I have not been content to suffer alone. I have always had followers, and all those who have come to this place are my rightful prey. I have gathered them all to me. Now I give you to them. They remember what it is like, to live. Their appetites have been starved these long years, but they will awake again if I give the order. You may possess your strength, Beetle girl, but I will wager that here I can hold you down while they slake their lusts on you. And I have many hungry servants these days – *many*! You are proud, Beetle girl, just like the little Wasp is proud, and I will break you both as proud slaves should be broken. I shall return in a day or so, as the time shall seem to you. For now, I go to rouse my servants to the heights of their vigour. Enjoy the wait, Beetle girl, for it shall be the last peace you will know for some time.'

He boiled away into nothing, leaving her staring at the dark that he had gone back to. She could feel fear hovering at the edge of her attention, in case she had need of it, but her mind was working as analytically as if she was faced with a logic problem back at College. That Argastos intended to carry out his threat, she had no doubt. She was no helpless girl, though, and his mastery of her was reliant on her being unable to use her strength properly.

Her surroundings had now changed from the caverns of his memory to something better fitting the fate he intended for her: a small cell, but with its walls formed of knotted roots as if she was buried beneath some colossal tree. Perhaps this, too, was some place Argastos recalled from his long-ago life.

She tried to change the walls, but they would not bend for her. In her mind they were unaccountably slippery, impossible to bring her strength to bear on. Well, then, that was only her most obvious and crude application of power. He would have anticipated that. She must keep one step ahead of his imagination.

She heard movement from without, and for a moment her mind threw up an image: a column of dead Mantis men approaching, their hollow eyes hungry for even the cruellest memento of life. Fear clawed at her, but she stepped back from it, holding tenuously on to her calm. And she moved her cell.

This was no physical place, of course, even though it imprisoned her. It was set within a matrix of Argastos's thoughts. There were no hard laws that determined the relationship of one mind-place to another. If she could not escape her cell, she could relocate it, sliding the idea of it through Argastos's mouldering mind, and thus giving herself more time.

It was a temporary solution, but one that she could perhaps repeat a few times before he realized what she was doing. He had not prepared for it. She had the idea that, just as his backdrops were always gloomy and enclosed, so his ability to think like a human being had been decaying for a long time. He would find it hard to predict her.

With a little time in hand, she cast her mind out, reaching for anything she could use, and found a familiar mind reaching back to her.

She recoiled in shock, but a moment later she was groping forward again, worried that she might have lost him entirely. He was still there, though, and she envisioned him behind closed eyelids: a gaunt man with a high forehead, hair grey like iron, skin like bronze, a figure owning to no particular kinden the modern world would recognize . . . save that she did.

You are Cheerwell Maker, the girl the Empress hates, he identified her.

Although the Empress and I appear to have made common cause, if you can believe that, she replied.

He digested that. *I would ask you: do not tell her of me. I tried to kill her – tried and failed, but I tried. Because of you.*

She did not need to question him. He had been in her mind, as one of her pieces. She understood. *So, who are you? And how are you here, even?*

There was a pause before he answered, and she guessed he was weighing up the merits of being honest. *My name is Esmail. I was a spy placed near the Empress, but I lost my way. As for here, I was drawn here with the rest of you, when Argastos came. But I was already trying to hide from the Empress. I am good at hiding. It is in my blood and my training. Besides Argastos was not interested in me. He wanted you.*

You're hurt, she understood.

By the Empress. I'll live.

She had a sense of him moving with a freedom denied her. *Where are you now, if the question means anything here?*

I am . . . behind the scenes, perhaps. A dark place, but untended, untenanted save for myself. I can feel . . . my magical skill is just enough to know that there are other places just next to me, and yet unreachable. But I'm working on them. You must be imprisoned in one of them, the Empress in another.

There were others as well, she told him. *My friends and the Empress's bodyguard.*

I found them. A pause. *Or where Argastos put them,* he added. *I saw him take them . . . They are like statues, now, where they are: statues of wood, grown into the floor. I think he is only keeping them at all because they may be useful to work on you. I had thought your halfbreed would resist him, in the end but, though she is clever, she is weak. He overpowered her.*

She shifted her prison again, whilst maintaining her link to Esmail. The sound of approaching feet diminished, but did not fade away entirely. *Can you help me?*

I don't know. I am trying to locate you but . . . the internal architecture of where I am seems . . . broken down, falling apart. There is no logic here.

The mind of Argastos, she considered, and then the tenuous connection with him was severed, gone in an instant, at his will, and a moment later a very different voice sounded loud in her head.

Beetle girl!

Seda? Che flinched, because if Argastos was carrying out his threat, this might be an agonized cry for help, a window onto the other woman's pain.

Instead, the Empress's tone sounded properly imperious. *Listen to me, while you can. No doubt the creature has made the same threats against you as he has to me. Focus on me and I will tell you how to defend yourself.* Che had the mental image of . . . fighting, blade on blade.

Argastos has his legions of slaves, Seda said contemptuously. *But he was a fool, and he has taken on more than he knew or understood. Seek them out: there will be those you can suborn to your purpose.*

Che blinked, trying to discover what the woman meant. The exasperation of the Empress at such slow uptake came through to her clearly.

Just look! And for a few seconds she had the Empress's eyes, and she was watching a vicious melee where the grey-faced, dead-eyed Mantis-kinden that Argastos had sent were kept away from Seda's person by a handful of Imperial soldiers. Che recognized some of them as those who had come with Seda herself to this place, and died at the hands of Che's own people. But there were others, too, in a motley selection of black and gold

546

uniforms, Wasp soldiers who must have marched with General Malkan and the Seventh in the last war, and gone too far into the wood.

They are mine, Seda declared proudly. *In life, in death, they are mine. You must find your own protectors from amongst Argastos's collection.*

But why?

I will need you to destroy Argastos, Beetle girl. Our truce holds until then. Quickly!

Che felt an innate revulsion at the idea: disturbing the dead who were already held in unnatural imprisonment here. And who amongst them could she move? She was no magician-empress to command loyalty beyond the grave.

And yet the sound of feet was coming nearer, and the darkness admitted movement closing in on her cell. The long march of Argastos's servants was nearing its end.

Do they still feel lust? she wondered emptily. *Or is it just cold loyalty to him that drives them?*

A tremor within her, and for a moment she was almost crying out for someone to help her . . . anyone. And perhaps that was just what Argastos had hoped for. Then she gathered her resolve and plunged her mind into the charnel house that was Argastos's realm, like thrusting a hand into a rotting carcass. With a convulsive effort that seemed to turn her entire mind on its side, she drew forth a protector.

Seeing him, all she could say was, 'I'm sorry. This is my fault. I'm sorry I brought you to this.'

The expression on his charcoal-grey face was one of mild reproach, but only because of the apology, not for her part in dooming him to this. He squared his shoulders, and she saw him not in his Company uniform, but in the armour he had worn in Khanaphes, that impenetrable suit of fluted plates that Totho had made for him. In one hand was his shield, in the other his leaf-bladed Khanaphir sword. This was Amnon prepared to do battle.

But he was not alone. To her surprise she saw that she had

hauled up others, too – those whose faces she did not even know. There were a couple of aviators, and a woman in a College robe, and there were a dozen at least sporting the same sort of garb Helma Bartrer had worn when serving at dinner: clothes fit for a slave before the Revolution. Many were Beetle-kinden, but some were Ants from various cities, and they had knives and clubs and staves, all the makeshift weapons of the downtrodden.

None of them looked at her, but when the Mantids, the oppressors, emerged amongst them, Che's guardians fell on them with a determination and a fury that startled her. Amnon was at their centre, immovable and unyielding, and the ghosts of the Apt – *and what an irony!* – flowed about him but held their line, and kept her safe.

And the voice of the Empress spoke to her once again. *Good, but we won't have much time now before Argastos realizes something's gone wrong with his tawdry little plan. We need a weapon to use against him. All this around us is born of his own mind. We need something outside of him to distract him. Just a moment should be sufficient for us to break away from here, and then we will see if the two of us together can crack him.*

He has had centuries to perfect his skills, Che cautioned.

What do you suggest we do, then? Seda demanded. *Give in to him and become his creatures, even as these slaves are? No, we fight. Even if we must lose, we fight.*

I haven't been able to find anything solid here to break out from, Che admitted. *When I try to focus my strength, it's just like fog.*

He is like a swordsman fighting stronger opponents. He cannot afford to pitch his might directly against ours, but he is fast and skilled. He can deflect where he cannot block. There was a particularly expressive pause, and Che received the impression that Seda's defenders were hard-pressed.

She delicately stepped back from her link with the Empress, seeking out Esmail instead. *We need to distract Argastos*, she told him. *Can you reach him from where you are?*

She thought she had lost him, but after a moment his voice

came to her distantly. *No. I am inside, as you are. I am just in . . .* *a suite of abandoned rooms, not set for visitors. Or maybe the servants'* *quarters that run all the way through an Arista's house. But, no, I* *cannot find him.*

Che took a step back, because Amnon was being forced to give ground, no matter how determinedly he tried to hold it.

Seda . . . she relayed carefully, because it seemed fully possible that Argastos might seize on any incriminating thought the moment it had left her head.

Speak, the Empress snapped back, tensely.

I have it, Che revealed. *I know how it can be done.*

Thirty-Seven

The good merchants and artisans of Stockwell Street had been talking longer than Serena was happy with, at least twenty of their finest crammed into the backroom of the Helleren Patch taverna. The Fly-kinden had assumed they were moved by the leaflets she had handed them, and by now everyone seemed to know that the Empire was fighting a war on two fronts within the city. *So rise up,* she had said to them. *Cast off your chains while you can! Drive the Empire out of Collegium.*

And they had seemed to go for it, right then. There had been plenty of people around – workers, apprentices, refugees from more embattled districts of the city – and some of them had been armed, and she had thought, *This is an army in the making.* And then the local magnates, the men and women whom everyone would follow, had closeted themselves in the Helleren and . . . and just talked. And were still talking, whilst Serena herself shuffled her feet, and Averic kept watch at the window. They were an odd pair to be out soliciting resistance to the Empire, she had to admit. She had assumed he would be doing the talking, denouncing his own people, telling of their atrocities in words that much more convincing coming from one of their own. Instead he just hung back, sullen and silent, and let poor Serena do all the talking.

And he haunted the window like last month's cut flowers, staring out towards the conflict, towards the College library and his friends, and Serena was beginning to wish that they had sent her out with Gorenn the Dragonfly, because at least that long streak of exoticism had something appropriately harsh to say about the Empire.

What's the matter, Averic? Wondering if you picked the right side? Which was a mean thing to think, but he *was* a Wasp, and it had been hard to accept him at the start.

Then she heard the door of the backroom open, and one of the local big men – maybe it was Vollery the plumber – was shouldering his way out, a slice of argument from within still to be heard as he shut the door.

'You're all set, then?' Serena asked him brightly, in absolute defiance of his expression.

Vollery glanced about. 'You'd better get going,' he told her.

'That's fine. When can we expect you?' She could read it all on his face – having been put there specifically for her to read – but yet she was cursed if she would accept it just like that.

'We . . . Just go now. It's not going to happen,' Vollery replied heavily.

'You must be mistaken. It *is* happening.' *Our people are out there, fighting and dying right now, while you've made me wait for this?*

'No, it's not.' Vollery sighed, a tradesman confronted with something he couldn't fix. 'Some students have got some stupid idea that it's not too late. It was too late as soon as the gate fell.'

'It's not just some students, it's the *Company*,' Serena insisted. 'Averic, come over here. Tell him.'

But Averic barely glanced at her, and she ground her teeth in frustration.

'Students,' Vollery repeated, and she read so much into that one word: how it was not just the Wasps who had overlooked the existence of the Student Company, or at least failed to take it seriously. 'Students, what do they know? They really think calculus and philosophy are going to get anyone out of this?'

'They're your own people, your sons and daughters, and they're fighting for your freedom *right now*!' Serena hissed.

Vollery's expression turned hard. 'My son died defending the gate,' he said. 'My daughter was raped by the Wasps on that first night.'

She stared at him, flinching in the face of his lack of expression. 'Then surely you . . .?'

'What do you know?' he asked her. 'You understand nothing. Fly-kinden? You lot can always just leave, can't you. And him? I'm sure there's a place waiting for him back home, when he stops playing.' And even that barb failed to hook Averic's attention. 'But me? I have a home here, and a trade. I have a wife and a daughter who need me. And I should take up a crossbow and fight the Empire's armies on the say-so of some fool students who think they know anything?'

Serena opened her mouth and closed it, her words had unaccountably dried up.

'Go,' Vollery told her. 'Go, and be thankful I care enough to come out and get rid of you before they finish debating whether to hand you over to the Wasps.'

'We have to go,' Averic declared. Serena looked between the two men for a moment, realizing that Averic had not been paying attention to a word Vollery had said, that his focus had been elsewhere entirely.

'We're going,' she confirmed, already backing towards the taproom door, and a moment later she and Averic were out on the street.

'It's changed,' he told her hollowly.

'What has?'

'The sound of the fighting. Come on.' His wings flashed from his shoulders and he was in the air in an instant, leaving her to catch him up.

They had held the Light Airborne off with some success for most of the morning. The students had thrown a barricade across

Albamarl Street and put snapbowmen at every window, and on the roofs, with more snipers dotted in buildings halfway to the College. When the Empire had dropped soldiers behind them, the Wasps had found themselves being shot at from every direction, and for hours now they had been driven off, over and over.

Word from the neighbouring streets had been encouraging. Everyone was holding their ground, and the Wasps did not seem to have the sheer manpower to force the issue. A bloody stalemate had gripped the streets around the College library.

Straessa was commanding the Albamarl barricade, for want of anyone better. Gerethwy, standing beside her, had a repeating snapbow leaning on the barricade as he fiddled awkwardly to fit a new tape of ammunition into its feeder. Since the last such device had blown his fingers off, she'd have thought he wouldn't want to touch the thing, but apparently he had new plans. A bulky pack of machinery rested beside him, and he was murmuring an explanation of what it was that he intended doing with it.

'There's no reason for any of this barbaric spectacle,' she caught him saying. 'This is just sheer atavism. We've scarcely moved on from the Days of Lore. But devices like ratiocinators have shown us that there's no limit to the tasks a machine can be set, which might have required a man to handle just a few years ago. Even fighting wars can be left to them, so long as we can work out sufficiently complex calculations fitting the task . . .'

'Shut up now, Gereth. They're coming.'

His head snapped up. 'But I'm not ready.'

'So sorry, I'll tell them to come back in an hour, shall I?' She looked at the heap of loose pieces inside his pack or scattered about him. 'Or would tomorrow suit you better? Inbound, everyone! Looks like grenadiers are back, too!'

All around her, the soldiers of the Student Company, plus a few veterans of her own Coldstone troops, levelled their snapbows or their pikes, whilst a few checked the always delicate mechanisms of their nailbows in preparation for close-in work. The Wasps were massing three blocks away from the barricades, and snapbow shot was already being exchanged, inaccurate on both sides. Straessa saw Castre Gorenn draw back her bowstring, kneeling under cover of the barricade, and then launch an arrow up at a ridiculous angle. The Antspider was quick enough to see it descend, striking a Wasp who looked as if he had been giving orders just a moment before from the shelter of a doorway.

Gorenn selected another arrow, her expression all business, devoid of pride. The fact that, at full draw, she could outrange a rifled snapbow with an accuracy that Straessa could not have matched at ten feet, had become a tenet of faith amongst the Collegiate insurgents.

'They're coming!' someone shouted, helpfully announcing what was evident to absolutely everyone.

The Antspider levelled her snapbow, butt to the shoulder to steady it, sighting down the barrel and then up a little to adjust for the range, leading the Airborne as they took wing. Her own shot was lost in the general explosive release all around her, like a round of spontaneous applause for the Wasps' grim perseverance. And that was the thing, because they were not going away, not even slightly. The Empire had been prodding at them all morning, taking light casualties, dealing considerably lighter ones, and all that while the bulk of their forces were not even fighting the Collegiates at all, but brawling with their erstwhile allies four districts away.

This latest attack turned out to be more tentative than most, and the score of grenadiers, whose approach the Airborne had presumably been intended to cover, lost four of their number almost immediately and broke off. Not a single flying assailant's shadow crossed the line of the barricade, and one Beetle student of agricultural economics took a bolt through the arm and was ordered to get herself off to the infirmary. The massing Wasps down the street had not gone, though, although Gorenn was still making their lives unpredictable and interesting.

Then someone was shouting her name, and she turned to see that Fly friend of Stenwold Maker's – Laszlo? – spiralling down towards the barricade amidst Wasp snapbow shot zipping past him.

'Get down!' she ordered him, 'What's . . .?' But the look on his face shook her, transformed from the usual easy-going man she remembered.

'You've got to get out!' he told her. 'Pull back for the College right now!'

'What? No, we've—'

'Shaw Street's gone. Half of them are dead and the rest are running.'

'That's—' *That's right next to us.* Shaw Street ran parallel to Albamarl. 'Gone how?'

'Just pissing *move*, will you?' the little man yelled at her. 'How much time do you think you have?'

And if they flank us, they can just come over the roofs anywhere they want. 'Everyone pull back! Get out of the buildings and head back for the College!' She saw Gerethwy frantically packing up his kit, gathering all those delicate gears and pieces. 'Gereth, there's no time!' But he would not be dissuaded, his hand and a half moving as deftly as he could to get everything back into his pack.

The thoroughfare behind her was emptying swiftly, her soldiers retreating further down the street, whilst keeping their eyes fixed on the sky. Those at the barricade, however, were ignoring her orders, and she belatedly realized this was because she herself had showed no signs of going.

Hold for another minute. Give the rest a chance to make some distance. 'What in the pits happened in Shaw Street?' she demanded.

'It's not just Shaw Street . . .' he started, and then pointed: 'That.'

A familiar metal bulk was moving smoothly onto the far end of Albamarl Street. The sun reflected off its articulated carapace, that one blind eye.

'Gorenn, got grenades?' Straessa called.

'Only works if I can get it in the eye,' the Dragonfly replied tersely.

'They're wise to that, believe me,' Laszlo told her. 'It can shove this whole barricade aside and mow the lot of you down with its piercers. It doesn't need its leadshotter at all. Now are you bloody leaving or what?'

The Antspider stared at the gleaming flanks of the Sentinel as it settled itself to face the barricade. The soldiers around it were obviously preparing to advance, but the way they were massing showed that the war machine would provide their vanguard.

She had seen how fast those things could move.

'Back,' she ordered, just the one word. She had a hand on Gerethwy's shoulder, but the Woodlouse was already straightening up, his toys all cleared up.

The Sentinel shook itself with a clatter of metal and she heard its engine roar even at that distance.

'Run!' she decided, and followed her own advice.

By the first sight of evening, the insurgents held the single College building from where their revolt had started, and no more.

They were the students, in the main. The neighbouring townsfolk who had risen alongside them had fled for their homes and workshops, those of them still alive to do so. The Wasp response had been brutal. Any Collegiate had been fair game for the snapbows, armed or not. Street by street, with their Sentinels at the fore, they had crushed any resistance until only the College itself was left.

The students still held the courtyard wall, their line of snapbows defended by more archers at every little window, and the Wasps seemed to think they had achieved enough for the day. They had built some barricades of their own, gutting a score of nearby buildings for material, and cordoned off every street surrounding the gate, out of easy snapbow range of the students but well within sight.

They were still fighting the Spiders, by most recent accounts. The soldiers of the Second had not even broken stride, it seemed.

The early evening quiet was broken now only by sporadic demands from the Wasp barricades that the Collegiates surrender, and that any non-combatants trapped on the wrong side of the barricades give themselves up now.

Anyone within our cordon at dawn will be treated as an enemy of the Empire and no mercy will be shown, came the warning. Since the call had gone out, a steady trickle of locals unfortunate enough to live too close to the College had been emerging: men, women and children shuffling hesitantly towards the Wasp lines with their heads bowed, not looking back at the College.

In the corridor outside the infirmary, Stenwold was laboriously pacing, despite the objections of the medical staff, working strength into his ragged muscles, his stick clacking and clicking on the floor.

'Any ideas from the War Master would be much appreciated,' Eujen observed.

The sound of the stick stopped. 'I have none,' Stenwold admitted. 'We could try to break out, but the cost would be terrible – their barricades will slow us far more effectively than ours ever slowed the Wasps. We could hold out here until they bring some artillery to bear. Or until they decide the lives of their soldiers are cheap enough for them to force entry. Or we could surrender.'

'On what terms?' Eujen asked bitterly.

'Whatever they offer, which aren't likely to be attractive,' Stenwold admitted. He looked the student leader in the eye. 'I'm sorry it's come to this, Eujen. You deserved better.'

'And you?'

Stenwold was silent for a long while. 'Perhaps this is what my life has been leading to. If I was a Wasp commenting on the life of Sten Maker, I'd say it was a fitting end.'

'This isn't just about you,' Eujen pointed out, clearly nettled.

Stenwold leant heavily on his stick, hearing it creak. 'I'm glad I can walk with some confidence now,' he remarked.

'Well, I'm happy for you, Master Maker,' Eujen replied acidly.

'It means I could walk out of the College doors and hand myself over to the Wasps.'

The silence between the two men dropped like a curtain, and held for some time,

'I'm right there at the top of their list,' Stenwold observed. 'I've earned that, frankly. I know there are others within these walls they want – probably everyone by now – but I'm the man whose name has been on the lips of the Rekef for ten years. I'm the notorious War Master. And our one bargaining counter is that, if they want to come and get me, they know full well my loyal followers will make them pay in bodies. And the Wasps are not quite so heedless of their lives that they would welcome the chance to cover every inch of this building in blood when there is another way.'

Eujen's expression was almost frightened, as he looked on Stenwold. 'And when the Rekef get you?'

'Then I'll regret we ever had this conversation. If I don't get the chance to do myself in first, of course. I've not had the chance to find out how quickly I can open my own veins, but there's always a first time. But if taking me alive will buy anything for everyone here, then I will go, Eujen. Because I am responsible.'

'Again, it's not just about you—'

'Eujen.' A reprimand within the utterance of the name, not War Master to soldier but College Master to student. 'I have been fighting the Wasps for more than a decade, and I have been inciting my city to fight them, also. I believed that it was the right thing to do. I am the man who built the Lowlands' resistance to the Empire. And, you know, it seemed to work. It seemed . . .' His arm was shaking, with the effort of just standing there, but he took a deep breath and calmed it. 'But they came back, despite everything. They kept coming, swarm after swarm. And I can't imagine how it must be to be General Tynan, just throwing an army at a problem over and over, machines and men and all the bloody waste of it, until you *win*. And if I'd known that before, known what an Imperial general – an Imperial army – was really like, then what would I have done?'

He looked at the silent Eujen and managed an ashen smile.

'And some idiot student was saying only recently, should we not have been treating with the Wasps, working on them, trying to work *with* them, to change them from within rather than resisting them from without. Maybe someone should have listened, eh?'

'Master Maker,' Eujen said, almost a whisper. 'I don't know. I no longer know what's right.'

'I think we can both drink to that.' Stenwold took a shuddering breath. 'You yourself have to bargain with them, Eujen. Tell them they can have me. If they . . . any concession is better than none. Tell them I'll come out alive, if they let everyone else just go home. I don't know . . . Tell them something.'

Eujen stared at him for a long time, and then looked away. 'I'll think about it,' he said. 'You need to go sit down now, War Master.'

The sky was already heavy with evening when Serena dropped back into the College courtyard. She had been gone the best part of an hour and Eujen had been as taut as a wire every minute of it, wondering if he had sent her to her death.

'Right, Chief,' she said to him, sounding shaky. 'Well, that went about as well as it was ever going to.'

She had not been the first to volunteer as messenger to the Empire. Castre Gorenn had put herself forward, but Eujen reckoned the Wasps would shoot a Dragonfly far quicker than they would a Fly-kinden and, besides, the Commonweal Retaliatory Army was nobody's idea of diplomatic.

'Report,' he told her, fully aware that these might be some of the last words he ever spoke as chief officer of the Student Company.

'Their officer in charge will meet with one of our leaders, Chief. To talk terms.'

It would not be fair to say that a great weight fell from Eujen's shoulders, but at least it shifted position. 'Now?'

'Well, I don't think they're going anywhere until dawn, you know, but I reckon they're expecting you sooner than that,' Serena observed.

Eujen nodded. He wished now that he presented a better image: a breastplate that was clean and undented, a buff coat that wasn't holed and stitched. Perhaps a more heroic physique. *Perhaps a better man entirely, to handle this more adeptly.*

But there was only him.

'Then I think it's time I went. Get ready to open the gates. Close them the moment I'm through.'

'Eujen!'

He closed his eyes. He had hoped to avoid this moment.

The Antspider stormed across the courtyard towards him. 'Have you been *avoiding* me, you child? What are you doing out here?'

He just looked at her. In fact he drank her in, those halfbreed features that were beautiful, to him, even flushed with annoyance, and the way she carried herself, the long-limbed grace of her.

'I'm going to talk to the Wasps. I won't be long.'

She made a strange noise that had probably started off as a word.

'I'm going to see what can be salvaged. I've got a few things to bargain with. Otherwise nobody's going to do well out of tomorrow, but least of all us here.'

He saw the sea-change pass across her face, Straessa automatically reaching for antagonism, because that was how she dealt with the world when she caught it cheating. 'You're doing *what*, now? Tell me I misheard you, Eujen, because that sounds about the most stupid thing I ever heard said on College grounds – and, believe me, that's including the entire philosophy department.'

560

He did not smile. He denied her that. 'The city hasn't risen, Straessa. The Wasps are mopping up the Spiders right now and, even without that, they've got the men and the machines to beat us. It hasn't worked.' He said it softly, reasonably. He knew it would provoke her but he could not help that.

'And you putting yourself in the hands of the Wasps will make everything all right, will it?'

'Of course not, but it might help. There are lives at stake. If I can do anything . . . They made me chief officer, Straessa. You remember, you brought me the note yourself. I'm *responsible.*'

She bit at her lip, and he thought she would break, but then she spat out, 'You intellectual cripple, Leadswell. You self-righteous turd. And it's all about you, is it? You nobly sacrifice yourself, and that somehow *helps*, does it?'

'I'm not sacrificing—'

'Bollocks, you aren't.' Her fists were clenched, perhaps to keep her hands from straying to her sword. 'Anyway, I'm coming—'

'No.'

'Yes.'

'That's an order, Officer Antspider. From your Chief.'

She looked at him as though he had stabbed her. 'You think I'm soldier enough for *that* to work?'

'Straessa, don't take this the wrong way, but what would I do with you there? You'd stab the first Wasp you saw of major or above, and piss on the whole thing. Look at you. I can't rely on you. You stay here.' *Sorry, I'm so sorry, but you're not coming with me, not this time. Forgive me later, but believe me now.*

She was trying to speak, and failing, the intended words just coming apart in her mouth, and he saw her shaking, shoulders, hands, all of her. In the lamplight her eyes were bright and shining.

'Open the gates,' Eujen ordered, and he heard the bars lifted off, the creak of reinforced wood. Stepping through them was a hard thing, perhaps the hardest thing he had ever done.

Behind him, he heard Straessa hurl a scream at him – wordless, frustrated, agonized, loud enough that the Wasps must be wondering what horrors were going on inside the Collegiate camp. *Just the usual, the way we always go about things.* It was a single, short, ugly sound, but it stayed with him.

There was a whisper of wings before he was twenty feet from the gates, and he thought for a moment it would be some overbold Light Airborne come to escort him in, and about to get shot for his pains. Serena dropped down beside him, though, matching his pace.

'Chief,' she acknowledged.

'Get back inside.'

'What're they going to think, if you just pitch up on your own, Chief?' she asked. 'Man needs staff, a retinue, or they won't take you seriously. We thought at least we should show them you're worth listening to.'

'Are you serious? Wait – "we"?'

'Eujen.'

The expected Wasp face, but set above a Collegiate uniform. Averic strode out of the shadows.

'Not a chance. Back behind cover, the both of you.'

'I'll be able to help you. They're my people.'

'And you're a traitor to them. That means . . . what is it, crossed pikes?'

Averic sighed. 'I'm not Straessa.'

Eujen frowned at him. 'I didn't think you were.'

'So insult me, tell me I'll spoil things, call me out for my kinden or my character. I'm still going with you.'

Eujen opened his mouth, but there was something in the man's voice, his face, that rendered any response he could make seem trivial. And he had already parted from one of his friends on poor terms. And he had no way of making Averic go, even if he tried to insist on it.

And, anyway, we're coming back. This is a diplomatic errand, like when Maker met with their general outside the walls.

He nodded, not trusting himself to find words, and continued on towards the Wasps with Serena to one side of him, and Averic to the other.

He had thought it hard to leave the gates. He had been wrong. *Hard* was approaching the Wasp-made barricades, seeing that long stretch of snapbowmen all giving him and his escort their undivided attention, seeing the great shell of a Sentinel reflecting the light of their sentry lamps, its scratched metal hide flaring silver. They all seemed unnaturally quiet and still, and he realized that it was because of him. He had their utter concentration. If he had been Stenwold Maker himself, in that moment, he could not have commanded the focus of the Wasps more completely.

As he neared them, two score soldiers dismantled a section of the barricade in front of him, with an efficiency that put his own troops to shame. He looked at their faces – Averic's kin, pale, tough-faced men, soldiers and conquerors. They did not spit at him or call insults, but there were thirty stings and as many snapbows trained on him at all times, and the same on his companions. This was what professional soldiers looked like: men whose entire livelihood was the uniform and the Empire's orders. How different from a Collegiate tradesman-turned-soldier, or even the Ant infantry who were citizens before they were warriors. War was what these men were made of.

He stepped on past them, Averic and Serena crowding closer without meaning to. There was a fire ahead, burning in the lee of a machinesmith's shop front to retain the heat. The only clear path through the Wasp troops led to it.

For some reason he had expected General Tynan. That bald, stocky old man, seen only once, had become the face of the Wasp command for him. Instead the officer he found there was a little younger, taller, vaguely familiar from that meeting outside the walls.

'You are not Stenwold Maker, I see,' were the first words out of the man's mouth. Apparently he had been labouring under a similar misapprehension.

'My name is Eujen Leadswell, Chief Officer of the Student Company.'

'I am Colonel Cherten of Imperial Intelligence,' the Wasp told him. He glanced briefly at Eujen's two followers, eyes lingering on Averic. 'Tell me, before we start, do you *have* Stenwold Maker, back there?'

All Eujen could think at first was, *Curse me, it really is all about him.* But, of course, it was just as the man himself had said. There was a list, but his name topped it. *And I have his permission to conjure with that name.* Eujen had thought long and hard about that, before embarking on this foolishness.

'We do not,' he replied, with the utter candour of the student debater. 'I thought he had escaped the city.'

If he was expecting Cherten to fly into a rage at being thus thwarted, he was disappointed. The man simply nodded curtly. 'Very well.' Barely a moment's more consideration on the colonel's part, then: 'Take them.'

Eujen's mouth was still open to speak when three soldiers grabbed him and slammed him to the ground hard enough to rattle his teeth. He heard Averic snarling, had brief glimpses of scuffling feet. A sting went off – he heard the crackle but saw barely a flash of it – but then the Wasp beside him was down, his hands pinned behind his back.

Eujen gave a great wrench and half threw off the men leaning on him. It was then he saw Serena drive a knife into the leg of the man who had laid hands on her, and a moment later she was in the air, wings driving her as hard as they could back towards the barricade and the College beyond.

He heard a sharp retort, without seeing the shooter, but Serena's scream was unmistakable. And then Eujen was shouting, fighting, throwing awkward punches at everyone within reach, clutching for a sword already taken from his scabbard. A Wasp punched him in the face, the Art-grown bone spike jutting from the edge of the man's hand laying open Eujen's cheek, and then he was being forced to his knees, arms twisted back as far as they would go, looking up at Colonel Cherten.

'We came to talk!' he spat, aware of how weak the words sounded. 'We came to make a deal.'

Cherten's face succumbed to contempt. 'The Empire may negotiate honourably with enemy combatants, *boy*, but your city has surrendered. That makes this a rebellion. That makes you all traitors to the Empress's rule. No negotiation, no mercy. Now get them back to the gatehouse. I have questions to ask.'

Thirty-Eight

Helma Bartrer came from an old, old family.

Of course, everyone came from an old family: nobody's family was older than anyone else's, but hers was superior to the rest, she knew. Her family had remembered the traditions and remained true. Generation to generation they had told the stories of their own heritage, all through the time of forgetting that followed the revolution in Pathis and the breaking of the Days of Lore.

Collegium, Pathis-that-was, had forgotten, but she remembered, as did some very few families else. Down through the harsh, bright centuries they had not abandoned their purpose or their faith.

And all it said in the Collegiate history books was that the Beetles had been slaves once, and the Moths had been their masters. They made that sound like such a bad thing. They compared it with being a slave for the Ants, for the Wasps, just hard drudgery in service of the uncaring, of the banal. They had forgotten how it was.

But Helma knew better, for the secret annals of her family made it plain. Perhaps even the Moth-kinden these days did not know the truth, mired as they were in their inward-looking squabbles. But there really had been a golden age: a golden age of night.

True, the Moths of Dorax did send word now and then,

praising Helma's kin for their ongoing service, offering some scrap of lore in return for intelligence on the internal workings of Collegium. She was cynical enough to recognize that for what it was: mere espionage, the regular business of modern nations. In itself that was an admission of failure: confession that their ancient skills had withered to the extent that they had to ask, and could not simply *know*. Helma's kin remembered what they had once been, better than the Moths did themselves.

And true also that Helma was Apt, and her family had been Apt for many generations, though the secret histories suggested that their Inaptitude had survived at least a century beyond the Revolution. There were wonders written there that Helma could not truly understand, just as she could not quite grasp the meaning of the old Moth scrolls in the College library, but that had not stopped her trying. She had steeped herself in Inapt lore from an early age, thus becoming, almost incidentally, one of the College's great scholars of history. She had even sought to take the chair for Inapt studies, but her Aptitude had shackled her, and even the halfwit Fly they had brought in for the post had that crucial advantage over her.

But she had learned, even if only by rote and in ignorance, and thus been vindicated spectacularly. She had come here to the forest with only the dusty old tatters of understanding and the name of *Argastos*, a great name from the Days of Lore.

And she had shed Moth blood, and so she had got in. It was her crowning achievement, to mimic Inaptitude with such sincerity that she had crossed the line, that once. She had become a fit servant for her masters.

Rather, for her *master*. Because whatever the Moths of today had devolved into, Argastos represented that kinden at its height, a man – and such a man! – who had strode a world that knew nothing of Aptitude, a world in which great things were still being done.

And she had come to him here, in his place, and knelt before him, and sworn to be his right hand, his servant, his ambassador, whatever he required of her. This was the culmination of centuries of familial ambition.

And now she stalked through the cramped, buried chambers of his home, the very surface layers of his mind, and experienced discontent.

Yes, she now had what she wanted. No, it was not what she had wanted, after all. She did not mind the darkness, having never much cared for the sun. What irked her was that she had worked so hard and come so far, and yet others were set over her who had done *nothing*, who had been handed the world on a plate. Others who knew less than she, whose kin had not kept the dark flame burning for so many generations, were valued more than she was.

It was not fair. It ate at her like a grub.

Argastos had gone to play with them again – to *woo* them, as he termed it. She was here, willing and ready, and he had gone in search of younger flesh to taste. Younger and more ignorant.

She could feel him at the heart of things, and she wanted to go to him, but he had forbidden it. *Await my commands*, he had told her, and she would be so happy to do just that if only she felt valued and appreciated.

And, as she brooded on that a while, a new wave of thoughts seemed to insinuate itself into her mind. *He does not deserve me.*

That was a shocking thought. She froze as it came to her, as surprised as if it had issued entirely from outside her. Yet did it not mesh with the gears of her own train of thoughts so perfectly?

This thought of gears, so ugly and inappropriate, threw her. *That* was why he did not value her, because her Aptitude clung to her like a stench. She was not worthy of Argastos, and yet he had taken her in . . .

Because he had no other servants. What sort of a master lives like this?

Again that intrusion into her mind, and yet was it not true?

You are Helma Bartrer, Mistress of the Great College, after all. You are a rare gem, one to be valued, and he does not appreciate you. You have been deceived in him. He is not worthy of a servant such as you.

She shuddered, feeling for a moment that her thoughts were not her own. But surely her own thoughts had been leading her in just such a direction ever since she had come here. It was just the speed and the distance she had travelled that had startled her.

There are other masters, if you must have one, she found herself considering. *But Argastos is a broken thing. You must confront him.*

Now she was frightened. Confront Argastos? The thought of his wrath was terrifying. He could destroy her, unmake her. He would hang her grimy robes among his trophies and forget her. No, no, she was his servant, and lucky to be that. She could not ask for more. She was not fit to be more.

And for a moment there was a new voice in her head, sharp as the smell of acid, and it said, *Oh, give it up. You don't have the faintest idea how to go about this.*

She froze, in that half-place, in that half-light, thinking, *Am I going mad now?* And this was her own thought, beyond contest. And even after that: *Would that make me more what he wanted?*

But then the assault of new thoughts resumed, and their tenor had changed. *Yes, I am not worthy. I am a slave, Argastos's slave. Yes, he does not value me, but I'm a slave and he's my master. It's not my* place *to complain.* And it was as though there was some other voice inside her mind protesting this, but being overruled. *But if I'm unworthy, what about the girl, hm? How much more is she undeserving of the honours he has given her? She doesn't even* want *them! That idiot child Cheerwell Maker has done nothing in her entire life to earn his love, and yet he woos her, he offers her the world. More fool her if she won't take it.*

I hate her. She realized this was true. *In all the world I hate nothing more than I hate Cheerwell Maker, who has stolen Argastos's affections from me.* It was strange to hear herself lay out her thoughts so clearly, but it was true, so true. That loathsome girl who did not know her own luck, *she* was the undeserving one.

She had come here to steal Argastos away.

Yes, of course she has. Oh, she plays at being unwilling, but she's a clever whore, that one. She will lead him on and lead him on, and then she'll turn on him when she has run him ragged, strip him of his power and destroy him – and then waltz back to Collegium, never caring what she has destroyed. I have to save him from her. I have to make him understand what she is.

She opened her eyes, having realized they had been closed. Everything was so very clear to her now.

Slowly, step by step, she began navigating the buried maze towards Argastos.

That's it, her mind whispered to her. *And when you have shown him what the Maker girl is, that scheming little witch, how he will reward you! How he will finally see you for what you are, for who else will his affections light on, if not you?*

A warm feeling suffused her, despite the chill of her surroundings. Argastos, broad-shouldered and brave, warrior-hero of legend, would look on her with his beautiful white eyes and finally know her for what she was. That image of him was strong in her mind, the war leader in his pale mail and dark cloak, the man who had fought back the Worm.

Her feet led her without error, twisting and turning through the root-snarled tunnels of his barrow. She only half-saw the skulls embedded in the walls, eyes and mouths stopped with earth, the bones and rusted shards of armour underfoot. She had eyes only for the visions of her own mind.

And she was suddenly before him, as he sat at the heart of his domain, and she let her eyes feast on him, strong and silent and wise, and then something wrenched within her mind, something seemed to fall from her eyes, and for a brief second she saw him as he really was.

Not merely a corpse, but what a corpse would become if it were buried forever underground and not allowed to rot: a peat-black, bone-hard, withered thing, and yet those eyes, those white and living eyes, rolling in the gaping sockets . . .

She screamed, recoiling, and something unfurled in her mind, striking at that withered thing from an ambush swift and fierce as any scorpion's sting or mantis's reach.

Argastos was abruptly standing, dragging his facade of a living man about him, but reeling, hurt, furious, and yet he barely saw her. Even then, he hardly noticed her presence at all, save as he might notice a gnat singing past his ear.

He lashed out. It was a reflexive gesture as much as anything. Even as he destroyed her, Helma Bartrer was wretchedly aware that this was not *personal*.

And as she fell into darkness, as his ancient mind extinguished hers, she realized that they were no longer alone. The girl, that despised girl, was there with them, having appeared from nowhere, and the Wasp bitch was with her. And, even as the two of them attacked him, Helma's last thought was that Argastos still valued them more than he had ever valued her.

'This place was once the hub of my new trading cartel,' the bearded Fly-kinden announced grandly. 'I took the good stuff out when we set sail. The rest, the Wasps got.'

Those words caught the notice of his audience, a couple of hundred pairs of eyes lifting towards him, if they had not been on him already.

'Which means,' he went on, 'that they won't be back soon to search it, I'm wagering. Eventually, yes, but not soon.'

He was standing halfway up the steps that led to the upper level, in order to be better seen. The ground floor was not quite full, not quite standing room only, but it was close. When Tomasso had acquired the lease on this warehouse, he had reckoned that it included more space than his family would require in this generation. He had not planned on storing Spiderlands merce-naries, who took up more room than expected.

Their leader was a pale, lean Spider in dark mail that Tomasso could tell was good quality, despite the battering it had taken. His name was Morkaris.

Up top, on the roof, Despard was keeping watch, hidden as best she could and relying on her good night vision in the encroaching darkness to warn of approaching Wasp patrols. The fighting itself was not close, now. Morkaris and his people had broken away from the main Spiderlands contingent early, and moved from cover to cover until Tomasso had spotted them and brought them here.

They looked at him with naked distrust, which was understandable in the recently betrayed. They were beaten and bloodied – Morkaris himself had a bandage about his forehead which was dark with drying blood. Many of his followers looked worse off.

Hard men, though. Tomasso knew the type, for he had done business along the Spiderlands coast for years and, with a Fly-kinden crew, he had hired muscle often enough.

'You want thanks, or you want paying?' the Spider leader asked him. The ragged pause before he said it showed just how tired he was. 'Or you want to see how much you can get for us from the Wasps?'

'I have a modest proposal.' Tomasso put his hands on his hips, surveying the mercenaries proprietorially. 'It's not much, I warn you, but in this market a handful of beans makes a wealthy man, as they say. You're for hire, or you were. And you signed on with the Aldanrael to come and sack Collegium.'

'Not Collegium, specifically,' Morkaris answered, mangling the name slightly. 'But, yes, what of it?'

'And because you're for hire, rather than sworn to the Aldanrael, when everything turned inexplicably to turds you got right out and left your paymaster mistress to it.'

The Spider shrugged, while his men remained silent, listening to every word and watching their chief for a lead.

'And you're in Collegium still, but they're rounding up all the Spider-kinden they can get their hands on – not just your lot either, I saw men and women who've lived here all their lives getting grabbed on sight. So you're well and truly pissed on, and no mistake.'

'Is this going anywhere?' Morkaris demanded sharply.

'Yes, it's going as far as this: I can't help you. The Wasps are going to get you sooner or later.' Tomasso shrugged. He registered the impact of his words on many faces. 'I think your men are loyal to you, Morkaris. They're still by your side, rather than just each man for himself. Are you as loyal to them, I wonder?'

'What's that supposed to mean?'

Tomasso clasped his hands together which, in much of the Spiderlands, was the archetypical gesture of a merchant putting forward a deal. 'I said I can't help you, Morkaris. Them, I can help. Maybe, I hope.' His gesture took in the far end of the warehouse, where certain groups of the mercenaries had set themselves up. Tomasso was used to quick counts, and he reckoned he had two hundred and sixteen Spider-kinden here, with thirty-nine Scorpions and a score of other assorted miscellany. 'No Spider within these walls is safe, but what about the rest? I've spoken with a merchant of the city whom I deal with. He runs big overland caravans – good stuff, lots of guards – and it's a dangerous time. No surprise he'd have a lot of guards on his payroll. Naturally, the Wasps won't want a large private militia of sellswords in the city, so our man will agree to get shot of them, kick them out of the city quick as you like. Of course, we'll get you out of that Spiderlands kit and into something a bit more local. We can sort that.'

Morkaris's expression was eloquent on the subject of how uncertain this plan sounded.

'I know, I know,' Tomasso admitted. 'But it's that or – what? Maybe you tell me your own plan, and we can compare notes?'

He sensed the mood, having been a leader for a long time. The non-Spiders had suddenly been given the gift of hope where they had none before. The rest . . .

Looking at those faces, pale, bruised, lean, yet drawn in every line with the elegance that Spiders took for granted: men and women in equal number, and all of them hearing that death sentence confirmed, it was an effort of will for Tomasso to face them with equanimity.

And Morkaris asked, 'What do you want, Fly? What do you want from the rest of us?'

Tomasso smiled slightly. 'Nothing but what you make a living at. I need you to fight – fight the Wasps specifically. Does that sweeten the deal?'

Morkaris glanced back over the disparate mercenaries, his followers. No doubt his mind was working hard, trying to prise more options out of their situation, but in truth Tomasso wasn't sure there were any.

'You want us to die for you,' the Spider leader said bitterly.

'Wouldn't you rather die for *something*?' Tomasso asked him.

Over the years, Ant tacticians had devoted much time to the unfolding of an army, the perfect elegance of thousands of soldiers moving as one, representing the highest expression of Ant-kinden culture.

So it was that the Sarnesh came in sight of the Imperial Eighth Army towards evening, and began ordering themselves by pitching a cursory camp from which they could mobilize within moments, assembling their artillery, arranging themselves in a widespread formation in case the Empire decided to bring its greatshotters to bear. It was a sight to make an Ant poet weep.

Tactician Milus was unmoved. The purest expression of the Ant way of life meant nothing to him unless he *won*.

It was entirely possible that the Wasps would have a go at any moment with their superior artillery – the Sarnesh were well within range. A lot depended on whether the Wasps wanted to fight now at twilight, when nobody was at their best but when the Ant-kinden's superior discipline and linked minds would add up to a significant advantage, or whether they would wait until morning. It was a decision Milus was not happy leaving in the hands of the enemy, but he himself did not want to try an immediate attack. Therefore it would be the decision of General Roder instead.

Lissart had known something about Roder, at least, and he would question her again after he retired to his tent. He had ordered her brought along for a number of reasons: she could advise on anything unexpected the Empire might do, or she could even be used as a bargaining counter, perhaps. In the hidden darkness of Milus's mind, where his fellows were not allowed, there was also the reason that she made him feel better: a tame Imperial agent he could bully and intimidate, and yet a woman who possessed a quick, biting conversation that none of his kin was likely to reward him with. And also expendable – useful but ultimately expendable. What more could a man ask for?

His commanders were reporting in, one by one, confirming their readiness, their part within the plan – whether that plan called for a battle now or tomorrow. Milus himself had obsessively pored over the reports of the first clash between his people and the Eighth at the siege of Malkan's Folly. There the Wasps had been securely dug in, and the Ants had tried their traditional frontal assault against that well-defended position. Here, however, the Eighth had been marching to meet them, so would have only the most cursory fortifications. Here also, the Ants were ready to disperse over an enormous area and come at the Wasps from all sides, giving no target for the Wasps to mass their superior artifice against . . . well, perhaps one target, but that was all part of the plan. Attacking in open order like that would be suicide for any other kinden and, because he was not so trapped in the usual thinking of his kinden, Milus was still concerned about the rush of casualties that his men would suffer when they did form up in the moments before they struck. Even with perfectly linked minds, it was a formidable piece of manoeuvring to get right, and there would be an uncomfortably long period when the Ants were still not quite together, and yet were packed close enough for the Wasps to unleash everything they had.

But that was the plan, and he had no better one. If he was lucky, his distraction would draw a lot of Imperial attention and buy his soldiers a little more time, saving a few lives. Sarnesh lives, of course.

There was one section of his army that would not be attacking in open order – because it lacked the hard discipline required for such niceties. They would go marching in shoulder to shoulder – or as close to that as non-Ants could ever manage. They would form the centre of Milus's attack. If he could have painted targets on them, he would have done so.

Tell me about Roder, he had encouraged Lissart. And, with a little encouragement, she had. Was he a clever man? She wouldn't say clever, precisely. Not a stupid man and nobody's fool. He was a solid planner of battles but not a man to rely on untested ingenuity. That had proved to be a strength when he had been fighting the Spiders at Seldis. It was a fool's game to try and out-weave Spider-kinden, after all – your clever plans would turn out to be part of their even more devious ones. Instead, he had trusted to the known capabilities of his troops and his armaments, and beaten them on the field deftly and brutally, before moving to invest their city. He had left precious little room for all their vaunted plots and trickery.

Milus could predict, therefore, that Roder would understand exactly how the Ants intended to come at him. And yet, at the same time, a tempting target for the Wasp artillery would not go unheeded, for even if those close-grouped soldiers were not Sarnesh, they were still a threat. All those Mynans, all that rabble from Princep Salma, they would still kill Wasps if they got close to them. Roder could not ignore them, therefore.

That they would die in their droves did not concern Milus. It was a battle, after all, and non-Sarnesh casualties did not overly worry him.

And there was one more thing he had learned from Lissart. Roder carried a grudge born from a narrowly failed assassination attempt outside Seldis.

Every Spider-kinden that Princep had vomited up for military service – and there were quite a few of them – would be positioned front and centre in that nice, tempting block of miscellaneous infantry. Oh, probably Roder was too much the professional to let that sway him, but Milus lost nothing by offering such a bait.

By nightfall it appeared that Roder would be spending the hours of darkness digging in, putting up what makeshift fortifications he could. The scouts of both sides would have a busy night of it, with Fly-kinden trying to dodge each other's attention to get a good look at the enemy. The entire Sarnesh force would be sleeping in its armour, ready to wake at a moment's notice, but by then Milus reckoned he had the measure of his opponent. He told his commanders to move the artillery three hours before dawn, and to expect the Wasp engines to start pounding them an hour after that.

History in the making, Milus knew. *On such decisions rests the fate of Sarn and, by extension, all the Lowlands.*

It was a shame – a predictable shame – that Collegium had not been able to hold out, but, if tomorrow's battle gave him the opportunity, he would enjoy the gratitude on the Collegiates' faces when he came to their aid. Sarn had been following the Beetle lead meekly for far too long. It was now about time that they renegotiated the details of their partnership.

Thirty-Nine

They left Averic in an interrogation room – not strapped to the table, yet, but with his wrists chained to the wall above his head, his hands bound palm to palm to stifle his sting.

He and Eujen had been marched under heavy escort across half the city to the district around the north gate, which was securely Wasp-held. Despite Imperial caution, there had been almost no sound of fighting on the still night air – and what little he had noticed came from the wrong direction, presumably the ongoing squabble between the Wasps and their erstwhile allies.

He was detained in a counting house off the market square, which the Second Army had seized for its use – appropriated seeming too polite a phrase. He assumed that the paraphernalia of interrogation that he had been left to ponder on had been installed recently. It seemed unlikely to have been a previous fixture.

They wanted him to reflect on all the ways they could persuade him, he knew. Even though he had never operated such machines himself, nor even watched another subjected to their mercies, he still had a clearer idea than any Collegiate as to just what extent his interrogators would go to. The physiology he had learned here at the College further established his grounding in just how much varied damage the human body could sustain.

But they had given him time. As a student of the College, solving intellectual problems was supposedly something he could do. So he stared at the table, at the rack of implements – none of them exactly spotless, for he was not the first citizen to find himself at the sharp end of the Empire's inquiries – and he considered his options.

After half an hour, by his best reckoning, an engineer came in to glance cursorily over the tools, while an officer came to look similarly over Averic. A captain, he noted. That told him precisely how important or otherwise the Empire felt he was.

'Well, now,' the captain remarked, eyes studying Averic, assessing tolerances. 'I'm going to ask you a set of questions, boy – once as you are now, and once on the table. After that I'll go and consider your answers, and then perhaps we'll go over everything again and put the table to some use, just to ensure that there's nothing you're holding back. But, then, I'd guess you already expected that, being what you are?'

'To be honest I expected a debriefing,' Averic said. His voice was steady, almost conversational.

The engineer stopped, a tool under his hand clicking metal on metal.

The captain's face remained without expression. 'Repeat.'

'I apologize. I expected a debriefing, sir. I've been amongst the Beetles for a year, sir. Proper procedure is hard to hold on to.'

'You expect me to believe that you're on the books?' The captain's insignia marked him as Army Intelligence, but he could easily be Rekef Inlander as well.

'My name is Averic, sir. You'll find it there.' Still so very steady, every breath measured carefully and his fear fought down. Because he might just live. Because they might just leave him intact. Because it might be *true*.

They had approached him, when the Second had marched on Collegium the time before. First a Wasp woman, then a Beetle man, calling him one of their own, telling him that he had been sent into Collegium under cover, the best sort of cover. He had believed himself a student but instead he had been intended as a spy.

They had told him the time had come to betray his fellows. He had believed them then. Perhaps he still did. Perhaps it was true.

He was unlikely to find out any other way than this.

His family, he had believed, were liberals who disagreed with the Empire's belligerent relations with its neighbours. He had therefore been sent to Collegium to learn the Beetles' ways, so that he could bring them back to the Empire.

Or else he had been sent to Collegium as an agent, living a lie all unknowingly, but the purpose was the same: to learn the Beetles' ways and bring them back. The seeming and the real danced about each other like Spider-kinden Aristoi, and he could not say which was true. For sure, he had turned aside from the Black and Gold when called on, but that bridge might not be burned. He could yet live. *They might not torture me.*

The captain's face was still as blank as glass. 'Why didn't you come forward once we took the city?'

'There wasn't the chance, before this kicked off,' he found himself saying. 'And when it did, there was no chance of getting word out.' A lie, an unbelievable lie. 'So I did what I could, sir.'

A snort. 'And what was that?'

'I brought their leader to you, didn't I, sir?'

The captain considered him like an anatomist regarding a cadaver. 'Did you,' he said without inflection. 'Averic, is it? Well, perhaps we'll get you to the table right away, boy, just in case, mind. Because if you turn out to be trying to save your worthless hide by lying, I'm going to take it out of you a finger-joint at a time. You don't mind, do you, soldier? You don't mind my going to make sure?'

Despite his position, Averic managed an awkward shrug. 'I'd expect it, sir.'

A couple of soldiers marched in at the captain's direction and, without complaint, Averic let them strap him to the table, his hands secured palm-down on the metal surface, where he would burn only himself if he tried to sting.

Then they left him to his thoughts.

He thoughts were mostly, *Eujen, I'm sorry.*

Eventually the captain came back, engineer and all, and stared at him, and Averic met his stare levelly, all his fear and regret pushed deep down. There was nothing more he could do for himself now.

'You,' the captain told him, 'are now going to have to answer more questions than *anyone* actually lying on the table.' Responding to an irritable gesture, the engineer began releasing him, a band at a time, grumbling under his breath. 'Such as what the pits you've been doing all this time. And don't give me that rot about your precious cover. A spy that won't break cover *ever* is no use to anyone.' From the man's disgusted tone, it seemed that Averic's case was only reinforcing the man's past experience with agents. 'For now, get yourself cleaned up. Get some food inside you. We can go over your sorry story in the morning.'

Something rang leaden in Averic's heart, on hearing that. *So it's true,* he thought numbly. *I was a spy after all. And my family: were they victims of this trick, too? Or did they know? Perhaps my own family didn't trust me enough, but let me come here still believing that I was merely seeking peace and understanding.*

And that is what I found.

Small wonder, then, that I became what they intended me to feign.

He swung his legs over the side of the table, gripping his hands together to work the stiffness out of them.

They must have reckoned that weak, insipid Collegiate philosophy could never overcome my kinden's love of Empire.

'Thank you, sir,' he said. 'I'd like very much to return to uniform.'

The nod the captain gave him was proprietorial and pleased, and it made Averic hurt inside.

He didn't have time to go rouse a quartermaster for some armour, but they found him a uniform tunic that fitted well enough, and then he received directions to the barracks which, as soon as he was out of sight, he totally ignored. Instead, he circled back to the repurposed counting house, doing his best to look like a soldier who had every business to be there.

The rear door was left unguarded – a low little affair meant for deliveries, leading to a cramped backroom store that the Wasps had cluttered with furniture removed from elsewhere in the house. Averic stepped lightly through it, constructing in his mind the layout of the place. The clerk's room he had been taken to could not be too far from here, and if they were now questioning Eujen . . .

Ahead of him, someone crossed the main counting house floor, an engineer from the look of him. Averic ducked back out of sight, realizing he would not have the nerve to bluff this out. Stealth it must be.

There came voices from outside, but just the usual murmur of soldiers in a camp, he guessed. The thought of what he would do once he had Eujen out of the building was something he was staving off, moment to moment. They were a long way from anywhere that could be called safe, and even though there were Beetles in the Imperial army, Eujen would never pass for one . . .

In front, a line of four doors, two of them standing open. If Eujen was to be found easily, it would be here. Averic inched closer, ears alert for the sound of anyone else entering the building.

He heard a clatter of metal from behind one of the closed doors.

Before his thoughts could deflect him, he was at the door and hauling it open, a hand extended to sting. The suddenness of his action surprised him, leaving him bewildered and shaken.

There lay Eujen, right there.

They had him secured to a table, and the injuries he bore so far were shallow and superficial, the result of a precise art that aimed at combining longevity with pain. They had not got to that later stage, where a subject's willpower is broken by irreversible damage. Two fingers of one hand were splayed at broken angles with exacting care, but the rest of the work had mostly been pressure on joints and a little surface cutting.

Eujen was weeping quietly. He had been stretching the fingers of his other hand towards the torturer's tools – knives and clamps and irons – that had been left almost within reach. One was on the floor, nudged perhaps by the furthest extent of one finger. His eyes were pressed closed, his body shaking with misery.

Averic set to work instantly, loosening his friend's bonds, ignoring the blood on Eujen's dark flesh. The Beetle's shuddering calmed, as he worked until the last manacle loosened. Then Averic met his eyes.

'You're here,' Eujen whispered, his eyes flicking to the black and gold uniform.

'Don't you doubt me, not ever,' the Wasp told him. 'We're getting clear now.' An awkward pause. 'Can you walk?'

'Going to have to.' Eujen lurched off the table, grabbing one-handed at it for support, and stood a moment with his face twisted in pain. After a deep breath, he forced himself to stand upright. 'I've had worse.' And the patent untruth of it almost made Averic weep. 'We're moving?'

'We are.' Averic was already at the door leading to the counting-house floor, and still nobody had come to continue their work on Eujen. They were leaving him to stew, of course, to consider his fate, and the door was unguarded because . . . well, because Averic's kinden were contemptuous of anything a manacled Beetle might achieve.

'Averic,' Eujen whispered. 'I'm sorry, I told . . . I told them . . .' His eyes glinted bright with fear and the memory of pain.

'It doesn't matter,' Averic told him, and led him by the arm towards the rear door. At every moment he knew that someone would walk in, that he would have to fight: kill or be killed. His luck, stretched beyond credibility, would snap back at him, surely.

He opened the door and they stepped out into the night, and his luck snapped there and then, and irrevocably.

They left Eujen standing, but the threat of Averic's sting meant that three men jumped him immediately as he stepped out into daylight, wrestling him to the ground with professional viciousness, wrenching his arms back at the joints to keep him down.

Half a dozen soldiers were what he and Eujen rated, he saw. There was the captain, too, and no less a man than Colonel Cherten himself had come to witness the entertainment, but there was no indication that either intended to get their hands dirty. Half a dozen soldiers, two of them standing back with levelled snapbows, all waiting outside the back door.

'Well done, Captain,' Cherten acknowledged. 'I applaud your instincts.'

'Thank you, sir.' The captain looked moderately pleased with himself, but not over much. It was not so great a triumph as all that. 'Back to the tables with them?'

'No, I have another use for them, and I need them for it now,' Cherten told him. 'I think we need to break the morale of their friends in the College. Have them secured and I'll take them off your hands.'

By the time the Antspider ascended to the courtyard wall there was already quite a crowd there, jostling and craning, and most of them with snapbows loaded and directed towards the Imperial lines.

'Are they mustering?' she demanded, though she could hear no sound of it. Surely there would be the rumble of the Sentinel engines; surely the movement of a large number of men could he heard on such a still night.

'Lighting up the place, is what they're doing,' Castre Gorenn told her.

Straessa opened her mouth to question that, but it was true. On a rooftop just overlooking the Imperial barricade directly facing the College gate, the Wasps had set out lanterns and lamps as though they were celebrating something.

'What does it mean?' she asked quietly.

'Nothing good,' the Dragonfly guessed, and Straessa had to agree.

Out of uniform, wearing only a nightshirt that hung short of his knees, Gerethwy stumbled into place beside her. He carried his snapbow, for what it was worth, and for a moment she was tempted to order him straight back down again. His face was drawn, hollow-cheeked through lack of sleep and from the recurrent stabs of pain he felt from the fingers he no longer possessed. Right now, he was plainly of no use to anyone.

But it would shame him, she knew, and so she left it. *See, I'm a terrible officer. Why does nobody else realize that?*

'Is that a flag they're bringing?' someone asked, and her attention returned to the rooftop. There were a fair number of soldiers there, and they carried some sort of bundle of staves. Her stomach went cold, wondering what new kind of weapons the Empire's engineers might have dreamt up.

'Should I try a shot?' Gorenn asked.

'At this range? Too far even for you, surely?' Straessa pointed out.

Gorenn shrugged irritably, and Straessa was about to suggest she try it anyway, when a Fly-kinden piped up, 'Spears. They've got spears.'

'Have to be bloody long ones, then,' a Beetle youth remarked. Whilst he earned himself a murmur of laughter, Straessa felt something grip her far beyond the nebulous threat of a new invention.

Not new . . . A real old-fashioned Wasp tradition, isn't that right?

'What are they doing?' More than a few people were asking the question, as the Wasps began setting out the long, barbed-headed weapons in pairs, fitting them to sockets they had already set in the flat roof. Four spears, forming two crosses.

Straessa was gripping the edge of the courtyard wall so tightly that her knuckles were white. Her whole world had contracted to that one bright spot ahead where the Wasps had cast out the darkness so that they could put on a show.

'Crossed pikes,' someone observed, and the conversation died, word by word, until almost everyone was silent. Of course, there were a few who had neglected their studies, but Straessa did not feel like educating them just then.

She remembered Averic talking about this, once – he had so seldom spoken about his home. He had been a little drunk, his pale face discoloured with bruises from a beating he had received, but had not risen to. She – or was it Raullo? – had said something about wagering that sort of thing wouldn't go on back where he had lived. He had then explained to them just what did go on. It had been a lapse, of course, and once the over-hasty words were spoken he had plainly wanted to take them back.

There was a skill to it, he had explained. To drive the spear-head into the side of the abdomen by careful degrees, so that whatever damage it did would agonize without killing – to lever it through the ribs without gashing the lungs, and then to ram it into the tricep and biceps, so that, once the crossing was complete, the victim hung from the spear-shafts, with the hooked heads embedded in the solid flesh of the upper arms. A soldier who could perform all that reliably was guaranteed a sergeant's rank badge.

Someone – either slow on the uptake or just absurdly optimistic – now moaned with horrified realization, as two new figures were led up onto the roof.

Eujen. Averic.

'I can't see Serena,' someone was saying, some friend of the Fly-kinden officer's.

'Then she's the lucky one,' Straessa whispered. 'Gereth . . .'

The Woodlouse was staring out at that illuminated rooftop, fingering his snapbow, but even on his best day he couldn't have made the shot.

. . . rammed through the body, inch by searing inch, an anatomy lesson for sadists, then hung . . .

The officer in charge seemed to be taking some pains

explaining to his prisoners what was going to happen to them. Of course, Averic must already know in great detail . . . while Eujen always did have a quick imagination.

Straessa levelled her snapbow, sighting it on those distant figures. The previous day's exchange had demonstrated that she could not possibly hit her mark, or probably even make the roof at all, and she would get in only one – perhaps two – shots, before the Wasps made sure she could not spoil their fun.

And she couldn't shoot Eujen. She didn't have it in her, despite everything. How many times had she joked that the thing he needed most was a shot in the head, and here they were . . . and she couldn't.

'Gorenn, you said . . .' She watched as Eujen and Averic had their hands freed, but of course you would have to have unbound wrists to go up on the pikes. 'You said you could manage the shot. Can you?'

The Dragonfly looked round as though noticing Straessa for the first time. 'Of course. Why not?'

Straessa saw them unsocket the spears again, in preparation for their bloody work. Setting the weapons up in advance like that was part of the ritual: to make the victims – and the onlookers – understand and know fear.

'Founder's Mark, do it,' she spat. *I'm sorry. I'm so sorry, Eujen. I wish you a clean death. That's all I can do now.*

Atop the roof overlooking the barricade, Cherten peered into the night, over at the College, seeing movement without detail along the wall.

'Well, why not?' he addressed his prisoners. 'After all, you came to negotiate a surrender. I will now show your fellows what terms they can expect if they continue to resist the Empire.'

Eujen did not look at him, staring at his own feet, but Averic glowered, twisting in the grip of the soldiers who held him.

Cherten favoured him with a cold smile. 'Yes, the greater of the two traitors first. Put the pikes in him now.'

He turned back to regard the dark bulk of the College and

opened his mouth to shout something at his audience there, and an arrow pierced his throat, through to the fletching.

And on the College wall, Straessa cursed and demanded, 'What did you *do*?'

Castre Gorenn stared at her. 'Wasn't that . . . Wait, what did you *mean* for me to do?'

There was a moment when that single arrow became a full-scale attack in the minds of most of the Wasps there, and Averic seized on it.

He tried to put an elbow in the throat of the man holding him, but slammed it painfully into the soldier's chest instead. It was enough, sending his captor reeling away from him, and then Averic's hands flashed, knocking down the man with the pike who stood right next to him, still staring dumbly at Cherten's body. The barbed spear ended up in Averic's hands, and he lashed it across the face of the man holding Eujen.

'Go!' he shouted, and because Eujen plainly had no idea how or where to go, he grabbed the Beetle student tight and threw them both off the roof towards the splintered architecture of the barricade.

His wings flashed, but Eujen was heavy, and the two of them barely cleared the barricade at all, before tumbling to the ground. There were shouts from behind and above – at least some of them directed at the escaping prisoners and—

Averic's heart soared. Eujen was on his feet and already beginning to lumber towards the College, stumbling at first, but gaining momentum as he went. And Averic flew after him, turning in the air to spit a scatter of stingshot at those he knew must be following.

'Get the doors open!' Straessa yelled. 'Get . . .' and then she had simply vaulted the edge of the wall, hanging by her hands for a moment and then dropping. Gorenn was with her, and a couple of Fly-kinden, and she heard the rattle and groan as the doors were unbarred and opening behind her.

Her feet pounded the flagstones, and she was already trying to level her snapbow, but it was a futile effort. Ahead she saw bright flashes that must be Averic's sting – and they were answered in kind, for the Wasps were in the air and descending fast on the fugitives. The distance between them – from Straessa to the escapees – seemed immense and ever-growing however fast she ran, like in some terrible dream.

Beside her, Gorenn was loosing another arrow, yet barely slowing.

She saw Averic turn again, kicking into the air, hands on fire with golden light. Then he had lurched sideways, and she realized he had been struck. There were snapbowmen still on the roof, and they had a clear shot. Averic was down on one knee, and she saw Eujen falter, slowing as if to turn – slowing to be caught.

'Run!' came Averic's high, clear voice. He had not even looked back, but his hands flashed and flamed, burning up his life in crackling Art.

He was down. It was so sudden Straessa did not even see the transition, but her Wasp friend was a motionless heap on the ground when her eyes found him again . . . and Eujen was still labouring towards her. He had spotted her now, and his expression was like a drowning man's.

There were Wasps behind him, practically hovering over his shoulders. One spun away with an arrow punched through his mail. The other dropped down to the ground, snapbow levelled.

'Eujen!' Straessa shouted. 'Go left!'

He lurched – it was nothing more than that – but she was already bringing her own weapon up, pulling the trigger, her hands so steady they should have belonged to someone else. The Wasp soldier stood up suddenly, then fell back down, and Eujen . . .

Eujen was picking himself up unsteadily, weaving oddly. His

lurch had not been in response to her call. He had been shot.

She tried to run faster to reach him, to compensate for the fact that he was no longer running at all. The next two bolts that struck him, she saw only in the shuddering of his body before he collapsed.

She was screaming, and there were other Wasps ahead, but she had brought a boiling mass of students in her wake, and now the snapbow bolts were flying in both directions and the Wasps had not been ready for a Collegiate sally.

She reached Eujen's body, saw him still moving, still clawing to stand up, and she took his hand, took his arm, but the sound he made when she tried to get him to his feet curdled her insides, and she let go.

'Gereth!' she called out, and of course the Woodlouse was there, without even a snapbow in hand. But he had come after her, and now he was gathering up Eujen, lifting the Beetle's bulk as though it was nothing, while soldiers of the Student Company flanked him and loosed their bolts at the Wasps to keep them back.

Straessa spared one look for Averic, but he was too far away, and lying too still . . . and she knew that to go after his corpse would be to run into a killing ground.

'Fall back,' she spat. 'Back for the College.'

The surgeons had been and gone before she was allowed to see him, coming and going behind closed doors as if they were merely ghosts or rumours. When Straessa finally forced her way in, after she had exhausted the protests of the staff, she found the same two Fly-kinden tending him as had watched over Stenwold Maker earlier. Sperra, the woman from Princep, and of course Sartaea te Mosca, her friend. Eujen's friend.

There was such grief on the little woman's face that Straessa thought he must have died.

When she crouched beside him, though, kneeling on the floor by his mattress, she could just hear his breathing, picking it out from the laboured breath of the other casualties there because she recognized it, even diminished as it was.

'Tell me,' she whispered.

Te Mosca shook her head slightly. 'We can't know, dear one, I'm sorry. There's hope . . .' Her tone belied her words.

'They said if he hadn't been a Beetle, he'd not have made it as far as the walls,' Sperra explained, briskly businesslike because Eujen was just one more injured Collegiate to her. 'They've dosed him up with Instar but sometimes it doesn't take, and sometimes it makes things worse.'

'It seems that medical science has come full circle, until it's as vague as my magic,' te Mosca murmured.

Sperra bent over Eujen's chest and listened carefully, before noting something down on a scroll. 'Don't do anything stupid. Just let him lie there . . . and let whatever happens happen. Make a nuisance of yourself, and it'll make him worse.' She stood up for a moment, swaying slightly, and Straessa wondered when this woman had last slept.

Te Mosca squeezed the other Fly's arm – small support but all she could wring from the situation – and Sperra nodded and moved on to the next bed, where her big Ant friend was sitting halfway up and sipping gingerly at a jug of water.

Eujen's dead weight lay beside Straessa, and she would have needed the instruments of the Apt to register his chest rising and falling. His colour was a ghastly greyish hue, as though the blood had congealed inside him. His exposed skin bore at least a score of lacerations, many still weeping.

She took his good hand, finding it clammy and too cold, and she sat there beside his bed for as long as she could stand it, listening to the weakening falter of his breath. Nobody was counting, but she reckoned that she lasted less than twenty minutes before she wanted to scream out her anger and frustration at the vaulted ceiling.

She stood up without warning, and te Mosca looked up at her, concerned.

'Straessa?'

'I'm sorry, I can't just . . . I can't just sit here and wait.'

The Fly took in her expression. 'Please, he needs you.'

'I can't. Not for him, not for you.' She was shaking a little, with a chill that had come from his cool hand.

'Straessa, please, don't go and do anything—'

'I can't just wait for him to die!' she burst out – heedless of the other patients, or of Eujen himself. But it was a true confession, and every moment she spent there, wondering if there would even be a next breath, was winding her up like a clockwork, tighter and tighter, until she could not remain still any longer. Until she had to act.

Out on the courtyard wall again, with the night sky above her – was it only a couple of hours past midnight? – she stared out towards the Wasp lines. She had escaped Eujen's deathbed, but the scratchy, failing whisper of his breathing had come outside with her, as though his comatose body was hung just behind her, whichever way she turned.

And she knew only this one thing: *I have to act.*

Castre Gorenn, who seemed to need no sleep at all, was eyeing her doubtfully, but then she used that same expression for so much she encountered in Collegium. She had left her home and come to an alien world of Beetle-kinden politics and artifice, and for her the Wasps were probably the only familiar faces in the whole city.

'I'm going over the wall,' Straessa told her, and the look that appeared on the Dragonfly's face was one of pure understanding. 'I'm going to fight the war.'

No objections, no raising of the alarm. Gorenn just nodded because it made sense to her.

'I've fought as an Ant for long enough,' the Antspider stated, unbuckling her breastplate. 'Now I'm going to fight as a Spider.' She set the metal down carefully and stripped away her buff coat as well, leaving only her dark tunic beneath. 'Besides, I'm far better with a sword than I ever was with a snapbow.' She took a deep breath. 'I'm going to kill General Tynan.' There, the words were said.

'Do you want me to come with you?'

Straessa stared at the Dragonfly. She had already considered the likely outcome of her mission, and it was plain that Gorenn concurred, but that offer had still been made.

And it seemed so tempting, but Straessa wanted no more weighing on her conscience, not just then. 'You hold your post, soldier. I'll be back before morning.'

And then she was over the wall and away, with assassination on her mind.

In the extensive cellars of the College library building there was one spur of rooms never used to store books. The chill was insidious there, far more so than any obvious factor could account for, and the walls ran perpetually with an acrid condensation. The College had tried to use the little chambers there as an ice room, but the resulting ice always smelled odd. People reported hearing strange scratchings sometimes. It had become a standard student dare to spend the night there: the Inapt claimed it was haunted, and the laughing Apt found it a safe place to titillate themselves with daring thoughts of the old days once the lanterns were put out.

But, being a place of education, among each generation of students there had always been a few inquiring minds who had been curious and analytical enough to work out precisely what was going on, to solve the mystery and declare it anything but supernatural, although they were largely ignored.

As luck would have it, a couple of such inquiring minds were in the Student Company garrison trapped inside the College, even then.

Forty

Milus had barely slept, or perhaps not at all. That was another thing that marked him out amongst his people – placed him on that razor-edged line between prized thinker and freak. His troops slept soundly, and would wake in an instant. Only he felt compelled to run his plans over and over, to build increasingly redundant fallback scenarios for remote possibilities. *What if they . . .?*

He went to speak with Lissart, because he could kick her awake at any hour, but she stared at him sombrely as though death had entered the tent alongside him.

'Come morning, is it?' she asked.

He nodded, his eyes on her but his mind working elsewhere.

'Good luck, then. I'm sure you Ants don't put faith in mere luck, but my people live by it.'

'I would have thought your wishes would be with the other side,' he said drily.

'That, Tactician, is because you're a humourless bastard and you don't understand me. You won't, either, however much you twist and pry.' She was in one of her brave moods, and that lifted his spirits. When she was too miserable with her lot, there was no talking to her. Her emotions seemed to swing wildly, and at their nadir they were more of a torment to her than anything he had inflicted.

'Your people out there,' he pointed out.

'Not my people now. The people I used to work for, yes.

Several minutes of inquiry teased that one out of me. I'm no Imperial. I was born in the Spiderlands.' She grimaced.

'Also the enemy,' he observed.

'Well, Tactician, let me put it this way, shall I? If the Eighth beats your army and sacks your camp and gets their hands on me, and if I can't persuade them otherwise – if they recognize who I am – then what the Rekef have at their disposal will make all your instruments and freezings and beatings look like the work of amateurs, believe me.'

She said it quite matter-of-factly, and he found her conviction genuine.

'Believe me, Tactician,' she went on, gathering speed a little, her heavy shackles clinking as she leant forward, 'I will go and act against the Wasps, I will. Set me free and I'll be yours. I'll go into their camp, I'll sabotage their machines and burn their supplies. You know how I can.'

He studied her for a long time, and into his mind crept a seditious thought, *Is that it? Have I misused this piece all this while?*

The barrier he would have to clear before trusting her to go about with her hands free was high, but had he been given enough time to think, then perhaps he could have surmounted it with sufficient safeguards. At that moment, though, he felt the ground shake and heard the distant thunder of the Wasp greatshotters.

Awake and to arms! Go rouse the cursed Mynans and that rabble from Princep! To battle, my siblings! And he was already striding out into the grey pre-dawn, with the leadshotters stalking their shells across the land, whilst his men were awake and in motion, thousands of them like gears in a perfect machine.

Behind him, Lissart's cry of frustration went almost unnoticed.

His soldiers would remain dispersed, even widening their front, daring the Wasps to sweep them aside; whilst the others – the foreigners he could not rely on – would be forming into solid ranks because they lacked the Art and the discipline to do anything else. Let the Imperial engines track them down and reap them like wheat as the Sarnesh advanced.

He strode through the effortlessly mobilizing camp, drawing his cloak tighter about him against the chill.

The battle for the Lowlands was beginning.

Tactician, change in the situation, a hurried report from one of his sentries, and an image – the hours before dawn still grey enough that he could not discern what the man was looking at. There were the campfires of the Wasps, and that blackness was . . .

Was something he had not foreseen.

He froze, letting the wheels of his mind spin, and trusting them to come up with the best solution in the seconds he had before he was required to give an order.

General Roder listened to the greatshotters as they found their rhythm, pounding out their percussion against the distant Ants. He knew what his opposite number was about, of course. The Ants would stay spread out as long as they could, to deny him a good target. Those huge engines were not really made for field battles, but he was looking forward to giving them their head before the walls of Sarn. Afterwards, perhaps, he would write a brief report on the relative merits of Mynan and Sarnesh architecture.

But, for now, the Sarnesh had made the sound decision to test him on the field, and the Eighth Army had nowhere near the fortifications it had been able to rely on at Malkan's Stand. He had set out his lines as best he could, nevertheless, with enough trenches and sharpened stakes to make any movement by the enemy a constant trial. He was also guessing that the Ants would have to mass up as they neared the Wasp lines, and that they would want to engage in close fighting, where they had an undeniable superiority. In that case the Wasps would trust to their own manoeuvrability, using the Light Airborne's wings to simply relocate the battlefield again and again, refusing to lock swords.

His fliers were taking off: some veteran Spearflights and half a dozen of the new Farsphex loaded with bombs. The Ant orthopters would be able to keep an impressive discipline and coordination in the air, but their machines were a generation out of date, by Imperial standards, and Roder was looking to secure control of the air relatively swiftly.

If the Ants stayed back, then the fighting would get bogged down into a long-range pissing contest with snapbows, which Roder reckoned he would eventually win, given his superior numbers and what he predicted would be a Wasp advantage in speed and accuracy. That would be a costly way to bring the battle to a close, though, and one that would be likely to allow the Ants to disperse and meet him again before their walls – or even attack him from behind as he invested the city. The painstaking progress the Eighth had made towards Sarn, with the Ants using minimal forces to cause maximum delay, had given him a new respect for whoever was planning their war.

Still, the Sarnesh resistance was all for nothing, since a messenger had arrived from Tynan's Second to confirm that Collegium had capitulated. The reinforcements that Sarn had presumably been hoping for were not coming. Sarn now stood alone.

There was a concentration forming in the centre of the Sarnesh lines, but his scouts suggested these were Auxillian troops, not the Ants themselves. *A distraction for the greatshotters, then.* But each death would still be one less enemy on the field, and so there was no reason not to oblige the Ants rather than attack their wide-spaced forces and squander the potency of the engines. It was as if he and the Sarnesh commander were following the same textbook, both seeing a different advantage in the same tactic, so that there were really no losers. Or nobody important, anyway.

A messenger landed nearby and ran up to him. 'General, word from the forest!'

For a moment he could not imagine what the man meant, but then it fell into place. 'The Mantids?'

'One of their women is here to speak with you, General.'

He peered through the unrelieved grey, trying to pinpoint her, but spotted her only when she was almost within a spear's reach: a lean, weathered, hard-faced woman, dressed in a chitin cuirass.

'You're of the Nethyen? How do things stand in the forest?'

'I am of the Nethyen,' she confirmed. 'The fighting is over.'

His heart leapt. 'Can you bring your forces to bear on the battle?'

'We can.' A small smile that made him uneasy. 'We have put aside our differences, the Etheryen and ourselves. From now on there is but one hold in the wood. Netheryon, it shall be called.'

Roder shrugged off the nuances of Mantis nomenclature. 'When can you strike?' he asked, acutely aware that the Ants would be closing the distance to his lines already.

'Now,' she explained, and went for him.

She nearly had him, too. Her blade rammed into his armour, biting into the metal but not penetrating, yet still knocking him from his feet. She wore one of those claw gauntlets, and he had not even noticed.

He thrust a hand out, but the soldiers around him were creditably alert and, even as she drew back her arm to finish him off, three or four snapbow bolts and a sting had found her, battering her from both sides so that she twisted and fell in a spray of blood.

'Pits-cursed Inapt!' Roder swore furiously, as one of his men helped him up. 'What was that . . .?' There was shouting, he realized. *Within* the camp there was shouting. In the pre-dawn he could make out nothing of it. 'Someone find out what that is!' he ordered.

But even as he said the words, he understood what it must be. He saw that the Mantis woman had not come alone; that her people, the Netheryen, were indeed ready to strike.

They had reached almost to the edge of the camp itself, and not one sentry or scout had spied them. All eyes had been focused on the Ants.

They had come, all of them, in their steel-edged hundreds.

Roder opened his mouth to cry out some command – *any* command – that might save the situation, and the might of the forest surged into the heart of his army, like a tide.

In that fractured second, Milus weighed many commodities within his soul, not least his surprisingly strong attachment to the original plan, however inappropriate. The Mantids had finally made their move; they were attacking the Wasps even now. They were hopelessly outnumbered, and yet when had that ever bothered them? He could now let them spend themselves against the black and gold, then strike at his own convenience. Or he could take full advantage of this unlooked-for intervention and hurry his men over to the Wasp lines as fast as they could be shifted, and construct a new battle plan while the fighting continued. It was another advantage of being an Ant, of course: he could change his orders at any time and the whole army would know and understand.

He made his decision in that same fraught second. *Forwards, all speed. Close with the Wasps as swiftly as possible.*

And Seda took one step forwards and threw out a stingshot at the seated figure of Argastos.

It was supposed to be that simple. However he chose to appear, the gnarled-stump body of the Moth War Master was there and had always been there, at the root-hung, earth-ceilinged centre of the barrow. This was the chamber they had dined in. This was where they had been imprisoned and threatened. This was the entirety of Argastos's world.

But he was quicker to react than that, and more clever. For all that he had atrophied into, he had been one of the great magicians of his people, with a millennium of scheming even after that. The space around them became instantly folded and convoluted so that, although he was physically almost close enough to touch, he had contrived a mile of tangled forest between them, and dropped Seda and Che inside it. And it was not empty.

'His ghost-soldiers are here with us, all around,' Che recognized.

'Keep them back. Misdirect them. Lose them within the landscape,' Seda directed, taking command because . . . who else was there? Gratifyingly, she felt the Beetle girl's immediate acquiescence. *Perhaps there is some potential in her that I missed. If I can make a servant of my enemy, what could we not do together?* And then she was pursuing Argastos, even as he tried to widen the apparent space between them, hauling swathes and handfuls of mismatched, misremembered land from his mind to cram into place.

But Seda had assessed his limits: his imagination was as dried-up as his body. Everything he raised up was brooding forest, fragments of ruined castle, clods of the deep underground. She had seen it all before and she flew through it like an avenging ghost, fire trailing from her hands.

Yet his memories, however limited, encompassed his days as War Master, his military campaigns, the great battles of the Inapt, and suddenly she was veering away, falling back, because she had met Argastos's armies.

The actual ghost soldiers, the remains of Argastos's real victims that could take on enough form to injure or kill her and the Maker girl – just as she herself had given Tisamon's ghost such form – were still being kept away, led into the dense, gnarled thickets of Argastos's own mind, constantly turned away by the Beetle's will. But that could not last forever. Seda had to tear her way past all the mummery that Argastos had thrown up, before those dead killers fought through Che's diversions enough to cross the few feet of actual real space that separated them from their intended victims. The two women became hunter and hunted all at the same time.

And here now was what kept her from her quarry: Argastos had ransacked his mind and cast up this recollection of the war-host of the Inapt. She had seem some fraction of it in the visions he had shown her, while wooing her, but this was it entire or as close as his memory could call forth. The forest was filled with moving soldiers: Moth, Mantis, Spider, Dragonfly, Woodlouse and others, great loose formations of them, armoured and armed, a dark glass being held up to the glory of another age.

Hurry! came Che's voice, in her mind. The Beetle was losing ground.

Useless creature. And Seda stood before Argastos's recreated host and called out, 'I am Seda, Empress of the Wasp-kinden. Do you presume to teach me about armies?'

She took a deep breath and clawed power out of the very tapestry that Argastos had raised to stop her, and she gifted him with her own thoughts on the subject.

She gave him the Barbs, General Alder's Fourth Army; she gave him Malkan's Winged Furies and Tynan's Gears. She gave him the Eighth, which General Roder was even now leading against Sarn. She gave him the artillery of the Engineers and the flying machines of the Aviation Corps. She gave him the Rekef assassins she had once lived in fear of. She gave him snapbows and the bright dawn of the new Apt age.

His remembered soldiers, a thousand years dead and obsolete, began their work, butchering her followers by the thousand, slaughtering the Wasps wholesale as she watched, and not all her powers or inspiration could inspire into that ersatz Black and Gold any semblance of the discipline and indomitable might of the Imperial armies that she recalled.

She had miscalculated. There was a hollow, clutching feeling inside her, and at last she was forced to recognize it as fear.

Hurry! Che Maker again, not realizing how Seda's plans had just collapsed in upon themselves. And then Seda was forced to confront two equally unpalatable options: lose to Argastos; confess to Maker that she was failing.

But she was not like her brother. She was not so insecure.

I need your help. A bitter confession, yet she shoved the situation facing her into Che's mind, and the girl understood immediately. *What can you give me?*

601

In the real world, the Wasp armies would have destroyed Argastos's barbaric rabble without slowing. Their orthopters and automotives, greatshotters and snapbows would have reaped that enemy like wheat and turned an army into an abattoir within two hours. But Seda had no understanding of such devices. She knew that they existed, but she left the details to her generals and her engineers. Here, with only her own mind to draw on, all the great machinery of the Wasps, their tactics and their innovations, might as well just be theatrical props. Argastos had led armies: he knew full well the strengths and weaknesses of his troops.

Change places with me, Che told her instantly, and Seda swallowed her pride and fell back, taking on the task of throwing Argastos's real soldiers into confusion, whilst Che hunted the man himself. It was the only chance they seemed to have.

In the midst of this twisted landscape that Argastos had summoned into being, Che could not see her own physical body, but she had the uncomfortable feeling that some of the Moth's dead slaves were practically standing over her with blades raised. She had tried all she had – misdirection, flight, lengthening the imagined terrain that they must cross, even calling on Amnon once again, and having him throw himself against their blades – and it was foul work, to do so, but she was dead if she did not.

In passing that task to Seda, she could only hope that the Empress would put her ruthlessness and her Wasp minions to good use, because Che herself had played that game as far as she could.

Here was a different battle, though, and one she had a new perspective on. She saw exactly what Argastos had thrown between them to protect himself – his great remembered army – and she understood why Seda had failed.

And what do I have?

She reached into her mind and peopled Argastos's battlefield with her own forces, marvelling at the irony that she should be more suited to such an attack than Seda herself. Here were the Dragonflies that she had seen in the Commonweal; here were the Moth-kinden of Tharn; here were the Mantids of the Nethyon and Etheryon – Argastos's own people turned against him by her will. And here . . . here was the Grand Army of Khanaphes, the great host of her own kinden, with chariots and cavalry and Amnon's heroic guard at its centre. And if they were Apt, it mattered little, because they were still waging war in a way that had barely changed since the Bad Old Days.

These were her troops, and she sent them off to war.

Argastos's own forces outnumbered hers to the extent that she reckoned his memories had multiplied the actual numbers who had ever fought under his command. Still, this was his battle, and played by his rules. Even if his mind was a liar, he would still manage to destroy her soldiers in time.

But that was not what she was trying to accomplish. She had another reason to take the initiative from Seda: a secret weapon.

The tide of battle swayed, and washed back and forth, her Khanaphir legion driving forward into the heart of the enemy, a bold thrust to get even a single arrow as far as Argastos himself. He countered perfectly, of course, concentrating his forces to block her at every point, but at the same time she was leading him on, stripping him of his reserves and his bodyguards, until he had committed everything he had in order to meet her threat.

And she called out, *I know you're there. Time for you to do what your people do.*

The bitter thorn of Esmail's mind revealed itself to her: *Do not believe all the Moths wrote in their histories.*

I don't care, she told him. *That reputation is what I need now. Be a scholar or a poet some other time. Can you reach him?* And if Esmail's answer was 'no' then everything would be for naught.

But then she felt him inching his way through the interstices of Argastos's mind, stepping behind and within, but never directly interacting with it: like a spider raiding another's web, each step desperate not to start the vibrations that might trigger an alarm.

603

And she continued to throw her soldiers at the enemy with a reckless disregard for their lives, suicidal and ludicrous enough to shame every general or tactician there had ever been. But either Argastos took it for her inexperience, or perhaps back in his day that was all battle had been about. He met her and crushed her forces, almost forgetting himself, losing his real purpose in this excuse he had manufactured to play War Master one last time. And, as he committed his imaginary troops to the fray, complicating and convoluting the distance between him and Che, so the ground immediately around him became simpler and simpler to traverse until one could have just walked across it.

I'm here, came the voice of Esmail in her mind. *But . . . I need to break into the real, where his body is. I –* he sounded shaken – *I hadn't thought – I can't get out myself. I'm not strong enough.*

Strength is something I have, and she watched the last of her forces torn apart, felt Argastos exalt at his apparent triumph, and reached out to un-seam his world and let her assassin out.

Hurry! This time it was Seda who was pressing her, but Che just sat back, imagining herself staring at Argastos over a chessboard. Her pieces were gone, he had achieved the perfect victory, and yet he had not won.

She sensed his confusion, aware that he had missed something and yet unable to conceive of what it was. Was he not the War Master, after all?

Esmail struck.

Through him, she saw the blade of his bare hand shear through preserved flesh that had become as hard as wood, so that a withered, blasted thing hunched in an overlarge throne was abruptly lacking a head.

It went. All of it went. The mind-forest became like mist, evaporating and gone in an instant. The dark heart of the wood stopped beating.

All those hundreds, all the trapped dead – from Argastos's original guard all the way up to those she and Seda had brought with them – were gone as though they had never been, like knots unravelling when the string is tugged. And she knew that Amnon was now free – destined for oblivion or for another life, however the universe might order such things.

And she was standing in a dome-ceilinged chamber beneath the earth, where a broken dead thing had fallen from its mouldering throne.

Che looked up from it, and she locked eyes with Seda.

That was a tense moment, the two of them, each waiting to see what the other would do. Wasp Empress; War Master's kin. Only now that she had met Argastos did Seda appreciate that the two of them composed their own legend: the two rival sisters who would fight until one of them was destroyed.

But if there was one thing she was not, it was a slave – not to Argastos and not to some Moth idea of fate, either.

The others, the survivors, were cautiously standing up around the chamber. Seda saw Maker's Spider Weaponsmaster retreat to her side, eyes on Tisamon, who was already at his accustomed position between her and danger. The tatty little halfbreed magician Maker had picked up from somewhere was taking a more sensible position behind her mistress.

There was another man there, the man who had done for Argastos in the end. After a moment's concentration, she understood who he must be: the assassin, the man who had fooled her, and who had worn Ostrec's face. The killer of her beloved Gjegevey. For a moment the flame of anger burned hot within her, but she conquered it – she was no slave to *that* either. If he could be kept on a leash then surely even he might prove a useful tool. Now she realized what he must be – no Spider as he had shown himself to her, but a kinden – and with a profession – out of the myths.

He flinched when she set eyes on him. That was a good start.

And over there was Thalric, hunched off to one side as though trying to avoid her notice. It was almost endearing.

'Cheerwell Maker,' she began, returning her attention to her rival. 'Here we are.'

The Beetle girl was waiting for her to strike, as well she might, although obviously not prepared to attack first. Seda forced herself to relax, and the slight smile that came to her face had a touch of the genuine to it.

'Cheerwell Maker,' she repeated. 'Look how far we've come, two Inapt girls. Is there a Moth Skryre in the world who would not tremble at our approach, either of us? The great terror that dwelt here is undone by us. His power is ours for the taking.'

Che was regarding her suspiciously, which Seda conceded to be a sensible stance.

'Ours, is it?' the Beetle replied.

Seda shrugged. 'I won't deny we've been enemies, and we have every right to be so. The very world seems to have gone to great lengths to cast us as eternal adversaries. And yet together we defeated Argastos, and neither one of us could have done it without the other. Does that not suggest something to you?'

Che's eyes flicked about the dim chamber, seeking out the faces of her friends. There was still a fading fire there, a guttering corpse light left over from Argastos's tenure.

'What do you want, Seda?' she said at last.

'I want to live without threat and fear,' the Empress told her. 'And that's no more than any other woman in this world wants. But, being who I am, I had to plot the death of my brother, engineer the destruction of a great magician, and have a Rekef general murdered before I could even begin to breathe easily. And since then I have set out to conquer the known world because, while it remains free, my body will be at risk from the machines of the Apt, and my mind from the magics of the Inapt. And both from you.'

'Me?' But Che could not quite make her surprise sound sincere. 'Yes, well, I won't say I don't understand you.'

'But what might I do if I could know you as something other than a threat to me?' Seda pressed. 'I had an adviser, until recently, an old man who knew much of the world, and who tried to steer me as best he could. Your creature there killed him.' And she could not keep her voice level, the bitterness forcing its way into those few words. 'Who do I turn to for counsel, now?'

The Beetle was looking at her, and Seda had the impression that she *wanted* to find a reason to trust her opposite. They led odd, privileged lives in Collegium, after all.

And surely that was her hidden weapon, to bring out into the open now. 'Che, General Tynan's Second Army has taken your home city.'

The Maker girl went completely still.

'I do not know how matters stand there. A great deal will depend on what your people do. Tynan is a rational, cautious man. Furthermore, he has one with him to whom I can speak, after a fashion. Cheerwell . . . you could be governor of Collegium. My very word could make it so.'

'And a subject of your Empire?'

'Would it not be *our* Empire? For all that I am Empress, you are my sister. If you spoke to me about Collegiate ways, would I not listen?'

And Che was backed into that corner, with the fate of her people in the palm of her hand, offered a future wherein she might temper Seda's Wasp steel and find power for herself. She might deny it in her own mind, but Seda had felt Che Maker's ambition. It was an indivisible part of becoming a powerful magician to want *more*.

'Good,' the Empress said softly. 'This is it, Cheerwell. If all of *this* was for anything, then this is what it was for: to bring us together, to show us that hand in hand we are more than we could ever be while at war with one another.'

And even as Che was nodding, she beckoned archly. 'Thalric, to me.'

There was a fraught moment: the Wasp man had taken a

single step, but no more, and he was now looking at the Maker girl.

'Thalric,' Seda repeated. 'You are my consort, have you forgotten? You were saved a traitor's death for no other reason than that. You are mine.'

She extended her power – the lightest touch should have sufficed against his Apt mind – but found an opposing push of equal strength: Cheerwell Maker.

'Don't be ridiculous,' the Empress stated, cold and regal. 'He is mine. He has always been mine. How could it be otherwise?' The contest was not for the man himself, that perennial renegade she hardly knew. For the principle of it, though, she must fight. Here was something they had both laid claim to, and if she was to have a sister working by her side, she must still be the wiser, the stronger. Thalric was the man both had claimed. He was their battlefield.

But, step by faltering step, Thalric was retreating from her, until he stood beside the Maker girl.

Something began to fray, inside her, and Seda called out, '*Her*, Thalric? I understand why you went to her once you were out of my sight. She has power, of course, and it is akin to mine, but I am here now.' But he would not move, and so she turned her narrowing eyes upon Cheerwell. 'Stop this,' she demanded. 'Release him.'

Che shook her head slightly. 'I don't believe in using chains to hold anyone.'

'Then withdraw your power from him, and I will take him. He doesn't know what he's doing.'

Che's chin jutted stubbornly. 'No.'

'Cheerwell, if we are to work together—'

'No,' for a second time. Three would be final.

'I hold your city in the palm of my hand, Maker. Give up Thalric, now, or the history of your kinden in the Lowlands will be a book of torment.'

A terrible, harsh expression came over the Beetle's face, even

608

as she shook her head. She took Thalric's arm in exactly the possessive manner that the Empress herself might have used, in claiming some thing she owned, and for the last time she said, 'No.'

'Thalric . . .?' And Seda saw him shake her head, and the words came spitting from her mouth: 'For *this*? When I'm ready to forgive you, to welcome you back, you turn to *this*? This, stunted, dark, ugly creature, instead of me?' And she realized that fate would have her after all, for surely all the legends sang the same song, and what else should two rival sisters come to blows over but this.

A rage welled up inside Seda, not merely the inherent temper of her kinden but the fury of a magician thwarted, and in that instant she had all her strength at her fingertips, and had ripped up everything left of Argastos too, holding it above her like a boulder, desperately reaching for her self-control before she—

The words came from her mouth unwanted, as though reading from a script: 'He's *mine*!'

And she released it all, a monstrous, bludgeoning expenditure of power hammering down upon Maker and all around her, screaming as she did so.

And she felt the ground crack beneath them – not the earthen barrow floor, but what lay beneath.

She had time for one brief, despairing thought: *The Seal! The Seal of the Worm!* And then the darkness rose up with many mouths, and swallowed them.

Forty-One

'There are two hundred and seventeen of them, sir. The rest are either dead or scattered throughout the city, hiding or holding out.'

'And *her*?' No need for General Tynan to qualify that, for he had made his liaisons no secret. Everyone in the Second Army knew whose company their general had sought out on the road to Collegium.

'Not yet, sir. She evades us, still.' The watch officer was standing with his back to the prisoners, all two hundred and seventeen of them. Many were wounded, and all were bound firmly and on their knees, out here under Collegium's morning sky in some square boasting the jagged stonework and broken metal of what had once been a fountain before the bombs fell.

To Tynan's eyes, how unsuited they looked to be soldiers! All so young and so delicate, handsome where their wounds hadn't marred them and proud still, despite it all. Even when defeated. Even when captured and lined up for execution.

'General.' It was Vrakir's voice, which Tynan had begun to loathe.

These men and women – yes, *women*! – had recently fought alongside his own. Spider sailors had brought his army food after the Collegiate pilots had made his airships their playthings. Spider troops had taken the brunt of the Felyal when they attacked, exposing themselves to the blades of their greatest enemies to give their Wasp allies time to regroup. They had stormed the wall using only their climbing Art. Their spilled blood had brought him here, as much as that of his own soldiers.

'General, it seems appropriate that a sufficiently public spectacle be made of this,' Vrakir murmured. 'Crossed pikes along the walls, perhaps. After all, they betrayed the Empress, did they not?'

'Did they?' Tynan stared at him, stony-faced.

'Do you doubt it?' The Red Watch officer looked unmoved.

If Cherten were here, he would agree with him. He would tell me to do the right thing, the Imperial thing. But Cherten had got himself killed by a student, somehow, in an unforgivable lapse of discipline. *I had not thought the time would come when I would lament the lack of Colonel Cherten, but I would he were here to do this business instead of me.*

'They are soldiers,' Tynan stated. 'We owe it to them to give them a soldier's death.'

'A *traitor's* death, General—' Vrakir stated, moving in too close, and Tynan smashed him across the mouth, backhanding him into the wall.

He was onto the younger man instantly, a solid punch driving Vrakir to the ground and then hooking his boot into the man's stomach. And though the banded armour had taken the brunt, the Red Watch man skidded five feet across the ground, rolling and coming up on one knee, hand out and palm open.

Tynan was just the same, ready to sting, and for a moment the two of them were frozen in place, before the horrified stares of the soldiers.

'Do it, or stand down,' Tynan growled, and Vrakir bared his teeth, but lowered his hand.

'The Empress will know of this,' he hissed.

'Take Captain Vrakir somewhere he can calm down and perhaps remember that most officers who threaten a superior get a pair of pikes for their own personal use,' Tynan spat. His gaze swept around to the ranks of defeated Spider-kinden.

This is where I free them, isn't it? Exile them from the city, tell them never to go near the Empire again, and everyone keeps quiet, a conspiracy of mercy, and the Empress never knows. But orders were orders, and the Empress had left him no leeway. And she would get to know, he had no doubt of it.

'Have them shot, quick and clean,' he ordered the watch officer. 'They've earned that much.'

He stalked away, and heard the killing start.

There was a counting house, or something similar, that Cherten had commandeered for interrogations, and the engineers had removed all the paperwork and the remaining money from the cellars and converted them to holding cells, probably without being asked to, just standard work for junior artificers wherever the Empire established itself even for a short while. Tynan had some business there now, left over from the previous night. *Another loose end that Cherten should be picking up.* He found that he did not feel particularly upset that the intelligencer had met his end, but it was undeniably inconvenient.

The interrogators were not at work – it would clearly take them a while to get back to routine without Cherten – and Tynan found he had the place to himself, his footsteps echoing back from the stripped walls.

Probably I should keep a bodyguard about me, he considered. *The situation remains fluid, after all, and you never know who might choose to have a go.*

He glanced about the counting house's interior, and reflected that he might almost welcome an assassin just about now.

But some great traditions could simply not be relied on these days.

He descended to the cellar, firing up a chemical lantern on the way, and casting a spitting white light ahead of him. Word had reached him just around dawn: there had indeed been an assassin, just not a very good one.

She was now the sole resident, hunched in the corner of the furthest cell as though driven there by the intrusion of the light.

The artificers' work allowed her no privacy: just a set of bars cordoning off one corner of the cellar, padlocked to eyebolts set in the stone walls on either side.

She was not a Spider, as he had been told, but a halfbreed with a lot of Ant blood in her as well, pale of skin and with dart-like blemishes on cheeks and forehead. She had been caught sneaking across the rooftops by sentries from the Airborne, where-upon she had apparently put up a fierce struggle to defend herself. She had injured two men before they got her sword off her, and they had not been gentle in subsequently expressing their grievances. He could see where her left hand had been stamped on, swollen and ugly, and the surgeon had merely knotted a strip of cloth over her bloodied right eye after cleaning out the wound.

When the soldiers had taken her down, she had called out Tynan's name, they claimed. That was the only reason she still lived: because it was personal.

'You're the best the Spiderlands could send, are you?' he asked. 'Did . . . did *she* send you?' *And what would I prefer to hear, precisely?* He almost found he wanted her to say yes, to confirm that Mycella was still thinking of him, if only to dispatch this half-trained killer.

The prisoner mumbled something through bruised and bloody lips.

'Louder!' he snapped, not going closer to the bars, just in case.

'Not Spiderlands,' he made out. 'Collegium.'

Tynan gave a surprised grunt. 'Didn't realize the locals did that sort of thing. Or maybe it's just you, is it? Well you're piss-poor at it, you know? Even as a murderer, you fail.'

That got a reaction and she bared her teeth impotently at him, her one good eye staring wildly.

'What did you hope to accomplish?' Tynan asked her. 'Killing me wouldn't free your city, anyway. Unless you were going to work your way down the chain of command, from the top.'

'You killed Eujen.'

He frowned. The words made no sense to him.

'He was my friend. He was the best man I knew. And when he came to talk to you, you took him and tortured him . . . and then you shot him.' As she spoke, her voice was low and dull, but her eye flashed fire when she looked up. 'You killed my friend. You killed lots of my friends, but Eujen . . . Coming to kill you was easier than staying to watch him die.'

When he came to talk . . .? 'This isn't that student nonsense, is it?'

He could have put another knife in her, and it would have hurt less. The dismissal of everything there ever was about her cause and her friends, this man who would write the history books deeming them a trivial irrelevance.

'Well, never mind about them. We'll wrap them up today,' he told her, thinking it more to himself than to torment her. 'As for you, though, I'll give you a choice. How much do you want to keep on living?' Recognizing that traitor – hope – in her eye, he shook his head. 'Oh no, don't start down that road. There are two fates for you, girl. One is that we gift you a pair of pikes of your own, and you'll die today, eventually. The other's if you think you know something that we might be interested in. That way you live much longer, though, given the circumstances, you may come to regret it. That's your choice, and that's all of your choices.' His voice had become rough and ugly, saying it. 'I've just had two hundred good soldiers executed, assassin. Their deaths were quick and underserved. At least when I see your corpse, I'll know yours was neither.'

Stenwold was managing to walk more easily now, although occasional waves of dizziness still swept over him, so he kept his stick handy. He had even been out to climb the courtyard wall at dawn, to look at the size of the problem.

It was a suitably large problem, too. There were plenty of Wasps out there, and some Sentinels, and it seemed likely that they would stir themselves soon, and then matters would get awkward.

If the Wasps were of a mind to break the building open, then a little artillery – perhaps even the leadshotters of the Sentinels – would suffice to do it, and then the students' defence would last only minutes under the descending host of the Light Airborne.

On the other hand, the Wasps had declined to do any such thing so far, although similar tactics had been used against entrenched insurgents elsewhere in the city, and so there seemed some chance that the Empire might have to do things the old-fashioned way, and take the building by storm. In that case, it was possible that the students might still be in possession of it by dusk, for the main door was the only real approach, and there were plenty of small windows overlooking it that student snap-bowmen might use. But the next day would probably see the end, Stenwold realized. They were short of ammunition. The Empire was not short of men.

The Dragonfly Castre Gorenn was in charge up on the wall – any command structure had come down to strength of person-ality, and the Commonwealer had become a near-mythic figure amongst the students owing to her feats of aim.

'I want only people who can fly stationed on this wall,' Stenwold told her. 'So yourself, Flies, any Beetles who've got their wings. When their advance comes you need to pull back to the main building in good time – get inside so we can shut them out. Or else, if you can't get in, just take off, get clear of the fighting.'

Gorenn nodded coolly.

'And no fool heroics. I mean in good time, Dragonfly.' Stenwold had heard a great deal about the Commonweal Retaliatory Army.

She met his eye warily, as if ascribing some legendary char-acteristics to him herself. 'Understood, War Master.'

Stenwold took another look over the wall, noticing movement about the Wasp lines, but a lazy sort of movement suggesting they had a little time in hand before any assault.

Then Laszlo landed close to him. 'Mar'Maker, you need to come now.'

Trouble, was his first thought, but Stenwold could read Laszlo well, and the Fly was excited rather than worried. Something had happened.

There was a gathering in one of the rooms off the infirmary – a band of about twenty, but they were the leaders. Stenwold marked Berjek Gripshod, now in a buff coat and carrying a snapbow, and a couple of other College Masters. The rest were students wearing their purple sashes, save for Gerethwy the Woodlouse, who still wore the colours of the Coldstone Company.

And in the middle of all this, a newcomer. A Fly-kinden with a riot of black beard, whom Stenwold had assumed was long shipped out of the city.

'Tomasso?'

'And here's himself!' the ex-pirate declared. 'Right then, let me speak my piece, for we've not much time.'

'How did you get in here?' Stenwold demanded.

Tomasso looked pained but said, 'Your little windows here will fit one of mine, just about, Master Maker. And fear not, your lads and lasses had a bow trained on me as I came in. They're sharp enough. Now, time for you to be going, though, don't you think? I can't imagine what you're waiting for, but it hasn't appeared.'

'That's not much of a joke, Tomasso,' Stenwold told him.

'Nonsense. I've a distraction lined up. Your people here look light on their feet. They can nip out and lose themselves in the streets. Meanwhile, you can come with me.'

'You obviously haven't seen how things are looking on the ground out there,' Stenwold replied flatly. 'The Wasps have a cordon set about the entrance to the College, and you'd need a remarkable diversion to stop them simply shooting us all down.'

Tomasso was nodding, a grin flashing from amidst his beard. 'Oh, that you can bet on. You'll all just need to be nimble in getting out.'

'And the wounded?' The voice came from the doorway: Sartaea te Mosca was standing there in a bloodied apron. 'We have eleven who can't walk, some who shouldn't even be moved.'

'Better to move them than let the Jaspers have them,' Tomasso pointed out.

'Nobody's nimble when they're carrying a stretcher,' she told him.

Tomasso looked exasperated, as though his audience didn't quite understand what he was offering. Nobody actually voiced the idea of abandoning the wounded, although it must have done the round of most heads there.

'Excuse me,' one of the students piped up eventually, a broad Beetle girl in chemical-stained overalls. 'We can get out another way, I think.'

Everyone stared at her and she shuffled back a little, obviously not happy with being the centre of attention.

'Cornella Fassen, isn't it?' Berjek Gripshod said kindly. 'Tell us what you mean, please.'

'Well, Master Gripshod, do you know the Cold Cellars?'

There was a murmur of bafflement and even laughter at that, as though she had told a joke just to defuse the tension. Those cold, slick, allegedly haunted chambers had been a part of student folklore for many years.

Even Berjek raised half a smile. 'What of them?' He remained painfully polite and correct, for all that there was an army gearing up outside even as he spoke.

'Last year, some friends of mine worked out that it's just . . . they're adjacent to the Natural History vaults underneath the Living Sciences faculty. That's where they keep the samples, and where all the preservatives tanks . . . and the cooling machinery.'

Stenwold and Berjek exchanged glances.

'What are you saying?' the War Master asked.

'For the last day we've been working on the wall there. We reckon there can't be that much that separates the two cellars.

We had acids on it, and we were chipping away. If we could just get into Living Sciences, we could come out through the Old Workshops, and that means outside the Wasp cordon. We thought it would be useful, but we didn't seem to be getting anywhere. But this morning there's a crack . . . In the wall, Masters. I think we must be almost through.'

A shudder went through them on hearing that. It meant the insertion of hope, like a needle. *A way out?*

Almost immediately there was shouting upstairs, and moments later a Fly skidded down, calling out to them, 'They've started! They're moving for the wall!'

'Get through to Living Sciences any way you can!' Stenwold almost shouted at Fassen, who was out of the door the next instant. 'Everyone else . . .' Wheels spun in his mind. 'I need a detail to man the windows – cover for the wall guards. And then . . . and then . . .' *And then hold your ground until they kill you,* he thought, as he realized what he was asking.

'I'll take volunteers for that,' Berjek said calmly.

'No—'

'Oh, shut up, Maker. Give someone else a chance.' The old man smiled wanly. 'Less to lose here, and less of a loss. Who needs one more historian, eh?'

Stenwold took a deep breath. 'I need a detachment ready to go through the breach in the wall as soon as it's made. We don't know who might be on the far side – the place could already be packed with Wasps.'

'I'll sort that,' someone volunteered, and Stenwold nodded in gratitude. 'Te Mosca, ready the wounded for movement. Yes, I know you don't want to move them, but you must. Tomasso's right. And, as for your distraction . . .'

'You make the call,' Tomasso told him, 'and I can signal them, no problems.'

'What are we talking about?'

'Suicidal counter-attack on the Wasps. Spider-kinden lorn detachment.'

Stenwold shook his head, impressed despite himself. 'We will have to talk about how you managed that.'

'Well, on the same subject, I have a whole bunch of former Spiderlands mercenaries hiding out with some trading friends of mine, at great expense, who will be getting themselves out of the city as soon as the Wasps open the gates to trade. I recommend you get your wounded, and anyone on the Empire's lists, to hook up with them. Best chance they'll get, believe me.'

'And me?'

'Master Maker, you're with me and Laszlo. We've got a boat to catch.'

'General!'

Tynan found that he had been expecting it, even as he sat taking reports and checking over the seemingly endless details of the Second's assimilation of Collegium. He looked at the sergeant who had burst in on him, here on the second floor of some ousted magnate's townhouse.

'An attack?'

'Yes, sir.' The sergeant took a deep breath. 'Best guess, about four hundred, sir. They must have been sneaking as close as they could, but as soon as we spotted them, they formed up. Sir . . . my lieutenant said you'd want to see.'

Did he, now? But Tynan put down his pen and shoved his chair back. *Four hundred, formed up, and I have a thousand snapbowmen right here, right now, and so many more ranged across the city. Is this all you could manage?*

'Send out orders – to keep all eyes out for lone archers and assassins,' he instructed, though if none was found it would not surprise him. An attack of any kind was madness. *Surely she could have escaped over the walls? We can't watch everything all of the time. Did I not leave even that much of a gap for you?* In his heart he felt he knew. What would she be returning home for, if she escaped? Already in disgrace in the Spiderlands, her family humiliated and brought low, this campaign had been her last chance to redeem herself in the eyes of her peers. Tynan had crushed that hope – Tynan and his orders.

'Let me see her,' he said.

The Spider-kinden had not attacked, and the Wasps of the Second had held their positions, waiting for their general's command, and so it was a motionless tableau that awaited him, as perfect as if they were holding still for some artist of epic talent, come to capture this moment in history.

They had their banners up, too. That was something the Spiderlands troops had eschewed while fighting alongside the Wasps, for perhaps Mycella had believed it would appear old-fashioned. Now, with nothing left to lose, flags billowed over the Spiderlands ranks, the bright silks of a dozen houses, with the Aldanrael at their heart.

She has come to say goodbye, Tynan thought. He could not see her, and it would have been perfect Spider planning for the woman herself to be elsewhere, perhaps sneaking over the walls even now, but he believed fiercely that she was somewhere in front of him, that she had chosen this way to finish their relationship with true Arista style.

'I want her alive,' he said, at first too quietly for anyone to notice, and then louder so his officers could hear.

'Sir . . . with a snapbow volley . . .' one of them ventured.

'Do what you can,' Tynan instructed. 'Two volleys, and then send the Airborne in and, if she lives, bring her before me.'

'Think your skipper can pull this off?' Stenwold asked, just because he needed to say something.

'Tomasso? There's nothing he sets his mind to that he can't do,' Laszlo declared loyally.

The stench of chemicals was overpowering as Fassen and her friends worked on the wall. Even far down the corridor, Stenwold kept a rag to his mouth and nose to block it out. He had stopped asking how much longer. Nothing he could do would achieve anything but to distract the artificers. Around him, the vanguard force shuffled and rechecked their snapbows or fingered swords ready in scabbards. Laszlo shuffled from foot to foot.

Word had come, soon after the start of the attack, that the courtyard wall had fallen, Gorenn pulling back as instructed, for once. The main gates had been punched in by a Sentinel's lead-shot, and the machine had muscled up to the wall and sent a shot through the gateway to stave in the College building's inner doors as well. Since then, Berjek Gripshod's lorn detachment had been keeping the Wasps off, making the final approach a nettle that the Empire was still steeling itself to grasp.

Beyond the wall, Tomasso's distraction had now arrived, a ragged band of Spider-kinden hurling themselves at the rear of the Wasp position, massively outnumbered but pushing as far as they could with the benefit of surprise, so that Laszlo had reported fighting deep within the Wasp camp. The Empire had drawn its forces back to eliminate these new challengers, whereupon the students had dragged out all manner of broken furniture to block up the doorway and the courtyard gate.

Then the Wasps had come back, the Spiders clearly dealt with. The sands were running fierce and fast in the glass now.

'Maker!' It was Sperra barrelling down into the cellars, her eyes wide. 'They're in! They're through the doors, Maker!'

A cold weight settled itself in Stenwold's gut.

'How are the wounded?'

'We're still getting them ready to move,' Sperra reported. 'Tell me we have somewhere to move *to*.'

He opened his mouth to confess that he stood between her and nothing but a dead end, that the end had found them.

There was a whoop, a veritable howl of triumph, from Fassen back in the Cold Cellars. 'Through! We're through!' followed by 'Hammer and tongs, what's *that*?'

'Vanguard forward!' Stenwold snapped. 'Sperra, get the infirmary cleared. Get everyone down here as quick as you can. Get . . .' but she was already gone.

And whatever Fassen's found, don't let it be another wall, he begged, as he pushed forwards with Laszlo at his heels.

He skidded down into the gripping chill of the cellar, and saw the wall ahead of him almost completely fallen, enough space for two people to squeeze through side by side. The work of the acids was plain, but there was a great deal of physical cracking that made him wonder if there had somehow been some movement of the earth that had touched only here. Or had Fassen other methods at her disposal than the chemical?

Whatever the reason, there was certainly a gap there, and it led *somewhere*.

The vanguard had waited for him, and he unslung his snapbow as he glanced around at them, at Fassen and her artificers, at Laszlo.

'Master Maker,' Fassen started.

'Let me see.' And he pushed his way to the edge of the hole.

He could see the cellars of Living Science, pungent with the reek of preservative because a lot of the jars and canisters there were broken open. That explained the chill and the smell that had tainted the Cold Cellars, and, for it to have done so, those cellars must have abutted here precisely, only this single thickness of wall separating two distinct College buildings.

He stepped across, and it took a long stride, because there was a gap below him, an impossible gap, and that was what Fassen had exclaimed about.

It was not large, just six inches in width, but for a long moment Stenwold stared down into it, and tried to understand what he was seeing. Darkness, yes, and the barrel of a snapbow poked into it encountered no resistance. Just a flaw in the earth, then? And yet . . . if he strained his eyes were there *lights*, at some unfathomable distance down below? As though this little crack gave onto a vast, echoing cavern extending impossibly beneath Collegium itself.

He drew back, feeling sudden vertigo. He had no idea what this was, whether it had always been there or had only manifested during this last night, in time to help Fassen in her work. He had more prosaic matters to hand.

'Living Science cellars look clear,' he announced, trying for his old booming Assembly voice, but low enough in the end for his words to have to be relayed back. 'Come on, we need to secure the floors above.'

Behind him, as they crossed, there wasn't a member of the vanguard who didn't pause and shiver a little, while crossing that inexplicable gap.

The narrow corridors leading down to the lower levels had never been intended for stretcher-bearers. Te Mosca and Sperra had got the wounded out of the infirmary easily enough, but navigating them to the Cold Cellars was an agonizingly slow business of knocks and bottlenecks, whilst everyone else in the building was desperately trying to hurry to the same place.

The sounds of fighting – and dying – were closing in on them. The Wasps were inside the building, and Berjek's gallant few were fighting them from room to room, spending blood and buying time at whatever rate of exchange they could get.

Another flight of stairs, but the stolid stretcher-bearers knew their business now – mostly Beetles, and many of them former wounded now strong enough to help their comrades. One stretcher at a time they descended as swiftly as was safe, their faces tight with concentration, blotting out the shouting and the fighting from just a few rooms away.

Sperra had gone on ahead, a faithful escort to Balkus's stretcher, but at the rear was Sartaea te Mosca, who perhaps had planned to provide an infinitesimal barrier between her charges and the Empire.

She brimmed over with exhortations to hurry that were utterly pointless. Nobody knew better than the men and women with the stretchers just how little time they had, and it was to their lasting credit that none of them cast aside their burdens to safeguard their own lives.

Most of the wounded were now on the level below, the last stretcher just about to begin its descent. Its rear bearer was Raullo Mummers, bag-eyed and hungover, but he had volunteered quickly enough.

'Please go,' he asked her, setting his foot on the top step. There was room for her to slip through above him, if she flew nimbly enough, but she shook her head.

'I shall see you to the foot of the stairs, Master Mummers, and then I shall be right behind you.' She risked a glance at Raullo's burden: he had insisted on carrying Eujen, and she hadn't had the heart to deny him the task. The chief officer of the Student Company looked . . .

Dead, he looked dead, and in Mummers's shaking grip there was no chance of detecting that infinitesimal rise and fall that earlier had betrayed some spark of life yet clinging to him. Simply shifting him might already have finished him off.

Running feet, and te Mosca wondered if there was any wretched magic that this heart of the Apt world would permit her, or if she had ever known any trick that could salvage a situation such as this.

'Knife . . . I've got a knife,' Mummers gulped out, stumbling on the stairs but keeping his balance. She just shook her head. One knife against the Empire was not going to tip any scales.

Rounding the corner came a couple of soldiers in Collegiate colours, but neither of them locals: Gerethwy and Castre Gorenn.

'You need to make better time!' the Dragonfly shouted at her.

'I am well aware of the situation, thank you,' te Mosca said tightly. 'We are evacuating as quickly as possible.'

'I'll hold here for them,' Gerethwy announced. 'This is a perfect position for my surprise.'

Gorenn gave him a nod. 'There will be no more of us coming this way. Those that remain are drawing the Wasps away, for as long as they can.'

'Perfect.' Gerethwy had dropped to one knee and unslung

his kitbag, dragging out his repeating snapbow and a tangle of mechanism.

'Gorenn, what about you?' te Mosca asked. Behind her, Mummers had wrestled Eujen's stretcher down to the foot of the stairs, sparing her one last look back before he went lurching off with it.

'I shall fight the Wasps,' the Dragonfly said, and all the fires of the Twelve-year War leapt in her eyes. 'And then, when that bores me, I shall leave, for there is no son of the Empire alive who can pursue me in the air. And I shall go to Sarn, and from there I shall fight them again.'

'May the sun be in the eyes of your enemies,' Gerethwy told her, his hands fitting components together deftly now, practice compensating for his lost fingers. Already the repeating snapbow was mounted on a low, bulky tripod, with some viciously toothed mechanism set in place to feed in its bolts.

Then the Dragonfly was gone, and Sartaea te Mosca was left staring only at the hunched back of her friend. 'Gereth, come with me now, please.'

'Not just yet,' he told her. 'But I will, believe me. Because I've solved the war problem.' A momentary grin appeared over his shoulder. 'Believe me, you won't catch me sticking around for the Wasps, but I won't need to once this is ready. My weapon will fight here without me.' Abruptly a dozen slender wires lashed out, unspooling themselves down the corridor. 'Ratiocinators, Sartaea, the future of artifice. Machines that can do things by themselves, react, calculate, even fight. And so simple – we could have done it ten years ago, if only anyone had thought!' His hands flickered over the mechanisms, making minute, final adjustments. 'Wars without soldiers, how about that? And we're done!'

Then a Wasp appeared at the far end of the corridor, with snapbow levelled. There was a frozen moment of shock on both sides and then the Wasp, seeing an enemy with a weapon directed at him, shot Gerethwy through the chest.

He rocked as the bolt tore through him, eyes wide, a single

625

audible breath escaping from him. Then the Woodlouse fell back with a perplexed expression. Sartaea dropped beside him, keening with loss because he was dead. She could see instantly that he was dead.

'You, away from the weapon, halt there!' the Wasp shouted at her. And then she was up, wings flashing about her shoulders, screaming at him for giving the warning one death too late.

Face fixed, he sighted on her and took one step forwards, and Gerethwy's snapbow twitched on its mount and shot the man two or three times, spilling him back against the wall.

She stared at it, then at Gerethwy. It was as if his ghost was animating the weapon, in some impossible bridging of the Apt and Inapt.

Then another half-dozen Wasps were there, also shouting at her, and she flew back from the weapon and watched as it attacked them, barrel jerking precisely left and right, spitting out handfuls of bolts at a time, the chattering gears feeding through the tape of ammunition with meticulous economy.

She left Gerethwy there and set off after the stretchers, knowing that her friend, even dead, was guarding their retreat.

Her bodyguard had been the last man standing.

With all the rest dead around him, Jadis of the Melisandyr had stood over his wounded mistress's body in his gleaming mail, shield up and sword ready to defy the entire Second Army. A Spider Sentinel, something out of another time, he had shown no fear nor even acknowledged the possibility of defeat. The sheer temerity of his defiance, backed by all the Spider Art he could muster, had held back the snapbow shot for a long count of ten.

And then they had gone amongst the bodies, giving the Spider wounded a swift, merciful death rather than have them fall into the hands of Vrakir or the interrogators. Save for Mycella – she, they had left for Tynan.

She had taken a snapbow bolt through the leg, he understood, but even then her sheer force of personality – the Art of her kinden – had held them back beyond the reach of her rapier. She had made laying hands on her person unthinkable, a sacrilege.

The word had come to Tynan that they had her, though, and so rather than wait for her to be dragged before him, he had gone to her, as a true penitent should.

The Spiders had fought fiercely, but like a war band from the Bad Old Days, and he understood that this had been deliberate. Like the banners they carried, this engagement had not been about winning. Trapped in Collegium, her army destroyed and her family disgraced, what choices had lain before Mycella of the Aldanrael? Surely she could have found a way to escape if she had truly looked for one, but then what? A beggar in some strange city? A renegade without status or power? What fate, for one who had misstepped in the Spider dance?

And so she had turned her back on survival at such a cost. For her, there was more merit in this ending, entering battle like mummers from some ritual drama, all bright colours and heraldry whose meaning had been lost to the world for centuries.

Seeing her there, on one knee with her sword in one hand, bloodied and bruised but unbowed, his heart was broken. He wanted to weep in that moment. He wanted to throw himself on her mercy, to beg her forgiveness. He wanted to howl out his bitter anger to the sky.

An Imperial general was denied all these things.

He could not say her name, yet looked her in the eye even so, felt her Art wash over him and then ebb, the force of her will fading before him until she was just a woman after all. Just another victim of his campaigns. He knew then that she truly had not betrayed him, that whatever the Empress intended, the Spiders – and what historian would ever believe it? – had not earned their allies' wrath. He knew that Mycella had been true to him, after all.

He felt as though the whole of Collegium was watching him as he lifted his arm, the palm of his hand directed towards her.

How can I live, after this?

The expression on her face was infinitely sad, and he knew it would remain there in his mind, sleeping and waking, for the rest of his days.

His hand flared as his sting discharged.

The refugee students broke away from the Living Sciences building in a rush. Stenwold stood by the door, leaning on his stick and hoping he looked like a stern warden guarding the retreat of the others, whilst trying his best to catch his breath.

The plan was simple, and encapsulated in the phrase: *It's a big city.* All those students able-bodied enough to do so were now going to ground. The Wasps could not know who had been in the contingent that had started the insurrection, and either they would round up every student of the College or they would not. Some would leave the city as soon as they could. Others – and by far the majority – would stay and wait their chances. Collegium would need them, Stenwold had promised. Their time would come.

The words had almost choked him, because their young faces had been so full of trust and hope.

The badly wounded were another matter – unable to move from place to place and with too much chance of their injuries being linked to the insurrection. They, and an escort, were going to join Tomasso's mercenaries. Word had been sent to the bearded Fly's mercantile contacts to smuggle them out of the city, posing as guards or servants, hidden within goods wagons, stowed away on ships. Tomasso had been working hard since his return to the city.

For Stenwold himself there were other plans.

The stretchers were coming out now. Tomasso had a quick word with the first bearers, to ensure they knew where they were going. It was not far but they must hurry, he was saying. The Wasps would—

Even as he was saying it, the Wasps had discovered them – a dozen of them bundling hurriedly from a side-street and stumbling to a halt at this sudden exodus of students. Stenwold felt the snapbow kick in his hands and a man in the centre of the squad went down, and then a handful of students were shooting too. *But it only takes one Wasp to raise the alarm!* And the last of the wounded was only just being brought out of Living Sciences.

Then the reason for the Wasps' initial hurry caught up with them: a handful of Spider-kinden, led by a lean man in black armour, ploughed into them and cut down two or three in those first moments. The Wasps scattered, some trying for the sky, but a couple of Spiders carried bows and, between them and the students, the entire squad was accounted for.

'Morkaris!' Tomasso called over. 'Still alive?'

The armoured Spider eyed him bleakly. 'There are more coming,' he said. 'We are the last. I hope you've spent our lives wisely.' He glanced at the last stretcher rounding the corner, at the handful of students even now backing away, about to run for their hiding places.

'Curse you all, Wasps and Flies and Beetles!' Morkaris declared, but a wild exaltation seemed to have taken hold of his expression, and a moment later he brandished his axe high in the air and went charging back the way he had come, his meagre handful of followers right behind him.

'Laszlo, pay attention, boy,' Tomasso barked. 'Get your wings up, and get off with you – the *Tidenfree*'s out past the sea wall, waiting for my word, so you go tell them we're on our way.'

'Right, Skipper.' And Laszlo was airborne in an instant, darting away at roof level.

'Come now, Master Maker.' Tomasso turned to Stenwold. 'The rest are trusting to their luck, so we must trust to ours.' He regarded Stenwold doubtfully. 'You're up for a brisk run, Maker?'

No! 'Going to have to be,' Stenwold replied curtly, and then Tomasso was off, half running and half in the air, leaving the Beetle War Master to lurch after him.

He was not up for even a brisk walk, so Tomasso had to keep returning to him, and Stenwold began to see the first spark of worry in the man's eye, fearing that he had miscalculated, ignorant of how badly Stenwold had been hurt. From the College to the docks proved a long haul, especially while avoiding all the city's biggest thoroughfares.

Tomasso had plotted their course in advance, leading Stenwold from Life Sciences to the river, and then through the rundown and unregarded streets that led along its course towards the sea. The Collegium river trade had been killed off almost entirely by the rails and the airships, and those parts of the city that had once relied on it had been dying for decades. There were plenty of shadowed places for Stenwold to fight for breath.

Sometimes they saw Wasps in the air above them, and once a Farsphex, and there were the occasional patrols on the ground too, and all the while they had to stop to rest more and more frequently.

Stenwold never knew whether the Wasps had spotted them from the air – a Fly and a Beetle out in daylight was surely not the most suspicious sight in Collegium that day – or whether one of the riverside locals had recognized his face and betrayed his own city's War Master, but, as they neared the docks, there seemed to be more and more of the Light Airborne overhead, until their progress was a punctuated series of hops and dashes from cover to cover – more and more suspicious by the minute until, if any Imperial *did* see them, he would guess instantly that they were fugitives. Tomasso was cursing now, under his breath but Stenwold could hear him. He had obviously intended to be out of the city by now.

'You go to the ship,' Stenwold told him. 'It's not as if I can't find the docks myself. You get going.'

'Not a chance, Maker. I made a promise I'd see this through, and I've been paid for it. When I give my word, I see it's kept.'

They were holed up no more than three streets from the docks by now, ducked into a storage shed that held nothing but scrap metal.

Then there was a hollow knocking sound that both of them recognized at once: the discharge of a leadshotter.

Tomasso was out of the shed immediately, with Stenwold lurching in his wake. There seemed little doubt about what the Wasps might be shooting at.

Stenwold shambled along the river's course for another warehouse-length before following Tomasso's abrupt left turn, cutting eastward for the main sea docks. There were fliers overhead, and shouting from somewhere behind. A noose was drawing tight, and he wondered if they had specific orders to keep him alive, or whether he was just some faceless fugitive to them.

Sooner than expected, he lurched out within sight of the docks, his lungs hammering with the strain and his head swimming with nausea. Whatever good work the Instar had done, he thought he might be undoing it with all this exertion. He staggered forwards again, then stumbled almost instantly to one knee, the world spinning about him.

Hands found his arm, hauling him upright. Tomasso was shouting in his ear: 'Almost there, Maker. Don't you give up here, you fat old bastard. Come on!'

Tisamon, in Myna, came the thought from somewhere, and it gave Stenwold a sudden new lease of strength, able to push himself to his feet and weave towards the sea and the piers and . . .

And no ship. The docks were empty.

Behind the sea wall? For that had been the *Tidenfree*'s trick before, and what Wasp would think to look there, that even the Collegiate Port Authority had contrived to overlook.

Except there was a Wasp leadshotter positioned out on the sea wall already. And, even as he spotted it, an exhalation of smoke burst from it, with the sound following like thunder soon after.

Out across the harbour, out on the open sea, a tiny ship was riding, forced well out of artillery range.

'Tomasso!' he gasped.

'I see it. Just keep going, you fool!'

There were Wasps coming now – not many, not just yet, but a dozen was more than enough. Stenwold found he no longer even had his snapbow. He had abandoned it some time during their trek.

'I understand.' And he was still running, forcing himself forwards one stride at a time, onto a pier now, a ramshackle old one with a storage hut at the far end, a place he had gone to before.

'Good!' Tomasso cried – and then he was abruptly no longer at Stenwold's side. His small body spun under the snapbow bolt's impact and then he was gone, knocked off the pier into the water. Two more bolts fell past Stenwold, like errant drops of rain.

And Stenwold had run out of places to go.

He stopped there, with the heels of his boots at the furthest edge of the pier, and watched as the Wasps feathered down out of a clear sky. Some of them must have known who he was, and communicated it to the rest, because the shooting had stopped now. They were just advancing across the docks, snapbows levelled.

Behind them, he saw his city as if for the first time: the newest subject state of the Wasp Empire, the furthest encroachment of the Black and Gold, despite all the blood and tears that had gone into keeping it free.

He raised a fist in the air. 'Liberty!' he cried.

As they reached the landward end of the pier, he took one step back, and let the water take him.

Epilogues

The Antspider

They had kept her imprisoned for more than a day, with a little brackish water but no food at all. The pain in her eye, where a sword-guard had been rammed into her face, had fallen into its own stubborn, unvarying rhythm, fading until she almost forgot about it, then flaring up just as she did. She had not dared to take the matted cloth from it to see . . . to see if there was anything to see.

Her hand felt better: if she did not move it, then it was almost painless. The Imperial surgeon in charge of fixing her up enough to be worth torturing had done his job well there, at least.

Sometimes, soldiers passed by, and she found herself flinching away from them, despite herself, pain from her eye and hand stabbing at her together.

There was almost no light down here, and it was damp, and sometimes she could hear cries and begging from above, where the interrogators plied their trade.

She had discovered in herself a terrible fear of yet more pain and, although she tried to shrug it off flippantly and find some quip or dismissive remark to distance herself from it, she could not.

When at last she heard heavy footsteps descending to her cellar, and saw the sway of a lamp as one of her jailers approached, she shrank back into the corner they had penned her in, hearing her own breath grow ragged, and hating herself for it.

The lamp was hung up on the wall, to cast its uncompromising light across them both, and she saw that General Tynan himself had come to give her the bad news.

'Your friends failed,' he told her, 'but you knew that.' She could not fathom his expression, for none of the pieces seemed to fit together to make the man she had seen before.

'There's peace in Collegium tonight,' he said. 'First time in a while. We won. We won it all. We beat all of them.' He sat down heavily across from her, the light gleaming on his bald head. He looked anything but triumphant. 'What d'you think about that, eh?' He yelled it without warning, as though the Wasp victory was a crime and she was somehow responsible.

She had shrunk away from that yell, but now she turned her wide eye back to him and found him still staring at her, apparently wanting an answer.

Something surfaced in her that had been buried for too long. 'Should I be saying hooray for the Empire?' she whispered, her voice hoarse.

'Hooray,' Tynan echoed, and put his head in his hands. With a sudden lurching of perspective, she realized that he was the sort of pure clear drunk that even Collegiate students seldom aspired to, and comfortable enough with it that he had been walking straight and speaking without slurring his words.

'I killed her,' he stated, without qualification. 'I followed my orders. What else was I supposed to do? You can't go against the throne. Who would obey a general who hadn't obeyed his own orders, eh?' Looking up again, his reddened eyes challenged her. 'I couldn't have just walked away, could I? I couldn't have just said no.'

And then, losing focus on her. 'I thought *she* was going to kill me, when she summoned me back to Capitas. When she said she was giving me my Second back, I felt so proud . . .'

Straessa was now completely lost, unsure even how many

women the general was talking about, whether he was claiming to have killed the Empress herself, or any of it.

'When we were at the walls the first time,' he rambled on, 'I captured Stenwold Maker. You remember that? I had his woman, and he walked out to save her from the pikes, gave himself to me. I had him in my hands. And then the orders came to head for home, but I could have had him shot. I could have rid the world of Stenwold Maker!' A theatrical gesture, as though he had an audience of thousands. 'But I let him go – and you know why? I liked him. I respected him. He had the sort of courage a Wasp should have . . . and that I've seen a good few officers lack! He abandoned his city, put himself in the jaws of the trap, just to save his woman pain. She betrayed him later, he told me. And she died for it.'

Tynan reached around, fumbling at his belt, and she thought he was going for a weapon – absurd, as he could have stung her through the bars with ease. Then there was a flask in his hand and he knocked back a long swig of it, and held it out to her as if she was just another soldier he was drinking with.

She took it with her uninjured hand and drank from it cautiously, recognizing a fiery brandy that sent a jab of pain down her parched throat.

She handed it back, shaking only a little.

'And now we find,' Tynan remarked, 'that I am not as brave as Stenwold Maker. That I would not walk away from my city to save my woman. That is what we learn.' He drained the flask and threw it away, so that it clattered on the steps. 'Tell me about him.'

Straessa started. 'What?'

'Your man, the one I killed. What was he, to you?'

She took a moment trying to collect her thoughts but they were scattered all about her head, defying order. 'He was a fool who meant well,' she said at last. 'He never knew how to keep his mouth shut. He once almost got killed by Stenwold Maker. His best friend was a Wasp. He wanted there to be peace, and

635

the fact that he hadn't the faintest idea how to make that happen hurt him more than anything – more than almost anything.' Her voice remained level only through a great exercise of will. 'He would have been the best Speaker the Assembly ever had,' she went on. 'He could have healed the whole world.'

General Tynan, master of the Gears, stared past the bars at her. 'And when he was on the point of death, you came here for me, rather than staying by him,' he observed.

She nodded, but at that point could not trust herself to speak.

'Then we neither of us have the courage we should have had,' was his verdict, and next a great sigh. 'And now I have orders still: every Spider in Collegium who's still alive and hasn't fled, every Spider must die. The Empress, she now hates Spiders *so* much, and nobody can tell me why, not even her creature Vrakir. I have my orders.' And he stood up abruptly. 'Not one Spider must remain alive in Collegium.'

'I see,' Straessa acknowledged.

'But perhaps half a Spider, nobody will miss.'

When he unlocked the bars, fumbling messily with the keys and then lifting the whole cage section away with more strength than she would have credited him with, she was not sure what to do. Here was General Tynan, the man she had come to kill. Here he was, drunk and off-balance, and surely he had a knife somewhere she could snatch. She could cut the head off the whole Second Army.

But the injured parts of her cringed away at the thought of it, and besides, *We neither of us have the courage we should have had*. And how true.

She tried to slip past him, not trusting her luck to bear her weight another moment, ready for the inevitable reversal. And he seized her wrist – her bad hand – dragging her back with a screech of pain.

In that moment, all her defiance was overwritten by a desperate begging need to live, and to be free from pain, and nothing else was real to her but that.

He tried to stuff something into her broken fingers, obviously not understanding why she was writhing and twisting in his grip, but at last she grabbed at it with her good hand, finding an untidy fold of papers.

'Pass,' he managed to explain. 'Or you'd not get ten yards from here. But, more, you're my messenger now. You're going to Sarn – official Imperial courier.'

Sarn still stands? If there was ever a point in her life when she had needed the feeblest spark of hope, it was now.

'Just go,' Tynan gave her a shove towards the stairs. 'Get out of my city before I change my mind.'

She went.

Jen Reader

The message had been written in haste, perhaps intended for the hand of some messenger already halfway out of the door on a greater errand.

Jen
Safe in Sarn and hoping against hope this reaches you.
Sarn safe for now. Eighth Army driven off at cost. Another Wasp force somewhere out there, so no immediate chance of marching to liberate Collegium, but hold on! A lot of expatriates here, and Sarnesh must come south sooner than later, before Empire can reinforce. That's my understanding, anyway. Meantime sorting out Ants' air power, of course.

Any word of Stenwold Maker much appreciated. Lot of people say he is dead, like poor Jodry.

If you get this, tell little Jen I'm fine, and coming home as soon as I can.

Will send more word.

W.

The message had been slipped under the door of her store cupboard at the library, and she could only assume that a reply might be dispatched the same way. When she tried to put pen to paper, her hand shook too much. Willem was safe, and in Sarn! That was enough.

She had thought life in Collegium was settling down. Having destroyed all resistance, the Wasps seemed to be lapsing to a sullen, constant oppression. Those few who were still foolish enough to aggravate them paid the price, but the business of the city was slowly resuming, each move tentative and wary of repercussions. There had been some trade with Helleron, although the prices were horrendous. In the markets, traders set out their pitiful wares and charged the earth. The Wasps, who had initially just taken what they wanted, were now supplied by airship and seemed to have actual money to spend, becoming the clientele that every Collegiate business must be ready to cater to. The boldest restaurants and tavernas and even theatres had reopened their doors, gingerly sounding out the Wasps' tastes. The city was not thriving, but it lived.

And she had returned to the College library, dreading what she might find there after the fighting, after its occupation by the city's valiant, doomed defenders. The shelves and their precious burdens, the stacked cellars, all of them seemed intact, and she had been able to pass through all those familiar halls and turn a blind eye to the dark stains on the stonework, or the black charring left by stingshot.

The College itself would reopen soon, someone had claimed. She was not sure about that, but the library needed her.

Then, today, she had found an intruder there.

The fright had nearly killed her. She had been walking between the shelves, pushing a trolley of books that had needed filing since before the gates fell, and there he was: a tall, arrogant-looking Wasp soldier wearing red armour at his shoulders and neck.

'You are the librarian?' he demanded.

She had been about to give her name, but decided against it, settling for a nod.

'I am Captain Vrakir, and I am the voice of the Empress,' he told her, as a statement of fact. 'You are in a position to serve my mistress. Rejoice, therefore. Your loyalty to the Empire will be noted.'

He wants me to betray Willem, she had thought instantly, gripped rigid by terror. *What will he do? What will I do?*

He thrust a scroll at her. 'Here is a list of works known to be in your collection somewhere.' His other hand encompassed the entire library, the gesture of a man who had no patience with her elaborate cataloguing systems. 'You will find them quickly and present them to the main barracks.'

She cast an eye down the list, then looked up at him, frowning. 'You're sure? Only these are—'

'You will address me as *sir*!' he snapped. 'And you will *not* question me. This is the Empress's will. These volumes are to be shipped to Capitas immediately.'

The sacrilege of that, to remove such volumes from the library, from the very *city*, almost had her protesting, but she realized just in time how close he was to violence. And, besides, these titles were mouldering tomes of ancient lore, worm-eaten histories of the Bad Old Days. Considering the alternative, she could almost convince herself that she would not be betraying her trust by letting them go to the Wasps. Odds were that they probably had not been read at all in living memory.

But nonetheless it was wrong, though she knew she had no choice but to comply. Amid the shock of carving off pieces of the College's collection at the whim of a Wasp, the question of why the Empress should require such reading matter wholly passed her by.

639

Bergild

With Collegium finally secure, the Second Army settled into what was anticipated to be a temporary custodianship of the city until the newly appointed governor and his occupation forces arrived.

Save for Wasp forces, the streets of the city were dead for the first tenday after the fighting finally ended. The locals stayed inside, and hoped that the next door to be kicked in would not be theirs. Imperial soldiers were out on the streets, trying to search the entire city for Spider-kinden and suspected insurgents. There were some executions, but surprisingly few by Bergild's reckoning. Still, everyone knew the Collegiates were soft, so they would probably never realize the disconcerting leniency with which they were being treated.

As the pilot understood it, the problem lay at the top. General Tynan, who had been expected to mastermind whipping the Empire's new possession into line, was ill. Or some said not ill but just brooding. His officers and men waited for him to let them off the leash, but such orders as did come simply reined them in. Even now, there were probably rebellious students and fugitives hiding in the garrets and the cellars of the city, yet Tynan would not give the requisite orders. Bergild had heard that, after setting out the limits of the army's conduct prior to the students' revolt, he had given relatively few orders since. She had also heard he was practically at war with Captain Vrakir of the Red Watch. She had heard far too many things for them all to be true. Her pilots, with little enough to do, were getting restless and uneasy, well aware of how they were regarded by the regular army as something of a necessary freakshow.

So it was that she had been deputized by her followers to go and seek out her best source of information within the army: Major Oski.

The little engineer was remarkably difficult to track down, but she eventually found him sitting outside a taverna near the Gear Gate – as the Second now called the entrance to Collegium which it had forced. She recalled the place had been damaged in the fighting and then sacked by soldiers after the surrender, and certainly the taverna was no longer opening its doors in any meaningful sense. And yet here was Oski sitting on a folding stool outside it as though he was enjoying the weather, a bottle of wine beside him.

'Captain,' he remarked, as she approached.

'You seem to have time on your hands,' she noted.

'I'm making vital Engineering Corps calculations,' he told her, and took up the bottle with both hands to offer her some. 'Anyway, last I heard, nothing needs fixing or blowing up, so here I am.'

'Tynan doesn't need you?' she ventured.

'Don't know what the man needs, but it's clearly not me,' he confirmed. 'That's all, is it?'

'We want to know what's going on,' she ventured.

'Doesn't everyone?' As he spoke, she became aware of a faint murmur of voices from inside the taverna. She leant closer to eavesdrop, but abruptly Oski rose before her, wings flickering.

'So let's go and discuss,' he said, a little too loudly. 'I'll wager I've got something for your pilots to chew on.'

'Oski, what *is* going on?' she asked, not moving.

'Nothing, *Captain*. Engineering Corps business, therefore none of yours.' He was right up close to her, forcing her to step back out of instinct, for fighting room.

'Major—'

'Bergild,' he told her. 'Never you mind. Not your concern. You know what your lads want to hear? About how Sarn kicked the arse of the Eighth Army all of a sudden. About how our pissing relief column, Collegiate governor and all, is now stuck out at Malkan's Stand to keep the Ants pinned down. Meaning we're not going anywhere, and Tynan's acting governor – which you can be sure he's just mad about.'

And that *was* what her people wanted to know about and, of

course, if a superior officer said it was none of her business, then that was true. Yet something in his manner, some furtive guilt, had communicated itself to her, so as she stepped aside with him, she was already detailing one of her pilots to get a glass and keep a more distant eye on the derelict taverna.

She was not disappointed. A half-hour later, as she saw it through her man's eyes, a unusual half-dozen crept out of the place, one by one, and headed off in separate ways. She recognized Ernain the Bee-kinden, and there was a Beetle there, and another couple of Flies, and all of them in uniform, though she suspected few were actually attached to the Second. The last one out was a Grasshopper-kinden, though, and that set the seal on her suspicions, because she was sure enough that the Engineers weren't recruiting from the Inapt these days.

A conspiracy, she decided, but that thought she kept to herself.

Sartaea te Mosca

Nobody was entirely sure who had dared go to General Tynan and ask if they could resume lectures at the College. Had it been someone possessed of great courage, or with a keen eye as to the mood of the reclusive acting-governor? Or had it simply been one of those academics so wrapped up in their studies that the perils of the world beyond their books failed to register?

But General Tynan had taken a moment away from his introspection to give the proposal the nod, and a tenday later there were students cautiously creeping into the College's halls once again.

Of course, things were not the same. How could they be? Even with Tynan himself practically a recluse, Collegium had a new administration. All the Consortium factors and clerks and bureaucrats that the Empire had sent to take over the running of Collegium had arrived on schedule, and the Imperial machine had long experience of taking conquered cities in hand with brutal efficiency. What had not arrived, of course, was the garrison that had been due to take the weight of Collegium off Tynan's shoulders. Instead it – and the colonel originally awarded the governorship – had been diverted in order to counter any move by the Sarnesh, and to reinforce the surviving strength of the Eighth Army, and so Tynan had been denied his chance to march away towards Vek and leave this city he plainly detested behind him.

The classes were now smaller: this was te Mosca's unavoidable observation as she moved through the College. There were missing faces – dead or fled – and everyone was quieter. Where before those students out of lectures had been raucous in their debate and merriment, now they went about their business with a soft step and whispered voice, because nobody wanted to be noticed any more.

Faced with Tynan's unexpected acquiescence, the administration beneath him had done their best to stamp the entire venture with black and gold. Every class would include an observer, nominally there to allow the Imperials to understand their new subjects better. In some classes, indeed, this unwanted new addition was very attentive indeed, more so even than the students themselves. When the College Masters gathered together behind closed doors, those who taught artifice agonized at the fact that they must either cripple their own teaching, or pass Collegium's mechanical knowledge piecemeal to the Engineering Corps. Teachers of social history had a worse time. One of them had simply disappeared early on, after forgetting herself during her lectures. The only sort of philosophy and political theory that the Empire would tolerate was its own.

Other observers seemed to be simple soldiers drafted in to make up the numbers, especially for such subjects as the Empire plainly had no use for and considered trivial. Their impact on classes was disconcertingly random – some simply knocked off for a drink at the start, or sat there and read, or just stared into space. Others took too much of an interest, such as the sergeant who had decided he was an art critic and used his sting to torch an entire class's life-painting efforts.

One of the Living Sciences lectures on anatomy had supposedly been commandeered by a Wasp who displayed a knowledge of the human body, its breaking points and tolerances, far in excess of the lecturer himself.

But Sartaea te Mosca, Associate Master and teacher of Inapt studies, was lucky, and she had pushed that luck a very long way indeed. After all, she was teaching a subject that the Wasp-kinden could not understand and did not care about. So far, her observer had been a Wasp soldier who had plainly been bored to tears by her ramblings, so usually just fell asleep.

And, all the while, she and her students spoke treachery. They spoke in the language of the Moths, who used the same words as everyone else but employed them very differently. They conferred about events within Collegium as though they were dry old histories, nicknamed living men and women with the monikers of ancient heroes. At first her class had been the usual handful of awkward Inapt and clueless Apt, but by now she was 'teaching' to a score of the city's finest, who came and mastered the conventions and the subterfuge they employed because nowhere else could they talk freely under the noses of their oppressors.

Sartaea te Mosca had never dreamt that her insignificant little class might ever provide so much of a service to the world.

She stepped into her classroom now – still the same cramped, high-ceilinged room as before, although it was getting difficult to fit everybody in these days – and she halted.

The expected bored Wasp soldier was not there. Instead, she faced a lean Moth-kinden man in grey robes, who looked at her with disdain.

'You are the lecturer in "Inapt studies", called te Mosca?' he inquired.

'Yes, that's me.' Sartaea had been trained by Moths, accepted into their halls because she had some magical talent, and yet never truly made welcome because that talent was not great. This man's arch and penetrating scrutiny brought those cold and unhappy days back to her with a vengeance. 'Can I help you?'

'I have been sent to Collegium from Tharn to assist our allies in the Empire with matters that Wasps themselves might not quite comprehend,' he said, pointedly offering her no name. 'I will be sitting in on your teaching, although what could possibly pass for true learning in a den of the Apt such as this eludes me. Perhaps you will surprise me. Perhaps your students are all budding magicians. We shall see.' His blank, white eyes seemed to see into every corner of her. 'I look forward to your words, te Mosca. And, rest assured, I shall be reporting to the administration on your fitness to teach.'

After her students had filed in, she stood before them, and began stammering her way through an old lecture, some genuine tangled Moth-kinden philosophy that most of those assembled there would never be able to grasp. Every time the Moth coughed, or shuffled, or just looked at her in a certain way, she trailed off into silence.

The day after that, she cancelled her classes.

General Roder

It could have been worse.

For Roder himself it almost certainly would become worse. The Eighth had been facing nothing short of extinction when the Sarnesh had barrelled in to catch his forces between themselves and the Mantis-kinden. And it had been *all* the Mantis-kinden, as far as he could work out, the Eighth's mere presence having apparently mended a rift that had stood between Etheryon and Nethyon for longer than histories recorded.

The defences that his men had put in place had slowed the Sarnesh charge and, had the Wasps been able to concentrate their efforts, then Roder was confident that the Ants would have been scythed down in their ranks and thrown back, just as they had been before Malkan's Stand. By that point, though, there had been several hundred Mantis-kinden running rampant behind the lines – and they were swift and deadly, able to fly or just leap over any trenches or barriers the Wasps had put up. They had the same grasp of tactics that Roder had marked in their clashes with the Eighth before the supposed alliance with the Nethyen – making effective use of their archers to bedevil the Wasp Light Airborne, continually disrupting any attempt to contain or flank them.

Had it been just the Mantids, or just the Sarnesh . . . but the two of them together had squeezed and squeezed until the basic ability of the Eighth to coordinate and function as an army had come apart at the seams, individual officers and detachments being swamped and destroyed, or falling back without orders.

Even then, Roder had done his best, sending out messengers by the minute to turn a threatened rout into a halfway disciplined retreat. He had saved as much as he could of his men. He had pulled the Sentinels back, and even salvaged some of the lighter artillery pieces.

He had been forced to abandon the greatshotters, however, those marvels of Iron Glove Cartel artifice, and now the Sarnesh engineers would be all over them. He had thus given one of the Empire's greatest weapons into the hands of the enemy. At least General Tynan, when he had been forced back from Collegium that first time, had possessed the decency to have his artillery destroyed by aerial bombardment.

He wondered where the Empress was now. If she was dead, then he might yet get to live, though hardly in glory. Did this new Mantis business mean her own insane errand into the forest had been fatal for her? Was the Empire even now rudderless?

The Eighth had pulled back south-east, away from the forest, away from Sarn. Subsequent scouting suggested that his forces had, against all odds, inflicted sufficient damage on the Sarnesh that the Ants were leery of immediately renewing hostilities, and the Mantids had not ventured far beyond their forest borders. Probably the two kinden were cautiously feeling out just where they stood with each other.

He had dutifully sent word to Capitas that he had failed, and asking for fresh orders. The temptation to falsify his report had been strong, but he suspected that the Rekef would have people amongst his officers who would ensure the truth was told back home, and hence honesty became perforce the best policy.

Yesterday those orders had arrived. The Empress's personal seal was missing, but the word was brought by one of those Red Watch types, stating as always how he was the Empress's own mouth. There was no suggestion that the Empress had gone missing, and Roder sensed that to ask the question would be even more hazardous than losing a battle to the Sarnesh.

From a lack of contrary word, he could only assume that he was still in command, and still in the war.

That night he had slept better than he had for a tenday, only to be woken before dawn by a commotion that he knew could mean only one thing. The Sarnesh were attacking. They had fooled his sentries and scouts somehow. He could hear shouts and screams already within the camp.

There was no time for armour, but he grabbed his sword from its scabbard and stumbled out into the grey half-light, demanding reports.

For a moment he could only see his own men rushing about, hear the crackle of stingshot, panicking cries from all around. He had no sense of which direction the attack was coming from.

Then he saw a man fall ten yards away, just tripping on nothing, then a moment later he had half-vanished, the ground beneath him caving in, tents nearby collapsing as their guy ropes flew free. Roder gaped, any words dying in his mouth, trying to understand what he was seeing.

Another soldier rushed forwards to help the stricken man, but something lashed out at him, a lithe, whip-like strike from the pit, and the rescuer fell back and then collapsed, convulsing and screaming.

Roder found his feet taking him nearer, despite a horrible atavistic fear that had sprung up in him. He had to know; he had to see.

The earth was falling away and there was a tunnel there, and surely this meant the Sarnesh had found some new way to employ their ant minions . . . or they had some new machine, or . . .

A knot of things was writhing within, long and twisted, segmented, and bristling with legs. Some raised their heads as he approached, barely more than two whipping antennae and a pair of curved, poisonous claws.

The world was full of venomous creatures, of course. There were spiders and scorpions aplenty, and many of them pressed into service as riding or draught animals, guards and even pets. There was one beast that no one had tamed, however, and those were killed on sight as often as not. There were stories and legends regarding them that the Apt scholars scoffed at, and that the Hornet-kinden told one another about their campfires in their superstitious, credulous way. Those stories were all running through Roder's mind right then, watching this writhing mass disentangle and uncoil itself. And, beyond them, in the pit . . .

He saw them, the kinden, as they emerged from the earth in a rapid column, one after another moving with a sinuous coordination, each practically on the heels of the one before. They were like no people he had ever seen, and a dreadful similarity occupied all their faces, enough to make an Ant shudder.

For all their discipline, they made a weirdly primitive show. They had armour of chitin plates and short blades and some were wielding slings, not even a crossbow amongst them. A laughable threat, said those rational parts of Roder's mind that were currently in the minority.

He saw his soldiers reacting, and most of them held snapbows – and surely these soil-dwellers wouldn't even know what a snapbow *was*.

And yet his men were not shooting. Most stood there and held their snapbows as though they had never seen them before, jabbing them at the enemy as though they knew the devices were weapons, but not what to do with them. Others were already resorting to their stings, but by then the subterranean warriors were upon them, and there were more crawling from the earth all around, snaking lines of them issuing from tents or just rising from the dusty ground, along with their murderous beasts.

Someone ran past Roder, one of the Bee-kinden that drove the Sentinels, and the general grabbed for the man's shoulder, spinning him round. 'Get in your machine!' he demanded, for surely those killer automotives would serve to scatter these attackers.

But the man just stared at Roder as though some part of his mind had been excised. 'My . . .?' he mouthed. 'Machine . . .?'

And Roder stared at him and realized that he now had no idea of what he himself meant. He and the Bee-kinden gaped at one another, while all around them the remnants of the Eighth Army disintegrated.

Raullo Mummers

And life in Collegium settled and found its new level. The Wasps had turned from a threat to a terror to a fact that must be lived with.

There were arrests still. A month after the final quashing of the student insurgency they were no longer common, but not a tenday went by without word of someone's broken door found hanging open, someone vanishing into the Imperial administration district that had been established around the Gear Gate. Some few were next seen on the crossed pikes, others were not seen again at all. Some were released again, and it was a different kind of horror to see their family and colleagues and acquaintances react to them: *What did you tell them, that they let you go?*

649

Raullo Mummers had expected to be arrested before this, because he had been in the College library building, because he had been part of the crowd that had lynched Helmess Broiler, simply because he had been *there*.

Two tendays later, he had finally come to terms with the fact that nobody cared. Nobody had been making a list of names back then, and in any event he had not been on the walls with a snapbow. Carrying a stretcher had been the greatest blow he had struck for the freedom of Collegium, and even that experience had terrified him close to death.

The only tangible upshot of his ineffectual, inebriate presence during the fighting had been this room he now occupied, situated over a taverna: a low-ceilinged garret a fraction of the size of his old studio, which had burned down during the bombing of the city. The taverner had a daughter, a student who had played a rather more active part in the insurgency, and she had spoken up for him. Otherwise, Raullo would have found himself without even a roof over his head.

His landlord's tolerance was a limited resource, though, just like any commodity in Collegium right now. Raullo knew that the man would come muttering for rent soon enough. There were plenty of other dispossessed in the city, and most of them better able to pay their way than an artist who no longer painted.

He had not put brush to canvas since his studio burned, save that one crude sketch for Eujen's doomed pamphlet. His life had been contained there, in the sum accumulation of his sketches, roughs and drafts curling and cindering from the walls in the wake of the incendiary. His entire career had burned, quite separate from this lumpen body of his that Eujen had dragged from the building. Apart from that, when he reached into himself for that piece of him from which inspiration grew, he found only a cracked, charred void.

Last night, though, he had dreamt: the first dream he could recall since the fires. He had woken shouting, fighting against the thin blanket, seeing it all ablaze, his careful linework, his life studies, his friends.

He had dreamt of Gerethwy and Averic, of Straessa and Eujen. But his dreams had given them all over to the flames. He had abandoned them there and fled the building, only to find the city outside roasting on the same pyre.

Now he stood with a canvas before him, in the poor light of the garret room, holding a brush in his hand. He had begged these meagre materials, drained the city of any residual good-will it might hold for him, because there was a new flame lit in that burnt-out core of him – and it hurt, and it seared him, and he had to get it out.

He took some black paint up on his brush and set to work.

What he made of the canvas was not art, at least not any art that he recognized. Collegiate patrons had always known what they liked: imitate life, capture the truth of a likeness or a landscape, and the plaudits would follow. Everyone knew that.

What Raullo created that day was something even he would barely own to. It was a horror of jagged shapes, the black of shadow, the red of leaping flames, twisted faces merging half into fallen walls, and the press of rushing human forms. Not what life looked like, but how it felt.

When it was done, he felt that he had vomited something up, purged himself painfully of a corruption that would only well up again in time.

He took it down to show the landlord, and the man and his daughter both stared at it for a long time.

'I can't look at it,' his landlord admitted at last; still staring. 'What is it?'

Raullo could only shrug.

'Take it away,' the man insisted, but he stopped Raullo when the artist tried to leave. 'Hammer and tongs, what have you done?'

He hung it up in the taverna's taproom two days later. He

claimed he could not stop thinking about it. He even bought Raullo more canvas, without being asked.

Two days later the landlord knocked at the door of the garret. 'Mummers, come out. There's someone here.' His voice sounded strained.

Raullo put his head round the door blearily – late rising and wine were two habits, at least, that had survived the ending of the war. 'What is it?'

'Someone wants to see you.' There was a warning note in the taverner's tone. 'He wants to buy your painting.'

The taproom was silent, when Raullo descended. Those few drinkers still present would not look at him.

'You are the artist?' The man at the bar had been staring at his painting, but now he turned. The captain's rank badge on his uniform flashed as it caught the sun.

'Yes, sir,' Raullo breathed raggedly. Everyone knew the correct way to address Wasps these days.

'How much?' the Wasp asked him. And Raullo was about to refuse to sell, or say something even more rash, but he looked the man in the face and saw what he had missed the first time: that gaunt, hollow expression about the eyes. Here was a man, of no matter what kinden, who had seen enough of what the artist had seen to understand.

Raullo named a sum.

Eujen Leadswell

When he awoke, there was a hand in his that he knew.

She screamed when he squeezed it, for all that it was a faint and pitiful motion, and was across the room from him, shaking and choking, staring at him as though . . .

As though I've come back from the dead.

The eyepatch suits her. Such a random thought, at such a moment.

Later on she would tell him everything: how they were now in the Sarnesh Foreigners' Quarter, which was thronging with Collegiate expatriates and Mynan exiles, all agitating to take back their own and each other's cities; how Castre Gorenn was now calling herself the Collegiate Retaliatory Army, and she wasn't the only one. She would tell him how the Mantids of the forest – the Netheryon it was now – had suffered some kind of radical change of policy, and were now negotiating with the Sarnesh high command.

She would explain how the Sarnesh had chased off the Imperial Eighth, but got a bloody nose in the bargain, and how a new force of Wasps appearing from Helleron had led to a complex chess game between the Ants and the Empire which neither side was ready to bring to an endgame, especially now that fighting had erupted between the Wasps and the Spiders down along the Silk Road. Seldis was ablaze, they said.

And about the raids, of course: villages not far from Sarn that had been found empty, with not a witness, not a body, only disturbed earth – so that people were talking about some terrible new Imperial weapon, save that some scouts had found Wasp camps similarly deserted.

And, at last, she would tell him that he had been lost to the world for almost three tendays, while the Instar fought against the injury within him, although she would never tell him how she had despaired, back in Collegium, and had abandoned him. And she would tell him of Averic, and Gerethwy, and all their other friends who had not left Collegium. And she would tell him that Stenwold Maker himself was believed dead, though nobody would admit to having seen a corpse. There would come a time for all these revelations.

But, for now . . .

'Hello, the Antspider.' His voice sounded faint in his own ears.

'Hello, Chief Officer Eujen.' Her smile seemed the most fragile thing he had ever seen, himself included. 'Where the pits have you been, eh?'

The Others

Across the Lowlands and the Empire and beyond, cracks had begun to show.

Tiny fissures, hairline fractures in stone, like the unexpected gap that those students had crossed to escape the doomed College. But they were deep. Look down into that sliver of abyss, and there might be distant lights, movement.

Sometimes the cracks were more than that, chasms rupturing wide into caves, the earth abruptly hollow . . . and then things came out.

They took the living and the dead. They left no bodies. They cared nothing for Empire or Lowlands, Apt or Inapt.

They had been away a long time, but they had not forgotten.

Glossary

Characters

Aagen – renegade Wasp, now of Princep Salma
Akkestrae – leader of the Felyen Mantids within Collegium
Amalthae – forest mantis
Amnon – former First Soldier of Khanaphes
Argastos – ancient Moth mystic
Arvi – Fly-kinden secretary to Jodry Drillen
Averic – Wasp student at Collegium
Balkus – renegade Sarnesh Ant, now of Princep Salma
Bergild – Wasp Air Corps captain with the Second Army
Berjek Gripshod – Beetle-kinden lecturer in history at the College
Brant – Wasp engineer lieutenant, Second Army
Castre Gorenn – Dragonfly archer with the Coldstone Company
Ceremon – Nethyen Mantis, consort of Amalthae
Cheerwell Maker – Inapt Beetle magician
Cherten – Wasp colonel, Intelligence Rekef, Second Army
Cornella Fassen – student at the College
Dariandrephos (Drephos) – master artificer and leader of the Iron Glove
Despard – Fly artificer, *Tidenfree* crew
Elder Padstock – Beetle chief officer, Maker's Own Company
Ellery Heartwhill – student at the College
Elysiath Neptellian – Master of Khanaphes

Ernain – Bee engineer captain, Second Army

Esmail – Assassin Bug spy masquerading as the Wasp Ostrec

Eujen Leadswell – Beetle student and leader of the Student Company

Gerethwy – Woodlouse student at the College

Gjegevey – Woodlouse adviser to Empress Seda

Gorrec – Wasp Pioneer sergeant, Eighth Army

Grief – formerly Grief in Chains. Butterfly Monarch of Princep Salma

Hanto – Fly Pioneer, Ninth Army

Helma Bartrer – Beetle historian and diplomat

Helmess Broiler – Beetle Assembler, Wasp sympathizer

Howell Graveller – Bettle student at the College

Icnumon – halfbreed Pioneer, Eighth Army

Jadis of the Melisandyr – Spider bodyguard to Mycella

Jen Reader – Beetle College librarian and wife of Willem Reader

Jodry Drillen – Beetle-kinden Speaker for the Collegiate Assembly

Jons Allanbridge – Beetle aviator

Jons Escarrabin – Beetle Pioneer, Eighth Army

Kymene – Mynan commander in exile

Laina Mowwell – Beetle soldier of the Student Company

Laszlo – Fly agent and occasional pirate

Lissart – Firefly agent and arsonist

Madagnus – Ant-kinden chief officer, Coldstone Company

Maure – halfbreed magician from the Commonweal

Milus – Sarnesh Ant tactician

Morkaris – Spider-kinden mercenary adjutant for Mycella

Mycella of the Aldanrael – Spider noblewoman

Nethonwy – ancient Woodlouse adviser

Nistic – Hornet-kinden captain

Oski – Fly engineer major, Second Army

Ostrec – Wasp Rekef major, Esmail's disguise

Paladrya – Kerebroi adviser of the Sea-kinden

Parrymill – Beetle-kinden Collegiate Assembler

Peddic Gorseway – Beetle-kinden soldier of the Student Company

Remas Boltwright – Beetle chief officer, Fealty Street Company

Roder – Wasp general, Eighth Army

Sartaea te Mosca – Fly lecturer in Inapt studies at the College

Scorvia – Sarnesh Ant sapper-handler

Seda I – Empress of the Wasps

Sentius – Sarnesh Ant commander

Serena – Fly officer, Fealty Street Company

Sperra – Fly of Princep Salma

Stenwold Maker – Beetle-kinden, War Master of Collegium

Storvus – Beetle-kinden Collegiate artisan

Straessa – the Antspider, officer of Coldstone Company

Syale – Roach-kinden diplomat of Princep Salme

Taki – Fly aviator of Solarno and Collegium

Tegrec – Wasp magician, ambassador to the Empire from Tharn

Terastos – Moth agent from Dorax

Termes – Vekken Ant commander

Thalric – renegade Wasp

Tisamon – dead Mantis Weaponsmaster raised by Seda

Tomasso – Fly-kinden pirate and merchant, captain of the *Tidenfree*

Tynan – Wasp general, Second Army

Tynisa – halfbreed Weaponsmaster, Tisamon's daughter

Vendall – Beetle Collegiate magnate

Vollery – Beetle Collegiate artisan

Vrakir – Wasp Red Watch captain

Willem Reader – Beetle Collegiate artificer

Wisden – Beetle Collegiate Assembler

Yraea – Tharen Moth diplomat and magician

Zerro – Fly scout working for the Sarnesh

Places

Capitas – capital of the Empire
Collegium – Beetle city-state
Commonweal – Dragonfly domain north of the Lowlands
Darakyon – Mantis forest, formerly haunted
Dorax – Moth retreat
Etheryon – Mantis hold
Felyal – Mantis hold and forest
Helleron – Beetle city-state
Hermatyre – Sea-kinden city
Kes – Ant island city-state
Khanaphes – ancient Beetle city-state
Malkan's Folly/Malkan's Stand – battlefield, former site of Sarnesh fortress
Myna – Beetle city-state, formerly part of the Empire
Nethyon – Mantis hold
Princep Salma – city founded by refugees of the last war
Parosyal – Mantis-kinden sacred island
Sarn – Ant city-state, ally of Collegium
Seldis – Spider city
Solarno – Beetle city on the Exalsee
Spiderlands – large domain south of the Lowlands
Tark – Ant city-state
Tharn – Moth retreat
Vek – Ant city-state, recently at peace with Collegium

Organizations and Things

Amphiophos – Collegiate centre of government
Arcanum – Moth secret service
Aristoi – the Spider-kinden ruling class
Army Intelligence – Imperial army corps

Assembly – Collegiate ruling body

Aviation Corps – Imperial army corps, part of the Engineers

Battle of the Rails – battle in which Malkan's Seventh defeated the Sarnesh

Coldstone Company – Collegiate Merchant Company, motto: 'In Our Enemies' Robes'

Consortium of the Honest – mercantile arm of the Empire

Engineering Corps ('the Engineers') – Imperial army corps

Esca Magni – Taki's orthopter

Farsphex – new Imperial model of orthopter

Great College – Collegiate centre of learning

greatshotter – new Iron Glove-developed artillery

Imperial Eighth Army – commanded by General Roder

Imperial Fourth Army – 'the Barbs', destroyed by Felyen Mantids in the last war

Imperial Second Army – 'the Gears', commanded by General Tynan

Imperial Seventh Army – 'the Winged Furies', Malkan's command, destroyed by Sarnesh in the last war

Iron Glove – artificing cartel led by Drephos out of Chasme

lorn detachment – soldiers sent on a suicide mission

Maker's Own – Collegiate Merchant Company, motto: 'Through the Gate'

Malkan's Stand/Malkan's Folly – Sarnesh defeat of the Empire, now Sarnesh fortress

Outwright's Pike and Shot – Collegiate Merchant Company, motto: 'Outright Victory or Death'

Prowess Forum – Collegiate duelling school

Quartermaster Corps – Imperial army corps

Red Watch – new Imperial corps, the mouth of the Empress

Rekef – Imperial secret service, divided into Inlander and Outlander

Slave Corps – Imperial army corps

Spearflight – Imperial model of orthopter

Stormreader – Collegiate model of orthopter

Student Company – newly formed Collegiate unit, motto: 'Learn to Live'

Twelve-year War – Imperial war against the Commonweal

*Continue reading for an
exclusive short story set in
the world of the Apt from
Adrian Tchaikovsky.*

Heart of the Green

It was the storm that tipped the balance. Everything else could be accounted for as just bad luck. By Sergeant Corver's estimation, bad luck was his lot in life, as if by a decree of the Emperor himself. The storm, though: that was through the other side of his luck and into a whole different country.

Bad enough to be on this little airship in the first place, let alone without clear orders to tell any of them where they were going. Worse still to be under the command of a slimy, self-interested creature like Captain Ordan of the Rekef Outlander, roped into some secret mission. Worse even than that to be in this piss-pot defenceless little craft headed westwards of that north–south line that the Empire's armies had drawn across the Lowlands, on one side, 'ours', and on the far side – the side the airship was flying over – 'theirs'. Sandric, the pilot, had been keeping up a steady, wretched muttering for hours now, waiting for the dots of Sarnesh orthopters to appear. Then the sky had gone from blue to grey, from grey to a thunderous, angrier grey, the wind had picked up, and Corver's luck had simply taken the day off. *You don't need me any more*, it had told him. *You're now so thoroughly pissed on that I can't possibly make things worse.*

There had been an abortive conversation between Sandric and Captain Ordan with the pilot insisting that they needed to set down, and Ordan pulling rank: 'This is enemy territory! What do you think we'll see if we set down here?'

663

Well, quite, had been Corver's unspoken thought. *And so where the pits are we going?*

A day before he had been sitting in the quartermaster's tent, dicing with an off-duty engineer and the duty sergeant, when Ordan had commandeered him to load an airship. The loading had been of a single metal-bound chest, and Corver had commandeered Vrant, one of his regular squad – and even then the two of them had struggled. It was noticeable that the two other soldiers following Ordan like his shadow had not lifted a finger to help, neither had the shifty little Fly-kinden in a Consortium greatcoat, who was either the captain's secretary or his overage catamite. By the time the chest was ensconced in the back alcove of the cabin that made up most of the airship's below-decks, Ordan had given Sandric orders to lift off, and Corver and Vrant had simply never been allowed off the ship, unwillingly seconded to the Rekef Outlander.

Sandric had become increasing panicked as the wind picked up – meaning as the wind picked up the airship and started throwing it about the sky. There was no way he could hold a course, the pilot had insisted. They could end up anywhere. Ordan had shouted at him to do his job. That was really just the final brick in the tower of suspicions Corver had about Ordan – a piece of mental construction finished behind time, far too late to do any good. By then it was plain that not only did Ordan have no idea about flying airships, but also that his plan appeared to be mostly to do with moving *away* rather than specifically *towards*. Away, in this case, from the camp of General Malkan's Seventh Army.

There had been a shake-up in the Rekef – everyone had heard the rumours. They said there were purges going on. Corver, like any sane man, had as little to do with the Empire's secret police as possible, but his luck, once again his luck, had found a way to get him stuck right in there with them.

Ordan had retreated to the rear of the cabin as the wooden walls around them began creaking and shuddering, the gondola jumping like a puppet as the battered balloon pulled its strings. The engine kept chugging, but its propellers might as well not have been there. They had all become the wind's playthings, despite Sandric's best efforts.

Behind Ordan: the chest in its alcove, shifting against the ropes that held it there, ready to become the sort of missile suitable for siege warfare the moment its restraints broke. To either side of the chest, Lucen and Tarvoc, Ordan's two silent accomplices, ensuring that nobody as untrustworthy as a sergeant of the Seventh Army should so much as get a look in. The wretched little Fly, Sterro by name, was clinging on for dear life somewhere, looking pasty and about to throw up, whilst Sandric held futilely to the controls and pretended he had some influence on where they were going. Corver and Vrant were left to their own devices.

Corver's own devices took him to Sandric's shoulder, peering through the glass of the ports at the sky ahead and the land beneath. 'Stab me,' was his immediate reaction. 'Should there be all that *green* down there?'

'No, no there should not,' Sandric spat back, any other words lost in the instinctive whimper as the airship took another battering, every part of it creaking and straining and trying to break free from the rest. Corver tried to picture what the land west of the Seventh's camp looked like – a sergeant didn't get to see the campaign maps, but he knew that there was the city of Sarn there somewhere, and north of that . . .

He felt cold all over: the Mantis forest, the name of which he could not recall, but he had enough jagged memories of their kinden from the Twelve-year War. For a moment he was clinging to the back of Sandric's seat, seeing the dark between the trees, hearing the whoops of the Mantids and the screams of their victims, of Corver's own men . . .

Then something struck the airship hard, making it lurch far more than the mere wind could account for, and Sandric let out a high, panicked cry. Fleetingly the gondola and balloon were in serious dispute as to which of them should be above the other.

'What? What is it?' Captain Ordan was demanding, shouting over the gale.

The face that Sandric turned back on him was white with dread. 'There's something on the canopy, sir!' The entire airship lurched again, drunkenly. 'We've got to get it off, whatever it is!'

Ordan blinked at him for a moment, then jabbed a finger at Vrant. 'You! Get out there and see what's going on.'

For a moment Corver thought that Vrant wouldn't do it – not through fear of the weather or the unknown but just because Vrant was like that, but then the big soldier stomped over to the side hatch, braced himself and unlatched it. He had to lean into it with some force to push it open, but then the wind caught it and slammed it out against the hull, its invisible claws rushing into the cabin and whipping every loose thing about the enclosed space, dragging at everyone, the great void of the sky hungry for them to join it. Vrant bared his teeth, and then bundled himself through the hatchway.

He was a bad soldier, Vrant. In a fight, under pressure, none better, but without something to focus his attention on he was first in line for any disciplinary charge you cared to name. Half his military career had been spent undoing all the good the other half had won through hard fighting and bravery. Men like Ordan, Rekef men with big mouths and no backbone, got right up his nose.

We will have a reckoning when I'm done with this, he promised himself, and hauled his body onto the top of the gondola, his Art wings a constant blur as they fought to counter the tug and push of the wind. The balloon was a great bloated moon immediately above him, impossible to see what was supposed to be wrong with it from here. For a moment he couldn't even work out how to go about this – taking flight would be a sure recipe for ending up miles from the airship. Then he spotted that some of the lines holding the canopy to the gondola were made into rope ladders, presumably for some arcane engineer business not normally carried out in the teeth of a pox-rotten *storm*.

I am going to kill Captain Ordan with my bare hands.

He set to climbing, with the same bloody-minded stubbornness with which he approached most things. Immediately the wind tried to snatch him, but he was a strong man, and his angry thoughts made him stronger. One hand, one foot at a time, and he ascended, bouncing and dancing with the strumming ropes like a webbed fly with the spider coming. He did not look up, or anywhere except at the rope ladder itself, closed his ears to the storm, brought to the task the single-minded vigour he normally reserved for thwarting his superiors. At first he was climbing half-upside down, up the underside of the balloon, but then he was righting himself, creeping over the curve, feeling the wind only stronger as it sought to brush him off the great rounded expanse of the canopy.

Right then, what—

But as he lifted his head it was immediately obvious what. They had a new passenger, hitching a belligerent lift atop the balloon. Vrant, not a man prone to fear, felt it touch him nonetheless, before angrily shaking it off.

There was a praying mantis twenty feet long lying along the top of the balloon, the weight of the beast deforming the silk into a sagging bowl-shape. Its legs were spread wide, claw-feet digging for purchase, and it stared right back at Vrant with more self-possession than he himself could muster just then. The huge, glittering eyes that made up so much of its triangular head kept a steady hunter's gaze on him, even as its slender antennae were lashed about like whips by the wind.

Its wing-cases were part-folded, the wings themselves protruding unevenly from underneath, and he guessed that the storm had caught it in mid-flight, cast it through the air until this unhappy meeting of aircraft and insect.

But it was staring at him like a man stares, with that shock of contact, consciousness to consciousness, that Vrant had only ever known looking into the eyes of another human being. Impossible: it was only an animal, no matter how dangerous, but as it clung to the balloon, shifting its spread-eagled pose slightly as the wind howled, it watched Vrant with a calmly malign intelligence.

'Pits with you,' he snarled, and shot it: holding tight with his left, he whipped his right hand up, palm outwards, spitting a bolt of golden fire straight into the thing's face. He had an instant's image of one huge eye caved in, a scorched ruin. In the next moment, rather than rearing up or going for him, the great insect just flung its wings wide open, as if readier to trust the storm than his sting.

But he thought, in that moment, of the way it had looked at him, the depths of understanding that gaze had spoken of.

The wind grabbed at the mantis immediately, the wings like sails hauling it back along the balloon's sagging length and away, and the insect's barbed forearms, which had been dug into the silk, unseamed half the canopy as it left.

Abruptly the motion of the airship was not a valiant struggle against the hostile elements, but a lurching, shuddering descent, barely slower than falling, towards the great, grim green beneath.

At the end of all the screaming and shouting and wild plummeting, Corver's head was ringing hard enough that there was a blur at the edges of everything he looked at, whilst some part of the gondola's inner hull had fetched him a crack to the ribs hard enough that just drawing breath seemed a privilege reserved for higher ranks. He was wedged near the pilot's seat, bracing himself as best he could against the curve of the hull and waiting for the next lurch to send him the length of the cabin. The inevitability of it, the sudden dislodgement, the bone-breaking impact, crowded his mind and monopolized his attention. Only slowly did he become aware that the much-abused airship was no longer moving.

No longer moving at all, that was – neither that mad, murderous fall nor the gentle sway of its proper operation. They had come down at last.

There was a boot close to his head, and he clutched at it, and nearly got himself kicked in the face for his trouble. The rush of relief at this surprised him: he had not appreciated it, but some part of him had plainly written off everyone else on the airship already. He had taken himself as the lone survivor.

It would not be the first time.

'Sergeant?' came a hoarse voice from the other end of the boot.

Corver levered himself out, holding onto the pilot's seat and – as it turned out – the pilot. Sandric was still in place, the battered emperor of a broken world, one of the control levers snapped off in his hand. Aside from a great florid bruise across his forehead he seemed in one piece. His vessel was less lucky.

Everything was tilted, enough that Corver would have found himself sliding towards the stern hold had he let go. They had come down, but on nothing level. It was hard to get any idea of the damage, for the only light was a broad splash of it from the open side-hatch – the cover now forever torn away – and a little peering in from Sandric's viewport, which was mostly occluded by trees. The rear of the cabin was in darkness. *So, survivors? Is it just Sandric and me?* Vrant had been outside, Corver recalled, and he felt a sudden stab of loss at that. The two of them had served together for some years.

Then someone groaned from down there, and Corver remembered that he was a sergeant of the Imperial army.

'Sandric, get a lantern going.' He was trying not to think about that mess of green beyond the viewport, that forest landscape he had seen in the storm. *I've had enough trees to last me a lifetime.*

'Sergeant?' came a voice from the darkness, and Corver reflected that men like Captain Ordan had a staying power that roaches and beetles would marvel at.

'Here, sir,' he called dutifully, at around the time that Sandric found that the second lamp stashed by his controls was still intact. Abruptly the cabin was filled with a burned smell and the hissing and crackling as the white chemical fire threw a cold radiance across everything.

Ordan was down the far end, as unscathed as could be, glowering up at his subordinates. Beside him – and below him, now – the hold alcove had plainly taken the brunt of their descent – or at least shared it with a couple of trees. The combined shattered woodwork – natural and artificial – was such a mass of splinters, jagged edges and spars that Corver only saw the blood and mangled bodies a moment later. Lucen and Tarvoc, Ordan's two cronies, had been in the midst of all that when the airship had met the forest the hard way.

Ordan followed Corver's gaze, and swore furiously at the sight. For a moment he had almost redeemed himself by showing an iota of sorrow over the two dead men, but then he was shouting, 'Get down here and free the chest, Sergeant!'

'Sir?'

'You heard me!'

The chest – that one apparently filled with lead from Corver's recollections – had taken a fierce blow that dented one metal-bound corner, but it was still there, plainly visible amongst the bloody wreckage.

He glanced at Sandric, his expression plainly indicating that no amount of a-pilot's-place-is-at-the-controls was going to keep the man from pitching in, but then something darkened the hatchway.

In that moment, all three of them, even Sandric, had a palm directed at the intruder.

'No way to welcome a war hero,' the newcomer muttered, and Sandric's chemical lamp lit on the brutish features of Vrant.

Corver just stared at him for a moment, noting the cuts and bruises that had made the man's face, none too lovely to begin with, a child's nightmare. 'Present yourself for duty, soldier,' was all he said, but there was no keeping the relief from his voice.

'Just get down here and move the cursed chest!' Ordan spat at the lot of them, and then, 'And that goes for you as well, you sniveller!' He was jabbing a finger up at the canted ceiling, and they saw Sterro the Fly-kinden there, clinging to a bulkhead.

The chest had been hard enough to shunt into its alcove. Slick with the remnants of the dead men, wedged in amongst the splintered wood, it was a nightmare to haul the weight of it out, but the Imperial army was nothing if not bloody-minded about things, and eventually the dented, battered object was in the centre of the cabin, courtesy of three Wasps' efforts and in spite of Sterro's getting in the way.

'Now get it out of the wreck. We'll need to carry it overland,' Ordan decided.

'Excuse me, sir, but we haven't looked at salvaging the airship yet,' Sandric spoke up, unexpectedly.

Ordan, halfway to the hatch, stared back at him as if he were mad. '*Salvage?* Look at the thing!'

'But, sir!' Sandric tried, but Ordan had already hauled himself outside. The pilot glanced about, plainly unhappy with any orders that would take him out of the airship's sheltering hull and into the green beyond. It was a sentiment that Corver could only sympathise with.

'Get the chest out here!' Ordan bellowed from outside.

Corver looked at the malignant weight of the chest, and then at Vrant, whose expression was murderous, and who looked as though he was about to have one of his occasional lapses of military discipline. Swearing to himself, Corver abandoned the chest and followed Ordan outside.

He was met with the immediate and expected, 'I thought I gave you an order!' Ordan looked pale and unwell – not the crash nor the walls of over-arching forest that rose on all sides, Corver judged, but the man's own inner fears gnawing at him.

'Sir, have you thought this through—?' he started, and Ordan rounded on him furiously, a hair's breadth away from violence.

'An order, Sergeant! You remember those? I need that chest up here, right away! I need—' And for a moment, as Ordan choked on the word, it was evident that, whatever he needed, it had driven him to his absolute limit. The next instant there was a slender shaft quivering in his throat, flaring his eyes wide with shock, and yet suddenly unseeing. The captain pitched back-wards over the sloping rail and Corver dropped back through the hatch with a yell.

The next few moments were brutal. The attackers were right behind Corver, and two of them got in through the hatch before the Wasps could even think of holding it against them. They were swift and slender, a man and a woman, angular-framed, one with a spear and one with a dagger in each hand, ferocious as beasts. Vrant had his sword in his hand immediately, but the spearpoint was already at him, skittering from his banded mail more by luck than judgement. The blow knocked him back, though, and he was gritting his teeth against a sudden pain – not the spear but the battering he had received in the storm.

The woman with the daggers shrieked and leapt for Corver, but the soldier part of the sergeant's mind was working smoothly. He fell back, cutting at her with his own blade – in his grip without him having any memory of drawing it – and his left hand coming up open-palmed to sting, burning her across the body and throwing her back, twisting and hissing.

Sterro shouted out a warning, and Corver turned to see another lean man twisting in through the wreckage at the cabin's rear, leading with a long, slender blade. The Fly fled before him, hands covering his head, and Corver's stingshot flew wide as the new assailant lunged in.

Vrant found himself fighting over the spear-shaft with his opponent. He was the bigger man, and stronger, but he was trying to work around some cracked ribs, and the fierce-faced enemy was trying to lance the spines of his forearms into the Wasp's hide, scraping and scratching as they dug at his mail. Then Sandric turned up behind the man and put a bolt of crack-ling energy into the small of his back, which solved that problem. Corver fell back to join them, only inches ahead of the rapier's point, and Sandric surprised all three of them by turning and reflexively killing the swordsman too, searing half the man's face off.

The quiet that followed stretched out for a long time, as the Wasps waited to see whether there would be any more of them. Vrant and Corver had a soldier's stillness, but Sandric was pale and shaking in the aftermath of his heroics, and it was plain that he had gone a long time, as a pilot, without having to dirty his hands with actual killing.

'Mantis-kinden,' Vrant grunted, as though it was some great revelation. The three bodies looked ragged and half-staved, to Corver, and one had surely been no older than fourteen, but Mantis-kinden nonetheless, and therefore the enemy.

'We must be in the middle of the Nethy or whatever it's called,' he said heavily. 'So of course Mantis-kinden. And more than just three out there. Sandric.'

The pilot watched him warily.

'Get out there and find some cover. We need a lookout,' Corver told him.

'Me? Sergeant, it's solid forest out there, you can't see a thing.'

'Then you'd better keep a really good watch, is all.'

Sandric's eyes darted madly about the cabin until they found Sterro. 'Him, Sergeant! Why can't he go?'

This was a classic command decision, as far as Corver was concerned. Sandric was probably right: as a Fly, Sterro had better eyes than any of the Wasps. Still, the little maggot had even less nerve than Sandric – and besides, Corver had given an order, and stopping for debate was not what they taught you in the army.

'Just get on up there and do what you're told,' the sergeant snapped, and Vrant loomed in to back him up, so that Sandric cringed away, and then clambered through the hatch very much under protest, muttering to himself.

'Right.' Corver took a deep breath, and the words he did not say were, *What the pits are we going to do?* Instead he stared down at the chest balefully. 'Get this thing open. Let's see what's so important.'

Sterro began to squawk an objection, but Vrant was already

673

laying in with a will, stamping where the wood was already damaged, his hobnailed soldier's standard issues thundering down in a solid rhythm and finishing what the crash and subsequent manhandling had already started. The eighth or ninth kick stove in one side of the chest, and ruptured two of the cloth bags inside, so that an insidious little trickle of bright metal spilt out onto the cabin floor.

Sterro stopped making noises, his hands twitching. They probably taught the expression on his face to all Consortium men under the heading of *naked greed*.

'Oh, stab me,' Vrant groaned, and took hold of the broken wood, tearing away three sides of the chest to reveal the hoard within. That the little sacks were all stuffed with gold coin, nobody doubted for a second. It was all Imperial mint, and Corver wondered just how much of the Seventh Army's pay was sitting there in front of them.

Sterro lunged forwards as though the gold was dragging him, but the sergeant cuffed him off. 'So what was the plan? Where were we headed with – with *this*?'

'You think I know?' the Fly demanded. 'You think he told me anything?'

'I think you were his creature, and that's why he brought you,' Corver pointed out.

'He wanted someone to hold his piss-pot and open bottles for him. Not like he actually let me in on anything!' Sterro protested, but under the grim looks of both Wasps he shrugged. 'Look, you know about the lists, right? Bad time to be on the Rekef books right now – Insider or Outsider, open agent or hidden in the army, they'll come for you with their lists and then a quick death is the best of it. Look then, Captain Ordan, he made a piss-poor job of keeping friends.'

'You surprise me,' Corver grunted, but the pattern seemed eminently plausible. So this was the grand secret mission Ordan had dragged them on: nothing short of desertion, theft and probably treason. Where would he have ordered them to? Collegium?

Sarn? Somewhere he reckoned he could buy himself an amnesty with gold and information. Being dead on the end of a Mantis arrow was too good for him.

It was then that Sandric began to holler.

Some years ago, the Empire's Twelve-year War against the Dragonflies had been brought to an end when the Ants of Maynes staged a rebellion, cutting off the Wasps' supply lines into the Commonweal. Sandric had been part of the punitive force sent to teach the Ants a harsh lesson in Imperial policy, which he had effected by overflying them in a boxy armoured heliopter whilst his crew dumped shrapnel grenades on the revolting populace through the floor hatch. That had been his sole stint as a combat pilot. The balance of his career had been ferrying supplies and men to one army or another, and although he had cut close to many a battle, none of them had ever required his personal attendance. Yes, the soldiers of the Empire spoke loud of the glory of combat, the crackle of stings and reddening of swords, but Sandric's philosophy was that there always had to be someone to carry the freight, and no army could march without it. Sometimes it took one man with his head in the clouds to keep ten thousand men with their feet on the ground.

This business with Ordan was not what he had looked for in a career. His professional life would have been complete without having killed two Mantis-kinden – would most certainly have been so without crouching at the rail of the airship, half-hidden in the fallen branches that had come down over the raised bow, and straining his eyes against the impenetrable shadows of the forest.

It was gloomy beneath the trees, and he suspected that Mantids were one of the many kinden that nature had equipped with better eyes than his own. Even beyond the threat of them, the forest was busy with life, from the mosquitoes that were after his blood to the six-foot-long segmented chain of a centipede that had come prowling about the hull, pincer-fangs gaping hungrily as it lifted its head towards him, surely venomous enough to kill a man stone dead with a single bite.

He had just about given up the entire business for lost, was already thinking of himself in the category of *never heard from again*, when he saw it.

From the vault of the heavens came the promise of salvation. The sight was so startling that Sandric stood straight up, and cover be damned. It was another airship.

Another casualty of the storm, he decided, that had only now given up its fight with gravity – it was a rotund little craft, a small merchantman perhaps, handling badly and plainly in trouble, but the envelope looked mostly intact. He could hear the moan of its engine as it fell sideways overhead, seen through the gap in the foliage punched by their own descent.

A moment later his wings coalesced about his shoulders, and Sandric threw himself straight up, desperate to follow the stricken vessel's flight and already fumbling for his pilot's instruments. He was in time, too – although the craft had moved further than he had thought it would in the moments it was out of his sight, and away from the line he had thought it was taking. Still, he saw it come down, far off in the forest, and he knew that they had to reach it – it was pure, distilled hope.

Then he was yelling, and a moment later Corver and Vrant spilt out onto the canted deck, swords in hand and ready for trouble.

Neither of them understood what he meant, at first. The import of it escaped them.

'So some other poor bastards came down, so what?' was all Vrant thought of it. 'You want to go conquer them for the Emperor, or can we just get out of here?'

'Yes, yes we can get out of here,' Sandric said, his voice shaking with the effort of talking down to these army thugs. 'But not as we are. Our envelope – the *balloon* – is completely opened up – just rags of it left. But it looked as if this other ship, it had a fair spread of canopy left – maybe it even carried a spare.'

Corver was frowning. 'But . . .' He waved his hand at the shattered stern

'Seriously, sir, give me a balloon I can patch up, and some time, and I can float us out of here – it won't be pretty, but we've got the gear and the chemicals to brew up some more gas, and it doesn't matter if the hull's full of holes – it's not as if we're going to sink because of it. Getting to the other crash is the most important thing in the world, right now.'

'If their balloon is intact,' Corver finished. 'If.'

Sandric's shrug managed to indicate all the violent green about them and the great distance to anything resembling Imperial civilization.

'Bit weird, having another airship about,' Vrant muttered.

Sandric shrugged. 'It was a big storm. Probably downed ships all over this part of the Lowlands. *Please*, sir.'

Corver nodded, looking up at the sky. Late morning already, not long before noon. 'How sure are you that you can find the site?'

'I took a compass bearing when I saw it go down,' Sandric confirmed.

'Then we go now.'

Back in the Twelve-year War Corver had been ordered to chase some fleeing Commonwealer troops into a forest, which had turned out to be a Mantis-kinden hold not marked on any of the ink-still-wet Imperial maps. The Mantids, who had not so much as lifted a finger to help the Dragonfly troops in the battle just concluded, had taken the invasion of their privacy very seriously indeed.

It was not the fighting that had marked Corver, but what came after. As they had hunted him through the trees, as his wounds had run fever through him like a hot knife, he had heard the screams of the men the Mantids had captured – probably soldiers from both sides for all he knew. He had staggered through a night strung with other people's torment and then . . . and then . . .

They had herded him to one of their places, where a worm-eaten idol had been reared up, crooked arms grasping wide. He had turned at bay then, the world about him a fever-dream of whispering voices and blurred images, but they had not come for him. Instead he—

He had not. He had *not* heard the voice. That had been his wounds and his delirium.

Now he was back in the green again, back in the land of the Mantis-kinden. Before Sandric's revelation some part of him had already given up – surrounded and besieged, there had been no hope for them. Now the pilot was offering him a slender lifeline, but it involved going *out there*, and facing . . .

If he had not made the call to depart then and there, reflexively and without thought, then his fears would have got the better of him, and he would have crawled into the airship's wreck and never come out. He knew that he was not thinking clearly, as an officer should, but he had no other options.

'Sterro!' he snapped out. 'Get your scrawny arse out here, or we leave you behind.'

There was a hurried scrabbling from within, and then the Fly hauled his skinny little frame out of the hold, making suspiciously heavy weather of it. When he presented himself before Corver, his leather coat hung with the bulked-out heaviness of mail. Every pocket bulged.

Seeing the sergeant's glower, the Fly scowled furiously. 'What? So we're supposed to leave it there?'

'It's the army's money,' Corver stated.

'And how's the army going to see it again?' Sterro demanded. 'Look, sir, we're in the latrine here, right in it. It's just us, no Emperor, no Rekef, no generals. We have to look after ourselves.'

Corver opened his mouth, but Vrant had already made a move for the hatch. At the sergeant's challenging stare he shrugged. 'Just a purse-full, eh? Think of it as a bonus for having to put up with Ordan.'

'Be quick about it then,' Corver snapped. Part of him was

raging at the poor discipline, the rest just bitter because he had left himself no dignified way to back down and grab a double-handful of retirement fund himself.

Sandric had made no move to follow. 'Sir, movement in the trees.'

They were crouching low in the next moment, using the rail and the slope of the airship as cover. Corver squinted and stared, and after a while he began to see it too – nothing so identifiable as a human form, but he knew they were out there, and in force this time.

'Think they're working up the courage?' Sandric asked him.

'Mantis-kinden don't need to do that. They're stupid enough to charge artillery.' He remembered the war, though – when the Mantids fought it was seldom as part of the Commonweal battle host. They came and went by incomprehensible rules of their own, attacking when least expected, but passing up on some obvious opportunities too. Rituals and superstition, Corver supposed.

'Get up here now, we're pulling out,' he called, and Vrant had appeared the moment after, sword in hand even as he clambered out of the hatch.

'Sandric, which way?'

The pilot consulted his compass and pointed.

'On three, then,' Corver decided, and then an arrow sprouted from the deck near his hand, almost magical in its suddenness, and he was going, sliding down the slope of the airship and over the rail, and the rest following him, jumping and gliding to catch him up.

The Mantids moved on them immediately: a scattered flurry of fleet, lean bodies moving through the trees from behind and both sides, spearheads and swords glinting momentarily as they crossed stray shafts of sunlight. Corver had meant to move into the trees like a soldier, alert and wary, but he was running almost immediately, and the others struggling to keep up. Sterro flapped along at the rear complaining, getting briefly off the ground with desperate stutterings of his wings before the weight of his sudden enrichment brought him down again.

An arrow cut past Corver, from nowhere and into nowhere, existing for him only in the moment that its swift flight crossed his path. There were whoops and yells from around them – then the crackle of stingshot as Vrant turned his Art on them – directing a palm backwards and lashing out blindly to make the enemy keep their distance.

And yet they *were* keeping their distance, and this frightened Corver more than anything. It was the Commonweal all over again. The Mantids were playing with them. Had they wanted the Imperials dead then a few well-placed arrows would have accomplished it, and Corver knew full well how good a shot the average Mantis archer was.

Abruptly he stopped, Sandric almost cannoning into him, Vrant barrelling past before skidding to a halt. Sterro practically dropped at his feet. Corver had his sword in hand, his off-hand directed outwards, and the other Wasps quickly joined him, standing shoulder to shoulder and facing away from one another.

'Sir?' came Vrant's taut question.

Corver peered between the trees. There was a complete canopy above them, and it was as dark as twilight down here. For a moment he could see nothing of the Mantids, just the overwhelming undersea gloom of the space between the trees, the shimmer and dance of flying things and the scurrying in the undergrowth.

Then he saw one: a tall, lean man in clothes the colour of the forest, bearing a bow as tall as he was, standing motionless, watching. Abruptly he could pick out at least two dozen of them, men and women bearing bows and swords and spears. They were unarmoured, probably barely counting as warriors by Mantis reckoning, but they were quite enough to make an end to some lost soldiers of the Empire.

They began stalking forwards – not running, but a slow, deliberate advance, and wherever Corver looked, in that quarter, he saw them slipping between the trees, bowstrings being drawn back, spearheads dark and thirsty.

'Go,' he decided. The word forced itself from him without his consent. A moment later he was on the move again – less of a frantic rush, because he was too tired and bruised for it now, but hurried even so. He knew without looking that the Mantis-kinden would be effortlessly keeping pace.

Ahead, the forest grew only darker, the trees closer together and the branches overhead just heavier and more intricately inter-leaved.

They battered their way another few hundred feet, tripping over roots and dodging about trunks, and each of them feeling an arrow aimed at the small of their back. In Corver's mind was the demand, *How far do they want to drive us, before they strike?* Certainly they would strike – probably to pick off one or two of them before running the survivors further. They were a cruel people, the Mantis-kinden. Every Imperial soldier knew it.

Sandric tripped and fell, cursing, tangled in briars, almost vanishing into an abundance of undergrowth that was abruptly about them past knee-height. The trees around them had become larger – trunks broader than a man was tall – and further apart to compensate. As Vrant hauled the pilot to his feet, Corver glanced up, seeing patchy sky for the first time in what seemed like two hours. Clouds rolled there, although it seemed impossible that there could be another storm brewing so soon.

'We left them behind,' Sterro declared.

Corver opened his mouth for a scathing denial, but he was scanning the trees back the way they had come, and the pursuit – which should have been on them by that time – was nowhere to be seen. Then he saw that the Fly-kinden was pointing.

They were there, the Mantis-kinden, but they were holding their ground – at least two score of them now, clustered between the trees, watching.

Vrant swore wearily.

'Sandric, do you have the first idea where we are, relative to that new crash?'

'Well yes, sir, I . . .' The pilot consulted his compass. The fact that they had surely gone madly off course in their flight was present with them, unspoken but universally acknowledged.

'Get yourself up there and take another look,' Corver ordered him.

Sandric looked as though he was about to argue, but then his wings whisked him up, kicking and twisting to avoid the branches.

Sterro sat down, dragging a water bottle out from one of his many pockets. After a deep swig he surprised Corver by handing it around.

The Mantis-kinden did not disperse, but kept their distance – not a bow was drawn back, despite Corver's estimate that they were still within longbow range. *Just waiting to make sure we don't double back*, was the miserable thought in Corver's mind right then.

A minute passed before Sandric dropped clumsily back down again, indicating a new course.

'We'll make it by dark?' Corver asked him.

'I'm sure of it,' said the pilot who had no experience of long treks through forest.

It had not escaped Corver's notice that the direction Sandric had indicated was into the thickest undergrowth, and more heavily shadowed, but perhaps that was just his luck coming into play once again. That the shadows seemed oddly independent of the canopy cover above . . . he shook himself. This wasn't the Commonweal. This wasn't *that* forest, and besides, there had been no voice, not then, not now . . .

Making off at the whim of Sandric's compass proved one thing: the Mantis-kinden had not been simply keeping their distance. They really had stopped, and in a very short time indeed they were out of sight, taken away by the trees and the underwater gloom. At that point Corver just knuckled down and marched, because there was no way at all that giving himself a chance to think about things was going to help.

Kicking and pushing through the ever-denser undergrowth played havoc with any sense of time or distance, and the forest that loomed on every side seemed always the same. When Vrant called out his warning, Corver realized he had no idea how far they had come.

'Movement!' the big man had snapped out, and Corver peered between the trees frantically, trying to spot . . .

Nothing, there was nothing.

Then they were upon him. He saw just a flurry of motion, barely anything registering of the body that made it, and a blow clanged off his upraised sword. His hand flashed in instant response, and he felt in his gut that he had scored a hit, but the undergrowth swallowed any body hungrily, and then there was movement all about them. Vrant roared and struck – he had always been good with a sword – and Corver saw the shadowy forms of two lean men attacking him – then falling back as the furious Wasp soldier hacked at them. An arrow struck Sterro in the flank, knocking him sideways with a yell, then he righted himself, his ill-gotten gains acting as a coat of mail. A moment later the Fly simply vanished into the ferns, very little discretion required to overcome his meagre valour.

Corver lashed out at anything that came near him. The Mantis-kinden were dancing from tree to tree, moving swiftly, using every part of their forest home to hide them. He caught not a straight glimpse of any of them, not a single face – just the murderous rushing movement as they lunged at him and then skipped away.

One darted past him – a momentary impression of hard, empty eyes, a sinuous form shrouded in grey – and Sandric went down, struck hard. He made a sound like a man dying, and Corver had heard enough of them in his time. He stabbed at the attacker, then tried to bring his sting to bear, but the Mantis was gone.

They were all gone. Corver straightened up, feeling quiet return to the forest. As swiftly as they had struck, the Mantis-kinden had fled – some part of their game, no doubt. *One by one, they'll come for us, just like . . .* but then Sandric sat up, his head just clearing the ferns. He looked pale, his face washed out and drawn in the fickle light, but he was alive, and Corver helped him up.

'Hurts, sir,' he said, but the leather of his pilot's cuirass had turned the blow just enough.

'We need to move,' Vrant stated. 'They'll be back. Where's—' But Sterro had already made his reappearance.

'Yes, yes,' he snapped at the big man. 'Don't pretend you care.'

'Sandric, go up and take another look.' Corver glanced at the sky and saw to his surprise that much of the gloom around them was evening stealing upon them.

The pilot ascended wearily, clutching at his side where the Mantis had struck him, and the other Imperials crouched in the ferns and waited. Then Vrant let out a long, low hiss, hefting his sword.

'What is it?' Corver asked him, tense as a wire and waiting for the Mantids to come back for a second sitting.

But Vrant just pointed. 'There's the bastard,' he said.

Corver tried to follow the man's finger, seeing it shake slightly. Still, Sterro saw it before he did, and only after a long time of staring did he pick out the shape of the beast that Vrant had spotted: a praying mantis, and a big one, fifteen feet if it was an inch, poised like an executioner, arms drawn up in contemplation of its next victims. One eye was a charred and ruined mess.

'That was on the airship,' Vrant grunted. 'That brought us down.'

'A mantis?'

'*That*,' the soldier insisted. 'It was that.'

'What are you saying, soldier? This *animal* followed us here?' Corver growled. The lopsided look the mantis had turned on them was considering, reflective, anything but bestial.

'I'm not saying anything, sir. Look, can we move—'

Then Sandric had descended in their midst, which failed to startle Vrant but almost saw Corver kill the pilot by reflex.

'We're right on course,' Sandric confirmed, pressing the compass into Corver's hand and showing the direction, 'but look, sir, I saw . . . hard to say but I saw what looked like – I don't know, buildings maybe? Or something.'

'Buildings . . .' Corver exchoed.

'Or something,' Sandric repeated, shrugging. Between us and the crash. And there was what looked like . . .' His face twisted wretchedly. 'Something bigger, a hall or something, I could just make it out – something further in.'

Further off, surely, Corver corrected for himself, but Sandric's words seemed entirely and unwelcomingly appropriate. 'We press on,' he told them. 'But watch for any sign of construction, is all.'

'Night soon,' Sterro muttered. Nobody dignified him with an answer.

Vrant took the lead, chopping and shouldering his way, from time to time in the ever-waning light consulting the compass that Corver held. The physical activity strained his abused ribs, but he was glad of it. In a long history of stupid assignments, this business was surely the worst. What was happening to the Imperial army these days? Surely things were simpler back when they were fighting the Dragonflies?

Building, the sergeant had said, as if anyone would really build anything in this place. Surely the Mantis-kinden slept in trees whilst their beasts roamed free and attacked innocent Wasp airships.

And that was another thing he didn't like. That *had* been the same mantis, bearing the scars of their previous encounter – but it had not attacked, and then Corver had been all 'press on' and Vrant had lost sight of it. That it was still out there was no hard conclusion to reach, though. *Hunting us*, he decided, but they were already so lost and so foreign to this louring place that he had to wonder just what sort of opportunity the monster was waiting for.

'Wait!' Sterro's voice hissed abruptly, from waist level. The little man had taken to travelling right at Vrant's heels, to his great annoyance, mostly to take best advantage of the path the Wasp was forcing through the undergrowth. *And since when did you ever get a forest like this – so much underfoot and yet so little sky above, eh?*

'Report.' Corver's voice sounded ragged.

'Light, sir. A fire.'

Vrant glanced up, barely able to distinguish scraps of sky from the branches that barred it out. The fabled buildings were starting to seem less a threat and more of a promise. *Roof over our heads wouldn't go amiss, no matter how many Mantids we had to kill for it.*

The Wasps squinted in the direction Sterro was pointing. Was there a faint suggestion of red there? Vrant couldn't tell.

'Move,' Corver decided, and they muddled on another hundred yards – by then they could all see it – a sullen glow that outlined the low, curved entryway to a hut. 'Hut' was almost an over-statement. The thing seemed mostly woven from branches, and one side of it was just latched onto a tree trunk. Aside from the doorway the only external feature was where the weave of its root projected up into an unpleasantly anatomical-looking spout, from which a light trail of smoke could just be seen as they approached.

Then Vrant looked to one side, and stopped, putting out a hand to halt the sergeant as well, with Sterro pattering on another few feet.

'Sir, we're surrounded,' Vrant murmured, sword clearing its sheath in what he hoped was a subtle way. He waited while the others took stock and came to the same conclusion.

The hut was a Mantis hut, no doubt about that, but that was because they were in the middle of a Mantis village. Of course, unlike civilized people the world over, the wretched Mantis-kinden didn't deign to undertake such menial tasks as clearing the ground around where they wanted to live. Instead, Vrant and the others had been walking through the Mantis community for some time. Now that they looked, they could see similar misshapen structures between and around and halfway up the trees in all directions, as though the forest had erupted in monstrous tumours.

There was not a sound save for their breathing, until Vrant finally said, 'So where are they? Are they here?' He had an open palm out, threatening the darkness.

Sterro had crept forwards towards the lit entrance. 'Someone lit the fire. Place isn't abandoned.'

'Maybe it was someone like us. Doesn't have to be locals,' Vrant opined, 'Hey, perhaps it's people from the other crash come to borrow *our* balloon, eh?'

Nobody seemed to think that was funny.

Sterro was at the entrance to the hut, the firelight reflecting on his pale features and making something corpselike of them. 'Reckon it was locals all the same, though,' he muttered, and Vrant went over to argue with him.

Inside, the fire revealed itself as embers in a bronze bowl, the wood there more than half ash, with a faint scent of herbs or incense on the air. At the hut's back wall, where it meshed itself with the gnarled trunk of a tree, there was a thing. It was hunched and crooked, an abstract sculpture in wood, piece upon piece tied and pegged in place to give it form, and all of it porous with rot, gnawed at by beetles and holed by their young. The sight of it sent a shudder through Vrant's innards, disproportionate to any concrete property of the icon. Even when he realized that the two branches were in fact crooked arms, that it was a representation of the Mantis-kinden's own totem, it was still instinctively disturbing in a way he could not account for.

'Lovely,' was his considered opinion. 'Let's not wait until they get back.' He turned from Sterro to see Corver plainly keeping his distance, his face legible enough in the firelight that Vrant could have read the man's whole haunted history there had he cared to. 'Sir?' he prompted.

The sergeant snapped back to them visibly. 'We move on,' he agreed.

'Sir, the place is empty. Couldn't we wait for morning?' Sterro pressed, although he was probably more motivated by the weight of gold he was dragging about than any actual strategy.

Corver's face froze for just a moment, his mind catching up with his senses.

'Swords!' he shouted.

They were surrounded. Vrant had the right of it after all. The Mantis-kinden had never left.

And yet some part of Corver's mind was insistent: *They were gone. The village had been abandoned, save for this one fire. The very huts themselves were ragged and piecemeal, eaten away by neglect!*

It was too dark to see them clearly, but he could sense them, all around, Vrant had gone almost back to back with him, Sandric to their flank. Sterro was crouching at the hut's edge, caught in the firelight and yet trying to be unseen.

Corver's eyes raked the darkness. Hidden as they were, lost in the night and in their Art, he sensed them still. They stood before each hut, between the trees, tall and proud and armed, regarding the trespassers in their midst. Slowly they let him see them: their ornate carapace mail, crafted with centuries of skill into elegant flutes and crests; their slender blades, the spines of their arms; their haughty, autocratic features like the ghosts of kings.

'Come on,' he murmured, sensing the other two Wasps shifting their footing, readying themselves for the rush that must surely come. They were growing more and more tense, and he could hear Sterro's whimpering breath, the Fly a moment from bolting for some mythical safe place away from here.

Still the Mantis-kinden stood there, in all their antique grandeur – no tension there, but some feeling between them

688

that Corver had no name for – some ineffable melancholy that had been lost to the rest of the world before the birth of the Empire.

'Come on,' he said again, but they were not coming. These four specimens of the new were too trivial to hold their interest. They were fading away between the trees – not turning, but simply evading his sight, falling back into history.

'Did you see that?' asked Corver eventually, when not a single Mantis remained in his sight.

Vrant let himself relax only very slowly. 'Sir,' he said. 'I didn't see a cursed thing.'

In the end they pushed on for another fumbling, tripping, blind half-hour before Corver at last consented to let them stop. Then they rested for a few miserable hours, spending more time keeping watch than sleeping. By that time the leaden light creeping into the forest suggested morning, and Corver ordered the march. He himself had barely slept at all, staring into the darkness with Sandric whilst the other two dozed fitfully.

By mid-morning they came across the other crash-site.

Sandric gave out a whoop of triumph and began bounding through the trees towards it, with Sterro on his heels. Corver brought up the rear with Vrant, considerably more cautious. Ahead, in the clearing it had gouged for itself, was the gondola of an airship a little smaller than their own. It had obviously been strongly made, for the bulk of its structure was still intact whilst the trees it had come down on had given way. Its sloping deck was greened with moss, and vines had clutched their way up its curved side to colonize the railings. The keel was buried entirely, invisible beneath accumulated soil and leaf litter.

'This . . . can't be the right one,' Vrant said slowly.

Corver nodded, and doubled his pace, reaching the gondola's near rail as Sandric was about to try the deck's central hatch.

'You say you saw this come down?' he demanded.

The pilot opened his mouth to answer in the affirmative, and then glanced about him. A flicker of doubt crossed his face. 'Must have been . . . another crash . . .?' he started.

'Another crash?' Corver echoed.

'What, and we got right to it with that compass?' Vrant demanded. The big man was jumpy, sword out again, starting out into the trees.

'The balloon's long gone, anyway,' Corver noted.

'This is a Collegiate design,' Sandric told him. 'The Beetle-kinden are a practical lot. Probably they had a spare. Help me with the hatch, sir.'

Corver signed and hauled himself up and over the rail with some difficulty to join Sandric in prising the hatch open. Inside was far darker than the night had been. The morning sun illuminated a jumbled, decaying rubble of wood, earth and a shocking flourish of fungus, showing that the hull's underside had mostly disintegrated. *Rotting, like the idol,* thought Corver, before he could stop himself.

They had not thought about making their own light overnight for fear of drawing the ire of the forest, but now Corver was cursing himself for not bringing a lantern from their airship. Still, they had one superior pair of eyes amongst them. 'Sterro, get down there.'

'Me?' the Fly-kinden demanded.

'You. Get in there and look for a light, or if there's no light just see what you can see.'

'I'm not going in there.'

Corver practically shoved the palm of his hand in the little man's face. 'You'll obey orders.'

Sterro's lips drew back from his teeth in a furious grimace, but at the end he did not dare brave the sergeant's temper. With a single backward glance, full of rage and fear, he ducked into the hatchway.

I will have him kicked down to common soldier, Sterro told himself grimly. *I will have him flogged. I will have him on crossed pikes.*

Oh, not now, certainly. Sterro's current capacity for revenge upon Sergeant Corver was limited to wishing him the plague. Once they got back to camp, though . . .

He held on to that *once*.

He had never been a big noise himself, Sterro – using others and being used in turn, that was how the wheels of the Consortium were greased. Patronage and nepotism all the way, hence Sterro had found himself attached to an odious creature like the late Captain Ordan. There had been drawbacks – namely virtually every aspect of the aforementioned deceased – but the good captain had been a man assured of his command of his underlings – namely Sterro – and that confidence had overlooked a great deal of embezzlement over the years. Sterro had enough money stowed in safe places to ensure that Sergeant Corver led a very miserable life for years to come. In fact he had enough money right now on his person for that – but until he could get anywhere civilized enough to spend it, he had no choice but to suffer Corver's abrasive and temperamental leadership.

He clung to the underside of the deck, wings stirring slightly for balance and the weight of his coat dragging at him, letting his eyes accustom themselves and leach every last speck of light from the near-darkness. It looked as though this doomed ship had been more compartmentalized than their own – at least one cabin fore and one aft as well as the compact chamber he had crawled into. The surface beneath him – which given the tilt of the room meant part of the floor and part of one curved wall – was a mess of rotten wood, earth and sprouting mushrooms, the forest working diligently to conquer the work of man from beneath. *This sure as orders isn't whatever ship Sandric saw.*

He reached into his coat, located one pocket by touch and pulled out his steel lighter, flicking at its wheel until the fuel caught, with a small but steady flame that gave his eyes quite enough to work with. This chamber appeared to be picked clean, certainly, and he descended with a shimmer of wings, touching down and heading aft.

Unlike their own, this craft had not slammed down stern-first, and the rear compartment seemed mostly intact. There was the rusting hulk of an engine here, cogs forever seized, and what might have been a galley, stove and all. There were compartments tucked up near the ceiling, some open, others closed, looking as though they belonged to the engineers' mystery, rather than anywhere someone might stow valuables. *Leave that for others to mess with.* He padded back into the central room and headed forwards.

There were smaller rooms forwards, cabins probably, all being reclaimed by the earth like the rest. Whoever had crashed here appeared to have made themselves scarce and taken the best of their loot with them, Sterro considered, or else the Mantids had come and carried off crew and goods.

He ducked into the narrow triangular room at the bows, one hand holding the flame up, the other reaching about the bulkhead, and his hand fell on something soft and furry that moved slightly at his touch. For a moment his mind was full of a bizarrely atavistic loathing at what he might have disturbed, some sense of an impossible creature from another time lurking here in wait for him. After his instant recoil he thrust the flame forwards, and was vastly relieved to see nothing but a huge tarantula carpeting one wall, no doubt intending to rest out the daylight here. It was most of his own size, but he knew the type well – placid, retiring and preferring far smaller prey even than he. Satisfied, he found a stick and prodded the unfortunate arachnid until, after raising its legs and showing its fangs a few times, it gave up and crept off to hole up in another cabin. Sterro wouldn't have bothered it even that much, save that beyond its furry bulk he had seen a little casket.

He shoved the box to one side, out of sight of the door, and then let his wings carry him back to the central compartment and out into the open air to make his report.

The Wasps conferred, and then Vrant went over to the rear of the deck and started stamping enthusiastically on the softened wood until he had made a scatter of rough-edged holes. Then, skylights installed, there was a general Imperial expedition to the ship's aft compartment to check out the lockers.

Sterro, overlooked once more, went off for the casket.

It was locked, but another pocket disgorged his picks and a tiny flask of oil, for the skill was surprisingly well known amongst Consortium factors. In just over a minute he had the tumblers lined up – thanking the good Collegium steel for being proof against rust. *What have we here then, eh? Some Beetle airman's retirement fund, maybe?* The fact that his pockets were already stuffed with gold was not lost on him, but there was always the chance that the Empire might confiscate *that*, whilst the contents of the chest were surely his by right.

His disappointment, when the bulk of the chest's weight turned out to be the chest's own sturdy construction, was keen-edged. Inside there were a handful of coins – Helleron mint, and of trivial value – and a scroll that the damp had just started to make inroads into. He almost abandoned it without reading, but the thought of returning to the Wasps' company was sufficiently unpleasant to him that he carried the document out into the beam of sunlight in the central hold and spread it out.

Autumn 34th Day, he read, set down in regular, careful handwriting.

So, new life, new journal. I am putting 'Kernels of Truth in Pathaian Folklore and Language Use' behind me. Perhaps, when I return from this voyage with something unarguable then I'll re-title it and re-present it, and nobody will know any better. For now, I am a new woman, and my life is a new life, and I have a new project.

Sterro almost gave up then. *How pissing jolly for you,* he thought. Only the fact that his current environment showed that the writer had come to a nasty end kept him reading.

I am somewhat late commencing this journal as we set off a day ago. However, I am now starting my record, like a good scholar. So, let it be known that I have, with the last of my funds, chartered the Plain Sailing to travel to Etheryon and make a study of certain archaeological sites there, assuming the locals will permit us. I have certain more desperate plans in mind if they do not, but I understand from my Sarnesh colleagues that the Mantids of Etheryon are relatively hospitable, for their kind, and I have high hopes for the success of our voyage.

I should say that the Plain Sailing is a compact little vessel, barely sufficient to fit my few belongings and myself. She has a crew of two: Master Magnus Patcher is the owner and helmsman, or pilot, or whatever the correct term is, whilst Solamon is the engineer. He is from Kes, and I suspect he is a renegade, but the topic is not one I feel prepared to bring up, so I will have to let my curiosity rest. I am invited tonight to Master Patcher's cabin to dine, although I expect the room will be sufficiently small that we will end up touching elbows as we eat. The food here is also not enthralling, being whatever Solamon cooks up over the burner, with a heavy emphasis on flatbread.

Autumn 38th Day

We were going to stop at Sarn, but Master Patcher has decided to go straight to the edge of the forest Etheryon for, as he says, various reasons of his own. I'd have thought it might be Solamon, had not Patcher's tone suggested some prior incident in his own life. The man is a bit of a rogue, I believe. He is also remarkably forward, and I rather feel that I shall end up spending valuable research time fending off his advances.

I am becoming more and more excited about the prospect of viewing Argax, or what remains of it. After talking to Master Patcher about the Etheryen I realized that the Mantis-kinden may still dwell there, or may have moved to dwell there, which will complicate matters, and

694

may have obscured much of the original material. However, Mantis-kinden are noted for being protective of the past, and for not building much in stone, and my accounts insist that Argax, whether it is described as a town or a hold or a hall, was of stone and wood, and I hope to find at least the original stonework intact. The description in Tenrathaea is very vivid, although no doubt the infamous Walk of Statues has long gone, let alone the Cold Gates. One must allow for Inapt poetic licence. Perhaps I will find nothing, but even then I can hope that the locals have preserved some manner of oral history, as I have found so many of the Inapt races do so skilfully. If I can return to the College with a collection of hitherto-unheard Mantis-kinden ballads and sagas it will go some way to repairing the damage. From the accounts given in Tenrathaea and in the Prados coda I cannot believe that they do not still sing of Argastos.

Sterro shivered, and lifted his eyes from the paper. He had never come across the name before, though he would guess it to attach to a Moth-kinden, from its form – and hadn't it been the Moths who used to lord it over the Mantis-kinden in these parts, way back when? Still, something about the name, even seeing it there in the workaday writing of some Beetle academic, sent a chill through him. He shrugged off the feeling, though, and returned to his reading.

Autumn 46th Day

The Etheryen are not cooperating, but it is the manner of their lack of cooperation that is remarkable. We are moored at the forest's edge, at a Sarnesh logging camp, and today a delegation of the Mantids came to speak to us. I explained to them who I was, and that I was an authority on pre-Revolution mythways (I put it in a manner more palatable to their pride, though!) and that I wished passage to Argax in order to study its ruins. No sooner had the name come from my lips than the entire Mantis party, some eight or so men and women, were on their feet and backing away, staring at me. Being as they were Mantids, everyone thought we were in for a fight, and half the Sarnesh nearby were suddenly making space and reaching for weapons. When it became clear that nobody was going to attack anybody, I asked them again. Their reply was 'We do not go to Argax,' and 'Nobody goes to Argax.' I couldn't believe it. Here we were, centuries after, and the legend of Argastos is still going. There is a part of the forest Etheryon where the locals apparently don't go – or at least don't go there casually – because of the reputation of a man who was dust before the revolution. And – note – whatever remains of Argax must be undisturbed, untouched and unseen, or at any rate treated with a great deal of respect. I knew then and there that I had to see it, with or without the natives. Tenrathaea gives a good enough idea of where the hall was, with reference to other forest landmarks, and I have some hope we may even be able to spot the place from the air. Of course, I then had to convince Sol and Master Patcher, particularly Patcher. He wasn't keen, notably because he thought the Etheryen wouldn't like it, and might just kill us out of hand for flouting their superstitions. However, with sufficient application of wine I had him mocking the unsophisticated forest-dwellers, and swearing that he'd take me wherever I wanted to go. I did make certain promises against the department bursary, which I hope I will be able to sort out when the time comes. Still, if I find what I hope, then funding should not be an issue.

Autumn 51st Day

I am getting somewhat desperate. I had not realized that it was possible for forest to be so dense. It is impossible to see anything but green from any height, and twice now, when we ventured low enough to make out details, parties of Mantis-kinden erupted from the trees and tried to board us. It was only by Sol's quick thinking that we were able to ascend swiftly enough to avoid them, and I am glad they are not strong fliers by habit. I have no telescope. I am, after all, in a profession that normally looks at small things from a very close distance. I had not thought that I would need one.

Master Patcher's temper is growing fouler by the moment, but I cannot go from the Etheryon without something to show the department, or I'm ruined. So far I am staving off Patcher, but I am concerned that he may have his suspicions about Sol and I, and this will worsen his temper. So far I have managed to fend him off, but each day's search is a daily effort in handling his deteriorating moods.

The next entry – the last entry – was different, the handwriting wild, trailing off into a shaking scrawl at the end:

There is a storm. Sol says it's like nothing he's seen. We've lost our way. I am writing this in case the journal is found. I would like my research notes given to the library for posterity. Please remember me as someone who died in the name of scholarship.

'And what's that?'

Sterro looked up sharply. He had grown too absorbed in the account, and now Corver was staring at him from the aft doorway.

'Just some diary that got left behind,' he said defensively, although it wasn't as though he had done anything *wrong*. 'Some Beetle from Collegium. She was coming here to study the Mantids.'

'She got more than she bargained for, then,' came Vrant's voice, as he shouldered his way out after Corver, dragging a huge canvas sack in his wake.

'So what's that?' the Fly asked.

'Spare balloon,' Corver told him. 'Looks like Sandric had the right idea of it after all. We take it back to our ship. We try to get the gas machine working, so we can float out of here. Worst case, we let the wind carry us away from the forest then just come down. Anywhere's better than here.'

'No argument from me, sir,' Sterro said, heartfelt, then Corver was reaching for the scroll, and for a moment he was about to be possessive about it, for no other reason than that he had been the one to find it. It was just trash, though, useful to no one, so he gave ground with the best grace he could. Corver's eyes flicked over the scroll, bleak and uninterested, and Sterro caught the precise moment that they stopped dead, muscles crawling on the man's face. The Fly was uneasily certain that it was that same Moth name that had halted his own progress.

'Right.' Corver wrenched his eyes from the writing and shoved something into his hand, and Sterro saw it was the compass.

'What's this for?' he demanded.

'You know what it's for,' Corver told him sharply. 'Now go and get aloft, take a reading for our own crash site.'

'Why me?'

'Because I'm *telling* you!' the sergeant yelled at him, nerves finding the same aggressive outlet that everything always seemed to, for Wasps.

Sterro added another few items to his mental list of what he was going to arrange to happen to Corver – and Corver's family, should he have any – and then kicked off for the hatch above, having to make a couple of tries before he could manage it against the drag of his illicit riches.

Corver stared at the scroll he had confiscated from Sterro. *Argastos.* Every time his mind touched on the name it was like a loose tooth: something moved and shifted within his head. From somewhere cavernous and distant he thought he heard a voice, whispering secrets to him. He so desperately did not want to hear.

'Sandric, you're sure you can get this balloon filled up, when we're back at our own ship?'

'No problems, sir,' the pilot confirmed.

'Good. Because we're getting out of here.' Corver wasn't sure who he was trying to reassure. 'Vrant, let's get this thing out into the open.'

Between them, the two of them manhandled the heavy bag out of the hatch, although the effort of it had Corver wheezing and Vrant pale and holding his injured ribs. It seemed perverse that something so fundamentally connected with lighter-than-air flight should be so heavy.

Then Sterro screamed.

They were standing instantly, letting the canopy bag roll down the sloping deck. A moment later, Corver picked out the little man pelting through the trees for them, and after him . . .

He could not quite believe that a mantis of such size could move so fast. Where the space between the trees allowed it, it flexed its wings for a sudden hop forwards, and then it was just striding – its stride leisurely but its long, arching limbs eating up the ground. Sterro was struggling, trying to get into the air, and Corver even thought, *The gold will be the death of him*. But without a moment's regret the Fly had shed his coat and kicked off desperately, wings a-flurry. In that moment the mantis struck.

Its forearms lashed out, extending and unfolding to the limit of their appalling reach, the hooked tips catching Sterro at the very apex of their arc to swat him out of the air.

Then Vrant was charging it, half on foot, half flying, roaring and sending searing bolts of Art energy at the creature. Its triangular head cocked towards him and it reared up – Corver caught his breath – arms outstretched like the jaws of a barbed trap, wings snapping out to flare their warning colours at him. Even back on the airship's deck Corver could feel the sheer force of it – a savage, furious presence where no presence should be – and Vrant skidded to a halt, sword drawn tight into his body, his stinging hand crooked into a claw as he fought against the sheer wave of fear that emanated from the creature.

It had one good eye, Corver saw. The other was a blackened ruin. The sight filled him only with a kind of resigned dread.

Then the wings thundered forward in a single beat that threw Vrant to the ground and shuddered the mantis into the air, and moments later it was gone.

'Sterro!' Corver called, clambering down from the airship with Sandric backing him up – both of them on the advance with sword and sting now the monster was actually gone. Vrant was standing off, watching the sky and waiting for a reprise, but Corver was only relieved to see the Fly-kinden man sitting up, examining the rents in his tunic. There was a little blood, but the wounds had been shallow, Corver saw.

'Get up,' he ordered. For once Sterro did not argue.

'My coat . . .' he muttered.

'Forget it. Vrant, we need to get the new balloon! We're getting out of here. We *are*.'

The big soldier stomped over. 'It'll be back for us.'

'Then let's not *be* here. Where's the . . .' He glanced at Sterro. 'Compass . . .?'

The Fly grimaced and shook his head, still seeming dazed.

'Get aloft and take a bearing on our crash,' Corver told Vrant, and then, 'Do it!' when the man wanted to argue. 'We'll just have to keep hopping up for a look.'

Vrant took to the air reluctantly, because his ribs were already pressing a hand of pain against his lungs each time he drew breath, but right now he reckoned that one more questioned order would send the sergeant over the edge entirely. *Man's owed some time back home.* Back in the Twelve-year War that had become a running joke.

He let his wings carry him up through the hole that the Collegiate airship had made when it came down, which the forest would take many decades to close. He was not a strong flier – certainly not now at any rate – but he was able to wobble and lurch in the air until he could make out some landmarks. *There* looked like that creepy village they had gone through during the night – he could even see a faint line of smoke, as though someone had been stoking the brazier there. Beyond it must be their own crash, although he was cursed if he could make it out.

He wheeled in the air, trying to keep an eye open for the killer mantis that was probably watching him right then, and saw something else.

Hadn't there been something said about buildings and construction? And surely the hovels of the Mantis-kinden hardly counted as that. Across the roof of trees, Vrant saw something that reared out of their clutches: stone and wood thrust together to make something substantial – not civilization, quite, and yet head and shoulders over anything a Mantis ever made.

By then his Art was failing him, and a measured descent was the best he could make of it. He took a final look towards the abandoned village, his landmark, and then returned to Corver, indicating their path.

Between them, they shouldered the heavy canopy bag, and set off into the trees without further words. Nobody wanted to point out how vulnerable they would be to attack.

The Collegiate crash had vanished behind them into the trees by the time the screaming started.

They dropped the bag at once, when they heard it: a long, raw, agonized sound, not a man injured, but a man systematically being injured by his fellow men. Every soldier did a stint bringing prisoners to the interrogation table: they were more than familiar with the sound. For a moment they were motionless, listening to that long drawn-out wailing, the sobbing gasp for breath, and then the shriek again.

Then Corver got a look on his face that Vrant didn't like, and a moment later he was leaping off into the trees – and what to do then, but follow?

The canopy-bag was abandoned behind them, but Corver had forgotten it for now. Let Sandric and Sterro hang back to guard it, cowards that they were. Corver was rushing through a different forest, hearing the screams of yesterday – his men in the Commonweal, whom the Mantids had taken alive.

He caught scattered glimpses ahead: the great idol the locals had raised up, that rotting wooden figure with its hooked arms, and, within its grasp, a human figure held there by wooden pegs or nails driven through his body, hanging in the arms of their totem, his blood soaking into its raddled frame and feeding the thousand scions of decay that lived within.

Not a soldier, he realized. Not a Wasp. He had a moment's clear glimpse as he tripped down a hollow, seeing a Beetle-kinden man in aviator's leathers, howling and thrashing against his own pinned flesh, against the shadowy tormentors who bent over him . . .

And Corver burst out into a clearing, and it was there.

Chest heaving, he stared, and knew that he was truly going mad.

The idol was there, all seven foot of it, but so fragile and worm-eaten that it seemed the slightest push would see it crumble and fall, The body that it held was still in place, the pins and pegs clearly visible amidst the bones and withered, part-eaten tissue, but the man had not been screaming these last months. Vacant sockets regarded the sky out of a jawless skull, but the clothes – holed and ragged but more durable than the man who had worn them – they were surely the canvas and leather of an aviator, just as he had seen.

'Vrant.' Corver turned, expecting the dour expression the man habitually wore, but this time the soldier's look was shaken, utterly undone.

'Sir, I thought I saw . . . I heard . . .'

'Back, back to the canopy,' Corver cut him off fiercely. 'Come on! Move, now! This is nothing, nothing for us at all!'

Vrant swallowed and nodded, and they fought their way back to the dropped bag, where Sandric and Sterro were waiting for them wanly, true to form. Corver had halfway thought that he might never find them again, once separated.

'Take another bearing,' he told Vrant.

The man looked aggrieved, but laboured up into the air again.

Corver looked at the other two. Their mute gazes seemed to accuse him. *You led us to this.* He wanted to beg for their under-standing, to ask what he could have done, in the end. Imperial sergeants did not say such things.

Then Vrant was down again, and there was a dreadful, haunted look on his face. 'We're off course, sir.'

'Explain.'

'I swear, sir, we were heading for that village place – I reckoned we'd see our ship from there, you know – it was on the way. Only . . .'

Corver just waited, although he almost felt that he could finish the man's report himself.

'There was this place – some big hall, or a mound or something – stones, some sort of gates . . . I saw it before.' Vrant got the words out through a visible effort of will. 'We're closer to it. We've gone off, somehow.'

Of course we have. Of course. 'You took another bearing? Good, then let's go.' Because those were the words a sergeant said, for all that they were no part of the wheeling turmoil within Corver's head.

After that they were waiting for the next shock, each one of them on edge as they pushed through the forest, Vrant and Corver stopping frequently to rest from the weight of the canopy bag. Somewhere close, the great scar-headed mantis was stalking them invisibly, ghosting between the trees. They knew it, and none of them said anything.

'Another bearing,' Corver ordered, after a time, and a distance, he seemed completely unable to keep track of. A muscle pulled at Vrant's mouth, but the man lumbered up into the air again, the others staring after him.

They were being watched, First Sandric felt it, then Sterro, and at last Corver saw a faint flutter of white in the corner of his eye. He did not want to look. Whatever it was, he had no wish to see it, and yet something, some machinery within his neck, was grinding his head round to take it in.

Vrant landed then. When he said, 'Sir . . .' his voice was shaking like that of a man on the rack.

'I know,' Corver told him softly.

'Sir, we're off course, sir.'

'I know.' Corver was looking at a Beetle-kinden woman, and she was looking back at him. Short, dark, wearing a tattered robe of that Collegiate style that even Imperial diplomats had started adopting. There was a look on her face like . . . Back in the war Corver had seen that expression on a soldier caught by the insurgents in the Maynesh rebellion. The man had been staked out as bait, looking as though he was just standing there, but the locals had put a wire noose about his neck, razor-sharp and tight enough to draw blood. He had just stood there, not daring to move or speak, as his comrades had approached. Then the ambush had been sprung and one of the Maynesh Ants had yanked on the handle, and the man's head had just come clean off.

They had made the Maynesh pay tenfold for every act of rebellion. Corver didn't think that there would be any such retribution here.

Slowly, he approached the woman, finding it hard to tell how far she was, how many trees away, through the forest. Vrant trod carefully behind him, his breath ragged, sword quivering in his hand. Corver felt oddly calm, though. They were off course? Of course they were. What else had he expected?

When something crunched under his foot he looked down, knowing that the woman would be gone from his sight in that moment. There were bones down there, and through the brittle ribcage a centipede moved sinuously, lifting its head almost to waist height to gape its fangs at them. Vrant's hand spat fire, incinerating those jaws and two sets of legs, and sending its long, segmented body into spasms of rage as it died.

Corver knelt down, staring at the remains. Enough of the robe had survived to confirm what he already knew. *Just another victim. Gone and yet still here.* He looked for some semblance of reason amongst the bones, some clue that would allow him to unlock this situation and find his way out into the world that he knew.

In one bone hand still flaking with dried skin there was a scroll case, clutched to the broken ribs as though this had been the woman's promised salvation. Corver's mind flicked to the account that Sterro had found, to the name it had contained. *I don't want it*, was on his tongue, but how would that look, before a soldier under his command? Every sergeant knew that you had to be braver, tougher, bloodier than any of your men.

Vrant was shuffling, eager to go, but Corver twisted open the waxed chitin of the case to reveal the account within. The writing was uneven, the lines trailing off, the letters larger and more uneven as the balance of the account descended towards its inevitable conclusion. Standing there over the remnants of its author, he followed her through her last few entries, undated, sporadic, inconclusive.

We are down, and all three of us alive, although the Plain Sailing *will never sail again. We are in the midst of the Etheryon. I have suggested that we should light a very smoky fire and wait for the locals to discover us and guide us out. Master Patcher was most uncomplimentary, and said that if the locals had not seen our vessel crashing then nothing would bring them out, and that it were better for us that they never found us. He wanted to leave at once, but Sol wanted to salvage more from the wreck, and they have argued a lot, nearly coming to blows on one occasion.*

It was another world, and one that Corver could barely have imagined even before coming here, even before the war. *How the rest of the world live, outside the Empire.* He read on.

We have been attacked. Mantis-kinden came from the trees at night and drove us from the wreck. Patcher has taken an arrow through the leg. We are hiding in the trees. Movement everywhere. Mantis-kinden, dressed in full armour. Archaic in look. We keep moving. They are all aro

And then a blank turn of the scroll, as though the woman was playing some literary joke, the writing tailing off into blots, but eventually, in ever degenerating script:

Magnus Patcher is dead. They caught him. I saw it all. He could not keep up, and at last they caught him. There was a statue, some kind of wooden thing, stylized mantis? They took him to it. They had skewers, steel. They hammered them in, pinned him to the idol while he was still alive. We could not get to him. Sol took me away. We could hear him screaming. They kept him screaming all night.

The forest around them seemed very silent, as intent on the words as Corver himself was. Vrant alone was restless, shuffling from foot to foot, wanting to be off even if they were so irredeemably off course, but Corver would not be rushed.

I have lost Sol. There is nothing but the forest. Something is hunting me. I am close now.

Patcher and I searched everywhere for some sign of Sol, but he is gone. The green has eaten him.

Frowning, he turned back, comparing entries. Of course, the writing by now was wild and spiky, the hand behind it trembling as the mind that guided it came undone.

I know I will never see the College again now. Nobody will find this journal. I shall be just one more academic who never came back. I cannot even remember if I said where I was going. They will remember me for one derided study of folklore. Folklore. I do not believe in folklore. There is no folklore. There is only the real.

Argastos. I hear Argastos.

It was the last of it. She had heard Argastos, and she had died. Corver stared down at the skull, flensed to the bone by all the myriad agents of decay that peopled the forest floor. Did he feel a kinship with the dead woman? If so, it was something they could never have shared while she was alive – before they had both come here, they would have been enemies, from different worlds. Now . . .

When he heard the clatter of steel, Corver did not even look up. He said nothing, made no attempt to stop Vrant as the man ran for the sound, hunting fervently for something he might understand. Corver just stood there, with the bones and the last words of an unknown Collegiate scholar.

By the time Vrant came back, the other two had come looking for them, to stand staring at Corver and his unwelcome find, silent and watchful. With the big soldier returned, unspeaking, the silence between the four of them grew quickly unbearable, and Corver forced himself to speak to forestall some other voice breaking it, perhaps that of the dead woman, perhaps of someone else entirely.

I hear Argastos.

'Report, soldier,' he snapped.

'I saw fighting, sir.' Nothing but the ghost of Vrant's usual voice, hushed and uneven.

Corver just stared down at the bones until the inevitable thread of the other man's thoughts drew the rest of the words out.

'There was an Ant-kinden, sir,' Vrant explained, and Corver nodded, for he had expected that. The report, such as it was, dragged on: 'He looked like from that place, what's it called, off on the island off south of here. He was fighting, I think it was Mantis-kinden, sir. I think.'

They would have been just shadows and movement, in the dark beneath the trees. Corver nodded again.

'He saw me – the Mantids were gone by now, sir. He saw me, looked me right in the eye. He . . .' For a moment Vrant's voice lost its way, fading into a shaking breath like that of a dying man. 'He put his sword through his own throat, sir. Just rammed it straight in there. Never took his eyes off me, sir.' There was something childlike in Vrant's tone that wanted Corver to reassure him that everything was going to be fine.

'We had better get moving,' the sergeant decided.

'Yes, sir. We'd—' Vrant made to head off for where they had left the canopy bag, but Corver lifted a hand to stop him.

'Not that way.'

'But sir, the—'

'Do you think we'll find our way back to the crash?'

Vrant stared at him dumbly. They all did. Corver felt that he should apologize for somehow bringing them to this, but that was another thing that Imperial sergeants never did.

'What do you think is happening right now, soldier?' he asked, mildly, and watched the expressions shunt and jostle on Vrant's face until the man finally found some way of saying it that made sense to him.

'Someone's pissing us about, sir.' Don't ask who or by what means, but that simple sentiment was like a lifeline.

'So we need to go sort them out,' Corver finished for him. A Moth-kinden name echoed in his head like distant thunder but he would not voice it. 'This hall, this mound or whatever, we're closer now than we were, yes?' *Despite all our efforts to avoid it.*

'Yes, sir.' Barely a tremble, barely a flinch.

'Then it looks as though we're going there, so let's go. Come on, swords out, stings ready. Soldiers of the Empire, right?' And if his own voice faltered behind the false courage, there was little Corver could do. Certainly the sentiment seemed to buoy Vrant a little, if not the others.

Corver drew his own blade, seeing an answering glint of steel in the hands of the others, even a dagger in Sterro's tiny fist. He was about to ask Vrant to take a bearing, to see which way to go, but then he remembered: it didn't matter.

The going was easier, then, the very forest standing aside to let them past, and they moved faster and faster, breaking into as much of a run as Corver's armour and Vrant's ribs would allow, until at last they burst out of the trees and saw the hall before them.

Hall. Tomb. Something.

A great hill had been raised here – too regular and singular to be natural, and roofed with flat stones, irregular and yet fitting together to make a weirdly makeshift dome. Grass and weeds sprouted in the cracks, and in places the paving had come away entirely, levered up by roots and the grasping hands of ferns, and fecund sprays of shapeless yellow fungus. There were designs of sorts cut into the slabs, stylized figures, abstract geometries, spirals on spirals repeated over and over. Corver had no wish to inspect them closer.

Facing them, as though mere chance had brought them unerringly on the correct approach, were the gates: standing almost as tall as the dome's apex, the mound's contours deforming outwards to accommodate them, they were framed in vast slabs of grey rock, but the doors themselves were faced with thousands of scales of wood, chipped and worm-chewed and discoloured, seeming less a barrier than the hide of some unthinkable monster. There was no breeze, and yet the scales seemed to shiver as the Imperials approached.

'Argax,' Corver said softly, and when the others stared at him he explained, 'The Beetle woman wrote it, in her diary.' He did not say that the name, the knowledge, had seemed to come to his mind unbidden – that the Beetle woman's journal had occurred to him only a moment later.

She had written of a 'Walk of Statues' too, and 'Cold Gates', and surely these were they.

'He's in there, is he?' Vrant demanded, clinging to belligerence for all it was worth, 'Whoever's pulling our chain?'

'That seems certain,' Corver agreed. In truth he could almost feel the presence within, beating like a heart, waiting for him.

There seemed nothing else to do. He put his hands to the gates, searching for some way to push or pull, feeling the fragile shards of wood break free under his touch.

Something squirmed beneath his fingers.

A moment later Corver was yelling – a sergeant's dignity be damned – as the broken fabric of the doors exploded beneath his hands in a seething swarm. In seconds he was elbow-deep in a writhing, knotting host of grubs and centipedes and beetles, boiling about his hands, dripping in twisting clots to the ground, spraying in individual looping bodies to scatter through the air. Corver fell back, flapping his hands to be rid of them, watching the entire front of the doors crawl with voracious life, forming patterns and words and hideous images second on second, as though some composite thing was trying to make itself known. A hand, eyes, a face . . .

'It's all right, sir! It's just bugs, nothing but little bugs!' Vrant was shouting, sweeping the crawling things off him. 'No harm in them! It's all right, sir.' The other two were backing away, and so nobody was keeping watch.

The strike, when it came, was a blur, a moment of discontinuity and then Vrant was simply not there. Corver started from his horror into a new one, scrambling to his feet to see *it,* the mantis, right there overhanging them, clinging to the very curve of the mound, and with Vrant clasped in its thorned forearms.

The solder was bellowing, but it was more rage than pain, hands outstretched and loosing his sting wildly at the creature that had him. In that moment, seeing Vrant's mail buckle where the creature gripped, Corver threw off all the leaden despair that had dragged him to this place, all the helpless resignation that had walked him here like a slave to the auction block. Instead he thrust out his own hand and let his sting crackle and spit, searing across the great insect's thorax and leaving dark smears of char.

He knew how mantids took their prey: a single surgical bite at the neck to kill off all resistance before it fed. He heard something crack as Vrant twisted in the creature's grasp – armour or bone? – and saw the angular head tilt, one eye glittering green and the other dark and dull, as it searched for its opening.

Corver hacked at its nearest leg, at the clawed foot where it rested on the gate's lintel, and with lunatic strength he sheared straight through. The mantis lurched forwards, abruptly off balance, and he put a stingshot into its other eye.

It reared up, wings snapping out again and Vrant tumbled clear from its grip as its arms were flung wide. Corver was still shooting, bolt after bolt, and the leap it took into the air went awry, bringing the colossal beast down not ten feet away, just clear of the treeline, on its back with limbs flailing.

Probably it had already been dying then, but Corver advanced on it, stinging and stinging even though the drain of it made him stumble and stagger. By the time he reached it, its only movements were a spasmodic twitching. Smoke rose faintly from its ruined eyes.

For a moment he thought that was it: kill the mantis, escape the trap. Even as he turned back though, even before he saw that the gates stood open now, he felt that presence once again, in the depths of the mound, and knew that nothing he had done here had accomplished anything other than to amuse it.

'Vrant?' he called.

The man groaned, and Corver lurched over to help him to his feet. He could not stand straight, and there was blood at the corners of his mouth. His armour, the banded mail of the Light Airborne, was creased and dented, the metal holed and gashed where the barbs of the mantis's arms had bitten.

Sandric and Sterro moved in, but neither made any move to help, and Corver struggled in silence until he had Vrant's arm over his shoulders, and his own about the man's back, feeling the jagged edges left in the metal. All the while the great dark gape of the gates breathed cold air before them, but they could wait. They had waited a long time, after all.

'Ready?' Corver pressed, and Vrant nodded, face taut with pain. Nobody asked where they were going. Nobody asked why.

When they crossed the threshold, there was no light whatsoever within the mound, and they stepped into a featureless midnight void where their scraping footsteps struck distant echoes from walls that seemed miles distant. Then Corver's straining eyes caught a faint suggestion of illumination from ahead – nothing so healthy as firelight, but a cold, green-white corpse light, the luminescence of decay. Still he laboured forwards, hearing Vrant's pained and halting breath in his ear, the weight of the soldier dragging at him both a burden and a reassurance.

With each step, by subtle gradations, the light grew stronger, until Corver could see that there were figures all about then, rank upon rank standing in a military order. For a moment he imagined pale, gaunt faces, hungry eyes, but then he looked again, and saw the truth. He was treading a straight clear path between stands of armour, row after row of it, receding into a distance that the mound surely did not contain.

He saw Mantis-kinden work, above all, and, had he been a collector and possessed of any illusions, he might have been thinking about how rich even one such suit might make him back home. It was the old carapace plate, an elegant, sharp-edged creation of another time, enamelled and gilded, sculpted into crests and whorls. Each vacant suit that he passed represented years of an armoursmith's life back in the days when everything was made only once and by hand, before the Apt world of factories and mass production.

There were others, mixed in with those silent Mantis husks: he saw cuirasses of time-rotten leather, in designs he did not recognize, or hauberks of orange chitin scales painted over with hatched spirals. There were great heavy suits of overlapping plates and light harnesses of scintillating metallic shine such as he had seen stripped from Dragonfly corpses in the Twelve-year War. Most of all, though, there was Mantis armour, surely more fine and delicate mail than was worn by all the living members of that kinden together in the present day.

He glanced ahead, and saw that he was nearing the hall's end, and what awaited him there, and he looked away again. Now the suits that flanked him had lost something of the earlier pieces' elegance and craft, practicality starting to outweigh artistry, and he knew that he was witnessing the history of a decline. Here and there he saw chitin and steel that had been punched in, holed by the crossbows of the Apt. Now the mail of the intruders was more familiar: he knew Ant-kinden work when he saw it, and Beetle too. Despite all he had been through and all he was, he could feel the fading echo of loss about him: a mourning for a world that had passed, the defeat of the formerly invincible, the end of a dream.

And he was almost there.

When the edge of the dais was creeping into his sight he gave in, and lifted his head to the throne.

Above it was another suit of armour, though none that the hand of man had ever made. The vacant, slightly translucent carapace of a mantis hung there, great arms gaping wide. One of its eyes was a fractured ruin, but the damage looked centuries old, as antique as the desiccated carcass itself.

The throne, an age-weathered lump of stone that barely seemed a seat at all, was still just about empty, but Corver could see a darkness gathering there, proof against the unhealthy light that fell on everything else and came from nowhere at all.

At his side, Vrant gave a long sigh and fell away, kneeling awkwardly, his strength spent. Corver sensed Sandric and Sterro at his back, pressing close as the darkness closed in, but he could not take his eyes off the throne.

First there was just the one, the scuttling shadow of a tiny woodlouse disfiguring the pristine grey, but then his eyes were pulled left and right, the creatures seeming to emerge from the very stone itself: worms and millipedes, deathwatch beetles and their fat, white larvae, all the things of rot and reclamation that had infested the Mantis-kinden icons, fed upon the Collegiate scholar and seethed from the material of the gates. Spiders descended on filaments picked out by that bleached light, blood-coloured centipedes coiled and reared, and all of them, every mote of that host, coming together in a nest of twisting bodies and sheets of dirty silk, until something mounded and composed

713

itself upon the throne, weaving itself into the form of a man, building and anatomizing from the inside out, bones, organs, thoughts and all. Then one by one the little architects were gone, and Corver found himself meeting the blank white gaze of a Moth-kinden man.

Corver thought he knew Moths: they were the pale, effeminate bookish creatures, comically superstitious and fearful, whose world had been taken from them centuries before by strong, Apt kinden like Wasps and Ants and Beetles. They were tatty fortune-tellers, beggars promising blessings or threatening empty curses, or figures of ridicule in a hundred jokes and stories. The few he had ever seen had been weak, starveling-thin, bewildered almost to death by the technological world the Apt were building.

This man – *Argastos*, Corver's mind insisted – was not the same. He had the broad frame of a warrior, and beneath his open-fronted robe he wore armour of leather and chitin, and if that mail was enamelled in black and edged with gold, Corver knew for a certainty that the man had taken those colours for his own long before there ever *was* an Empire to contest them with him.

His lean, hollow-cheeked face was grey, the eyes the featureless white of his kind, His chin was spiked with a sharply pointed beard such as Corver had not seen anyone wear in his lifetime, and the Moth's pale hair fell long onto his shoulders. He seemed a figure from an ancient portrait, a statue of the Bad Old Days brought to life . . . or perhaps not life, for Corver was bitterly sure that this revenant before him had surely not drawn breath these five centuries or more.

'Keep close now,' he whispered, ostensibly for the benefit of his men, but mostly because he had hoped that the sound of his own voice would banish some of the crippling fear that was running wild through him. Any temporary relief was dispelled when the Moth's own voice came to him.

I have waited for you.

Corver's lips moved, but no further sounds came from them.

It was the same voice that had been murmuring just beneath the threshold of hearing ever since they left their crash site. It had been the same voice that . . .

In the Commonweal, yes. The voice of Argastos did not require anything so mundane as lungs or breath, but gusted about the great space, making the standing armour shiver and rustle. There was less humanity in his gaunt, grey face than there was in the chitin mask of the great mantis mounted above him.

I have brought you here to bear a message for me back to your Empire, warrior.

And a wretched little croak of laughter finally escaped from Corver, because the thought that he might ever return to the Empire, in whatever capacity, was surely nonsense. He, whose disbelief had been stabbed at and stabbed at until it lay dying on the floor, could not bring himself to credit that.

Oh, fear not; nothing will harm you when you leave this place, came the icy voice of Argastos. *No beast of the forest, no ghost or spectre, most especially not the Mantis-kinden, who will know well whose mark you bear. I lay the way open for you all the way to the edge of the trees, and from there you will have to find your own way home.*

'And my men?' Corver whispered, and when there was no response he repeated himself, almost boldly, almost desperately. 'And my men? What of them?'

Oh, warrior . . . Those blind-seeming eyes might have been looking anywhere, but the man's head tilted, ever so slightly, and dragged Corver's own gaze onto the nearest armour trees.

Ragged aviators' leathers, he saw there; a tattered robe hanging from one stand, cut in the Collegiate fashion; buckled mail in the black and gold bands of the Light Airborne; a cuirass with an Imperial pilot's insignia; a Consortium greatcoat with its pockets still leaking stolen Imperial gold: all rusty with blood from the wounds that had done for their owners.

Corver's hand came up to sting, but shaking so badly that he could not aim. Instead he brought it back until it was before his

715

face. His Art was locked within it, that had killed the Empire's enemies since he had first donned the black and gold. He reached for it, felt the warmth of his sting building, staring into his own hand, willing it to become his executioner.

But: *Oh, warrior,* whispered Argastos's voice once more, and Corver knew that he did not have the will. He was no tragic Mantis hero to die on his own blade. All his human sensibilities could not eclipse that animal part of him that desired life, at whatever cost.

Go to your Empress, Argastos instructed him – and despite it all Corver found himself echoing, *Empress?* – but Argastos was continuing, that dry voice etching the words on his mind, *Go to her and tell her: I am here, and ready for her. When she seeks me, she shall find me waiting.*

Who knows? Perhaps she will bring you with her, when she comes.